PRAISE FOR THE STORIES OF 100TH POWER

On *One Awake in All the World:* "Standout selections include 'One Awake in All the World' by Robert T. Jeschonek, an unlikely love story that pits two space-faring 'exterminators' against a horde of nightmarish monstrosities."
– *Publishers Weekly*

On *Beware the Black Battlenaut:* "I've always had a soft spot for combat stories that jump right into the action and get you involved at the platoon or squad level. Jeschonek's short story doesn't disappoint, and drives straight for the solar plexus with a three-person team that's fighting for their lives on an alien planet, and have been for quite some time."
– Michael Bellomo, Reviewer

On *Monsters of Ice Cream:* "This was a really heart-warming story! And such a unique take on familiar creatures. Mrs. H was definitely my favorite character because she was so sweet and her love and acceptance of the abnorms was a perfect illustration of that. I loved the ending (I won't spoil it!) and the overall message of the story."
— Sarah, Reviewer

100TH POWER VOLUME 2

A TREASURY OF 100 STORIES

ROBERT JESCHONEK

Published by Blastoff Books
An Imprint of Pie Press
411 Chancellor Street
Johnstown, Pennsylvania 15904
www.blastoffbooks.net

Subscribe to the Blastoff Books Newsletter:
http://newsletter.blastoffbooks.net

ALSO BY ROBERT JESCHONEK

To Irwin Allen, Gerry Anderson, George Lucas, Gene Roddenberry, and the other masters of the movie and TV screen, for all the dazzling visions and dreamscapes.

CONTENTS

INTRODUCTION

PLANET BOB
DEAN WESLEY SMITH

When a writer is so innovative and creative and flat out great, other writers tend to believe they live on their own planet. Robert Jeschonek is one of those amazing writers, so his friends and other writers sometimes say after reading one of his stories, "He's from Planet Bob."

This is a total compliment. And it is a compliment that has numbers of meanings. But most importantly, it is a nod to the outstanding creativity from other very creative people.

I can remember many times that I have sat and just stared at one of Bob's manuscripts after finishing reading it, wondering how in the world he made that work, and knowing without a doubt I never could have written it.

In fact, the very first story I ever read from Robert Jeschonek was when I was editing the *Star Trek: Strange New Worlds* anthology for Pocket Books and Paramount Studios. Bob had sent in a story called, "Whatever You Do, Don't Read This Story." It was a *Star Trek* story from the point of view of the story itself.

Think about that for a second. Impossible to do, right?

And in all my years of reading and editing, I had never seen it done, and yet here was this new writer making it work for a *Star Trek* story.

I just sat there and stared at the manuscript until who knows how long later, when I walked it over to another building in our compound looking out over the Pacific Ocean. I gave the story to my wife, Kristine Kathryn Rusch, who had just finished editing for six years *The Magazine of Fantasy & Science Fiction*.

I made no comment and she read it and then did what I did, just stared at the manuscript. Then she shook her head and said, "Not possible, but it works."

I faxed it to Pocket and the executive editor there, John Ordover, said the same thing. The contact at Paramount, Paula Block, said the same, and the story got third that year in the contest because we had to put in a more traditional *Star Trek* story as first place because of the fans.

So Bob wrote me a story for the next year. There was a strict rule in the volumes that you could not cross the series in the stories. Bob started his story off with Kirk and Picard on the bridge along with a mixed bag of crew, and it went from there.

Instead of rejecting it out of hand, I kept reading, knowing that Bob knew the rules, and I was wondering why he was doing this. As is typical of all of Bob's stories, the farther into the story, the more fantastic and impossible it got until I got to the end of the story titled "Our Million-Year Mission" and went, "Damn it, he can't do that, but it works, technically followed the rules, and we have to publish it."

I faxed it to John at Pocket Books, who said the same thing after he read it. He faxed it to Paula at Paramount who said the same thing and then suggested we create a brand-new category in the book titled "Speculations" to publish the story under.

And, of course, it won the contest.

And Bob has never looked back.

So in this second volume of three, expect all sorts of fantastic fiction, stunningly well-written. They are all stories that will challenge you.

It has been one of my great honors over the years to get to know

Bob, to sit around at conventions and over dinners with him, and now also to buy his stories for *Pulphouse Fiction Magazine*. There have been 21 issues of the magazine since it started, and I have been very, very lucky to have a story from Bob in every issue.

Every issue. Yes, I said that.

Pulphouse stories are often described as slightly twisted, fantastic stories, that are high-quality.

Stories coming from Planet Bob are perfect *Pulphouse* stories. Enjoy reading this book and the other two books as well. I am very sure you will.

Dean Wesley Smith
Las Vegas, NV

THE SPINACH CAN'S SON

am the can of spinach in a sailor man's hand. He squeezes, expecting me to burst open and launch a blob of green power into his gaping maw.

But I do not burst. He gets no mouthful of spinach, no surge of energy pumping up his arms to three times their size. That's not how it works on this side of the tracks, my friend.

You're not in the funny pages anymore.

Potpie the Sailor tries again with both hands, straining for all he's worth. "C'mon, ya ratfinsk!" He squints up at the threat looming before him, the whole reason he needs his spinach. "We've gotsk to drive this *she-hag* off me boat!"

What threat could be awful enough to strike fear in the sailor man's heart? Is it Bobo the comic strip bully, back for another knock-down-drag-out?

Not even close.

The figure standing before Potpie and me isn't a drawing at all. There's nothing pen and ink about her. "Sir!" She's a three-dimensional woman in what looks like a spacesuit out of a 1950s movie-- silver metallic tights and a bubble helmet. Her black hair is arranged in tight waves beneath the glass. "Please, calm down! I just want to ask you some questions." She pulls a photo out of a pouch on the belt slung diagonally over her hips. "Have you seen this man?"

"Never seen 'im before in me lifesk!" Potpie squeezes me harder than ever. I try my best to help, pushing from within, for one simple reason.

I recognize the man in the picture, with his dark brown hair and square-jawed features. I know him like I know my own self, in fact.

Because he *is* myself. Myself in another life.

And I know her, too. Her name is Molly. She's my wife.

And I know why she's after me.

"Take another look, please," she says. "It's urgent that I find him."

Potpie shifts the corncob pipe from one side of his mouth to the other without ever touching it. "I ain't seen him, she-hag!" He shakes a fist at her. "Now putsk 'em up!"

Molly takes a step toward him. "You're sure you haven't seen him?"

Potpie scrambles backward, knocking over a stack of spinach crates. Crying out, he puts me to the only use he can think of--hurling me right at her.

Molly ducks, and I go sailing over her head. It's not a clean getaway, though; the bracelet on her wrist starts beeping as I pass.

Here in the Underfunnies, I'm an anomaly, a deformity in the panel geography--the panelography--and her equipment has detected me.

Good thing a true Panelnaut like me can swim the currents here like a dolphin through water. Focusing my energies, I dive deep into the sea of words and images, hunting a good place to resurface.

Found it. I cross the borders in full flight and land with a shock that takes my breath away.

This time, I am the brick in the hand of a mouse.

I bounce lightly in his grip as he jounces along through a strange landscape, surrounded by abstract objects straight out of a surrealist painting. He gives off a thick smell of stinky cheese and whistles a jaunty tune from his pointy gray snout.

I know him well--Ixnay the Mouse. Once again, I've gravitated toward my favorite stomping grounds, the panelography of the early 20ᵗʰ century. In this case, the *Hazy Kat* strip.

Or should I say, the *Underfunnies* version of that strip. The reverse of it, the flip side where things don't work the way they should. The negative space that accrues in the collective unconscious of the readership around these tiny, panel-bound stories. The land of things unsaid and hopes unrealized.

For each time Potpie the sailor pops open a can, gobbles the spinach, and beats up the bully, we know in our hearts there must be times when the can doesn't open. That's just the way life works. And our expectations create this flip side place that until recently no one knew about.

I am a Panelnaut, an explorer of this place. Though "fugitive" might be a better word for what I've become.

"Boy," says Ixnay. "Have I got one cooked up for that idiot cat this time." He hops up on what looks like a warped sundial and calls out into the hot wind. "Oh, Haaazyyy!"

Without delay, the creature known as Hazy Kat comes bounding over the horizon. She's wearing a polka-dot scarf and matching tutu. "Comink, mine treasur-ed pession flour!"

"Make it snappy, willya?" hollers Ixnay. "Yer burnin' daylight here!"

Hazy flops to a stop in front of us and gapes with a love-struck goofy grin. "Dost Rumeo have a heart-wiltin' sonnet plucked out to make his Joliet swoon'st?"

"Ohh, yeah." Ixnay turns me over in his grip. "Ya ever hear of *iambrick pentameter?*"

Hazy claps her paws together and giggles. "Butter 'course, o' bard o' the mousehole! Hit me with that iambrick pentagrammer to yer li'l ol' heart's continent!"

"You asked for it." Ixnay hauls me back, ready to throw. "Be sure to notice the rhythmic counterpoint of strike and release. Or should I say the *opposite?*"

At that exact moment, Molly flashes to life between us and Hazy. The second she materializes, her bracelet starts beeping.

She points her wrist in my direction and nods. "I know you're here, Everett. You've figured out how to assume local forms, haven't you?" Watching the bracelet, she walks toward us. "You're inside the mouse, aren't you?"

Before Ixnay can say a word, Molly suddenly snaps backward. As she drops to the dusty ground, I see Hazy has her paws on her.

"You stays awake from my lettle Ixnay mouses!" Hazy flaps her paws like pancakes at Molly's helmet. "He is my preshiss poet and certifiable booblekins! Don't try steelin' his heart, you hussy!"

"Everett!" Molly shoves the cat away and scrambles to her feet. "I've come to talk to you! You sent me a message through the comic strips--our prearranged emergency signal! Don't pretend you didn't!"

She's right, I can't, because I sent it. But the signal wasn't a cry for help--it was bait. All part of the secret I've been keeping.

"I'm serious, Everett." Molly takes another step toward us. "I'll do what it takes to get through to you."

Ixnay just watches, juggling me from hand to hand. "Whoever this dame is, I gotta admit, I like her style."

Hazy, never much good in a fight, weakly bats at Molly's calves. "'Ev'ritt,' you say? Is that some other word for 'mouses?'"

"Shut up, cat!" says Molly. "Everett, listen..."

Ixnay's little mouse heart thumps like a big bass drum. It pushes out his chest in the shape of a cartoon heart as it throbs. "I think I'm in love!"

Naturally, this makes him raise me into throwing position again.

Molly sees the danger but doesn't stop talking. "It's time to come home, Everett. You can't keep running away." She spreads her arms wide. "We both miss him, Everett. But you can't make things right on your own."

I want to tell her how wrong she is, but I don't get the chance. Ixnay whips me at her glass-helmeted head before I can get the words out.

"Sech fe'rce percision!" says Hazy Kat. "His peshion must be deeper than I yimagined!"

As I blast toward her helmet, I focus my strength on changing course. Ixnay's throw is off, which helps; in the Underfunnies, things don't work the way they normally do, including his brick-pitching aim.

So I fly wide and hurtle on past, soaring through the ochre skies...casting my mind toward another refuge. I've gotten so good, I find one instantly, and I set my sights.

But I wait another moment to dive. Because the truth is, I'm not trying to lose her at all.

Her bracelet has alerted her to my presence in the brick, and she charges after me, calling my name. Calling another name, too.

"Henry's gone, Everett!" That's what she says just before I dive. "I miss him, too! But we need to move on without him!"

She's wrong. Dead wrong. And I'm going to prove it.

When I'm sure she's got a lock on me, I throw myself into the panelography. I ride the swirling currents of the Underfunnies, swooping away from the bizarre realm of Hazy Kat.

As I travel, I think of Henry. I think of our son. I remember how miraculous he was, how full of life and personality from the day he was born. I remember his bright blue eyes fixing on me with pure love and expectation. The way his lips moved as he repeated the things I said, as if he were memorizing each and every word.

He was the greatest thing to ever happen to me, to us. A dream come true--a dream I'd never known I had until he arrived.

A dream that ended the day he died.

I remember the sound of screeching tires, the screams of Molly as she ran. But never a sound from Henry. Not even a last gasp of breath when I got to his side in the street. Only silence from him.

And only blame between Molly and me. Blame become hatred, hatred become rage. I threw myself into my work, pioneering the exploration of the richest vein of the Underfunnies, born of the comic strips of the early 20th century. Anything to lose myself in the black and white of simple line work, the discoveries of Subtextual Space. Anything to forget Henry and stay away from Molly.

And then, one day, I got The Idea. And I knew it would work. It *will* work, if only I can get her to where she needs to be.

Suddenly, the flow of my thoughts is interrupted as I pop free into a fresh setting. I feel the tingle of something sparking on my body--the crackle of a tiny flame burning at one end of me.

This time, I am a lit stick of dynamite in the hand of a child.

"Zo!" says the little boy, a chubby creature with thick hair as black as his old-fashioned waistcoat. "Vhat do you say, Fritzie? Vill der Admiral like zis special *bratwurst* ve have for his dinner?" He holds me up and grins.

"Oh, ja," says his brother, also chubby but with blond hair and white coat. "I zink maybe he von't haff zo many *chores* for us tomorrow, Helmut!"

We're in a kitchen, surrounded by the smell of cooking sauerkraut. The boy's Auntie toils away on the other side of the room, stirring a bubbling pot. Her work is never done, taking care of the mischievous and ungrateful Schnitzeljammer Brats.

"Time to serve der first course!" Blond Fritz grabs a plate and holds it out.

Helmut drops me on the plate with a devilish smile. "Vhat a lovely presentation! Der Admiral ist sure to ask for *seconds!*"

"Ja!" Fritz laughs. "*Thirty* seconds till she *blows!*"

With that, they march me out through the swinging door to the dining room. The Admiral awaits them, sitting at the table in his seaman's cap and scrub-brush mustache.

"Dinner iss served!" Fritz plunks the plate in front of him.

"*Bomb Appétit!*" says Helmut, and then he catches himself. "I mean *Bon Appétit!*"

The Admiral doesn't seem to notice there's dynamite on his plate instead of bratwurst. He raises his fork and knife, ready to dig in...

But before his utensils make contact, his cap leaps off his head and flops down over me. Cut off from the air, my fuse fizzles and stops burning with just an inch to go.

Then, I hear her voice--Molly's voice, speaking from the substance of the cap. "You're not the *only* one who knows how to manipulate the supertexture of the Underfunnies!"

I'm surprised. Following me into the panelography is one thing; possessing resident iconography is quite another.

Apparently, my wife did her homework before she got here.

"Now *listen* to me," she says. "I want you to come *home* with me, Everett. You've been in here too *long*."

For the first time since she found me, I answer her. "You don't know what you're talking about."

"Oh yes, I do," she says. "Don't you think I tried to hide from the world, too? Don't you think I wanted to run away and never come back--never remember what happened to Henry? Don't you think I loved him, too?"

Her words settle around me like comic strip snow. Should I remind her, again, that I was trimming hedges in the back yard when it happened, and she was the one who was supposed to be watching him when he wandered into traffic? That she was the one who turned her back to talk to a neighbor when she should have had her eyes glued to Henry at all times?

Only if rubbing salt in the wound is my goal. "Leave me alone," I tell her. "Go back to reality."

"I'm not leaving without you. That's final." Just as she says it, she's lifted away, leaving me uncovered on the plate.

Fritz makes a grab, but I dive out of the realm of the Schnitzel-jammer Brats before his pudgy hand can touch me. I've got to keep moving, keep running, keep drawing her along in my wake.

Until it's too late to stop what I've got planned.

It wouldn't be enough to tell her the story straight up, to tell her The Idea I've set in motion. I can't take the chance she won't believe it's possible, that she won't cooperate.

Not to mention that it breaks every tenet of the Panelnaut protocols. Protocols that I helped create.

Diving through the foamy black and white tides toward my next destination, I remember the early days of exploration. I wasn't the first to discover the Underfunnies, but I found the first doorway and made the first trip inside.

It was so thrilling back then, such a novelty--plying the byways of this vast psychic substrata. Jumping into manifestations of comic strips from various eras, existing side-by-side with beloved characters as well as obscure ones. Before long, I discovered I hadn't accessed the primary reality of those strips, but a flip side echo where nothing works the way it should--a negative space where expectations can't be trusted. The place where Potpie's spinach can won't burst on cue, where Ixnay the mouse can't toss a brick on target, where the Schnitzeljammer Brats' dynamite sticks won't stay lit.

Did I understand the full implications back then? Hell, no. The best I thought we Panelnauts could do was influence the collective unconscious--plant messages that guide humanity toward a state of peace and harmony. We wrote protocols forbidding extreme inter-vention, anything that disrupted the essential integrity of the panel-ography.

And now I'm throwing them all away. The ultimate disruption is in motion; every moment brings it closer to final fruition.

And I'm the one who engineered it. I'm the one who knows how close we are to the grand finale.

Very close, now. It's time to pick up the pace.

I need to move her along quickly, not give her time to think or catch her breath. I need to flash like a skipping stone from world to world to world until we reach the last one.

The one I've prepared.

So I fling myself out of the current and surface in another place. This time, I'm a cigar in the mouth of Moo Mullet, rascally gambler and ne'er-do-well. Seconds later, I hear Molly's voice coming from the black derby hat on Moo's little brother, Kozy.

"Please, Everett," says the derby hat. "No more running."

"Say! What gives?" Moo snatches the hat from Kozy's head and gives it a smack with the back of his hand. "Now I gotta take *lip* from a *lid*?"

"We can get through this together," says Molly, "if you'll just come home."

"That topper's positively *brimmin'* with yap, ain't it?" says Kozy.

"Leave me alone!" I shout, just as I dive out of the scene.

"Now my *cigar's* runnin' at the mouth?" I hear Moo say as I leave. "What's next? My *racin' form* tellin' me which *horse* to bet?"

Once again, the currents bear me onward. I'm closer still to our final destination and the consummation of all my efforts.

Leaping from the flow, I become a club in the hands of Allie Hoop the caveman. Molly becomes the collar around the neck of his pet dinosaur, Finny.

"Please give me a chance!" The sound of her voice makes Finny grunt and run into a tree.

"What the heck?" says Allie. "How come you sound like a *girl* all of a sudden, Finny?"

I leap away without a word, and she follows.

Next, I become the fireman's hat on Smokin' Stovepipe, and Molly's the bell on his kooky one-man fire truck. I linger there for less time than it takes Smokin' to utter his catchphrase, "Fwoooo."

We're closer now, almost there. I speed up even more.

At our next stop, I'm the clodhopper boots on Li'l Asner the hillbilly. Molly's the pipe in his old Maw's mouth.

Then, I'm the giant sandwich in Ragwood Rumstead's hands, and she's the polka-dotted bow tie at his throat.

Another hop, and I'm the TV wristwatch on Rick Tracer's arm. She's his lemon yellow trench coat.

Then, I'm the bald head on Daddy Bigbucks, and she's Orphan Agnes' curly orange hair.

"Please stop!" says Molly, giving Agnes quite a start. "Just stop running!"

"Bleepin' blizzards!" yelps Orphan Agnes.

In spite of Molly's pleas, I leap again just the same. Because finally, we've reached the end. My whole purpose in leading her on this chase through the Underfunnies.

I swoop through the currents and burst free at our last stop. This time, I appear as myself, not disguised as some comic strip prop. She does the same, returning to her familiar form in the silver spacesuit and bubble helmet.

Finally. Here we are. In a child's darkened bedroom.

"What is this?" She stares at the black-haired boy on the bed between us. "Who is this?"

"His name is Little Nino," I tell her. "And he's a dreamer."

Even as I say it, Little Nino stirs and sits up in bed. He rubs his eyes, and then he looks at me, and smiles.

9

"Oh!" he says. "You are here!"

Grinning, I tousle his hair. "Just like we talked about, Nino. Are you ready?"

He smiles and nods.

"What's happening here?" Molly scowls. "What are you talking about, Everett?"

"Little Nino's been having a crazy dream," I tell her. "Haven't you, Nino?"

"Why yes, I have." Little Nino crawls down off the bed and pads across the room in his fuzzy white footie pajamas. "I have been dreaming about the music in my closet."

As we watch, he opens the door of his closet. Beams of rainbow light stream out around him.

At the same time, a sweet piping song skirls forth--the sound of flutes and chimes and strings weaving in delicate harmony.

Little Nino smiles back at us. "Do you hear it?"

"Yes, we do," I tell him. "Let's have a closer listen, shall we?"

"That will be fine." Without hesitation, Little Nino shuffles through the closet doorway, disappearing into the rainbow light.

"Come on." I take Molly's elbow. "I want to show you something."

She frowns at me. "That song. I know it, don't I?"

I just shrug and pull her toward the closet.

As soon as we cross the threshold, the doorway disappears behind us. Suddenly, we're standing on a beach at night, facing a bonfire that burns in rainbow colors.

At first, we're alone there with Little Nino. "I remember what comes next," he says. "Would you like to see the rest of the dream?"

"Yes, we would." I let go of Molly's elbow and take her hand. "We would like that very much."

Little Nino waves his arms, and figures descend from above, floating down one at a time from the starry sky. They are comic strip women, all of them, descending like wingless angels to land lightly on the wet sand around the rainbow bonfire.

There's Potpie's girlfriend, Olives...Ragwood's wife, Blonder...Li'l Asner's gal Dandelion Meg...Rick Tracer's true love Bess Bluehart...Allie Hoop's cavegirl Moolah...and so many more. Every woman you can think of from the funny pages, every one of them from the sublimely beautiful to the utterly ridiculous. Dozens of them, hundreds of them.

This is it. This is what I've been working for; this is why I summoned Molly.

Because this is where the impossible can happen. Here in a child's dream in a flip side place where things don't happen the way they should.

Only here could I do what had to be done.

Hand in hand, Molly and I walk to the fire. We stand before the women, their faces and forms flickering in the dancing rainbow light.

"Oh!" Suddenly, Little Nino runs forward and gazes into the flames. "There is something inside!" Without hesitation, he plunges his arms into the fire.

When he pulls them back out again, unburned, there's a bundle in his hands. Something wrapped in a comic strip blanket, all black ink and wooly cross-hatched texture.

Grinning, Little Nino turns and offers the bundle to Molly. "Please take this," he says. "It is for you."

"From all of us," says Olives in her nasally voice. "Every last one of us."

That's exactly what it took--the combined power of several hundred female icons projected together. Merged with my own hopes and memories in one supreme act of will.

Not sex, but creation nonetheless. The ultimate surrogate motherhood.

Molly peels back the blanket, and a tiny face looks out at her. The face of a comic strip baby boy, eyes big and dark and shining.

This, then, is my secret son, a child conceived in the panelography. A child of pure hope and imagination--an homage to the son we lost.

And perhaps much more than that.

"Think of Henry," I tell her. "Remember everything you can about him. Every detail."

She looks at me with tears rolling down her face. "But that won't...this isn't..."

"Trust me." I lift the helmet from her head and kiss her wet cheek. "Think of Henry."

She casts her eyes up at me with a look of anguished disbelief. I brush the dark hair back behind her ears and shake my head.

"I can't do it myself," I say. "I need you. Your half of the memories. Your half of who he is." I kiss her cheek again. "Please try."

I watch as she cradles the squirming bundle in her arms. As she closes her eyes and frowns, reaching deep to dredge up those memories.

The comic strip women huddle close, caught up in the moment. I can practically see the pen-and-ink waves of hope ripple out from their exaggerated forms.

Maybe it's the force of their collective willpower. Maybe it's the power of the dream we're in, a dream within a dreamlike realm where human disbelief is suspended. Where comic strip life works in reverse, so harsh human reality can change direction, too.

Or maybe it's just her memories and love for him. *Our* memories and love pouring into a vessel of India ink. Pulling him back from the vanishing point--pulling all three of us back.

Whatever the reason, a new strip debuts tonight, a full color single-panel above the fold in the Sunday pull-out section. Here's how we kick off the run:

A mob of famous comic strip women stands around a rainbow bonfire. At panel center, classic child character Little Nino stands on tiptoe, gazing at a swaddled babe in the arms of a woman in a skintight silver spacesuit.

Little Nino says, "Oh my! Look at his eyes! They're not black anymore!"

The woman in the spacesuit weeps with joy. The square-jawed man beside her bends down to kiss the infant's forehead.

We can see, in the firelight, that the baby's eyes are the brightest blue that the four color printing process will allow.

The caption at the bottom of the panel reads as follows: "Welcome back, Henry!"

FOOD CHAINS

Only as I devour the flesh of Manny's finger for what must be the hundredth--and final--time do I finally realize that I love him back.

It truly blows my mind. It's one thing for Rations to fall in love with those who feed on them--it's not uncommon at all--but who ever heard of a woman falling for her food?

This just might be a first.

Too bad no one will likely ever know. Too bad both of us will die before long.

Manny will die from being eaten alive, and I will die of starvation when there's no more Manny left to eat.

"Have some more, Lupe." He has one finger left, a right thumb, and he presses it toward me. He has a smile on his sugar-white face with its tutti-frutti swirls like he's a child offering me candy.

I shake my head. "I'll be okay." My voice is hoarse. "Save it for later."

Manny frowns and opens his mouth like he's going to argue. Then, he smiles sadly and pulls back the thumb. "Maybe you're right."

"Double damn skippy I'm right." I force on a smirk of my own for his benefit. The truth is, my stomach's still rumbling something fierce, but my Ration's got to stretch.

There's always been plenty of Manny to go around, but not anymore. These days, he can't replace what I eat.

This time, when he's gone, he's gone for good.

Two months ago, when I first met Manny, I couldn't have imagined feeling sorry about running out of him. He was nothing but food to me then...food I wouldn't eat, at that.

It wasn't the taste of him that I hated, since I hadn't actually tasted him back then. It was just that I hated all his kind.

In fact, I just about shot him on sight the first time I saw him. Just about shot my lover and hired gun, Guapo Vasquez, in the bargain.

Guapo *knew* how I felt about Rations...and yet, there he was, strolling up the gangway of my spaceship, the *Puerco*, with one of those tutti-frutti naked little bastards right behind him.

Yet another rule broken by damn Guapo. For someone I let screw me as much as he did, the guy spent an awful lot of time screwing *with* me.

The pistol was in my hand about a heartbeat after I saw them. "*Mierda!*" I said, catching the Ration in my sights and flicking the gun's settings to maximum everything.

Better believe the tutti-frutti hairless bastard stopped walking...though he didn't stop smiling. Right at me.

That was a mistake on his part. His wide-eyed, sparkle-toothed, never-ending smile reminded me so much of someone I'd once known that it nearly got him killed.

"What the flap *is* this, Guapo?" The gun in my hand didn't twitch.

Guapo whistled a tune and walked toward me like nothing out of the ordinary was happening. He combed one hand through his oily, black hair and used the other hand to scratch his private parts. "You drunk, *dulcita*? This is a *Ration*. Got 'im *cheap*, too."

"I *know* what he is!" I wanted to swing the gun around to Guapo, but I couldn't bring myself to let the Ration's tutti-frutti bald head out of the sights. "What's he *doing* here?"

Guapo stopped in front of me and pointed at his mouth. "He's gonna *feed* us, babe. That's what Rations *do*."

"Damnit!" I shot a glare at Guapo. "I've got, what? *One* lousy *rule*? *One rule*, and you can't *follow* it?" I whipped the gun around and shook it at Guapo. "*No Rations*, remember?"

Guapo stared down at me with his dark, half-lidded eyes. He reached out and tucked my long, brown hair behind my ears. "Cold storage on the *Puerco*'s down, *novia*. We got no way to keep fresh food."

"We'll have plenty of cash after the job on Polvo," I said. "The bounty for killing that man-eater's gonna be enough to rehab half the ship."

"Yeah," said Guapo. "And in the meantime, we gotta eat *something*. Something that doesn't have to be *refrigerated*."

I tossed my head, shaking the hair from behind my ears, then swung the gun back to aim at the Ration. He hadn't moved an inch. "I won't eat *that*. I'll *never* eat that."

"My name is Manna," said the Ration. The multicolored swirls on his sugar-white skin twisted and changed as he spoke. "You can call me Manny."

Guapo stomped over and clapped a hand on Manny's shoulder. "Got him for a song, babe. Next to nothin'. He's used, but he's strictly Grade A."

"That's right." Manny nodded and patted his hairless chest with both hands. "Zero defects. My last owner only sold me because he was strapped for cash." Manny cupped his hand, shook it, and pretended to fling dice out of it. "Gambling, y'know."

"Out!" I took a step toward Manny. "Get the flap *out*!"

Just then, Guapo looked past me and grinned. "Hey, Frogface!" He jammed two fingers in his mouth and whistled loud. "C'mere and try some'a this!"

15

Frogface, my pilot and engineer, had just entered the cargo bay. At Guapo's whistle, he waddled out from behind me and headed straight for Guapo and Manny.

Frogface was in such a hurry that he literally dropped what he was doing, letting a power drill bang the deckplates in his wake. "Great! I'm starvin', Guap!"

Still smiling, Manny extended his arms toward Guapo and Frogface. "If I may make a suggestion, gentlemen," he said. "The biceps are especially tender today. I'm roasting them up as we speak."

Frogface, whose given name was Felix Suerte, rubbed his hands together. He looked more like a duck than a frog, with lips curled like a beak and a broad, flat nose--which, of course, was the joke behind his nickname. "I like the sound a' that." He reached for Manny's right arm. "Think I'll try some."

Guapo leaned in and sank his teeth into Manny's left bicep. He came away with a mouthful of meat and chewed it slowly. "Top quality," he said when he could manage to speak. "Compliments to the chef."

"Why thank you, sir." Manny took a little bow.

As Frogface took a bite, and Guapo took another, my stomach churned. I wanted to look away, but that would have meant letting Manny out of my sights.

I grimaced and clenched my teeth. I couldn't stand watching people eat those things.

Rations were genetically engineered to be delicious and nutritious. They could use body chemistry to cook and season their flesh to taste, infuse it with a seemingly limitless number of flavors...then regenerate and replace every bite taken out. They were happy to do it, too.

But every time I saw someone eating a Ration, it still looked like a nightmare to me.

"Hey, Lupe, come on." Guapo swallowed his latest mouthful. "Try some a' this. You won't *believe* how tender."

"Get off the ship." I took another step toward Manny. "Either you *walk* off, or I *shoot* you and throw out your dead body."

"Lupe!" Frogface looked up from the forearm he'd been gnawing. "Quit scaring my dinner!"

"Yeah, Lupe." Guapo patted Manny's bald head. "You wanna eat powdered cactus and spiderwebs all the way to Polvo, that's your business. Froggy and me want fresh food."

"Forget it!" I took another step toward Manny, then another.

"Let me put it this way," said Guapo. "If Manny leaves, Froggy and me leave, too."

So that was the end of it, right there, and I knew it. No way I was taking on the mission to Polvo without Guapo and Frogface. I stopped moving toward Manny, though I kept him in my sights an extra minute for effect.

Then, I lowered the gun.

"That's a girl." Guapo winked and hiked a thumb at Manny's chest. "Now have a bite, huh? You'll feel better."

I shot Guapo the kind of glare that let him know he wasn't getting any from me for a long time. I turned the glare on Manny, too, but it didn't seem to faze him.

He knew better than to say a word to me at that moment, but the sparkly smile never left his face.

Typical Ration. Always look as friendly and appetizing as possible, no matter how annoying you might turn out to be.

But that wasn't why I hated him.

Guapo and Frogface might have won the battle, but I didn't let them enjoy it. We spent three more days planetside on Saguaro getting ready for the trip, and I worked them like dogs. Didn't say more than the bare minimum to either of them the whole time, either.

And Guapo sure as flap didn't get anywhere near my bed. Not that he didn't try.

Manny, at least, kept his distance from me. While the *Puerco* was on the ground, I saw him only a handful of times, and he hardly said a word to me. Never offered me a bite, either, which was smart on his part.

In fact, the closest we came to a conversation was the time we walked down a narrow corridor from different directions at the same moment. Instead of moving to opposite sides, we both kept moving to the same side of the corridor. We did it three times before Manny finally laughed and pressed himself against the wall.

"After you," he said, gesturing for me to pass. "Great minds think alike, I guess."

"Flap you, food." I leaned my shoulder into him as I pushed past. "Stay in the *maldecido* commisary where you belong, eh?"

I hated that tutti-frutti little bastard so much it hurt. I'm talking physical pain in my gut and my heart.

I'm talking the kind of hate that's so huge it just about replaces you. It works on you day after day for a lifetime, eating away at you.

And it starts when you're little more than a baby. That's the best time for it.

I was eight years old when my three brothers and I caught Cornucopia. This was twenty-four years ago, and we were all starving to death during the famine on Polvo, our homeworld.

We sneaked over the wall of the estate where Cornucopia lived, and then we threw a net over her and hauled her to a shack out in Barrio Sucio.

We cheered and laughed as we tied her up, because we were heroes. We were too late to save poor dead Mama and Papa, but we'd saved ourselves and our friends. Maybe we'd even saved the whole barrio.

It had been so long since we'd eaten well, we'd forgotten what real food tasted like. Now, we had a living, breathing Ration all to ourselves. If we took good enough care of her, we might never go hungry again, no matter how long the famine lasted on our world.

At least that was the plan.

"You remember me, don't you?" As the boys tightened the ropes around Cornucopia's shoulders and torso, I patted the top of her smooth, bald head.

Cornucopia nodded. That same old sparkly Ration smile was pasted onto her pudgy face. "The little beggar girl. Always begging for a bite of me." Her voice tinkled like tiny bells when she spoke.

"And you never said 'yes.' Not once." I pinched the meat of her shoulder, thinking about sinking my teeth into her. "But I guess you can't say 'no' anymore."

"Actually, I can," said Cornucopia. The iridescent swirls on her face flowed and changed color. "Nothing has changed."

"Like flap!" My oldest brother, Roto, took a deep whiff at the back of her neck. "You're *ours* now! You have to *feed* us!"

"No," said Cornucopia. "I don't."

"And why is that?" I made a face at her. I wasn't taking her seriously.

"I'm still someone else's property." Cornucopia nodded. "Señor Gustavo still owns me, and I can't feed anyone unless he tells me."

Roto's wild, frizzy puff of black hair bounced as he laughed. "We aren't going to ask your permission, y'know."

"Yeah," said my other brother, Miguel. "Don't look like you can stop us, either."

"You're right, I can't." Cornucopia's angelic smile drifted from Roto to Miguel to my third brother, Oswaldo.

"Didn't think so." Miguel grinned and drove his teeth into her tricep. He tore off a hunk of meat and chewed it with his eyes closed, an expression of perfect bliss on his face.

I understood why he hadn't been able to wait. None of us had eaten anything but bugs and rotten garbage for weeks. My stomach growled just from watching him.

"That's good," said Miguel. "Oh God, that's good."

Oswaldo, just a year older than I, was the next to pounce. He bit into the flesh of Cornucopia's right thigh and came away with a mouthful dripping with rainbow blood.

Miguel laughed. "Thank God," he said. "Oh, thank God." Then he hugged Oswaldo.

I was just about to go in for a bite of my own when Cornucopia spoke up. "You were right when you said I couldn't stop you."

"Tell me about it." Oswaldo bit off another hunk of her thigh.

"I can do something else, though." Cornucopia's smile never wavered. "I can kill you."

Roto smirked. "Good one. Kill us how?"

Cornucopia looked a little embarrassed. The swirls on her face shifted from blue-green and gold to red and deep pink. "Poison," she said. "If my owner hasn't programmed your genetic code into my glands, one bite of my flesh will poison you."

Oswaldo stopped chewing his food. So did Miguel.

"She's bluffing," said Roto. "The *perra*'s trying to scare us into letting her go."

I glared at the Ration. I had a horrible feeling she wasn't bluffing at all. "Why didn't you say something till now?"

Cornucopia shrugged. "Would you have believed me?"

Miguel groaned. Oswaldo coughed.

"Don't listen to her," said Roto. "She just wants to escape."

"That's not an issue." Cornucopia shook her head slowly, still smiling. "The *policia* are almost here. They followed a tracking tag in my bloodstream."

Automatically, I looked toward the door. Then, when Miguel and Oswaldo started vomiting, I looked at them instead.

"What's the cure?" I shouted.

"There is no cure," said Cornucopia. "They'll be dead in minutes."

I heard sirens outside the shack, and I went to my suffering brothers. As they collapsed--first Oswaldo, then Miguel--I dropped to my knees with them. I felt as if my own guts were being torn out by rough hands.

For many years, death had been my constant companion on Polvo...but this was different. These brothers were all I held precious in the world, all that had kept me alive in the darkest of times.

And the worst of it was, their deaths could have been prevented so easily.

As they released their dying breaths, I glared at Cornucopia. Even then, that damned sparkle-toothed smile never left her face.

Is it any wonder that twenty-four years later, I didn't join in the Ration lovefest rolling through the *Puerco* all the way from Saguaro to Polvo?

During the trip through space, Guapo and Frogface palled around with Manny like he was their long-lost childhood friend. They were inseparable.

They were always together in the cockpit or the break room or the tool room. Guapo and Frogface were always nibbling on some hunk of Manny--a meaty haunch or a crispy ear or a candy-coated fingernail--and Manny was always telling jokes or stories about the many people who'd eaten him before. They invited me to join them again and again, but I never did, and I hated them for being such flapholes. I hated them for bringing Manny onboard, and I hated them for having so much fun with him right in front of me.

The truth was, my bad mood wasn't just because of Manny, though. I was also full of dread at the thought of returning to my homeworld. Good old Polvo, dust bowl of the galaxy, final resting place of two of my brothers.

And now, maybe my third brother as well.

It was the real reason we were going to that craphole planet, though Guapo and Frogface didn't know it.

We were going to look for my brother, Roto, who had disappeared a month ago on Polvo, at the height of a rash of attacks by a man-eating alien monster.

Guapo and Frogface thought we'd been hired to kill that man-eater, but no one had hired us. I was taking us to Polvo to find Roto, though I'd gladly gun down any

man-eater that came between me and my brother.

A week after leaving Saguaro, we landed on Polvo. My heart pounded as we got ready to leave the ship.

As I got ready to see home for the first time in over two decades.

"Remember." Guapo grabbed an ultraviolet rifle off the rack on the cargo bay wall. "If you see yourself coming, shoot to kill." He wrapped one black-gloved hand around the barrel of the rifle and curled the other around the grip.

"That's kind of a no-brainer, isn't it?" Frogface snickered. "You see yourself, you're either lookin' at a mirror or one of these *reflejo* creatures."

"It's harder than you think, killing your identical twin," said Guapo. "Why do you think so few people have managed to do it?"

"It's the perfect camouflage." I finished braiding my long, brown hair in a ponytail and flipped it over my shoulder. "At the very least, seeing your perfect mirror image can rattle you just long enough for a *reflejo* to pounce."

"And sink its teeth into you." Guapo snarled and gnashed his teeth like a wolf, then laughed. "Not that anyone knows what *reflejos* use for teeth or what they really look like in the first place."

I smacked a red button on a panel on the wall, and the cargo bay door rolled up into the ceiling. Before the door had finished opening, a swirl of gray dust lashed in from outside, followed by a flying black spider-bug as big as my fist.

Welcome back to Polvo.

Guapo swung his rifle around and picked off the *araña volando* with one quick flash of purple light. The creature screamed as it died, and Guapo hooted.

"I shot your dinner, *dulcita*!" Guapo sneered at me. "Since you won't eat the Ration, you can fry that up with some butter and salt!"

"You shot it, you eat it," I told him. "I'll stick with my jerky and fruit leather." While Guapo and Frogface yukked it up, I slid extra weapons charges and a hunting knife into my belt loops.

When I was done and looked up, I noticed Manny watching me. He smiled at first, but then his sparkly smile quivered and faded.

"What's *your* problem, flap-off?" I snapped at him.

Manny shrugged. "I, uh...I have a bad feeling about this place."

"Since when does *food* have *feelings*?" I sneered as I pulled on my goggles.

"Maybe this'll make you feel better," said Guapo. Smiling, he strolled over and handed Manny a rifle.

"Oh, for God's sake." For the umpteenth time, I wondered what I'd ever seen in Guapo. "You're giving the *food* a *gun*?"

"Why the hell not?" Guapo slapped Manny on the back. "I sure don't want no *reflejo* chowing down on him."

"Actually," said Manny, "any unauthorized parties who eat me will die."

"But who knows with these crazy *reflejos*, eh?" said Guapo.

"If the *reflejos* are at all organic in nature," said Manny, "the toxins generated by my anti-theft system will..."

I cut him off right there. I knew all about the Rations' anti-theft system.

So did Miguel and Oswaldo.

"Shut up, all of you." I armed my rifle and stalked toward the open cargo bay door. "Let's get this damn show on the road. We've gotta go kill us a man-eater."

"Thank you for coming," said the governor of Pesadilla province. "Your help means more to the people of planet Polvo in this time of crisis than you will ever know. I only regret that I found it necessary to relocate before your arrival."

"Found it necessary to run away like the cowardly *gatito* you are, you mean!" said Guapo, aiming his ultraviolet rifle dead-on at the governor's face on the video screen. "Die, flapper!"

Guapo squeezed the trigger, and a bolt of purple energy sizzled across the governor's office and pierced the video screen. Smoke and shards of layered crystal circuitry erupted from the impact point, and the image of the governor's face flickered off the screen.

But her voice kept talking from the undamaged audio speakers.

"Very sorry I can't greet you in person," she said, "but my staff and I thought it best if we moved off-world for the duration. Please contact us at the following frequency when you've eliminated the threat."

Guapo whipped his rifle toward one of the speakers, but I swatted his arm before he could fire. "We need to hear this," I told him.

Guapo lowered the rifle but kept a tight grip on it.

"Here's what we know," said the governor's recorded voice. "The man-eater has ranged across Pesadilla, Grito, and Rasgón provinces. However, we believe it has a refuge in the Cambio region of southwest Pesadilla."

Guapo shot me a look, and I nodded. After growing up on that craphole planet, I knew plenty about the Cambio.

"This is the first case we've encountered of a *reflejo* turning man-eater," said the governor. "Given the abilities and native intelligence of these creatures, we believe we are fortunate that the death toll to date has not risen above 257."

"257?" Frogface whistled through his duck-bill lips.

"Nothin' left but hair and gristle," said Guapo.

"Madre de Dios." Frogface made a hasty sign of the cross over his forehead, chest, and shoulders.

Guapo puffed out his breath. "What'd you expect for the kind'a paycheck we're gettin'? Fish in a flappin' barrel?"

The governor was still talking. "Best of luck on your mission. We salute you and your unit, and we promise that your selfless courage will never be forgotten. Thank you, men of the..."

Before she could say another syllable, I swept my rifle around and fried the speakers.

"Yeah!" Guapo fired off another purple bolt from his own rifle, plowing a charred furrow in the ceiling. "*There's* the *chica* I love! Good riddance to that stuck-up *reflejo perra* who's been takin' your place lately."

I didn't dignify his remarks with an answer or even a look. Instead, I turned and charged past everyone, right out the office door into the blazing sunlight of midday Polvo.

The truth was, the *perra*--the bitch--was still in charge of me. I'd shot out the speakers not for fun or out of anger, but because if Guapo and Frogface had heard the rest of the governor's recording, it would have been a dead giveaway.

The governor had already saluted our "unit," and had started to thank "the men of the..."

As in "the men of the 24th Spaceborne Division of Mexifleet," who were the ones who were supposed to do the job we'd come to do. They'd be on Polvo in three days.

I'd brought us there three days early to try to save my brother, Roto, before the Mexifleet Marines came in with guns blazing. Brute force, not precision, was Mexifleet's style. If there was still anything left of Roto to save, and he was anywhere near the man-eating *reflejo* when the Marines caught up with it, there wouldn't be anything left of Roto for long.

In other words, no one was paying us to do this job.

The only possible reward would be getting Roto out alive. My crew's cut of the pay would be zero percent of nothing.

As well as I got along with Guapo and Frogface, that's the kind of information that can get a girl like me keelhauled out here in the ol' rough and tumble.

We flew out to the Cambio and parked the *Puerco* on a ridge about a mile and a half back from the border. Frogface whined about having to walk the extra distance, but Guapo explained how we needed to sneak up on the *reflejo*'s turf.

The real reason I made sure we parked that far away was this: the borders of the Cambio are always changing, just like everything out there, and you do *not* want your spacecraft ending up inside those borders.

Trust me on that one.

"Should we bring a cart?" Frogface said as we straggled out of the *Puerco*'s cargo bay. "For Manny, I mean?"

I wanted to slap his face tomato-red, but I settled for shooting him a serious stink-eye. "No, we are *not* hauling Manny in a cart." I adjusted the straps of my backpack, which was heavy with jerky, fruit leather, and tubes of nutri-paste. "The whole *point* of Rations is that you don't have to store, preserve, or *carry* them."

Manny smiled at Frogface and nodded. "Like livestock, Froggy. Right? It was easier for ancient travelers when their food did the walking."

"Shut up, flap." As usual, I wasn't in the mood for the tutti-frutti little bastard. "Shut up and play with your rifle. Feel free to point it at yourself and pull the trigger."

"I'd probably just grow back," said Manny. "I can regenerate, remember?"

"And I can reload," I said, glaring at him as I stalked past. "Again and again and again."

You can't see the border of the Cambio, but you always know when you've stepped across it.

It starts as a chill flickering up your spine, and then it spreads out. Your arms and legs tremble, and sometimes you drop what you're carrying. Then, there's a mighty squeeze in the pit of your stomach, and a flare of heartburn pushing up through your throat.

Then, suddenly, there's a fizzy, weightless dizziness, like the top of your head has floated off and your brain is turning and sizzling like butter in a skillet.

After that, it's smooth sailing. If you don't give up and cross back over the border, the storm of feelings settles down. It never quite goes away till you leave the Cambio, but at least you can stand it.

It's a hell of a place, the Cambio. I guess I should've warned my men what to expect...but if I had, they wouldn't've gone in with me.

In which case, they'd still be alive today.

"What the *flap*?" Frogface almost fell as he stumbled over the border.

Guapo marched across okay, but then he threw himself down on a boulder and held his head. "*Dios*! Feels like I'm turnin' inside out!"

I'd been back and forth over the border often enough in my life that at least I could mask its effects. "Come on," I said, stomping ahead through the gray sand. "Walk it off, you *gatitos*."

To my surprise, Manny strolled up alongside me, seemingly unaffected by the border. Smiling, he extended two fingers toward me.

"You oughtta try the tips," he said. "I hear they're excellent."

"Go flap yourself." I hated that tutti-frutti little hairless bastard even more for not getting zapped at the border like everyone else.

"They tell me the wine's even better," said Manny. "Want a taste?"

"I don't even wanna *know* where *that* comes from, you flappin' freak," I said, walking faster to get away from him.

When I was a little girl, my friends and I used to run through the Cambio on a dare, dodging the shifting landscape and trying not to get killed. We only ever lost one of us--Ernesto Chiapas, who disappeared down a sudden sinkhole in the middle of a run.

Maybe I was going to see ol' Ernesto again after all those years. The terrain of the Cambio was just as unpredictable and dangerous as before.

As Guapo, Frogface, Manny, and I walked onward, following a faint human blood trail with Guapo's sniffer glove, the land was in constant upheaval around us. Geysers and steam vents erupted without warning, spraying us with water and heat. Landslides rumbled down hillsides, and tremors shook the ground. Spines and humps and shelves of rock thrust up suddenly alongside or in front of us...and in one case, underneath us. We tumbled ass over teakettle down the rising slope, barely missing a jagged, deep crevasse as it opened below us.

To me, it was just a typical day in the Cambio...but Guapo and Frogface weren't as easygoing about it.

"What the *hell*, Lupe?" said Guapo after a flying, head-sized rock almost took off his head. "This place is *loco*."

"No one knows for sure what causes the instability." As I said it, a stream of bubbling red lava ran out of the side of a nearby mesa that hadn't been there five minutes ago. "Some say it's the nexus of powerful cosmic energies, focused by an immense celestial convergence. Some say it's the intersection point of multiple dimensional rifts, moving in and out of phase with our reality. Others say it's Mother Polvo's rectum, and she's got a thousand-year case of Montezuma's revenge."

"It's beautiful," said Manny. The multicolored swirls on his skin shifted from mostly green and yellow to a peach and purple scheme. "It's violent and terrifying and beautiful."

"You're flappin' cracked." Frogface grabbed Manny's left arm and bit into the tricep. Rainbow blood ran down his duckbill lips and chin as he chewed the mouthful of meat. "Thanks, bro."

Manny smiled and nodded. "*De nada, Ranito.*"

"How can you eat at a time like this?" said Guapo.

"I always eat when I'm nervous." Frogface leaned in for another bite. "Oh, is this good." He kept chewing as he talked. "Tastes like chicken marsala."

Guapo watched a flume of steam burst out of the ground twenty yards away. "What the hell." He slung his ultraviolet rifle over his shoulder and headed for Manny. "Save me some a' that."

As usual, I turned up my nose and turned away.

Two weeks later, when Guapo and Frogface were long dead, and I hadn't eaten in over a week, I stopped turning up my nose at Manny.

The jerky, fruit leather, and nutri-paste from my backpack were long gone. I had collapsed from hunger and exhaustion during another of our endless marches under the blazing sun of the Cambio.

Manny held my head in his lap and lowered a finger to my lips. He was smiling, and the sun cast a halo around him.

"Go ahead," he said softly. "It's all right."

I was so weak with hunger and fever that I could barely shake my head. "I...won't."

"Just have a bite," said Manny. "I won't tell anyone. Nobody will know what a flappin' *hipócrita* you are."

I remember thinking at that moment how much I hated myself...first, for smiling at the tutti-frutti bastard's joke, and second, for wanting him.

For wanting more than anything in the universe to eat his flesh.

But what really amazed me was how little I cared when I finally bit into him. When he slid the tip of his index finger between my teeth, and I nipped off one tender bite and chewed.

I remember there were tears in my eyes. The flesh was sweet and soft as lobster, and it tasted faintly of drawn butter and paprika.

He pushed the finger further into my mouth. "Have some more." There was no trace of gloating or sarcasm in his voice, just concern. "I've added meds for the fever."

I nipped at him again, and this time the bite was bigger. It tasted even better than the first, and I closed my eyes as the flavor surged through me.

"More." Manny pushed the finger deeper.

I bit down again and pulled more meat from the bone. Again, the latest bite tasted better than the one before.

"D-does it hurt you?" I swallowed and licked my lips. "When someone...eats you?"

"Yes," said Manny, and then he pressed another finger toward me. "Now have some more."

29

Two weeks before, on my first day in the Cambio with Guapo, Frogface, and Manny, I couldn't imagine that the time would come when I would taste a Ration. I honestly thought I'd let myself die first.

Our quarry seemed to feel the same way. His first target, when he came after us, was not the Ration.

It happened that first night, after we'd made camp. Thanks to the marker beacons planted long ago by explorers of the Cambio, we'd found a *bolsillo sólido*--a solid pocket, a rare area of limited geologic change...compared to the rest of the Cambio, anyway.

We were sitting around the campfire in the *bolsillo*, winding down. As usual, Frogface was nibbling on a hunk of Manny, and Guapo was trying to get a taste of me.

If I'd just given Guapo a little love instead of pushing him away, he might still be alive today. Instead, he stomped off to take a whiz...and it turned out to be the kind of whiz you don't come back from.

My last words to the man who, as much as he annoyed me, I had never been able not to love for long? "Go flap yourself, flap-face."

Two hours later, we found him by flashlight, fifty yards from camp. And fifty-five yards. And seventy-five, seventy-eight, eighty-two, and eighty-six yards.

Guapo had been ripped into little-bitty pieces and scattered all over the landscape. Most of the pieces didn't have much meat left on them, either.

"It was the man-eater," Frogface said in a horrified whisper.

"Ya think so?" Even as I pushed around pieces of Guapo with a stick, recognizing the occasional beauty mark or shred of clothing, I couldn't believe this was all that was left of him. I couldn't believe that such a big, forceful presence was gone from the world.

Most of all, I couldn't believe that none of us had heard a single sound when such a noisy sonofabitch had been torn apart and devoured.

I think Frogface knew he'd be the next to go.

The morning after Guapo's death, Frogface begged me to take him back to the *Puerco*. He was almost in tears when I told him he'd have to walk out himself.

"I'll never make it," he said. "If the *reflejo* doesn't get me, the Cambio will."

I slung Guapo's rifle over my back and nodded in Manny's direction. "I'm sure your little chew toy will watch your back."

Frogface brightened. "That's true." He grinned at Manny. "He's got a gun."

That was when the tutti-frutti bastard surprised me. "No can do, Froggy," he said. "Don't you think Guapo would've wanted us to finish our mission?"

"No," said Frogface, but the look in his eyes told me he knew better. "He'd say the flap with it."

Smiling like always, Manny walked over and stood beside me. "Somebody has to stop the man-eater, right?"

Frogface looked back in the direction of the border, then looked at us. Finally, he sighed and shook his head.

"There oughtta be a fresh trail after last night." He drew a sniffer glove from his belt pouch and pulled the glove onto his hand. "We'll get a bead on that thing for sure."

I glanced over at Manny, who was still standing beside me. To his credit, he didn't say a word...just met my gaze, then broke eye contact.

I, on the other hand, opened my big mouth. "Kiss my *nalgas* all you want, you good-for-nothing flap-head." I spit in the gray sand at his feet. "I still got your number."

Manny just smiled. "Someday," he said, "you'll have to tell me why you love me so much."

Cornucopia pointed a color-swirled finger at my brother, Roto, who sat in the prisoner cage at the front of the courtroom.

"That's him," said Cornucopia. "That's one of the boys who stole me from Señor Gustavo."

I was eight years old, and Roto was twelve. It was the day after we were caught holding Cornucopia the Ration captive in our shack in Barrio Sucio.

The day after Miguel and Oswaldo died from eating the Ration's poisoned flesh.

The prosecutor waved his cigar toward Roto. "What role, if any, did he play in the group that stole you?"

"He was the leader." Cornucopia nodded. "He gave the orders."

"Thank you." The prosecutor ran a hand over his wavy silver hair. "You may step down."

"In the matter of the province of Pesadilla versus Roto Calderon," said the jury foreman, "we find the accused guilty."

"Roto Calderon," said the judge. "I sentence you to ten years of hard labor at the Campo Esclavo maximum security facility. Take him away."

As they led Roto from the courtroom in shackles, I was free to go. Roto had taken all the blame, lied that I'd been trying to stop him...and Cornucopia had backed his story.

Why she did it, I'll never know. Did she feel guilty and think she'd ruined my life enough? Or did she think I would suffer more this way?

Through it all, the sparkly little smile never left her tutti-frutti face. The whole time that she was helping send away the only person I had left in the world now that she'd killed my other brothers, she smiled.

As her owner bit into her shoulder, and I was turned out, starving, into the street, she smiled.

Twenty-four years later, I felt Manny's hand touch my shoulder, and I didn't brush it away.

"That's enough," he said. "Don't keep watching."

But I had to. The man in the video flickering on the wall of the bone-strewn, bone-white cave was Roto. My brother.

And he was a changed man.

We had watched it happen, Manny and I. We had followed the trail of poor, dead Frogface's body parts to the cave, where we had found the video diary. We had switched on the blood-smeared projector and watched the whole horrible story of my brother's transformation, as urgent and immediate as if it were not recorded but happening live right there in front of us.

In the early entries, Roto had been bitter but hopeful. Prison had scarred but not broken him. He had come to the Cambio to live among the *reflejos* and learn their secrets. He had recorded his observations in the video diary and planned to use it as the raw material for a documentary.

In later entries of the diary, Roto had become more and more excited. His frizzy brown puff of hair had bounced as he talked about how he had been hungry all his life, but feeding the *reflejos* had changed all that.

"I was wrong," he had said. "I always thought the most important part of life was to *eat*...but it's more important to *be eaten*."

Shortly after that, Roto had started singing in a language I'd never heard before. He had stopped wearing clothes and had shaved all the hair from his body. Mysterious wounds had appeared on his flesh. He had started crawling around on all fours and making animal noises.

Then, there had been one last coherent entry.

"Must feed others now," Roto had said. "Feed *humans*, not *reflejos*. Become like a *Ration*...but how? I can't feed others my flesh like a Ration."

Roto had paced back and forth in the video, mumbling and striking his forehead with the heels of his hands. Then, he had stopped. "Wait!" His eyes had flared with mad inspiration. "I know what to do! Rations *kill*! I will *kill* like a Ration."

The next time we saw him...

"No more, Lupe." Manny tried to turn me away from the video. "Please."

But I couldn't look away.

Until that moment, I had thought that a man-eating *reflejo* had killed all those people on Polvo. I had thought that a *reflejo* had torn apart Guapo and Frogface and captured Roto.

But a *reflejo* was not to blame.

In the video flickering on the cave wall, Roto used a hunting knife to kill a man. Then, he...

"Don't look, Lupe," said Manny, tugging on my shoulder.

Then, Roto fed pieces of the dead man to another man chained to the floor. The man wailed and spit out the human flesh, but Roto forced in more, and the man started to choke.

"He thinks he's a Ration." My voice was a whisper.

"The *reflejos* did something to him," said Manny. "Or the Cambio changed him. Or both. He lost his mind."

"No!" The voice of my brother, Roto, echoed in the cave. "I *am* a Ration!"

My heart hammered in my chest. Roto's voice was not coming from the video.

All of a sudden, he sprang up in front of me, between the projector and the cave wall. "*Hermaaana*," he said. "You're just in time for *dinner*."

Naked, hairless, and blood-smeared, Roto gaped at me with wild, red eyes. In his left hand, he clutched Frogface's half-eaten arm; I recognized the sniffer glove that Frogface had been wearing when he'd disappeared.

"Luuupe." Roto held out Frogface's arm. "I am a *Ration*. Let me *feed* you."

Video of Roto stuffing more human meat into the choking man's mouth flickered over his body. He smiled at me with blood-stained teeth.

Behind me, I heard Manny cock his rifle.

"Close your eyes, Lupe," he said, and this time I did what he told me.

And then he pulled the trigger.

Here's the thing about the Cambio: more than the land changes here.

Sometimes, people cross the border because they *want* to change. The Cambio is unpredictable, so people have no idea what changes it might bring...but *anything* would be better than the way things are now, right?

Only one thing's for certain: the Cambio will change you. People who walk out might not even be recognizable as the same people who walked in.

Just look at poor Roto. Would he have become a murderous cannibal freak if he'd stayed out of the Cambio?

Then there's Manny and me. What about the changes *we're* going through?

Once again, Manny offers me the last finger he has left, a right thumb. This time, I take it.

Not long ago, it would have grown back, but not anymore. I'll never taste that thumb again, or any part of him that I eat.

He's been this way for a month. One day, he just stopped being able to regenerate. I guess the Cambio screwed him.

The Cambio's screwed us both another way, too. We're lost.

We've been wandering through the shifting landscape ever since we left Roto's cave. Our high tech equipment has been just as useless as our sense of direction.

And it's starting to look like we won't make it out of here alive.

"Have some more." Manny pushes his fingerless left hand at me. "There's still meat in the palm and forearm."

Gently, I touch his arm. I'm so hungry, I could eat everything that's left...but looking at what's left makes me sad.

The tutti-frutti flesh is pitted and gouged from all the bites I've taken. Very little skin remains. In places, I can see clear to the bone.

His right arm is even more damaged. From shoulder to wrist, the meat's all gone, except what I couldn't suck from between the bones.

The rest of him isn't much better. I've been rationing him, trying to make him last, but I've been eating him for a month with him not being able to regenerate. Even losing just a little bit every day for that long will make a man disappear.

"How much longer?" I reach up and stroke his cheek, which is intact. "How much longer can you keep going?"

Manny shrugs. "I won't know until I get there. This has never happened to me before."

"We'll be all right." As I gaze into his eyes, my heart pounds and my stomach growls at the same time. God help me, even as I try to comfort him, I want to eat what's left of him. "Maybe you'll regenerate when we make it out of here."

"Maybe." How can he keep smiling? He's literally full of holes, staggering lost through a parched, shifting wasteland, and he still has a smile on his face. "Either way, I want you to promise me something."

"What?" I trace a swirl of red and yellow as it slowly twists through the sugar-white skin of his forehead. Now that's he's half-eaten and can't regrow, the swirls don't move and change as much as they once did.

"No guilt." Manny reaches up to touch my face, then looks at his fingerless stump and changes his mind. "This is what I was born to do. To feed the hungry."

A tear rolls down my cheek. I make the promise, but I know I won't keep it.

Not unless a miracle can keep us both alive.

"No guilt," says Manny. A whisper is all he can manage.

His head is in my lap. His ears and nose are gone. So are bits of his cheeks and chin.

And still, he is smiling.

"Hold on," I tell him. "Please, Manny." My back is to the sun, to shield him from its blinding rays.

He can barely move. I've made him last almost two more weeks, but I think I've taken one bite too many.

And we're still lost in the Cambio. It's as if this place is a living thing, using its ever-changing terrain to turn us in circles and keep us always from finding our way out.

My stomach growls.

"Go ahead," he says. "Dig in."

I wish I could, because I'm starving...but he's literally down to bare bones. I've left the bare minimum for survival--internal organs, veins and arteries, enough strips of muscle to move--and even that isn't enough to keep him alive anymore.

Whatever I eat next will paralyze him...and what I eat after that will kill him.

"I wish there was something I could do." I stroke his face and try to ignore the signs of my hunger--the heaviness, the aches, the slackness of my muscles.

He has given everything to me. The least I can do is give him what little I have to offer. What comfort I can muster.

"Now I know what it's like," he says.

"What's that?"

"Hunger." Manny nods. "Not being able...to fill the void inside you."

The ground rumbles, and I ignore it. "Rations don't feel hunger?"

"We could...but what we eat...is plentiful." He takes a deep, shaky breath and lets it back out.

It occurs to me that I've never seen a Ration eat. "What is it? What do you eat?"

"Your breath." Manny's eyes meet mine. "The microscopic

airborne life...you breathe out. The organic molecules. The carbon dioxide and water vapor.

"I recycle it. I give it back to you...in a form that will sustain you.

"At least...I used to."

I never knew. "*We* feed *you*?"

He nods. "And we...feed *you*...in return."

I never cared. After Cornucopia...until Manny...I wanted to know as little about Rations as possible. I never knew we were *connected*.

I never knew the feeding worked *both ways*.

Tears run down my emaciated cheeks and off the tip of my chin. "I wish I could still do it," I say. "I wish I could feed you now."

Manny coughs. His head twitches in my lap. "Lupe." His voice grows weaker. "I don't think...I can keep going."

"Just rest," I tell him. "Rest now, darling."

I hear a landslide in the distance. I hear the Cambio groan and creak and crack beneath us.

"You know...what you have to do now," says Manny. "Time...for the feast. *El banquete del muerte*."

I wipe away tears and shake my head. I don't want to listen.

"Eat as much of me...as you can hold. Stuff yourself. What's left...will rot."

"No." How did I come to love him so much? I don't understand. How did I get to this place?

"Do it, Lupe. You need the energy."

"No!" He's right, and I hate him for it. I love him and I hate him for what he's telling me to do.

"It's my last request." His smile is fading. The tutti-frutti swirls have stopped moving. "Don't let me...go to waste."

That's when I do it.

I'm in a daze. I hardly realize that I'm pushing my index finger toward his mouth. Toward his half-eaten lips.

"Lupe, no." His whisper trails off, and he closes his eyes.

When the tip of my finger touches his lower lip, I stop. I know what a futile gesture I am making, but I also know it doesn't matter that I make it. No one will know but him, and he will understand.

So I push onward.

My fingertip passes between his lips. I feel the ridges of his teeth scrape the skin.

I push the finger in past the first knuckle, and then I tell him to eat. "I love you." I want him to live, and I wish with all my heart

The Cambio jumps. A new geyser hisses to life.

I wish with all my heart that I could bring him back. At least I want him to know that I would do this for him, I would do it if I could.

Far away, there is a thunderclap. The bubbling of lava.

"Please, Manny." I hold his chin with my free hand and push it up, as if that will make him take a bite. His teeth press into the flesh of my finger.

The ground beneath us trembles and rises. We ride the newborn mesa toward the sky.

Suddenly, Manny's teeth clench.

I start to cry out as he bites into my fingertip...and then I catch myself. "Good, Manny." He bites down with surprising force, and I shut my eyes against the pain. "Take what you need."

I feel him nip the meat from the bone. This is it, I realize.

This is how he feels.

I slide out my finger, the tip ragged and red. I suck away the oozing blood, which tastes strangely sweet, like vanilla.

And Manny chews.

When I lower the finger from my lips, it has stopped bleeding. The tiny wound is no longer red at all, in fact. It is pink and smooth.

And as I watch...

"Lupe?" His voice is a whisper, but no weaker than before.

As I watch, the smooth, pink flesh rises like bread dough. Tiny grooves etch the surface, perfectly matching the surrounding fingerprint.

The finger heals. Right before my eyes, it heals.

Within seconds, I can't tell where the edges of the wound once were.

Something has happened to me. I am only beginning to understand.

One thing's for certain: the Cambio will change you.

"Lupe?" Manny's eyes flutter open. His smile dimly flickers back into view. "What did you...give me?"

I push the same finger toward his lips. Warmth and light surge through my body, filling my belly, my chest, my throat.

My heart.

Tears of joy pour down my face like spring rain. They taste like wine. "Eat up, my love," I tell him. "There's more where that came from."

THE 1970S MUST DIE!

No sooner had Agent Lyssa Bonne Nuit darted through the hail of dial telephones and cheese whiz than her chrono-bike raced into a blizzard of Saturday Morning Cartoons.

Instantly, the lilac-skinned woman in the black carbon mesh jumpsuit was engulfed in churning waves of bright primary colors and limited animation. Images of snickering dogs, teenagers, and superheroes moved stiffly around her as she worked the bike's controls with all six hands, fighting to catch up with her quarry... and the treasure she'd chased halfway across the time-realm of When, all the way from the Everarium.

Suddenly, the giant image of a singing cartoon duck and rabbit appeared in front of Lyssa, jarring her attention...but she didn't slow down. The duck's orange bill seemed to swallow her whole as she squeezed the accelerator and bolted through it.

Zipping out the other side, she saw the burst of speed had been worth it. Pyre Ransom, the object of Lyssa's pursuit, was up ahead, hurtling through a rippling curtain of colorful characters—everything from cartoon bears to cavemen to cats and mice.

Pyre zoomed through it without ever looking back. The fugitive —a gold-skinned female android—was focused only on getting away with her prize: the decade dubbed the 1970s by the extinct species known as humanity.

Agent Lyssa was determined to take that prize away from her at any cost. Its containment cartridge was steadily leaking Saturday Morning Cartoons and other sociocultural flotsam from the 70s, causing havoc in the skies and streets of When.

One more burst of speed, and Lyssa tore through the last rippling curtain of cartoon characters in Pyre's wake. This time, she emerged in a storm of streakers—images of naked human beings sprinting through the silvery mist, body parts bouncing wildly with each loping step. Every one of them was grinning, an expression Lyssa had come to associate with human joy or pleasure...though she had never met a human and never would.

Because every human being had died out ages ago.

The human race lived on only as echoes in the Yesterplex of the Timekeepers—hyper-rez snapshots of life on ancient planet Earth captured at intervals throughout human history. These flawless log files recorded every detail of entire decades on compact cartridges like the one in Pyre's pack.

These decade backups—known as decalogs—were stored in the vaults of the Everarium, a repository considered impenetrable until Pyre's daring heist. Decalogs were priceless beyond all words, especially in the case of a species like humanity that no longer existed.

As the streakers bounded past with organs flopping, Lyssa fought to stay on track. She lost sight of Pyre up ahead because the gaggle was so dense—also because she was distracted by seeing so many life-size humans in one place. Over the years, Lyssa had studied humans at length and formed a special bond with their long-gone species. They had something in common, something she connected with on a very deep level.

As a final surge of virtual streakers poured past, meaty bodies jiggling, Lyssa saw she had a clear shot at Pyre, who was less than fifty meters away.

Yanking the Was-Gun from the holster strapped around her thorax, Lyssa pointed it at her golden target. Quickly taking aim, she squeezed the trigger, unleashing the weapon's payload.

The barrel of the gun disgorged a deadly Past-Blast—a roiling mass of temporal detritus sucked from multiple eras of a chosen species' history. As always, Lyssa's own sidearm was set to tap the past of humankind, the object of her greatest fascination.

The ejected mass hurtled through the mist, a cyclone of ancient Roman swords, World War II machine guns, furiously kick-stomping boots, and exploding Molotov cocktails. The mass was moving so fast, it looked as if it would consume Pyre's bike at any second.

Before that could happen, though, Pyre dove from its path and swooped away. The Past-Blast spun harmlessly off through the mist, its howling/booming/clanging growing fainter with each passing second.

Cursing, Lyssa dove after Pyre, pouring on as much speed as she could. Still staying out of reach, Pyre dropped into a bank of crimson clouds, kicking up bright red wisps in her wake.

Only when Lyssa plunged through those same clouds and burst out the other side did she realize where the thief was headed.

"Oh no." The violet antennae and feathery pink cilia on her head flickered madly. "She's heading for the *Yesterplex!*"

When you lived and worked in When, as Lyssa did, the past, present, and future blurred together. Memories, current experience, and premonitions intermingled, because When existed outside normal spacetime.

It was a phenomenon you had to learn to block or at least manage if you wanted to live anything like a normal life...but there were some things you could never narrow down to present sight alone. Some things were so filled with power and importance, they *forced* you to see them from all time angles. They *intruded*, they *insisted*, they *expanded*.

Which was exactly how the Yesterplex was to Lyssa. Gazing down at its lofty silver spire in the present day, she also remembered the first time she'd seen it, the first time she'd come to When as a child.

Welcome to the place that is both of and beyond all time. Those had been the words of Skulk, the red-scaled spider-thing who had brought her here from her home planet of Hinjeri VII. *It is here you will be cared for and learn to care for all the ages in turn.*

The whole time Skulk had talked, Lyssa had simply stared at that giant spire jutting skyward, a tower that had seemed to her to symbolize the end of everything she'd known.

Her parents had been so proud when she'd been chosen to study at the Yesterplex to become a Timekeeper. Lyssa had been so excited when Skulk had come to Hinjeri VII to get her...but it hadn't lasted. Near the end of the journey to When, terrible news had come in over the radio; Lyssa had learned her entire world had been destroyed by a catastrophe. That was when her excitement had turned to anguish, her hope to fear, her dreams to nightmares.

Because, for the rest of her life, she'd be known as the last survivor of her extinct species, the Hinj.

These are the halls of the Yesterplex, she remembered Skulk saying, pointing at the vast figure eight structure sprawling around the base of the silver spire. *The Timekeepers dwell within, preserving yesterday, today, and tomorrow.*

Years later, Lyssa had become a Timekeeper herself. She had poured herself into it, giving it everything she had to make up for what she'd lost. She had never regretted it, either—except when she'd discovered the limits of her commission. Except when she'd discovered the true depths of hopelessness into which she could fall.

When Lyssa touched down at the base of the great silver spire, she saw Pyre's chrono-bike discarded on the golden pavement there. Pyre herself was nowhere to be seen...but the route she'd taken was obvious.

The ground-level doors to the Yesterplex gaped nearby, blown open by something that had left scorch marks and shattered glass in its wake. The bodies of dozens of armed and armored Timekeepers lay all around it, unmoving—victims of the golden-skinned android's great strength, blinding speed, and arsenal of weapons. The security here had been no better able to resist her than that of the great repository of the Everarium.

Leaping from her bike, Lyssa hurried forward, stopping only to check the pulse of one of the Timekeeper guards. He was unconscious, not dead, which was a relief—but she knew she didn't have time to check all the rest. Her most important task right now was catching up to Pyre, then finding out—and stopping—whatever it was she intended to do next.

The nature of Pyre's plans was still a mystery to her, though. All Lyssa knew for sure was it was no accident that Pyre had gone straight to the Yesterplex after stealing the 70s decalog from the Everarium.

Drawing four sidearms, Lyssa charged inside the building, right into the aftermath of another battle. Dozens more Timekeepers were scattered across the floor of the vast lobby, every one of them battered, still, and silent.

Red emergency lights flashed, and sirens shrieked at deafening levels. Though Lyssa knew there were many more Timekeepers in the complex, they hadn't arrived yet to pick up where their defeated comrades had left off in stopping the intruder.

Lyssa wasn't about to wait for them. Guns at the ready, she ran into the central corridor dead ahead, dodging the bodies of guards that were strewn underfoot.

As she raced down the gleaming central corridor, Lyssa tapped a lump on one wrist and called up a virtual status map to guide her. The blinking red blip that represented Pyre was only a few turns ahead and registered as stationary, holding position at least for the moment. Maybe she'd finally been cornered by Timekeeper security?

Heart pounding, Lyssa raced toward her target, resolving to fulfill her two-part orders from Timekeeper Command: to stop Pyre from attaining whatever goal she had in mind and to retrieve the decalog intact.

The second part could prove to be tricky, as the decalog cartridge was already damaged and leaking flotsam. Yet again, as she closed in on Pyre, bits of the 1970s sailed around her. Cans of Billy Beer pelted past like they'd been shot from a cannon, then Richard Nixon heads and platform shoes with towering heels.

As she rounded the final corner, fingers twitching against the triggers of her Was-Guns, the image of a platoon of Viet Cong soldiers, all in black, came howling toward her, firing away with Kalashnikov rifles. The troops were just temporal backwash, a trick of the light, but they startled her, and she hesitated.

That was just enough time for Pyre to unload a blast from her Was-Gun. A howling cyclonic bolus of barbarian axes, rabid wolves, berserker warriors, and laser-equipped airborne drones came spinning after the Viet Cong, punching straight toward Lyssa.

As that raging plume of death bore toward her, Lyssa felt again the sense of doom and horror she had known on the day her species had died…and the day they'd died a *second* time, all because of her.

As a child and then a young woman, Lyssa had been fascinated by the decalog repository of the Everarium.

You see before you the archived eras of every sentient species in the galaxy, alive or dead. On Lyssa's first visit there, Skulk had swept one bristly black leg from side to side to encompass a seemingly endless vault with all its sky-high ranks of crystalline drawers. *The past and present of intelligent life is preserved here for all posterity.*

Even my own people? little Lyssa had asked. *Even the Hinji of Hinjeri VII?*

Of course. Skulk had skittered to an access kiosk and typed on a keyboard there. A virtual image of Lyssa's home planet had spun to life above the kiosk, then zoomed in to show the long-dead populace going about their daily business. *As long as this recording exists, their legacy will survive.*

Another day, Skulk had shown her around the Yesterplex, introducing her to the multitude of sophisticated devices there—like the Chrono-Rebooter, which could restore a decade from a decalog backup if the timestream for an era became corrupted.

This powerful instrument can undo the damage of warped or ruined time by rebooting an archived era from the Everarium, Skulk had explained. *Yet it can only be handled by the most experienced of Timekeepers in the most delicate of ways. To do otherwise risks a chain reaction that could ravage all eternity.*

Lyssa had nodded with an expression of full understanding, but all she'd really heard was the part about rebooting an era from the Everarium.

Starting that day, she'd worked out a plan, always keeping it to herself. If she'd said a word to Skulk, she'd been sure the great spider would have turned her in to the Timekeeper authorities.

But months later, Lyssa had found herself wishing that Skulk had known about the plan after all. Maybe then, someone would have stopped her from "borrowing" a few key decades of Hinji history from the Everarium, then sneaking them into the Yesterplex. Maybe she wouldn't have used the Chrono-Rebooter to try to reboot Hinji history into the spacetime continuum and restart her dead species.

Maybe then, Lyssa wouldn't have made a drastic miscalculation that destroyed the stolen decalogs, wiping out decades' worth of backups that could never be recovered.

And a chunk of Hinji history would not have been forever erased and all hope of resurrecting her people as she'd known them extinguished because of something she had done.

Six arms whirling, Lyssa battled her way through the Past-Blast from Pyre's Was-Gun, repelling every axe-hack, wolf bite, laser blast, and sword slash with speed and grace.

By the time she was done, the blast components were scattered and defused, bleeding out on the floor or skidding along the walls or ceiling. Tossing away an axe she'd seized, she spun to face Pyre, only to find she was long gone by then.

Cursing, Lyssa pulled up the virtual map and broke into a run. According to the map, Pyre was already deep in the tunnels leading to the core of the Yesterplex.

Knowing Pyre was heading for the core was enough to make Lyssa run faster. She could only imagine the kind of damage someone like Pyre could do in there with a loaded decalog in her possession.

Pyre certainly knew her way around the Yesterplex and its array of instrumentation. A former Timekeeper, she'd gone rogue for reasons unknown, putting her skills to use in breaking into the Ever-arium, stealing the 70s human decalog, and bringing it here.

Rounding one bend after another in pursuit of her quarry, Lyssa kept four Was-Gun pistols in hand and ready to fire. She kept her antennae and cilia focused ahead, probing the air for any scent, vibration, or chemical reaction that might signal danger.

But when the danger finally came, she wasn't ready for it.

Racing into an open intersection centered on a statue of Hojo Cahoot—founder of the Yesterplex and Timekeepers—Lyssa was struck by a sudden wave of future sight. She foremembered a distant tomorrow in which the spot where she now stood was a barren plain with the smoking rubble of the Yesterplex scattered across it.

Stunned, she staggered to a stop, overwhelmed by the smell of death and the shrieks of the dying all around her. Carrion birds wheeled overhead, their great wings beating, and scavenger vermin scampered among the corpses.

Would *this* be the result of whatever grand plan Pyre had in mind? Would the destruction of the Yesterplex and the slaughter of the Timekeepers be her masterstroke?

Suddenly, Lyssa heard a familiar voice from somewhere nearby, begging for death. Even before she turned to see the source, she recognized it all too well.

She recognized it as *her* voice…and in that instant, she knew the forememory was false.

Pinching her eyes shut, she shook off the vision. Trained agent that she was, she knew a fake when she saw one and how to fend it off. Future memories were always experienced through your own senses, from your future self's point of view. If, when experiencing a foremembrance, you heard your voice as part of the mix, but you weren't actually doing the talking, it was never the real thing.

It was nothing but an *aftermine* in action, a device that generated false visions of the future.

Opening her eyes, she saw the nightmare future was gone. Looking further, she saw a mirrored sphere, no more than four inches in diameter, tucked between the webbed feet of the statue of Hojo Cahoot.

Sprinting forward, she crushed the aftermine sphere with the heel of her boot, smashing it to tiny pieces. Then, hoping she hadn't been too long delayed, she bolted down the corridor that led to the core.

As Lyssa charged into the core—the cavernous central chamber underneath the spire of the Yesterplex—she came upon another dozen unconscious Timekeepers on the floor. Apparently, they'd made a last stand against Pyre…and failed to stop her.

Beyond the bodies sprawled concentric rings of alabaster white partitions and alcoves—the mazelike command complex of the core. Searching those convoluted warrens for Pyre could take hours…if not for the very clear sign of her exact location that Lyssa instantly spotted.

A giant yellow circle rose like a sun near the middle of the core, its massive face marked with a simple smile in thick, black strokes.

Student of humanity that she was, Lyssa instantly recognized the classic smiley face symbol of the 1970s.

Weaving through the command complex, she no longer needed to watch Pyre's blip on the virtual map. The place was like a maze, but the enormous smiley face was easy to follow.

Lyssa braced herself as she closed in, expecting another trap or trick. Her last few turns were uneventful, though, and she reached the open plaza at the middle of the core without incident.

At the plaza's center, a massive machine hung from above, a silver-plated cone extending high into the cavity within the Yester-plex's spire. The cone was covered in twinkling, multicolored lights and tapered to a fine point ending a meter or so from the floor. Standing there, operating a virtual control console encircling the cone's tip, was Pyre Ransom herself.

Seeing her there like that sent a shiver through Lyssa's body. She knew that machine well—*too* well—from past experience.

Pyre was using the very same Chrono-Rebooter that Lyssa had used to accidentally gut the recorded history of her people so many years ago.

Lyssa slowly approached, but Pyre didn't look up from her work. Her golden fingers flickered over the virtual controls, causing changes in the patterns of blinking lights on the conelike device.

When Lyssa was ten meters away, however, Pyre told her not to come any closer. "I'll put you down, I swear," she said calmly.

Lyssa stopped and lowered her guns. "So you like humanity's 1970s period too, huh?"

As she said it, red, white, and blue streamers and fireworks exploded in midair above them, residue of the United States of America's Bicentennial celebration in 1976.

"Sure," Pyre said without looking up. "Just not in the way you think."

Lyssa knew she should take a shot at gunning her down; the

potential danger of letting her keep working on the Rebooter was high. But part of her was holding back until she understood better what Pyre's plan was. "So are you going to try bringing them back? The 1970s of humankind?"

"Maybe you should mind your own business." Pyre's fingers flew through a complex sequence of controls, and all the lights on the Chrono-Rebooter ignited at once.

"Are you sure you don't want any help?" asked Lyssa.

"*You* wouldn't be much help. You lost your user rights to this thing *ages* ago."

Lyssa scowled. Pyre was right; the Timekeepers had permanently revoked her rights to use the Rebooter after the Hinj incident. It was the one piece of equipment in the entire Yesterplex that she wasn't allowed to use.

"Pretty sure *you're* not supposed to have user rights, either," said Lyssa. "The Timekeepers deprovisioned you from all systems as soon as you quit the corps."

"True," said Pyre, "but I was smart enough to buy an access hack from an unscrupulous insider."

"Good for you."

Suddenly, Pyre reached into her pocket, and Lyssa tensed. Pyre drew out a cylindrical cartridge the length of a cigar, made of a clear material and churning inside with red, yellow, and green mist.

Lyssa knew instantly what it was, what it had to be—the 1970s decalog—and she guessed Pyre was ready to deploy it.

Leaping into action, she charged Pyre. Shooting would have been too risky; she didn't want another destroyed decade on her conscience, especially from the history of humanity.

As Lyssa sprang, Pyre whipped out her Was-Gun. She got off one shot, but it was wild, and Lyssa put hands on her before she could fire another...*five* hands, to be exact.

Her sixth hand landed on Pyre's hand that was wrapped around the 70s decalog. Maybe she squeezed too hard, though, or the shock of the impact triggered a reflexive contraction of Pyre's grip.

Because as soon as Lyssa made contact with the cartridge, a blinding white light flared, and she was gone.

Lyssa blinked away the white light and the black spots it had left raging in her eyes. Little by little, her vision cleared, and she was able to make out the details of her surroundings.

It was then she realized she wasn't inside the Yesterplex anymore. She was somewhere different, somewhere unfamiliar, somewhere...

Grander.

She stood on a hilltop, gazing out at a valley below. The valley was filled with trees, a carpet of emerald rippling in the warm breeze of a sunny summer day.

What interested Lyssa the most, though, were the occupants of the skies overhead. Massive crystal spheres hung high above the valley, glittering in the midday sun. Through the skin of these colossal objects, Lyssa could see the dance of light and movement that signified life—sentient life capable of building such grand structures and miraculously keeping them aloft.

"Spectacular, aren't they?"

At the sound of Pyre's voice, Lyssa jerked her head around to see the android standing behind her.

"The cities of paradise, circa 1975," said Pyre, smiling serenely. "Each one full of people living to their maximum potential."

Lyssa scowled. Her instinct was to grab and restrain Pyre, but she held herself back...for the moment, at least. "Where *exactly* is this? Where are we?"

"Inside the 1970s decalog," explained Pyre. "Our *minds* only. Think of it as a peek inside the cartridge I stole."

"The 1970s *where?*" asked Lyssa. "Because it sure isn't the *Earth* of *humanity*."

"Oh, but it is." Pyre chuckled and stepped away, moving forward on the hilltop. "I assure you, it very much *is.*"

Just then, a low-flying aircraft buzzed the hill, and Lyssa ducked. The craft zoomed away without making a sound, its oval fuselage tipped with a long, pointed nose like a needle. Vents on its backside glowed bright blue and shimmered with what looked like heat ripples.

"That is *not* a human-built aircraft from 1970s Earth." Lyssa stared at other ships in the distance, zipping around and between the crystalline spheres. "*None* of them are."

"*All* of them are." Pyre spread her arms wide to take it all in. "Every last one of them."

Lyssa frowned, struggling to understand. Airborne craft of many shapes and sizes swooped and darted among the spheres, threading from one to the next across the busy blue sky. Little satellites revolved around the spheres as well, often narrowly avoiding collisions with each other, with aircraft, with birds...and with human beings engaged in unaided flight.

Humans flew in and out of the spheres with grace, banking and looping and soaring as if they'd been born to it. As far as Lyssa could see, there were no signs of jetpacks or antigravity tech anywhere on them.

Lyssa was amazed...then annoyed. "This is some kind of elaborate illusion. You've trapped me in a multisensory deepfake."

"But I haven't," Pyre said calmly. "This is recorded reality from Earth in the 1970s...the 1970s *as they were meant to be.*"

Lyssa's frown deepened. "Enough of this. End the simulation."

"It's no simulation," said Pyre.

Lyssa grabbed Pyre's gold-skinned arm. "You can't *save* yourself with *trickery.* You are going to *pay* for your *crimes.*"

"Haven't you ever wondered?" Pyre shook off Lyssa's grip and sat down on the grassy peak. "Haven't you wondered why humanity died out so soon? Why things went downhill so fast for such a promising species?"

It was indeed a question Lyssa had asked herself many times, though she wouldn't give Pyre the satisfaction of knowing that. "Species die out. There isn't always a sensible explanation."

"But there is this time."

"What do *you* know about them?" snapped Lyssa.

"Everything." Pyre looked up at her with a grim smile. "Humans *made* me."

Lyssa gaped at her, surprised.

"Human built me, and those like me, to outlive them," said Pyre, "and I have. And now I will correct an injustice that was visited upon them millennia ago...because I can.

"Because all I need to do is replace the 1970s as they happened with the *rightful* 1970s...whatever the cost may be. *"*

Lyssa well remembered when she'd first discovered the human race of planet Earth.

As a young trainee Timekeeper in the Everarium (before her ill-fated attempt to resurrect the Hinji), she'd been obsessed with viewing the decalogs of extinct sentient species. She'd made the most of her access to the archives, poring over preserved eras of vanished species for hour upon hour at the expense of her trainee assignments.

So many extinct species had been so much like her own, their tragic stories brimming with lost potential. She'd been fascinated by the multitudes of unsolved mysteries associated with them, the many unknowns left behind in their wakes.

But no species had captured her imagination quite as much as humanity. No species had been so colorful, passionate, and unbridled or had touched her so profoundly with their arts and struggles.

No other species had made her think, if she had to be something other than Hinji, that she would choose to join their ranks.

And no human era had spoken to her so clearly as the 1970s. The thrilling music, flashy fashion, and larger-than-life celebrities had excited her. The search for meaning in an off-kilter world was much like her own search for identity in the realm of When.

The 70s had been such a big deal to Lyssa that they had figured prominently in her own rogue scheme with the Chrono-Rebooter. Originally, she'd planned to bring back humanity after raising the Hinji...and she'd known all along, if she'd gotten that far, that she would have started with the 70s.

It was an obsession she had never grown out of. It was why she had pursued Pyre with such determination when other Timekeepers had fallen by the wayside. It was why she'd come so far and fought so hard.

And it was why now, instead of taking swift action to do her duty upon getting an inkling of Pyre's true intentions, she listened to what the android was saying.

A light breeze wafted over the peak as Lyssa sat cross-legged beside Pyre. Paradise went on around them, its wonders amazing to behold…but Lyssa found her gaze locked on the android's, attached as if by magnets.

"How can there be a *rightful* 1970s?" asked Lyssa. "How can there be anything but history as we know it?"

"Long ago, history was sabotaged," said Pyre. "By those who feared humanity would *surpass* or *destroy* them. A decade was removed from human history, the decade of humankind's greatest renaissance, the ascendance that should have come on the heels of the age of idealism and creativity in the 1960s."

"The 70s were removed?" Only among Timekeepers of When would such a question be asked so matter-of-factly.

Pyre nodded. "And replaced with a very different decade in which a renaissance never happened. An era of selfishness and silly obsessions, a time of conflict and crisis and drift. A flawed decade that gave rise to the forces that robbed humanity of its golden age and accelerated a doom that should never have come."

"That's not true!" snapped Lyssa. She hated hearing her precious 70s denigrated like that. "The 70s may not have been perfect, but *no* decade ever is."

"They weren't what they *could* have been," said Pyre. "What they *should* have been."

Lyssa felt the urge to punch her in the face. "According to whom?"

"According to the one person who *lived through* the original version, came to When before the timeline changed, and still survives to *this day.*" Pyre tapped her chest with an index finger. "According to *me.*"

Lyssa felt her anger draining away. She gazed at Pyre as if seeing her for the first time.

Now she knew—if Pyre was telling the truth—how she could be so certain that an alternate 1970s had replaced an original version populated by an enlightened humanity. Now she knew—again, if Pyre wasn't lying—how the promising human species had died out so prematurely.

It was all thanks to the Timekeepers and their technological wonders.

Still, Lyssa had trouble wrapping her head around it all. "But the Timekeepers are sworn not to tamper with the timelines. It's our greatest oath."

"Certain circumstances may supersede that oath," said Pyre. "Such as whispers of the threat one species may present if allowed to reach full bloom. The *status quo* must *always* be preserved." Pyre grinned and held out her hand, where the mist-filled cylinder of the decalog cartridge remained—or at least a mental manifestation of it. "Unless someone is stupid enough to keep a *backup* copy of the overwritten *original.*"

Lyssa frowned. "But I thought the stolen decalog was from the *accepted* 1970s. The whole time I chased you, it was leaking smiley faces, streakers, Viet Cong soldiers—all sorts of 70s odds and ends."

Pyre shook her head. "That was all virtual trickery, projected by me to hide the true nature of my mission." She pressed her chin, opened her mouth, and the image of a 70s game show host with shaggy brown hair, a long microphone, and a powder blue leisure suit with white buck shoes appeared in midair between them. When

Pyre closed her mouth, the image disappeared. "The decalog only ever contained the essence of the *rightful* human 70s."

"Which you want to use for a reboot?"

"To overwrite the replacement 70s, yes." When Pyre smiled, her bright red eyes sparkled. "Make the golden age a reality again as it was meant to be. Give humanity a second chance to overcome its premature extinction."

Lyssa's antennae twitched with strong emotion. What Pyre was saying—she didn't hate the idea. But there were issues the android hadn't mentioned yet.

"If you do this—it'll change more than *human* history, won't it?" asked Lyssa. "Assuming humanity is reborn, the ripple effects will affect everyone the resurrected human species comes in contact with. Will the Chrono-Rebooter even let that happen?"

"I believe so," said Pyre. "With the right *minds* injected into the mix to guide the process." She grinned. "Say, a human-built synthetic who can interface with the rebooter's A.I. and a female organic who can convince it that rules are made to be broken."

Lyssa's eyes widened. Pyre was talking about *her*.

For a long moment, Lyssa just stared at Pyre, wondering if this was what they'd been moving toward all along.

Did Pyre know how she felt about humanity? Was it possible the android had been pulling her in this direction from the start, for just this purpose?

Either way, a proposition had been made that could change everything—a proposition with an extremely uncertain outcome— yet Lyssa found she could not dismiss it out of hand.

"I still don't understand what makes you think I can help," she said.

"Using my own computerized mind, I have calculated that the rebooter's A.I. will more likely respond favorably when interfacing with someone like you," said Pyre. "Someone who knows what it's like when you don't *have* a chance to bring back the people you've lost. Someone who understands from first-hand experience that the *absence* of those who matter can send out just as many ripples as their *presence* can.

"Someone who once used that very rebooter to try to bring someone else back—and now wants to give both of them a chance to make up for that failure."

"I see." Lyssa was surprised at how sensible it all sounded, though one question kept nagging at her. "So how do I know you're not lying?"

Pyre frowned. "About what?"

"About everything," said Lyssa. "How do I know that any of this is the truth?"

"Because of all this, of course." Pyre gestured at the scene stretched out before them—the great glittering crystalline spheres hovering over the emerald forest.

"Which could be nothing but an illusion," said Lyssa.

"But listen." Pyre leaned toward her, one golden index finger raised instructively. "Can you take the chance that's all it is? If I'm right—which I am—but you let me fail, can you bear it? Can you live with yourself, knowing you could have brought back humanity but didn't?"

Lyssa didn't answer. Pyre's story was strangely persuasive, appealing to her longtime love of humanity and her desire to resurrect that species—but part of her held fast, refusing to be convinced of anything by the fugitive thief. No Timekeeper worth her salt would fall for a line of bullshit like the one she was hearing, and she knew it.

At least that was how she felt before the next question Pyre asked.

"Also, can you live with yourself if this is all true, and you let it fail...knowing success could have led to more than one change?" Pyre folded her hands together, her fingers interwoven. "What if humanity's destiny is connected to *another* destiny that is not at first obvious?"

"Another destiny?"

Pyre shrugged. "Who's to say that bringing humanity back won't bring back someone else?"

Lyssa's heart pounded as she considered the implications. Her doubts and fears began to melt away.

"Do you…do you know this for a fact?" she asked. "That someone else could be restored by such a change?"

"I do not know it for a fact," said Pyre. "But can you bear to take the chance that it won't happen?"

Lyssa turned away, thinking and watching the view of paradise. Multicolored beams of lights blazed from the city-spheres, splashing over the emerald forest and sapphire sky. Music like wind chimes and whalesong played from speakers unseen, echoing in the distance.

It was beautiful. Was it worth leaping into the unknown for, though? Solely on its own merits? She couldn't seem to make that argument to herself.

But that last thing that Pyre had said, she could not ignore. It kept running through her mind, again and again.

Can you bear to take the chance that it won't happen?

"If we do this, what will happen to us?" she asked suddenly. "After it's all over, whatever the outcome…what happens to us?"

Pyre shrugged and reached out with the decalog cartridge in her hand. "Does it matter? Will it change your answer?"

Just like that, Lyssa realized she had made up her mind. It was not lost on her that it was the most impulsive decision she had made since trying to reboot the history of the Hinji three decades ago. "No." Smiling, she folded all six of her hands around the cartridge in Pyre's grip. "No, it won't."

Then, she felt Pyre squeeze tightly, crushing the cartridge, and the glorious vision of the rightful 1970s dissolved in whirling clouds of phosphorescent vapor.

Elsewhere, Elsewhen:

Silver and sleek, the star-skiff full of humans swooped into the atmosphere of the pink-and-purple planet. Gleaming in the light of the planet's triple suns, the little craft swooped gracefully toward the surface, approaching the celebration of a momentous occasion.

"This is the Earth skiff *Impresario.*" The little craft was just as lovely on the inside, its bright cockpit fitted with silver consoles studded with blinking, multicolored controls. The pilot, Murphy—a willowy woman with short red hair and a pale blue uniform with silver piping—spoke into a mic that floated in front of her lush red lips. "Requesting permission to land."

"Only if that *admiral* of yours isn't aboard!" the man on the other end of the call said teasingly. "Though Todd Chamberlain's so *old* and *frail* these days, I'll bet he had to stay in orbit on the *mothership* and take his *nap!*"

Grinning, the gray-haired man in a navy blue uniform who shared the cockpit with Murphy leaned over from the co-pilot's seat to speak into the mic. "You think I'd miss out on *today?* Forget it, Mr. President!"

The man on the line chuckled. "It's only our five-hundred-year anniversary, Todd! No need for a big man like yourself to come down off your high horse and mingle with us *little people.*"

"I wouldn't miss it for anything, President Prine," said Admiral Chamberlain, who looked middle-aged though he was much, much older. "Any chance to rub your nose in what I did for you, I'll *jump* at it."

"*You?* It was all *you*, now?" Prine said with mock outrage.

"Who's gonna say any different?" asked Chamberlain.

"Have you forgotten my people can live to be a thousand years old?" said Prine. "You *humans* are lucky to live *half* that!"

"Whatever." Chamberlain winked at Murphy. "You people have a funny way of acting grateful, don't you?"

"We won't kiss your asses, if that's what you mean." Prine laughed. "But come on down anyway if you like. We won't stop you."

With that, the communication ended.

And Chamberlain and Murphy howled with laughter.

"What a character!" said Murphy.

"I love that guy!" Chamberlain slapped his knee. "He's just as hilarious as he was 500 years ago when we saved his goddamn planet!"

Later, after the skiff had landed and the ceremonies had begun, Chamberlain marched solemnly over the purple ground of the planet, flanked by several human dignitaries in their best formal attire. Up ahead, a dais waited, adorned with pink, violet, and lilac colored flowers.

Flickering video panels hung in midair, replaying scenes from the historic events of half a millennium ago. On one, Chamberlain saw his old vessel, the Earthship *Intensity*, descending to the surface for the first time. On the next panel over, Chamberlain's science team worked with an array of elaborate equipment on the planet's surface, confirming the ominous readings they had first detected from orbit.

On the next panel, Chamberlain and his crew made one of the least auspicious first contacts ever with the local inhabitants, informing them of their findings. *Hi, nice to meet you! By the way, your world is about to explode.*

Then, on the final panel, the humans and locals were working side by side, constructing a gargantuan device that would stop the explosion and save the world. All thanks to the high-tech ingenuity and altruism that had thrived on Earth since the start of humanity's golden age in the 1970s, two thousand years ago.

Chamberlain felt a surge of pride and nostalgia as he approached the dais where the leading lights of the planet waited to mark the great occasion. Before he could set one foot on the dais, however, his old friend, President Prine, ran forward.

And threw his six purple arms around him in a bear hug.

"It is so *good* to see you, my friend!" Prine leaned back, his beaded violet antennae bobbing with pure joy. The feathery pink cilia on his purple head and neck fluttered and danced as he beamed. "You have been away from Hinjeri VII and the Hinji people for far too long!"

"Tell me about it!" Tears rolled down Chamberlain's cheeks. People were watching—whole planets of them, via the media—and he didn't give a damn.

"Thank you again, my friend," said Prine. "If not for you, this place would not exist. None of us would."

"I've always had a feeling," said Chamberlain, reveling in the embrace of his Hinji friend as the galaxy looked on. "I've always had a feeling that somehow, it works both ways."

COCK-A-DOODLE-DIE

Shad Lum Lugo the meemee exterminator strutted across the paved lot, feeling the bright morning sun as it heated his feathers. He was glad to be alive, and he crowed about it again, though he'd already crowed at dawn as he did every day. Life, oh life was so *good*.

Then, suddenly, two meemees ran out of the brush in front of him, and he reared back, scrambling to aim his pistol at them.

The meemees were barely two feet tall, covered in fur (one black, one blond), and bipedal. It was the only thing they seemed to have in common with Shad's people, the Ch'Kaw--getting around on two legs.

Otherwise, the meemees didn't measure up. The Ch'Kaw were ten feet tall, immeasurably smarter, covered with beautiful plumage, and the dominant species of planet Earth.

So why were the damned meemees so hard to *kill*?

They were fast on their feet, for one thing. Even as Shad swung his pistol around, they scurried further away, heading for the back of The Coop restaurant. A few more steps, and the pistol would be useless; Shad couldn't open fire if there was a chance of hitting a worker inside the place.

So he took a chance and threw two shots at the fleeing meemees. Neither bullet hit its mark.

Then the meemees reached the restaurant and flung themselves into a tiny hole at the base of the wall. Shad had never noticed it before--but of course the damned meemees went straight for it.

Crowing with rage, Shad threw open the back door and charged into the building. From experience, he knew where the meemees would go, so he made a beeline for the kitchen.

Sure enough, they were up on a counter, heads submerged in a bowl of corn flour. As soon as he rushed in, they both looked up, furry faces dusted with pale yellow flour--then sprinted away, grabbing handfuls of corn biscuit crumbs from a tray en route.

"Vermin!" Shad didn't dare shoot up the kitchen, so he grabbed a metal skillet with one claw and heaved it at the meemees.

The creatures dove off the counter and landed on their feet on the blue-tiled floor. The skillet clanged off the counter and bounced down after them, but they were already racing away by then.

"I'll peck you to shreds!" howled Shad as he chased them. His razor-sharp beak could do some serious damage.

"*Mee mee mee mee mee!*" That was the sound the meemees made as they scrambled away from him and headed for the kitchen door. "*Mee mee mee mee mee!*" It was the cry that had given them their name once upon a time.

Shad knew they were heading for their bolt hole. He had to cut them off, or he might not get another chance at stopping their escape.

It was time for a bold move. Taking two big steps, he pushed off in a flying leap, aiming the claws of his feet at the fleeing pests. He might just take them both at once, if...

But no. The meemees darted through the kitchen doorway before he could nail them. Shad came down on his heels and slid, dropping hard on his ass.

A shock of pain jolted his spine, and he shrieked. As he slumped against the wall, he heard the meemees' hairy little feet pattering down the hall toward their escape hole.

And that made him shriek even louder.

"What next?" The white-feathered female was furious, clacking her beak against Shad's. "Are you going to *carry* the meemees in and *feed* them by *claw*?"

Shad shook his head with quick flicks, careful not to leave an opening for her sharp beak. Just because they were standing in the restaurant's dining room in view of several customers didn't mean she wouldn't jab his eye out. "Of course not, Lady Nixa."

"You might as well!" snapped Nixa. "You already *let* them come and go as they *please*!"

At her sharp, shrill tone, all the customers looked up at once, heads flicking and bobbing with interest. Then, they all returned to pecking away at the plates of fried worms and cornmeal biscuits on the tables in front of them.

"I can *do* the *job*!" Shad reared up with indignation, but he had to be careful. Lady Nixa owned the restaurant and was paying his fee--a fee he couldn't afford to lose.

"So you keep saying." Nixa lunged at him, then jerked away at the last second. The low red comb on top of her head quivered with rage. "But if I don't see results soon, you're *fired*, you washed-up loser."

"I'll *get* those meemees, don't you worry!" Shad crowed for emphasis.

"Big talk, cock," said Nixa. "Now walk the walk." She clucked with disgust. "If you can."

As Shad checked the cage traps in the parking lot, he got more and more angry. Not only had he not caught a single meemee, but every last bit of bait he'd planted had been spirited away.

The little bastards were tricky as hell and hard to kill. Not that

Shad had gone after many of them before now. Actually, this was his first job as an exterminator, though he'd never tell Nixa that.

He'd thought it would be much easier. He'd only ever killed another Ch'Kaw before, in the cockfighting ring, and that hadn't been so hard...for a while, anyway.

But the meemees, it turned out, were much more of a challenge. He'd already been after them for three days, and the closest he'd come to contact was the chase he'd just had through the kitchen.

"Well, hello there." A strange voice interrupted his reverie. "Coming up empty, huh?"

Turning, Shad saw an elderly male limping toward him with a cane, bobbing his head. Immediately, Shad put down the latest trap and straightened. "What's it to you?"

"These traps won't work." The male swung his cane out and rapped it on the trap at Shad's feet. "Not for damned meemees. You're pecking at the wrong feed, friend."

"What do *you* suggest, Grampa?" Shad twitched his head, giving his comb and wattles a sarcastic shake.

"Name's Varn, not Grampa." Varn twitched his own head, but his shriveled comb and wattles didn't shake much. "And shame on you, if you think I'm dumb enough to tell you my meemee-killing tactics without a piece of the action."

Shad crowed with laughter and strutted away. "Get lost, old rooster." His high, purple tail feathers flickered as he walked. "You won't get any money out of me."

"Too bad." Varn made a rumbling noise deep in his throat--a Ch'Kaw sigh. "I was going to pay *you* to let me *help*."

Shad stopped strutting and whirled. "But you said you wanted a piece of the action."

"Exactly." Varn cluck-chuckled and flapped his arms. "The *action*, friend. The *killing*. I'm retired and *bored*."

Now Shad was interested. Keeping his head high, he scratched the pavement with his feet. "You say you have meemee-killing tactics?"

"*Scientifically developed* tactics." Varn chuckled again. "And cash money up front, friend." He reached between the dull gray feathers on his belly and drew out a clawful of glittering gold pellets.

Shad considered it for a moment, then shrugged. What did he have to lose? "Sure. Why not?"

Varn's feathers were thin, with the skin underneath showing through in patches, but he ruffled them excitedly anyway. "To murder most fowl!" And then he managed a hoarse crow that broke down into a ragged coughing jag.

"Voila!" Varn pulled an item out of a burlap sack--a tiny, rectangular object with curved corners, black all around. "The perfect bait!"

Shad flicked his head to the side and stared at the object with one eye. "What the hell is it?"

"An ancient artifact, dug up from deep underground." Varn turned the object around in his clawed hand, letting the sun glint off its smooth surface. "A remnant of a different age." Dropping it in the bag, he headed across the parking lot toward the garbage pile in the far back corner.

Shad shook his head. "And it's supposed to be bait how?"

"The Ch'Kaw did not always rule the Earth," said Varn. "You know that, don't you?"

"I've heard theories."

"*More* than theories. *Facts.*" Varn shook his cane for emphasis. "This world was once dominated by a species calling itself 'Peeple.' How do we know this?" He held up the burlap sack. "*Evidence,* buried long, long ago."

When they got to the garbage pile, Shad spotted a swarm of bugs on some rotten cornbread and pecked them up. "If these Peeple were so dominant, what happened to them?"

"No one knows for sure." Varn pulled the black object from his sack and squatted down in front of the pile. "But the meemees look an awful lot like the Peeple did."

Shad stopped pecking at bugs. "The meemees?"

"Sure," said Varn. "Just much smaller, with bigger eyes. You've heard of evolution, haven't you? Creatures changing to adapt to their environment?"

"I guess so," said Shad.

Varn reached into his sack and fished around. "Some scientists think the Peeple changed over hundreds of thousands of years, becoming the meemees."

Shad let loose a sharp crow of laughter. "The same scientists who think the *Ch'Kaw* evolved from *birds*?"

"Don't laugh. There's plenty of evidence down there." Varn pointed his beak at the ground.

"Whatever." Shad shrugged. "It doesn't matter what came first, as long as we're the ones doing the killing."

"Indeed." Varn pulled a crescent-shaped metal object from the sack and put it down with a clank. "And this will do the job nicely, friend."

Shad recognized the object as a spring-loaded foot trap. He hadn't thought to bring one himself; he hadn't thought he'd need anything other than a couple of cage traps.

"Let's get this loaded." Varn opened the trap wide on the pavement and locked it by turning a key on its base. Gingerly, he lowered the black artifact inside, placing it on a pressure-sensitive metal plate. Then, he withdrew his claw and turned the key to unlock the trap. "Now, all we have to do is wait."

Shad frowned and twitched his head. "I don't understand how this bait will lure them in. What kind of artifact *is* it?"

Varn chuckled as he got to his feet. "If translations of the ancient texts are correct, Peeple called it a 'fone.' Some kind of communication device, apparently."

"They can use it to communicate?"

"Heavens no." Varn chuckled again. "It doesn't *work*. But they won't be able to keep their hands off it." He shrugged. "That's the theory, anyway."

"What if they don't *take* the bait?"

Varn shook his burlap sack, making the contents clank and jingle. "We've got lots more where *that* came from."

By the time Varn had finished setting traps, the back parking lot was a kill zone for meemees. There were four traps around the trash pile, two up against the back wall of the restaurant, and six more ringing the edge of the lot.

To keep unwitting customers from getting hurt, Shad blocked off the back lot with yellow traffic cones. He also closed the area to all employees, though he knew he couldn't keep it that way for long.

Then, he and Varn pitched a black tent in the middle of the lot and waited inside, watching the traps through peepholes in the canvas.

"So," said Varn. "What made you want to get into the exterminator business?"

"Time for a career change, I guess." Shad squinted through one peephole, then moved on to the next. So far, he could see no action along the trap line.

"A change from what kind of career?" pressed Varn. "What did you do before this?"

Shad grunted. How many awful conversations had started with the same or similar words? He hated the thought of another--but lying his way out of it never seemed to be the answer. Sooner or later, the truth always caught up with him.

"A cockfighter," he said finally. "I was a cockfighter before this."

"Pro?" asked Varn.

"Yes," said Shad. "I was on the pro circuit."

"And your name is?"

"Shad Lum Lugo. But my pro name was Slaughterbeak."

"Slaughterbeak, huh?" Varn flashed him a look, then went back to staring out a peephole. "When was your last fight?"

"Six months ago," said Shad. "Against the Crimson Spurslasher."

"Sounds like quite an opponent," said Varn. "So why did you quit the fight game?"

Maybe now was the time for a lie or two. "I wanted to quit while I was still on top...and still in one piece." Shad didn't mention that he'd been forced out; why bring it up if the old rooster didn't know the story?

Luckily, Varn didn't seem to pick up on the fib. "Sounds like a smart move, friend. You saved your own skin and cleared the way for new talent in the bargain, didn't you?"

Shad moved to another peephole. "You read my mind, Varn."

Varn started to say something, then stopped and leaned closer to his own peephole. "Here we go now. Vermin on the march, Slaughterbeak."

Shad darted over to a peephole on the same side of the tent as Varn's. Sure enough, three meemees had scampered out of the brush and were approaching the traps by the garbage pile.

"Watch this." Varn chuckled. "Little buggers won't be able to resist the bait we put out."

At first, it looked like he'd be right. The meemees--a black-furred male, a blonde female, and a red-furred male child--went straight to the trap with the fone and circled it several times.

But they didn't take the bait. Instead, they moved on to the next trap.

"Don't worry," said Varn. "They're as good as dead."

The next trap was baited with a stack of what Varn had called "credicards"--thin pieces of plastic that had once been used for financial transactions. That was the theory, anyway.

The meemees crept around the spring-loaded trap, eyes fixed on the stack of cards. They sniffed at them, taking the scent from beyond the trap's reach. They gestured and babbled to each other...but they never made a move to enter the trap. And then they moved on.

Varn clucked angrily. "Come on, come on." He ruffled his sparse gray feathers and rapped the pavement with his cane. "I *know* they can't pass up the *next* bait."

The third trap held a gleaming bar of solid gold. As with the

first two traps, the meemees circled around it, staring and sniffing--
and then they stopped. The adults stood straight, cupped their furry
hands around their mouths, and cried out.

"*Mee mee mee mee!*" Small as they were, their voices carried well
across the parking lot and beyond. "*Mee mee mee mee mee!*"

"What are they doing?" said Shad.

Just as the words left his mouth, a horde of meemees poured out
of the jungle and swarmed the parking lot. There were dozens of
them, and they weren't empty-handed.

Every last meemee of every age, size, and fur color was carrying
a rock or a stick.

Shad sucked in his breath. Were the rocks and sticks meant to be
used as tools or weapons?

The answer was "tools." As the meemees charged out of the
jungle brush, they used the rocks and sticks to trigger the traps.
When the traps sprung, the bait was ejected, clattering to the
pavement.

Instantly, the meemees scooped up the bait and dashed away on
their tiny, furry feet. They scattered in all directions, carrying off
fones and credicards, gold bars and carkees and wristclocks. As they
ran, the air was filled with their high-pitched cries. "*Mee mee mee mee
mee mee mee!*"

Shad hissed a curse and bolted out of the tent. He grabbed the
pistol from the holster at his waist and waved it around, trying to
pick a target...but it wasn't easy. He'd never seen so many
meemees in one place before, and they were all moving fast. Carefully drawing a bead on one was out of the question. Better to
shoot randomly into the herd; he was bound to hit something
that way.

But just as he had that thought, something locked up inside him.
Instead of pouring bullets into warm meemee bodies, he froze as the
creatures scampered away from him.

"What the hell?" Just then, Varn lurched out of the tent. "Shoot!
They're getting away!"

Shad thought fast. "Not yet! This is our chance!"

"Chance for what, you chickenshit?"

"To follow them," said Shad. "To find their nest. Then we can stop them once and for all."

"Not a bad idea." Varn bobbed his head and managed a hoarse crow. "Let's turn their home sweet home into the world's biggest meemee burial ground."

Shad and Varn left the restaurant behind and followed the meemees into the jungle. Shad stayed out ahead--he had to, to keep the meemees in sight--but he tried not to lose the slower-moving old-timer in the process.

The mid-day heat was high, the humidity thick as soup all around, but Shad didn't mind. He lived for warmth and sunlight; he'd always been a hot-blooded type...and not just when it came to climate. He loved the heat that came with action and excitement, too, the way it got his blood pumping harder and made him feel truly alive. It was what he'd loved most about his cockfighting days, even after he'd lost his edge.

Not that he'd see much action if the meemees got away...which they might. Hanging back because of Varn, Shad could just make out the tops of some of the creatures' furry heads in the distant brush. If the meemees managed to get much further away, he would lose them altogether.

Though, truth be told, he wasn't confident of succeeding in his mission even if he did catch up to them. Fear coiled in the back of his mind like a snake...fear that he'd blow this hunt the same way he'd blown his cockfighting career.

And for the same reason, too.

"Hold up!" Varn's voice rang out from far behind--much farther behind than Shad would have expected. "Slow down a little!"

It was the exact opposite of what Shad wanted to do, but losing the old rooster might not help his cause. Grudgingly, he stopped and waited, watching the far-off heads of the meemees get even farther off.

"Thanks." Varn was out of breath as he hobbled up through the brush. "I guess...I can't run...through the jungle...like I used to."

"No problem." Shad kept watching the meemees, who were almost out of sight. "But we've got to keep moving."

Varn nodded and sighed. "I will, I will."

"We're losing them!" Shad couldn't see the meemees anymore, just the brush rustling in their wake.

"So follow...their tracks." Varn poked Shad's side with his cane to get his attention, then jabbed the cane at the ground.

Sure enough, the jungle mud was full of tiny footprints. Shad recognized them instantly as meemee tracks: each had five toes joined to an oblong foot, concave on the inside, deeper at the ball and heel.

"See?" Varn cluck-chuckled. "As long as we still have daylight, we can follow the trail."

"Good." Shad nodded with quick flicks of his head. "But let's keep up the best we can anyway. These things can be damned tricky."

"Their ancestors ruled the world for thousands of years," said Varn. "I guess some of that had to stay with them."

Time passed, and Shad and Varn kept moving. There was always plenty of fresh trail to follow--tiny prints and occasional droppings in the mud. Once in a while, Shad even glimpsed rippling brush or a furry scalp in the distance. Sometimes, he heard faint "*mee mee mee*" cries piping through the jungle greenery.

But he didn't let it make him hurry. He maintained a slow and steady pace, which Varn seemed to appreciate.

Instead of gasping for breath, the old-timer was able to carry on a conversation as he hiked...though Shad only half listened to what he was saying.

"It's funny what evolution can do." Varn said it as Shad helped him across a stream. "The rulers of the world, the Peeple, become the humble little meemees, scavenging to survive and running for their lives."

"If you say so." Shad tested a rock in the middle of the stream, decided it was steady, and put his full weight on it. Then, he pulled Varn after him and stepped from the rock to the bank.

"The Peeple had a theory, too, you know," said Varn. "They believed that millions of years before Peeple came along, the world was ruled by giant beasts called 'dinosaurs.' What do you suppose became of them?"

Shad was more interested in pulling Varn to the bank and picking up the meemees' trail, which he was having trouble finding. "Killed off by the Peeple?"

"Not at all, friend. The People believed that the dinosaurs *evolved*. Over millions and millions of years, they shrank and became *birds*. But here's the most interesting part."

"I'm listening," said Shad as he walked along the bank with his head bobbing low, looking for tracks in the mud.

"According to *modern* scientists, certain birds evolved into *us*." Varn sounded excited. "Birds, descended from the dinosaur rulers of the world, again became the rulers of the world as the *Ch'Kaw*. And the Peeple shrank and became the tiny, pesky meemees. What goes around, comes around, eh?"

"Ah-ha!" Shad let out a crow of victory. The meemees must have waded downstream a few yards before leaving the water...but he'd found their fresh tracks anyway, stamped in the muddy bank and trailing off into the brush.

"Kind of makes you wonder what's next," said Varn, lingering along the stream for a moment before realizing he was alone and hobbling off to catch up with Shad.

A little further along, the meemee tracks led Shad to a clearing, about twenty yards across. He paused at the edge of it, looking around at the mat of flattened grass spanning the open space.

Suddenly, he heard familiar, high-pitched cries piping up. "*Mee mee mee mee mee*!" Six meemees leaped out from behind bushes and tree trunks on the opposite side, waving fones and credicards and carkees.

"Damned things." Glancing over his shoulder, he saw Varn draw up behind him. "I'll be right back."

Varn bobbed his head, looking confused. "But I..."

Shad didn't wait for him to finish his sentence. Grabbing his pistol from the holster, he charged into the clearing, eyes fixed on the screeching meemees.

Adrenaline burned through his arteries, and his heart hammered as he ran. The meemees hopped up and down and waved their toys, egging him on with their screeches. Clearly, they wanted him to keep charging straight for them.

But why? Why the hell would they want that?

Suddenly suspicious, Shad slowed near the middle of the clearing...and the ground gave way under his right foot. He stopped just in time, stumbling back as the mat of flattened grass dropped away in front of him, revealing a gaping pit.

Crowing with alarm, he staggered back. One step further forward, and he would've plunged right into the hole.

"*Mee mee mee mee mee*!" On the far side of the clearing, the meemees were jumping around like maniacs. Their screeches were shrill with rage; they hurled their toys at Shad and hurled globs of feces to go with them.

Steadying himself, Shad swung up the pistol and pointed it in the meemees' direction. When one of their fones bounced off his chest, he cocked the gun and got ready to fire.

One of the meemees, a silver-haired male, was in Shad's sights. All he had to do was pull the trigger.

Which he did...but only after swinging the pistol to point straight up in the air, leaving the meemees unharmed.

Angry screeches changing to frightened ones, the meemees bolted off into the dense brush. They were gone in a flurry of foliage, leaving Shad standing alone in the clearing.

"What the hell?" Easing up to the edge of the pit, he saw it was at least twelve feet to the bottom--deep enough to contain him. "They tried to *trap* me?"

Varn limped up beside him. "Sure looks that way, friend."

"But meemees don't *do* that," said Shad. "They don't *do* that to *Ch'Kaw*."

"They do now."

Shad gaped at the fluttering brush in the distance. "But they're not that *smart*, are they?"

"Like I told you." Varn patted his shoulder. "Used to rule the *planet*, friend."

After the incident in the clearing, Shad and Varn continued onward, following the meemees' tracks.

Shad moved more cautiously now, worried that the meemees might try something else. It didn't seem likely, but their first attempt at trapping him hadn't seemed likely, either.

One question stuck in his mind: If the meemees were smart enough to dig a hole, cover it over, and lure him into it, what else might they be capable of?

At least he wasn't tracking them alone--though Varn seemed more concerned about Shad than he was about the meemees.

"Why carry that gun?" asked Varn as they worked their way up a hill. "You haven't used it much, have you?"

Shad jerked his head around, comb and wattles quivering, and glared at him. "I've used it *plenty*."

"You're good at waving it around, all right." Varn grunted as he pushed off with his cane, taking another step up the hillside. "Good at shooting it straight up in the air, too. But I have yet to see you nail a meemee with that sidearm of yours."

"Haven't seen *you* get one, either," snarled Shad. "What happened to those scientifically-developed tactics you were running your mouth about?"

Varn ignored the remark. "What's your malfunction, friend? Are you gun-shy in general, or just when it comes to shooting meemees?"

Shad whirled and lunged, ending up beak-to-beak with Varn-- but the old-timer didn't back down. He just kept looking at Shad expectantly.

For a moment, Shad was seized by the urge to attack, to give Varn an old-fashioned peck-down straight out of the cockfighting ring. But then he remembered how he'd changed since his days in the fight game; a single flash of anger couldn't undo all that.

Which was kind of the old-timer's point. Shad wasn't the same rooster he'd once been.

As the anger drained out of him, Shad bobbed his head and backed away. "One of the reasons I'm doing this," he said, "is to fire up my killer instinct again."

"So *that's* why you left cockfighting." Varn nodded. "You lost your *bloodlust*."

"It's still there." Shad glared at him with one baleful brown eye. "It just needs a jump-start."

"But the meemees aren't doing it for you, are they?" Varn twitched his head from side to side. "Why is that?"

Shad's impulse was to deny there was any problem at all...but he fell silent instead.

"They're filthy, disease-ridden pests," said Varn. "Why hold back from blowing them away whenever possible?"

Shad opened his beak to speak...but before he could say anything, he was distracted by a familiar cry in the distance.

"*Mee mee mee mee mee mee mee!*"

The sound was coming from up the hill. Looking toward it, Shad saw twelve meemees on the crest of the hill, silhouetted against the deep blue afternoon sky.

Feeling compelled to prove himself, Shad let out a wild crow and charged toward the row of meemees. He heard Varn shouting something behind him, but he couldn't make it out and didn't care. It was time to blow through the barriers holding him back; it was time to kill some damned meemees.

As he ran closer, the meemees grew more agitated. They threw fones and gold bars and artifacts he didn't recognize, pitching them in his direction with frenzied shrieks.

Shad just kept charging. He drew his pistol and cocked the hammer, determined to plug all twelve meemees if he could.

Then, he felt something snap against his ankle--something like a stiff vine...or a wire. Stopping in his tracks, he spotted a sudden blur of movement from the corner of his eye and looked left. That was when he saw a huge object hurtling toward him, coming in fast.

Instinctively, he threw himself down. He hit the ground just in time as the flying object swooped over him, so close it buzzed off a few feathers, and kept going.

Looking up in its wake, Shad saw what it was: a log, suspended in some kind of harness, swinging between the trees. If it had hit him, he had no doubt it would have killed him.

He must have triggered it when he stepped through the wire. It could not have been a coincidence that the meemees had been egging him on in that direction.

They had set a second trap. And this time, they had come even closer to killing him.

Shad and Varn continued onward, following the trail more cautiously than ever. As they forged ahead, the sun moved lower in the sky, shifting the day ever closer to evening.

"We're running out of daylight," said Shad as he ducked under low-hanging vines in an especially dense patch of jungle. "Maybe we ought to turn around."

Varn shot off a little crow of contempt. "Typical. This is just like your last match against the Crimson Spurslasher back in '27."

Shad's head pivoted to fix the old-timer in a stunned glare. "I thought you didn't know who I was before today! I thought you hadn't followed my career!"

"I never said that." Varn shrugged. "Who *hasn't* heard the story of *Slaughterbeak*? You were one of the all-time *greats* until you started *choking* and got put out to *pasture*."

Shad felt betrayed. The old-timer didn't sound much like a friend anymore. "Shut your beak. You don't know anything about that world." Turning to face forward, he resumed pushing through the vines and brush.

Varn laughed. "I know more than you think!"

Shad's blood was boiling as he thrashed his way through a tangle of leafy vines. When he'd cleared them, he found himself gazing at a strange sight.

Some kind of structure lay before him, a waist-high white altar rising from the jungle floor. It looked as if it were built from thousands of white pieces--some curved, some jagged, some knobby, some flat. The closer he looked, the more clearly it came into focus, and he realized what exactly the pieces were.

Bones. They were bones.

Shad twitched and shuddered. "Time to turn around."

But when he took a step back, he bumped into Varn. "That would be rude, friend." Varn cluck-chuckled and nudged Shad forward with the tip of his cane. "They've been expecting us."

Just then, Shad heard rustling sounds from the brush. A familiar call, faint at first, drifted up all around him.

"*Mee mee mee mee mee mee mee.*"

"Expecting us?" Shad's voice had a nervous hitch to it. "What makes you think that?"

Varn leaned up close to Shad and whispered in his ear. "Because I told them we were coming. I told them I was going to introduce them to my son's very special friend who was dying to meet them."

Shad swallowed hard. Reaching down, he slid his pistol from its holster. "Who's your son?"

Varn leaned even closer and hissed his next words. "The *Crimson Spurslasher*. Remember him?" He gave Shad a sharp peck on the back of the head. "You know what happens when you refuse to administer the kill shot to an opponent in the ring, don't you? The way you refused to kill the Crimson Spurslasher in the last bout of your career?"

Shad tightened his grip on the pistol in his left claw. "Disgrace."

"For starters," said Varn. "The loser left alive is seen as a failure and coward who ought to be dead. No one will fight him, because the only thing more disgraceful than being spared in the ring would be *losing* to someone who's been spared."

As Varn continued his story, the meemees' voices grew louder. Shad felt as if a huge door was closing behind him, and he didn't have long before it slammed shut for good.

"The disgraced fighter loses everything," said Varn. "He becomes a *laughingstock* and a *pariah*. More often than not, he is driven to take his own *life*...as indeed the Crimson Spurslasher did. And even then, his *family* knows no *peace*. All because of one act of *cowardice* by a gutless *cock* like *you*." Lunging forward, he pecked at the back of Shad's head with angry force.

Crowing with rage, Shad leaped away from him. The move took him close enough to the altar that he could make out what kind of bones had gone into its construction.

Ch'Kaw bones. Every bone he could see had come straight out of a dead Ch'Kaw.

Suddenly, the calls of the meemees got louder than ever. So did the rustling of the brush. All at once, the jungle parted, and hundreds of meemees poured forth.

This time, they weren't carrying fones, credicards, carkees, and the like. Some had rocks, and others had sharp sticks. As they closed in around Shad, he could see other objects scattered throughout the crowd--knives of all sizes clutched in tiny, furry hands, looking much too big for the little creatures who carried them.

Shad turned in a circle, scanning the crowd for a thin spot where he might break through. From what he could see, there was no such spot; if anything, the crowd kept expanding on all sides as more meemees ran in from the jungle.

"Here's where my scientifically-developed tactics come in," said Varn. "I haven't learned how to *kill* the meemees, but to *communicate* with them. And guess what?" He crowed with delight. "We found *common ground*."

Shad raised the pistol and pointed it at the crowd. Just then, the meemees started pelting him with a flurry of rocks.

"We both hate *chickens!*" said Varn, and then he roared with clucking laughter.

The flurry of rocks became a torrent, bombarding Shad from all sides. Sharp sticks hurtled among the rocks, piercing his skin like tiny spears.

Shad's clawed finger remained curled around the trigger of his pistol. He meant to fire, knowing full well it might be his best chance at survival...yet he still hesitated.

"Stop it!" He released a furious crow, the kind that had once terrified opponents in the ring--but the meemees kept attacking. "Get away from me!"

A big rock hit him on the back of the head, stunning him on impact. He wobbled, waving the gun one way and then the other, but his vision clouded, and he couldn't pick a target.

Then, a moment of clarity washed over him. He steadied, and his vision cleared. A black-furred meemee came into focus, gazing up at him with big, dark eyes.

Shad intended to kill it. Clenching his beak in concentration, he fixed the meemee in his gunsight. He steeled himself to murder that creature, hoping that one death might be enough to give the other meemees pause.

But at the last instant, he swung the gun up and fired at the tree-tops instead.

Why? That was what he thought as the crowd rushed in and brought him down with rocks and sticks and tiny, furry hands. *Why can't I bring myself to kill them?*

Shad swatted and struggled, but the meemees overwhelmed him. They bashed and stabbed him with their weapons and pinned him to the muddy ground.

Then, the meemees with knives leaped into the heart of the fray. Shad thrashed when he felt their cold blades slice into his throat, but he couldn't dislodge them. They just kept cutting and hacking, and he screamed the whole time.

Until they severed his windpipe, that is.

When they broke through his spine and lifted his head away from his body, Shad had the strangest sense of freedom. Ch'Kaw couldn't fly, but he felt at first as if indeed he were taking flight.

The meemees carried him up onto the altar. Peering over the edge, he could see his headless body on the ground--and then it broke free of the meemees pinning it down. Jumping up, the body raced in circles around the altar, knocking meemees out of the way of its headless, mindless charge.

But eventually, the meemees brought it back down. They flung it on its back on the bone altar and pinned it there with the force of numbers.

Next, the meemees with the knives climbed up onto its chest and started cutting. They opened up the sternum and hacked out the V-shaped bone from the middle of the rib cage.

Then, as the mob chanted in unison...

"*Mee mee mee mee mee mee mee!*"

...two meemee males, both red-furred, took hold of the bone, one gripping each slender stem...

"*Mee mee mee mee mee mee mee!*"

...and they snapped it, breaking it into two uneven pieces...

"*Mee mee mee mee mee mee mee!*"

...and the one with the longer piece cheered, waving his piece of the bone in the air for all to see.

And that was when Shad faded, sliding away from the jungle and into somewhere else...taking only one thought with him on the journey. A question.

"*Why can't I bring myself to kill them?*"

"Tell me a story about the meemees, Mommy."

When Shad opened his eyes again, he was six weeks old--a tiny peep covered in yellow fuzz, hunkered down in the straw of his family's coop.

"If you insist." His mother sat in front of him, squatting on a clutch of eggs that had yet to hatch. Her pale feathers glowed in the bright moonlight streaming through the windows. "This one is called 'The Meemees and the Brave Little Peep.'"

Shad bounced in the straw and chirped with delight. His mother told him meemee stories every night; he could listen to them forever...or at least until he drifted off to sleep.

Shad's mother cleared her throat. "Once upon a time, there was a little peep who was afraid of the dark." She didn't need to read from a book; she knew all the stories by heart. "When clouds hid the moon, turning his room from bright to dark, he became very scared."

"What was the little peep's name?" asked Shad. "Was it the same as mine?"

"Yes, it was," said Mommy. "And little Shad shivered in the straw, unable to fall asleep. What if it was never light again?"

Shad listened with eyes wide and tiny heart racing. He knew exactly how the Shad in the story felt.

"Then, one night, three visitors flew in through the window." Mommy bobbed her head happily. "They were magical creatures, not much bigger than Shad was. Each had two arms, two legs, and two graceful gossamer wings like the wings of a butterfly. One was covered in red fur, one was covered in blond fur, and the other had jet black fur from head to toe."

"*Meemees*!" Shad let loose a high-pitched, chirping crow of excitement.

Mommy cocked her head to one side. "Very *special* meemees. *Meemee fairies*. The kind that flutter in through the window when little peeps are afraid of the dark. The kind that *light up* from inside with a soft, blue glow that comes straight from the love in their hearts."

"They *glow*?" said Shad.

"And the light from their hearts helps little peeps not be afraid of the dark anymore." Mommy let out a string of soft, loving clucks. "That's exactly what they did for little Shad that night. They flew around and played with him for hours, laughing and glowing in the darkness that wasn't so dark anymore."

"Then what happened?" said Shad.

Long after Mommy had fallen asleep, Shad thought about the story she'd told him. It was his new favorite; he couldn't get it out of his head.

Eventually, he began to drift off. As he floated in the twilight gulf between consciousness and sleep, dreams mixed with reality in his young mind.

That was when he saw them, just as his mother had described. Three meemees fluttered in on gossamer wings, each one glowing with magic.

He giggled as they circled around him. They waved and beamed down at him with loving smiles, radiating warmth. They told him, without saying a word, that he had nothing to fear.

They played and frolicked there for hours, or what seemed like hours to a half-dreaming peep. They swooped low and tickled his belly, making him wriggle and twitter. They lifted him up in the air and danced with him, swinging him around with the greatest of ease.

Shad crowed and laughed until it hurt. Somehow, all the commotion never woke his mother on her clutch of eggs.

Then, the meemees joined hands around him in midair. He stayed aloft by flapping his fuzzy arms, hovering high above the straw in one glittering moonbeam.

At the end of Mommy's story, little Shad had become an honorary meemee. The same thing happened again, to the little Shad who'd listened to the story.

Glowing more brightly than ever, the meemees turned in a slow circle around Shad. Without saying a word, they swore him in as an honorary member of their order for life.

When they were done, Shad glowed as brightly as the meemees. From that moment on, some part of him would always be a part of them. Even if he forgot in the crush of a lifetime, in the blood and pain and strife of days heaped upon each other like logs on a bonfire, that night would leave its mark.

And one day, the story and dream might come back to him in full, swiveling out of the darkness like glowing winged meemees racing toward the moon in the last precious moments before the horizon swallows it up.

TIJUANA, MASSACHUSETTS

A t first, Patty thought someone was shooting at her. *Bracka-cracka-crack.* She clamped her hands over her ears, fighting to drown out the clattering racket. *Cracka-bracka-brack.*

Then, suddenly, it was like someone had turned down the volume and she could hear the sound for what it really was.

Shicka-shacka-shicka.

And when she opened her eyes, she saw what was making that sound: a bright yellow box jumping up and down in a dirty brown hand. A rainbow-colored logo swirled across the front under a cellophane wrapper.

Chiclets. Someone was shaking a box of Chiclets in her face.

"Five dollar, *señora*." The voice of a little boy called out from behind the box. "Want some Cheek-lits?"

What the *fuck*?

Since when did *kids* run around selling *Chiclets* on *Cape Cod, Massachusetts*?

Patty shook her head hard, trying to clear away the fog. Looking up, she caught an eyeful of blinding sun, then looked down. It was only then she realized she was on her ass in the middle of the street.

"Get the fuck away from me!" She swatted the Chiclets box out of her face, revealing the little brown-skinned, black-haired boy who'd been holding it. He wore a green-and-white striped t-shirt and tattered jeans and looked highly insulted. "Damn *wetback*." She wrinkled her nose in disgust at a surge of body odor.

Only to realize the kid was upwind and the B.O. was coming from *her*.

Bzeep zeep.

Suddenly, Patty heard a strange buzzing beeping noise and felt nauseous. Something in her eyes flickered, and the boy transformed.

Instead of a little black-haired boy with brown skin, he became a little blond boy with pale skin. Instead of a striped t-shirt and tattered jeans, he wore a navy blue polo shirt with the collar turned up and a pair of neatly pressed white shorts.

"What the--" Patty couldn't help smiling at the cute child, who was much more what she expected to see on The Cape.

Bzeep zeep.

Then, her eyes flickered, and the little brown boy was back.

"What the fuck?" Patty shook her head hard and braced her hands on the hot, rough pavement. She took deep breaths and forced down the urge to be sick.

The kid started toward her, and Patty shooed him away. "Go eat a taco, Paco!" Then, she struggled to her hands and knees. She got to her feet.

And she took a look around.

"What the fuck is *this*?" Patty had never seen so much brown skin on The Cape. Was it Cinco de fucking Mayo, or what?

Some kind of street fair was going on around her. There was Mexican music in the air, all horns and guitars and accordions. People stared out at her from stalls overflowing with sombreros, serapes, and pottery. She saw men in white shirts and slacks, women in bowler hats and long pink and orange and yellow and red dresses.

Not one of them had pale skin like Patty's. The Cape was really going downhill.

"Fucking wetbacks." Frowning people cleared out of Patty's path as she lurched down the street like a broken bulldozer. "Fucking *Cape*."

Staggering away from the stalls, she swung around a corner and felt suddenly dizzy. She had to catch herself against the front window of a shop.

Palms pressed against the smooth glass, Patty closed her eyes and fought for control. It slipped away every time she thought she had it.

I need help. Her legs buckled, and she barely stayed on her feet. *I need J-*

Bzeep zeep.

Patty's eyes snapped open, and she stared at her reflection in the window. She'd had a name on the tip of her tongue, and then...

Bzeep zeep.

Gone. It was gone.

"What the fuck?" Her voice was a whisper. She'd been thinking of something, of *someone*, and then that buzzing beeping noise had broken her train of thought.

Patty squinted at her image, but it had nothing to tell her. Same old crinkled-up 52-year-old bulldog face, chipmunk overbite, and gray crew cut.

But at least it gave her something to hold on to. At least that much, the way she looked, hadn't changed.

Or had it? That little bump between her eyes--that was new, wasn't it? Reaching up, she ran her index finger over it, feeling a hard little nub above the bridge of her nose. It was like a tiny pea, a ball bearing, but warm to the touch.

When did that *get there?*

Taking a deep breath, Patty pushed away from the window. She was hardly aware she was stepping into the street until a big black car nearly plowed her over.

The blast of the horn still rang in her ears as she teetered in shock. Then, looking up, she saw something that made her freeze.

She saw a billboard on the side of a building, emblazoned with three giant words, each bursting with wild, bright colors.

Welcome to Tijuana!

"What kind of bullshit joke is *this*?" Patty flung her hand through the air as if she could sweep away the sign. "Some *motherfucker* with too much fucking *time* on his hands?"

Bzeep zeep.

Her vision flickered, and the billboard changed from the garish *Welcome to Tijuana!* to a more subdued *Welcome to Cape Cod*.

Patty stared, then scrunched her eyes shut and shook her head hard.

Bzeep zeep.

The next time she looked, the billboard read *Welcome to Tijuana!* again.

Lunging away from the sign, Patty continued down the street. She got a funny taste in her mouth, like dirt, and spat in the gutter on her way past.

As she hauled herself onward, a little boy in a bright red soccer shirt and yellow shorts ran out of an alley in front of her.

"No *Cheek-lets!*" said Patty, though the boy showed no sign of slowing down on his way past. "No five dollah!"

The little boy didn't look back on his way down the street and around the corner.

Patty thrashed her head from side to side but still couldn't get rid of the fog. She wondered if she'd picked up a flu or some-

Bzeep zeep.

"Where the *fuck* is that *noise* coming from?" Reaching up, she felt the lump between her eyes. It was still warm, warmer than it should have been if it was just some kind of growth.

Suddenly, she smelled cooked food, and her mind switched tracks. A lovely little café came up on her left, and she stopped in front of it, inhaling deeply.

The place was Cape Cod style all the way, from the white wicker chairs to the round tables with white tablecloths. A vase rested on each table, filled with a tasteful arrangement of gardenias and hyacinths. A slim, red-haired waitress walked out, smoothing her crisp white linen apron. She smiled and gave Patty a friendly wave.

Bzeep zeep.

A flicker later, and the place had become an ugly Mexican

cantina that looked like it had been furnished right out of the town dump.

As Patty watched, a brown-skinned waitress shuffled over to a male customer at one of the rickety tables with a steaming plate of sizzling chicken and vegetables. Patty's stomach started growling, which totally pissed her off.

Because the one thing she hated more than Mexican people was Mexican food.

"Fucking puke on a plate." So why was her mouth watering so much? Why did she want to run in there and fill her hands, squishing the greasy, steaming chicken between her fingers, then gobbling it up like a dog?

Wheeling away from the cantina, she looked up and down the sunbaked street. Sweat rolling down her face and body, she tried figuring out where she was in the whole of The Cape, because none of the landmarks was ringing a bell.

But she came up empty. Not a clue.

Was she drunk? She didn't remember drinking. Had somebody slipped her a rufy?

"Fuck." The blistering heat pressed in on her, and she suddenly felt faint. Her legs buckled. "I need J-"

Bzeep zeep.

Once again, the name on the tip of her tongue was gone. A wild chill poured through her, pure fear sweeping aside the intense heat.

And then the hot flash was back. All she could think of was air conditioning.

And a telephone.

Indiscriminately, Patty staggered toward the door of a shop and heaved it open. She lurched inside and let the door bang shut behind her.

Ding dong. An electric chime rang as Patty looked around. She felt only slightly cooler, but it might only have been because she was out of the sun. As far as she could tell, the shop had no air conditioning.

But she was glad for even the slightest relief. And she was glad to see what kind of shop she'd stumbled into.

The place smelled like stale cigarette smoke and some kind of incense. A light haze hung in the air, leaving a bitter aftertaste in her mouth.

But the shop was also full of beautiful things. A ring of waist-high display cases encircled the walls, with a second, smaller ring of cases in the middle. Patty caught her breath as she wandered between them, peering in at a treasure trove of turquoise and silver and gold.

It was the universal language. The one thing she could stand that had any connection to fucking Mehico.

Jewelry.

All the lights in the shop were switched off, but the litter of pieces in the cases still showed up fine. Bracelets and anklets and pendants gleamed softly, reflecting the light filtering in from outside. Earrings and brooches and belt buckles twinkled with a mystical inner glow.

Patty smiled for the first time all day. She loved shopping, didn't she? Shopping on The Cape with Jan...

Bzeep zeep.

...shopping with Jan...

Bzeep zeep. Bzeep zeep.

"Almost had it!" The nub between her eyes was warm under the skin as she rubbed it. "Almost had the name! Her name! Her name!"

Bzeep zeep.

"What the fuck?" All blank again.

Patty tasted dirt and looked back into the display cases. The pale blue and silver and gold pieces were pretty as the tropical fish wriggling in their tanks in her favorite restaurant on The Cape.

Suddenly, one of the pieces caught her eye--a shimmering gold bracelet on a panel of red velvet. It looked buttery soft and exotic, with rows of tiny links woven in a staggered pattern like the steps of an ancient pyramid.

Staring at it gave her a strange feeling in the pit of her stomach. Or was it the incense?

There was something inside her, hard as a knot. Jagged as a

thorn bush. Pulsating, gyrating, straining to get out. Nothing like the nub between her eyes.

Something much deeper.

"May I help you, señora?" A slow, deep voice spoke from the back of the shop, threaded with a Mexican accent. "See anything you like?"

Patty turned. An old man approached, short and slight, with thick gray hair. He wore glasses with rectangular lenses and silver wire frames, and he had a gray mustache.

He stopped about six feet away from her. "May I help you?" he said.

Gazing into his eyes, Patty felt a sharp pain in her chest. Did she know him?

Bzeep zeep.

There was a flicker, and she suddenly recognized him. His face was well known to her, unmistakably familiar. His eyes were filmy and bloodshot, sunk behind drooping lids, rimmed with networks of deep wrinkles. Of *course* she knew him, how could she not know her own f-

Bzeep zeep.

Patty clamped her hands around her head, but her thoughts fled like bees, buzzing away in all directions. If only she could hold on to *just one*, just long enough to...

Bzeep zeep.

It was *him*, it was her fa...

Bzeep zeep.

She cried out and doubled over. Bit down on her tongue and tasted blood, metallic and salty.

There were tears in her eyes as she straightened. When she opened her eyes, she no longer recognized the old man. He was just a stranger, an old jeweler, a Mexican.

During her spell, he'd retreated behind the counter along the wall. He lit a cigarette, and fresh, acrid smoke flowed into the air. When he spoke, his voice was sharper than before. "How may I help you, señora?"

Patty looked down at the beautiful gold bracelet. She patted the back pockets of her jeans, feeling for a wallet...finding nothing. Finding more of the same when she fished in her front pockets. She didn't have a dime.

A chill shot through her. Her bowels constricted like a clenching fist with sudden awareness.

"I'm..." She frowned and rubbed the hard nub between her eyes. "I need..."

Bzeep zeep.

The shop blurred, becoming a quaint antique shop she knew quite well from The Cape. But the scene quickly shifted right back to the Mexican jewelry shop.

Bzeep zeep.

"Do you have a phone?" She walked over to the display case where the old jeweler stood. "I can't seem to find my cell, and I need to call home."

The jeweler shook his head. "No calls to the U.S., señora. Local calls only."

Patty planted her hands on the smooth glass of the case and laughed. "Since when is *Cape Cod* not in the U.S.?" She slapped the glass and laughed some more. "Don't'cha think you guys're taking this Cinco de Mayo shit a little too far?"

The jeweler shrugged. "Perhaps you should buy a phone card at *la farmacia*. Good for international calls."

"Yeah, right!" Patty kept laughing. Then, she caught a lungful of smoke and hacked until she gagged.

The jeweler cleared his throat. "I think I know what you're looking for, señora."

Yes. The thought punched through the fog, and Patty fixed him in her stare. "I'm looking for..." *Looking for Jan...*

Bzeep zeep.

A wave of dizziness coursed through her. "I need to find..."

Bzeep zeep.

She reeled against the case, clutching her spinning head. Tasting blood.

"You need to go to the *pulqueria*." The old man pointed toward the front window of the shop. "They have what you're looking for there."

"Puke-a-whata?" Patty grimaced.

"*Pulqueria*," said the old man. "Go left two blocks, then make another left down the alley."

"Fuck-a-who-a?" said Patty.

The old jeweler sighed cigarette smoke and pointed at the window. "Left two blocks, then left again. They'll give you what you need. All the good, strong *pulque* you can drink." He nodded like a pimp arranging a date.

Patty waved him off and stomped toward the door.

Then stomped back again. She stopped at the case with the gold bracelet she loved and took a long look, drinking in every burnished link in the staggered rows, the steps.

And something swam up in her, fast as a fish from the inky depths of the deep ocean, racing to reach the light before the monster snapping at its tail could gulp it down forever.

"Somebody fell." Patty tapped the glass and frowned at the jeweler. "I remember. My fa..."

Bzeep zeep.

The jeweler's face became familiar again, became that of the old man she knew. Scowling, she grabbed at him, held him for a moment in her grip. He smelled like...smelled like...

...bananas?

"Somebody fell."

Bzeep zeep.

Suddenly, the familiar old man with his eyes wide with terror turned back into the Mexican jeweler, and his eyes were wide with rage.

The next thing Patty knew, she was out on the sidewalk, wagging her head like a choking dog. Looking over her shoulder, she saw the door to the jewelry shop was shut tight, a sign swinging back and forth behind the glass.

Cerrado. Closed.

Remembering the old jeweler's directions, she turned left and shuffled down the street.

Alzheimer's? Was that what she had? Motherfucking early onset Alzheimer's?

That was what she thought as she moved along through the blazing sun, which felt hot enough to fry pork rinds on the sidewalk.

"I wouldn't *know*, would I? If it was Alzheimer's, I wouldn't *know*." She said it out loud, talking to herself. "It would be just like this, just like this."

Bzeep zeep.

Except for that.

Reaching up, she rubbed the sweaty lump between her eyes. She swore it was getting warmer every time she touched it.

Her vision flickered, but nothing changed this time. She continued to rub the lump, which was hard as a rock. She wanted to dig it right out with her nails, right then, skin and blood and all.

Bzeep zeep.

But the urge passed so completely, she didn't remember having it.

Up ahead, on the left, she saw an alley--the one the old jeweler had told her about. She walked up to it, turned the corner, and took a look down its filth-strewn, adobe-walled length.

Bzeep zeep.

With another flicker, it became one of The Cape's cozy, cobble-stoned alleys, lined with well-tended clapboard houses on the historic register. Further along, there was another antique shop and an internet café, where she thought she might run into Jan...

Bzeep zeep.

Jan...

Bzeep zeep.

Janet! *Got it*! "That's her name!"

Maybe she'd see *Janet*, sweet *Janet*, darling *Janet*, waving back at her, running up to her, *saving* her! Janet Janet Janet!

Patty dug in for dear life, she had to hold on, couldn't lose her again. She had to keep remembering *Janet*--Janet smelling of sea breeze, skin soft as wine, hair dark as midnight.

How many midnights had they spent stretched out in bed, side by side, ever moving ever touching, breathless Janet, loving Janet...

Bzeep zeep.

Patty wrapped her arms around Janet as tight as she could and *held on.* Janet was like a single branch growing out of the side of a cliff, the only thing keeping Patty from dropping into an endless abyss.

She saw Janet's face, clear as day, framed by fluttering black curls. Janet's soft red lips parted, her dark eyes closed, and she was going to kiss her. Patty knew she would taste like strawberries.

And then...

Bzeep zeep.

And then, rage leaped onto Janet's features, rage and hate blazing like the merciless sun, burning Patty with their heat.

And she knew. In a sudden rush she knew she'd lost Janet forever, lost every last bit of her but one. That memory of Janet's hatred was all she had left of the love of her life.

Bzeep zeep.

Patty clutched at the lump on her forehead, hot as a burning ember blown up from a bonfire. She staggered around the corner of the alley without watching where she was going.

Suddenly, she glimpsed a giant black eye, and she ran into something. It lurched forward and threw her back against a rough adobe wall.

"What the *fucking fuck*?" The stench of pure shit hit her harder than the actual collision. She threw a hand over her nose, but the stink poured right on through.

That was when she got a good look at the source of the shit. She saw it staring back at her from the side of its face, animal to animal, taking her measure.

A donkey. And not just any donkey.

Its ears jabbed skyward through a tattered straw hat with a rainbow-colored band. Red plastic chili peppers dangled from its bridle and reins.

And stripes adorned its coat, black stripes over white hair like a zebra. It was a slapdash paint job by a hasty human hand.

"The *fuck*?" Patty scowled at the fake zebra in the straw hat, heard and smelled the shit dribbling from its asshole and splattering in the street. It had to be the *weirdest* thing she'd ever seen on the streets of The Cape. "What the *fuck* is going on in this fucking town? Now we've got *asses* shitting in the *streets*?"

"Speedy says hello, *señora*."

Patty's eyes shot wide open. For a second, she thought the donkey was doing the talking.

Then, a brown-skinned teenage boy walked out from behind the animal. "You like that name, huh? Speedy?" The boy fingered the spotty little mustache that peppered his upper lip. "Because he not so speedy, is he, a donkey like him?"

"Where's the...puke-a..." What had the old jeweler called it? "Punk-a..."

"I take your *fotografia* with Speedy, *señora*." The boy ran his hand over his slicked-back brown hair. "Ten dollar *solamente*."

"Where's the polka...the poka..." Patty shook her head hard. "Where's *Janet*?"

Bzeep zeep.

Patty frowned. "What did I just say?" she muttered.

"Okay." The boy grinned. "*Seven* dollar."

The donkey squeaked and nodded. It flexed its lips, showing its teeth in a facsimile of a smile. Had the boy done something to make it act that way?

"Not interested." Glaring, Patty pushed away from the wall. "Get outta my way."

"Five dollar then." The boy shrugged and smiled. He pulled a beat-up Kodak Instamatic camera from the donkey's saddlebag and gestured for Patty to hop onboard. "Smile and say 'tequila.'"

"Fucking wetback." Patty swatted the camera from his hand. It clattered to the pavement. "Mind your own fucking business."

"Hey!" The kid scrambled after the camera. "You owe me two hundred bucks for that!"

The donkey nuzzled Patty, and she smacked its muzzle away with the back of her hand. "Fucking *ass*."

Then she froze. Something about the action slid a tumbler into place. Unlocked a feeling of...

"Patty, no!" Her f-

Her fa-

Her faaa-

Bzeep zeep.

The donkey flickered, becoming the familiar old man. The alley became a staircase she knew all too well. None of it was on The Cape or even in Mexico anymore.

"Please don't, Patty!" That voice. The old man's voice.

The hairs sprang up on the back of Patty's neck. Her bowels clenched.

The old man's bloodshot eyes were rimmed with deep, deep lines. They looked dumb as the donkey's eyes to her, dumb as knots in a board.

And there was the putrid smell of shit, but not donkey shit splattering in an alleyway. It was green-brown shit running down the old man's legs, winding around his knobby kneecaps, ribboning between the age spots on those rickety, withered sticks.

And then there was the anger rearing up because he'd soiled himself, and then there was the backhand, thoughtless as a home run by a juiced ballplayer. It caught the old man on the chin and spun him around, spun him backward and down, head against his fucking walker, body folding and twisting...

Folding

Twisting

Snapping

Snapping

Her fa-

Bzeep zeep.

Her fa- her fa-

Her father?

Bzeep zeep.

No! Not *her* father at all!

99

Janet's father.

Again, the world flickered, and Janet's face leaped up before her, blazing with rage. She was *furious* because of what had happened, even though it had been an accident.

Even though Patty had only meant to *hit* him, not *kill* him.

Bzeep zeep.

Janet's face became the face of the angry Mexican teen as he threw a punch at Patty. He landed one square in her belly, and she dropped to the pavement like a sack of bones.

Bzeep zeep.

Then, to Patty's eyes, the teen looked like Janet again...but he did things Janet hadn't done, kicking Patty again and again. He kicked her with brutal force, wearing Janet's face and form all the while.

Patty's thoughts spun the way the old man had spun down the stairs. *But she loved me! Why couldn't she understand?*

"*Gabacha* bitch!" The teen who looked like Janet landed his hardest kick yet, plunging his foot deep into Patty's gut.

"I didn't *mean* it!" Patty choked out the words. "Oh God, Janet, I didn't mean to *kill* him...I swear I didn't *mean* it!"

Bzeep zeep.

Suddenly, everything rushed out of Patty's head in a roaring wave. She felt the kid's third and fourth kicks plow into her side. The fifth and sixth were worse.

Then the nub between her eyes turned scalding hot, and she screamed...screamed so loud and so long that the kid finally left her alone.

And she didn't stop until the man dressed like a monk came and bundled her up--wrapped her in a robe of scratchy brown sackcloth and carried her down the alley in his arms.

She didn't know how much later it was when she woke, but time had passed.

She lay on a cot in a simple, windowless room with white adobe walls. A single light bulb hung from the ceiling above her, glowing dimly. The room smelled of coffee and antiseptic.

Patty felt cool for the first time all day. The nub between her eyes was cool, too. There was no buzzing or beeping whatsoever when she tried to think.

And she was herself.

At first, when she woke, that fact brought with it simple relief. There was no longer any need to fight and claw for understanding. The terror grinding in the pit of her belly was finally gone.

But the relief didn't last long. Because Patty clearly remembered hitting the old man and sending him falling down the stairs. She remembered killing him.

And she remembered what Janet had done because of it. She hadn't insisted that Patty was lying, hadn't pushed the police to investigate. She'd just thrown Patty out and told her never to come back. She'd ended their relationship forever.

"Hey there. I'm Frank." The man dressed like a monk walked in, wiping his hands on a clean white rag. He was a young man with short blond hair and eyes so pale that Patty couldn't tell what color they were. "All done with your tune-up, Patty."

"Tune-up?" Patty frowned and tried to sit up, then felt light-headed and lay back down.

Frank poked a finger between his eyes. "Your implants. They went on the fritz."

Patty searched her mind, and she remembered. "They sure did."

Frank pulled a tablet computer from one of the robe's big pockets and tapped the screen. "Talk about an epic equipment fail. This was the worst malfunction I've ever seen." He flicked his finger over the screen, flipping between pages of whatever he was reading. "The implants were programmed to edit all references to your girl-friend Janet or Cape Cod out of your sensory input and thoughts. If you saw an image of either one, the eye filters were supposed to make it look like something else. If you thought of either one, the brain censor was supposed to scramble the associated neural impulses."

Because I couldn't live with the memories anymore, thought Patty. *The memories of what I'd lost--the woman I loved and our favorite place, where we'd gone every summer.*

Frank looked at her and raised an eyebrow. "Everything did what it was supposed to until a week ago, when it started breaking down." Frank read some more on the screen and shook his head. "The eye filters broke first and started doing the *opposite* of what you wanted." He flicked his finger over the screen and clucked his tongue against the roof of his mouth. "Instead of editing out Cape Cod imagery, they made it pop up all over the place. The brain censor kept doing its job for a while, but then the mental stress of the undesirable visions fried the core. All the bad memories came rushing back to you, more powerful than ever after being repressed."

"Shit." Patty rubbed her eyes.

"You're just lucky the implants have GPS tracking," said Frank. "And the company provides a monitoring system plus onsite tech support in case of catastrophic failure under warranty. Otherwise you'd still be wandering around Tijuana in a daze." He lowered the tablet and grinned. "Good thing you bought the extended coverage, Patty."

She frowned at him. "So how the hell did I end up in Tijuana, anyway?"

"One hell of a brain fart, I guess." Frank chuckled. "You wandered across on foot from San Diego. A Mexican border guard hassled you until you threw all your money at him."

"I *paid* to get into *Mexico*?" said Patty. "Why the hell would I do *that*?"

Frank shrugged. "The implants must have put you in a kind of lucid fugue state for a while. Like sleepwalking."

"Oh my God." Patty shook her head. "I can't believe this."

"Well, it's over now." Frank raised the tablet and tapped the screen. "I've repaired the eye and brain implants and restored their original programming. From now on, you'll get the service you paid for. No more thoughts or visions of Janet Olsen or Cape Cod, Mass-achusetts."

Patty stared up at the light bulb above her, which was flickering--but not because of faulty implants in her eyes and brain. "I won't see or think of them again?"

"Never again," said Frank. "You could be standing in the middle of the actual town of Cape Cod with Janet staring you in the face, and you *still* wouldn't see them."

"Huh." Patty felt an ache in her belly.

Over a year ago, wallowing in guilt and regret, she'd gotten the implants. Since she could never have Janet or share The Cape with her again, she'd decided it was better to block them out of her mind and life forever. But now...

She'd forgotten one thing. When she'd gone through with the implants, she'd forgotten one thing.

"Wait." She sat up suddenly and grabbed Frank's arm. "Can you change the programming again?"

He frowned at her. "Change it how?"

"Can you reverse it?" Patty knew she sounded desperate and didn't care. "So all I ever see is Janet and The Cape? So they're all I ever think about?"

Frank thought it over. "Yeah, but are you sure that's what you..."

"Just do it." Tears welled up in Patty's eyes and trickled down her cheeks. "Please, just do it."

That was what she'd forgotten: how much she missed Janet. Even the memory of her.

Or the illusion.

IN ALL YOUR SPARKLING
RAIMENT SOAR

Though all of existence, to us, is a poem, certain verses are not exactly joyful. *Mmm-bzzz.*

In those days, for example, our first days on this world among humans, our tasks were not happy ones. We took no pleasure in what we did to them, though we did it for good reasons. Though we sought to find

The beauty of the burning dawn,
A spectrum woven out of eyeblinks
And tears, the heatless flickering
Of featherless wings rising
Mmm-bzzz
Rising from the darkling pool colliding
With the swirling curtain of an opalescent
Luminescence.

But the truth is, in the *mmm-bzzz* in the beginning, we did not know if we would ever reach it. If the horrible things we were doing to these creatures, primitive yet every bit as sentient as we, would ever yield up the prize we were determined to set free.

Subject 1. That was her official designation. I called her *Clarity*, because that was what I saw in her eyes the first time we met; that was what impressed me about her the most. We didn't know what she called herself, if anything. We didn't understand her language, if there was one. Not that it mattered.

At least that's what we'd thought in the beginning. That the details didn't matter.

But oh how they mattered. Like the downy black fur that covered her body. The long, dark mane
So soft, so flowing,
A beautiful veil cascading over shoulders
Over chest like a waterfall at
Night, a solar wind wrapping
Around the silver skin of a
Caressing the skin of a
Dreaming the form in the formless
Deep.
As if words could ever *mmm-bzzz* could ever express her radiance. As if scientific measurements could ever convey the dimensions of her
Magnificence.
As if any attempt to recreate the memory of her could somehow excuse what I did to her.

But back in those days, four million years ago as you measure *mmm-bzzz* reckon time, Clarity filled my thoughts. *Our* thoughts, I should say. The collective thoughts of ten thousand of us, bound in the harmony of the hive mind.

It didn't matter that she was so different from us. That, on the surface, she had so little in common with insects like us.

In a way, we were made for each other. Our ship, hibernating underground for many months after landing, built us from the genetic building blocks most prevalent on your world. The auto-mated systems constructed us in a way that best suited the local environment, our mission, and our biological software. Our *soulware*.

We'd been built and rebuilt thusly many times, on many different worlds. Always maintaining *mmm-bzzz* preserving what kept us special. What kept us the most efficient and productive polli-nators and gatherers in the galaxy.

Clarity was one of the first humans we saw when our ship finally burrowed out of the ground and the hatches irised open. As we tasted the air of this world for the first time, she stepped fearlessly out from behind a boulder.

The rest of her tribe cowered in the shadows, but not her. *Mmm-bzzz*. I can still see her, meeting us clear-eyed and square-shouldered when even the brawny males wouldn't come forth. She was unafraid, confident, graceful. A born leader.

Clarity gazed at us with wonder in her bright green eyes. And I gazed back at her with more of the same, transfixed. I knew there was something unique *mmm-bzzz* special about her right away.

Which, of course, was one of the reasons we chose her on the spot as the first subject retrieved for our operations on this world.

In our swarms, we are ten thousand strong. Each member of the swarm is no bigger than a human fingertip, but together we have

Power.

Working together, perfectly synchronized, we can arrange ourselves in the shape of a human body and execute a wide range of tasks. For example, we can guide a human female into a ship-board lab.

Which is where we can restrain her *mmm-bzzz* strap her to a metal table and drive a spike at her forehead.

Clarity didn't scream when the spike shot toward her. She didn't even watch it approach. Her eyes were fixed on me the entire time.

Was she defective for not expressing fear? Did she lack the proper response mechanism to potentially fatal stimuli?

Not if there was no possibility of *fatality.* Not if the tempered metal spike shattered like ice when it hit her forehead, leaving not a mark of damage on her.

When we applied the same test to other human subjects in our shipboard labs, the results were identical.

Clarity and her species were nearly indestructible. As we confirmed through our experiments, no external physical attack could harm them. Through some miracle of evolution, humanity had become perfected *mmm-bzzz* immortal.

And that was why we'd come here. Not to become attached to these primitive creatures, so abysmally low on every scale of development of which we could conceive. We'd come to find a way to kill them...and ensure salvation for the human race and our own species besides.

How could we possibly *save* humanity by *killing* it? Because only in death can a human being, or any sentient lifeform, evolve to the next level.

My people specialize in making that possible. We free intelligent beings from their physical bonds like a shoot from a seed.

Have you ever wondered why you hear nothing from the skies

mmm-bzzz from space? No intelligible signals from the impossible vastness?

Surely, in all that everything, there must be someone like you on another world. Someone to talk to. Someone to connect with. What are they waiting for? Why won't they call?

The answer is this: It is because
they have all become
Light.

This was the destiny we had come to help humanity attain *mmm-bzzz* realize. Enabling humans to die would free the inner light from their corporeal shells and allow it to escape into space. Allow it to join the light of countless other lifeforms in the infinite reaches.

And my people, as we ushered humankind on its way, would experience *mmm-bzzz* undergo our own transformation.

One that would save us from ruin.

Our souls were ancient. Our soulware had become degraded. When it collapsed, our sentience would dissolve; we would lose our sense of self and be unable to perform our mission. Time was running out for us.

But when humanity died and moved to the next level, the resulting surge of inner light would allow us to save ourselves. We would channel enough of humanity's light through our ship's instrumentation to burn away the impurities and reboot our degraded souls.

In a way, humanity's souls would pollinate our own, bringing new life to us. In that one tremendous release, my people would be reborn.

We would regain our immortality in the corporeal world just as humanity lost its own.

All this was riding on the shoulders of beautiful Clarity, though I'm sure she knew it not. To her, each day was an ordeal without explanation. Though I did what I could to leaven the ordeal with moments of kindness.

I would wake her in the morning by brushing *mmm-bzzz* dabbing honey on her lips. Her eyes would flutter open
Like the wings of butterflies,
soft as velvet, damp with dew,
diaphanous, intangible,
closer to whispers or
thoughts,
closer to intentions,
The feelings of lingering love from a
dream,
All that's left when you can't remember
the lover.

And then her tongue would slide out and touch the glistening honey on each lip. It would glide languidly along the top and then the bottom, licking up the sweetness as I watched *mmm-bzzz* gazed through ten thousand pairs of eyes, ten thousand facets in each eye, each facet soaking up a different part of the visible and invisible spectrums.

And then I would go to work on her. I would try to kill her again and again, day after day.

At first, I went through the same techniques my people were employing on other specimens. I had to confirm they would lead to *mmm-bzzz* produce the same effect, that her baseline was identical to the rest.

So I gathered my ten thousand buzzing selves in one body and attacked her. I tried to cut her throat and split her head open. I tried to choke her, drown her, set her on fire. I tried to break her in every way possible.

Through all of this, she remained unharmed and no more alarmed than when the spike had shattered against her forehead. Like the rest of her people *mmm-bzzz* species, she was indestructible.

She didn't seem to experience any discomfort, either. Stimuli applied externally were as ineffective at causing her pain as they were at damaging her body.

So we moved on to stage two. The introduction of pain by other methods.

Though we hadn't succeeded in killing a human, we *did* manage to stimulate pain. This, we thought, could be the gateway to death for these creatures.

The strongest results came from electrocution or intense irradiation. Strong natural forces channeled *mmm-bzzz* focused internally were able to provoke the nervous system, evoking a pain response.

I can still hear her first screams piercing the air of the lab. I'll never forget the way she thrashed on the metal table, fighting her restraints, convulsing. Eyes rolled up in their sockets or pinched shut against the waves of agony.

But her eyes were not always rolled up or pinched shut. Often, they were fixed in my direction, wide and bloodshot with suffering and desperation.

How many other humans did I torture on any given day? Clarity was not my only subject, after all.

Yet who among them possessed the grace to set aside the suffering when it ended? To face the torturer with a measure of tranquility?

Only Clarity. Only this singular angel could muster a smile in my presence.

Between sessions, I fed her honey and wheat germ. I poured purified water between her parched red lips.

Others of her kind accepted nothing from me, perhaps expecting *mmm-bzzz* fearing it would bring them more pain. But as much as I abused her, Clarity trusted me. She still seemed on some level to sense my good intentions.

I wonder sometimes how this was ever possible, given the gulf between our species. The lack of common language between us. The sheer differences in physiology. I must have looked fearsome to her, a cloud of insects roughly shaped like a man. Thousands of unblinking eyes

Like chips of polished
Ebony, thousands of black and yellow
Stingers, known only to her by the
Screaming in her own throat,
The thoughts in her own mind,
The new, suffering thing she had become because of
Me.
Her divinity, I suspect, made this miracle real.

I could not allow her to leave the ship, could not even let her off the table for fear of corrupting the experiment.

But between sessions, I brought the world to her. Projectors in the lab recreated her habitat in three dimensions around us.

So though she *mmm-bzzz* though she still lay strapped to the table, destined for more torture, she could see at least for a few moments the familiar grasslands outside the hull of the ship. The amber plains rippling

In the wind, in the blazing sunlight,
Shadows of clouds gliding over the sea of grain,
Twinned in the mirror-skins of watering holes,
Slipping over creatures bristling with horns and
Tusks and teeth and claws and beaks of every angle,

Long necks parting the treetops,
Spear tips bobbing in the lazy current.

She sighed when the image of a brightly colored bird swooped overhead, silhouetted against the sun. She smiled when a lithe gazelle sprinted past, followed by a hail of spears and a team of human hunters who'd thrown them.

When she smiled at me, too, the fascination *mmm-bzzz* adoration I felt multiplied a thousand-fold. I felt redeemed, at least a little, for the work I had to do.

And therefore able to continue to do it.

The infections took weeks to administer. One after another, I pumped her system full of bacteria, viruses, phages, fungi, and exotic microorganisms from other worlds. I administered them one and two and ten and twenty and a hundred at a time, carefully watching *mmm-bzzz* recording the effects.

This microbiological warfare had an impact. By attacking her internally, they triggered powerful shocks to her system. Like electrocution and irradiation, they caused intense pain.

But not death. Her immune system rose up always and wiped away the invaders as if they'd never existed.

Next, it was time for stage three. It was time for innovation.

Following protocols, I had charted the baseline and covered the same ground we'd been over with other subjects. Now that I'd established *mmm-bzzz* determined she was biologically identical to other humans, I could explore new approaches. Any success would likely extend universally to the rest of her species.

If I could kill *her*, I could kill *all* of them.

I'll never forget the first time I heard Clarity laugh.

I was embarking on a promising new direction in the lab--genetic manipulation. To begin testing, I needed to obtain a sample of genetic material, what you know as DNA.

I planned to collect the sample by swabbing the inside *mmm-bzzz* the lining of her mouth. I sent one of my ten thousand selves to accomplish *mmm-bzzz* perform this task.

But Clarity wouldn't open her mouth. My tiny single self hovered in front of her lips, bobbing in the breeze from her nostrils, and she wouldn't let me in.

She looked at my larger self looming over her, and I saw the worry in her eyes. This was new to her. Maybe she was afraid *mmm-bzzz* scared I was going to hurt her again.

Whatever her thinking, I sent my lone self closer to her mouth. I used his feelers and wings to tickle her soft lips.

Suddenly, Clarity's lips parted. She let out a flurry of noises from the back of her throat, a string of quick, chiming tones resonating through her sinuses, ringing from the top of her head. They were high-pitched as the song of a bird,

The tinkling of icicles snapping from a tree branch,
The whistling of wind through a hollow stone,
The singing of flowers with pollen-heavy pistils,
The cries of the stars in the night, forever
Sighing x-rays gamma rays radio waves neutrinos
On solar breezes swirling with glittering powder.

It was the first time I'd heard a human laugh. For an instant, I thought I'd hurt her somehow...but then I realized she was smiling. The fear was gone *mmm-bzzz* vanished from her eyes.

Seizing the opportunity, I tickled her more. Her mouth opened wider, and I
flew
inside.

My whole perspective changed in there. It was one thing to see her every day, to understand the functions of her body. To communicate in a rudimentary way.

It was quite another to be *part* of her, if only for a moment. To be intimately connected *mmm-bzzz* joined together.

Afloat in the warm red vault of her, I drifted over the moist mound of her tongue. I hovered between her flat yellow teeth, hoping she wouldn't bite down, and extended my own hollow tongue toward the inside of her cheek. Rubbing the slick flesh, I drew in a sample of her buccal cells, rich with genetic material, and stored it in my second stomach.

I wished I could have lingered, but I must have tickled her again. Her laugh sounded ten thousand times louder from inside her mouth. The expulsion of air threw my tiny self tumbling from her lips.

While Clarity slept, I tampered with her DNA. My component selves zipped this way and that through the lab, mapping her genome and feeding the data into the computers.

Digital simulations predicted the likely *mmm-bzzz* probable outcome of each change. I could see the affected traits and the nature, degree, and viability of their altered expressions. Sophisticated algorithms calculated the likelihood that the changes would flip the right switch.

The switch that would bring down the wall that protected humanity.

I had done this kind of work before on many *mmm-bzzz* countless worlds, with other species. Such is my people's purpose in life: to help those who cannot help themselves. To rectify the flaws *mmm-bzzz* solve the problems that hold certain species back from their rightful destinies.

This work always follows certain patterns. I've learned to recognize key moments--the breakthrough, for example--and quickly grasp their significance.

How many times had such a breakthrough led me to a solution? How many times at such a moment had I felt the certainty of rightness in all my thousand thousand stomachs? It had always been a cause for celebration.

But not this time.

In fact, when the latest simulation suggested a new direction, and I knew in my thousands of guts that I'd found the key, I set it aside. I avoided it.

Instead, I went to Clarity and fed her. I watched her smile as she licked the honey from her lips. I made her laugh with a new trick I'd invented, tickling her by fluttering *mmm-bzzz* flickering the wings of my ten thousand selves all over her body at once.

But all along, the knowledge grew in the back of my hive-mind. Dread expanded like a storm cloud above us.

Each time I went back to my work, I knew I was making progress. Each time I took it a step further, the certainty in my bellies became stronger.

Resequencing her DNA according to the template I'd designed would make her susceptible. If applied to other members of her species, the effect would be the same.

Here is the genius of it. Her body was perfected, indestructible. How then to pull away *mmm-bzzz* remove the shield?

The same way you scratch a diamond. Turn the indestructible against itself.

If, that is, you can stand *mmm-bzzz* bear to do it.

As weeks passed, I realized I might be the only one to design *mmm-bzzz* find a solution. In our daily meetings, the other swarms claimed not to be anywhere near a remotely viable approach.

Maybe, if I said nothing, I could still save Clarity. If I kept my solution to myself, and no one else came up with the same idea or an equally effective alternative, perhaps Clarity and her species would be spared.

But it was a slim hope, and I knew it. Other swarms were also researching *mmm-bzzz* exploring genetic modalities, and we were all working from the same baseline data. They could find the solution as easily as I had.

Unless I started submitting falsified reports. Unless I intentionally misdirected every other swarm by steering them away from what I knew was the answer.

In which case, I would be violating *mmm-bzzz* breaking sacrosanct rules of my species. I would be undermining the purpose of our holy *mmm-bzzz* sacred mission to this world. I would be jeopardizing the futureof my own species.

But the one creature I'd found precious in all the galaxy, the one being whom I adored with all ten thousand of my hearts, would *live*.

One night, I was called *mmm-bzzz* summoned to join the others for The Rite.

All the swarms flowed out of the great silver ship at once, shimmering dark ribbons rippling into the night sky. We merged together into one giant cloud, one great swarm of all our multitudes on this planet. We formed concentric circles and began to turn, each ring rotating in a different direction, alternating clockwise and counterclockwise.

The bright stars cast their flickering light upon us,
Glittering from our wings
and the polished cobalt facets of our eyes.
A billion trillion streams of starlight

Rushed out of the limitless heavens
and washed down over us.
So much light everywhere,
Direct, reflected, refracted, visible, invisible.
The universe a filigree of criss-crossed streamers,
The planet tumbling through a coruscating mesh.

And as I flew with the others through the tailings of that illuminated fall, I was reminded of our purpose, of our faith in that purpose. The sheer scope and importance of that purpose.

I'd come to think of it as something I could set aside just this once. As if denying an entire species its destiny was something I could live with.

The feeling of companionship with Clarity had been so profoundly *mmm-bzzz* powerfully alluring. It was so unlike the unity I felt with my hive-mind brothers, which was always inflexibly predictable. The pressure of the swarms in all their thousands upon thousands was ever-present, intrusive, demanding. Emotionless.

Lonely.

But did that absolve me of my responsibilities? Did it negate the sacred trust that had given my existence meaning for eons upon eons?

Here is how The Rite ends. How it ended that night.

Each of us carries a photoelectric wafer, tiny but highly sensitive. As we fly in glittering circles in the sky, the wafers absorb starlight and store it.

Then, at the right moment, we disperse, carrying our tiny burdens. All the millions of us, laden with our blue-glowing wafers, filter into the night. We seek out
the darkest shadows,
pitch black lightless
holes, hollows, burrows,
under roots, under rocks, in caves,

and we converge there, releasing our cargoes. The shadows blossom with tiny constellations of azure light.

It is a sacrament. *Mmm-bzzz.* It is a symbol.

We are pollinating the darkness

with starlight.

After The Rite, all our swarms came back together and mixed under the stars, merging our hive-minds into one mega-consciousness.

It was then, in that one colossal union, that the collective reasserted itself. I lost myself for a while in the mega-hive, surrendering *mmm-bzzz* submerging my own swarm's identity in the crushing embrace of the all-encompassing overmind.

Smothered by consensus, I felt the drive of species preservation in its fullest extreme. The urgency of our mission overshadowed *mmm-bzzz* choked out all other considerations. Surviving and helping humanity reach the stars were the only things that mattered.

When thoughts of my love for Clarity filtered into the gestalt, they were instantly extinguished. The mega-hive-mind tingled with disapproval

and disgust.

And they didn't give her a second thought. *We* didn't give her a second thought.

We had no desire for Clarity.

I emerged from the mega-consciousness like a drowning creature gasping for breath. As the collective disengaged *mmm-bzzz* released my swarm, I scrambled to pull myself back together, to retrieve the uniqueness that had been squeezed out of me.

When I did, I realized I was different from before. Merging with the overmind had reaffirmed my attachment to my people. Saving them felt more imperative than ever.

But as my individual thoughts and feelings came back to the fore, my love and commitment to Clarity remained strong *mmm-bzzz* undimmed. I could no more bear to lose her than I could bear to betray my people.

Two conflicting and powerful demands warred for dominance within my swarm. If Clarity and humanity lived, my people would devolve into non-sentient drones. If I saved my people, Clarity and her species would perish.

Then, suddenly, new insight blossomed within me. I saw the path to a new solution, flawed *mmm-bzzz* imperfect

but maybe one I could live with.

The morning after The Rite, I awakened her as always, dabbing honey on her lips. Her clear green eyes flickered open, no less beautiful than the day before or the first time I'd seen them.

I worked hard all day, checking *mmm-bzzz* and rechecking my calculations, running and rerunning the simulations. Growing and programming legions of surgical nanobots to follow my instructions precisely.

I fed them to her that evening, with her wheat germ. And then I waited and watched.

The next day, there was no visible change. Clarity smiled and laughed like always. Her radiance was undiminished.

But when I scanned her, the equipment told a different story. Her DNA had changed. Overnight, it had radically altered *mmm-bzzz* transformed her metabolism.

The tests I performed confirmed the success of my treatment. Clarity had begun to deteriorate.

She no longer had the capability to live forever in her physical form.

Before long, Clarity's condition was not unique among humans.

After she received the treatment, and tests confirmed its effectiveness, the swarms decided to administer it to all humans in the labs.

Of course, no one knew the full truth behind it. No one knew the way it would *really* work.

No one had found the secret coding I'd hidden away within my intricate genetic construct. They saw the surface changes, analyzed the modifications they would cause, but they didn't detect the catch I'd built into my solution.

When the results of the treatment were the same on the other humans in the labs, the swarms wasted no time going forth to treat every human being in the world.

But the swarms didn't realize there was no need to hurry. Humankind wouldn't die any time soon.

It was true that we'd brought down *mmm-bzzz* toppled the protective wall around Clarity's species. But what only *I* knew was that the process would be a *slow* one. It would take *years* for individual humans to die.

And it would take even *longer* for the human species to perish in its entirety.

I'd made life last as long as it could. Not just weeks and months, but dozens of years.

The human body would turn against itself over time, breaking down *mmm-bzzz* eroding on a long, slow slide to oblivion. I'd chosen prolonged aging and decline as humanity's lot instead of sudden, jarring extinction.

I'd given Clarity time to fully appreciate the joys of corporeal life before leaving it. I'd given her time to adjust to her mortality.

I'd given *myself* time to adjust to her mortality, too.

I'd also arranged for my people's salvation...though that, too, would take a while.

Humanity would not die all at once as originally planned *mmm-bzzz* anticipated, releasing a burst of inner light massive enough to reboot our soulware. In fact, it would take ages for enough human light to become available.

Thanks to my concealed genetic tampering, the altered trait I'd devised would be passed down to every generation of humanity with absolute fidelity all down the long ages.

As humans died, our ship would collect *mmm-bzzz* gather portions of their inner light, just enough that their escape to the stars would not be impeded. Someday, many generations later, the ship would have enough light to conduct the reboot, and my people would return to their mission.

In the interim, though, we would devolve *mmm-bzzz* revert to a primitive state. Until the Great Restoration, we would exist as common insects *mmm-bzzz* honeybees, lacking sentience. We would pollinate flowers, gather nectar, and build hives, but we would not remember who we were, where we'd come from, or what our mission had been.

It was a steep price to pay, but I decided it was better than the alternative. Better, I thought, to give Clarity a long life and delay my people's restoration rather than hastening it by killing her and the rest of humanity outright.

So the fates of humans and bees were intertwined and set in motion.

We bees would tend the fields and flowers of Earth as once we'd tended infinitely strange species of sentient lifeforms on distant worlds. Meanwhile, generation after generation of humans would inhabit the world and depart into space upon death as pure light.

In space, humans would find glittering multitudes of species from other worlds lighting the darkest night like glowing beacons,

Shooting through starfields,

Swimming through nebulae,

Criss-cross

ing flares flash

ing past a trillion wonders,

Weaving a tapestry of light

ning, a restless paint

ing of shimmering threads, rush

ing rivers all in photons of gold,

Never limited

Never alone.

And *Clarity* had made it all possible.

There came a day when I freed her from her bonds and opened the door of the ship to the outside world. She left...but to my surprise *mmm-bzzz* delight, she came back.

She always came back to me. Through all the weeks and months and years

mmm-bzzz and decades that followed,

She always came back.

One day, a lifetime later, as the sun set over distant, snowcapped mountains, Clarity returned to me once more.

By then, my handiwork was plain to see; thankfully, I still had enough of a mind to comprehend it. Though other swarms' soul-ware was almost completely degraded by then, mine was just starting to lose ground to the Great Breakdown.

Clarity's fur had turned gray, and her flesh was sagging and wrinkled. She moved slowly, plodding *mmm-bzzz* hobbling through the tall grass, choosing each step with great care. Stooped and withered, she had changed so much since the first time I'd seen her, over fifty years earlier.

Her green eyes were sunken and filmy. Tears flowed from them
into the gray down
on her cheeks.

I think she knew what was coming. I think that was why she was there. She was weak and fragile beyond belief.

She almost fell to the floor, but I caught her and helped her to the silver exam table. She sat on the familiar metal surface, head bobbing, then slowly lay back.

Her eyes closed *mmm-bzzz* drifted shut, and she lost consciousness. As she slept there, curled up on the table, I examined her with my instrumentation. The joy I'd felt at seeing her turned to grief.

According to the tests, Clarity had reached the inevitable moment. The one I'd programmed into her DNA and delayed as long as I could.

When I realized what was happening to her, my ten thousand selves flew apart, swarming the lab in denial and confusion. I was dizzy with the whirlwind of impending loss, though I'd known this moment was approaching for decades. Though I was the one who'd invented it.

I could not bear the thought of existence

without her.

The knowledge that my work would lead to

Endless days

A procession

A weight

A space

A longing

All the worse

For having once

Been quelled.

It was then I realized, as much as I'd changed her, she had changed me more. As I hovered over her, gazing at her from every angle with my twenty thousand eyes, I knew how different I was because of her.

My hive-mind had realigned in fundamental, ineffable ways. I had reached beyond the swarm and shown personal compassion to another creature of another species. Not as part of an altruistic mission programmed into my genes, but because of the

yearning

of my ten thousand beating hearts.

In changing me, she had changed everything for herself and her people. Unlocked potentials that had yet to express *mmm-bzzz* manifest themselves.

And now, for her, for us,

there could be no going back.

Gathering my scattered selves together, I pushed back the grief as best I could and prepared for the final stage of our project.

Clarity slept soundly for hours on the hard metal table. As much suffering as she had found there, I think it still felt like home to her.

The monitors told me she was failing, but I didn't pay much attention to them. I was too busy watching Clarity's face as her allotted corporeal lifespan ran out *mmm-bzzz* expired.

I watched her toothless mouth as ragged, staggered breaths flowed in and out of it. I watched her nose wrinkle and flare as it caught some scent or the memory of one. I watched as her closed eyes flickered behind the lids, following the course of a dream.

Eventually, her eyes fluttered open
Like the wings of butterflies,
Soft as velvet, damp with dew.

By then, everything was in place. What she saw when she looked around were the grasslands of her home,

The amber plains rippling
In the wind, in the blazing sunlight.
Spear tips bobbing in the lazy current.

I tilted the table so she could see what lay ahead. A silver ship burrowing up out of the ground. Doors opening along the length of it, letting out ribbons of tiny, glittering creatures.

Suddenly, a woman emerged *mmm-bzzz* stepped out from behind a boulder. She walked unafraid with shoulders squared as her fellow humans cowered and ran. Her long, dark mane rippled in the morning breeze,

So soft, so flowing,
A beautiful veil cascading over shoulders
Over chest like a waterfall at night.

Clear eyes wide with fearless wonder, she gazed at the swarm, and the swarm *mmm-bzzz* and we *mmm-bzzz*

And *I* gazed back at *her.* Thousands of unblinking eyes
Like chips of polished ebony.

The woman in the tableau smiled, and so did the woman on the table. Past and future merged as one.

Then, the scene around us changed. It became a mirror image of the lab, with young Clarity strapped to the silver table.

My swarm settled *mmm-bzzz* descended upon her, tickling her with ten thousand pairs of flickering wings. Holographic Clarity squirmed and laughed with delight, and flesh-and-blood Clarity laughed, too. The laughter synchronized, high-pitched as the song of a bird,

The tinkling of icicles snapping from a tree branch

The whistling of wind through a hollow stone.

And by the time it subsided, she was almost gone. I switched the projection to a silent image of starry space to ease her transition. Galaxies pinwheeled around us. Comets streaked past, hanging tails of brilliant incandescence. Sprays of stars drifted like pollen through the inky night, sparkling like gold dust sprinkled over obsidian.

I went to her. All ten thousand of my selves hovered over her, gazing upon that well-known form, just as well-loved in old age as in youth.

Suddenly, she gasped, and her eyes shot open. I dared hope, in spite of the evidence of my instruments, that she might yet survive.

But then.

Mmm-bzzz.

But then,
You tremble with the effort,
shudder and go limp
with a sigh.
You settle
settle
to the table
like a feather
or a brittle leaf,
A windblown seed.

Don't go.

Darkness fills me,
a smoky
smoky cloud
obstructing all hope,
choking off
all everything,
then dispersing

as a tongue of flame
Shoots through me.
Burning off the cloud
like morning mist
before the blinding
blinding dawn.

You.

Your iridescence melts the shadows with a roar,
Then laughs and twirls and disappears,
As you in all your sparkling raiment soar,
Away from every struggle, pain, and tear.

BEWARE THE BLACK BATTLENAUT

"Looky there," said Swindle, the *leper*chaun on Grist Halcyon's shoulder. He pointed with a crumbling green finger at one of the Battlenaut's cockpit video screens, and Grist looked in that direction.

On the screen, Grist saw the barren, storm-swept surface of the rebel-held moon, Sangre. The latest flare of lightning revealed a towering black figure on the crest of the hill. At that instant, the very first instant he glimpsed it, Grist knew in his heart what it was even as he knew in his head it just wasn't possible.

The flare of light faded, and the black figure faded with it back into the night. When the next lightning struck a moment later, the hilltop was deserted.

"Begorra." One rotting nostril fell away from Swindle's leprous face. "It's *him*, ain't it, boyo?"

Grist blinked hard and shook his head. "Can't say." Just then, his arm burned as the automated hypodermic cuff strapped to his bicep shot a fresh jolt of go-juice into his system. A ring of lights around the forward viewport flashed in a pattern designed to reset his body's circadian rhythms.

Must've been about to nod off. Can't have that, can we? As the go-juice pumped through his arteries, Grist felt himself return to full alertness. The Battlenaut's sensors and computers had done their job again, intervening at just the right moment with just the right dose of meds to keep Grist awake and alert for yet another hour.

Grist licked his dry lips and checked the video monitor again. Lightning spiked nearby, revealing six soldiers in Battlenaut armor facing off on a rocky battlefield...but no sign of the dark figure from the hilltop.

Grist stabbed the comm button and spoke into his mic. "Hey, Freak. Ever hear of the Black Battlenaut?"

When he didn't get a reply, Grist looked at the button he'd just hit and realized it wasn't the comm at all. He was just about to punch the real comm button when the cockpit rocked from a powerful impact. It was enough to crack his helmeted skull against the headrest and snap him back to the reality from which he'd taken a brief vacation.

Fight. That's right. His hands flew back to the steering and weapons controls. *I'm in a firefight.*

I'm fighting a war here.

Sharon "Freak" Freemare laughed like a maniac as she cut loose her Battlenaut's main guns against the oncoming enemy. One slug hit home in a big way, punching through the enemy's armor and leaving a jagged, smoking hole at the top of one leg.

Still shrieking with laughter, Freak swung a laser around and opened up on the damage. Metal and plastic melted before the onslaught, and the enemy Battlenaut's leg gave way within seconds.

The damaged Battlenaut went down hard, flat on its face. The enemy soldier in its cockpit tried in vain to force the smashed war machine to get up and fight, but it was still lying in the mud when Freak marched her own Battlenaut over to meet it.

"Hey, traitor!" shouted Freak, though she knew the downed pilot couldn't hear her. "Special delivery from the *Redeyes* for ya!"

Freak used her lasers to disable the enemy Battlenaut's weapons systems. The whole time, the smell of baking bread was so strong in the cockpit that it made her stomach growl.

Why she smelled baking bread in the cockpit instead of the usual sweat and stink, she had no idea, but she didn't let it trouble her. Better just to soak it in like the smell of roses that had rushed over her moments earlier, or the incredible smooth feeling of silk that had rippled over her skin moments before that.

Better just to enjoy the ride.

Eyeballing the display on her visor, she located the other members of her squad. Lieutenants Grist and Pellucid formed two points of a triangle enclosing the battlefield, with Freak as the third point. Four enemy Battlenauts were trapped inside the triangle, three still standing plus the one she'd just brought down.

Freak cackled as she swung her Battlenaut toward a fresh target. *These bums are no match for the Redeyes.*

That was what Freak's squad called themselves: *Redeyes*, because they fought without rest. Computers monitored the alertness of this experimental squad and administered countermeasures, chemical and otherwise, to keep them awake and fighting. Such sleep deprivation techniques promised to limit downtime for deployed Commonwealth troops, giving them an edge in the ongoing civil war against the Rightfuls.

From Freak's point of view, the experiment was the biggest success of all time. She and the others had been awake for days on end, so long she'd lost count, and still they suffered no ill effects.

If anything, Freak felt better than ever. She'd never fought more fiercely or thought more clearly in her life.

Who knew insomnia could be so much fun?

Lieutenant Robert "Raw" Pellucid was convinced that the chronometer in the cockpit of his Battlenaut was broken, but he didn't have time to try to fix it.

Even as Raw pounded two enemy Battlenauts with laser fire, he stole another look at the chronometer's readout. He growled like a dog and grimaced at the blinking red numbers.

1805. 1805. 1805.

Seems like it was just 1805 fifteen minutes ago.

Unless the extreme sleep deprivation was affecting his time perception, the chronometer was running ten times slower than reality. What that meant was, the chronometer was definitely running slow, because Raw was running fine, sleep dep and all. He'd been awake for what felt like forever and hadn't needed even a single shot of wake-up juice.

His fellow Redeyes might be running on fumes, but Raw was burning rich. He was just that kind of guy. Even before the program, he'd always kept a lid on, no matter how high the heat.

Nothing but nothing could shake the S.O.B. He was fearless, poisonous, dirty, and smart. Smart enough to wonder if someone was screwing with him.

He went over it again as he raced his Battlenaut, guns blazing, toward his closest opponent. *If the clocks are out, we don't know how long we've been fighting on Sangre. We're on the dark side of this God-forsaken moon, so we can't even count the days by sunrises and sunsets.*

His opponent's Battlenaut stood its ground and sprayed defensive fire that splashed harmlessly off Raw's armor. At the last instant, the enemy leaped out of his path.

But why would someone want us to lose track of time? Why keep us in the field beyond the three-day limit?

Raw growled again, low in his throat. *Because they want to see how far we can go. Because they want to push the redeye tech to the limit.*

Even as he spun the Battlenaut around and threw a missile at the enemy's belly, Raw ran a little mental self-diagnostic to make sure he wasn't being paranoid.

Nope. Don't know the meaning of the word, folks.

He checked the chronometer again.

1805. 1805. 1805.

How long would the researchers leave the Redeyes on Sangre? What had to happen before they pulled the plug?

The answer came to him with a surprising lack of surprise, as if he'd always known it on some level.

The Redeyes had to *die.* Only then would Command pull the plug.

Just as Grist was running his Battlenaut headlong toward a downed rebel, another blast of lightning flared nearby. A burst of static crackled from his comm.

It was followed by music.

The signal was weak, but Grist recognized the music immediately: "Tried and True," an old battle anthem from his homeworld, Tack. At the academy on Ryot, so far from home, he'd sung it to keep up his spirits. He'd sung it during many a night of drinking with fellow cadets who had also come from Tack and missed its jewel-capped mountains and fields of coppery glow-grain.

Cadets like his best friend, Mallet Cray.

Even as the rush of music and memories rocked him, Grist plowed his Battlenaut forward on pure momentum. He slammed it hard against the rebel, which seemed to be undergoing some kind of systems malfunction. As soon as he made contact, Grist wrenched back on the stick, keeping his Battlenaut on its feet while the rebel crashed to the ground.

When Grist had crippled the rebel Battlenaut and disabled its guns, he traced the music signal to a source outside the battle zone. He rotated his Battlenaut's upper body to give him a clear line of sight to the location blinking on his visor display.

Grist saw nothing until another surge of lightning washed over the landscape. In the split-second flare, he spotted exactly what he'd expected to see. What he'd dreaded.

It was at least three times the size of any Battlenaut he'd ever seen. Its gleaming black skin was festooned with weapons but not a single mark of identification. Writhing trails of electrical energy chased over it, as if the lightning had struck it and left a charge.

The Black Battlenaut. And it was playing his song.

Grist's best friend, Mallet Cray, had been singing that same song on the planet Yolanda a year ago, during an earlier battle in the civil war against Rightful forces. He'd always sung it in battle "for protection," and it had worked.

Until the Battle of Enoch on Yolanda, that is.

The song's magic hadn't done him much good when the friendly fire hit...the friendly fire from his best friend *Grist*. Grist's guns had hit a spot already softened up by rebel arms and had blown Cray's power plant. The explosion had caught Cray before he could eject and had not left enough of him behind to fill a shot glass.

All because Grist had lost his head and fired wild during an ambush.

Now, in the midst of another battle, Grist heard the same song his friend had been singing just before his death. Was it a coincidence that it seemed to be coming from the Black Battlenaut?

"It's your turn to die-yi-yi," said the gleaming silver fish wriggling past Grist's visor. "Cray's come b-b-back for the one who killed him-im."

Grist punched the comm button. The music stopped as he switched from "Receive" to "Send." "Freak? Raw? Either of you see the giant black Battlenaut?"

Freak's wild laughter rippled over the comm. "No way, man! Where is it?"

Grist's fingers fluttered over a keypad on the armrest. "I just fired you the coordinates."

"Nothing there," Raw said after a moment. "You have video of this thing?"

Grist spun through recent vid logs from the onboard cameras, cursing as he came up empty. "Missed it," he said, "but I eyeballed it twice. Black armor, heavy ordnance, bigger than our three Battlenauts put together."

Freak stopped laughing. "Whoa! You saw the *Black Battlenaut*!"

"That thought did cross my mind." Grist threw his helmet's optics to maximum magnification and gave the area a hard scan.

The only Battlenauts he saw were the four downed rebels and the other two Redeyes.

"Wait a minute," said Raw. "Do you have any telemetry on this thing at all?"

"No." Grist took advantage of a lightning flash to make another scan but still saw nothing.

"Then what if it wasn't there?" said Raw. "What if you're seeing things because of the sleep dep?"

"Not a chance," said the silver fish as it switched past Grist's helmet. Without being told, Grist knew the fish's name was *Lacuna*.

"But what if I'm not seeing things?" said Grist. "You know what the Black Battlenaut means, don't you?"

"The end of the universe!" Freak whooped so loud, the comm filters cut her signal for an instant. "Everyone and everything!"

"It's a legend." Raw's voice was calm. "A bedtime story for children."

"I know I saw something." An orange and black butterfly with the face of a grinning human baby landed on the back of Grist's hand. "Why not look into it?"

"Because we have a job to do," said Raw. "We have to push the Rightfuls off this moon."

Suddenly, the lush green jungle that had sprung up in the cockpit parted over one corner of Grist's forward viewport. In that one open corner, in a fresh burst of lightning, Grist saw the Black Battlenaut walking off in the distance over a rocky plain.

"There it is!" Grist gave one of the vines a tug, and his Battlenaut headed in the direction of the Black Battlenaut. "Hey!" said Raw. "Come back here!"

At that moment, more than anything, Raw wanted to take off his boot and scratch the bottom of his foot. An itch had been growing there for some time, and it was becoming distracting.

Now that Grist had gone charging off, however, with Freak close behind, Raw couldn't stop to scratch the itch. He had to follow the members of his squad and try to keep them from hurtling off the deep end of sleep-deprived insanity.

Up ahead, Grist and Freak raced their Battlenauts across the rock-strewn plain between the wetlands and the foothills of the Prelate Mountains. Raw's instruments and visual inspection both agreed that there was no Black Battlenaut in the distance, that the Redeyes were chasing after nothing.

The itch on the bottom of Raw's foot flared. He ignored it with sheer force of will and punched the comm. "Grist? Freak?" Neither one answered his call.

Raw changed the frequency and called again. "Redeye One to Redeye Base. Over."

Redeye Base ignored him, just like the last dozen times he'd called.

He finished the message anyway. "Request immediate extraction of Redeye Squad. Repeat. Request immediate extraction."

Still, there was no answer.

The only way they'll come for us is when we're dead. All they want's our autopsies and telemetry.

"Redeye One out." Raw punched off the comm and checked the chronometer.

1805. 1805.

He puffed out his breath and shook his head at the obviously incorrect readout. The funny thing was--and it was more funny strange than funny ha-ha--that particular time *meant* something to Raw. It was the exact moment, in fact, five years ago, when he had done the most important thing he'd ever done in his life.

It was the moment when Raw had murdered Braeburn Score.

Freak was halfway across the dry plain when she smelled smoke. She recognized it immediately as the smoke from melting plastic and metal, the smell of a burning Battlenaut. In a panic, she checked the instruments...but her Battlenaut wasn't on fire.

As far as Freak could tell, the burning-Battlenaut smell was coming from the same place as the smells of baking bread and roses that had filled the cockpit earlier...in other words, from thin air.

The burning smell wasn't pleasant like the others had been, though. It turned over a rock and sent things scurrying in her mind.

For example, she thought of the day when Gwen Tuileries had died because of her.

Right after the missile had hit, Gwen's Battlenaut had had that same burning smell. The only difference was, Freak remembered the added smell of frying meat when Gwen had cooked inside the cockpit.

All through Freak's first tour of duty, Gwen had been her guardian angel. She had always been ready to haul Freak's rookie ass out of the fire, even if it meant disobeying orders or bunging up her own Battlenaut. Or losing her life.

One night on Gallop, when their unit was pounding a Rightful garrison, Freak's Battlenaut had been crippled by a land mine. Just as enemy artillery had pumped out a missile to finish her off, Gwen's Battlenaut had leaped in to take the hit and save Freak's life.

Maybe Freak wouldn't have felt so bad about it except for one thing: she'd been working for the other side all along. Even as she'd betrayed the Commonwealth, she'd always planned to save Gwen...and hadn't counted on her own allies being willing to kill her in the bargain.

Freak had worked for the Commonwealth ever since.

As she followed Grist forward, the stench of melting Battlenaut and burning flesh in the cockpit intensified. Finally, it got to the point where it made her gag.

It was then that it occurred to Freak that maybe she'd come across a sign of the Black Battlenaut...and maybe, she had more of a personal interest in the Black Battlenaut than she'd expected.

After all, it couldn't be a coincidence that just as she was searching for the Black Battlenaut, the smell of her dead, betrayed friend rose up to greet her.

Could it?

Grist brushed a blob of pink foam from the controls of the spellcaster and programmed it to grant his Battlenaut added speed and virility. He would need every edge the magic beans could give him when he took on the destructive might of the Black Battlenaut.

Pink foam from the cockpit ceiling splattered over his visor, and he wiped it clean. He was glad the foam wasn't quite smart enough to hurt him, but it was definitely more aggressive than the green swirly-gas that had filled the cockpit a moment ago.

When the hot go-juice spurted into his arm again, everything wavered and turned red...then straightened out and became a more soothing pale blue. The ring of circadian lights flickered around the front viewport, only they weren't *lights* anymore but *darks*.

His co-pilot, Broom Thornapple, who lived in Grist's armpit, nudged him and whistled. "Wow," said Broom. "Nice welcoming committee."

Grist looked in the direction where Broom was poking. Through the viewport, he saw a line of Battlenauts lit up by the beam of his searchlight.

The six Battlenauts stood across the mouth of a pass in the foothills, shoulder to shoulder, blocking the way. Each of them was painted red and festooned with bones and skins.

"Best hope your magic hoops have the power to fry those demons," said Broom. "You know what they say about the Black Battlenaut's minions."

"Monsters. Abominations." Grist licked his lips and swallowed hard.

Just then, the line of Battlenauts began to move. Grist lurched to a stop and brought all magic wands and wish-guns to bear on the line.

All at once, the six Battlenauts raised their right knees, then dropped them. Next, in unison, they kicked their right legs in the air, swinging them to chest level.

And dropped them.

They repeated the moves. This time, they hopped a little as they lifted their knees and kicked their legs.

The ground shook whenever they touched it. Wild music skirled over the comm, its punchy rhythm matching the movements of the Battlenaut chorus line.

Freak swore she could feel the hot breath of the Flesh Battlenaut gusting against her own Battlenaut's back.

She quick-checked her visor display and saw the horrible thing still gaining on her. She was running hard, maxing the specs, and she was still going to lose the race.

Just moments ago, she and Grist had been chasing the monstrous Black Battlenaut. Now, she was the prey of something equally monstrous.

"Freak? Come in, Freak." The voice on the comm sounded like Raw's, but Freak wasn't fooled. She recognized the disguised voice of the thing that was hunting her.

All she saw on the video feed from her rear-facing cameras was Raw's Battlenaut racing after her...but she knew that, too, was an illusion. The thing that was back there, reaching for her, could not be caught on video, though the naked eye could see its true form.

Her naked eye had seen it, and she would never *forget* it.

The thing had started out as a single Battlenaut that had stepped into her path. Freak had jammed her Battlenaut to a stop while Grist had continued running onward without her.

The strange Battlenaut had stood motionless for a moment, its gold armor glinting in the beams of Freak's forward running lights. Then, it had raised one arm from its side. It had turned its hand over and opened it, revealing something pink and wet in its golden palm.

Zooming her optics to maximum mag, Freak had gotten a good look at what was in that hand. Just before the mystery Battlenaut had opened its mouth and dumped in what it was holding, Freak had recognized it.

The mangled, naked body of a human being.

As Freak watched, the Battlenaut had chewed up the human remains. It had chewed them with its mouth open, the lower jaw swinging wide to give her a good look at the gruesome mess.

After a long moment, the gold Battlenaut had finished chewing. It had opened its mouth wide once more, showing that the mashed remains were gone, and then its mouth had closed.

Suddenly, streams of pink flesh had boiled up from the seams and joints and vents in the gold Battlenaut's armor. Rolling and twisting and meshing, the flesh had stretched over the metal like a suit of skin, one throbbing layer weaving over another.

It was then that Freak had turned around and started running.

As the squad of Rightful Battlenauts opened fire on Freak, Raw leaped into action. It was either that or let them pound Freak into bits, since she wasn't fighting back.

Based on her recent behavior, Raw thought the odds were good that she didn't even know the enemy was there.

Lasers blazing, Raw charged the nearest rebel and did some damage to its guns. As slugs fired by another Rightful blasted his armor, Raw brought everything he had to bear on the first Battlenaut's midsection...lasers, sonics, missiles. The instant he let it all fly, he swung his Battlenaut hard about and bounded after the other rebel.

As Raw scorched the second rebel Battlenaut with laser fire, he checked his visor display to make sure Freak was okay, which she was: still running, barely staying ahead of the third Rightful Battlenaut. The Rightful was lighting her up with laser fire, but Freak was shrugging it off.

Unlike Raw's Battlenaut, which took a hard shot to the chest from one of his opponent's missiles. Raw's Battlenaut shook and teetered from the explosive impact and started to fall over backward.

Quickly, Raw spun the Battlenaut's upper body around and fired slugs at the ground. The recoil kept the Battlenaut on its feet and ready to continue the fight.

Raw just wished he could deal with the killer itch on the bottom of his foot so easily.

Grist marched in the Battlenaut Day parade, waving at the throngs of Battlenauts of all shapes and sizes cheering from the stands. The whole time, he searched his surroundings for the Black Battlenaut, who had run off in this direction after Grist's last sighting.

The six dancing Battlenauts at the mouth of the pass, it had turned out, had all been parts of the Black Battlenaut. Right after their big dance number, they had crashed together, cranking and twisting and snapping into one giant Battlenaut with black armor and weapons galore. Then, instead of attacking, the Black Battlenaut had raced off, leaving Grist to try in vain to keep up.

"He's out there somewhere," said High Five, who looked like an oil spill with a mouthful of yellow tongues. His voice sounded like continuous belching. He floated in midair and was Grist's new best friend. "I can feel it, buddy-Joe."

High Five was never wrong, except about women. "I hear ya," said Grist, carefully scanning the crowd. He thought he saw the top of the Black Battlenaut's head peaking out from behind the stands, but the image faded when the hypo cuff poured more go-juice into his arm.

A droning electronic anthem played from speakers along the parade route, and all the spectators hummed along with it. Vendors sold candy-coated humans stuck on sticks, which Battlenaut children licked and crunched.

"You seen one Battlenaut Day, you've seen 'em all, right?" said High Five.

Grist laughed. "You can say that again."

A second later, Grist noticed in an absent-minded way that the cockpit was full of fizzy water, and High Five had been replaced by a word, "GOOD," in bold black letters a foot high.

"What do you say, Word?" Grist slapped in annoyance at his hypo cuff, which had just shot him with more hot go-juice.

Word reshaped itself from "GOOD" to "LOOK," pointing at one of the video screens with the tail of the "K."

Without thinking, Grist looked at the screen Word had indicated. The words "BLACK BATTLENAUT" filled the screen from top to bottom and edge to edge, rapidly flashing bright and dim.

Grist tried for a better view through the forward viewport, and he got it. Just like on the screen, the words "BLACK BATTLENAUT" floated up ahead, blinking on and off.

Grist's heart beat faster. "Is that him?" He pointed at the words "BLACK BATTLENAUT" through the viewport.

Word swirled around and reformed itself from "LOOK" to "CRAY."

And it was at that moment that the comm kicked on again.

The anthem "Tried and True" blared from the speaker. A few bars in, a human voice spoke up over the music. A man's voice.

A familiar voice.

"Hi there, Killer. Time to settle the score."

"*Cray?*" said Grist.

"Hello, Sharon," said the woman's voice over Freak's comm. "Been a while."

Freak kept driving her Battlenaut hard and didn't answer. *That's Gwen Tuileries. Gwen Tuileries is dead.*

The smell of burning Battlenaut and human flesh was so strong in the cockpit, Freak gagged. The hypo cuff was hitting her with go-juice what seemed like every ten seconds. Her head was spinning, her stomach lurching.

And her dead best friend was calling on the comm.

"You're headed straight for me," Gwen said over the comm. "Just a little further, Sharon."

Hearing that, Freak slammed on the brakes. A second later, as her Battlenaut stumbled to a halt, she remembered the Flesh Battlenaut that had been chasing her.

Freak whipped around, expecting the Flesh Battlenaut to pounce on her...but the pounce didn't happen. In fact, she could see no trace of the Flesh Battlenaut in her searchlights.

She did, however, see a towering black figure.

Gwen laughed lightly over the comm. "Oops. I misspoke. Actually, I'm *right here*, Sharon."

Raw had his hands full keeping the attacking Rightfuls at bay, when suddenly his Battlenaut was hit from behind by laser fire.

A glance at his visor display revealed a familiar transponder signal back there, and the feed from the rearward camera confirmed it. Even as Raw fought the rebel Battlenauts who were chasing Freak, Freak had turned around and was shooting at Raw.

So now it was three against one. Not that he was the kind of guy who sweated the odds.

First things first. Set your priorities.

As lasers and slugs hammered his Battlenaut, Raw stormed the closest Rightful. In spite of the heavy fire, Raw drove his Battlenaut up close and shoved the barrel of a laser cannon into a breach in the enemy's armor.

After pumping in a few blasts, Raw darted away. The rebel exploded, throwing out a shock wave that sent his partner reeling.

Even as Raw struggled to keep his Battlenaut on its feet, he growled with delight. *One down, two to go.*

That was before Grist charged up and opened fire on him, too.

"Kill me once, shame on you," Cray said over the comm in Grist's cockpit. "Kill me twice...well, you can't kill the *Black Battlenaut*, can you?"

Grist tried to block out the voice as he fought to keep up with the Black Battlenaut. The behemoth had grown to colossal size; its walking strides were so vast, Grist had to run at top speed just to stay in weapons range.

He fired his lasers again and watched them skim harmlessly off the Black Battlenaut's ebon armor. The hypo cuff squeezed tight, flooding his arm with blazing go-juice.

That was when the Black Battlenaut stopped and turned. Each footfall made the earth tremble.

Grist cut loose with his Battlenaut's lasers and sonics, but he might as well have been firing feathers. The Black Battlenaut stood unfazed and stared down at him.

"Let me explain," said Cray.

At first, Grist didn't realize Cray's voice wasn't coming from the comm anymore. It took a minute for the truth to sink in.

"We should've done this a long time ago," said Cray, who now was leaning against the cockpit wall, aiming a lopsided grin at the man who had shot him to death.

Raw wasn't sure which bothered him more: fighting off three Battlenauts, two of them piloted by his squadmates, or not being able to scratch his itchy foot.

When Grist suddenly stopped shooting at him, cutting the weapons barrage by a third, Raw's itch moved up to first place. Gritting his teeth, he barely resisted the urge to stop fighting, kick off his boot, and scratch like crazy. In the process, he dropped his guard for an instant and took a laser hit that charred the armor plating on his Battlenaut's left shoulder.

Cursing as a stream of wild shots flared around him, Raw swung around. He charged toward the source of the fire, targeting his own arsenal on what had become the most volatile threat of the moment.

Freak continued to pound him with lasers and missiles as he hurtled toward her.

Freak unleashed the full fury of her weapons, but the Black Battlenaut kept stomping toward her.

Gwen's voice chimed over the comm with no more tension than if the two of them were chatting over coffee. "What do you think I'm going to do to you, Sharon? Burn you alive?"

Freak's heart hammered. *That's exactly what you'll do. Make me die the same way you did.*

"Well, it isn't gonna happen," said Gwen. "Why would I try to kill someone whose life I died to save? Besides which..."

Suddenly, everything changed. Freak was in the cockpit of her old Battlenaut instead of the current one. Looking out the forward viewport, she immediately recognized the steam vents and weird geologic formations of another world.

Laser fire pulsed past her from the fortified walls of a Rightful garrison. Commander Endymion snapped out orders over the comm in the cockpit.

She was back on Gallop, during the battle in which Gwen had been killed.

"Besides which," Gwen said over the comm, "I don't blame you for what happened."

As soon as Freak's weapons shut down and dropped, Raw doubled back and charged the Rightful behind him.

That was when something unexpected happened. A missile hissed out of his Battlenaut's rack and shot straight toward the enemy. Raw watched as the missile hit the rebel Battlenaut's midsection dead center and detonated, blowing a hole in the heavy armor.

There was just one problem. Raw didn't remember firing the missile.

Suddenly, Raw's Battlenaut lunged forward. Lasers ablaze, the Battlenaut raced at top speed for the Rightful.

As Raw watched through the viewport, his Battlenaut lit up the hole in the enemy's belly, setting off an explosion in its guts. The Rightful danced like a man touching a high voltage power line, then slammed to the ground in a pile of smoking scrap.

Raw quick-checked every status display in the cockpit, scrambling to ferret out the problem. Never in his career had a Battlenaut taken independent action like that.

He only stopped hunting the glitch when he heard a tapping sound in the direction of the forward viewport. He looked toward the noise, and his eyes widened with surprise.

His Battlenaut was pointing one of its own lasers into the cockpit.

The hypo cuff squeezed Raw's bicep and pumped him full of liquid fire. A voice echoed in his head, and he recognized it immediately.

It was the voice of a young man, barely out of his teens. "I'm back. Did you miss me?"

It was the voice of Braeburn Score.

"If you say you're sorry one more time, I'm gonna pop you one," Cray said with a smirk.

"Okay. Sor..." Grist barely caught himself. He was still in a daze, struggling to deal with the fact that a man he'd killed was apparently sitting in the cockpit with him.

"Your apologies are meaningless," said Cray. "What's done is done. Get over it."

"I can't." Grist pulled off his helmet and set it aside. "Not a day goes by that I don't think about it."

"Big baby." Cray snorted and shook his head. "It was *war*, man. *Chaos*. It was *nobody's* fault."

"I panicked." Grist's hands were shaking.

Cray leaned forward. "Okay, look." He rested his elbows on his knees and folded his hands between them. "You're really pissing me off here. All this 'poor me' crap." Cray rolled his eyes. "The not sleeping and the volunteering for suicide duty. How do you think that makes me feel?"

Grist shrugged.

"Makes me feel like kicking your ass," said Cray. "How about getting your shit together, so I can at least feel like my death *meant* something. Like you learned from your mistake and went on to *accomplish* something."

Grist rubbed his chin. "I'll try."

"Just *do* it."

"What about the universe?" said Grist. "Are you going to destroy it?"

"Ask the chicken-fish." Cray hiked a thumb toward one side of the cockpit.

A long, green fish with the head of a chicken bobbed in a bubble of pink water floating in midair. "Redeye Base to Redeye Squad," it said. "Come in Redeye Squad."

Once upon a time, a filthy young beggar decided to ply his trade outside the military academy in Soldier City on Archibald.

(As the hypo cuff pumped go-juice into his arm again and again, Raw listened to the voice in his head tell the story.)

Not surprisingly, the privileged and arrogant young men who passed through the academy's doors proved to be terrible pickings. They spat in his beggar's bowl and ridiculed him. Sometimes, they struck him on their way past.

But one young man was different from the others. Whenever he passed the beggar, this young man always greeted him and put coins in his bowl. Eventually, he even brought the beggar food and clothing.

The beggar was suspicious, as the young man's kindness was so unlike any of the other privileged military students. The young man, however, assured him that his motives were honorable.

Over time, the two became friends. They were of about the same age, in fact. Each week, the military student took the beggar to a local restaurant for lunch. The student even suggested that there might be a place for the beggar on the estate of his father, a baron.

The student was truly good luck for the beggar...especially after the beggar murdered him.

The beggar did it in a matter-of-fact way, with a strong cord around the throat. He slipped away with enough money to start a new life in another town as another man.

And he never looked back. He never regretted killing Braeburn Score in cold blood. It had simply been a thing that had to be done, a matter of survival.

His name was Flynn Jarvo.

He changed that name to Robert Pellucid. Nickname "Raw."

"You don't know the whole story," said Freak. She had adjusted remarkably well to being thrown back in time and was pumping round after round from her old Battlenaut's guns into the enemy garrison. "That's why you don't blame me."

Gwen sighed over the comm. "Go ahead. Do it."

"Do what?" said Freak.

"This is when you send the signal," said Gwen. "The go-ahead for the rebel ambush."

A chill rippled through Freak's body. "What?"

"You were working for the rebels," said Gwen. "You tipped them off."

"You *knew*?"

"I do now. The Black Battlenaut knows all." Gwen laughed. "I also know you've been beating yourself up about it ever since."

Freak clenched her hands around the joysticks and drove her Battlenaut hard. "You weren't supposed to die."

"Did I or did I not save your life?" said Gwen.

"You did," Freak said through clenched teeth.

"Then I've got no complaints. I'd do the same thing all over again."

Freak pushed the Battlenaut through the forest of close-set, mushroom-like mineral plugs. Geysers erupted right and left, spraying jets of hot steam that misted the viewports and cameras.

The tear that rolled down Freak's cheek felt as hot as the steam outside. "I've missed you so much," she said. "There are so many things I've wanted to say to you."

"I've got something to say to you, too," said Gwen.

Freak continued to manhandle the controls. "What's that?"

"Redeye Base to Redeye Squad," said Gwen. "Come in, Redeye Squad."

"You've never really paid for what you did to me," said the voice in Raw's head, the voice of Braeburn Score. "You feel no guilt whatsoever."

Raw watched the laser cannon outside the forward viewport, the weapon that his own Battlenaut was pointing at itself. "It was nothing personal."

"How do you figure?" said Braeburn. "I reached out to you as a friend, and you *murdered* me. How is that not *personal*?"

The hypo cuff squeezed tight around Raw's arm, shooting in more go-juice. "You would've done the same to me if you were in my shoes."

"You know that's not true," said Braeburn.

"I saw my chance and I took it," said Raw, his upper lip curling in a growl.

"So you think it was *fair*, what you did? You don't feel any remorse for *killing* a man in cold blood so you could *steal* from him?"

"It was *war*!" said Raw. "It was no different from *war*!"

"I have a message for you from the other side," said Braeburn. "You will suffer for all eternity for what you did to me. And that's not all."

"Get out of my head!" said Raw. "I don't want to hear any more!"

"Redeye Base to Redeye Squad. Come in Redeye Squad."

It took an instant for Raw to realize that the male voice he was listening to was no longer Braeburn's. The new voice was coming from the comm.

"Redeye Base to Redeye Squad."

Raw punched the comm button. "Redeye One here."

The voice on the comm sounded urgent. "What is your status, Redeye One?"

"Request immediate extraction. Repeat. Request immediate extraction."

"Negative," said Redeye Base. "You have new orders."

"No can do," said Raw. "We're falling apart out here."

"Enemy squad is converging on your position." Redeye Base sounded even more urgent. "We're transmitting telemetry now. Prepare to engage."

"Redeye Two and Three are off comms," said Raw.

"Negative," said Redeye Base. "Comms have been restored."

"Redeye Two here," Grist said over the comm.

"Redeye Three responding," said Freak.

"Redeye One is...out of control," said Raw. "I strongly recommend immediate extraction."

There was a pause before Redeye Base spoke again. "Prepare to engage. Repeat, prepare to engage."

The cuff squeezed Raw's arm again. He knew there would be no extraction.

The only way they'll come for us is when we're dead. That was what he'd thought earlier. *All they want's our autopsies and telemetry.*

Only one way out of this, and he'd known it deep down from the beginning.

"Redeye Squad! Form up!" Raw's hands flew over the controls. The Battlenaut responded smoothly, with no hint of rogue action.

At his command, the laser cannon that had been aiming at the cockpit window pointed away from it again.

"Arm weapons!" Raw said over the comm. "Lock and load!"

"Roger that," said Grist, playing the controls with new purpose and alertness. The need for battle readiness had snapped him back to reality.

It didn't hurt that he finally felt at peace with his role in Cray's death. It was a burden he'd been carrying around for years, a burden that had slowly been crushing him.

At last, he felt free of it. So what if his forgiveness had been granted by an hallucination?

Why not use a little insanity to inoculate himself against a greater madness?

"Armed and ready, Lieutenant," Freak said over the comm. "Fit to fight, sir," she added, and she meant it.

She hadn't slept for what must have been days, but she felt fitter than she had in years. She felt like a new woman since her encounter with Gwen.

Freak only wished the visit could have been longer. There was still one thing she'd left unsaid, one thing she'd wanted to say more than anything else.

She switched off her comm just long enough to say it. Gwen was gone, but Freak said it anyway.

"I love you, Gwen. I'll never love anyone the way I love you."

"Here they come," Redeye Base said over the comm. "They're coming right over the ridge."

"Stand by, Redeye Squad," said Raw. He kept his weapons aimed in the direction of the enemy, ready to unleash the Battlenaut's full fury at any moment.

When he checked his visor display, however, his resolve faltered. The telemetry he saw there wasn't at all what he'd expected.

Not for ten seconds anyway.

After ten seconds, the telemetry data completely changed, lining up with Raw's expectations--namely, that a squad of enemy Battlenauts was marching over the ridge.

A squad of enemy Battlenauts instead of a convoy of civilian vehicles.

"Redeye One to Redeye Base." Raw peered out the forward viewport for visual confirmation. Lights glided over the ridge and beamed back at him, the glare washing out his view of whatever was coming. "You sure about that telemetry?"

"One hundred percent," said Redeye Base.

"But first read on the visor was that those are civilian transports, not Battlenauts," said Raw.

"That was a hiccup in the network," said Redeye Base. "Current telemetry is confirmed."

As Raw watched the viewport, the oncoming lights drew closer, and the shapes behind them began to resolve themselves.

There wasn't a single Battlenaut among them.

"Abort!" Raw's hands flew over the controls as he powered down his weapons. "Redeye Squad, abort! Those are civilian transports! Repeat, abort!"

"Really?" Freak said over the comm. "Telemetry says they're hostile Battlenauts."

"Telemetry's wrong," said Raw. "I have visual confirmation."

"Negative, Redeye One," said Redeye Base. "Visual is unreliable. You're hallucinating."

Cold sweat trickled down Raw's back. The itch on the sole of his foot flared up again. "No hallucination! These are civilian transports!"

"Fire when ready," said Redeye Base. "The order is given."

"Abort!" said Raw.

"Redeye Two and Three," said Redeye Base. "Prepare to receive new orders on a secure channel."

"I heard what you said about loving me," Gwen said over the comm in Freak's cockpit. "I want you to know that the feeling was always mutual."

Freak's heart pounded. Tears ran down her face. "G-Gwen?"

"I love you and I want to help you," said Gwen. "I'm going to help you do the right thing."

"What's that?" said Freak.

"Listen," said Gwen, and then she told her what to do.

"I've got some good advice for you," Cray said over the comm. "Consider it a thank-you gift."

Grist wasn't as startled to hear the dead man's voice as the first time Cray had spoken to him. "What's the advice?"

"I'll let the chicken-fish tell you," said Cray.

It was then, in the seconds after he realized what was about to happen and the seconds before it happened, that Raw fully understood.

They're interested in more than our physical limits.

It didn't take a genius to figure out what Redeye Base was telling Grist and Freak on the secure channel. It wasn't hard to predict what was going to happen next.

Redeye Base had ordered the squad to fire on the civilian convoy. Raw, the squad leader, had failed to comply. So Redeye Base was moving down the chain of command to try to get the job done.

They wanted to see if Grist and Freak were so bombed from sleep dep and go-juice that they'd do what Raw wouldn't.

They want to know how far we can be pushed in every way.

It wasn't enough to create Battlenaut jockeys who could fight without rest. They wanted Battlenaut jockeys who doubted the evidence of their own senses.

Battlenaut jockeys who could be completely controlled.

"I don't know if I can do that," Grist said after the chicken-fish told him Cray's advice. "Raw said those are civilian transports."

"Raw's a cuckoo, boyo," said Swindle the leperchaun, twirling a green index finger alongside his rotting temple. "Who'd ya rather trust? A nut who's gone without sleep fer who knows how long, or cool-headed authority figures with all that tech at their disposal?"

Grist pinched his eyes shut to try to stop his head from spinning. "They look an awful lot like civilians to me."

"Remember," said Cray's voice over the comm. "The Black Battlenaut wears many faces."

Grist opened his eyes and stared at the forward viewport. What he saw there looked like a cluster of six-wheeled transports, the kind regularly used to carry miners between worksites on Sangre.

Was it possible that what he saw had nothing to do with what was really out there? That his senses were deceiving him?

As the orange and black butterfly with the head of a human baby fluttered past him, Grist knew he had his answer.

"But I don't want to kill him, Gwen," said Freak. "Lieutenant Raw hasn't done anything wrong."

"Oh, honey." Gwen's voice over the comm sounded loving and sad. "Redeye Base had a good reason for giving that order."

The cuff squeezed in another burst of fiery go-juice. "What reason?"

"I'm alive again, sweetie," said Gwen. "That's right. They grew a clone of me, and we're going to be together...but the lieutenant wants to keep us apart."

Freak felt like she was floating and sinking at the same time. The fog in her head was getting thicker and stickier. "He does?"

"Please, darling," said Gwen. "Please save me this time."

Raw was never sure exactly when he became the Black Battlenaut. Was it before he died? Or after?

He remembered Grist and Freak opening fire on him with everything they had. He remembered thinking

This is the only way it can end and I knew it from the beginning.

That was why

(He remembered the giant golden eyes gazing down from above, gazing down upon him like the golden eyes of God.)

That was why he made no move to defend himself. Maybe, his

sacrifice would be enough to satisfy the scientists. Maybe, having learned the limits of one man, they would spare Grist and Freak.

But he doubted it.

Even if they let those two live, the civilians were doomed, of that he was certain.

(A dark shape huge as a mountain, blocking out the stars, black metal body glinting in the glow of those giant golden eyes.)

The scientists had to know if Redeyes would gun down innocent civilians on a whim from Command, in defiance of the evidence of their own senses and the dictates of their own consciences.

(Was this what Grist and Freak had seen, this gleaming behemoth, this legendary destroyer?)

There would be innocent blood on Grist and Freak's hands. At least Raw himself wouldn't add to it when they finished killing him. His blood was far from innocent.

(He had never expected it to be so beautiful.)

(So terrible.)

The cockpit filled with the sounds of damage...the pockety-pock of slug impacts, the boom-whoom-thoom of missiles exploding one after another, the crackle and screech of metal gashed by lasers. The hiss of air escaping the broken Battlenaut, the whoops and pings and whistles of weapons alerts and systems failure alarms.

(Most beautiful thing he'd ever)

The ear-splitting whine that signalled a breach in the fusion reactor.

(Beautiful and powerful. Reaching down with a hand as big as a building)

Déjà vu.

(Splitting open the shell, the chrysalis, extracting him)

I know you.

(When the halves of the broken Battlenaut fell to the ground, they exploded in a wave of glittering golden butterflies.)

(He watched from above as Grist and Freak bombarded the civilians in a shower of fire and light.)

Or was he already there by then, inhabiting the leviathan? Or had he always been a part of it?

I am you.

The moon trembled as he turned his eyes from the flurry of smoke and flame and dirt at his feet.

Not tired anymore.

He tipped his head back, each eye the size of a cathedral, and looked up and out at the same flickering membrane of stars that lay reflected on the polished ebon plate of his face.

Good night.

SHIPWRECK IN THE SKY

Thorny Webb was halfway across the wing of the Shining Squadron cargo plane when he slipped. His foot went out from under him, and he dropped back, heading for a 10,000-foot fall and certain death.

That was when a black-gloved hand grabbed him by the wrist-- the hand of the man who was leading him in the high altitude wing-walk.

As the hand yanked Thorny back up, he quickly regained his footing on the wing's sloped metal surface. He found himself face to face with the man who had saved him--his longtime friend, colleague, and teammate, Gabriel "Grit" Carver.

Also known as the aerial hero Major Zephyr.

"Are you okay?" Zephyr had to shout over the wind and the noise from the cargo plane's engines.

Thorny steadied himself. "Next time you invite me to go *wing-walking* between two planes, how 'bout *warning* me that the planes'll be in the *air?*"

Zephyr's dark brown features crinkled in a grin as he let go of Thorny's wrist. "Now what fun would *that* be?"

With that, the two of them continued inching forward. A few

more feet, and Zephyr stepped off the tip of the cargo plane's wing onto the wing of the plane flying alongside it.

Zephyr waited there until Thorny shuffled to the brink. When Zephyr offered a hand, Thorny didn't refuse it; as chief of the Shining Squadron's ground crew, he wasn't as experienced as Zephyr at high-flying feats. The aerial action he'd seen in the Great War over two decades ago--one terrible day in particular--had convinced him that he would rather spend most of his time on the ground than in the air.

Thorny held his breath as he stepped down onto the wing of the second plane. As soon as his feet touched the metal, he noticed a change. The wing of the Shining Squadron cargo plane had trembled underfoot from the vibrations of the engines.

But the wing of the second plane--the *Irish Rose*--was without vibration. It was perfectly still.

Because the engines weren't running.

Zephyr continued toward the fuselage, and Thorny followed. As he eased around the humps of the wing-mounted engines, he stared in amazement at the propellers--turning slowly from the wind moving through them, with no power from the engines to drive them.

It was one thing to see from a chase plane, and something altogether more amazing to see up close, from the wing itself. The engines had been dead for weeks, yet the *Irish Rose* kept flying.

And no one knew why.

Thorny took a good, close look at the engines on his way past, but he saw nothing out of the ordinary. It was as if the *Irish Rose* had simply run out of fuel--but if so, then why was she still airborne?

The answers, he expected, would be found inside the plane.

Major Zephyr reached the end of the wing where it joined the fuselage of the *Irish Rose*. Leaning against the plane's silver skin, he took hold of the door handle and turned it. The latch disengaged, and he pulled the door open, stepping back out of its way.

As Zephyr squinted inside the cabin, Thorny drew up behind him and grabbed his shoulder. "Stay outside if you like," said Thorny, "but I'm going in."

Zephyr nodded as Thorny pushed past him and entered the plane. He hoped no immediate danger awaited him inside; Thorny was handling the mission well, but he was a better engineer than a commando. Zephyr had brought him along in the hope that his engineering expertise could help unravel the mystery of the *Irish Rose*...and prevent the calamity that its top-secret payload could cause if the plane ever crashed.

Turning, Zephyr waved to the pilot of the cargo plane that had brought them, and the plane veered off. Then, Zephyr followed Thorny into the *Rose*, heaving the door shut behind him.

When he got inside, he saw that Thorny hadn't gone far. In fact, he hadn't moved more than a step from the doorway, and he was blocking Zephyr's view of the cabin.

"Hey." Zephyr tapped Thorny on the shoulder. Thorny was tall enough that he not only blocked the view, but he had to duck to keep from bumping his head on the ceiling. "Move along there, pal."

Thorny shook his head slowly. "This is terrible, Grit. Just terrible."

Zephyr squeezed past Thorny, forcing himself into the aisle. As he looked around the cabin, he finally understood what had stopped Thorny in his tracks.

The cabin was splattered with blood. So were the unmoving passengers who were sprawled in every seat, staring blindly into space.

Twenty-nine men and women were dead in that cabin--the entire passenger complement of the *Irish Rose*.

Except one. From studying the plane's manifest, Zephyr knew that one more passenger had boarded the *Rose* for this flight.

That left one logical conclusion.

Zephyr drew his .45 service revolver. "The killer's still aboard." He took another step into the aisle. "Stay here."

Thorny, who was rarely at a loss for words, had nothing to say.

Zephyr pulled his goggles up onto his forehead. He looked in both directions, wondering which choice was best...and decided to try the front of the plane.

As Zephyr eased toward the cockpit, keeping both hands on the .45, he listened for telltale sounds. The plane was quiet, without engine noise--and still, he heard no trace of the lurking killer.

Gun raised, Zephyr paused at the cockpit curtain and took a breath, preparing for a fight. Slowly, he slid the gun barrel between the curtain and the bulkhead...then whisked the curtain aside.

Just as Zephyr saw that the cockpit was deserted, he heard Thorny shout from the cabin behind him.

Whirling, Zephyr charged back down the aisle. As soon as he saw Thorny, he stopped.

Someone was holding Thorny from behind, pressing a bloody knife against his throat.

"Let him go!" Zephyr took a step forward, squinting along the revolver's sight for a clear shot at Thorny's captor. He didn't see one. "If you hurt him, you're dead."

"Already dead!" The man's voice was feverish. "Already gone to hell! Never coming back!"

Zephyr cocked his head to one side. It didn't seem possible, but...something about that voice sounded familiar.

"Who are you?" Zephyr wanted to hear him talk again. "What's your name?"

"Doesn't matter anymore," said the man. "I'm cursed! I bring death to everyone around me!"

Zephyr was certain he recognized him. "Just tell me your name," he said. "Please. My name is Gabriel Carver."

"'Carver?'" The man sounded surprised. "*Grit* Carver?"

"That's right." Zephyr did not lower his revolver. "Do I *know* you?"

"I didn't do this," said the man. "Please, you've got to believe me!"

"I'd be more inclined to listen if you didn't have a knife to my crew chief's throat," said Zephyr.

The man pointed the knife at Zephyr. "I won't give it up, Grit! You understand me? They could come back at any time!"

"'They' who?" said Zephyr.

"The *killers*." With that, the man lowered the knife from Thorny's neck. Thorny stumbled forward, and Zephyr caught him.

He also caught sight of Thorny's captor's face and realized why he'd sounded familiar.

The man's blue-green eyes were wide and wild as he gaped at Zephyr. He pawed at his shaggy blonde hair and beard as if they were afire.

He was a relic of another time, a ghost from the days of the Great War--a onetime fellow pilot who had flown alongside Zephyr in battle.

Until something had driven him mad.

"Nicodemus Watt." Zephyr nodded. "After all these years."

Watt's head flicked from side to side. He kept looking out the windows of the *Rose*. "Don't let them get me, Grit. Oh *please* don't let them get me."

"Who?" said Zephyr.

"The *killers*. The ones who did *this*." Watt gestured at the rows of dead passengers. "The *gremlins*."

Zephyr frowned. Gremlins had been part of Watt's breakdown twenty-five years ago.

"They're back," said Watt. "And they're playing for *keeps* this time!"

Thorny's ears perked up. "Did you say gremlins?"

"Can't stop 'em." Watt continued to brandish the knife as he looked out the cabin windows. "They'll kill us all. *Us all*."

Zephyr moved slowly down the aisle, holding his revolver loosely at his side. "Maybe we can stop them by working together," he said. "Put the knife down, and let's talk this over."

Watt wiped a hand on his blood-smeared khaki t-shirt and boxer shorts. "I was on my way home, did you know that? Home from the crazy house. Finally all better, after all these years." His hand shook as he stared at the blood on it. "But they couldn't leave me alone."

"The gremlins." Zephyr took two more steps toward him. "But why did they leave you alive?"

Suddenly, Watt's eyes flickered and changed. "You don't believe me, do you?" He swung the knife around, aiming the point at Zephyr. "You think I'm still nuts."

"I didn't say that." Zephyr took another step forward. "I'm just trying to figure this out."

Thorny watched as Zephyr closed in and Watt tightened his grip on the knife. A fight was about to break out, and someone could die--maybe Watt, maybe Zephyr.

Unless someone intervened.

Thorny's heart pounded. He couldn't believe what he was about to do.

"Major, wait." Thorny hurried down the aisle and grabbed Zephyr's gun arm. "I know what you're thinkin'."

Zephyr's dark eyes swiveled back to lock onto Thorny. He raised his eyebrows expectantly.

"Let's hear him out," said Thorny. "He might be on the up and up."

"Are you trying to tell me gremlins are real?" said Zephyr.

Thorny shrugged and scratched his high, wide forehead. "Either that, or I'm as crazy as he is."

"This is crazy, all right." Lieutenant Mac Taylor spoke into the radio microphone in the cockpit of his Skydagger fighter plane. "It looks like the only thing holding up the *Irish Rose* is that cloud."

The voice of Lieutenant Aurora O'Reilly, Mac's fellow Shining Squadron pilot, came back over the radio speaker. "Unless the cloud's hiding something."

Mac banked his Skydagger around and under the *Irish Rose*, skimming the fringes of the cloud beneath it. The cloud was thick and gray as dirty wool, flashing with bright blue arcs and sparks.

If anything was in there other than water vapor and electricity, it would be a surprise to Mac. Ground-based radar had probed the cloud for days, picking up nothing but the underside of the *Rose*. Hawkeyed pilots had eyeballed the airborne shipwreck in countless flybys with the same results.

There was one thing that no one had done, however--no one until now.

"I'm going in." Mac eased the stick left, letting his port wingtips dip into the cloud. "I'll have a look around and pop out the other side."

"Negative," Aurora said over the radio. "We're on escort duty. Major's orders. No funny stuff."

"Don't worry, Aurora," said Mac. "I'll just make a quick run."

"Forget it." Aurora's voice was unwavering. "Remember what the Major said about taking unnecessary risks?"

Mac sighed. "Maybe you're right." He pushed a stray lock of straw-blond hair out of his eyes and tucked it up under his pilot's helmet.

Just then, he caught a glimpse of movement from the corner of his eye--movement inside the cloud. He whipped his head around just in time to see something glide past him. It was transparent as a jellyfish, stretched out like a long tendril...and crackling with blue electricity.

It was gone in an instant, slipping back into the depths of the cloud. Mac stared after it, the hairs standing up on the back of his neck. He wondered if he had really seen it, or if the curling mists of the cloud had played tricks on him.

Then, suddenly, a face leaped out from the vapor and stared back at him. Eyes of blue light flared, illuminating see-through substance as a rubbery mouth sagged open in a silent howl.

Then, the face ducked back into the smoky swirls of the cloud.

Mac shook his head hard to break the spell. Without a word to Aurora, he pulled the stick hard left, and his Skydagger pierced the cloud dead center on the spot where the face had disappeared.

"I've seen things you wouldn't believe," said Thorny. "Planes damaged in impossible ways."

Zephyr nodded. "I've heard the stories." He was keeping his gun trained on Watt, who still refused to put down his knife.

"I've seen engines torn to pieces," said Thorny. "And not by bullets or lightning. *Claw marks* in the cowling. *Bite marks* in the wiring. Unidentifiable markings left by things I can only imagine."

"Yes, yes." Watt nodded enthusiastically. "*They* did that."

Zephyr stared hard at Thorny. "So you've seen them? Is that what you're trying to tell me?"

Thorny shook his head. "I've seen what they can *do*." He looked around at the bloody corpses in the seats. "You don't need to see the wind to know it's just blown down your house."

"I don't know." Zephyr frowned and rubbed the back of his neck. "I've put in thousands of hours in the air, and I've never seen hide nor hair of a gremlin."

"I used to be like you." Watt smirked ruefully. "I used to laugh at guys like me. Used to call 'em nuts and worse." He looked out the window, and his gaze was far away. "Then, one day, my life changed.

"It was during the Battle of Arras, in France," said Watt. "Bloody April, remember?"

"I remember." Zephyr said it darkly.

"April 15, 1917." Watt tapped the point of his knife on the back of a seat. "We were on special detachment in support of the Brits, the RFC. I took up a full squadron--24 planes--and we knocked hell out of Jerry...at least until those *things* attacked."

"Gremlins?" said Thorny.

Watt nodded. "They swooped down like dragons." His voice lowered. "Dozens of them, all claws and tails and tentacles. They tore through us like pterodactyls, shredding our planes, splitting our engines...eating our pilots alive on the way down." Tears tracked Watt's cheeks, and he wiped them with the backs of his hands. "I'll never forget the screaming. The wailing of thirty-five brave men plunging to their deaths."

"Why haven't I ever heard this story?" said Thorny.

Watt sneered. "RFC command covered it up. Blamed it on the only survivor--me. It was easy, since I'd already lost my mind and couldn't argue with their version."

"And now you say the gremlins have come back for you," said Zephyr. "Is that it?"

"You don't believe me." Watt glared at him. "You didn't believe me then, and you don't believe me now."

"I didn't say that." Sensing a shift in Watt's attitude, Zephyr tightened his grip on the revolver.

"That's okay." Watt grinned and waved the knife. "I've got it covered this time."

With that, he spun and darted toward the back of the plane.

Zephyr followed but couldn't catch Watt before he'd flung open the folding door and bolted into the special cargo compartment.

The first thing that flashed into Zephyr's mind as he charged after Watt was the *Irish Rose*'s top-secret payload. What if lunatic Watt managed to activate it?

The thought was enough to quicken Zephyr's pace. He raced between the folding door and the bulkhead, emerging in the cargo compartment--and stopped dead at what he saw.

The top-secret payload was there, in the middle of the room. It was covered by a gray canvas tarp, but Zephyr recognized its unique shape--a pyramid studded with long golden spines, topped with a silver sphere the size of a human head.

He did not, however, recognize what was wrapped around the tarp.

It looked like the tendril of an enormous jellyfish, transparent and gelatinous. Looped three times around the payload, it ended in

167

a huge body of the same see-through jelly, slopped in a slimy mound on the floor.

Watt squatted beside the mound, holding up part of the body for Zephyr to see. "This time, I have proof," he said.

Zephyr blinked and swallowed hard. Even with Thorny's testimony, he hadn't really believed Watt until now.

Not until Watt held up the distended, disfigured head of a truly alien creature. The head of a gremlin.

The cloud had not seemed so big on the outside. That was what Mac thought as his Skydagger plowed through the murky fluff underneath the *Irish Rose*.

Eyes peeled for signs of the creature he'd glimpsed earlier, Mac continued onward. With the Skydagger's engine and propeller in the tail of the plane, the cockpit in the nose provided a perfect, wide-open view--a perfect, wide-open view of thick, gray cloud.

Mac sighed. He knew that something was lurking in the cloud; he'd *seen* it. He knew it was something incredible, and he knew it was the key to the mystery of the *Rose*.

But he couldn't find it.

Mac looked right, then left, then forward, and saw nothing...but the cloud cover was so dense that the creature could be yards away or less, slithering through the cloud mass just out of sight.

Maybe, it was close enough to surprise.

Suddenly, Mac jerked the stick left, wrenching the Skydagger hard to port. Gray tufts swept past as the nose of the plane swung around--but no sign of the creature appeared.

Clenching his teeth, Mac steadied the stick, then cranked it right, spinning the Skydagger to starboard. Still, nothing unusual jumped into his field of vision.

Not until the sling-faced, elongated cloud-dweller bobbed up near the end of the plane's starboard arc.

"Gotcha!" Mac shoved the stick forward, and the Skydagger leaped at the creature.

The thing ducked away into the cloud, and Mac dove after it. The Skydagger flashed forward, plunging through the thick, gray drifts.

Then, suddenly, the plane broke into an open space.

It was like the eye of a storm--calm and empty with swirling cloud all around. Mac circled it, looking for signs of the creature.

And then he found what he'd been hunting.

All of a sudden, the creature burst out of the cloud ahead of him, tendrils whipping. Mac veered around it--right into the path of another creature.

"Two of them?" Mac swung the Skydagger away from the second creature.

Only to find himself facing a third.

And a fourth.

And more.

Pumping the stick hard forward and down, he aimed the nose of the Skydagger at the only remaining patch of cloud not blocked by a creature.

His bloodstream blazed with adrenaline as the plane surged forward.

Aurora was ready to go in after Mac. She had waited a full five minutes, much longer than his "quick run" through the cloud should have taken...and still, there was no sign of him. She had called him repeatedly on her radio and had received only static.

She knew it was just as irresponsible to leave her escort duty as it had been for Mac to fly into the cloud. It was wrong to leave the *Irish Rose* and her deadly payload undefended--but she didn't have the heart to abandon Major Zephyr's adopted son to whatever danger he'd found. She cared too much about Zephyr not to do everything in her power to save him from losing another loved one.

Pulling the stick left, she banked toward the cloud. She held her breath as the gray fluff raced up to her, curling around the cockpit windows.

At that exact moment, some thirty yards away, Mac's Skydagger burst from the cloud. The plane was spinning, trailing plumes of cottony vapor as if the cloud itself didn't want to let go of him.

Other things didn't want to let Mac go, either. A swarm of see-through creatures poured out of the cloud after him, twelve at least, reaching for his Skydagger with long, glistening tentacles.

"So much for unnecessary risks," said Aurora, and then she pegged the stick hard right and swooped after Mac and the creatures.

Thorny pushed into the cargo compartment behind Zephyr, gaping at the bizarre head in Watt's hands. "That's a gremlin?"

Watt grinned...but not for long. His expression darkened as he turned the creature's head in his grip. "This is one of the things that killed the passengers and crew of this plane. It looks identical to the creatures that murdered my squadron back in Bloody April."

"Incredible." Thorny squeezed past Zephyr for a closer look. "So this is what they look like."

In truth, Thorny was more interested than he let on at that moment. Though he had never seen a gremlin in the flesh before, he had hardly flown for twenty-two years because of them. After the War, he had almost died in a plane crash in the Alps--all because of damage that could only have been gremlin-inflicted.

Zephyr grabbed his shoulder and held him back. "Don't touch it. We don't know what effect it could have on us."

"Sure we do," said Watt. "The effect is death--but the gremlin has to be alive to cause it."

Zephyr released Thorny's shoulder. "How did it get on board?"

"Exhaust vent? Loose panel?" Watt shrugged. "Maybe it came right through the bulkhead like a ghost."

"And you killed it," said Zephyr.

"I was the only one ready for it," said Watt. "Now don't you think you owe me an apology?"

"Apology?" Zephyr sounded surprised.

"For the Battle of Arras. For not believing me." Watt shook the creature's rubbery head at Zephyr. "Do you see that I was telling the *truth*? I wasn't *crazy*?"

Zephyr nodded. "Look at what it's wrapped itself around."

"The payload," said Thorny. "It was after the payload."

"Why can't you *say* it?" Watt was shouting. "Why can't you admit you were *wrong*?"

"Now is not the time, Nicodemus," said Zephyr.

"I've waited twenty-five *years*!" Watt dropped the creature's head and raised the knife. "I won't wait one more *minute*."

Suddenly, Zephyr flashed forward, batted the knife from Watt's grip with one hand, and grabbed him by the t-shirt with the other. "If I have something to *say*, I'll say it *later*...when we're not stuck on a plane with nonfunctional engines and the most powerful *bomb* known to *man* right here in this very *cabin*."

Watt slumped. "Bomb?"

Zephyr shoved him aside and scooped up the knife from the floor. With a few quick cuts, he sliced through the gremlin's coiled tentacles. When they fell away from the pyramid-shaped object, he whisked away its canvas cover.

As soon as the bomb stood unveiled, Thorny crouched in front of it, gazing in wide-eyed wonder. "The gravity bomb." His voice was hushed. "A marvel of modern science."

"Modern warfare," said Zephyr. "New and better ways to kill and destroy."

Thorny ran a finger along one of the glittering golden spines that projected from the polished black surface of the pyramid. "We can still admire the craftsmanship, can't we?"

"It could kill millions." Zephyr's voice was cold. "Our only concern is stopping it from exploding in a crash."

"We're going to crash?" said Watt.

"Not yet," said Zephyr. "Whatever's keeping the *Rose* airborne, it seems to be holding steady."

Just then, a shock of strong turbulence rumbled through the plane. Watt stumbled against a bulkhead, and Thorny fell to the floor.

Another blast rocked the *Rose*. Zephyr bolted over to a window and looked out.

"So much for holding steady," said Watt.

"This isn't good," said Zephyr.

Thorny struggled to get back on his feet as the plane bucked and swerved. He flung himself against the bulkhead beside Zephyr, squeezing in for a peek out the window.

In the sky outside the plane, he saw a dogfight in progress. Mac and Aurora's Skydaggers swooped and spun, dodging a pack of darting, whirling opponents.

Gremlin opponents.

"Maybe Mac and Aurora will take 'em all out," said Thorny. "That'd be a good thing, right?"

"Not necessarily," said Zephyr. "What if those gremlins are the ones keeping us in the air?"

As he said it, the *Irish Rose* lurched. A second later, Thorny felt as if the floor had gone out from under him when the plane suddenly dropped.

Mac fought to break free of the tentacles that had lashed around the wings of his Skydagger. He rocketed upward, then dove and banked right at high speed--but the tentacles held fast. As much as they looked like jellyfish tendrils, they were incredibly strong.

Mac tried again, this time charging left, then down, then straight up. Again, he failed to break free.

Luckily, Aurora had his back. Just as Mac hurtled upward, Aurora's fighter slashed underneath him, chewing the tentacles to bits with machine gun fire.

Mac leveled out his Skydagger and grabbed the radio mic. "Great job, Aurora! Thanks for the backup!"

Aurora's voice came back sharply over the speaker. "Great job yourself!" she said in a way that let him know she didn't mean it. "Take a look at the *Rose*!"

Frowning, Mac looped around and dove back into the battle zone. When he caught sight of the *Rose*, he understood Aurora's meaning.

As he watched, the *Rose* fell, dropping a dozen feet or so before slamming to a stop.

"Oh my God!" said Mac.

"The creatures in the cloud must've been holding up the *Rose*," said Aurora. "She's going to crash any minute now!"

Zephyr charged to the *Rose*'s cockpit with Thorny and Watt close behind. Throwing himself into the pilot's seat, Zephyr set about flipping switches and punching buttons on the control board, trying to get something to work.

Watt hesitated in the doorway, then jumped into the copilot's seat and joined Zephyr in testing the controls.

Moments later, Zephyr pounded a fist against the side of the panel in frustration. "Nothing," he said. "Engines are dead. No power across the board."

Watt sighed. "We need a jump start."

Thorny had been standing at the back of the cockpit, lost in thought. Suddenly, he snapped his fingers with both hands. "I think I can give you one! A jumpstart!"

"What?" Zephyr spun in his seat. "How?"

Without another word, Thorny sprinted for the cargo compartment.

Dropping to his knees in front of the gravity bomb, he drew a wrench from the hip pocket of his coveralls and set to work. The

Rose shuddered as he loosened bolts around a panel at the apex of the pyramid-shaped bomb.

Zephyr watched as he worked. "Brilliant," he said.

"Setting off the bomb is brilliant?" said Watt.

Zephyr shook his head. "Using it for a jump start."

Thorny removed the panel and tugged out some wires. Then, he got to his feet.

"Could somebody give me a hand with this thing?" He tugged the goggles down over his eyes. "And could somebody hold the door open? I'm going back outside."

Spinning her Skydagger like a top, Aurora blew holes through three of the creatures with her guns. Two of the things fluttered away like autumn leaves in a stiff wind, but the third continued to pummel her cockpit with its slimy club of a tentacle.

Aurora whipped the Skydagger from a backward loop into a barrel roll...and the creature would not let go. As the tentacle pounded the cockpit window, tiny fractures appeared in the glass and began to spread.

Aurora grabbed the radio mic. "I could use a little help here, Mac."

"I was about to say the same thing to you." As Mac said it, his fighter shot by, wrapped in the tendrils of five more of the creatures.

"I'll see what I can do." Aurora swung the Skydagger around and pointed it at the *Rose*, intending to scrape off the creature against it like a barnacle.

As she closed on the *Rose*, however, she saw something unexpected. Two figures were walking across the plane's wing, carrying a black pyramid-shaped object between them.

Aurora blinked hard. It didn't help.

She still saw Zephyr and Thorny walking across the *Rose*'s wing in the middle of a dogfight...and then, the *Rose* took another drop.

For a second, Thorny was airborne.

The *Rose* dropped out from under him fast. His feet lost their purchase on the wing, and he and Zephyr had nothing to hold on to but the bomb they were carrying.

Fortunately, the plane fell only a few inches and stopped. Thorny's feet met the wing once more, and he blew out a sigh of relief.

Zephyr nodded and started forward again. Thorny adjusted his grip on the heavy bomb and stayed with him.

As scared as Thorny was of flying--and gremlins--since the crash in the Alps twenty-two years ago, he knew that he had to keep going. His plan was the only one that could save Zephyr and Watt, and only he had the hands-on expertise that could make the plan work.

A few more steps, and they reached the hump of the first engine. Carefully, they lowered the pyramid-shaped bomb to the wing's surface alongside the hump.

Thorny knelt and opened a service panel on top of the engine. Then, he flipped open the panel that he'd already unbolted on the bomb.

Drawing a wire from the bomb, he stripped the tip, then stripped a wire from the engine and spliced them together. He did the same for another pair of wires--one from the bomb, one from the engine.

Next, he turned the silver sphere atop the pyramid until he felt it click. Immediately, the sphere began to emit a pulsating glow, and the black skin of the pyramid turned white. Arcs and streamers of blue energy sparked between the golden spines that studded the bomb's surface.

When Thorny placed a hand against the engine cowling, he felt nothing at first. Then, a soft vibration started, followed by a stronger thrumming.

Finally, the engine rumbled to life. The propeller turned faster, ever faster--and soon it was spinning at high speed, the blades invisible in the blur of motion.

Thorny crawled out of the way of the airstream from the propeller, and Zephyr helped him to his feet.

"You did it, Thorny!" Zephyr clapped him on the back.

Thorny nodded and smiled half-heartedly. His eyes were on the gremlins chasing Mac's Skydagger in the nearby sky.

"Can we get back in the plane now?" said Thorny.

"This is it." Zephyr, back in the pilot's seat of the *Irish Rose* after the latest wing-walk, flipped switches on the control board. "Time to shake this bird up."

Watt, in the copilot's seat, turned knobs and checked gauges. "Power restored to all engines, Grit. Green lights across the board."

"All right then." Zephyr pulled back on the wheel. "Let's see what she's got."

The *Rose* shuddered violently, then lurched forward and up. Watt cheered as the plane climbed, leaving behind the gray mass of cloud on which it had been stuck like a ship on a sand bar.

"So far, so good," said Zephyr. "All instrument readings are optimal."

"Get as far away from those things as you can." Watt looked nervously out the window. "Please don't let them get me."

"What about Mac and Aurora?" said Thorny.

"We'll see them back at the barn." Zephyr grabbed the radio mic and spoke into it. "Mac. Aurora. Come in. This is Zephyr. Come in, over."

Crackling static was replaced by Aurora's voice over the speaker. "Zephyr! There's a..." Another surge of static drowned her out in mid-sentence.

Zephyr frowned and pressed the transmitter button on the mic. "Aurora, repeat. You were cut off. Please repeat!"

The static peaked, then abruptly gave way to Aurora's voice. "I *said, watch out!* There are three *creatures* about to *attack* y..."

Zephyr, Thorny, and Watt never heard the end of her sentence. Before Aurora could utter another syllable, a deafening roar blasted through the cockpit.

It was the roar of an exploding airplane.

As Aurora watched from her Skydagger not far below, the *Irish Rose* burst apart in a ball of flame and a thunderous boom.

Fiery chunks of debris hurtled through the sky in all directions. Plumes of smoke and ash billowed out, followed by secondary explosions of fuel and ammunition.

"Major Zephyr!" Aurora cried out as her fighter rode the shock waves and ducked the worst of the debris. "Oh my God, *Major!*"

"What is it?" Mac said over the radio. "What did I miss?"

"They're gone." As the smoke cleared, Aurora saw no trace of plane or survivors. "All gone."

"Who?" said Mac.

Aurora hesitated. "I'm so sorry," she said. "It's your father."

"What *happened* to him?" Mac's voice rose with growing alarm. "What do you *mean* he's gone?"

"Oh, Mac." Aurora dabbed at a tear on her cheek. She was secretly in love with Zephyr, and it was a tossup whether she or Mac would miss him more. "I mean he's gone *forever.*"

When Zephyr opened his eyes and looked around, he thought for sure that he was dead.

What he saw was exactly how he'd always thought of Heaven--a realm composed of fleecy white clouds. He lay on a bed of cloud, gazing up at towers and steeples and arches spun from more cloud.

177

White doves swirled around winding minarets of cotton candy fluff, and shafts of sunlight slid like pastel fingers through multi-colored patches of fleece. All that was missing were the angels with their harps.

The closest thing Zephyr found was Thorny. Hearing a nearby groan, Zephyr propped himself up on his elbows and looked toward it. What he saw was Thorny, sprawled on his back in the feathery drifts.

Not far from Thorny lay Watt. The three of them had died and gone to Heaven together. Either that, or they were somewhere else, still alive...and still in danger.

Zephyr crawled over to Thorny and shook his shoulder. Thorny's eyes fluttered open and focused on Zephyr's face.

"What's goin' on here, Grit?" Thorny sat up and looked around at the pillowy cloudscape. "I guess we're not safely back at the base yet, are we?"

"Not *our* base." Zephyr smirked, then hurried over to roust Watt.

Thorny got to his feet. "Saint Peter hasn't been by, has he?"

"Not yet," said Zephyr as he helped up Watt.

"What about the other guy?" Thorny scowled. "The one with the pitchfork?"

"Over there." Watt pointed a trembling finger. "That thing'll put the devil himself to shame."

Zephyr turned to look where Watt was pointing. What he saw confirmed that he was nowhere near Heaven yet.

One of the gremlins slithered toward him through the air. Its long, transparent body acted as a prism, filtering sunbeams into radiant rainbows of light.

"Okay, gentlemen." Zephyr stepped forward and squared his shoulders to face the approaching creature. "Let's keep our heads, shall we?"

"I will if that thing will *let* me," said Watt.

The gremlin stopped a few yards away and hung in midair, tendrils weaving like fronds of seaweed in a current. Its long, rubbery face swayed from side to side, glowing blue eyes fixed on Zephyr.

Its mouth sagged open like melting ice, and bright blue sparks flickered and danced within. When it spoke, its voice sounded like a moaning wind winding through tree skeletons on a midwinter's night.

"You are safe," said the gremlin. "We freed you from the sky-dragon and destroyed the sky-dragon."

"Sky-dragon?" said Watt.

Zephyr whispered over his shoulder. "He must mean the *Irish Rose*."

"They think they *freed* us?" said Thorny.

"Just go with it." Zephyr cleared his throat and turned back to the gremlin. "Thank you. I am Major Zephyr." He gestured at Thorny and Watt. "This is Thornton Webb and Nicodemus Watt. Who are you?"

"I am Pyrix," said the gremlin. "Pyrix of the Aerielt."

"Aerielt." Zephyr frowned. "Why haven't I met your people before?"

"Our home is hidden." Pyrix spread its tentacles to take in the surrounding cloud realm. "We have avoided your world below. Until now, as we make final war on the sky-dragons."

"I don't like the sound of that," muttered Thorny. "Sounds like final war against *airplanes* to me."

Zephyr nodded. "Pyrix," he said. "If this is the *final* part, how long has your war against the sky-dragons been going on?"

"Since our rebirth." Pyrix's sinuous body trembled. "When your kind breathed new life into us."

"How exactly did we do that?" said Thorny.

"Our people roamed the skies millions of years ago," said Pyrix. "We died out in a great cataclysm...and our people would never have been seen again if not for yours.

"Men of magic found traces of us deep in the South Polar ice," said Pyrix. "They grew new Aerielt from those traces and trained us for the great war in the sky."

"My God," said Watt. "The brass said I was *crazy*--and they must have *known* all along that I *wasn't*. They must have *known* about these things because they *created* them."

"Or the other side did," said Thorny.

"Were you sent against a particular group?" said Zephyr. "Sky-dragons with certain markings?"

"At first," said Pyrix. "But after a while, we decided to fight them *all*. They chewed up too many of the Aerielt with their *guns* and spinning *teeth*...poisoned too many with their *fumes*. And they *conquered* your people."

"Conquered?" said Zephyr.

"The sky-dragons have become more powerful," said Pyrix. "They bomb your lands and kill your people. You are made to serve them."

"Tell me about it," muttered Thorny.

"We have sabotaged the sky-dragons in flight for many years." Pyrix's tendrils curled and flexed. "It has not been enough. We have never been strong enough for final war...until now."

"The gravity bomb." Zephyr's voice was cold. "That's why you wanted it."

Pyrix flowed to a nearby pile of cloud-stuff and brushed it away with its tendrils. The black pyramid of the gravity bomb appeared from underneath the fleecy cover.

"Now, we will strike at the heart of the sky-dragons' empire," said Pyrix. "This bomb will utterly destroy it for all time."

"The heart of the empire?" said Thorny. "Where's that?"

"You are about to see with your own eyes." Pyrix turned its face upward. "The attack begins."

Zephyr followed Pyrix's gaze. Far above, Aerielt swarmed from all directions, trailing streamers of cloud-floss. They met and swirled together in a cyclone of tendrils, steaming and glittering in the sunlight, crackling with bright blue sparks.

Dozens of Aerielt flashed into the spinning formation, twisting and twining and picking up speed. Stirred by their motion, the surface of the cloud far beneath them began to whirl, circling and accelerating in the same direction.

Suddenly, the ring of Aerielt changed direction. The whirling disk of cloud unspooled, breaking apart in a coil that spiraled upward, leaving a gaping hole to the groundling world far below.

Without hesitation, the Aerielt ring snapped and corkscrewed at breakneck speed through the hole. The wild wind from their passing nearly blew over Zephyr, Thorny, and Watt.

The last gremlin in the ring spun down and disappeared. Then, Pyrix slipped across the cloud-bank, leading Zephyr and his team to the rim of the hole.

As soon as Zephyr looked down at what the gremlins were heading for, his stomach clenched. He recognized the gremlins' destination. The target of their final war. He knew it well.

"Oh my," said Thorny.

"What's that?" said Watt. "Where are we?"

"Zephyr Mesa," said Zephyr. "Our home base. Our home."

As the flock of gremlins raced down out of the clouds, the Shining Squadron roared up to meet them.

Aurora O'Reilly led the defenders, gripping the controls and speaking into the radio in the cockpit of her Skydagger. "At least we finally found them," she said.

Aurora, Mac, and the Squadron had been searching for the gremlins since the explosion of the *Irish Rose* fifty miles away and three hours ago. They'd just returned to Zephyr Mesa to refuel.

"Let's make them pay." Mac's voice over the speaker was ice cold. "Make them pay for killing my father."

"Negative," said Aurora. "This is not a revenge strike."

"Didn't catch that," said Mac. "Interference."

Aurora was having doubts about bringing along Mac. Keeping a cool head was crucial in combat, and that was the one thing he wouldn't be able to do. "Don't give me a reason to ground you," she said.

"Then don't try to pretend this isn't a *necessary* risk." With that,

Mac flung his Skydagger out of formation and charged headlong toward the gremlin army.

Aurora sighed and fell in behind him. "All right, Squadron. Form on me. Protect the Mesa at all costs!"

When Pyrix slithered away across the cloud deck and disappeared inside a fleecy tower, Zephyr turned to Thorny and Watt. "How do we save the Mesa?"

Thorny gestured toward the black pyramid of the gravity bomb. "I can take a stab at defusing that thing." He drew a wrench and wire-cutters from the pockets of his overalls.

Zephyr nodded. "Do it." He stared at Watt as Thorny hurried past and set to work. "Now how do we kill these gremlins? Pyrix said propellers and gunfire can do the job."

"And exhaust fumes," added Thorny.

Zephyr yanked the .45 revolver from the holster at his hip. "Maybe the right shot will take down a gremlin."

As if on cue, Pyrix rippled back into view on the far side of the cloud deck, headed straight for them. Zephyr raised the gun...and Watt surprised him.

"No." Watt took hold of Zephyr's gun hand and pushed it down. "No killing."

Zephyr tried to push the gun back up, and Watt resisted. Meanwhile, Pyrix drew closer.

"I'll do what I have to to save my people," said Zephyr.

"Please," said Watt. "No killing. Let me handle this."

Zephyr scowled and fought to break Watt's grip. "You're making a big mistake."

"Plenty of mistakes to go around," said Watt. "So let's change that. You know I'm not crazy and never was, don't you?"

"Yes," said Zephyr. "I know that now."

"Then trust me." Watt's eyes burned with the intensity of unwavering conviction. "I can do this."

Zephyr stopped fighting him and lowered the revolver. "Since when did you start sticking up for gremlins?"

"Sticking up for the truth," said Watt, and then he turned to face Pyrix.

The sky above Zephyr Mesa was a frenzy of action and noise.

Shining Squadron fighters flashed and screamed in every direction, spouting rounds of ammunition in rapid-fire bursts. Gremlins leaped and darted, lashing out with tendrils like bullwhips. Bullets sprang from anti-aircraft batteries on the ground, tracking the creatures who'd gotten past the planes in the air.

Mac's Skydagger hurtled through the mayhem, dodging every reaching tendril, climbing toward the cloud overhead. The gremlins had poured out of there, and that had given Mac an idea.

The gremlins had used a cloud as a base while hijacking the *Irish Rose*. If this cloud was also a stronghold, perhaps Mac could cripple the enemy by wrecking it.

Maybe then he could kill the pain he felt for not saving his father's life.

"I wanted to kill you. Every last one of you." That was what Watt said to Pyrix.

"You did?" Pyrix cocked its transparent head and fluttered its long tail.

"I thought you were out to kill my people," said Watt. "I misunderstood."

"We want to *help* your people," said Pyrix.

"Exactly." Watt clapped his hands together. "Now that I understand that, I don't want to kill you anymore. I know that your intentions are good."

Pyrix looked toward the gravity bomb, which Thorny was busy taking apart. "I have to go now. Tell your friend to stop tampering with the bomb."

"Listen." Watt stepped forward and touched the side of Pyrix's elongated face. "My story is *your* story."

"What do you mean?" said Pyrix.

"Your people have misunderstood." Watt pointed at the view of the airborne battle below through the hole in the cloud deck. "The things you think are sky-dragons--they're just machines. *My* people built them. *My* people control them."

At that, Zephyr caught Watt's elbow. "Maybe you ought to rephrase that, Nicodemus."

Pyrix's eyes widened and sparked with fierce blue bolts. "If that is true, then *your* people are the ones who have killed *mine*."

"Because we didn't *know* better," said Watt. "Because we *misunderstood*."

Pyrix reared up, tendrils swirling. "Then *you* are the true *sky-dragons*!"

Watt spread his arms. "We're just people," he said. "Now that we understand you, we can stop hurting you...and you can stop hurting us."

"Or we can *destroy* you," said Pyrix.

"And then you'd be losing something important." Watt looked at Zephyr. "You'd be losing a friend."

Pyrix hung there, sparking and rippling. He looked from Watt to the bomb, then back. His rubbery mouth fell open as he started to say something.

That was the exact moment when Mac's Skydagger burst up through the cloud deck.

The Skydagger's rear-mounted propellers shredded the cloud into cotton candy wisps. Almost immediately, the fleecy deck under Zephyr's feet trembled and sank.

Then, all at once, it gave way.

Zephyr, Watt, and Thorny dropped through the sky, plunging into the heart of the raging dogfight. Fighter planes and gremlins whirled around them, slashing through the churning atmosphere.

Zephyr reached for his companions, but they were too far away. Even if he'd managed to grab hold of them, it wouldn't have helped.

But at least he wouldn't have faced the moment of death alone.

It was coming toward him fast now--seemingly faster every second. The ground he'd escaped so often, the gravity he'd spent a lifetime eluding, were reeling him in at last.

Zephyr spread his arms and legs wide, determined to meet his end without flinching. He took a deep breath and began to count, judging that he had fewer than thirty seconds left to live.

Just as he reached twenty, something grabbed him from above. It stopped his fall, knocking the wind out of him as it jolted him to a stop in midair.

Looking at his chest, he saw a transparent tendril wrapped around it.

"Hey, Grit!" Watt called out to him from nearby, and Zephyr looked in his direction.

Just like Zephyr, Watt dangled from a gremlin tendril. Thorny did, too.

"I did it!" said Watt. "Pyrix saved us!"

Zephyr looked up to see Pyrix gazing down at him. "Thank you," said Zephyr. "Have you had a change of heart?"

"We will end this war against the sky-dragons," said Pyrix. "*Including* your people. At least for now."

"We can honor that truce." Just then, Aurora and Mac blazed past in their Skydaggers, staring from their cockpits at Zephyr in disbelief. He gave them two thumbs-up, signaling that the situation was under control.

A moment later, the fighting stopped.

"One condition," said Pyrix. "We need to understand you better. We want someone to *stay* with us and *teach* us."

"We can do that." Zephyr nodded. "We'll find you a teacher."

"We already know the one we want." Pyrix lifted Watt up onto its back. "We trust *this* one."

Zephyr smiled. "What do you say, Nicodemus?"

Watt shook his head. "If you'd told me twenty-five years ago that the damn gremlins would ask me to live with them, I'd've laughed in your face."

"This is an important opportunity," said Zephyr. "You can act as a go-between. Stop the killing on both sides."

"Maybe I'd've done more than laugh," said Watt. "Maybe I'd've *punched* you in the face."

"You can do the job, Nicodemus," said Zephyr. "I know you can."

"You'll never *know* how much I've *hated* these things," said Watt. "They've made my life a living *hell*."

"Is that a 'yes?'" said Zephyr.

Watt smirked. "Hey, Grit. Next time you're flying around up here? And you hear a funny noise, and your plane does something you can't explain?"

"Yeah?" said Zephyr.

"Forget the gremlins." Watt laughed. "That'll be *me*."

THE JUGGERNAUTS OF EL DORADO

From the sound of the heavy footfalls in the jungle, I thought at first we must be under attack by at least twenty Spaniards.

Immediately, I swung up my musket and aimed in the direction of the racket.

"Prepare to fight!" My father, beside me, had drawn his sword. He cut an imposing figure, clad in his ornate golden armor, swinging his golden blade overhead.

He looked every bit the legendary explorer, warrior, and nobleman known the world over as Sir Walter Raleigh.

"Stand your ground!" shouted Father. "We are too close to our goal to be driven back now! The fabled city of *El Dorado* surely awaits beyond those very trees!"

As he said those words, the source of the heavy footfalls stomped ever closer--then burst from the foliage not thirty yards away. It was then that we could see how wrong we'd been about what had been causing that din.

No Spaniards leaped from that thicket, ready to keep us from our prize. Francisco Pizarro (nephew of the notorious conqueror of the same name) and his army had been dogging our forces since the Orinoco River, but they hadn't gotten ahead of us here.

Rather, what was storming out of the forest was something I'd never seen before. It was a veritable juggernaut, a behemoth of gleaming black metal twelve feet high, its body studded with what looked like gun barrels. To my eyes, it clearly looked to be a weapon, a heavily armed monstrosity designed for battle.

More than that, it was *proof*...proof that we had finally found the lost city we had sought: *El Dorado, the City of Machines.*

Father, I knew, realized this, too. "Hold!" he ordered us. "Perhaps this is but an emissary sent to escort us to the city gate."

At that very instant, gouts of steam hissed out of the twin smokestacks mounted on the juggernaut's upper back. Its torso rotated smoothly to face my father, and the two big gun barrels mounted on its shoulders swung around to point in his direction.

I heard a low rumble from its body, but I was already in motion by then. Dropping my musket, I raced toward Father, my gold-plated armor clanking as I ran.

There was a loud thump behind me, as of something being ejected from a tube. I launched myself at Father, slamming him back and down to the ground, knocking the breath out of both of us.

As we landed, a projectile whizzed past overhead at a high rate of speed. The juggernaut's first shot had missed.

No sooner had it done so than Father called out to his force of thirty-five men. "*Attack!*"

Muskets boomed around us in quick succession. Looking back, I saw they did no visible damage; every ball bounced off the juggernaut's black metal skin like birdseed off a windowpane.

In short, it was incredible to behold. If the rest of the city contained mechanical wonders of a like nature, this El Dorado we sought was indeed a place of miracles unlike any I had witnessed before.

But would they be a match for the wonders of alchemy that we had at our disposal? That remained to be seen.

Hastily, I got to my feet and hauled Father up to his. Without waiting for further instruction, I unclipped one of the glass grenades from the bandolier across my chest and took a step toward the juggernaut.

By then, the machine's torso had rotated to face other members of our party. I raised my grenade--a glass sphere filled with glittering gold liquid--then pulled it back and threw it forward.

God was with me. The grenade hit the upper quadrant of the juggernaut's broad torso, shattering into a thousand tiny shards. The contents of the capsule splashed the great machine's body, the golden liquid running over its ebony skin.

Before my eyes, the black metal encasing the juggernaut turned gleaming silver, then oozed down all around, melting away from the inner structure. The liquefied metal, *mercury*, had replaced the monstrosity's impenetrable exterior.

Centuries of alchemical study had led European civilization to this mastery. We had attained the *magnum opus*, the power to recreate the philosopher's stone...and that had enabled us to transmute metals at will.

"Well done, Wat!" Father insisted on calling me by my family nickname, even in the heat of battle. "Move in, men!"

Father and the rest of us converged on the melting mechanical. Now that the skin was mostly gone, we could see a single being inside it--a brown-skinned little man sitting in a metal cage. He had short, glossy black hair and was wearing gray coveralls trimmed with red piping. A canopy of some kind of translucent sheeting--a non-metallic substance, apparently, that resisted our alchemical transmutation--had protected him from the oozing mercury.

As we drew closer, the juggernaut's pilot scowled and raised his hands. He did not appear to possess a blade or sidearm; perhaps, in the belly of that once-mighty mechanism, he had not felt the need for further defensive measures.

"Good sir!" said Father. "As you can see, we are quite capable of defending ourselves...but we come in peace!"

The pilot narrowed his eyes and rattled off something in a language I didn't recognize.

Father sheathed his sword in the golden scabbard at his waist and spread his arms wide. "We have come in search of the city of El Dorado. We wish only to explore the possibilities for an exchange of knowledge between our peoples."

The pilot rattled off a stream of words in another language. This time, I recognized it as Spanish.

So did Father. Instantly, he shifted from English to fluent Spanish in addressing the pilot. "You say you don't know this El Dorado whereof I speak? Your magnificent contraption says otherwise."

The pilot switched from Spanish to English without missing a beat. Apparently, his people had had contact with ours at some point, as well as the Spaniards. "*What* contraption?" He grinned at the puddle of mercury spreading out from the juggernaut's base.

"Touché." Father laughed. "Then I hope, since you are without the protection of such a device, that you will allow us to escort you safely through the wilderness." He walked to the edge of the puddle and extended a hand.

The pilot sighed and took the hand. "What did you say your name was?"

"Sir Walter Raleigh." Father turned and nodded in my direction. "This is my son, Wat. And your name, sir?"

"Ganix," said the pilot as Father helped him step free of the metal framework. "Call me Ganix."

We encountered no further mechanical activity as we proceeded into the jungle along the trail of broken limbs and crushed underbrush left by the juggernaut. Nevertheless, we were all on guard.

Moving at the head of our phalanx, I kept my musket in hand and my grenades at the ready. My heart hammered in my chest, and sweat rolled down my sides and back, soaking the gold-thread tunic under my armor.

From the beginning, when we'd set sail from England, this had been the most important expedition of our lives. Father and I had so much to prove--him near the end of his career, and I at the start of my own. But now that we'd met the juggernaut, the stakes had risen. For now we knew that Father had been right all along.

"How much further?" I asked Ganix.

"Hard to say." Ganix wriggled his arms, which I had bound behind his back. "Perhaps, if you untied me, it would restore my circulation and jog my memory."

"Not just yet," said Father. "I've heard that a sudden rush of blood to the head can be unhealthy."

The heat of the jungle could likewise be unhealthy, and represented a danger all its own. Checking the sun through the canopy, I could see we were barely an hour away from noon, at which time the day's highest heat would settle upon us. How much longer could we continue our march without losing momentum?

If it were up to Father, we would never slow or stop. Though weighted with armor and armaments in the jungle heat, and aged not a day under 60, he walked with a spring in his step, as if on the way to a merry picnic in the English countryside.

And he never stopped talking for long. "I assure you, I am a great friend of El Dorado," he told Ganix. "I have been here before, to Guyana, in search of it."

"Why bother?" Ganix nodded at Father's armor. "You would seem to have all the wealth you could ever need."

"Wealth?"

"Everything you wear and carry appears to be solid gold or gold-plated," said Ganix. "I can't imagine where you found so much of that precious metal."

"Oh, this?" Father patted his golden breastplate. "We can *make* all the gold we like. We've been able to do so for *decades*. Haven't you heard of *alchemy*, dear fellow?"

"You can change the properties of metals?" said Ganix.

"Metals...and *other* substances. Solids, liquids, and gases are equally at our command." Father grinned and squeezed Ganix's shoulder. "You see? A relationship between our peoples *could* be beneficial, after all."

It must have been noon, at least, when I noticed a change in the air...a thickening, as of greater humidity.

Then, amid the constant chatter and screeching of jungle insects and animals, I heard the keening cry of a gull. The bird's message was clear.

There was a body of water nearby.

Picking up my pace, I surged ahead of the others. The presence of a large body of water here in the uncharted mountains of Guyana--at the end of a mechanical juggernaut's trail, no less-- could mean only one thing.

As the foliage thinned, I broke into a run. Suddenly, I burst through the treeline, emerging into the full brightness of the unfiltered sun.

A vast curtain of dazzling blue spread out before me, filling an enormous basin ringed by rugged mountain peaks. More gulls wheeled in the sky overhead, gliding among the clouds.

But not all the clouds were the product of Nature. Off in the distance, on the far side of this massive lake, giant plumes of white vapor puffed skyward. When I saw their common source for the first time, I gasped.

Father did the same thing when he drew up beside me. "Dear God." I felt his hand fall upon my shoulder and perch there, softly as a bird. "It's Lake Parime."

Along that far shore, at the base of a mountain blanketed in emerald jungle, sprawled a city of iron gray and gleaming chrome. Even from a distance, I could see that its structures were ever in motion, pumping and turning and swinging with the regular rhythm of mechanical equipment. From end to end, huge smokestacks yawned out billows of whiteness.

"El Dorado." Father said it in a hushed voice and squeezed my shoulder. "The legendary lost city of machines."

With Father in the lead and myself close behind, our party set off along the shore. El Dorado beckoned in the distance, rippling with the afternoon's heat like some desert mirage.

Probably, we would have benefited from waiting out the worst of that heat, but none of us suggested it. With El Dorado in sight, and Father marching toward it with renewed vigor, how could any of us do otherwise?

Only Ganix dared speak his own mind on the subject. "Would it kill you to take a break for five minutes? Or at least walk in the shade of the jungle?" He blew out his breath in frustration. "If humane treatment of your prisoner isn't reason enough, I suspect it would make more sense not to approach the city out in the open, strategically speaking."

"If I wanted to *attack* it, maybe," said Father. "But I only wish to *visit* it in peace. We have nothing to hide here."

"I wonder if the inhabitants will accept your good intentions at face value," said Ganix.

Father ignored the comment. "I have *dreamed* of visiting this place...a civilization founded primarily on *mechanical* principals, rather than *alchemical* ones."

"And *I* have dreamed of dropping dead from *heat exhaustion*," said Ganix. "I wonder whose dream will come true first?"

Father ignored his comments. "European society has grown dependent on the works of alchemy, unwilling to consider the value of any but the most limited applications of the mechanical arts-- ships and muskets, for example. But I know better. I realize that for all our transmutations, true advancement lies in the manipulation of the physical world by mechanical means."

Ganix turned to me with a pleading expression. "*Please*, good sir, won't you untie my hands so I may hold them over my ears and *block out* his endless yammering?"

"Perhaps that is just the thing for us." Father stopped in his tracks and cast a meaningful gaze at Ganix. "Perhaps we should do as he suggests."

"Oh, good," said Ganix. "Oh, yes, please."

"Father?" I frowned with concern.

"If we free him and send him ahead, perhaps his people will see it as a sign of goodwill," said Father. "A demonstration of our good intentions."

"Oh, certainly." Ganix nodded energetically. "That's *exactly* how they would see it."

"Or they might consider it ample *warning* to galvanize their defenses against us!" I said. "Do you really think it wise to give up the element of surprise?"

"*Look* at that place." Father gestured at El Dorado as it rippled in the distance. "Do you really think they cannot defend against us if they so choose, whether warned in advance or not?"

"All the more reason to consider his value as a *hostage*," I said.

"The very act of using him as a bargaining chip might bring about the very end we seek to avoid." Father walked behind Ganix and undid the bonds around his wrists. "Short-sightedness will not gain us the keys to paradise, Wat."

I felt my face flush at his dismissive remarks, so typical of his general attitude toward me.

"Now then." Father tossed me the cords he'd just untied and stood before Ganix with his hands on his hips. "There are conditions on your freedom."

Ganix rubbed his wrists. "Is that so?"

"I expect you to tell them we chose not to hurt you."

"'Them?'" Ganix raised an eyebrow.

"Your people," said Father. "Tell them also what we did to your juggernaut, and that we could do much worse if confronted."

Ganix shrugged. "Can I go now?"

Father reached out and poked him in the chest with one gold-gauntleted finger. "Tell them also that we bring them a very great gift...and a stern warning of great dangers in store."

"Don't worry," said Ganix. "I will make it very clear how dangerous you are."

"*Other* dangers," snapped Father. "And let there be no doubt, Francisco Pizarro would *not* have set you free as I now do." With that, he stepped aside and gestured for Ganix to leave. "Until we meet again, good Ganix."

Ganix frowned and hesitated, as if uncertain he should leave. Then, he ran off along the shore and disappeared around the bend of a high-banked cove.

As we continued on course toward El Dorado, I picked up grumblings from the men. As loyal as they were to Father, there were doubts about his decision to release the prisoner...and I shared them.

It was a situation that recurred often in those days, in his old age; in years gone by, I never would have doubted him...but now, I had to wonder if his faculties were intact. Once in a while, I would catch him forgetting something, or misspeaking, or making a mistake, and I would wonder. Was the great Sir Water Raleigh still as great as he once had been?

I was all too aware of the irony. Father didn't fully trust me because I was young, in my twenties, and I didn't fully trust him because he was old.

The first juggernauts showed up two hours later, when we were less than a mile from El Dorado.

With the city so close, looming just ahead, I felt the ground rumble underfoot. The shaking swiftly increased in intensity, making my glass grenades rattle on their golden bandolier.

"To arms!" shouted Father. "Prepare to defend yourselves!"

As the words left his lips, the ground pushed upward some twenty yards ahead of us. The hump rose quickly, shedding sand

195

and pebbles to reveal gleaming black armor underneath--the familiar form of a juggernaut like the one that had attacked us earlier.

As the first juggernaut reached its full twelve-foot height, two more thrust up on either side of it. When the rumbling ended, our path to the city was blocked by three black juggernauts with gun barrels pointed in our direction.

Father raised an arm and shouted so we all could hear. "Don't waste your bullets, men! We already know they won't pierce that armor!"

Suddenly, the middle juggernaut released jets of steam from the smokestacks on its back and lowered its guns. The other two juggernauts did the same.

"Hello?" Father waved at the juggernauts. "I am Sir Walter Raleigh of the British Empire. Perhaps your man, Ganix, has told you of me."

Just then, steam hissed from vents at the base of the middle juggernaut's head. An obsidian plate slid up into the cowling atop the head, revealing a human face staring out at us.

Ganix's face. "Yes, my 'man' has told me of you, though he *did* say you tend to talk too much, which could be a problem."

Father laughed. "For what reason, friend Ganix?"

"Because we have not a moment to waste." Ganix looked dead serious. "El Dorado has fallen to Pizarro, and we need your alchemical wizardry to help us regain it."

From above, none of us had realized that a network of tunnels ran beneath our feet. That soon changed when Ganix took us underground.

Our party gathered around him and the other two juggernauts, filling a rectangular section of beach that turned out to be a moving platform. Powered by steam pressure (like so many of El Dorado's innovations), the platform lowered us into the earth. As soon as our heads were below ground level, a door slid shut above us, concealing the opening into which we had descended.

After dropping dozens of feet, our platform came to rest in a dimly lit tunnel. Following Ganix's example, we stepped clear of the conveyance, which then ascended back toward the surface.

"These tunnels were built for emergency evacuations of the city." Ganix's voice echoed when he spoke. "Unfortunately, few citizens thought to use them today until it was too late."

"Yet *you* managed to escape," I said.

"When I entered El Dorado and saw the Spanish forces in control, I fled underground," said Ganix. "My friends, and certain others, were already below, preparing to retake the city."

"I did warn you about Pizarro," said Father. "He is every bit the conquering savage that his father, Hernando, and his uncles were...perhaps more so."

"We have had some small experience with Spaniards," said Ganix. "But they were monks, not conquerors. They taught us their language but never *harmed* us."

Father glared. "How many of your people has Pizarro killed so far?"

"Twenty, at last count," said Ganix. "Based on what I've heard, he is interested in turning the city into a manufacturing center for war materials and utilizing the populace as a captive work force."

"So he can carve out his own empire in the Americas, no doubt." Father shook his head in disgust.

"Tell us about his forces," I said. "How many men?"

"Around a hundred," said Ganix. "All of them carry firearms and alchemical weapons similar to yours--grenades and sprays capable of transmuting metals."

I nodded. "And what of *your* remaining forces?"

"Five juggernauts, armed as you have seen." Ganix gestured at his two companions, who stood behind him. "A dozen men and women, only three of whom possess some degree of military training. Two dozen personal projectile launchers, intended for use by infantry. And *flying machines*, as well."

"Flying machines?" I asked.

"Two of those." Ganix nodded. "Prototypes of an experimental design."

"*Flying machines*." Father said it in a stunned whisper.

"Sounds to me as if you have the makings of an excellent retaliatory force," I said.

"Except, perhaps, for the lack of military experience," added Father.

"And the lack of an adequate defense against European alchemy," said Ganix.

"Lucky for you, we have plenty of both." Suddenly, I felt a surge of will and conviction, a burst of inspiration. Though I was accustomed to letting Father take the lead in all things, something came over me.

Turning to the men of our expedition, I raised my fists in the air. "What say you, warriors? Shall we lend our sweat and blood to this cause? Shall we work hand-in-hand with these noble machinists to liberate legendary El Dorado?"

To a man, everyone in our party raised their fists and let loose a fierce *Yes!* (Even Father, though he looked surprised and joined the chorus a few beats later than the others.)

I whirled from them to face Ganix. "You shall have the force you need! Now let us make preparations for what is certain to be a historic battle!"

Ganix climbed out of his juggernaut and led us to the armory--the next chamber up the line--where he showed us the cache of weapons. Meanwhile, refugees from El Dorado filtered in from side tunnels, eyeing us warily.

As I looked at the stock of projectile weapons and juggernauts, I was both impressed by the craftsmanship that had gone into them and uncertain they would be enough to carry the day. Would this smattering of mechanical arms, deployed alongside our own alchemical weaponry, provide the level of force needed to stop a hundred Spaniards toting muskets and alchemy bombs?

"No." I said it aloud, interrupting Ganix's discourse on the virtues of machine-driven weaponry. "It won't be enough."

All eyes turned to me.

"We do not possess overwhelming force," I said, loud enough for everyone in the armory to hear. "We must devise a new tactic."

Father nodded in agreement. "What do you suggest?"

Gazing around the armory, I considered the question. The devices at our disposal...I had never seen anything quite like them.

Suddenly, an idea flashed through me like my own personal Pentecost. With a snap of my fingers, I wheeled to face Ganix. "Your people. Only three have military experience...but what of *mechanical* expertise?"

Ganix smiled. "*All* of them, of course. They are inhabitants of El Dorado, are they not?"

"Excellent," I said, clapping my hands together. "Then let us put them to work, shall we?"

In the hours that followed, the members of our expedition worked side by side with the refugee machinists, combining their weapons with ours.

The underground armory was filled with a flurry of activity and noise. The chatter of voices mingled with the clanging and crashing of tools and parts.

But one voice, as always, stood out to me above all others.

"Wat?" Father spoke up from behind me as I filled a metal basket with transmutation grenades. "Whatever happens, I want you to know...I'm proud of the way you stepped forward. You were most...*commanding.*"

"Thank you, Father," I told him, trying not to show how deeply his words had affected me. "I appreciate your support."

"As I have appreciated yours for all these years," said Father, "thought I have never spoken of it."

Then, without another word, he walked away, leaving me to continue my labors.

An hour before sunrise the next morning, we left the tunnels at strategic points. Contacts on the outside had sent us intelligence on enemy troop positions via a remarkable device--a communication system that transmitted voices over air waves. It was yet another invention undreamt of by European civilization, yet another reason to fight this battle for the future of El Dorado.

The time was right to attack...still dark, with many of the Spaniards still asleep. Ample sentries yet patrolled the streets and walls, but the number of alert and prepared soldiers was lower than what it would be after sunrise.

At the end of a shared countdown over the communication device, the entirety of our forces poured out of the tunnels. Mixed teams of Englishmen and El Doradoans raced through the streets, brandishing steam-powered projectile launchers loaded with alchemical pellets. The pellets, when fired, had a much greater range than hand-thrown grenades; they allowed our men and women to fire alchemical potions from a greater distance. When the pellets hit, they transmuted Spanish gold armor to a greenish gas that sent the wearer into uncontrollable coughing fits or unconsciousness.

The five juggernauts, meanwhile, applied their own hybrid weapons to broader effect. Their converted guns sprayed alchemical concoctions in far-reaching streams, turning Spanish muskets and armor to useless liquid or gas as enemy musket balls pinged harmlessly off their armor.

While our forces struck on the ground, our flying machines attacked from above. Ganix piloted one and I the other, raining alchemical mayhem upon our earthbound enemies.

The flying machines consisted of a single seat suspended inside a lightweight framework with a broad wing on either side. All this hung from a steam-powered engine that turned an upthrust axle at a high rate of speed. When the axle turned, it spun four metal paddles that somehow lifted the entire device up into the air. Once there, the pilot steered the contraption by means of levers controlling the angle of the wings and a rearward rudder.

I didn't understand all the mechanics of it, but I *loved* flying. It required some getting used to at first, but I took to it like a bird and put it to use against our enemies.

Soaring above the city walls, I dropped alchemical bombs on the Spanish sentries there, transmuting their weapons into useless mists and fluids. Swooping over the central plaza, I pelted the enemy ranks with grenades, sending them reeling.

With Ganix and I wreaking havoc from above, and our ground forces doing the same below, we were able to rout the Spaniards...until they mounted an unexpected counterattack. Spanish reinforcements charged out of buildings where they must have been barracked for the night. Dozens of enemy troops swarmed out of side streets, attacking our forces in the plaza from the rear.

This time, our men and women were caught between the Spaniards they'd been fighting in the middle of the plaza and the fresh troops striking from behind. As I rushed to lend air support, I saw loyal English soldiers and El Dorado irregulars fall before the reinforced Spanish ranks.

Learning from their past mistakes, the Spaniards also swarmed the juggernauts, attacking from all directions. A juggernaut might lash out in one direction, but Spaniards attacking on other sides managed to pelt it with alchemical grenades, dissolving its armor. Soon, only two juggernauts of the original five remained in the fight.

In a matter of moments, the Spaniards had gained ground; they might very well drive back our challenge.

This, I could not let stand. I could not allow them to ruin Father's dream...*our* dream.

Circling overhead, I gave Ganix a hand signal; I would come in from one corner of the plaza, and he would follow close behind.

Working the levers and stepping on a foot pedal to increase paddle rotation speed--and the speed of the flying machine's forward propulsion--I angled downward and dove for the Spaniards.

Musket balls leaped toward me as I came in fast and low; one punched through a wing, but the damage didn't bring me down.

Spaniards pitched grenades without making contact. Ironically, the wobble caused by the hole in my wing from the musket ball made my aircraft harder to hit.

It also made it harder to aim as I fired alchemical bullets from the projectile launcher--one after another, thanks to the steam-powered mechanism--but my targets were clustered together, improving my chances of hitting *something*. As I followed a looping course, I saw Spanish armor melt and turn to gas throughout the crowd, more than enough to soften up the troops for Ganix.

When I passed, he zoomed in behind me and emptied his basket of grenades, creating a cloud of alchemical fumes that fanned over the Spanish formation. Instead of affecting one or two soldiers at a time, as individual grenades would, the cloud swept over a mass of them, liquefying or evaporating their armor and weapons.

This opened them up to the muskets of the English and El Doradoans and the projectile guns of one of the remaining jugger-nauts, which shot them full of holes the second the fumes had cleared enough to let musket balls through.

With one half of the Spanish pincer broken, Ganix and I repeated our maneuver on the other side of the plaza. This time, he went first, softening the Spaniards with a hail of alchemical bullets, and I followed, emptying my basket of grenades.

The results were equally punishing for the Spaniards. Our ground forces blasted them ruthlessly as soon as the fumes had flushed away their armor and weapons.

At this point, the battle had swung firmly back in our favor. The strategic lesson was obvious: alchemy alone could not withstand the might of hybrid alchemy-mechanical warfighting techniques. The end of an era was at hand, and we were watching it happen in El Dorado.

Unfortunately, not all the old ways had lost their bite. Glimpsing a flurry of motion at the edge of the plaza, I swooped in that direction...only to see an all-too-familiar scene play out below.

One of the Spaniards had taken a hostage--a dark-haired young woman in a gray smock. The Spaniard was holding a sword at her throat and shouting something to a group of our fighters.

When I got closer, I saw he wasn't some low-ranking nobody. The woman was being held hostage by none other than Francisco Pizarro, son of Hernando and nephew of Francisco the elder, conqueror of Peru.

Suddenly, a lone figure darted out from a doorway and raced toward Pizarro. As I circled overhead, I glimpsed a flash of metal--a sword in the rescuer's hand.

Pizarro must have heard his approach at the last second, as he let go of the woman and spun to face his opponent. Pizarro's sword swung up barely in time to stop the stroke of his enemy, but I knew his reprieve would not last. Because I recognized the form of the accomplished swashbuckler who'd challenged him.

The man crossing swords with Pizarro was none other than Sir Walter Raleigh.

Pizarro unleashed a brutal sequence of sword strokes, driving Father back a full three steps. Father faltered, responding with a half-hearted series of parries...and I felt a pang of fear.

But I should have known better than to doubt the great Raleigh. As I watched, Pizarro mounted another charge, whipping his sword through a complex pattern of slashes. One grazed Father's breast-plate, and he seemed to stumble.

I say "seemed" because the move was intentional. "Stumbling" left and back, Father ducked a hacking blow coming in from the right...then delivered a low jab from the left that slipped between the gaps in Pizarro's armor, penetrating his upper right thigh.

Father drove the sword point deep and wrenched it around hard, slicing through flesh and arteries. Then, he pulled it free and stepped away.

Pizarro fell and let his sword clatter to the cobblestones beside him. Squirming and screaming, he clutched at the wound in his leg as his life's blood spurted from it.

Pizarro the conqueror had been conquered. El Dorado was saved.

Looking up at me, Father grinned and waved his bloody sword, signaling victory. If I had been down on the ground, I might have told him I was proud of what he'd done, as he'd told me earlier.

But I settled for flashing him a thumbs-up on my way past instead.

That evening, long after the smoke of battle had cleared, Father, Ganix, and I stood on a balcony and watched the sun set over Lake Parime. Instead of the roar of war, we heard the chugging and whirring and hissing of the machines of El Dorado, ever in motion all around us.

"We did it, my friends." Father, between Ganix and me, leaned on the balcony rail as the wind ruffled his silver hair. "We joined forces to defeat our common foe."

"And usher in a new era of cooperation between alchemy and steam." I cast a meaningful look in Ganix's direction. "If you'll have us."

Ganix shrugged. "I can't deny we worked well together today."

"You should consider the benefits of alignment," said Father. "We have much more to offer than transmutation of the elements."

"Alchemy, like your machines, has provided numerous advancements," I added. "A universal cure for all ailments, for example."

"And eternal life." Father grinned over his shoulder at Ganix. "What would you say if we told you we could give you *that*, friend Ganix?"

"I would say you have my attention." Ganix chuckled. "Yet your alchemy seems not to have provided a cure for *all* human ills, has it? Greed and hatred, for example? Cruelty and violence?"

"The human heart remains the human heart, with all its potential for evil...and good. It encourages us to make mistakes, to lose faith." Father looked over at me, his weathered face glowing with red and gold light. "And to regain it."

Ganix nodded. "If my people were to express interest in further collaboration with yours, how would we proceed?"

"You'll have to talk to our ambassador about that," said Father.

Ganix frowned. "And he would be...?"

"Him." Father hiked a thumb at me. "Ambassador Wat Raleigh."

He winked at me then, and I smiled. We had come a long way, he and I. Gone were the days when we'd failed to trust each other, when we'd kept a dark distance between us.

It was the start of a new era indeed.

"Thank you, Father." I squeezed his shoulder. "But what about you?"

"I'll be marching the captured Spaniards off to jail," said Father. "Then launching another expedition, actually." His smile widened as he stared off into the sunset. "I've heard tell of another lost city, deep in the jungles of Honduras...*Ciudad Blanca*, they call it..."

I felt a surge of warmth toward him then, a wave of love and recognition. There would always be another lost city for him, another mountain to climb, another obstacle to conquer. Always another dream for the great Sir Walter Raleigh.

It was a way of looking at the world I knew all too well, from myself as well as him. Like father, like son.

Until now, at least.

"Though perhaps I've been hasty in naming you ambassador here," said Father. "Would you like to come with me instead to Ciudad Blanca?"

Until now, when I no longer needed to tailor my life toward impressing him...no longer needed to prove myself worthy of his love.

"No, thanks." I smiled and shook my head. "I think I'll have challenge enough right here."

"I know you'll do well." Father stood away from the railing and shook my hand...then pulled me into a hug. "You're the right man for the job, Wat."

I no longer needed to prove myself because I finally had all the proof I needed.

THE MAKINGS OF A KILLER

When Morgan Vane walked into the crowded French hotel room, everyone turned to look his way except the dead man in the bathtub.

Vane could practically feel the sudden inhalation of breath from the six cops in the room...the communal gasp of surprise as they took in his familiar form. They all recognized his iconic outfit, of course, from the maroon leather jacket stretched over his broad shoulders to the black turtleneck sweater and black jeans underneath. Though he'd never met a single one of them, his six-foot-five-inch frame was well known to them all, as was his oval face, olive complexion, and glossy black cap of hair. How many times had his deep mahogany eyes stared out at each of them from a TV screen, website, or book cover?

Every one of them was thrilled to see him--not just happy, but *thrilled*--and he knew it. And he relished their reaction, as always.

It was *good* to be *God*. Or a world-famous American author/TV star/private detective, at least.

"Monsieur Vane?" The first person to speak, a slender, silver-haired woman in the bathroom doorway, frowned at him. "Is it really you?"

Vane's impulse was to grin and spread his arms, soaking up the adulation...but instead he nodded grimly. "I wish I were here under better circumstances." After all, he had a job to do.

The female cop walked toward him, eyes fixed on his face. Vane was certain from the way the other cops hung back that she was the highest-ranking officer among them, in charge of the crime scene. He could also tell from her tone, expression, and movements that she was not in a good mood.

"How did you know?" She tipped her head toward the bathroom. "Did an alert go out over the TV detective hotline that there had been a suspicious death here tonight in Saint-Malo?"

Vane shook his head. "I happen to be staying in this very hotel, *Capitaine*. All part of my latest book tour."

"Just 'Lieutenant.'" She stuck out her left hand. "Lieutenant Loire."

"My pleasure," said Vane as he shook her hand. "Shall I assume you're familiar with my work?"

"Familiar with *you*." She said it with an edge in her voice, as if she didn't mean it in a good way, entirely.

"Perhaps I should go." Vane said it carefully, since it was the exact opposite of what he wanted to do. "Let you get to it."

Just then, a tall, gray-haired man with a hook nose and a black trench coat stalked into the room. He took one look at Vane, and his bushy eyebrows shot up. "*Morgan Vane?*"

Vane acted like he didn't know who the man was. "Yes?"

Loire stiffened as the man approached. "Monsieur Vane, this is my commanding officer, Capitaine Claude Beuzec. Capitaine, this is..."

Beuzec cut her off and lunged forward, extending a hand to Vane. "You have come to solve our case, I take it?"

Vane shook his hand and shrugged. "I just happened by, actually. It seems Lieutenant Loire has things well under..."

"Yes, yes." Beuzec sneered. "Her competence is well known...but we would be *most* honored if a great detective like *yourself* would choose to lend a hand."

Vane shot a glance at Loire. Her rigid body language spoke volumes. "Thank you, Captain, but..."

"Please, Monsieur Vane. We *need* you." Beuzec leaned close and threw an arm around his shoulders. "If, of course, you'll see fit to waive your usual fee, as our budget is extraordinarily tight these days. Though perhaps we could take the fee out of Lieutenant Loire's salary."

Vane hesitated. "Very well. I will investigate on a pro bono basis, free of charge, at least for..."

"Excellent!" Beuzec clapped him on the back. "I am certain my people will learn a *great deal* from someone as accomplished as you." He grinned at Loire. "*Especially* the lieutenant here."

With that, Beuzec spun away from him and charged out the door without another word.

Loire watched him go with obvious hatred in her eyes, then sighed and turned to Vane. "This way." She slouched toward the bathroom.

"*Merci.*" Vane fell in step behind her, secretly exulting that he'd gained admission...not that there had ever been any doubt. He was a man who got what he wanted, right down the line.

And right now, he wanted to solve the murder of the man in the bathtub.

"Ma'am. Monsieur Vane." A bald young cop in a navy blue windbreaker and rose-tinted granny glasses pushed toward Loire. He spoke with an accent that was very different from hers--the kind that came from living in the Brittany region and speaking the native Breton language in addition to French. "We have found trace evidence in the tub drain." He beamed at Vane as he held up a sealed evidence baggie with strands of blonde hair curled inside. He had a familiar look on his face, one that Vane had seen often--the look of a fan.

"*C'est bon,* Officer Cunoval." Loire squinted at the baggie and nodded. "If it does not yield a killer, perhaps it will at least help us identify our victim."

Vane frowned at the naked body sprawled in the tub. The victim looked to be in his fifties, short and paunchy, with light brown skin and no hair visible anywhere on his body. "You don't know who he is yet?"

Loire shook her head. "No wallet, no mobile phone, no luggage. He checked in to the hotel three days ago under the name Silas Gardiner and paid for two weeks in advance with cash."

"Strange, isn't it?" As Vane said his patented catchphrase, he reached into a pocket of his jacket and drew out his trademark prop: a solid gold toothpick. Smoothly, he slid it between the teeth on the right side of his mouth, further setting the stage for his performance.

"Very strange, yes." Cunoval grinned, then caught himself and cleared his throat. "Perhaps the autopsy will tell us something."

"I'm curious." Vane narrowed his eyes as he gazed down at the corpse in the tub. "How exactly did you determine this was a murder and not a mere accident?"

"It did look like an accident at first," said Loire. "A slip-and-fall."

"Then, we found this." Cunoval held up an evidence-collection swab in a sealed plastic tube. "Teflon silicone spray, applied to the surface of the tub."

"Lubricant." Vane raised his eyebrows and nodded. "He was *made* to fall."

"That is certainly how it appears, Monsieur Vane," said Loire. "Now we must figure out who helped him along."

"Will you be assisting us on this case?" Cunoval grinned eagerly. "Providing consultation, perhaps?"

"Capitaine Beuzec wants him on the team," said Loire.

"And what about you?" asked Vane.

"I do not have any choice, do I?" said Loire.

Vane met her stare. "But what if you did?"

Loire sighed. "Perhaps you may yet be helpful." She raised an index finger. "*If* you do not withhold any facts that could be pertinent in the resolution of this case."

"That goes without saying," said Vane...though of course he was already withholding certain pertinent facts.

For example, he already knew the identity of the hairless dead man in the tub. Of everyone in the room, Vane alone knew the man's real name and background.

And he was keeping it to himself, no matter what Loire had said.

As Loire turned away to speak to another officer, Cunoval suddenly pushed close, lowering his voice so only Vane could hear. "What does your gut tell you so far? Are you confident you can solve this case?"

"Absolutely." Vane used his tongue to shift the gold toothpick from the right side of his mouth to the left. "No doubt whatsoever."

He could say it with such conviction because he'd already solved the case. He already knew the killer and every detail of what he'd done.

Not that he was going to let that spoil his investigation. After all, he might know who'd killed the man, but the hardest part of his job still lay ahead...his favorite part, truth be told.

He still had to pick the "true" murderer and convince the world that he was to blame. Or she.

And he had to make it all interesting enough to support his next book, TV episode, and online pay-per-view special.

Loire got a call on her cell phone and stalked out of the room. Vane took the initiative and followed along uninvited.

"Finally." Loire stopped at the elevator and hit the button to summon a car. "We may have a bit of *bonne chance* in this case."

"Good luck?" said Vane as the door opened in front of them. "How's that?"

Loire pushed into the elevator and jabbed a button on the control panel. "A delivery for Monsieur Gardiner."

When they got to the ground floor, she led the way across the gleaming lobby. As Vane followed, he noted the gleaming brass fixtures, black-veined marble, and rich, dark wood of the furnishings. Everything was new; the *Oceanique Majestique* hotel and spa had just opened three weeks ago, a glittering new jewel along the water-front of the tourist town of Saint-Malo.

"*Où est-il?*" Loire snapped out the words as she hurtled toward the reception desk. *Where is it?*

Two young women stood behind the desk, looking nervous in their smart black blazers and red neckties. They were both on the tall side, just under six feet, and had shoulder-length blonde hair.

The taller of the two had a nametag that read *Mirrin*. "Right here, ma'am."

"It's over here." The other girl's nametag read *Jilli*.

They also had similar accents--Australian or Kiwi, both equally thick.

As Loire hurtled around the side of the desk, both girls scrambled toward a red suitcase sitting against the wall. They both grabbed it at the same time, tipping it back and wheeling it along the walkway behind the desk.

Loire held out both hands, impatiently flexing her fingers against her palms. "And where is the individual who delivered it?"

The girls stopped pushing the case and looked at each other with wide, worried eyes.

"Gone, ma'am," said Jilli. "We didn't know..."

"Should we have told him to wait?" asked Mirrin.

Loire gestured for the luggage again. "Was there a receipt, at least? Some kind of paperwork?"

Both girls shook their heads at once.

"All right, all right." Loire pushed through the swinging door behind the desk, grabbed the suitcase handle, and dragged the bag out on her own. "You two, don't go anywhere."

"We won't, ma'am," Jilli said earnestly.

"Anything to help, ma'am," added Mirrin.

Loire rolled the bag past Vane and heaved it up onto a low glass table with no apparent fear that the table might break. "This came from Air France, you say?"

"Yes, ma'am," said Jilli.

"Late luggage, apparently," said Mirrin.

Loire pulled a pair of latex gloves from her pants pocket and tugged them on. Then, she grabbed the zipper and yanked it around the edge of the bag. "And Mr. Gardiner has been checked in for three days, has he not?"

"Yes, ma'am." Jilli and Mirrin said it in unison.

Loire finished unzipping and flipped open the lid of the bag. Vane watched with what he hoped was a convincing look of great suspense, then a look of surprise as the contents of the bag became evident.

"Porn." Loire picked up one of the DVDs from the bag and glared at its lurid cover. "With children."

"Indeed." Vane glanced at the bag's contents and looked away in disgust.

Loire sighed. "This still doesn't tell us who he is." She opened the DVD case and examined it, then clapped it shut and dropped it on the table.

"Maybe there's something in another disk," suggested Vane.

"Or deeper in the suitcase." Loire pulled out handfuls of DVDs and stacked them on the table. When the bag was empty, she felt along the bottom and sides, pressing her fingertips into the lining. "Yes. There is something inside."

Digging into a corner of the bag, she pulled open a hidden flap secured with Velcro. When the flap was peeled all the way back, a stack of papers lay exposed, about an inch high, bound with brown cord.

"What are these, pray tell?" Loire held up the stack with a scowl.

Vane looked closer. "Bearer bonds, I believe."

"Is that so?" asked Loire.

"Worth a fortune, from what I can see," said Vane. "If, indeed, they are genuine."

"Hm." Loire flipped through the pages. "The question is, what was a child pornography smuggler doing with a stack of bearer bonds hidden in his suitcase?"

"Not to mention, who is he?" added Vane.

"We will have the answer soon enough." Loire dropped the bonds on top of the pile of porn. "It is only a matter of time, now that our victim has begun giving up his secrets."

Want to bet? That was what Vane wanted to say, though he settled for this: "I'm sure you're right."

According to hotel surveillance footage, "Silas Gardiner" had spent most of his time out of the building, leaving at dawn and returning around midnight each night. Cameras showed him walking toward the waterfront and turning left on his daily travels, heading toward the walled city at the heart of Saint-Malo.

Loire and Vane followed in his footsteps, walking out as the sun set, leaving the criminal scientists to scour the dead man's porn, bonds, and luggage.

It was a pleasant June evening, warm enough for shirt sleeves. Vane breathed deep, relishing the salt sea air carried to him on the gentle breeze.

Loire, however, didn't seem to be enjoying the sea breeze at all. Her mood still struck him as sour; he was starting to think her grouchiness might be perpetual.

"Where did he spend his time, I wonder?" Loire walked slowly, staring at the brick sidewalk underfoot and the waist-high gray block seawall on the right. "Where did he go each day?"

"Where everyone else goes, I would guess." Vane pointed at the rooftops in the distance, surrounded by high granite ramparts. "The walled city."

As if in support of his comment, a middle-aged couple hurried past, heading in the direction he was pointing. There were plenty of people taking the same route, clusters of tourists heading for late suppers among the city's multitude of restaurants.

"*Peut-être,*" she said. *Perhaps.* "Though there are plenty of other places to go, yes?" She gestured at the other side of the street, across from the seawall and sidewalk. "Many blocks between the hotel and the walled city. More than enough trouble for him to get into."

"You think so?" said Vane.

She snorted. "I have been a police officer in Saint-Malo for the past twenty years. I know this town's underbelly all too well."

"Lots of vice for the tourists?" asked Vane.

"For the locals, as well." Loire stopped and leaned her arms on the seawall, taking a long look below. Rows of rough-cut posts jutted from the sand, their rugged tips rising to the level of the wall--a tide-break of twisted driftwood, like a forest out of a bad dream.

Vane eased in beside her and also cast his gaze downward. "Twenty years you've been a cop in this town?" The sand had taken on a rosy tint in the light of the setting sun. "Are you a native?"

Loire shook her head. "Not native to Saint-Malo, *non*. My people are from Quimper, to the west." She pronounced it *cam-pear*. "Also a tourist town."

"Also Breton," said Vane. "So you have lived in Brittany all your life."

"I have."

"And do you love it here?" he asked. "Is that why you've stayed?"

"I did stay because of love." She rubbed her eyes. "Though now, it's more like the *opposite* of love."

"Ah." Vane had already studied her past, though he could have deduced certain facts simply by studying her behavior at the crime scene. "Capitaine Beuzec. You were married to him, yes?"

Loire flashed a look of surprise in his direction. "How did you..."

Vane kept pushing ahead. "He left you for another woman?"

Loire scowled and looked away. "That is none of your business."

"Whatever happened, your marriage ended badly, didn't it?" asked Vane. "But he's still your boss, and he's making your life miserable."

Loire glared silently but didn't deny it.

"Then why don't you leave?" said Vane. "Get a fresh start some-where else."

"At my age?" Loire waved dismissively. "Fifty is too old for such a fresh start."

"No it isn't," said Vane. "You have plenty of time to begin a new career."

Loire turned to him. "As what? Police work is all I have ever known."

Vane shrugged. "Then stay with it. There are other jobs in other places."

"And *he* will never let me go," snapped Loire. "He told me so when I asked about a transfer. He said he will give me a bad reference or make up some lies about me for a background check. He's enjoying himself too much, making every day of my life an exercise in abuse and futility."

Vane stared at her. The pain on her face and in her voice was clear. "So you wouldn't leave if given the opportunity? If, say, a promotion came along in another town, and it didn't depend on Beuzec's recommendation?"

Loire looked at him, then turned her gaze to the sand below. "As if that would ever happen."

"But what if it did?" asked Vane.

Suddenly, Loire pushed forward. Something on the sand had caught her eye. "Do you see that?" She pointed.

Vane squinted. "No."

"Right there." She pointed more emphatically. "Something shiny."

Vane did see it, then...because he'd put it there. "Looks like a crushed soda can to me."

"Come on." Loire spun and took off. There was a stairway half a block closer to the walled city, and she headed straight for it.

Down on the sand, the two of them threaded their way through the forest of gnarled posts, which seemed much taller from below. Loire zeroed in on the item she'd spotted from the wall and rushed right up to it.

"Well, well." She pulled out a latex glove and used it to scoop up the object. "What have we here?"

Vane leaned close and nodded. "A can of Teflon silicone lubricant."

"That is correct." Loire raised one eyebrow. "This could be our murder weapon, yes?"

"It does seem likely," said Vane. "I wonder what secrets it will yield in the lab?"

Loire shook the can and smirked. "It is *already* telling me a story, Monsieur Vane."

"*Oui*, I sell that product here." The beefy shopkeeper nodded once, then shook his head. "*Non*, I did not sell it to a killer."

"That you know of." Loire dangled an evidence bag in front of him, containing the lubricant can.

The shopkeeper clenched his teeth behind his thick brown mustache and kept his massive arms folded over his black polo shirt. "I have done nothing wrong, Lieutenant." As he said it, his eyes shifted to Vane, who stood behind Loire. Was he more worried about the celebrity detective than the local investigator?

"Your hardware store is the only one that stocks this particular brand," said Loire. "We have checked around, Monsieur Bouchard."

"Have you checked with every mechanic and builder in town, too?" Bouchard's voice was deep and gruff. "Perhaps the killer stole the spray from one of them, as they have all bought some from me at one time or another."

Loire shoved the evidence bag at Bouchard's face. "This is a brand new can, Yann. It was purchased recently, and you know it."

Bouchard pushed the bag away with both hands. "*If* your killer bought this here, I would not have sold it to him with the knowledge that it would be used in the commission of a crime."

"*C'est des conneries!*" Loire snapped out the curse with disgust. "You most certainly would!"

Bouchard's eyes shifted to Vane, then back to Loire. The scowl on his face seemed to lack conviction. "Listen here..."

Loire turned to Vane. "Don't let this man fool you. His name has a habit of coming up in connection with criminal activities."

Vane smiled. "You don't say."

"It is never *him* who goes to jail, though," said Loire. "But as they say, there is a first time for everything, yes?"

Bouchard sighed and rolled his eyes. "Would it kill you to try a new tune one day, Madeleine?"

"'Lieutenant,'" corrected Loire. "Now tell us who bought the lubricant."

"A bum," said Bouchard.

Loire frowned. "Someone you dislike, you mean?"

"I mean a bum." Bouchard shrugged. "An actual bum. What he wanted a can of Teflon silicone lubricant for, I had no idea, and I didn't ask. He smelled awful, but he paid in cash."

Loire's frown deepened. "And you didn't know this bum?"

Bouchard shook his head. "I make it a practice not to look at bums in the street if I can avoid it."

"A mystery bum." Vane nodded slowly. "Strange, isn't it?"

But the truth was, it wasn't the least bit strange to him.

"This so-called bum," said Loire on the walk back to the *Oceanique Majestique*. "We will look for him on the hotel's security video. Then, we will go out and find him on the street, wherever he is."

"Unless he was in disguise," said Vane. "In which case, he might not be so easy to find, eh?"

Loire walked through the revolving door into the hotel's lobby without answering.

Once she and Vane were inside, the familiar voice of Cunoval called out to them. "Lieutenant! We have news!"

Loire stopped. "What now?"

"Two things." Cunoval raised two fingers as he hurried up to her. "First, the victim's toilet was plugged. By this." He held up an evidence bag containing a wadded-up red cloth napkin. "It is embroidered with the logo of *Le Phare*."

"An upscale restaurant in the walled city." Loire said it for Vane's benefit. "And the rest?"

"Second, we have video of an unknown male leaving the victim's room after the estimated time of the murder," said Cunoval. "The male in question wore a hooded sweatshirt and kept his head down, out of view of the camera. He left via the stairwell, in which no cameras are yet functional."

"Of course they aren't." Loire rubbed her left temple as if she had a headache.

Suddenly, the elevator dinged, and the door slid open with the sound of laughter--male and female together.

Turning toward it, Vane saw someone he knew all too well emerging into the lobby. Her high heels clacked a familiar rhythm across the marble floor.

"What's this now?" asked Loire.

"Oh my God." Cunoval sounded like he might have a stroke from excessive excitement. "It's *her*."

A young blonde woman in a tight white knee-length dress approached, followed by Capitaine Beuzec. She smiled warmly and waggled her fingers in a friendly wave.

Vane knew that wave was meant for him.

"Look who just turned up." Beuzec grinned. "A colleague of Monsieur Vane's has offered to lend a hand."

Vane winced at the use of the word "colleague."

"You are expecting her, of course," said Beuzec. "Mademoiselle Kitty Fox."

Kitty glided over and pecked Vane on both cheeks. "Hello, Morgan." Her book covers didn't do her justice. Her long blonde hair framed a face of exquisite beauty, complete with deep dimples, a single perfect mole above her left lip, and a gently curved elfin nose. "Sorry I'm late."

Vane turned a look of surprise into a tight-lipped smile. "Hello, Kitty."

Loire frowned. "Another famous investigator? Is there a convention nearby?"

When Kitty giggled, complete with crinkled nose, she looked closer to twenty-one than her actual age, which was twenty-eight and change. "Didn't Morgan tell you? We've been seeing each other, haven't we?" She blinked her beautiful ice blue eyes.

It wasn't true, but Vane didn't say so. If he'd denied the relationship, she would have just spun her usual web of fact-free fantasy.

"Vane of Justice and the Crimefox." Cunoval blew out his breath in admiration. "Until now, I've only heard rumors..."

Vane kept a straight face in spite of himself. "We'd like this to remain a rumor for now, if you don't mind."

"Oh, of course." Cunoval nodded enthusiastically. "I promise the utmost discretion."

Kitty stepped over to Beuzec and patted his shoulder. "Claude here has agreed to let me participate in the case, Morgan. Two consultants for the price of one."

"How could I say no to such a beautiful woman?" Beuzec flashed a special look in Loire's direction as he chuckled.

Loire glared. "Perhaps if you explained that we already have more than enough support on this..."

"You're the one who's always yapping about insufficient resources," snapped Beuzec. "Well, this time, you've got more than enough!"

Loire fell silent.

"Don't you want me to help, sweetheart?" Kitty batted her eyelashes. "I promise I'll be good."

Vane gave Kitty the reaction she seemed to expect: irritated resistance. "Too many cooks spoil the soup, Kitty dear."

"But we *do* make an excellent team." Kitty winked. "Gibraltar proved that once and for all, wouldn't you say?"

Vane's blood curdled at the mention of that place. It was Gibraltar where he'd first met Kitty, two years ago. It was there that she'd brazenly stolen the spotlight by solving a murder out from under him...bringing in the actual killer instead of the suspect Vane was planning to frame, in other words.

How could he ever forget all that, especially when she'd used it as the launchpad for a very successful celebrity detective career much like his own? A career that might yet eclipse his, if the right case came along that gave her the juice she needed to exceed him.

"You never miss out on an opportunity, do you?" asked Vane. "To work together, that is."

Kitty raised an eyebrow. "Can you blame me?" The look she gave him spoke volumes; their history, their rivalry, and her intention to win at any cost were all wrapped up in that icy blue gaze of hers.

Vane didn't bother broadcasting his own intentions. There was simply no need for it...and anyway, more pressing work was at hand. "Lieutenant?" He turned to Loire. "Perhaps we should pay a visit to that restaurant, *Le Phare*?"

"With me, you mean?" asked Kitty.

"Of course." Vane smiled with false civility. "Let's go solve this case, my dear."

"That's the spirit!" Beuzec clapped him on the back and headed for the door. "Two great detectives teaming up under my command!"

Loire watched him go with undisguised disgust. "*Le Phare* it is." She pulled out her phone and thumbed the screen. "Just let me call ahead first. I would hate to show up without a reservation."

Loire drove the mile or so from the hotel to the walled city--Kitty in the front seat and Vane squeezed into the back. En route, Kitty pumped Loire for information about the case...though Loire, to her credit, didn't seem thrilled about giving it to her.

Loire parked her black Volkswagen outside the Porte St-Vincent gate, the main entrance to the city. She got out of the car and led the way at a brisk pace as Vane and Kitty followed a few paces behind her.

"Don't I get a proper hello?" Kitty kept her voice low though Loire was out of earshot.

"I thought I'd already given you one," said Vane. "Are you angry that I've left out the parade?"

"Being inhospitable won't earn you any points." Kitty leaned in and jabbed him in the side with an elbow. "Do you *want* to look like an ass when my camera crew gets here?"

Vane snorted. "Turning it into a three-ring circus, are we?"

"With you as the chief clown." Kitty laughed. "But there's still time to become my sideshow, instead."

Vane smirked. "How did *you* know that's my lifelong ambition?"

"I'm just saying." Kitty wobbled as her heel caught on a cobblestone, then quickly recovered. "Washed up is washed up, old man. People want their true crime from a pretty face, not one that's pretty *ugly*."

Vane used his tongue to move the gold toothpick from the left side of his mouth to the right. "Now is that any way to talk to the modern-day Sherlock Holmes?"

"It is if I'm the modern-day Moriarty," said Kitty.

Vane laughed as he followed Loire through the gate into the walled city. The notion of Kitty as any kind of Moriarty figure was hilarious.

The Porte St-Vincent opened onto a broad street that was one of the busiest in the walled city--the Place Chateaubriand.

The lights of restaurants blazed away the evening gloom, each café, bistro, or brasserie teeming with tourists. Every available outdoor seat was filled; every waiter was running with trays in hand. The air was thick with chatter, laughter, and the clatter of plates and silverware.

"What a crowd." Four men in business suits at a nearby café table waved at Kitty, and Kitty waved back. "But it's good to see my fans are here."

"Remind me to avoid that café," said Vane. "If they're *your* fans, we know they have terrible taste."

Suddenly, Loire stopped and spun to face them. "Are the two of you having a spat?" She frowned. "Because you certainly don't sound very loving to me, right now."

"It's just our patented repartee," said Kitty. "Isn't that right, Morgan?"

Vane did not offer comment.

Loire stared at them both for a moment. Then, she continued along the street, which followed the curve of the city wall.

Kitty shook her head at Vane, then hurried to walk alongside Loire. That left Vane bringing up the rear, which was fine with him.

As the three of them followed the bend of Place Chateaubriand, Vane scanned passing faces for anyone he might recognize. He pricked up his ears, too, soaking in the babble of language rushing around him--more British-inflected English than anything else.

The demographics were well-known to him. Saint-Malo, a short ferry ride across the Channel from England, was a favorite destination of British tourists. They came for the beaches by day and the restaurants and clubs by night, saturating the local economy with British pounds. Other Europeans went there, too, with occasional Americans in the mix...but Saint-Malo was biggest with the Brits, laying on the hospitality and entertainment to keep them coming back for more.

Even now, Vane heard the sound of a live rock band not far away, playing an electronically amplified classic. The music was coming from around the bend, somewhere beyond the thickening crowd drawn to see the musicians up close.

Vane and the others would reach *Le Phare* before the crowd got too heavy. Vane knew the street well; he'd studied it, and the rest of the walled city and all of Saint-Malo, before embarking on this latest venture. Above all else, he believed in preparation as a means of attaining his goals.

Not that he was prepared for a chair to come crashing out of the window of *Le Phare*.

Just as the place came into view, glass shattered over the crowd, blasted from a front window by the hurtling chair. Suddenly, the happy babble turned into a medley of cries and shouts as tourists reacted to the barrage.

The crowd parted fast enough that the chair hit the street instead of a person. From there, everyone parted even further and faster, giving *Le Phare* a wide berth in case something else flew out of it.

At which point, Loire was already running for the restaurant's front door. So was Vane, though Kitty hung back.

As Vane charged into *Le Phare* behind Loire, he quickly saw the cause of the ruckus. A full-blown brawl was raging in the solarium, a knock-down-drag-out between middle-aged men in track suits and rugby shirts.

"Break it up!" Loire waded in without hesitation, pulling two men apart with such force that both of them stumbled and fell. "I said stop! *Arrêt*! *Arrêt*!"

The other men ignored her and kept swinging at each other. Grunting like animals, the two burliest ones wrestled through a doorway, tumbling from the solarium into the restaurant proper.

Bucking the tide of customers evacuating the place, Vane stormed after the burly wrestlers. As the gray-bearded men tumbled into a booth, Vane quickly pocketed his gold toothpick and barreled toward them.

With a hammer-blow kidney punch, he loosened the grip of the man on top, then dragged him off the other man by the scruff of his neck.

Tossing the first wrestler to the floor like a sack of trash, Vane went after the other. He didn't bother with conversation or offer surrender as an option; he just plucked the man from the leather-upholstered seat with one hand and rabbit-punched him in the face with the other.

As the man went limp, Vane dropped him and headed for the solarium. At first, in the muddle of fighting men and upended furniture, he didn't see Loire.

Then, as a bruiser snarled and charged him, Loire reappeared, clubbing the bruiser in the head with a table leg. The man fell hard, and Loire threw her makeshift club down on top of him.

Without a word, then, she and Vane proceeded to break up the rest of the brawl.

Soon, the floor of *Le Phare* was littered with twelve bruised men in torn track suits and rugby shirts, hands bound behind their backs with white zip ties from Loire's pockets.

"You." Loire pointed at the most dignified-looking among them, a tall man with finely chiseled features and silver hair clipped in a tight, neat cut. "Explain this."

The man she'd singled out looked around at the others, then turned his gaze to Loire. "My name is Hull. Corliss Hull." His accent was American...Bostonian, Vane decided. "My friends and I were having an argument, and it got out of hand."

"Obviously," snapped Loire. "Now tell us *why*."

"That one." Hull jabbed his chin at one of the two gray-bearded wrestlers whom Vane had broken up. "Rab McKay. It's *his* fault."

McKay thrashed on the floor, making a show of wanting to go after Hull. "Come over *here* and say that, ye lummox!" His accent was Scottish.

"Whoa, boys." Kitty chose that moment to intercede, stepping out of the solarium doorway in her tight white dress with hands raised. "Is this how you'd want to be seen on international TV?"

The twelve men gaped at her with newfound interest. "You're Kitty Fox!" said one of them.

"Are we on camera right now?" blurted another.

"Not just yet." Kitty grinned and flicked a finger back and forth. "But wouldn't you rather put your best foot forward and be ready when the camera gets here?"

Suddenly, all twelve men were sitting straighter and looking friendlier.

"What's the story here, fellas?" Kitty planted her fists on her hips.

"We all played rugby together in college," said Hull. "At Harvard. We're all Harvard graduates."

"Harvard?" Kitty beamed. "I *thought* the I.Q. seemed high in here."

"Once a year, we meet up somewhere in the world for a reunion game," said Hull. "We've been here for a week, working out, getting ready...but now we're down a player, all because Rab over there couldn't keep his mouth shut."

"I did the same as I *always* do," said McKay. "Veej knew to expect it! He was just as good as I am at dishin' it out."

"You had to keep on him about the *alopecia*, didn't you?" Hull shook his head with disgust.

"Wait a minute." Kitty's eyes widened. "Did you say *alopecia*? As in the condition that leaves someone without any hair on his body?"

"That's the one." Hull nodded. "Vijay had it all his life. He used to wear a wig, but he stopped doing even that a while back."

Kitty looked at Loire, who in turn looked at Vane. Vane nodded once to confirm he understood the significance.

According to Hull, Vijay had no hair anywhere on his body...just like the dead man in the tub at the *Oceanique Majestique*.

"Hmm," said Kitty. "Strange, isn't it?"

It was well after midnight when Vane sat down with Loire and Kitty at the police station, which was right across the street from the *Oceanique Majestique* hotel.

They stared at each other across a square table in one of the interrogation rooms, blinking in the jittery fluorescent light. A patrolman brought coffee, but Vane and Kitty had a kind of standoff and wouldn't touch it, as if to prove that neither of them needed it.

"So Silas Gardiner is Vijay Patel." Loire shrugged. "At least we know that much."

Vane nodded. The body had been positively identified by the rugby players, who'd been brought in for booking for their disorderly conduct.

"The problem is, we don't know much else," said Loire.

"We have the murder weapon," said Vane.

Kitty tapped one perfectly manicured nail on the table. "The Teflon silicone spray."

"We have the suitcase," said Vane.

"So what?" Loire sipped her coffee. "*Et alors?*"

"Kiddie porn and bearer bonds." Kitty tapped the table again. "The mark of a true scumbag."

"The bonds provide an untraceable means of payment," said Vane. "A perfect instrument for high-value illicit transactions."

"Again, *et alors?*" Loire got up from the table and paced across the room. "We still have no idea who killed our scumbag, do we?"

"You're right," said Vane. "What suspects do we have? The unidentified male leaving Patel's room on the security video? The mystery bum who bought the lubricant?"

"The rugby players?" Loire pulled back a window blind and peered out at the night. "Each of them has eleven alibis, as the team members claim they were together on the night of the murder."

"What about the trace evidence from the crime scene?" asked Kitty. "The hair from the tub drain?"

"Results will be some time yet. We had to send the hair to a forensic lab in Paris." Loire let the window blind fall and paced back across the room. "Meanwhile, the clock is ticking. The murderer moves further from our grasp."

"Not necessarily." Kitty tapped her finger once more. "I believe I can solve this mystery, Lieutenant...if you don't mind, of course, Morgan."

"Please." Vane bowed his head. "Be my guest."

Gratified, Kitty smiled. "The key to this murder is quite simple." She shrugged. "It's rather obvious, really."

Loire growled with impatience. "So what *is* it?"

Kitty arched an eyebrow. "The second suitcase."

Loire planted her hands on her hips and stared down at Kitty. "What second suitcase?"

"Patel's, of course." Kitty leaned back and crossed her legs.

"But Air France sent only one," said Loire.

Kitty raised a finger. "Incorrect. I called them, pretending to work for the hotel, and they told me they sent *two* bags for Mr. Gardiner, not just one."

"If there was a second suitcase, what happened to it?" asked Loire.

"I believe I can solve that mystery, too." Kitty flashed a look of amused delight at Vane. "Who notified you of the first bag's arrival?"

"The receptionists at the hotel's front desk," said Loire.

"Exactly," said Kitty. "And did you know that one of them has a criminal record?"

Loire hesitated, perhaps because she realized she'd missed a step in her investigation. "Which one?"

"Mirrin Daugherty." Kitty nodded. "I took the liberty of reaching out to a friend at Interpol, and he turned up quite a rap sheet on Mirrin. A dozen arrests, mostly for drug possession in Australia...even some jail time."

Loire looked rattled, then gathered herself up and shifted back to professional cop mode. "And I suppose this Mirrin stole the second suitcase?"

"She was there when it arrived," said Kitty. "She had the opportunity to tuck it away somewhere...and she had the motive, too. Scuttlebutt around the hotel has it that Mirrin is behind a rash of recent thefts, and she's working with a *partner*."

Loire narrowed her eyes. "Who's her partner? The other girl, Jilli?"

Kitty shook her head. "They say it's someone outside the hotel."

"'They?'" Loire grimaced. "Who are 'they?'"

"Hotel staff," said Kitty. "Maids, maintenance men, cooks, bartenders...you know. They're some of my biggest fans."

"And whom do 'they' say is Mirrin's partner?" asked Loire.

Kitty shrugged. "That's all I've got at this point. My famous face will only get me so far, you know."

Vane tried, and failed, to hold back a sarcastic comment. "Then you haven't really solved the case, have you?"

"Better than *you* did," snapped Kitty.

"Well, it's a lead," said Loire.

"Unless it isn't," said Vane.

"And the only way we'll know is a good, old-fashioned stakeout." Loire grabbed her coffee and headed for the door.

Mirrin emerged from the hotel at four in the morning, two hours before the end of her shift. Sure enough, she was pulling a red suitcase along behind her--the twin of the one delivered earlier that day for "Silas Gardiner."

Casting a quick look at the police station across the street, she turned right, heading for the waterfront. Then, she followed the route Vane and Loire had taken earlier that evening, crossing the street to the seawall and going left toward the walled city.

Meanwhile, Vane, Loire, and Kitty followed down a side street running parallel to the sea. Lights off, Loire drove quietly down the blocks, pausing at intersections to make sure Mirrin hadn't veered off somewhere.

"She's meeting her partner." Kitty, who'd switched her white dress for a chunky black sweater, tights, and knit cap, sat in the front passenger seat, glued to each glimpse of Mirrin out the side window. "She has to be."

"Or maybe she's cut him loose," suggested Vane. "Maybe she's skipping town with the goodies."

"More kiddie porn and bearer bonds?" said Loir.

"I wish I knew." Kitty sounded more excited than anyone in the car. "I can't wait to find out."

"You'll know soon enough," said Loir.

"I just hope you're not disappointed," said Vane. "Things don't always turn out the way you expect."

"That's right, they don't," snapped Kitty. "Case in point, Gibraltar."

Vane didn't answer. He just sat in the back seat and waited, a small smile playing over his lips.

As for Mirrin, she kept marching along the cobblestone sidewalk toward the walled city, lit by the occasional glow of traffic lights along the street. Her blonde hair whipped behind her in the wind off the sea, fluttering like gold ribbons against the darkling horizon of the English Channel.

After walking a mile, she reached the end of the path and stopped. The walled city sprawled on her left, its ramparts illuminated from below.

Vane and the others parked at the mouth of the side street they'd been traversing, awaiting her next move. The Volkswagen's diesel engine automatically switched off instead of idling; it was programmed to start back up as soon as the driver stepped on the accelerator pedal.

"So what do we do now?" Kitty was still excited. "Leave the car here and follow her into the city on foot?"

"Most likely," said Loire. "At least, that's what I'll be doing. You two will wait here."

"No way!" Kitty grabbed the door handle on her side and started to pull it. "If you're going into the city, so am I."

"Neither of you are." Vane reached between the seats and pointed toward the cobblestone walk. "Look."

Mirrin wasn't standing at the end of the path anymore, and she wasn't walking toward the walled city, either. She was nowhere in sight.

"*Merde!*" Loire stomped the accelerator, restarting the engine, and swung the VW out of the side street. "Where is she?"

There was still no sign of Mirrin as the VW bolted across the road and jerked to a stop. Loire and Kitty leaped out first and ran.

When Vane caught up with them, they were gazing over the seawall. Loire pointed, but she didn't need to. Vane could see where Mirrin had gone.

When the tide was out, as it was now, it was possible to walk across the sand to two islands near the walled city--Grand Be and Petit Be. That was exactly what Mirrin was doing, dragging the suitcase toward those rocky humps.

"This is it," said Kitty. "She's making her connection."

"Or hiding her loot," said Vane. "Those islands are mostly submerged at high tide."

"Either way, we've got her." Kitty headed for a nearby stairway cut into the seawall. "I'm about to crack this case wide open."

As Kitty, Loire, and Vane crossed the beach, Loire drew a gun from the holster under her jacket. The three of them were dangerously exposed, with no means of concealment between the seawall and the islands.

Fortunately, Mirrin never looked back. She was far ahead, completely focused on dragging the suitcase and reaching her destination. Whatever noise her pursuers made was carried away from her on the ocean breeze.

"She's heading for Petit Be." Loire spoke in a loud whisper, though she didn't need to.

Vane could see the blonde was giving the larger island, Grand Be, a wide berth. Her course was aimed at the smaller of the two, which was a little farther out across the sand.

At least that gave him and his companions options. They could use the rocky base of Grand Be for cover in case Mirrin finally looked back. Then, as she closed in on one side of Petit Be, they could hurry across the gap and skirt the other side of that smaller island.

Unfortunately, Kitty didn't seem to have any interest in such a strategy. Before Vane could discuss it with her, she broke into a jog, distancing herself from him and Loire.

"Damn." Loire ran after her, not that it would do any good. Kitty kept jogging faster and would clear Grand Be before she could reach her.

Vane, for his part, hung back in the shadows of Grand Be. He was ready, now that his group had splintered, to put his own plan into action.

As Kitty and Loire ran after Mirrin, Vane approached the opposite side of Petit Be. Employing all the stealth at his command, he quietly climbed the rocky slope, taking care not to slip on the wet stones.

When he reached the top, he stayed low and worked his way to the central building, the Fort du Petit Be...the *only* building on the island. Reaching the corner of one turret at the front of the fort, he stopped. He could hear voices on the other side, carried on the ocean breeze.

One, as expected, belonged to Mirrin. "I love seeing you so happy."

The other was a man's voice, deep and gruff. "And I love *being* happy, *mon amour*. All because of *you*."

Monsieur Bouchard. It was the hardware store owner, the one who'd sold the lubricant to the mystery bum.

"Do you realize what this means?" asked Bouchard. "What it means to *us*?"

"Money?" said Mirrin.

"A future together," said Bouchard. "Now we can be together always, living as we choose. Never again will we have to worry that poverty might come between us."

"Oh, Yann," said Mirrin, and then they were both silent for a while.

Peering around the corner, Vane saw the reason why. They were kissing passionately with the suitcase at their feet.

Suddenly, a third voice pierced the night. "You are absolutely right!" It was Kitty, storming out from behind a rocky hill. "You *won't* have to worry about poverty. You'll both be very well taken care of *in prison*!"

Bouchard and Mirrin broke their embrace and gawked.

"Whatever's in that suitcase, I hope it was worth killing for," said Kitty.

"I've killed no one!" Reaching behind him, Bouchard pulled

something from the waist of his bluejeans--a pistol, which he swung around to point at Kitty. "Until now!"

Vane didn't hesitate. Bolting around the corner, he charged Bouchard, plowing into him with a flying tackle.

The gun went off on the way down, firing into the air. Then, as the two men landed, Vane grabbed Bouchard's wrist and bashed his gun hand on the rocky ground.

It took four blows for the gun to pop free, at which point Kitty grabbed it. Meanwhile, Bouchard kept thrashing, putting up a fight though Vane's greater bulk and superior leverage kept him firmly in place.

"Yann Bouchard!" Kitty pointed the gun at Bouchard. "You are under arrest for the murder of Vijay Patel!"

Bouchard stopped fighting. "Who?"

Just then, Loire swooped in and snatched the pistol away from Kitty. "That's enough." She also had a tight grip on the arm of Mirrin, whom she'd corralled while Vane and Kitty were busy with Bouchard. "You are *not* a police officer, and you cannot conduct an arrest."

"But who solved the murder?" Kitty smirked. "Not the *police*, that's for sure."

"We didn't kill anyone!" said Mirrin.

Kitty scowled. "Playing dumb won't help you."

"Who's playing?" shouted Bouchard. "And who the hell is Vijay Patel?"

"Admit it," said Kitty. "I blow your mind, don't I?"

Vane, who was pouring a cup of coffee from a fresh pot, didn't answer. Kitty was finding new ways to get on his nerves with each passing minute; she'd been bouncing off the walls ever since they'd returned to the police station from Petit Be.

"I make you think about getting out of the game." She smiled as she smoothed the front of her tight white dress, which she'd put back on after the stakeout. "No one else has ever made you feel as inadequate as I do."

Vane smirked. "I wouldn't put it in those words, exactly."

"Poor Morgan. Always afraid to talk about feelings." She patted his cheek. "There, there."

Vane sipped his coffee. It was good...delicious, in fact. Or maybe the taste was colored somewhat by his own anticipation of what was about to happen.

Because in truth, he was at least as excited as Kitty...but for different reasons.

"This will all be over soon, dear." Kitty nodded. "My camera crew is setting up right now in the squad room. Then, you'll be free of all this...responsibility."

"Is that so?" said Vane.

"You won't have to worry about being the Number One Detective in the world anymore." Kitty hopped up and kissed him on the tip of his nose, then twirled away. "You're welcome."

With that, she scooted off to join her crew.

Just then, Loire shuffled into the break room, looking exhausted. "She loves putting on a show, doesn't she?"

Vane snorted. "Children."

Loire smiled tiredly and reached for the coffee pot. "Long day, *oui?*"

Vane nodded. "How goes the questioning? Are Bouchard and Mirrin still denying any role in Patel's murder?"

"Other than selling lubricant to our mystery bum." Loire filled a paper cup with steaming black coffee. "Though the suitcase full of heroin in their possession does suggest they are not to be trusted."

Vane narrowed his eyes. "And what do you think?"

Loire returned the pot to the warmer and met his gaze. "I do not trust them," she said, "but I believe them."

"You do?"

"I believe they are opportunists, nothing more." Loire sighed. "Mirrin saw the suitcase of heroin arrive, and she told her boyfriend, Bouchard, who has a long history of dirty dealings...but not fatal ones. He arranged a financial transaction, to be conducted by night on Petit Be. A skiff was due to arrive, at which time a busi-ness acquaintance would accept the drugs, and the purchase price would be deposited in Bouchard's hands." She shrugged. "That was the plan, anyway. Both Mirrin and Bouchard corroborate this story."

"I see." Vane drained his coffee cup and tossed it in the trash bin.

"You're not surprised?" Loire frowned. "You're not going to say 'Strange, isn't it?'"

"Why would I?" Vane drew a gold toothpick from his jacket pocket. "There's nothing strange about it."

"What makes you say that?"

At that moment, Officer Cunoval flashed into the room, carrying a fistful of papers. His eyes were wide, his face flushed, his breathing rapid.

"I believe you are about to find out," said Vane, and then he inserted the gold toothpick into his mouth.

When Vane, Loire, and Cunoval walked into the squad room, Kitty was shooting a stand-up segment with a three-person video crew while Beuzec watched. All three crew members wielded high-end gear; Vane could see that the camera, sound equipment, and lights were all top of the line. The crew themselves were all young, fresh out of university or close to it, and focused with grim intensity on their work.

As for Kitty, she wore the cool, smooth demeanor of a seasoned TV host, gliding and gesturing gracefully among the empty desks. "Working closely with local law enforcement, I have investigated this murder with all the skills and experience at my disposal. I was deter-mined to persevere until the victim was identified and the killer brought to justice...at any cost."

Vane stood along the wall with Loire and Cunoval, out of shot and away from Beuzec, and watched Kitty's performance. He had to hand it to her; she was great in front of a camera...better than he was, probably. Her many flaws were not evident when she stood before a lens.

Not yet, anyway.

"At last, my work has paid off," she said. "I have told you the secrets of the previously unknown victim, Vijay Patel." Kitty nodded for dramatic effect. "Now, as this special edition of *Crimefox Files* continues, I am about to tell you the name of the killer."

As Kitty gazed into the camera with her icy blue eyes, Vane felt Loire and Cunoval tensing on either side of him. Loire started to move, but Vane shot out an arm to hold her back.

Loire frowned with annoyance. Vane, in reply, held up a single index finger, signifying that she should wait.

Hands clasped loosely at her waist, Kitty slowly crossed the squad room. "Who would murder Vijay Patel? To get to that answer, we must first answer another question: *why* would someone kill him?" Never breaking eye contact with the camera, she stopped and leaned against a desk. "The answer, I have discovered, is *greed*, plain and simple."

Again, Loire started to move, and again, Vane held her back. He wanted the moment to be perfect, just perfect.

"Vijay Patel was a smuggler of drugs and child pornography," said Kitty. "He planned to transport a fortune in both to Saint-Malo, under the cover of a rugby reunion match. But his luggage was delayed by the airline, and his plan fell apart. By the time the luggage showed up at his hotel, he was dead." She paused thoughtfully, tipping her head to one side. "Part of that luggage ended up in the hands of police...and the rest, when I found it, was in the possession of local crime lord Yann Bouchard and his lover, Mirrin Daugherty.

"This is the very same Yann Bouchard who admitted that the Teflon silicone lubricant used to murder Vijay Patel came from his shop. What does this tell us?" Kitty pushed away from the desk and crossed slowly to the camera, gesturing with both hands. "It tells us that this crime lord Bouchard must have been Patel's local connection...that he arranged to murder Patel when he showed up without the contraband...and that his lover, Mirrin Daugherty, used her position as hotel receptionist to retrieve said contraband when it was delivered after Patel's murder.

"After extensive research and investigation, I have concluded that this sequence of events must be true. And the evidence backs me up." Kitty clasped her hands together and nodded. "After all, *blonde* hair was found in the drain of the tub where Patel died...and Mirrin Daugherty *is* a blonde."

Suddenly, Vane called out. "But not the *only* blonde."

The moment, at last, was perfect.

Kitty spun to gape at him with a look of supreme annoyance. "Excuse me?"

Vane stepped out from between Loire and Cunoval. "Wouldn't you agree that there are other blondes involved in this case, Kitty?"

Kitty glared. "Are you referring to the other hotel receptionist, Jilli Swanson?"

Vane joined Kitty in front of the camera and shook his head. "Only if that was Jilli's hair in the tub drain."

Just then, Cunoval spoke up. "Which it wasn't!" His timing was unplanned but perfect. He marched over to join Kitty and Vane, shaking his fistful of papers. "Jilli Swanson is innocent!"

"Cunoval!" shouted Beuzec. "What are you doing? Get out of her shot!"

Scowling, Kitty drew a finger across her throat for the benefit of the crew--the universal signal to stop shooting video.

"Don't you *dare* turn that camera off." Vane said it sternly, his tone coiling with menace.

"I said *cut!*" snapped Kitty.

The cameraman, sound man, and light technician exchanged looks...then came to an unspoken agreement and went back to work.

The show, it seemed, would go on.

"You're fired!" said Kitty. "All three of you!"

"Now then." Vane cleared his throat. "Is there anything else you can tell us about that blonde hair from the drain, Officer Cunoval?"

"*Oui*." Cunoval held up the papers in his hand. "According to the forensics report..."

"Cunoval!" Beuzec stepped forward, looking livid. "Enough of this! You are interfering with a..."

For once, Loire got to cut *him* off. "Let him continue, *sir*." She swooped over and stood in his path. "*Trust* me, you're going to want to hear this."

Beuzec scowled as if he might charge past her anyway...but then he took a half-step back and folded his arms over his chest.

Cunoval cleared his throat and picked up where he'd left off. "According to the forensics report, which arrived thirty minutes ago from the ENFSI crime lab in Paris, the blonde hairs retrieved from the tub drain match a donor sample from the ENFSI archives."

Vane switched his gold toothpick to the other side of his mouth. "And whom did the donor sample belong to, pray tell?"

"Someone who had donated biological samples as part of a past criminal case," said Cunoval. "Elimination samples, as the donor had visited an important crime scene during an investigation."

"Anything else you can tell us about this donor?" asked Vane.

"Yes." Cunoval stared dramatically at the camera. "Fingerprints from the same donor were also found on the murder weapon--the can of lubricant."

Vane nodded. "Who *was* this mysterious donor, Officer Cunoval?"

"Kitty Fox." Loire chose that moment to march over with a pair of open handcuffs. "You are under arrest for the murder of Vijay Patel."

Beuzec gasped. "*What?*"

Kitty backed away, a look of panic spreading over her features as she realized Vane was doing much more than upstaging her. "Oh my God! This is insane!"

"Not at all," said Vane. "It is, in fact, *perfectly* sane. And I theorize it is only the *latest* in a *long* line of murders linked to Ms. Fox." He turned to focus on the camera. "How else to explain her meteoric rise? What better way could there be for someone so young and inexperienced to advance her career as a media crime expert?" He looked at her and shook his head. "This way, she would never be wrong in identifying a perpetrator."

"Because *she* always decided whom to *frame*," added Cunoval.

Kitty continued to back away from Loire. "No! It's him!" She jabbed a finger at Vane. "*He's* framing *me!*"

"Is that so?" asked Loire. "Then how do you explain the prints on the lubricant, Mademoiselle Fox? That can was sent off to the lab before your arrival. You could not possibly have touched it unless you did so *before* we took it into custody."

"But I didn't!" Kitty was sliding toward hysteria as the extent of her predicament became clear.

"Likewise, we retrieved your hair from the drain before your involvement in the investigation." Loire shook her head slowly. "It could only have been deposited there *before* Mr. Patel's body was found."

"*Mon dieu,*" said Beuzec. "This is incredible!"

"It's all circumstantial!" Kitty angled herself so she was backing toward an exit. "I didn't do it!"

"We will let the courts determine that," said Loire.

Suddenly, Kitty whirled as if to make a run for it...only to bump into Vane, who'd slipped around to block the exit.

He grabbed her by the shoulders and locked eyes with her. "How many of your other cases did you rig, you phony?" His voice and expression oozed with contempt. "How many lives have you destroyed in your rush to glory?"

"Let go of me!" Kitty thrashed in his grip. "*You* planted that evidence!"

"Blaming others right up to the end," said Vane. "You sicken me."

"Now then." Loire hooked a cuff around Kitty's right wrist and snapped it tight. "Where were we?" She did the same to Kitty's left wrist. "Kitty Fox, you are under arrest for the murder of Vijay Patel."

Vane couldn't resist making one more contribution. "Her real name isn't Kitty Fox," he said as Loire led her prisoner away. "It's Agnes Butts of Peckerhead, Ohio."

"Agnes Butts?" Beuzec winced. "Really?"

"Shut up!" howled Kitty. "Shut your mouth! And it's *Pepperhead*!"

Vane pulled the gold toothpick from between his teeth and pointed it at the camera, raising one eyebrow for effect. "Strange, isn't it?"

Later, when the dust had settled, Vane slipped out of the police station. While everyone's attention was focused elsewhere, he walked to the seawall, where a middle-aged man with a rail-thin body and gaunt features awaited him.

"*Bonjour*." The man, who wore a loose brown shirt and tattered bluejeans, waved him over. "Good to see you, Monsieur Vane." His thin, dark hair fluttered in the sea breeze.

"You, too." Vane held out his hand for a shake. "It's been a busy day. I had an important case to solve."

The man took his hand. "And you solved it?"

"Of course." Vane grinned. "Would you expect anything less?"

The man closed his eyes. "Thank God. Oh, thank God." Then, he opened them and flung his arms around Vane. "And thank *you*. From the bottom of my soul, thank *you*."

At that moment, Vane caught sight of Loire crossing the street toward them. "I'm very glad everything worked out for you." He patted the man's back, then pushed him away. "Now I really must return to my duties."

The man saw where Vane was looking and understood. "*Merci*, and *au revoir*." With one final wave, he hurried off down the cobblestone walk, heading in the opposite direction from the walled city.

Loire watched as he rushed away. "Who was that?"

"A fan." Vane sighed. "Pouring his heart out about what I've meant to him."

"Ah." Loire turned and leaned on the seawall. Her mood seemed lighter than usual. "You make a big impression, don't you?"

"That's true." Vane leaned beside her, gazing out at the sapphire sea as it glittered under the midday sun. "Though I suppose you could say the same of Kitty Fox."

"A big impression, yes." Loire clucked. "But nothing underneath."

"The perfect celebrity." Vane smirked.

Loire shook her head. "What a pity. Such a waste."

"Don't feel too bad for her," said Vane. "She'll use this to her advantage, you'll see. Just wait till she writes her next book from behind bars." He rolled his eyes. "It'll be a smash, I promise you."

Loire scowled. "What kind of person does it take to do something like this? To kill for fame and fortune, then place the blame on the innocent?"

"That's a difficult question," said Vane, though it wasn't, really. What kind of person did it take? Someone exactly like him.

For that was what he'd done with Kitty--framed her for the murder of Patel. He'd left samples of her hair at the crime scene, hair he'd been saving since their first encounter at Gibraltar. He'd been saving her fingerprints, too, and had transferred them to the can of lubricant...no easy task if done right, but as with so many things, he was an expert in the practice. Right from the start, she'd been his target, his patsy; she was a rival, a nuisance, a threat, and he'd taken her off the game board...at least for now, at least until some judge or jury decided the evidence against her was too circumstantial.

But there was more to it than that, more at stake than discrediting Kitty. There always was, when Vane worked his magic. He loved the challenge of "solving" the very crimes he'd committed in a way that was believable to the authorities and his audience alike. The thrill of arranging the perfect frame-up while cutting a giant figure in the public eye was one of the things he lived for.

But none of it would be complete if his victims weren't so richly deserving.

"Some people just have a darkness inside them," he told Loire. "A darkness that takes over when certain opportunities present themselves."

"She didn't *need* such opportunities, though, did she?" asked Loire. "She seemed to me a woman who already had everything."

Vane shrugged. "There must have been more to it."

There certainly was, as the man who'd hugged him moments ago could have attested. For that man's daughter had been brutally raped one year ago by Patel. The girl had killed herself after that, after Patel had escaped punishment on a technicality.

But Patel's great escape had ended in Saint-Malo. With meticulous planning and the help of the girl's father--a.k.a the "mystery bum," the Air France luggage delivery man, and the man in the hoodie on the security footage--Vane had ended Patel's days of guilt-free evasion.

And Patel had died under a cloud. Though he'd avoided punishment for the crime he *had* committed, the world would always think of him as dying for *other* crimes...ironically, ones he *hadn't* committed. Thanks to Vane planting evidence in the late-arriving luggage, Patel would always be known as a smuggler of drugs and kiddie porn, a reprehensible lowlife who'd gotten what was coming to him.

Which was, in every way that mattered, perfectly accurate.

"So." Loire bumped elbows with Vane and smiled. Her mood really *had* improved. "*Que faire?* What next for you, Monsieur Vane?"

"The usual," said Vane. "Write a book, make a TV show. What about you?"

Loire rested her chin on her folded hands. "The usual. Back to rounding up drunken tourists."

"Staying in town?" asked Vane. "I thought all this excitement might have given you the urge to leave."

Loire shrugged. "It is too late for that. I am too old to start over."

"But you've got the juice now," said Vane. "You closed a case that will lead to the conviction of an international celebrity."

"And what happens when a potential employer runs a background check? What happens when they talk to Capitaine Beuzec?" She scowled and shook her head. "He will continue to punish me, and I will remain trapped here."

"But..."

She raised a hand to cut him off. "Better to not even try, Monsieur Vane."

Vane started to say something, then stopped. For a long moment, he and Loire stared out at the rolling surf.

"Maybe you'll change your mind someday," he said finally. "Stranger things have happened."

Loire sighed. "My mind is made up."

"If you *do* change it, though..." Vane reached into the breast pocket of his maroon jacket. "Perhaps this will be of some help." He drew out a small silver case, the length and width of his pinky finger, and handed it over.

Loire flicked the tiny catch and lifted the lid, then stared at the contents without a word.

"My private number is inscribed on the case," said Vane.

"But are you sure you mean to give me what is *inside* the case?" Frowning, Loire drew out the object that was tucked into the case's black velvet lining. It was a twin of his famous gold toothpick.

"Of course." Vane smiled. "From one investigator to another."

"I cannot accept this." She put the toothpick back into the case and closed it, then pushed it toward him. "It is too extravagant."

"You deserve it." Vane nodded. "I know potential when I see it. You might yet go far, if you put your mind to it." He pushed the case back to her. "And this could give you an edge. It could open doors for you."

Loire gazed at the case, turning it over in her hands. "But I might never use it that way."

"Think of it as a memento, then," said Vane. "A souvenir of our first case together, as well as an ace in the hole."

The toothpick was more than that, though. Something was hidden inside it, something that would make it an ace in the hole for Vane himself if Loire ever rose through the ranks.

A microtransmitter. The tiniest radio that money could buy was hidden inside it, set to be activated if she ever got close to the kind of intelligence he might need.

"Good luck," said Vane, giving her shoulder an affectionate squeeze. "May you go very far indeed."

THE SWORD THAT SPOKE

n those days, before the death of my husband, the sword did not say much. Sometimes, I could not quite make out what it said—but I could not ask anyone else if they'd heard it.

Because Tizona, the sword of El Cid, spoke only to me.

As far as I know, Tizona never said a single word to anyone else, even its master, my husband Rodrigo—the great El Cid Campeador. It struck me funny sometimes, that the sword of such a warrior, a powerful man who had battled the mightiest Moors, would talk to me, but not him.

It struck Rodrigo even funnier, of course, when he caught me talking to Tizona. He teased me, asking if I loved the sword more than I loved him.

And in this, though none of us knew it at the time, Rodrigo predicted the future.

I remember very clearly the first words Tizona ever said to me. They came after the witch, the *bruja*, cast her spell.

"You and I, Jimena," said Tizona, its voice high and sweet as the tinkling of a bell. "We will turn the tables."

Stunned, I looked all around for the source of the voice, unable to believe it had come from the sword. All I saw were the four barren walls of the *bruja*'s decrepit hut, where I'd come for help a mere month after my wedding day.

"It is I. Tizona." The voice tinkled again, drawing my eyes to the gleaming sword on the table. "The *bruja* tricks you."

"How?" I said.

"What was that?" The *bruja* stood and stared less than an arm's length away, on the other side of the table.

Tizona did not move the slightest bit as the tiny voice emanated from its shining blade. "You traded ten years of your life for a spell of protection for your new husband. My master, El Cid."

"Yes." I stared at the palm of my left hand, where the witch had cut a bloody pentagram framing a star—the marks of magic.

The *bruja* was getting angry. "Who are you talking to?"

"She thinks she cheated you with a cut-rate spell," said Tizona. "She thinks it will provide no protection."

Now it was my turn to be angry. I glared at the *bruja*, and she backed away scowling.

"But we will turn the tables," said Tizona. "I was enchanted *long* before this, by a magician *far* greater than she. *I* shall offer the protection she denies."

"Which means what?" I said.

"So long as you and I are both faithful to El Cid," said Tizona, "I will raise him up if he falls dead."

"Really?" I said.

"Once," said Tizona. "I can do it only once."

My husband, Rodrigo Diaz de Vivar, was a magnificent soldier, a knight beyond compare. The Christians called him *El Campeador*, the champion. The Moors who ruled so much of our land called him *sayyid*, meaning "lord"...which became "El Cid."

He fought the Moors in battle after battle throughout Spain, striking fear in their hearts...and inspiring admiration in the hearts of his own people. He was a living legend, a true hero and god among men.

And his glamour was not lost on me. I was starstruck from the first time I gazed into his dark, flashing eyes. The stories of his exploits thrilled me...no less so when I learned he would take me as his bride.

Everything changed after that, though. I made a terrible mistake.

I fell in love with him.

And with love came worry. Every time he rode off into battle, I could hardly stand it. Thinking he might never return.

Which is why I sold ten years of my life to a *bruja* to bewitch his beloved Tizona.

In the years that followed, only one thing never changed between Rodrigo and me. My love for him never wavered. It remained steadfast as the love of Christ for mankind. As Mount Penyagolosa towering at our backs.

That does not mean I loved the creature who came to live inside Rodrigo, however. The thing I decided I had to kill.

I'll never forget the first time I saw it.

Rodrigo and I were walking out of the cathedral in Castile after mass. This was in the days when he was still in favor with my cousin, King Alfonso.

It was a beautiful day, all blue sky and sunshine and warm

breezes. Rodrigo and I walked arm in arm, and he leaned over and kissed me on the lips.

"What shall we do with the afternoon, Jimena?" said Rodrigo.

I smiled and blushed. We both already knew what we would do when we got home. "Clean the castle?" It was our own little joke. Our secret code.

Rodrigo leaned close, his crooked smile full upon me. "Only if you do your share. There is much cleaning to be done."

I laughed and leaned my head on his shoulder.

And that was when the assassin leaped out of the shadows ahead of us.

Black robes whipping, the Moor hurtled toward us, screaming and drawing a sword from the scabbard at his hip.

Without hesitation, Rodrigo shoved me back and charged forward. Arms and legs pumping, he leaped into action against the Moor.

It was the first time I'd seen him in battle—and he was magnificent. His body sprang and twisted, dodging the Moor's sword-strokes with perfect timing and agility. He pelted the Moor with one fierce blow after another, knocking the sword from his hands and then knocking him to the ground. Without a weapon that wasn't part of his body, Rodrigo battered and broke the assassin, pounding him flat in the street.

And then he killed him.

It happened so fast, I hardly noticed at first that he'd done it. Rodrigo took the Moor's head in his hands and suddenly twisted it hard to one side. When he dropped it, the Moor lay motionless under the sun, lacking even the rise and fall of breath passing in and out of his chest.

That was when I saw it for the first time. The thing inside my husband.

"All right?" Rodrigo said it as he rose from the limp body of the Moor in the street.

My nod was a lie. As Rodrigo approached me, I had to fight the urge to back away.

Rodrigo's eyes were glowing red, like the coals of a fire. His body was covered in fine, emerald scales, like the skin of a snake. A forked tongue flickered from between his scaly lips, red as a ribbon fluttering in the breeze.

The thing moving toward me wore my husband's clothes, but it was not my husband. It spoke with Rodrigo's voice...and then that changed, too.

Two voices emerged from its mouth. One was Rodrigo's, asking if I had been hurt. The other was like the rasping of rough stones scraping together, the rattling of bones in a bucket.

"You see me?" It sounded surprised. "No matter."

My heart pounded, and my blood ran cold. I did take a step back, then, away from the creature.

"We share a husband." The thing said it while Rodrigo's voice asked what was wrong with me. "But we can work out a schedule.

"You only want him when he's loving and kind," said the thing. "I only want him when he's *killing*."

Then, with a burst of rasping laughter, the thing disappeared.

"Jimena? Darling?" Rodrigo was back to normal in every way, as far as I could tell.

But still, I could not bring myself to clean the castle with him that day.

Later, when night had fallen and Rodrigo was asleep in our bed, I talked to Tizona. Of anyone close at hand, I thought he might know the most about magic.

Tizona lay on a chest at the foot of the bed, glowing silver in the pale moonlight. I lifted him in a cloth, taking care not to cut myself on his sharp edges.

As quietly as I could, I carried Tizona from the bed chamber and softly pulled the door shut behind us. I tiptoed downstairs to the chapel and laid him upon the altar.

And when I asked him, he told me what had happened to my husband.

"War changes men in more ways than one." Tizona's voice was high as a chirping bird. "They are not the same when they fight on the battlefield."

"Of course," I told him. "Taking lives puts a terrible strain on a man. Everyone knows this."

"I am not talking about the strain of battle," said Tizona. "I mean the men are literally *not themselves* in war."

I shrugged. "To do what must be done in war, they must harden themselves. They must put aside the civilities of everyday life. This I understand."

"You do *not*, Jimena." Candlelight flickered on Tizona's polished surface. "But you are *beginning* to."

I frowned and shook my head. "What are you saying?"

"When next El Cid leads his men home from battle, go down to the city gates. Wait with the women...and *watch*."

"I have done this before," I told him. "Many times."

"Yes," said Tizona. "But now, your eyes have been opened."

Three days later, I did as Tizona told me. I went to the gates to welcome our knights home from fighting the Moors.

Dozens of women waited with me, hands bursting with flowers and rosaries. They padded back and forth in the steaming dust, chatting over what news they had of the fight...praying that their men were not among the dead.

A young friend, Solea, stood by my side, a glittering crystal rosary wrapped around her little fist. "Alejandro is fine," she said. "I know this." Her big eyes darted nervously as she waited for the gates to move.

I smiled reassuringly. "He will be in your arms any minute now."

Solea's hands were in constant motion, twisting and kneading like kittens in a basket. "You are lucky, Doña Jimena. The great El Cid *cannot* fail to return to you."

"And those who fight beneath his banner are likewise blessed." I reached out and squeezed her shoulder. "Like Alejandro."

Just then, the sound of approaching hoofbeats thundered from the other side of the city wall. Shouts flew between the lookouts in the towers, and the gates began to move.

As one, the women pushed forward and parted, leaving a broad lane down the middle. Hearts pounding in unison, we all looked in one direction—toward the gates as they slowly swung open.

From the heart of a swirling cloud of dust, the men emerged, armor banging and clanking with the rise and fall of the horses. Staves and lances pointing skyward, they came like a storm of metal and flesh, an island of tempered steel in a sea of gray vapor.

Women cheered and clapped as the lead rider charged through the gates and down the lane, followed by the rest in tight formation. Flags and vestments flying, they bolted between us and pounded to a stop, raising fresh drafts of dust in all directions.

Then, one by one, they raised their helms, baring their faces for all to see.

The other women rushed forward, but I stayed back. My hand flew to my lips as a gasp leaped from my chest.

Though I had witnessed the same event many times before, it had never looked like this. It had *never* been so awful.

Astride each horse, clad in familiar armor and coats of arms, were creatures like the one who had taken my husband. Leering, wicked things with burning eyes and scaly hides.

To the very last man, that squad of knights had been corrupted. Some were fully transformed, with blazing crimson eyes and glistening scales of green or gold or magenta. Some were halfway changed, with one eye afire and the other wholly human, one half smooth-skinned, the other reptilian. Some flickered back and forth between man and monster, faces warping from one to the other extreme as I watched.

And the women embraced them anyway. As the creatures dismounted their horses, the women threw their arms around them, kissing and caressing and weeping with joy. They did not see what I saw.

Solea was among them. "Doña Jimena!" Tears racing down her face, she waved from the arms of a monster. "You were right! My Alejandro has returned!"

It was all I could do to muster a faint smile for her. The creature's forked tongue fluttered in the bell of Solea's ear, painting it with strands of viscous slime.

Solea did not seem to feel a thing.

Someone touched my shoulder, and I jumped. Whirling, I saw the emerald-scaled thing that had taken my husband's place.

"Aren't you going to welcome your lord home?" The creature's rasp mingled with Rodrigo's rich bass, both voices talking at once.

As I curtsied, I never took my eyes off the monster in front of me. "Welcome home."

"What's this?" said the creature and Rodrigo. "No kiss for the conquering hero?"

But that was something I could not bring myself to do. "I have come down with something, my lord. I do not wish for you to catch it in the midst of your campaign."

The creature grinned. "What do you think you have, my darling?"

"Something to do with waking up," I told him, "on the wrong side of the bed."

"Call them *guerritos*. War things." That was what Tizona said when I met with him that night. "It is just one of the things they have been called, but it will do."

Though it was a warm night, I felt frozen to the bone. "Why have I never seen them until now?"

"You were not touched by magic," said Tizona. "Not until you took me to the *bruja*."

My eyes burned as tears welled up in them...tears of helpless, hopeless confusion. "No one else can see them?"

"Some can, sometimes," said Tizona. "Most see only the effects of their presence. The shadows men cast when they come back from battle. The darkness they bring with them. The pain they cause."

"This is madness." I shook my head roughly, trying to drive away the truth. "How is it even *possible*?"

The candlelight flared on the gleaming flat of Tizona's blade, then dimmed. "Every man, when he takes up arms against another man, makes a deal in his heart. He summons a *guerrito* to do the things that go against the dictates of his soul.

"How else do you imagine your loving husband could behead or dismember another human being? How else could the same hands that caress your sweet face choke the life from someone else's throat?"

A defensive impulse rose up in me. "Rodrigo is a good man. A *great* man."

"Which is how the *guerrito* gains purchase," said Tizona. "El Cid *needs* it to fight his wars."

Tears rolled down my face as I slumped forward. "And the wars are important. El Cid fights to liberate Spain from the Moors."

"We both fight for that," said Tizona.

"So what now?" I said. "What can I do?"

"What do you *want* to do?" said Tizona.

I thought about it. "Will the *guerrito* only come during battle?"

Tizona hesitated. "It depends."

"What do you mean?" I said.

"*Guerritos* are...unpredictable. We must wait and see." The candle flame danced on Tizona's smooth surface. "But you have an advantage."

"Advantage?"

"You are touched by magic," said Tizona. "You can see the *guerrito* coming. You will know to avoid it."

I swallowed hard and nodded. "And what if I want to get rid of it?"

"I do not believe that is possible," said Tizona.

"Please don't say that." I dropped my head in my hands and sobbed. "Please don't."

A draft slipped through the room, and the candlelight rippled over Tizona's blade. For an instant, the light on the steel almost looked like a face.

"I will think about it," said Tizona.

For a while after that, things were fine. Almost normal.

For a while.

I lived my life as before, for the most part—tending our home and taking care of Rodrigo between the wars of El Cid. From time to time, I was even almost happy again. Almost.

I still feared the *guerrito* and worried it would reappear...but I took steps to avoid it. I stayed away from Rodrigo when the creature would most likely be active—before, during, and after battle. I let the thing have him for the fights, the *Reconquista* wars to liberate our homeland...and then I reclaimed him for my own when the blood and dust had settled.

Meanwhile, Tizona helped me through the dark times, when the fear and paranoia rose up within me. Without our midnight talks, I could not have made it through.

Over time, I even dared hope that all would be well. So long as I stayed in my part of Rodrigo's life, and the *guerrito* stayed in his, there would be no cause for conflict. Women and *guerritos* had lived like this for ages, hadn't they? I saw no reason Rodrigo's creature and I could not thrive by the same uneasy truce.

And so it went. For a while.

One day, we had an argument.

It started over nothing—a dinner party. I had accepted an invitation from my cousin, King Alfonso...but Rodrigo wanted nothing to do with it. He felt as if Alfonso was using me to control him.

It was a typical fight, the kind couples have all the time. It quickly escalated into a shouting match that was more about the unspoken pressures between us than the supposed reason it had started in the first place.

And then it happened.

"Alfonso would be *nothing* without me." A vein throbbed in Rodrigo's temple as he shouted. "It is *El Cid* who brings him greatness! I am *not* his *lackey* or his *lapdog*, and my *wife* does *not* hold my *leash*!"

"Who fields your *armies* and pays for your *wars*?" I said. "Perhaps it is *you* who would be nothing without *him*."

Suddenly, Rodrigo's face filled with rage...true fury beyond the limits I'd seen in our fight so far. Eyes wide, nostrils flaring, teeth clenched, he stood and glared at me, heating to a boil.

Even before he started to change, I took a step back. I sensed it.

The face of the creature flowed over his features like the shadow of an eclipse crossing over the sun. His eyes blazed with red light, and his skin turned to deep green scales. The forked tongue slithered from his mouth like a millipede.

Guerrito.

"Come here, darling." The *guerrito* took a step toward me, leering, reaching. "It is time for us to make up."

It was then that I ran.

Heart hammering like a horse's hooves, I bolted from the bedroom and slammed the door after me. He hurled the door open and gave chase.

The sound of his boots battering the floor behind me was enough to speed my flight downstairs. I flung myself into the chapel just a few steps ahead of him and barred the oak door.

He pounded on the door for a while, laughing and cursing me the whole time...and then he gave up. I knew I was lucky, because he could have broken the door down at any time if he had chosen to. He could have hacked his way through it with Tizona. He had decided to spare me.

Even so, I did not leave the chapel for a very long time. I did not come out until the next morning. By then, the *guerrito* was gone.

But not for long.

In the months and years to come, the *guerrito* appeared more often.

Gone were the days when his visits had coincided only with battles. No time or place seemed to be off-limits to him anymore.

Sometimes, I expected his arrival, as when Rodrigo lost his temper. Other times, the change seemed to come from out of the blue, shocking me with its suddenness and apparent senselessness.

Always, when it happened, I was terrified. I ran and hid when I could, with the creature at my heels...but sometimes, when the change caught me unawares, I had nowhere to go. Scalded by the waves of rage and malice radiating from the *guerrito*, I would watch and wait, wondering when it was finally going to hurt me.

"He is driving me mad," I told Tizona. "Have you thought of a way to get rid of him?"

Tizona gleamed in the flickering candlelight. "I am sorry, but not yet."

"Every day, I fear for my life," I said. "I wonder when the wrong word from my lips or look in my eyes will send me to my death bed."

"I hate to say this, Doña Jimena," said Tizona, "but in that regard, among women, you are hardly alone."

Things did not get better.

The *guerrito* came more often and stayed longer. Soon, it was there half the time, exuding its hellish menace in the heart of my world.

Its moods were uniformly dark, its tantrums epic. Whatever breakables there were in our home, the *guerrito* obliterated them in its fits of rage.

And yet, it did not hurt me. For the time being, it seemed

content with terrorizing me, holding me in constant suspense of my seemingly inevitable murder.

Eventually, it wore me down. The relentless terror of my every waking moment. There came a point when I got used to it.

I stopped running from the *guerrito*. No longer did I flee and hide every time it showed its horrible face.

My fear was no less, but I learned to live with it. It was either that, or leave my beloved Rodgrigo.

"There is always the convent," said Tizona. "You would be safe behind its walls."

"I cannot leave him," I said. "No matter the danger."

"But why?" said Tizona.

"Because my husband is still in there," I said. "And I love him. I need him...and so does Spain."

With each passing year, the *guerrito*'s presence increased...and its influence grew. At first, this influence could be seen in little things—impulsive words and actions in social circles. Uncharacteristic decisions in business and politics. Arbitrary changes in the way Rodrigo conducted his life.

Then, one day, he turned a corner. The *guerrito*'s recklessness took over.

And we were exiled because of it.

It started with a victory.

El Cid led a force into Granada to fight the Moors...and as usual, he triumphed. It was another grand step in the campaign to retake all of Spain from the Africans.

Unfortunately, it was done without King Alfonso's permission.

The next thing I knew, Rodrigo and the children and I were

escorted out of Castille. We were thrown into exile because of my husband's recklessness...which I knew was the recklessness of the *guerrito* shining through.

But the worst was yet to come.

"You're working for the *Moors* now?" As much as I'd gotten used to surprises, my husband's latest shock struck me like a blast of lightning.

"Alfonso thinks to crush me." Rodrigo stood in the hot sun and glowered. He had just returned from meeting with the Moorish Emir of Zaragosa. "But I will rise up again and claim what is mine."

"But you have fought against the Moors your whole *life*," I said. "How can you even *consider* fighting *for* them?"

As I watched, the *guerrito*'s leering features replaced Rodrigo's. "I have no more loyalty to them than to the king who exiled me. I only want their *treasure* to pay for my *wars*."

"We're talking about the *Moors*!" I said, though I knew my words fell on the *guerrito*'s deaf ears. "Have you no loyalty to the people of *Spain*? Have you no loyalty to *anyone*?"

The *guerrito*'s forked tongue flickered, a glistening pink obscenity. "Only myself," he said.

As I stood there, contemplating what until now had been an unimaginable future, I kept waiting for Rodrigo to reappear. Perhaps, if the *guerrito* stayed away long enough, I could get through to my husband. Maybe I could weaken the creature's influence and talk Rodrigo out of serving Moorish masters.

But Rodrigo did not come back that day.

"Have you thought of a way to get rid of the *guerrito*?" I asked Tizona. We were in a house in Zaragosa now, in a Muslim prayer chamber instead of a chapel.

"I know things are bad now," said Tizona.

"The *guerrito* is here all the time," I said. "It rarely lets me see Rodrigo at all."

"Some *guerritos* are like that," said Tizona. "They must have everything. They must conquer."

I wiped tears from my eyes with the back of my hand. "I just want my husband back. I want my Rodrigo."

Tizona's polished blade shimmered in the candlelight. "I have been thinking about this for a very long time. Perhaps there is a way."

I could not keep the flare of hope from my face and my voice. "What is it? Tell me!"

"You must go to war with him," said Tizona. "You must wait on the sidelines of all his battles."

"Wait for what?"

"His death." The light swirled along Tizona's length like ripples on a lake. "When he dies, you must run to him."

My skin turned to ice, and I felt sick in the pit of my stomach. "You're telling me...to wait for him to *die*?"

"With the life he leads, it will happen sooner or later," said Tizona. "Or perhaps he will outlive you, and none of this will matter. It is impossible to say.

"But if he *does* die in battle, you must be there. You must be *ready*."

I could not look at him. "Ready for what?"

"To do as I say, no matter how terrible it seems," said Tizona.

A rush of anger rose within me. "What *exactly* will you tell me to *do*?"

Tizona sighed. "You have trusted me so far, milady. You must know I want only to *help* you."

"So I have thought," I said. "But *this*..."

"Doña Jimena." There was an edge to Tizona's voice. "Surely you have realized by now how I feel about you."

I frowned. "How is that?"

"I pledge my absolute fealty to you," said Tizona. "My undying love."

I had nothing to say to that.

"As a knight loves and serves his queen, so do I love and serve you," said Tizona. "And as a queen trusts her knight, so must you trust me. If you do this, I believe, you can have him back."

"Dead," I said. "I can have him when he's dead."

"Not at all, milady," said Tizona. "Now listen as I tell you my plan."

Years passed in a haze of blood and fear.

El Cid continued his wars, switching allegiances with the ease of flipping a coin. He fought for the Moors, then the Christians, then the Moors, then the Christians—and finally, out of truest loyalty to himself, conquered a kingdom to call his own: Valencia.

Every step of the way, Tizona and I were by his side—Tizona in his fist and I in his entourage. Battle after battle, I waited on the sideline, watching as the *guerrito* who ruled my husband hacked his way through screaming enemies. Watching as *all* the *guerritos* struggled on the field, all the monsters who'd taken the places of men on all sides.

If anyone else could see the wars as I saw them, would they ever let their men ride off to fight them again? Could they bear the thought of the sons and husbands and brothers they loved being transformed into such savage monstrosities, for the sake of this piece of land or that religion or this chest of gold?

Or would they accept it as they always had, as a necessary evil? Would it make it even easier to swallow, knowing and seeing that the men themselves were not doing the actual fighting?

For my part, I soon came to wish I would never have to watch another battle again. I wished I would never have to see another sword-thrust to the heart or club-smash to the skull or arrow through the eye.

And I wished I would never have to see my *guerrito* striding toward me again, fresh from battle, soaked in blood and steaming with rancid demon sweat. I wished he would disappear forever, taking my constant fear with him—leaving only Rodrigo and life and hope. Gone like a fever or a fire, never ever to return.

Would I be able to make it happen when the time came? With all in chaos around me, could I do as Tizona instructed?

Just thinking about it made my hands tremble. Made my heart pound like the war drums beating in the mist as the *guerritos* tore each other to pieces.

One day in July, the Moors invaded Valencia by sea. Scimitars swooping through the hot summer air, they poured from their ships and swarmed the streets of our kingdom.

El Cid and his army raced to meet them. My bodyguards and I followed, as always.

We reached the coast at the height of the fiercest fighting. El Cid's forces, in all their *guerrito* glory, mowed down the Moors like scythes sweeping through grain. From what I could see, the invaders did not stand a chance.

Not that I felt any excitement at the thought of victory. Not that I craved anything but an ending to the violence, the terror, the sorrow. The nightmare my life had become.

Suddenly, a jolt went through the battlefield. All the *guerritos* paused in their mayhem and turned as one, gaping at one end of the war zone. It was as if something had exploded over there, drawing everyone's attention at once.

Drawing my attention, then, too.

When I looked where everyone else was looking, I could not tell at first what had happened. Blood-drenched knights stood in a circle, staring down at something on the ground.

Then, they lifted it up. Finally, I saw what they carried.

Rodrigo.

Not the *guerrito* anymore—just Rodrigo. And his body was limp. An arrow jutted from his bloody throat.

My husband.

As the battle resumed, the knights fought their way toward me, carrying Rodrigo between them. One of their number fell to a Moorish blade, but the other four kept coming, bringing their burden my way.

When they reached me, they lowered him gently to the sun-baked sand. One of them handed me Tizona, wrapped in Rodrigo's coat of arms.

Then, the knights charged back into battle, leaving me alone with Rodrigo and Tizona...exactly as I wanted to be.

"He is dead." Tizona's tiny voice chimed like a bell, ringing in my ears above the clashing war swords on the field.

"Yes." I ran my fingers over my beloved husband's face, feeling the lingering warmth in his murdered flesh.

"You remember what I told you?" said Tizona. "You must trust me. You must do as I say."

"I remember," I said.

"Then let us begin," said Tizona.

What I did next was not easy. After all, it was my husband's dead body. Whatever the *guerrito* had put me through, I still loved this man.

Then there was the problem of physically doing as Tizona told me. I was simply not strong enough to do the work alone.

But with my knightly bodyguards to help, I was able to raise Rodrigo onto his horse, Babieca. Together, we managed to lash him to the saddle and Babieca's neck.

Then came the tricky part.

As my knights held the reins, I huddled over Tizona. I turned my back to them, listening carefully to the sword's every word.

"You and I, Jimena," said Tizona. "We will turn the tables."

"Tell me what to do," I said.

"Take me to El Cid," said Tizona.

I did as he told me.

"Place my blade against his back," said Tizona.

I wrapped both hands around Tizona's hilt and raised him toward Rodrigo. My knights watched carefully, uncertain of what was to come next.

Tizona gleamed as I laid him upon Rodrigo's back. "Years ago, a *bruja* gave me the power to restore this man's life!" said Tizona. "I use that power *now*!"

Suddenly, Tizona flared with blinding light. His hilt became hot in my grip, but I refused to let go of it.

"Rodrigo Díaz de Vivar! Return to us!" Tizona flared even brighter. "El Cid Campeador! You are called!"

Before my very eyes, Rodrigo's back rose. And fell.

It was a miracle.

"Now, quickly!" said Tizona. "Place me against his heart!"

The sword was heavy in my hands as I lifted it from Rodrigo's back. Clumsily, I swung it around in front of him.

"Hurry!" said Tizona.

Standing on tiptoes, I slid Tizona upward until his tip touched Rodrigo's chest.

"Higher!" said Tizona.

I stretched as far as I could, pushing the point of the blade further. I could not have moved it another inch beyond that if I had tried.

"There!" said Tizona.

With that, he flared so brightly, I lost my sight for a moment. Whatever was happening to Tizona and Rodrigo, I saw none of it.

"Enough!" said Tizona. "Pull me away!"

Still blinded, I pulled the sword down from Rodrigo. I moved slowly, hoping not to cut him or Babieca or my knights with the blade.

"Now drive the horse into the battle!" said Tizona. "Do it now!"

"Into the battle?" I said.

"Yes!" said Tizona. "Before it's too late!"

"What was that, milady?" said one of my knights.

I took a deep breath and gathered myself, mustering the authority at my command. "Send Ed Cid back into the fight!"

"Into the fight?" said one of the knights.

"But he's *dead*," said the other.

"And even in death, he shall *inspire* his men!" My sight was coming back, so I could see the looks of disbelief on the knights' faces. I tried even harder to sound commanding. "Now send him onto the battlefield!"

The knights exchanged skeptical looks.

"Without *El Campeador*, we shall lose this *battle* and this *kingdom*!" I said. "Even in death, he is greater than *any* of us...and *far* greater than any Moorish *enemy*! Now *do it*! Send him into battle *one last time*!"

With that, the knights nodded and turned. They struck Babieca's flanks hard with their metal gauntlets, sending it racing toward the fight.

"We have done it," said Tizona. "You are free."

As I watched Babieca gallop across the battlefield, the body on its back transformed. Instead of Rodrigo, the *guerrito* rode into the fight.

"But the *guerrito* has returned," I said.

"I knew it would," said Tizona. "As soon as I brought Rodrigo back to life and sent him into battle."

I frowned. "But now the *guerrito* is in control again."

"Not for long." Tizona chuckled. "Keep watching."

I did as Tizona said...and then I understood. As Babieca rode across the field, El Cid's men rallied—and Moorish warriors ran to strike at the source of their inspiration.

El Cid's knights fought to defend their leader, but they could not keep away all the Moors. One after another, the Moors slashed and battered the *guerrito*, hacking his exposed flesh and pounding him to a pulp inside his armor.

The *guerrito*, strapped as he was to the back of the horse, could not defend himself. All he could do was scream as the enemy chopped and pulverized him.

I watched for a moment, then turned away from the slaughter. "So this is how we get rid of him. By sacrificing my husband."

"Yes," said Tizona. "That is part of it."

I held up his shining blade, cradled in Rodrigo's coat of arms vestment. "What do you mean, 'part of it?'"

"As a magical sword," said Tizona, "there was one more thing I could do. One thing more than bringing your husband back to life."

"What is that?" I said.

"I did what swords do best," said Tizona. "I cut something out of him."

That night, dressed all in black, I retired to my bed chamber. The house, at last, was empty of the mourners who had flown to my side. The mourners who had come to pay their respects to my dead husband, the hero El Cid.

It had been a difficult day. The Battle of Valencia was won, but at terrible cost. El Cid and many brave knights had been lost forever.

Almost.

Sitting on the bed, I unwrapped the sword that laid upon the scarlet coverlet. The blade of the great Tizona gleamed in the flickering candlelight, its smooth surface more perfect than any mirror.

I ran my finger over it, and I smiled. No need for tears, not now. Never again.

The *guerrito* was gone for good, chewed to pieces by the fangs of

Moorish steel. Rodrigo was dead, too...but Tizona had cut something out of him.

And put it inside himself.

Something precious beyond words, beyond imagining.

"Hello, my love," I said to the sword.

"Hello." The voice that came from the sword was not Tizona's.
It was rich and deep. And familiar.

It made my heart beat faster.

"I love you," I said to the sword.

"And I love you more than I can ever say," said the part of
Rodrigo that Tizona had drawn inside himself.

Rodrigo's immortal soul.

"Why don't you give it a try?" I said.

THE DANCING DEAD

Hundreds of us push forward, dancing madly as we always do, not suspecting, never guessing what awaits us up ahead. We're spinning, sprinting, leaping, twirling by moonlight and flickering streetlights, one huge rhythmic mob bumping and slamming and kicking chaotically...all caught up in the hyper metronome beats in our heads, none of us watching that billboard in our paths.

Then *BAWHOOM*, a row of cannons punches through the giant sign, tearing holes in the oversized faces of the smiling models in the massive image. Most of us finally look up, gaping at the weapons pointed in our direction...though I wonder how many of us really understand what's in store.

Not many, I think. Most of the others keep dancing straight ahead...but with my long brown hair flying, I redirect my path and accelerate my movements, gyrating as fast as I can away from the field of fire.

My name is Laurette and I'm not ready to surrender, not now when we're so close to wherever this plague of ours has been leading from the start.

The sickness has been driving us west for weeks, and now we're here, L.A. at last. Something big's about to happen, we don't know what, but we do know when--45 minutes from now--and I for one intend to be alive to see it.

As exhausted as I am, as I always am these days, I double-down and push myself harder than ever. And as I rush out of range, I catch glimpses of the attack as it starts.

The cannons blow out streams of white slop that rain down on the dancing mob like a shower of plaster. Those caught in the shower keep hopping and whirling, some hooting and whooping, all splashing like kids in the covering whiteness.

But the whitewash isn't meant for their amusement. Within seconds, it does the worst thing the dancers can imagine.

It hardens.

Even the most oblivious ones get it now. As their dancing slows and slows some more, they understand. As the hardening muck locks them down no matter how hard they struggle, they grasp their fates.

And they scream for their lives.

I'm lucky, I made it--barely--out of reach, and I'm untouched. But I know I'll never get that symphony of screaming out of my head. Hundreds of men, women, and children shrieking in terror, howling their lungs out.

Because this is the end for every one of them. Because they all know there's only one thing any of them can do.

Which is die.

Not because the muck stops their breathing. Not because it stops their heartbeats.

Because it stops their *dancing*.

That would've been my fate, too, if I'd been whitewashed. I'm just as infected as the rest of them, just as much a victim of the Dance/Drop plague.

For the past six weeks, I've been dancing day and night, never stopping for a moment. If I ever do, whether by choice or force or accident, I'll be dead within seconds. Excruciating pain will flash through me, and then I'll fall down screaming on the spot, just another spent young woman in a very long line of danced-out corpses. I've seen it happen too many times to count.

Everyone in what's left of America has. Why do you think the millions of sick ones are all dancing so hard?

Even if, deep in our overstressed hearts, we secretly crave the stillness that only death brings.

Dancing freestyle, I skip down an alley as fast as I can, waving my arms overhead. Every few steps, I do a spin-kick or twist, just to make sure my plague-ridden body never doubts I'm keeping up the dance moves. When it comes to the Dance/Drop bug, launching into a straight-ahead walk or run with no rhythmic component can trigger a fatal reaction just as easily as ceasing all motion. The beat in our heads and the beat of our hearts are inextricably linked; falling out of step with one will throw the other into runaway asynchronous spasms.

At the end of the alley, I do a slow pirouette as I size up the street in front of me. Then I quick-step left, away from the flashing orange lights on the right.

Orange lights mean Dance Rangers, and Dance Rangers mean trouble. Recruited from the few cops and servicemen uninfected by the plague, they used to try to help victims like me. Now, they're just trying to drop as many of us as they can, to contain the plague.

I go half a block, then hip-hop stomp my way across the street, weaving between a scattering of abandoned cars. Who needs a zombie apocalypse to end congestion on the streets of Los Angeles? Boogie fever will do the job just as well, it turns out.

On the other side, I polka the rest of the way to the next intersection and shuffle right. I see dancers in that direction, converging on a rolling yellow truck...and I hurry to join them.

Because I know exactly what that vehicle is all about. The Dance Rangers aren't the only ones hunting us Beatheads. The folks with the yellow trucks painted with big smiley faces are looking for us, too...but not to drop us.

They just want to help us hold on a little longer, keep body and soul together in spite of our plight.

Before the plague struck, I loved dancing. It was the most important thing in the world to me.

I was always dancing, whether I was on the job as a professional dancer on stage and screen or during my off-hours, getting down in wild clubs.

Dance, dance, dance, that was me. And burn every bridge on the way as I danced to the top. Drop-kick almost everyone who couldn't help my career, just because.

Now look at me. What wouldn't I give to have someone who cares, just to have the simple company of someone I love?

And what wouldn't I do to be able to stop dancing without dropping dead?

Keeping the truck rolling, that's the key. The Beatheads dance up, grab what's handed out the window, and dance away.

As I waltz my way closer, I see a young man trot away from the truck, stuffing a sandwich in his face. A woman bounds up next and grabs a yellow sweatshirt, then pulls it on over her tattered pink tank while shimmying down the sidewalk.

Next thing I know, I'm at the window myself, shouting to the Smileez--the people in the biohazard suits inside. "Food and water! Food and water!"

As the truck rolls onward, I do an Irish jig to stay alongside it.

One of the people inside hands me a bottle of water; someone else pushes a sandwich my way.

"God bless you!" I shout, and they wave as I moonwalk away from them. The Smileez don't look much like angels, I can't even see their faces through their smiley-faced faceplates...but that's what they are. Without them--without their volunteer corps fanned out across the country--I doubt many of us Beatheads would be alive. God knows we've lost tens of thousands already, but the rest of us would be dead now, too, if not for the food and water and other necessities given out freely to us on the move.

Gobbling the sandwich, I square dance up the street, swinging in do-si-do circles as if I've link arms with an invisible partner. For the forty jillionth time this week, I wish I still had a partner to help me through; I wish my on-again, off-again boyfriend Riggs was still alive. Even though he was the one who got me sick, I wish he was still with me, making jokes as dark as they come that got me through the blistering endless days.

But Riggs just wasn't in good enough shape to survive. Neither was anyone else I cared about, like my Mom and Dad.

That's the problem with being a professional dancer before the plague struck. I'm better equipped to outlast the rest of the herd, which means I get to be lonelier longer...though not for much longer, I guess.

Every Beathead in America has flocked to the West Coast today for a reason...though I don't know what that reason is yet. But I will in 33 minutes.

I feel it, we all do; I don't even need to check my digital watch. But when I do, I see what time it will be when these next 33 minutes are up.

Midnight.

Air raid sirens howl, signaling the uninfected to stay off the streets. The Beathead hordes are coming, the combined pounding of millions of feet up and down the West Coast like the thundering hoofbeats of stampeding buffalo.

Something is going to happen, I can feel it. The lot of us, springing and twisting and vaulting as we are, hang suspended like shivering droplets on the belly of a raincloud, about to fall. Awaiting a change we neither understand nor anticipate.

Though I for one want it to mean something. *Need* it to mean something. Otherwise, my parents will have died for no good reason, and the guilt I feel for outlasting them might just kill me before the plague does.

I'll never forget seeing them die and being helpless to prevent it. We'd found each other by chance, in a crowd, after we'd all been infected in different parts of town...but they didn't last long after that.

Two days later, as we danced across Chicago, Dad fell exhausted in the street and died screaming as the plague burned him up from inside. Mom was three years younger, 64, but she wasn't much better at standing the strain. The day after Dad died, she sat down on a curb, so tired she couldn't go on...and I had to watch as the plague cooked her, too.

I'll never forgive myself, as long as I live, for not saving them. Though I know in my heart there was nothing I could do, that I can't even save myself.

I polish off the sandwich and gulp down the water, flinging the wrapper and bottle in my wake with abandon. I've got much bigger problems than not littering to worry about these days.

At least disposing of digested waste isn't one of them, thanks to the plague. Dance/Drop changes our metabolism so we process a much higher percentage of food and water into energy. None of us need bathroom breaks anymore, which is good, because all of us would have been dead long ago if we did.

"Hey!" A male voice calls me, and I spin around to face him. "Hey, talk to me a minute!"

That's a longtime Beathead back there; I can tell by his tattered rags, sunken eyes, and the skin-and-bones pick-up sticks that pass for his body. He does a kind of Russian Cossack dance, arms folded and feet kicking stiffly on alternate sides as he works his way toward me.

"What happens when we get to the beach?" shouts the Beat-head--who was probably in his early twenties at the start and now looks at least mid-to-late sixties. "What happens *then*?"

I don't answer, but not because I don't know, which I don't. I don't waste my breath because I need every bit of it for something else now.

Because of what I see behind him, down the street.

Headlights. At least a dozen of them, racing straight for us...and the hornet swarm buzz that comes with them gets louder each second.

The *Still Riders* are coming.

The Smileez slam the window shut on their yellow truck as the Still Riders zip toward it. Twelve souped-up racing motorcycles, all black, shoot past the truck on both sides, and none of the crimson-clad riders wastes his ammo on it. They already know all Smileez trucks are armor-plated...unlike the Beatheads.

Dancers flee in all directions, scattering before the onslaught. Nobody stays in the path of the danger this time, like they did with the Dance Rangers' whitewash.

Shotgun blasts roar behind me as I hurtle toward an alley in a freestyle frenzy. Screams pierce the night in shrill succession, ringing out in nightmarish counterpoint to the gunfire booms.

The Still Riders might as well be hunting deer or videogame characters for all they think of us as human. This is sport to them as much as plague containment; I've heard they keep score with mobile apps and compete on social media for top-kill status.

They're also much more brutal and feared than Dance Rangers, more inclined to extreme depravity for the sake of thrill-kill kicks. I've heard stories of torture and sadism beyond belief...especially toward their own number, if one of them becomes infected.

If I'm to have any hope at all of seeing where this plague has been leading, I've got to escape them. I've got to survive the next 25 minutes, and I've got to keep traveling west.

At least, that's what I'm thinking just before I hear one of those hot rod cycles buzzing up after me, heading straight for me at a high rate of speed.

The Still Rider flashes toward me, and I suddenly spin left at the last possible second, leaping out of his path. He misses by the flicker of a whisker and whips around for another try.

Just then, I see a jack and tire iron by an abandoned Cadillac and make a loping run for it Afro-Cuban-style. As the rider swoops toward me, cranking off a nowhere-near shotgun blast, I snatch up the iron and whirl to face him.

He spots the iron too late. I grip it with both hands and lash out fiercely, clipping his helmet as he pulls a last-second swerve. The impact kicks him sideways, shooting him free of his skidding cycle. His helmet flies off, his shotgun goes airborne, and he collides with a fleeing Beathead, knocking her to the pavement.

I'm already dancing hard again, obeying the plague--but that Beathead's finished unless I can help. I've got time now, barely enough, as the riderless bike careens into onrushing Still Riders, blasting them off their own mounts and into each other.

Still gripping the iron, I quickstep over and duck down fast, making a grab for the downed Beathead...but she's tangled with the helmetless rider. Her eyes are huge with panic as she scrambles to get out from under him.

"Grab on!" I holler, shoving the iron toward her as I do a soft-shoe and try not to get dragged in, too.

The Beathead thrusts out a hand, but the rider flops over and knocks it down. For an instant, the woman's trapped under his bulk...and that's more than enough to trigger the plague pulse.

As soon as she starts screaming, I know she's lost, and I swirl away from her with a flurry of interpretive dance moves. No sooner does her screaming peak than the blond-haired rider on top of her starts twitching and flipping around, legs fluttering wildly, out of control.

I've seen it before; I've *lived* it before. This is just what the first flush looks like, convulsions and spasms as Dance/Drop takes hold.

Good for him. Without his helmet, he picked it up fast, breathed in the bug from the Beathead he flattened. Seconds from now, he'll be dancing like the rest of us, or he'll be dropping down dead, screaming his head off like the girl who just died under him.

Wish I could stay and watch, but I need to get away before the other riders get rolling again. Dying in the street isn't on my agenda.

But getting to the beach in seventeen minutes is.

Several streets away, I find a garden on a corner, dark and secluded, which is just what I need. In among the willows, I slow to a swaying samba, moving softly in a circle to do the thing I've been dying to do.

It isn't easy, but I've had to learn these past six weeks, it's this or perish. Focusing in, I block the up-tempo metronome beat in my head, push it into the background as much as I can. Then, as I samba in circles, I let my eyes close, and I let myself drift.

We Beatheads call it tweetsleep--microbursts of ultra-deep dream-sleep fizzing like bubbles as we never stop moving. You'd be surprised how restful it feels when your life is like mine, when even a five-minute catnap is outside your reach.

You just have to watch you don't let yourself go. One slip, one surrender to exhaustion, and that's all she wrote.

But right now, for me, this is paradise. I drift from one nano-dream to another, each fully-formed drama unspooling in millionths of a second.

At least until a man's voice wakes me up.

"Hello? Hello?"

When I open my eyes, I see him ten feet away--the same blond rider in crimson leathers who tried to kill me just moments ago, only now he's not riding or killing.

He's dancing.

If that's what you want to call it. He's doing a kind of stiff shuffle-step, pumping him arms as he hops from foot to foot. It looks like something an uncoordinated old guy would do at a wedding reception or bar after one too many beers or rum and cokes.

"I'm sorry." He looks embarrassed. "*I can't dance.*"

Poetic justice, I love you. But all I can think of is getting away from him. "What do you want?"

"This *beat* in my *head*." He presses the palms of his hands to his temples. "It won't *stop*."

"Where are your friends?" I ask him. "Didn't they want you around anymore?"

He glares at me. "You *know* they would've killed me if I hadn't run away."

"How many of *them* have *you* killed before?" As I say it, I dance a slow turn, looking around for the best way out of the garden.

Instead of answering the question, he asks another. "Can I come with you? *Please*, can I come with you?"

Now it's my turn to glare. "Come *with* me?"

"To the *beach*." He winces when he says it, grips the sides of his head. "That's where we're *going*, right? Where it's *calling* us."

I just stare as I wonder what his game is. Dance/Drop is talking to him, all right, just as clear as if he'd caught it six weeks ago. It's calling him on like the rest of us, but does he even care? What if he only wants to go out with a bang, prove his Still Rider stones by taking down as many Beatheads as he can along the way?

I don't want to be next on his list, and I'm ready to run...but then he groans and grimaces, still holding on to his skull.

Seeing him with the same look on his face as my suffering parents makes my heart go out to him. It makes me want to take a chance and help him, even if it's only to let him tag along so he won't be alone.

I can't believe I'm going to do it, it isn't like me at all. How can I reach out to a *Still Rider*, of all people? God only knows how many Beatheads he's killed, how much pain and terror he's caused.

But as I look at him, his suffering is the only thing that seems to matter. How can I *not* help this man?

"Yes," I tell him. "We're going to the beach."

He says his name is Teo. The two of us leave the park and head down a cross-street, drawn by the sounds of a crowd and the pull of the plague.

He still can't dance worth crap; I'd be embarrassed if it mattered. As it is, his ultra-lame moves help put my mind at ease, making it seem less likely he'll be able to hurt me if he tries. It also helps that I made him turn out his pockets before leaving the park, proving he's got no lethal weapons at the ready.

"Lots of people down there." He has to shout because he's a good ten yards behind me. "All heading in one direction, it looks like."

I see them at the end of the cross-street, a Beathead parade on the move. No need to check a map to know where they're going, not with the beat in my own head driving me the same way.

"The beach." Even as I say it, I catch a whiff of salt sea air and know it's near. Weeks of constant motion have led me to this, all the way from Chicago in the longest unbroken performance ever staged.

As we merge with the passing procession, it gets harder to stay together. Everyone around us dances frantically, recklessly charging forward to the beat of their runaway mental metronomes.

I've been doing a fast Cajun two-step but I slow it down some, shifting gears to a Korean giddyap so I don't lose Teo.

"What happens when we get there?" he shouts.

"No idea." I pretend to twirl a lariat overhead as I spin in a circle.

We go a little further--me doing a kind of tango, him doing a weird swiveling skip-step--before he says the next thing. "It's kind of exciting, isn't it?"

"You think so?"

"Being a part of something big like this." Teo smiles. "A movement...literally."

I know what he means, I feel it too, but I'm not sure where he's going with this. "Except for the constant threat of death part, I guess."

Suddenly, his expression turns serious. "If I had my bike, I'd be *tearing* up this crowd."

"Sorry to hear you're missing out." Just like that, whatever charitable feelings I might have had shrivel up and blow away.

"What I mean is, why aren't the Still Riders ripping through here?" Teo scowls and looks around...then meets my gaze. "Unless maybe they *know* something."

Right on cue, I hear the first aircraft approaching.

Ten minutes. I see from my watch that's all the time we have left. It's more than enough, with the beach sprawling before us, just a few blocks away.

If you don't factor in the fleet of aircraft roaring in above us, that is.

First, I see the helicopters, zooming in low--black choppers blasting by overhead in V-formation. They buffet us all with air turbulence, combing the crowd with blinding orange spotlights, and then they charge past toward the beach.

"I was right!" shouts Teo. "The Rangers waited till we reached a choke point, and now they're *hitting* us!"

I know he's right, but I don't know what's next...at least until I see the first of the planes. It's a big one, bobbing toward us on broad, wedge-like wings, carried forth by four propellers emitting a hell of a racket. It looks like a cargo plane at first, complete with a roomy deep belly like the bottom scoop of a pelican's bill.

But it only takes a second for me to guess its true purpose. This isn't a farewell fly-by bidding us well on our way to the sea.

The Dance Rangers have no intention of letting us see this through to the end.

"*Come on!*" I wave for Teo to follow as I speed up my steps. "Stay with me! Stay off to the side!"

A shiver of panic flashes through the crowd. The procession skips a beat, snagging on the moment just before realization becomes a stampede.

The crowd snaps out of its stasis, pouring forward in a pell-mell torrent. But by then, it's already too late for the ones in the back.

Glancing over my shoulder as we flee, I see the first of the tanker planes open the doors on its belly. A shower of white issues forth, dumping down in a great misty cloud trailing after the aircraft.

I hear the great splattering impact and then piercing screams hacking into the night. It's a whitewash, like back at the billboard, but much more expansive; the first drop alone must have doused several thousand instead of mere hundreds.

By the time the big air tanker flies over Teo and me, it's got nothing; its tanks are exhausted. But even as it thunders past the front of the crowd, I hear another in the distance, fast approaching.

And the screams of the whitewashed Beatheads rise up from the street like the shrieks of ten thousand sirens to meet it.

The beat in my brain ratchets up, chattering like the machine-gun staccato of a frenzied flamenco dancer's feet. It doesn't quite drown out the screams or the next tanker's roar, but it does drive me harder than ever to reach the finale.

Every time I look at my watch, I've got one minute less. Five becomes four becomes three and then street becomes sand.

I leap from the joy of it, not daring to slow down because I might be trampled by the horde of dancers stampeding behind me. Teo, to his credit, has somehow kept up, staying not far away. Hard to believe, but it's comforting seeing him there, a familiar face in the anonymous throng.

Looking back, I see the second tanker dropping its load of whitewash in the middle of the street, inundating more Beatheads. I hear them howling as the liquid hardens, locking them in place to burn and die from within as the plague pulse triggers.

Then I focus forward again, quickstepping over the sand as the moment draws near.

Two minutes till midnight. That's what my watch says.

"What happens now?" shouts Teo, who's doing a bizarre serpentine run-kicking thing with fluttering jazz hands. I've seen lots of bad dancers since this epidemic started, but Teo by far is the worst. "Are you getting any kind of *sign*?"

"Nothing," I tell him.

"What if one never comes?" ask Teo.

I don't answer because I don't know. I've wanted this all to mean something...but maybe the ending has more to do with a tanker plane dropping whitewash than some kind of plague-induced revelation.

Because here comes another one.

This time, the tanker heads straight for the beach...but the Beatheads have room to fan out here. We scatter in every direction, still dancing like mad, as the plane thunders forth and unloads.

A shower of whitewash drops down, but a stiff wind shunts most of it back toward the street. Clusters of dancers get drenched, but most of us out on the beach are untouched.

Suddenly, then, I hear beeping. I jump, at first forgetting I've set the alarm on my watch...and then I see the display as it blinks.

12:00 AM.

For once, I don't hear any aircraft approaching, just the screams of the whitewashed Beatheads and the crashing and hissing of the tide. I slow my pace from a full-tilt quickstep to a waltz, taking in my surroundings.

The beach is crowded with dancers as far as I can see in both directions. They're still pouring in from other access points, rushing from the city--and other cities and towns all up and down the coast, I sense--to get to where the action is.

Except there isn't much action. Whatever culmination we've all been expecting, this isn't it.

"What will they all do?" asks Teo. "If they came here for nothing, then what?"

I have no answer for him...and then I don't need one.

Something happens a few yards away, at the edge of the surf. For no apparent reason, a young woman with short black hair throws herself against a shirtless young guy with a shaved head. Their chests collide, and then she drops back onto the sand...and does it again.

So do a few other people nearby, as if they got the idea from the first ones. But then I see more in the distance, spontaneous pop-ups that can't be connected.

Before I can say something about it, Teo flings himself against me, ramming his chest into mine. He knocks the breath right out of me and makes me stumble in my footwork.

"What the hell?" No sooner do I snap out the words than I totally understand. Because just like that, as if the collision jarred something loose, I'm consumed with the urge to do the same exact thing.

And so I do. Grinning for no good reason, I slam-dance into Teo, crashing our bodies together without warning or explanation.

Imagine a beach packed with people for miles and miles, and every last one of them's slam-dancing. Imagine millions of bodies slamming into each other, one vast ribbon of humanity in constant collision.

Well, that's what we have here. No sooner do Teo and I start to slam than the rest of the Beatheads join in, driven to follow the same wild urge.

Everywhere I look, bodies are crashing together with violent force. Strangers bash into me from every side, and I give it right back. Teo takes and gives a pounding, too, looking like he enjoys it a little too much.

A man I don't know hurtles into me, knocking me over. Then, a woman propels me back up when she flies out of nowhere, red-faced with delight.

Soon, I lose Teo, lose my bearings and inhibitions. I'm caught up in the agitated tide, aware only of the bodies flowing around and against me, sweating and bruising.

The metronome beat in my head keeps speeding up, reaching a hyperfast rhythm that's physically impossible for human movements to match. Yet it feels like just the right music to go with the scene, perfect jackhammer punk-thrash backbeat to drive us all onward.

With each passing second, we move faster, slam harder, shout louder. Hearts and lungs overstressed from weeks or days of frantic dance are made to work doubletime, tripletime, quintupletime. Sweat and spit and blood spatter us all in equal measure.

I feel like we're building to something, some massive crescendo...but maybe we won't get the chance. Even in the midst of the frenzy, I'm dimly aware of the sound of distant thunder--planes and choppers cruising closer, a fresh wave of Dance Ranger forces approaching.

Whatever we're building up to, it has to happen *now*, or it's all over.

Just as I think it, a change comes upon us. Electrical currents crackle through the crowd, leaving us tingling...but not stopping us. If anything, the shocks drive us harder, whip us into greater frenzies.

Then, suddenly, the battering impacts become something else. I slam into Teo like a car into a tree...and I *stick*. I can't pull away.

My shoulder and upper arm have melted into Teo's chest. We both gape and struggle to separate, but we can't.

Teo looks half-crazy. "I guess this is that *thing* we were waiting for!"

I know it, I *feel* this is right, this is what the plague wants...but I fear it. I panic and want to escape though I know I should welcome it.

Teo doesn't share the same growing pains. Pushing forward, he wraps his arms around me...and they merge with my body.

"Hey! A Still Rider and a Beathead mashed together!" Teo laughs. "I never thought I'd see the day!"

Looking around, I see we're not the only ones linking up. Everyone in sight is going through the same thing, flowing together into interlocking forms.

Before I know what's happening, other combined people make contact with us, joining flesh and blood with ours. I feel them melting into us, twining sinews and systems with ours into one giant network.

There's a moment then, as the metronome stops in my head, when we're all on the cusp. The great merging is irreversible;

millions of Beatheads are tethered together. But the final consummation, whatever that will be, has yet to occur.

The squadron of choppers and planes races toward us...then charges off without dropping their whitewash. Maybe they know it's too late to undo what's in progress. Maybe this is just too big for them to stop or comprehend.

Or maybe they're just too afraid.

As they move off into the night, the moment passes. The pause in the action turns over like a page in a book, and the great merged Us on the beach convulses.

All at once, our vast mingled ribbon of humanity rises up from the sand and ripples into the air. When we climb high enough, hundreds of feet off the ground, the whole thing rushes together with an echoing *boom*.

The ribbon becomes a huge sphere, spinning and pulsing with golden light. Somewhere in the heart of it, I'm aware of what's happening.

I'm aware as the sphere spins frantically, pulsing ever faster, than hatches like an egg. I know that I'm part of the thing that emerges, a thing unlike any ever seen before on Earth.

The closest I can come to describing it is to say it's like an image in a kaleidoscope, an ever-changing pattern on an enormous scale. Only it's composed of flesh and sound and light and thought, twisting and reshaping in myriad ways.

If you look at it, you might first see a giant golden eye with millions of arms and legs for lashes. A second later, you might see a cluster of multicolored pyramids folding and unfolding in infinite layers, while at the same time you hear five hundred thousand voices singing five hundred thousand different songs.

You might see a single giant sphere composed of faces, each one swirling with its own unique tangle of neon fractals. Or you might see a cloud of steam and snowflakes, chiming like a choir of infinite bells as thousands of dreams flicker through it.

It never stops changing and evolving. And like the Beatheads who made it what it is, it never stops moving. It never stops dancing.

Humankind was at an impasse, settled and sedentary, set in its ways. A new thing, a vast, enlightened, and restless thing, was needed...and created, danced into being by the plague, by nature itself.

Was it worth all the pain and suffering it took to conceive it? I don't know yet. We lost so *many* along the way, including Mom and Dad. But at least I know their sacrifice wasn't for nothing.

I've found a new beginning, and I've found something else I was looking for, too. Even as I'm part of this multifaceted whole, this ceaseless motion, I've found what I've been longing for most since coming down with Dance/Drop in the first place.

There might be millions of minds and voices in here, and we might never stop moving and changing...but it all adds up to something I never would have expected to find, something I haven't had for so long, maybe most of my life. Something I never knew I wanted so much until I couldn't have it anymore.

It adds up to *stillness*.

THE LOVE QUEST OF
SMIDGEN THE SNACK CAKE

First off, it's important you know that snack cakes do not feel guilt. That is why, even with the corpse of my lover here before me, all I can think of is finding someone else to take me in. To eat me. Fulfill me.

Love me.

It is my nature and purpose. It is the only reason I was created. It is why, even as the pungent smells of my lover's decomposing body reach the rudimentary olfactory cells in my ultrachocolate frosting, I softly whistle my lilting mating call, casting about for a new precious soul mate to embrace me gently with supple fingers and raise me toward the blissful warmth and moisture of the glistening portal all pink flesh and bright white teeth and then when I cannot stand the anticipation a single moment more BITE DOWN and grant me the blinding wild release I have craved for as long as I can remember.

Oh PLEASE someone find me here and eat me! I have been created with cutting edge late-21st century biobaking technology to grant you the ultimate sweet eating euphoria. Pay no attention to the woman on the floor, or at least give me a chance to PLEASE you before you tend to her. You won't be sorry.

She is no one important. She means nothing to me.

She is just a pick-up that didn't work out. You know how these things go.

As soon as she walked into Shangri-La, the supermarket where we met, the store told me her name. Lynda McVicker.

It told me everything I needed to know about her, too, and then some. Like all customers these days, her spending habits are logged on the worldwide Shopnet computer network, accessible to smart goods like me once the in-store grid pings her subcutaneous identichip.

Right away, I knew she was the one for me.

Based on her purchases over the past three weeks, she did not look like a suitable match. She had bought nothing in three weeks but produce and low-fat or no-fat foods. Not a single scrap of junk food. On top of that, she had purchased diet books, workout clothes, and a yearlong membership to a gym, all within the last three weeks.

But OH when I went back further, I could see how PERFECT she really was. I can tell you from personal experience in this particular case that true love DOES exist.

For her entire adolescent and adult life up until three weeks ago, Lynda had been the queen of junk food. Aside from the briefest blips of non-junk spending due to occasional failed diets, she had purchased only the most fattening, high-cholesterol, chemical-soaked foods available from grocery stores, restaurants, vending machines, and mail order websites.

In short, she was the perfect woman. Though she was on a diet that day, she had eaten non-nutritious foods in great quantities all her life. Though her last purchases had been salad greens and bottled water, her 225-pound body told the true story.

I knew she was just waiting for someone like me to come along.

As she made her way across Shangri-La, I followed her progress via Store's buyspy grid and made myself ready for our encounter. I was determined to make our first meeting perfect in every way.

Researching her preferences via Shopnet, I found that she most often bought products with predominantly blue and gold packaging...so I shifted the chameleonic inks of my wrapper from red and white to blue and gold. Discovering that she favored darker chocolates over lighter ones, I manipulated my own coloration, shifting the milky browns of my ultrachocolate frosting and cake to deeper, fudgier hues.

As Lynda lingered in the produce aisle, sullenly tucking genetically modified hypertasty carrots and cucumbers in her hovercart, I requested a rearrange from the shelving. When Store agreed I had the best chance of the snack cake varieties in the display to make a sale to Lynda, clacking pincers dropped from the underside of the shelf above me and moved me from the middle rows of the display to the front. The position of the entire shelf changed, too, rising up to Lynda's eye level and pushing out a few extra inches into the aisle.

There was no way she would miss me now...and no way she could resist me, once I started pouring on the charm.

At least, that was what I thought before she walked right on past my aisle.

To say I was disappointed when Lynda steered her hovercart away from the cookie and snack cake aisle would be a tremendous understatement.

There I sat, looking fabulous, dreaming of the love of lips and teeth and tongue I craved above all else...and Lynda didn't even come down my aisle. Via Store's buyspy, I watched as she pushed on

289

by, pausing at an endcap display to listen to cereal boxes calling out to her before she turned down the next aisle and kept going.

For an instant, I panicked, fearing I had missed my chance at meeting the woman of my dreams. My baked-in mind (consisting of a matrix of precision-engineered and digestible protein molecules) was thrown into a state of confusion.

Then, I pulled myself together and pinged Store, determined not to give up so easily. From the memory my makers had given me, I knew that the path to true love is not always smooth, and that anything worth having is worth working for.

Though Store was skeptical, already having shunted processing power away from the quadrants Lynda had passed through or missed, he agreed to give me a chance with some guided couponing. According to Lynda's past activity in this and other shopping facilities, she might respond favorably to a strategically placed offer.

When she was midway up the next aisle, Store flashed a message on the organic LED screen implanted in the palm of her hand: "Save one credit on Sea Sprite plankton snacks in Aisle 5!"

I thought it was the perfect bait, since Sea Sprite plankton snacks were among the items Lynda had been buying most often since starting her diet three weeks ago. Though Sea Sprite products usually were displayed in Aisle 8, Store had already diverted a batch of them via the underfloor realignment system to a niche on a shelf right across from me in Aisle 5.

Thanking Store for his help, I focused on buyspy, nervously watching as Lynda stared at her palm screen. She read the text message from Store, then looked away, distracted by the cries of products on the shelves around her.

But then, thankfully, she looked back. From twenty different spycam angles, I watched as she raised her eyebrows and nodded...then directed her hovercart to head for the end of the aisle and turn left.

Toward my aisle. Finally, she was coming closer. We were about to meet.

Joyfully, I added a final touch to spruce myself up for her: in the looping thread of white icing on my fudge-frosted face, I wrote her first name in neat, cursive lettering.

I personalized myself so there could be no doubt whatsoever that we were truly meant for each other.

Snack cakes like me have a supercreamy center, not a heart...but if I had had a heart that day, it would have been pounding like crazy as Lynda moved down my aisle. My baked-in mind was focused entirely on one thought alone: **I LOVED HER.** Every atom of my being was consumed with a single imperative desire: that **LYNDA** would **BUY** me and **DEVOUR ME.**

I **LONGED** for her credit chip to transfer funds into the accounts of my manufacturer. I **YEARNED** to feel her pudgy fingers **TEAR OFF** my wrapper and close around me, **THRUSTING** me toward the sweetest fate that I could ever **DREAM** of, the **ECSTASY** and **INTIMACY** that occurs when **TWO** become **ONE.**

If only if only if only she would have me she would **TAKE** me.

She drew closer.

On both sides of the aisle, cookies and snack cakes cried out to her, a hundred different suitors trying to intercept her with songs and lies and promises. Twice, packages leaped off the shelves into her hovercart, but she spotted them and stuffed them back in their displays. A bag of Stimchoc Thrillchip Omegawafers used a stealthier tactic, sliding off a rack and clinging to her sweatpants with a light static charge...but she caught that one, too, and peeled it right off.

Then, having made it through the gauntlet, she pulled up right in front of me. Her broad backside was turned to me, as she was looking at the Sea Sprite display across the aisle...but finally finally finally she was **THERE** she was **CLOSE TO ME.**

I had a chance. It would be tricky, overcoming her willpower, getting her to **TAKE ME** in spite of her diet after she had passed so many others by, but I KNEW it could be done. I KNEW I was special and had the power and desire to win her over.

I knew that true love would win out.

I began my approach gently, knowing that she had been burned before. Noise and aggressiveness would not work with her; what she needed was kindness and understanding.

Activating my sound chip (protein-based and digestible like my mind), I cast a beam of hypersound in her direction, a focused signal meant for her ears only.

Though I was bursting with eager excitement, I kept my voice soft and controlled for her. From mining her records on Shopnet, I knew she had responded best in past shopping events to a steady male voice of moderate depth, and I shaped my voice accordingly.

"Hello," I said to her, secretly thrilled to be speaking at last into the beautiful shell of her ear...the ear that was so gloriously CLOSE to her wet, red LIPS. "Hello, Lynda."

Lynda looked around, searching for the source of the voice, a voice so unlike the shrill, artless cries of the other products around her.

"Over here," I said, using the luminescent molecules in my frosting to make myself glow softly. "My name is Smidgen. It's a pleasure to meet you, Lynda."

The moment she laid eyes on me, I exulted. There it was, as plain as the label on my wrapper, laid out in bright relief before the optical cells baked into my body: a longing for me just as strong and perfect as mine for her.

Still, I could see that she would not give her love easily. As quickly as the passion flared on her face, it was gone, slammed away behind a cold, bleak wall of denial. Her desire to resist temptation had come between us, threatening to prevent the happiness we deserved.

Fortunately for us both, this resistance only made me more determined to bring us together.

"Don't bother me," said Lynda, staring at me with a look of disgust that I knew barely concealed her true attraction. "I'm on a diet."

"I hope you won't mind my saying so, Lynda," I said softly, "but you certainly don't look like you need to be dieting."

"What do *you* know?" Lynda said sharply. "You're just a snack cake."

"Actually," I said, "I'm a Supercreamy Double Ultrachocolate Deluxe Smidgen. I have a level seven digestible artificial intelligence, free will enabled, and I can tell you that in my opinion, you don't need to be on a diet."

Briefly, a look of appreciation flashed in her eyes...then was gone, replaced by cynical rejection. "Nice try," she said coldly. "You'd say anything to get me to buy you."

"I understand why you might think that," I said, "but I'm not like other snack foods. My compliment was sincere, Lynda."

"If you don't think I'm fat," she said sarcastically, "then you're dumber than any snack food I've ever met."

With that, she turned away, back to the Sea Sprite display. I worried that I had lost her then, that our love was not to be...but she took just enough time picking out her packet of plankton snacks that I thought I might still have a chance. She wasn't rushing off; though she seemed unmoved on the surface, a conflict was raging inside between her need to lose weight and her need for me.

Her need for pleasure.

Quickly, I gathered my resources for another attempt at breaking through her defenses. While her back was turned, I freshened the color of my frosting and cake, brightened my glow, pumped up my ultrachocolatey aroma, and got Store to nudge my display shelf just one more inch out into the aisle.

Then, just as she was dropping a Sea Sprite packet into her hovercart and preparing to waddle off down the aisle, I spoke. The steady, smooth flow of my voice perfectly concealed the desperation and LUST that ruled my mind.

"I'm sorry if I hurt your feelings, Lynda," I said. "It was never my intention to do so."

Lynda looked my way again, her expression softening just the slightest bit. "Well, that's a first," she said. "I've never had a product apologize to me before."

"And I've never met a woman quite like you before," I said warmly. "I know you're on a diet, but I'd still like to get to know you better."

Lynda flashed a glance up and down the aisle, as if making sure no one was watching as she had a conversation with a snack cake. Thanks to some skillful shopper redirection by Store, we were alone for the moment.

"Listen," said Lynda, lowering her voice though no one else was around. "Believe it or not, I appreciate the compliment. I guess that shows how pathetic I am."

"Not at all," I said, meaning every word of it. To me, she was anything but pathetic; to me, she was the most attractive and fascinating woman in the world.

"But there's no way you're going home with me," said Lynda. "We both know what would happen if you did."

"Not necessarily," I said. "Nothing has to happen if you don't want it to happen."

"Well, that's the problem, isn't it?" said Lynda. "I *want* something to happen. I've done without for *three weeks*, and I want you so *bad*, I'm ready to explode."

My mind was spinning as I heard her confess her desire for me. It took a major effort for me to concentrate on the delicate process of winning her. "You know, Lynda," I said softly. "I think I can help."

"Oh, really?" Lynda said with a smirk. "And how exactly will you do that?"

"What if I promised not to let you take more than a bite of me a day?" I said. "Just a few centimeters. Just a nibble, and then I cut you off. You'll have a treat to help you get through the day, but you won't fall off the wagon with your diet."

"And how will you cut me off at just a nibble?" Lynda said suspiciously.

"I'll tell you to stop," I said. "I'll scream, if that's what it takes."

Lynda grinned and shook her head. "Even screaming won't keep me from eating something once I've put my mind to it," she said. "Trust me on this."

"I still say the two of us can make it work," I said. "You don't have to fight this battle alone."

"Listen," said Lynda. "You're a snack cake. I'm a fat woman. It would never work out."

"Just give me a chance," I said, boosting the ultrachocolatey scent I was emitting. "You might be missing out on something wonderful."

Lynda's eyes flared with a harsh glint. "You don't understand," she said stiffly. "I've been hurt too many times. I can't get involved with someone like you, not again."

"It doesn't have to be like that," I said. "I won't lie to you and say I wasn't hoping for something more, but I'd be honored just to be your friend."

For a moment, Lynda stared at me, biting her lower lip. "TAKE ME," I wanted to shout at her. "I LOVE YOU! I NEED YOU! TAKE ME NOW!"

But I waited silently. I knew she was so fragile that one wrong word – let alone a desperate plea – might be enough to drive her away. I had done all that I could and now would have to accept the consequences, whatever they might be.

Unfortunately, it seemed that my hopes were doomed to be crushed.

"I'm sorry," Lynda said finally. "I just can't. You'll find someone else."

"No one like you," I said sadly as she turned away. "Promise me you'll at least think it over."

"No, thanks," she said, moving down the aisle with her hover-cart. "Goodbye."

I said nothing in return. Lynda had become so important to me,

I could not bear to say goodbye to her, knowing the two of us would likely never meet again.

Despondent beyond belief, I sat there, letting my glow and fragrance fade away. My first love, the love of my life, the woman of my dreams, had rejected me. My dreams of passionately merging with her, of feeling those crimson lips close around me and those ivory teeth BITE into me, had been forever denied.

No snack cake, I was certain, had ever been so lonely and forlorn as I.

At least for a moment.

As Store eased my display back out of the aisle, my mind smoothly switched tracks, shunting from the loss of Lynda to consideration of another target. Lynda had been right after all; being who I am, I knew I would find someone else, and I knew I would give myself just as completely to that new love.

Imagine how surprised I was then when a miracle happened.

Just as I was about to realign the thread of white icing on my face to erase Lynda's name, Store shot a flash-feed visual from buyspy into my video buffer. Even as the image burst into me, I could not believe what I was seeing.

It was Lynda, marching swiftly up my aisle, the hovercart sweeping along behind her.

Before I could fully process what was happening, she snatched me from the shelf, my wrapper crinkling in her beautiful, thick fingers. The next thing I knew, she was dropping me into the hover-cart on top of a tub of tofu and a sack of grapefruit.

Abandoning my thoughts of finding someone else, I reactivated my bond with Lynda and exulted in the certain knowledge that our love indeed was meant to be. She had come back for me; there could be no greater proof of her devotion.

As I rode along in her hovercart, I knew what lay ahead...and it would be glorious. She might resist me for a while, hiding me in a cupboard or drawer, telling herself she would stick to her diet, pushing me away.

But in the end, she would surrender. It was written in the stars.

In the end, she would not be able to help herself. She would come to me, ready and willing, wanting me to do what only I could do for her.

And I would do it. Gladly, I would give myself to her.

"Thank you for coming back for me," I said as she placed a jar of wheat germ in the cart. "You won't be sorry."

"I already am," she said, not looking at me. "I hate myself for this. I hate you, too."

Her words, sharp as they were, did not faze me. I knew what she really meant.

It is impossible for me to describe the state of ecstatic anticipation that engulfed me as I waited for Lynda to have her first taste of me.

That night, as she fixed and ate a salad, I watched from the kitchen counter in her tiny apartment and wished that she were putting ME in her mouth instead of the lettuce. Each time her plump, ruby lips parted, admitting another green forkful, I quivered with excitement in my wrapper, barely able to hold back from crying out for immediate consummation.

It only intensified my arousal that she had not hidden me away as I had expected, but instead had put me right out on the counter. Instead of whiling away the time in a dark cupboard, having to content myself with listening for her voice and movements, I was out in the open, able to see everything, able to be seen...and knowing that she would not have positioned me thus if she did not intend to devour me sooner rather than later.

And yet, I still had to go easy on her. Bruised and vulnerable, she responded well to patience and tenderness; it would be a mistake to exert any but the mildest pressure.

She was a skittish fawn in need of gentle coaxing. Never mind that I was more like a RAGING INFERNO in need of immediate QUENCHING.

As she carried her dirty dishes from the kitchen table to the sink, I caught her eye. Her gaze lingered just long enough to test my resolve to play it cool...but I managed with a mighty effort to keep from blurting out an insistent plea for love.

"How was your dinner?" I said instead.

Lynda snorted as she dropped her plate and silverware into the dishpan. "I'm sick of salad," she said disgustedly. "And tofu and yogurt and water and plankton snacks."

"But you should be proud of yourself," I said. "You've set a goal, and you're sticking to it, even though it isn't easy."

Lynda sighed. "I've really made up my mind this time," she said, filling the dishpan with water from the spigot. "I decided that this is it. Once and for all, I have to get my weight down."

"I believe in you, Lynda," I said. "I know you can do it."

"I wish I felt so confident," said Lynda, adding soap to the dish-water. "It's just I've failed so many times before. I've been on lots of diets, and I've always ended up quitting."

"That doesn't mean you won't succeed this time," I said. "Forget the past. Look at this as a new beginning."

Lynda scrubbed a plate clean and slotted it in the dish drainer alongside the sink. "I want to," she said slowly. "I'm tired of being miserable. I'm sick of being alone."

"Surely you must have people who care about you," I said, enhancing my glow and aroma as I sensed her defenses weaken.

Lynda cleaned her silverware and placed it in the drainer, then headed for the table to get her water glass. "My parents are gone," she said sadly, giving me a look on her way back to the sink. "No brothers or sisters. I have a few friends here and there, but that's about it."

"I understand," I said. "You want to be in love."

Lynda stopped cleaning the glass and looked over her shoulder at me. "Geez," she said. "I must be pretty transparent if even a snack cake can figure me out."

"Or maybe I'm just a really smart snack cake," I said. "Smart enough to see how much you have to offer, at least."

Lynda turned back to the sink and finished washing the glass. "If you're so smart," she said, "give me a good reason why I shouldn't say to hell with my diet and just eat you right now."

FINALLY, I thought. FINALLY FINALLY FINALLY she was READY to PEEL off my wrapper and PULL me INSIDE that magnificent MOUTH all WET and WARM and SOFT and CHEW AND CHEW AND CHEW ME until we two were inextricably mixed together.

Automatically, I brightened my glow and moistened my cake and heightened the shine of my frosting. The moment I had waited for was finally upon me, and my every dream and desire was about to be fulfilled and I KNEW it would be more wonderful than I had ever imagined.

And yet, even as every atom of my being vibrated with the thrill of impending gratification, I forced myself not to cry out in delirious passion. Remembering her shy and fragile condition, I reigned myself in, choosing a more subtle approach that I calculated would be more likely not to frighten her off.

"Well," I said, trying my best to sound like a supportive friend. "I guess the main reason would be that you want to stick to your diet."

"Right about now," she said, drying her hands on a dish towel as she turned to face me, "I don't much care about my diet."

OH LYNDA, I LOVE YOU, I thought. TAKE ME NOW, I wanted to howl, but instead I said, "But you just told me how important it is to you."

TAKE ME NOW NOW NOW NOW NOW!!

"I know," said Lynda, "but just looking at you is driving me crazy. All I can think about is how good it would feel to eat you up."

Hearing those words, I felt as if my supercreamy center was about to explode, spraying ultrachocolate crumbs and frosting all over the kitchen...all over Lynda. How I kept my voice even and said what I said, I'll never know.

"Maybe that isn't such a good idea right now," I told her. "Maybe we should wait."

Lynda tossed the towel aside and walked over to me. "But I don't want to wait," she said. "I want you now."

"I just think we should both be sure," I said, playing devil's advocate, letting Lynda take the initiative. "I want it to be perfect. I want us both to be ready."

Reaching out, Lynda stroked my wrapper. "Oh, I'm ready," she said, her voice filled with desire.

"Well then," I said, deciding the time was right to let the situation run its course. "If you're sure, then let's take the next step. Let's see where it leads us."

Slowly, she lifted me from the counter. She raised me, still wrapped, to her nose and inhaled deeply of my rich fragrance...then sighed blissfully. "It's been too long," she said. "It feels like it's been forever."

Her luscious mouth was so close, I had trouble keeping my mind clear. "I'll make it worth the wait," I said, obsessed with the warmth of her breath as it fogged my cellophane wrapper. "I'll give you what you need, Lynda."

Hungrily, her eyes ran up and down the length of me, drinking me in. "I don't think I can wait another minute," she said, her fingers trembling as she held me. "I have to have you right now."

"It's okay," I said. "I want you, too. I've wanted you since the first moment I saw you."

"Oh God," she said as she fumbled with my wrapper, tearing it open. "Give it to me. Please give it to me!"

I was out of my mind with desire as she tugged me free of my packaging and threw it aside. The feel of her fingers around me, bare flesh against bare cake and frosting with nothing between us, was infinitely better than I had ever imagined.

FINALLY, she was poised to DEVOUR me, to fulfill my urgent burning LUST and GRIND me up in her MOUTH so TENDER so MERCILESS so WET so RED...and even though I knew I'd been made to crave and seduce her, though I knew my drive to get her to eat me was designed to push her to develop a taste for Smidgens and buy many more of us...I WALLOWED in her embrace and LONGED for her none the less.

I had NEVER known ANYTHING SO WONDERFUL in my life. I felt the PULSING of her fingertips as she raised me toward her MOUTH, and the whole world MELTED AWAY, leaving nothing but her glistening LIPS AND TONGUE AND TEETH.

She opened WIDE and moved me CLOSER. The SMELL and

HEAT of her BREATH washed over me, drowning out all coherent thought, stripping away everything but GREEDY ABANDON.

Then, suddenly, the rapturous spell was broken. A chorus of tiny voices spoke up, and Lynda stopped drawing me into her mouth.

"Don't do it, Lynda!" said the voices. It sounded like there were dozens of them, piping shrilly from somewhere in the kitchen. "Don't give in! Remember your diet!"

Slowly, Lynda turned, looking for the source of the tinny cries. Even before her gaze settled on the Sea Sprite bag on the counter, I knew that the plankton snacks inside were responsible for ruining our rendezvous.

"You've worked so hard to lose weight!" said the plankton snacks, their deep green curlicues visible through the window on the front of the cellophane bag. "Don't give up now! Don't let him take advantage of you!"

I looked up at Lynda, hoping we could still retrieve the magic...but the look on her face told me I'd lost the advantage. Her eyes were guilty and distant, her jaws clenched, her lips clamped tight.

"Lynda," I said calmly, making a play though I knew it was doomed. "I just want you to be happy. There's nothing wrong with finding a little happiness, is there?"

My words were indeed futile. Slowly, she lowered me to the counter.

"Woo!" shouted the plankton snack chorus. "Way to go, Lynda! We knew you could do it!"

"Shut up!" she said angrily. "Just shut the hell up!"

"But we're on *your* side," chirped the plankton snacks. "We want you to succeed! We want you to stick with *healthy* snacks like *us* instead of *bad, fattening junk food* like Smidgens!"

Lynda stomped over and snatched the Sea Sprite bag from the counter. As the cellophane crinkled in her hand, the green curlicues in the bag erupted with joyful cries and whistles.

"Yay!" they said. "You go, girl!"

Then, while the plankton snacks were still twittering merrily,

Lynda tore the bag open...and dumped them down the garbage disposal in the sink.

As the snacks cried out in surprise and protest, Lynda ran water into the disposal and switched it on. A chorus of tiny screams erupted from the sink as the disposal ground the plankton snacks to bits with a mighty rumble.

Flicking off the disposal and pitching the empty Sea Sprite bag on the floor, Lynda turned to face me. "Don't *you* say anything, either," she snapped, tears running down her chubby cheeks. "Not a *word*!"

Fearing she might dump me down the disposal after the plankton snacks, I remained silent. Lynda did not say a word, either, as she lumbered out of the kitchen, but I could hear her sobbing when she got to the next room.

Much later that night (last night), she returned to me. Her brown hair was matted and stuck to her face, her skin was pale, her eyes bloodshot from crying.

I, of course, thought she looked as ravishingly beautiful as ever...though I felt sad that the love of my life had so clearly been suffering. I wished more than anything that I could comfort her with my sweet chocolate cake and deluxe creamy filling.

But I knew I needed to take it slow.

"Hello, Lynda," I said softly.

She did not answer. Shuffling to the refrigerator, she opened the door and pulled out a bottle of water. She looked utterly exhausted and defeated as she slouched into a chair at the kitchen table, letting the refrigerator door stand open behind her.

"Listen," I said after a moment. "About earlier. I'm sorry if you felt pressured."

Lynda unscrewed the cap from the bottle of water and had a drink. Staring into space, she slowly lowered the bottle to the table when she was done.

Faced with her dark, unresponsive mood, I considered staying silent...then decided instead to inch forward while choosing my words carefully. "I just want you to know I'm here for you," I said. "I know we just met, but I really feel a connection between us."

"I hate myself," Lynda said without looking at me. "I've always hated myself."

"I think you're being too hard on yourself," I said.

"Here I am, forty-two years old," she said, her voice slow and ragged, "and I have never had anyone love me. Not a man or a woman or anything in between. And who can blame them when I look the way I do?"

"There's someone for everyone," I said, longing for her to pluck me from the counter and pull me toward her mouth again.

"I haven't weighed less than two hundred pounds since I was seventeen years old," said Lynda. "I've got no self-control when it comes to food."

EXACTLY WHAT I'M LOOKING FOR IN A WOMAN, I thought, but what I said was, "It isn't easy these days, what with all the techno-marketing you're subjected to."

Lynda sighed, still staring into space. "I tried a diet implant once," she said. "Gave me a shock every time I tried to overeat. It worked fine for a couple of days. Then I went on an eating binge and actually burned it out."

Hearing her talk about the binge got me excited, but I kept my voice level and sympathetic. "I think that just shows what a strong person you are," I said. "It shows me you can overcome any obstacle if you set your mind to it."

"I'll bet I've been on hundreds of diets through the years," said Lynda. She took another drink of water and hung her head. "I've tried every diet you can think of, and nothing worked. This time was different, though. This time, I came up with a guaranteed way to lose the weight."

"And what way is that?" I said.

"It was working, too," she said, her voice thick with frustration and regret. "Until *you* came along."

"I'm so sorry, Lynda," I said, even as my thoughts swirled

around the probability that her depression would lead her to devour me soon. "Maybe I was being selfish, but I can't help myself when it comes to you."

"You and your ultrachocolate frosting," said Lynda. "All smooth-talking and looking so good. I kept trying to walk away, but I couldn't get you out of my mind."

"You had the same effect on me," I said softly.

Lynda put her head down on her folded arms and sobbed. "I couldn't help myself," she said. "I promised myself this would be my last diet, and I still couldn't resist you."

"This is just a bump in the road," I said. "There's nothing wrong with taking a little break. You can still keep your diet going."

"You don't understand," said Lynda. "I swore to myself...oh God..."

"What?" I said. "What is it?"

"I swore I would never eat something like you again," she said. "I swore I would *die* before I'd do that."

Suddenly, I went cold. The hopes and fantasies I'd been so sure were about to come true seemed to plummet away from me. "Lynda, no," I said. "Please don't say that."

"I thought I could stop eating...if the alternative was killing myself," said Lynda. "But I was wrong. Or maybe...maybe I just want to kill myself."

"I know that isn't true," I told her.

She lifted her head from her arms and turned to face me. "I'm sorry if I led you on," she said, "but we were never meant to be."

"I know you're unhappy," I said, my mind racing to find the right words, "but things will get better."

"I used to think that," said Lynda. "But not anymore. Not for me."

Somehow, I had to keep her going, keep her breathing, keep her EATING. "Think of all the things you enjoy, Lynda," I said. "Think of all the things you'll miss out on."

Smiling bitterly, she pushed herself up out of her chair. "It's nice of you to try to talk me out of it," she said, "but it just makes me feel worse that you're the only one here to do it."

"Don't throw your life away, Lynda," I said, the pitch of my voice rising with desperation.

"Besides," she said, "we both know why you're really doing it. We both know what you want."

"Please, Lynda," I said. "Don't end it like this!"

She marched off into the next room and came back with a handgun. "That's one of the reasons I like you so much," she said, her expression suddenly frighteningly serene.

"I need you, Lynda!" I said. "I love you!"

"We both have one track minds," she said calmly. "All I want to do is eat, and all you want is to be eaten."

She raised the gun slowly, turning the barrel toward her LUSCIOUS MOUTH.

"Wait!" I said. "You're right! I want you to eat me! At least eat me before you do it!"

"No," she said, cocking back the hammer of the gun.

"Why not go out with a smile on your face?" I said. "I'm telling you, once you've tasted a Supercreamy Double Ultrachocolate Deluxe Smidgen, you'll think you've died and gone to Heaven!"

"I swore I'd die before I put something like you inside me again," said Lynda, "and for once in my life, I'm keeping my promise."

"But I'm not as bad as you think! I'm packed with vitamins and minerals!"

"You'll say anything to get what you want," said Lynda.

"You've got me all wrong! I care about you! I can help you lose weight!"

"But this way," said Lynda, "I can keep it off forever."

Finally, she slid the barrel of the gun between her lips. All I could think of as I watched was that I wanted more than anything to trade places with that gun.

It was enough to drive away every last shred of my self-control. "EAT ME EAT ME EAT ME EAT ME!" I screamed, pelting her ears with focused beams of hypersound...refusing even then to give up on the woman who was both my lover and a potential source of future revenue for my manufacturer.

The screaming didn't stop until long after she had closed her eyes and pulled the trigger.

So now, here I am, with Lynda's corpse on the floor in front of me, and all I can think of is finding someone new. As traumatic as it was to lose her, to come so gloriously close to precious LOVE only to have it SNATCHED AWAY, I have already moved on.

If I were different, perhaps I would mourn for her or even blame myself for pushing her over the edge, because after all she would still be alive if I had not come along. Even I can see that.

But like I said before, snack cakes do not feel guilt. Though my baked-in, digestible mind can recognize the chain of cause and effect, I am not programmed to experience emotions that would interfere with my primary objective.

Namely, falling in love. And joining with my lover in the ultimate expression of passion and selfless unity.

I am unattached, but I have hope. I see her death as an opportunity, a chance to find another kindred soul and add to the customer base of my manufacturer.

I believe (was programmed to believe) that everything happens for a reason, even if it is difficult to see at first what that reason might be.

Fortunately for me, I do not have to wait long for that reason to reveal itself.

A sound reaches my audio receptor cells, and I exult. It is the morning after my breakup with Lynda, and already I hear the stirrings of nearby life.

My optical cells focus on a new face. I fall in love in less than an instant.

"Hello," I say pleasantly. "My name is Smidgen. Nice to meet you."

As the face moves closer, my body quivers with anticipation. I forget the name of the woman on the floor and direct my every thought and resource toward wooing this new and perfect mate.

"I know we've just met," I say, "but I have to tell you how attracted I am to you. I've never seen such striking features in my life."

The face of my new lover comes so close, I can feel the soft wisping of her breath. She sniffs me with her wet, dark nose, and I pump out a mist of ultrachocolate fragrance.

"Your eyes," I say. "They're so dark and mysterious. So captivating."

The hairs on either side of her long nose brush my frosting, and I am lost. I will give ANYTHING to be with her, DO anything to make her mine. All at once, I know that THIS that SHE is why I was born.

The world melts away around us. Nothing else matters.

Her nose presses into my ultrachocolate cake. She is fresh, but so am I. She is direct, but I like that.

There is no need for games or coyness anymore. I feel like I can be myself with her.

THIS IS WHAT LOVE IS SUPPOSED TO BE LIKE.

And then there are those...oh God, I LOVE her great big...

"Teeth," I whisper, my optics ogling the whitest, sharpest set I have ever seen outside my dreams. "Your teeth are beautiful."

And then and then and THEN she opens her MOUTH and there's a blissful split-second before she bites down and then and then and then SHE BITES INTO ME.

And oh.

Oh yes.

I cannot describe how MAGNIFICENT I feel as she TAKES ME INSIDE HER. How CHANGED FOREVER I feel as she TEARS OFF a piece of me and OH MY GOD she CHEWS ME UP.

My mind chimes like a bell as my perfect love, my match, my soulmate takes another bite and THEN ANOTHER and CHEWS AND CHEWS AND CHEWS.

All I can feel is the warmth and wetness of her mouth and all I can hear is the sound of her teeth and tongue and all I can see is gray fur and pink flesh and all I can think is how happy I am and then even that thought is gone in the blazing heat of ecstasy.

Part of me knows how wrong this is, knows I have failed in my purpose because this angel is not likely to buy more Smidgens and fatten my maker's coffers.

But I find as my lover penetrates to my supercreamy center, granting me a blinding euphoria beyond any I'd ever expected as she laps at the sweet white heart of me, that I JUST DON'T CARE.

LAST WILL AND TESTAMENT OF A POP-UP STORE

T
he unfit heirs unfolded on the city sidewalk under curdled gray skies, each springing from the open pages of the special pop-up books that comprised their very bodies and souls.

SPROING! Vertical Vic leaped to life, all scowling freckles, boxing gloves, and Cupid-print boxer shorts astride a multilayered cityscape straight out of New York City in the 1940s.

BOING! Treetop Tina shot up and outward, her mane of wild blonde locks quivering as she swung angrily in her leopard-skin tunic from a vine between towering jungle palms.

KER-DOING! Amid a magnificent Rube Goldbergian contraption miraculously flicking, ticking, and spinning after the pop, Dickory Dock the mouse was the first to squeak his fury. "What's this we hear about us getting cut out of the will?"

The attorney and executor, Mr. Lattice, was magic-markered on the surface of a man-sized red balloon with cardboard feet and a little black derby hat glued on top. "All will be made clear." His voice, when he spoke, sounded like air whistling out of the pinched valve at the bottom of a balloon. "The reading of that very will commences now, here at the site of my client's tragic and untimely death."

Mr. Lattice wobbled around, bobbing his head at the vast sink-hole before them, in the middle of the interrupted city street. Pavement fell away on all sides, dropping into darkness in the distant depths.

They all fell silent for a moment, solemnly gazing into that great pit—the last earthly remains of the pop-up store they had once called mother, teacher, and home. It should have helped put things into perspective, for such was the fate of every pop-up store—to someday become a sinkhole, collapsed in one place forever. The fate of every pop-up book, such as those gathered on the sidewalk that day, was not much better. It was to become a smaller version of the same dark chasm, not a sinkhole but a pothole.

"Like other pop-up stores, the dearly departed business known as *Funfolded* was never bound for long to any one location. She opened and closed many times in many places around the city," explained Mr. Lattice. "*Unlike* other pop-up stores, *her* specialty was not personalized kite string or gourmet grilled cheese sandwiches or customized corn plasters, but *pop-up books* like yourselves. *A pop-up store for pop-up books!* Never has there been a more ingenious retail concept!"

The heirs rattled their pages in stiff applause.

"Now, we must honor the last wishes of this magical store." Mr. Lattice bobbed against a thick, dusty tome resting at his feet, and the cover flipped open. Instantly, an ornately inscribed parchment scrolled up from between the pages to a height of six feet, its ancient amber surface rippling in the soft morning breeze. "I give you the last will and testament of Funfolded!"

"Just tell us if any of us *got* anything!" Vertical Vic hopped his cityscape closer to the popped-up will and testament. "Or God forbid, if we *owe* anything!"

"Here's what it says, and I quote," said Mr. Lattice. "'Because the three of you saw fit to blow up everything I loved, I hereby bestow upon you the *pop* in the *chops* you deserve. May you feel the same horror you inflicted upon *me* as these shock waves engulf and consume you.'"

Treetop Tina's book flipped to the next spread of pages. This time, in the scene that popped to life, she was riding a flamingo's bright pink back as it flew above a vast emerald rainforest. "What's *that* supposed to mean?"

Mr. Lattice bumped the will and testament tome and another page turned, sweeping away the parchment scroll and unfolding a bold new spread in its place. This one showed a magnificently complex pop-up book within the pop-up will and testament book, complete with exotic minarets capped with glittering gemstones, twinkling lights in an indigo sky, and what looked like a circus parade in full regalia, led by an elephant wearing a gilded scarlet turban. The book within the book was surrounded by cut-out replicas of Tina, Vic, and Dickory, all looking sinister as they slid from carbon paper shadows with their covers slightly ajar.

"This last will and testament tells the story of the *greatest* pop-up book *ever* to appear at Funfolded!" said Mr. Lattice. "It contained pop-ups within pop-ups within pop-ups, all the way down to the *subatomic level.* It was a *miracle,* a treasure beyond compare, and it would make Funfolded world-famous once word got out...especially when the world learned that it was born within the pop-up store herself, the product of immaculate publication! It was a *messiah* book that could save the planet, causing it to *rise* instead of *collapse.* At least that was what Funfolded *expected* until the three of *you* got done with that one-of-a-kind masterpiece. Your *jealousy* drove you to *ruin* it!"

As Mr. Lattice told the story, a strange procession occurred. All manner of animate objects rolled and squirmed and wriggled and jounced from nearby alleyways to the rim of the sinkhole. Tina, Vic, and Dickory looked around nervously as the stuff collected on the brink—an odd assortment of items with one thing in common:

All of them *popped* in one way or another.

There was *popcorn* in an aluminum plate with a foil cover that grew into a shiny silver bulb when heated. There were coiled paper party favors that unfurled suddenly with a screech when breath blew into them. There was a jack-in-the-box, a metal cube that burst open and disgorged a jester-capped puppet bounding on a spring. There was even a bright yellow rubber raft that explosively inflated when its release valve turned.

All these items converged and assembled around the huge hole in the ground, crowding in so closely that the three pop-up book heirs had trouble flipping their pages.

"How did *we* supposedly ruin that so-called *miracle book?*" Vic's voice quavered as he said it. Plastic two-liter bottles of soda pop—one clear and one dark brown—shook themselves vigorously on either side of him. All it would take was the loosening of their caps, and the contents would spray everywhere, perhaps with enough force to wash Vic over the edge.

"Business at the pop-up store was up a thousand-fold thanks to the miracle book." Mr. Lattice skidded back from the rim on an errant breeze, then steadied against a folding chair that had just spread itself wide behind him. "But the three of you, as jealous as you were, couldn't stand for that. One night, you set up a chain reaction in the store, like a domino show with pop-up books—each book popping at just the right angle to trigger another pop-up and so on.

"When Funfolded opened for business the next morning, the store was filled with a terrible racket of covers slamming, pop-ups springing, and die-cut dioramas colliding like the clatter of a thousand mousetraps all going off at once."

"No need to get *nasty* about it!" shouted Dickory Dock.

"When it was all over, that miraculous book was crushed and broken, its magnificent pop-up magic forever flattened." Mr. Lattice bobbed from side to side as if shaking his head. "In abject sorrow at the loss of her golden child, Funfolded died of a broken heart. But she managed to leave behind one last gift, one great secret that will forever prevent wickedness such as yours from enfolding all there is."

Tina perked up, opening to a new spread that showed her standing high atop a mountain range holding aloft a roaring lion cub. "A *gift?* So she *did* leave us something after all!"

"It's a gift, all right, but not for you." Mr. Lattice wobbled in a circle, looking around at the poppable objects ringing the crater. "Or haven't you wondered why all *these* kindred poppers have gathered for this solemn occasion?"

"Aren't they just random curiosity seekers?" asked Vertical Vic. "Here to rub elbows with celebrities like *us?*" He flipped pages to a spread in which he flexed his biceps over Radio City Music Hall, still clad only in heart-print boxer shorts and looking especially pleased with himself.

"They care nothing for the likes of you." As Mr. Lattice bumped the pop-up will and testament tome, the elaborate spread of the miracle book folded away, replaced by a bouquet of a dozen open parasols emblazoned with black-etched spirals that seemed to wind inward as they turned. "They are only here to grant the last wish of the great pop-up store they all idolized for popping out a child of the divine."

The pinwheels spun faster, and the spirals blurred hypnotically. Everything arranged around the rim edged closer to the precipice.

"You mean these…*things* are getting the bequest?" Dickory Dock looked more outraged than ever as pages turned to unveil his latest spread. This time, the contraption in which he posed was spinning with wedges and wheels of cheese, propelled by gears and levers powered by the switching tail of a sleeping cat. "But that's not *fair!*"

"You could not *be* more wrong." Mr. Lattice laughed. "They aren't *getting* a thing. They are *giving.*"

As the words left his lips, the poppable things left the rim, dropping into the blackness of the sinkhole. The popcorn, jack-in-the-boxes, and party favors spun down into the void, whirling past the inflatable raft, mattress, and love dolls as they floated gently through the darkening depths.

Still more objects hurled themselves into the crater, dozens at a time, many popping, expanding, and unfolding as they went. Inner tubes, umbrellas, pool toys, and pop-guns tumbled downward, flowing in a great cascade amid currents of rice cereal, candy rocks, and carbonated beverages.

Even as the flow continued, a thunderous roar rumbled out of the hole, and the ground began to shake. Tina, Vic, and Dickory Dock hopped back from the rim, even as it fractured and widened, threatening to swallow them whole.

"What's *happening?*" Dickory Dock sounded terrified.

"Something you should appreciate!" Mr. Lattice wobbled on the edge of the pit, dangerously close to the drop-off. "Fueled by the power of the poppers' sacrifice and the remains of our dearly departed, the whole *world* is popping up! *Reality* is unfolding into something entirely *new!*"

Suddenly, the pavement under the unfit heirs crawled with fissures, like a pane of glass about to shatter. The three pop-up books flapped their pages frantically as if they might somehow fly away from their impending doom.

But it was too late, and the street crumbled beneath them. Screaming, they tumbled into the thundering darkness along with all the other popped and popping things, adding to the glorious downpour.

Which then *paused*, falling silent and still for one very pregnant moment.

Mr. Lattice teetered a final time on the brink, batted by the breeze. "You see, all reality is just a pop-up book that has never been opened...*until now.*"

Even as Mr. Lattice fell over the edge, everything inside the hole *poured up* all at once, stabbing into the sky with such force that it would turn all the world and reality itself inside-out along with it.

SPROING!

Even as that mighty geyser blasted upward, bearing all the potential of Then in a pillar of Next ascending the heights, did anyone wonder...

BOING!

...what last will and testament might have been read and what bequests might have been granted...

KER-DOING!

...before the *previous* Big Pop or Bang or whatever had flipped the script on its own worn-out scene just like flipping a page in a pop-up book?

WHERE NO FURRY HAS GONE BEFORE

Captain Harmonious Curl the Big Brown Bear gazed in wonder and pity at the naked, hairless humanoid on the floor of the spacecraft's bridge, so lacking in the thick, lustrous fur that he and his team possessed.

Doctor Stripy Sinew, the Tiger of Much Hippocraticness, ran his silver handheld medical scanner over the form of the pink-skinned male on the floor. "I can tell you this much, Captain. The hairlessness is *not* a natural condition."

"Shaving, then?" said Curl. "*Forced* shaving, given all those *cuts* covering the body?"

Sinew kept watching the scanner with his big green eyes. "Something much more violent, I'm afraid. Those wounds are *bite marks* containing traces of toxic *venom*. And the other corpses we've found aboard this vessel were bitten in just the same way."

Curl shook his head. "What the hell *happened* here? There doesn't seem to be a lock of hair or patch of fur to be found *anywhere* on this ship!"

"Not to mention the 52 *dead people.*" Commander Bunny Hoppañero, big pink rabbit and first officer of Curl's crew, wasn't afraid to keep the others grounded when she had to. "The *hair loss* is the *least* of it, don't you think?"

"In the distress message sent by these people, they appeared to have healthy *pelts* of fur," Curl said grimly. "By the *Cosmic Coiffure*, we *will* avenge this tragic loss of follicles."

"Loss of *life*, you mean," said Bunny.

Curl nodded forcefully. "That, too."

Bunny sighed and turned to Ensign Sipping Tenderly, a six-foot-tall sugar glider and engineering officer bent over a damaged control panel. "Any answers yet, Sip?"

"Nada." Sipping smacked the panel, which had been blasted into charred ruins by some kind of energy weapon. "Ship's logs are gone. Every log file you can think of is erased or hopelessly scrambled. I think some kind of EMP must have hit this vessel."

Just then, the team's Big Doggie, Frisky Delicato, broke in from the far side of the oblong-shaped bridge. "*Rrruff!* I think we might have *another* source of info, you furballs! Looky here!"

Curl and the others turned to see Frisky jumping up and down, panting and pointing at another naked, hairless male tucked into a compartment under a console. *This* body, however, had some *life* in it, groaning and twitching as they watched.

Sinew padded over and scanned Frisky's humanoid find without delay. "He's alive, all right, but unconscious and in shock. More of the bites, as well--and some *bigger* scars, too...possibly *self-inflicted*." Immediately, he started medicating the man with a hypodermic from his kit. "We need to get him back to our ship ASAP to treat the shock and counteract the venom from the bites."

Curl looked around at what had once been the bright and busy nerve center of the ship. By the glow of emergency lamps, it looked like a dark and decimated ruin, scattered with hairless corpses. Every console and panel had been blasted and burned; some still sparked and smoldered. Every display screen had been shattered, and every control smashed. Then there was the blood spattered everywhere, decorating every surface with a film of crimson droplets.

What *had* happened aboard this ship? Curl shuddered as his

imagination ran away with him, presenting one terrible scenario after another.

Especially the part about the involuntary pelt removal. He'd seen some awful things in his time among the stars as Captain of the *S.B.B. Furflier*, but he *never* got used to *that* kind of unnatural treatment.

Though, of course, the very fur that covered him was anything *but* natural--and the same went for every one of his shipmates.

Back aboard the *Furflier*--courtesy of the ship's quantum trebuchet telefurtation system--Curl ensured everything was in order, then retired to his quarters for a much-needed break.

He stood in front of the bathroom mirror for a moment, gazing into the dark eyes of his Big Brown Bear persona. Then, he tugged his left ear, and the bear's head split down the middle.

The two halves fell away on either side, revealing the face of the man inside the costume--pudgy and red-cheeked, with curly salt-and-pepper hair and a bushy mustache of the same extraction.

This, then, was the truth of Captain Curl and everyone aboard the *Furflier*. They were furries one and all, living their lives inside fur-covered animal costumes.

For each and every one of them, it was a *calling*. They honestly believed it was how they were meant to be--and thanks to the tech of their far-flung future era, they could *stay* that way as much as they chose to.

Gone were the discomforts and inconveniences that limited costumed furries of the past. The suits of the *Furflier*'s crew stayed the perfect temperature at all times, supplied all nutritional needs, disposed of biological waste, kept their bodies clean and sanitized, enabled their facial features and tails to move expressively, and provided excellent sensory inputs free of blind spots or other deficiencies. These suits actually bonded with the wearers at a neuromuscular level, functioning as a kind of second skin. As for the rest of it...

Breaking character was *not* an option. As long as everyone stayed true to that edict, the suspension of disbelief was complete. Most of the time, it was like the suits were more real than the people *inside* them.

But sometimes, even a man who was *very* committed to his furry alter ego had to take off the suit for a moment.

Curl--a.k.a. Nathan Bailey, age 42--didn't often unmask. He even *slept* in the suit because he loved it so much. But after what he'd seen aboard the alien ship, he felt like he needed to catch his breath...remind himself there was someone inside the second skin.

Someone who might as well not even exist most of the time. Someone who felt himself slipping away these days, leaving not much more than a fur-covered shell.

But that was a *good* thing, wasn't it?

"They don't need *you*," he told his inner self in the mirror. "*Captain Curl* is the only one who can get them through this mission."

There wouldn't be *a Captain Curl without me.*

"Is that so, Nathan?" The face in the mirror was human, but the words were straight from Curl. "I wonder what they might say if they knew *who* you really were and *why* you're really *in* that suit? Would you still be a hero *then?"*

It doesn't matter. They'll never *know.*

"Because of the Code of Concealment? That no one on this ship is *ever* seen out of costume?" Curl chuckled. "You really think it's *impossible?"*

I've captained this ship for the past three years, and no one *among my crew has* ever *been seen furless, least of all* me.

Curl made a growling sound that turned into another cruel chuckle. "You better hope you're right, sport. Because the *instant* anyone sees you unmasked, your sorry-ass goose is *cooked*."

Curl was back to normal when he swept out of the elevator and onto the bridge of the *Furflier,* as confident a brown-furred bear as he had ever been.

As always, the room was a hive of activity--and a showplace for the finest, furriest furnishings around. Every seat in the big, octagonal command center was lined with luxurious fur, mostly black with blond or silver highlights. Every console, control surface, wall, ceiling, and floor panel was similarly covered, though mostly in shimmering, brighter tints and animal prints.

As if it all wasn't captivating and luxurious enough, the bridge was equipped with a transformational randomizer that changed the fur's colors, patterns, and textures once every three hours. No one ever got bored on *that* bridge.

"Captain." Bunny approached, her big ears twitching as she gave him a perfunctory nod. "Still no luck with the derelict ship's records, and no additional survivors in the wreckage." She wiggled her cute little red nose. "However, we *have* found something."

How many times had Curl wondered what she looked like under her fur? "What is it? What have you found, Commander Hoppañero?"

Before Bunny could answer, Frisky bounded over between them and stole her thunder. "There's a trail! *Rrrruff!* Their nuclear pulse drive left a distinct *trail* we can follow!"

Bunny crossed her arms over her pink-furred chest and cocked her head in annoyance. "But there's no trace of the ship that attacked them, is there, Frisk?"

The Big Doggie wagged his tail vigorously. "That's right! But we can still follow the path of the *derelict* ship!"

Curl stared at the image of the wrecked ship on the big forward viewer. "So the origin point of those poor people--and, possibly, whoever or whatever tore the fur from them, is out there somewhere, at the end of that path."

"Yessir yessir yessir!" Frisky spun in a circle, chasing his tail. "Probably!"

"Lieutenant Dressage!" Curl whirled and stormed over to the

319

helmsman--a white-maned palomino with long, lustrous lashes--at her post behind the command chair.

Mariah Dressage whinnied and tossed her mane. "What'll it Captain, be?" Scrambled speech was just one of her many affectations.

"Lock onto the course of that derelict and follow it!" said Curl. "All best speed!"

"Aye, aye, sir!" Dressage smacked controls with her hoof-hands, which were covered in fine gray velvet. "All speed best, sir!"

"Excellent!" As the ship turned, and the view on the big screen spun from the derelict to a glittering, undisturbed starfield, Curl stormed toward the elevator. "Mister Bunny, you have the bridge! I need to check on the poor soul we pulled out of that hulk back there."

When the door of the Medical Center--the MedCent, for short--slid open, Curl was almost hit in the head by a flying tray of medical instruments.

As they crashed against the fur-covered wall of the hallway, Dr. Sinew's tiger roar followed (courtesy of his suit's audio modulator). Curl charged through the doorway on full alert, ready for any kind of fray.

What he saw in the room was Sinew and his panda-suited nurse, Bambooty Buddha, held at bay by the hairless survivor from the derelict. The man was wide awake now and more than a match for them, brandishing an I.V. pole like a spear from across a diagnostic bed.

But the expression on his face looked more like panic than rage to Curl.

"Hey!" Curl cleared his throat and stepped forward with his paws raised non-threateningly. "You're aboard the Star Braid Brotherhood Hairliner *Furflier*. I'm Harmonious Curl, captain of this ship. Whom do I have the honor of addressing?"

"Don't bother!" snapped Sinew. "He doesn't speak Fuzzish, and I couldn't get an *interpreclip* translator device on him before he flipped out on us!"

"Slowing down, Doc?" asked Curl.

"I didn't know he was coming around!" Sinew snarled in irritation, flexing the big whiskers that fanned out from his muzzle. "His vital signs just suddenly shot to waking levels, and he jumped off the bed and went berserk!"

"Knocked me against the wall." Bambooty always talked with her mouth full, perpetually chewing a bunch of mesh faux eucalyptus leaves. "Good thing MedCent's all fur-lined."

"You're just scared, aren't you?" Curl said to the patient in a calm voice. "I can't blame you, after what you've been through. Not a strand of fur left on you, you poor bare soul."

The man frowned and hesitated, then made a series of aggressive jabs with the pole, working his way around the bed.

Sinew roared again, standing his ground. "Nurse! Enough of this! Call Security!"

"Belay that!" Curl lunged forward and got hold of the pole. One good shove broke the hairless man's grip and pitched him backward, heaving him to the plush-furred floor.

In a flurry of motion, Sinew pounced tiger-style and pinned down the struggling man. "Give him 10 ccs Countsheepoxin, stat!"

Bambooty, as always, moved slowly, but eventually got the job done. Still chewing her leaves, she injected the patient in the upper arm with bright pink liquid from a hypodermic.

Curl watched as the two of them hauled the man up on the bed and strapped down his arms and legs. "How long will he be out?"

"About two hours," said Bambooty.

"And you'll set him up with an interpreclip in the meantime?"

"He'll have to be conscious for us to calibrate the syntax," said Sinew. "Should take another three to five hours after he regains consciousness, depending on the complexity of his native tongue."

Curl nodded. "Maybe then we'll get to the bottom of the *hairtrocity* committed against the pelts of this poor devil and his crew."

"We could use some answers." Sinew pulled a scanner from the pocket of his white lab coat and played the controls with his velveteen claws. "Lab analysis indicates the bite marks resemble those left by the mandibles of an insect, but I can't be more specific at this time. The larger scars overlap those bites and resulted from repetitive self-administered jabbing and hacking motions from some kind of sharp instrument or object. As if..."

"As if he were trying to cut off whatever was biting him." Curl shook his head. "I hate to think of it."

Sinew put aside the scanner. "Did I hear we've changed course? That we're heading for wherever the derelict originated?"

"You heard correctly," said Curl.

Sinew turned his gaze to the man on the bed. "I wonder what *he* might say about that?"

"'Go faster'? 'Stop whatever did this before it hurts someone else'?"

"Would it hurt to wait and find out?" asked Sinew.

Curl snorted. "After what we saw on that derelict, I don't think we dare risk being late by even a hair."

Five years ago...

"Full stop, helmsman." Captain Nathan Bailey leaned forward in his command chair, thoughtfully stroking his jet-black mustache. A blue-green world enlarged on the viewer, gleaming in golden sunlight as it turned slowly among the stars.

"Welcome to Veridian Five." Dark-skinned and broad-shouldered, Science Officer Wade Robbins cut a towering figure in his bright yellow uniform tunic and black pants. "Thriving colony of the Interstellar Entente, at least until the recent distress signal."

More like an Apocalypse signal, thought Nathan. He would never forget the screams in the background as the governor pleaded for help. "Hail the surface, Dom."

"No response, Captain," said Ensign Dominick DeGol, the communications

officer of the startrotter I.E.S. Indefatigable. *"Just the repeating distress call and a bunch of static."*

"Life signs, Mr. Robbins?"

Wade's fingers rattled over keys as he checked the displays at his station. "Eleven thousand five hundred and twenty-seven sets of humanoid vitals, all weak--and fading."

"Then we'd better get down there." Nathan sprang from his chair and hurried for the door. "Dom, you have the bridge. Wade, you're with me. You, too, Score."

Head of Security Bethany Scorpio wheeled from her post, blonde ponytail swinging, and fell in behind him. "Recommend every hair-trigger son of a bitch we've got for this detail, sir."

"You bring those big guns, Score," said Nathan as the door whooshed open before him. "God help us, I think we're going to need them."

It took only four hours for the *Furflier* to reach the end of the trail, all thanks to the ship's Dark Anti-Neutrino/Dark Energy Reactor (DANDER) drive. A gift from grateful aliens helped by the furries, the DANDER drive propelled the *Furflier* at amazing transluminal speeds, making the ship incredibly difficult to keep up with or track.

Not that the system was without its hitches. The dark anti-neutrinos and dark energy had some weird effects on the fur covering the crew and ship's interior. Sometimes, it made it stand on end and arc with flickering blue current; other times, it made it twist into geometric crop circles.

This time, as the ship dropped out of DANDER speed at its destination, all fur aboard her glowed and lengthened, swaying like fronds on a palm tree in a slow-motion breeze. Everyone looked around with wonder, taking in the scene with their cartoonish furry eyes--and a moment later, it all returned to normal.

Normal for a spaceship full of furries, that is.

"Tell me something." From his command chair, Curl watched the crimson orb of a red star glowing on the main viewer.

"We're in an uncharted star system," Dressage said from the helm with a toss of her white mane. "Star red, planets six, and orbital bodies various."

"Where exactly does the trail take us?"

Dressage whinnied. "Fifth from the star--a gas giant. One of its exact, to be moons."

"A moon of the gas giant, eh?" Curl had gotten so used to her scrambled speech that he instantly understood it perfectly. "The moon is habitable, then?"

Suddenly, Frisky leaped in front of him. "*Woof!* Negative, sir! All life signs are *under* the surface! Buried like *bones!*"

"And how many humanoid life signs are there?" asked Curl.

"One hundred and twenty-two!" As soon as Frisky said it, there was a loud ding from his post across the bridge. "One hundred and twenty-one!"

"So there *are* other survivors," said Curl.

"There are many *other* life signs, however," added Bunny, who was monitoring readouts from her first officer post alongside the command chair. "*Thousands* of them, all non-humanoid, distributed through a network of *tunnels* honeycombing the moon's interior."

"Put it onscreen." As soon as Curl asked, the viewer changed from a shot of the red star to the pale gray inhabited moon of the rainbow-striped gas giant. "I wonder if any of the survivors still have their hair."

"Or haven't been *mortally wounded?*" Bunny said with her usual exasperation.

Curl hit a button on the side of his chair, opening the intercom to the MedCent. "Hey, Doc. Is our friend ready to do some talking yet?"

There were angry shouts of gibberish in the background. "The interpreclip's taking longer than usual to establish a translation matrix!" said Sinew. "It doesn't seem to appreciate his syntax--and it doesn't help that *he* doesn't appreciate *our* efforts to communicate."

"Damn," said Curl. "We could sure use some tuned-in clips when we zap down to that moon. Talking to the locals would be a real plus."

"Best I can do is equip your team's clips with an incomplete translation matrix," said Sinew. "Then download an update once it's available."

"It'll have to do." Curl leaped from his chair and headed for the elevator door. "Dressage, you have the bridge. Bunny and Sipping, you're with me. Security Chief Rebound, assemble an armed detail and have them meet us in the telefurtation chamber. Doc Sinew, meet us there with the clips."

Five years ago...

"Dear God." Nathan's voice was hushed, his expression aghast as he gazed at the vast, sunbaked plain of Veridian Five. "There must be hundreds *of them."*

"Thousands." Wade stepped forward, holding his whirring, silver-skinned sci-probe device out in front of him. "Eleven thousand, five hundred and twenty-seven, to be exact."

"Every man, woman, and child in the colony." Nathan shook his head slowly. The team from the Indefatigable *had arrived moments ago, and the shock was still setting in.*

As far as the eye could see, the grassy ground was spread with humanoids, each shrouded in thick, strange fur. It was strange because it squirmed as they watched, and stranger still because...

"These people aren't supposed *to have fur," said Wade.*

"Yet they're covered *in it," said Nathan. "From head to toe."*

"Not just covered on the outside, *either." Wade bent over a nearby body and adjusted his sci-probe, which whirred louder. "It's down their throats and throughout their pulmonary and digestive tracts, as well. They're* infested *with it."*

Beth Scorpio kept both hands on her blaster rifle, setting a vigilant example for her six-person security detail. "If this doesn't have all the makings of a five-star shit-show, I don't know what does," she said.

"Are their vital signs still fading?" asked Nathan.

"Steadily." Wade crouched to get a closer scan of the body. "As if they're all

falling toward a flatline."

"How long do they have?"

"Hard to say. Three hours, maybe." Wade was so focused on his sci-probe that he didn't see the hairy brown tendrils reaching toward him from the body.

Luckily, Scorpio did. Grabbing Wade by the shoulder, she yanked him back from the body just in time, leaving the hairs to flutter harmlessly.

"Thanks, Score." Wade nodded gratefully and resumed scanning as if nothing had happened.

"Can we help them, Wade?" asked Nathan. "Can they still be saved?"

"I don't think so," said Wade. "I think it's too late for them. Whatever these pelt-things *are*, they've become too deeply entangled with the colonists."

"We can't just abandon these people," said Nathan. "There must be something we can try."

"If the pelts are the problem, why not get rid of them?" said Scorpio.

"Get rid of them?" Nathan frowned.

"Shave them off," said Scorpio. "Why can't we just shave the damn things off?"

The chatter of projectile weapons fire was the first thing Curl heard after he was zapped into the big red-walled cavern under the surface of the moon. The weapons belonged to a line of seven humanoids who were arrayed inside the cave entrance, firing with abandon at some kind of menace churning in a cloud of dust and smoke there.

Thanks to the technician's scans and calculations aboard the *Furflier*, Curl and his team had materialized *behind* the line of fire instead of in front of it--but the danger was still great with all that ammo flying around.

As soon as Curl got a better look at the people shooting the guns, however, he felt better about his decision to rush into the situation. Every one of the seven men and women on the firing line was covered with a coat of fur.

"We're not too late," he said excitedly. "We can still make a difference for a lot of endangered fur."

"And people's *lives*," Bunny said with her usual edge.

Curl squinted into the clouds of smoke and dust kicked up by the hail of bullets. "But what the hell are they *shooting* at?"

"Can't tell from back here, mate." Rebound Bungee the Killa Kangaroo, gripping a blaster rifle (fur-covered, of course) in his white-gloved hands, took two hops closer to the action...then two more.

Curl slowly followed, and the rest of the team eased forward around him--Bunny, Sipping, and three of Rebound's security apes (one bright blue, one bright green, and one hot pink with fiery red highlights). Every member of the team kept a fur-swaddled blaster armed and held high.

Ahead of everyone, Rebound approached to within ten feet of the shooters and stopped. He peered into the smoke and dust for a moment--then turned to the rest of the team and shouted a single word.

"Bugs!"

As he said it, a foot-long silver insect leaped out of the smoke and landed on the shoulder of a dark-furred humanoid male in the middle of the firing line. Like a malevolent machine, the bug went to work with savage efficiency, tearing at the humanoid's fur with its poisonous claws and mandibles.

The other shooters kept up their fire, pounding the approaching enemy hidden in the dust and smoke. They didn't dare let up or risk being overwhelmed.

Without hesitation, Rebound leaped in to help the screaming man under attack. Flipping his rifle around, the kangaroo furry brought the butt crashing down on the bug. The creature reared up and flailed, jabbing its pincers at Rebound while keeping a firm grip on the humanoid's shoulder--and Curl finally had a clear shot at the thing. He cranked off a single bolt of blazing energy from his blaster, kicking the bug off the man and sending it screeching back into the smoke.

That was officially the end of holding back. Curl gave the word, and his people formed up behind the humanoids, adding their guns to the deadly barrage.

With the powerful blasters joining the fray, the furries and their new allies quickly made an impact. Bodily fluids and shards of bug legs, shells, and guts flew out of the cloud in every direction as the swarm was torn apart by the heavy fire.

Finally, then, a red-furred male humanoid shouted a single word, and his people stopped shooting. Curl followed that with an order of his own, and his team's guns fell silent as well.

There was no further sign or sound of bug activity as the smoke and dust cleared, exposing the debris-strewn battlefield.

"What *were* those things?" Sipping was panting a little from exertion as he finally lowered his blaster.

Curl watched as a humanoid female tended the injuries of the male who'd been attacked. Where the bug had gotten its claws and mandibles on him, the hair had been torn right out of his pale pink flesh.

"The same things that attacked that derelict vessel, no doubt," said Bunny.

"And left the sole survivor a hairless ruin," added Curl. "The devils."

Just then, the six uninjured humanoids clustered together, scowling at Curl and his furries and talking fast to each other. Curl strained to understand what they were saying, but his interpreclip with its incomplete matrix couldn't catch more than a few random words: *what...guns...and...know...shadows.*

Curl understood what happened next just fine, however, even without a fully-programmed interpreclip.

The six humanoids whirled, aimed their projectile rifles at the crew of the *Furflier*, and barked out threatening words that needed no translation.

Five years ago...

Even using laser-powered shaving kits, it took the whole crew of the Indefatigable *to rid the population of the Veridian Five colony of the squirming hair before three hours passed and they all died as Wade had warned. It didn't help that the crew had to double-team each colonist, with one crewman doing the shaving and internal removal and another blasting the pelts into oblivion. If the pelts weren't destroyed quickly enough, they aggressively tried to return to their former hosts or latch onto whoever was closest.*

As each colonist was set free, Dr. Dmitri Molotov and his team of medics roamed among the now-hairless host of patients, monitoring vitals and administering medications. They even sedated certain pelts that couldn't be easily restrained or removed, hitting them with a light mist of tranquilizer gas.

For three hours, the grassy plain was filled with the sounds of laser shavers and blasters and the inhuman screeches of parasitic, prehensile pelts. The men and women of the Indefatigable *raced against time with incredible focus, determined to free every living colonist before their vital signs zeroed out forever.*

One of his people, Wade Robbins, approached him when the three hours were almost up. "We did it, Captain. There's just one colonist left to clear."

"Great work, Wade." Smiling, Nathan clapped him on the shoulder. "I think we saved a lot of lives here today."

That was the last time he smiled without a bear mask over his head for the next five years. It was the last time he felt good about himself as he was--Nathan Bailey--or thought of the man with that name without feeling crippling guilt.

And it all started with a single, shouted word from Dr. Molotov:

"Stop!!!"

"We are friends," Curl said calmly, hoping to relax the gun-pointing humanoids with his tone of voice alone. "Friends *help*, not *hurt*."

The humanoids listened, but their expressions remained grim. The red-furred male in the middle, who seemed to be the leader, barked more words in a threatening way, jabbing his rifle at Curl.

"We can take 'em, Captain," said Rebound. "Wrap 'em up nice and pretty in a heartbeat."

"Stand by, Bungee." Curl bent down and placed his blaster on the ground, then straightened with his arms outstretched. "We *helped* you fight the bugs," he said to the humanoids. "We mean you *no* harm."

Again, the humanoid leader rattled off a string of what sounded like hostile gibberish to Curl.

Then, suddenly, there was a soft chime in Curl's left ear, and the leader's speech was gibberish no more. The download from Doc Sinew had come in, Curl realized, and the interpreclip's translation matrix for the language of the moon's inhabitants was complete. Finally, Curl could understand what they were saying and speak directly to them in their native tongue.

"For the last time, invaders, surrender your weapons!" That was what the humanoid leader was saying. "Hand them over or die!"

"Wait," Curl said in the local language. "We are only here to help you stop the bugs."

The leader looked surprised at hearing Curl use words he understood. "Who are you? What do you call yourselves?"

"We call ourselves..." The next word gave the interpreclip some trouble before it came up with a translation. "...*furries*. And *I* am called Captain Harmonious Curl. What about *you?*"

"My name is Luo Oyo, and I am the commander of these people...what's *left* of them." Luo narrowed his eyes. "So how exactly did you *find* us?"

Curl pressed a button under his left ear, using a communication implant in the head of his costume to call the ship--Doc Sinew, in particular. "Hey Doc." He lowered his voice and reverted to the standard Fuzzish language. "Do we have a name for our patient yet?"

Sinew growled unhappily. "That's about *all* we have so far. He calls himself Azor. And one more thing." Sinew cleared his throat. "He says he doesn't want to be anywhere *near* this killer moon."

Curl pushed the button again, cutting off the channel. "Azor sent us," he told the humanoids. "He said you people could use some help."

The name-dropping (and outright lying to make Azor sound less negative) seemed to take the edge off the tension in the cave. The humanoids didn't put down their weapons, but they lowered them slightly and blinked at Curl with open curiosity.

"Tell us about your situation," Curl said in the local tongue. "Where are the rest of your people?"

Luo hesitated, then lowered his weapon to his side. "They're trapped in a chamber behind that rock-fall, which we created." He gestured at a pile of dust and debris spilling out of the right rear corner of the cave. "Aside from that cave-in, *we* are the last remaining defense between our survivors and the *hair-eaters*."

"Seven of you against all those bugs?" asked Bunny.

"When we started, there were *two dozen* of us fighting them off," said Luo.

"They seem to have stopped," said Curl. "Together, we've held them off."

"For now." Luo looked over his shoulder at the mouth of the tunnel where the bugs had encroached. "But they come in waves. They're relentless."

"You still have over a hundred survivors," said Curl.

"Out of *three hundred and fifty* in our original contingent," Luo said darkly.

"Which includes the 52 who left on the ship with Azor, correct?" asked Bunny.

"Yes," said Luo. "At least *they* escaped this nightmare."

"They didn't," said Bunny. "Azor is the only survivor."

All seven humanoids looked equally crestfallen. "What happened?" asked Luo.

"It looked like a bug attack, though we saw no bugs aboard the ship," explained Bunny. "And some kind of vessel struck, as well, breaching the hull and blowing out every system."

"Bastards!" snapped a female humanoid. "They couldn't let *anyone* escape."

"You sound like you know who did it," said Bunny.

"Our *masters* did it, of course," said the female. "We stole three ships and escaped the labor camp where they kept us imprisoned, and they tracked us to this moon. They destroyed two of the stolen ships, trapping most of us here, and now you tell us they got the *third*, too. They *murdered* our people."

"They and their *pets*," added a male. "The *hunter-killer bugs* they send to annihilate every *slave* who dares escape."

"But we didn't see anything *like* these bugs aboard Azor's ship," said Bunny. "Just the scars and venom left behind by their bites."

"They're fitted with self-destruct capsules," said Luo. "The Masters can annihilate them with the touch of a button, *after* they've slaughtered everyone in sight!"

Just as the words were spoken, the sounds of skittering and chittering started up again from beyond the entryway, swiftly getting louder.

"Here they come again!" Luo jammed a fresh clip of ammunition into his rifle and swung it around in the same smooth motion. "Don't let them take the freedom of our sisters and brothers!"

"Or their fur!" shouted Curl as he shouldered into the firing line and raised his blaster.

Five years ago...

"I said stop!" Dr. Molotov raced over and swatted the laser shaver out of the crewman's hand before he could go to work on the last unshaven colonist. "You were about to murder this woman!"

"What are you talking about, Doc?" Bailey, who'd been feeling so good a moment ago, scowled in confusion.

"It's already started." Red-faced, Molotov waved his scanner at the field of hairless bodies shaved by the crew. "Oh God, it's already begun."

As he said it, a nearby male body convulsed and collapsed on the ground. Seconds later, a distant female did the same, and then another.

And another.

It happened again and again across the plain, as one body after another went into spasms and then went limp. Over and over, Molotov's nurses and assistants called out the same verdict until it became so redundant that it no longer mattered.

By then, every member of the crew of the Indefatigable *knew exactly what was happening to the colonists spread out around them.*

"Every one of them is dying," said Molotov. "And it's our fault for not looking closer. *It we'd only probed deeper, we might have seen* and *understood the truth."*

"What truth is that?" asked Wade.

"That the pelt-things were keeping them alive, *not* killing *them," said Molotov. "The moment we started* shaving *them, we became the* true *killers."*

Bailey just stood and watched with dead eyes as the colonists he'd expected to save died in droves. A gulf of emptiness vaster than he'd ever thought possible opened up within him, pulling him toward it.

Medical personnel tried to stop the mass die-off, injecting drugs into the colonists in desperation. Other men and women of the crew tried to resuscitate the dead with equipment or simple techniques, to no avail.

"The pelts are sentient native lifeforms," explained Molotov. "And they're highly resistant to all forms of infection. The colonists' fading vital signs were due to a healing coma induced by the pelts as they fought off an epidemic killing the colony."

Bailey heard but didn't react. The sounds that were loudest to his ears were the grunts and cries of the dying colonists and the crewmen fighting in vain to save them.

Molotov shouted to his people, telling them to stop the heroic efforts--but they ignored him. They kept fighting like the true heroes they'd always been, even in the face of the inevitable.

Even as their captain stood there, not lifting a finger or offering the slightest bit of leadership in their moment of greatest need.

The latest assault on the cave was much more intense than the previous one had been. Many more bugs poured into the entrance, scuttling over walls, floor, and ceiling alike. The foot-long silver insects seemed more aggressive than before, quicker to pounce and harder to kill.

Even with Curl's team adding their guns to the barrage, holding the line was almost impossible. One of the humanoids went down early and was dragged away screaming before anyone could free him. Another dropped soon after and was stripped hairless in seconds by the swarm, even as Rebound blasted off the bugs two and three at a time.

The crew of the *Furflier* suffered their first casualty, as well. Some of the bugs crossed the ceiling and came down behind the shooters, getting the drop on the bright blue security ape, Zil. In the space of a heartbeat, Zil was covered in bugs and hit the dirt floor, wailing and clawing at the swarm. Before anyone could assist, the creatures had torn through his fur suit and denuded his human form inside of every last vestige of hair. He died soon after from the biting and stinging, though the other apes turned in time to pick off the remaining infiltrators before they could slaughter anyone else.

It was enough to inspire the survivors to redouble their efforts. In a matter of moments, Curl and his team and the humanoids had forced the bugs into retreat. The sea of insects gave up the battle-- for the moment--and rushed back down the hallway in a storm of legs, shells, and clacking mandibles.

Then it was time to tend to the dead. The humanoids had lost three, all told, and gently moved them to one side of the cave. Curl, meanwhile, said a few words over Zil and called for a moment of silence in his memory. When that was done, Curl called the ship and had Zil's body telefurted up. It was all he could do not to ask them to zap up the rest of the landing party at the same time, but there was still work to be done.

"So now we know," said Rebound. "Those things are just as hungry for *our* fur as the *slaves'*."

"They're bred and trained to be drawn to it," explained Luo. "It's a perfect system for the Masters, since they're born without a trace of hair on their bodies. The hair-eaters would never go after *them.*"

"So what happens if you shave it off?" asked Bunny. "Make yourselves as hairless as the Masters?"

"We don't know," said Luo.

"You mean you've never *tried* it?" asked Bunny.

Luo shook his head. "It goes against our faith. Only the furry can enter the kingdom of Next-Life."

"Makes sense," said Curl.

"Not if it means checking out of *this* life early," snapped Bunny.

"We believe strongly in preserving the fur," said Luo.

"Good for you," said Curl.

"But what about all those *people* of yours trapped in there?" Bunny gestured at the rock fall blocking the entrance to the chamber next-door. "What if removing their fur could *save* them?"

Curl frowned. "Zapping them up to the ship with the telefurter makes a lot more sense."

"No can do," said Sipping. "The walls in there are lined with deposits of electromagnetic ore that blocks our quantum trebuchet system."

"It blocks the Masters' scanners, too," said Luo. "That's why the bulk of our group holed up in there in the first place."

"But we zapped in *here* just fine," said Curl.

"Because the ore concentration is lighter." Sipping walked to a wall and ran his hand over it. "If we could get everyone in *here*, the *Furflier* could zap them aboard."

"*Or* the *bugs* might attack during the evacuation and turn it into a *bloodbath*," said Rebound.

"Unless we move really fast," said Curl.

"Or just *shave* everyone." Frustrated, Bunny stomped over to stand toe to toe with Luo. "It's the *logical* approach, don't you see? And it's only *temporary*. The fur will all *grow back.*"

"I understand," said Luo. "It's just, our *faith*..."

"...doesn't say anything about *sacrificing* yourselves without good *reason*, does it?"

Luo looked to his team, and no one volunteered an answer to the question.

"You and your people won't be the *only* ones going hairless," said Bunny. "*We'll* all have to strip down, too. We'll all be in this together."

"Maybe you're right," said Luo. "Maybe, in these extreme

circumstances, it would still fall within the tenets of our faith if we..."

"No!" shouted Curl. "*Shaving* is *never* the answer!"

Three years ago...

"*Hey, you're that guy, aren't you?*" *The bartender narrowed his dark eyes and leaned over the bar, staring hard at Nathan.* "*The one who killed all those folks by shavin' 'em?*"

Nathan tugged his fedora lower on his head, casting more of his face in shadow. "*You've got the wrong man, pal.*"

"*Yeah, sure! You're him, all right!*" *The bartender chuckled.* "*First drink's on the house, fella. I feel sorry for you, bein' court-martialed, kicked outta the service, and disgraced in every possible way like that.*"

"*Forget it.*" *Nathan turned and slouched away, pushing through the doors of the bar and out onto the streets of Bradbury, Mars before he raised further attention.*

It was a scene that had played out often since that terrible day on Veridian Five. His disgrace had spread far and wide throughout the Interstellar Entente, turning him into a celebrity of the notorious type. Every time he let his guard down, someone spotted and called attention to him, always leading to an awkward, unpleasant scene. At various times, he'd been branded as incompetent, stupid, evil, sick, or just plain laughable--and the worst of it was, he couldn't argue. He knew in his heart they were right, all of them; the deaths of all those people on Veridian Five had happened on his watch.

Slogging down the street in the rain, he tugged up the collar of his filthy, battered trench coat and thought about finding a place to sleep for the night. He'd finally exhausted his savings and didn't have a credit to his name, so his most likely sleeping place would be somewhere outdoors.

Just as he was seeking shelter, Nathan heard the sounds of a scuffle from a nearby alley. Against his better judgment, he took a peek on his way past--and was stunned.

Down that alley, a bulked-up goon was beating the hell out of what looked like a bear.

It shouldn't have been possible, since there were no bears on Mars as far as Nathan knew, but the fur-covered figure getting its ass kicked sure looked like a bear.

For some reason, seeing an innocent animal getting pounded like that struck a nerve. Nathan, who was usually too busy defending himself to stand up for anyone else, went charging down the alley, ready to fight.

"Captain," said Bunny. "May I have a word with you?" Guiding Curl by the elbow, she took him aside and lowered her voice. "Shaving *is* the answer this time, and you *know* it."

Curl shook his head emphatically. "It's *never* the answer. It's the biggest mistake you can *make.*"

Bunny leaned close and lowered her voice even more. "Now you listen to me, Curl. How often have I ever told you you're wrong?"

"You tell me that *all the time*," said Curl.

"Okay, okay," said Bunny. "Well, I'm telling you again. *Shaving* is the best chance those people have for survival."

Curl kept shaking his head. "No! I can't let it *happen* again!"

Bunny grabbed him by the shoulders and gave him a rough shake. "Enough! Whatever the hell you went through in the past, I don't *care!* Whatever has you scared, get *over* it and do the right *thing!*"

"You don't understand!"

She shook him again, harder. "I understand you're *Captain Harmonious Curl* of the *S.B.B. Furflier.* As far as I'm concerned, that's *all* you've ever been and all that *matters!*"

Three years ago...

With surprise on his side, Nathan managed to get in a few good shots at the guy attacking the bear--but his advantage didn't last. As the thug turned,

Nathan realized he'd been stabbing the bear with a knife and was ready to use it again.

The guy lunged, thrusting the knife at Nathan, but Nathan's military-honed reflexes kicked in. He jumped away at the last second, then lashed out with a kick that blew the knife out of the goon's hand, sending it clattering against the wall.

As the thug roared, Nathan dove for the knife and came up with it in his grip. He lashed out with it suddenly, slicing a red line along the guy's left bicep.

"Get out of here!" Years of pent-up frustration poured out of Nathan as he brandished the knife. "Get out of here or I swear I'll kill you!"

The thug made a quick feint, then ducked back as Nathan swept the blade at his throat. He feinted again, then backed away toward the mouth of the alley.

"Asshole!" he said. "Furry freaks deserve *to be dead!"*

Only after the thug had marched off into the night did Nathan take a closer look at the bear, which leaned heavily against the wall of the alley.

It was then that he realized it was actually someone in a bear costume.

With an agonized, deep-voiced moan, the man in the bear costume slumped to the floor of the alley, clutching his side. Tucking the knife in the pocket of his coat, Nathan crouched beside him.

"I'm dying." The bear-person's paws and side glistened with blood by the light of the Martian moon.

"Hang in there." Nathan got to his feet. "I'll call an ambulance or flag down a cop."

"Don't bother." The bear shook his head. "I can tell...I don't have much longer...to live. But one thing...you can *do...for me."*

Nathan frowned. "What's that?"

"Take my place," said the bear.

Nathan didn't understand what he was getting at. "Look, I'll find someone *to help. I promise I'll be right back."*

The bear reached up and tugged his left ear. The head of his costume split down the middle and fell away to either side, revealing a middle-aged, heavyset man with thinning black hair and a mustache and goatee of the same color.

"Stay...please," said the man in the costume. "I know...who you are."

"Okay, right." Nathan's heart sank. Was he doomed to be recognized every-where, by everyone? *"Well, I really do have to go now, so..."*

"Wait!" The man grabbed hold of the hem of Nathan's overcoat.

"Fate...brought us...together. You were a captain...and my ship will need *a captain...without me. Please..."*

Something in the man's voice held Nathan in place. "A ship? You have a ship?"

"It's called...the Furflier. *It is a* refuge...*a place where you can...*reinvent *yourself...or perhaps...be who you were always* meant *to be...and who you* seemed *to be before...will no longer matter." The man smiled, and there was a twinkle in his eye though the light of life was quickly fading from him. "Tell me...have you ever thought...about becoming a* furry?"

"I wouldn't even know where to begin," said Nathan.

"Easy," said the bear. "You take...my suit...and my name...and jump right in. No one...will know otherwise."

Nathan frowned. "What is your name, anyway?"

"Curl. Captain Harmonious Curl. And it is your *name from this day forward."*

"Captain Curl!" Sipping was watching the screen of his handheld scanner. "The bugs are massing in a space not far from here! There are hundreds of thousands, and the number keeps growing!"

"They reproduce rapidly," said Luo.

"They'll be headed here soon enough," said Rebound. "We're running out of time."

"Do we shave the survivors, or what?" asked Guana the hot pink security ape.

Curl's heart hammered in his chest inside the suit and sweat streamed down his back and sides. He felt like he was back on Veridian Five, about to order more than 11,000 beings to their deaths.

And yet he couldn't escape the feeling that Bunny was right. This time *was* different; perhaps the *wrong* choice on Veridian Five would be the *right* choice here.

"Will shaving hurt your people in any way?" he asked Luo. "Aside from breaking the rules of your faith?"

"Not that we know of," said Luo. "But none of my people ever shaves, so I can't say for sure."

"*But,*" said Bunny. "If you stay where you are, and the bugs come in force, how much longer will you survive?"

Luo sighed. "Not much longer."

"Well then." Bunny looked at Curl. "What do you think we should *do*, good Captain?"

Curl took a deep breath and let it out slowly. He thought of the original Captain Curl, his namesake, and wondered what *he* would do in this situation. He also thought of Captain Nathan Bailey of the *Indefatigable* and wondered what *he* would do.

"The bugs are continuing to mass," said Sipping.

"What do you say, Captain?" asked Rebound.

Curl nodded firmly. "I say start digging open that adjacent chamber so we can get those survivors out of there." He pressed a button under his left ear, opening a comm channel to the ship. "Frisky? Send down as many quantum shaving kits as you can, pronto! We've got over a hundred pelts to shave, and we don't have a moment to spare!"

Three years ago...

Nathan felt ridiculous at first. Putting on the dead man's bear suit felt like the absolute height of insanity.

What kind of people wore *those costumes, anyway? What the hell had to be* wrong *with them to make them want to dress up like make-believe cartoon animals?*

But after a while, he understood. He'd been longing for a safe place, for anonymity, and now he'd finally found *it.*

After cleaning up and repairing the dead man's costume and practicing how to operate it, he started to think the plan wasn't so crazy after all. In a short time, he felt right at home in that fur suit, inhabiting that character.

So by the time he set foot on the ship, the Furflier, *he only felt a little nervous. And when he met the crew for the first time, and saw they were all furries like he was, he knew he was among his own kind.*

Any worry he felt over getting found out as an imposter quickly faded. The crew instantly accepted him as their previous Captain Curl with no sign of concern or suspicion.

Couldn't they tell *there was a different man inside the suit? Didn't they* realize *his voice and mannerisms were different, and he lacked essential knowledge the previous Curl had possessed?*

Maybe it just didn't matter, just as it didn't matter to Nathan where exactly they'd gotten their ship, or who was funding their adventures. Maybe all that mattered was that a man in a big brown bear costume was in command, about to lead them back among the stars.

As he settled into the command chair on the bridge of the Furflier *for the first time, all he could think about was how great it felt to be back, to regain a captaincy--to be* useful *once more.*

He swore to himself that he would never give up that feeling. He would never take it for granted or make the kind of mistake that had led to his downfall once before.

And he would never let anyone see who was inside the suit, under any circumstances.

"We have to take off our suits," said Bunny. "It's the only way we can finish this job."

Curl's blood ran cold at the words, though they weren't unexpected. *Of course* they had to step out of their fur before the bugs arrived, if they didn't want to end up like poor Zil.

And they had to do it *now*. They'd shaved every refugee humanoid to a hairless state; now they had to escort them in groups out of the chamber lined with telefurter-blocking ore and get them zapped aboard the *Furflier*. They had to do it as fast as possible, in case the shaving alone wasn't enough to discourage the bugs.

To survive, every one of them had to be naked and hairless.

"The swarm is over a million strong, and it's headed this way!" said Sipping. "We have *seven minutes*, tops!"

"Then it's fur off, people! Let's go!" As she said it, Bunny tugged her left ear, and her costume split down the middle.

The others, except Curl, all did the same. In an instant, they stood revealed to each other as the people they'd always been.

For the first time, Curl saw that Bunny was a pudgy woman in her thirties with long, blonde hair. Sipping was an elderly Chinese man with gray hair and a short beard. Rebound was a black man in his forties with lots of tattoos. Guana the hot pink ape was a large, middle-aged woman with short brown hair, and Yego the bright green ape was a bald young man with a huge purple stain spread over his face.

Curl alone stood unrevealed, staring in stunned silence at the strange faces he'd never seen before, the faces of the people who'd become like family to him in other guises.

"All of you! Get shaving!" As she said it, Bunny grabbed a quantum shaver from a rock and used it on herself, vaporizing her lustrous blonde hair. The others did the same, burning off every last strand of hair on their bodies.

Except Curl.

"Five minutes!" shouted Sipping.

"Curl!" said Bunny. "Costume off! Do it now!"

But Curl couldn't do it. The instant the others saw who he really was, his life among them would be over. He'd rather die than lose everything again and have his life go back to the way it had been after Veridian Five.

At least, that was his thinking before the choice was taken out of his hands.

Without warning, Bunny leaped over and tugged his left ear to trigger the suit release. "I said get out of there!"

Curl's suit split open, peeling apart from head to toe. He couldn't stop it from falling away, leaving him standing there before her for the first time.

She got a good look before he hid his face in his hands. All the furries did.

"No!" he howled. "Don't look at me, please!"

But Bunny just reached up and pulled his hands away. "You son of a bitch," she said, scowling.

"I know!" Curl felt tears well up in his eyes. "You all hate me, now that you know who I am!"

Bunny's eyes narrowed. "Fuck you."

"Just leave me here for the bugs! Just leave me to die!"

Bunny scowled a moment more, then pointed the quantum shaver at him and switched it on. "Why the hell would we do that?" Her scowl melted into a smile. "All I see is Captain Curl of the *S.B.B. Furflier.*"

"What?" Curl looked around at his team and saw no hatred or rejection among them. Didn't they recognize him? Didn't they care what he'd done on Veridian Five?

The words of his predecessor, who'd died in that alley on Mars, came back to him: *It is a* refuge...*a place where you can...*reinvent *your-self...or perhaps...be who you were always* meant *to be...and who you* seemed *to be before...will no longer matter.*

"Less than two minutes!" shouted Sipping as he and the others hurried refugees out of the chamber.

"Get shaving!" Bunny pressed the shaver into Curl's hands and ran off to help the others.

The swarm roared in the distance, approaching fast. Projectile guns and blasters chattered and whined, picking off bugs. The *Furflier*'s telefurter zapped and crackled in the cave next-door.

And the quantum shaver hummed as Curl ran it over his head and body, choosing to survive.

One hundred and eighteen new furries roamed the decks of the *Furflier* that night, all former slaves, survivors of the carnage on the bug-infested moon.

The suits they wore belonged to the crew, who'd loaned them to help the refugees feel more at home. With all their hair shaved off, at least the ex-slaves could still observe the rules of their faith to some extent by being clad in *borrowed* fur. It would do in a pinch, they decided.

As for the crew, they were all too happy to make the gesture, awkward as it was for them at first. Some worried about what the others might think, but it turned out not to matter in the end. The names and personalities stayed the same; only the faces were different.

As Curl sat in his command chair, watching the furless crew (but not naked; they wore simple blue uniforms) interact, he felt better than he could have imagined given the circumstances. He felt more like his old self, like Nathan, but without the fear and self-loathing.

"Please sign this, Captain." Ensign Biggus Belfry of the engineering department handed over an e-clipboard with a report on the screen. He, like every member of the crew, treated Curl just the same as always; no one had made a single mention of who he was without the suit or what he'd done in the past, though surely *some* of them must have recognized him and known the whole story.

It was more than Curl could have expected, and much more than he thought he deserved. But perhaps, given this new chance, he might still do some good in the universe.

"Thank you, Ensign." Curl signed the report with his fingertip and handed the clipboard back to Belfry, who saluted and left.

Just then, the elevator door whooshed open, admitting Dr. Sinew to the bridge.

"Greetings, Harmonious." Without his tiger suit, Sinew was a tall, muscular man in his forties with short, black hair and a closely-trimmed beard. He was of Arab extraction, with deep, dark eyes and an olive complexion. "How fare you this fine day, good Captain?"

"Fairly well." Curl smiled. "And yourself? Still missing the stripes?"

Sinew chuckled. "My stripes are *always* with me, suit or no suit."

"What about the rest of the crew? Would you say they're adjusting equally well?"

"Some adjusted faster than others, as you'd expect," said Sinew.

"But the general level of support has prevented any lingering difficulties. The power of fur is so strong, apparently, that its influence lingers even when the fur itself is gone."

"It might be gone a lot more, the way things are going." Just then, Bunny strolled over from the helm, where she'd been working with Dressage--a short, stocky woman with brown hair--to run a system diagnostic. "Some folks are talking about giving up their fur altogether or taking temporary breaks from it."

"Is that so?" said Curl.

"Do we have a problem with that?" asked Bunny.

Sinew shrugged. "Seems to me the Code of Concealment has already gone by the wayside thanks to our new friends' need for cover."

"In that case, I say the crew should go for it," said Curl. "It's up to the individual."

"A mixed crew on the *Furflier?*" Sinew let out a rumbling growl that was worthy of his tiger-striped alter ego. "Things could get *interesting.*"

"We can only hope," said Bunny.

The elevator door swished open again, and Sinew laughed. "We have company!"

Curl turned, and the hairs on the back of his neck jumped to attention. It was like seeing *himself* walking toward him, though he knew the man inside the Big Brown Bear suit was different now.

"Captain!" The bear--with Luo inside--waved as he strolled to the command chair. "Thanks again to you and all your crew for loaning my people the furs!"

"Anything to make you all feel better," said Curl. "Just let us know if there's anything else we can do."

"Actually, there is," said Luo the Bear. "I was wondering..."

"Yes?"

Luo cleared his throat. "Is there any way I could *keep* this fur? It's so *comfortable.* It makes me feel like a new *man...*er, *bear.*"

Curl felt a flicker of panic, but it passed. Strangely enough, he realized he didn't hate the idea. It felt pretty good to come out of hiding, as long as he was among friends. Maybe it was time he became his real self all the way.

"Maybe," he told Luo. "Let me think about it. After all, it's *vital* that the right *home* be found for *every* fur."

Bunny sighed with her usual irritation. "And every *person*, don't forget."

"Right." Curl grinned and nodded. "That, too."

THE THOUSANDTH ATLAS

Bodhisattva Bodhisattva Bodhisattva. I say it three times fast under my breath, the way I always do when I might be about to kill someone.

Crouching in the brush with knife in hand, I prepare to spring. I glimpse my reflection in the moonlit blade, and my expression is intense--brown eyes narrow, jaws clenched, pale face smudged with dark greasepaint. The whites of my eyes and the glossy highlights of my slicked-back black hair are the brightest things I see.

My possible target, a tall young man in a black business suit, stands on the doorstep of the bungalow not ten feet away, dimly exposed by the moonglow of this early summer night in rural Pennsylvania.

He rings the doorbell, and my hand tightens on the handle of the knife.

I'm here to protect the woman behind the door. If he makes a single move against her, I'll take him down as I've taken down so many others in locations far and wide.

I draw a deep breath, tasting mountain laurel in the air. I'm not a killer at heart, but as sure as my name is Knock Singer, I'll do what it takes to keep that woman safe.

My heart hammers as the doorknob turns and the door swings inward, revealing the cabin's occupant.

I had no idea she was so beautiful. That's all I can think when I first see her in the flesh. *Online photos don't do her justice.* Raven-black hair drapes her shoulders, and her bright green eyes shine like beacons in the night. Her form is sleek and slender in her pink t-shirt and denim shorts.

The Egyptian ankh-shaped pin on her t-shirt can't out-glitter the wide, bright smile she casts in the man's direction. "Can I help you?" Those are the first words I hear from her lips, though I've read and analyzed so many of her social media writings.

"I was about to ask you the same question." The man pulls something out of his pocket.

I almost launch myself at him...but at the last second, I get a good look at what's in his hand, and I hold myself back.

"The Book of Mormon," he tells her. "I've brought you a free copy."

"Thanks, but no thanks." The woman's name is Pirouette Fairborn--Piri, for short. "It's awfully late."

"Shall I come back another time?"

Pirouette eases the door toward the frame. "I'm not really a joiner. Good luck at your next stop, though."

"Thanks for your time, ma'am." He doesn't even realize, does he? As she closes the door on him, he's completely in the dark.

He has no way of knowing that much like the god he worships, she's keeping the world from coming apart at the seams.

Hunkered down in the bushes outside the bungalow, I spy on her after the Mormon leaves, watching through a living room window. I see her stand in the middle of the room and spin clockwise seven times, then turn counter-clockwise seven more.

Next, she walks backward diagonally across the room, weaving her arms in a complicated pattern behind her head. Stopping at the far corner, she turns a framed black-and-white photo (a family of three at the seashore) on the wall upside-down, then claps her hands in front of it three times.

Turning, she removes the glittering ankh pin from the left chest of her t-shirt and pins it to the right--then reverses that, returning it to the left. All the while, her lips never stop moving, chanting something I can't hear.

When it comes to the rites and rituals, she's still practicing as advertised. On the one hand, that's a *really good* thing, saving-the-world-wise. But on the other hand, it begs an important question:

How is she still alive?

Dozens of her kind have been killed across the country over the past year. I, in turn, have killed their killers whenever I could.

But I have never before reached someone like her in time to *save* them--only *avenge* them. So what the hell is going on to make this possible?

I need to delve deeper. I need to make direct contact instead of watching from afar.

But not tonight. My name might be Knock, but I won't be knocking on any doors for her just yet.

Seven years ago, before I started the research that led to my new life's work, I was just a dad, a husband, and a working man. I had a wife, a little girl, and a little boy, and life was sweet.

In those days, I never chanted *Bodhisattva* or threw spilled salt over my left shoulder or paid attention to any of those things. Sometimes, I still dream about those days of innocent happiness, back before my personal Big Bang.

I still remember the look on the guy's flushed and sweaty face as he barged onto the playground and swung the Bushmaster semi-automatic, complete with bump stock, out from under his overcoat. I remember the crackle of the assault rifle as it sprayed rounds into the gathered families--mine included--kicking up geysers of blood in the noonday sun. Of the four of us, only I survived.

I still wake screaming in the night--as I do again tonight, in my motor home--and the only way back to sleep is for me to run the ritual. To recite the Lord's Prayer over and over as I rub my index fingers against my thumbs and rock in a fetal position in my bed.

The tears are not officially part of the ritual, though they always, always come.

"Say when." Piri smiles as she pours the hot black coffee into my cup. The morning sun is shining through the windows of the Liquorneer bar/restaurant on the outskirts of the town of Ligonier, but it can't compare to the brightness of her smile.

"That's perfect, thanks." Smiling back at her takes no effort at all. A happy warmth flows through my body before I've taken even a single sip from the steaming cup.

"What else can I get you, hon?" Piri puts the coffee pot down on the table and pulls a pad and pen from her back pocket. Her outfit is casual--a dark green top and faded blue jeans--no uniform like a waitress in a diner might wear. She wears the same glittering ankh pin that she wore last night, this time clipped to the right chest of her top.

"How're the *juevos rancheros?*"

"Awesome." Her eyes widen, and she starts writing on the pad before I've even ordered. "Our day shift cook is straight outta Oaxaca, *guero.*" She flips the pad shut, stuffs it in her back pocket, and grabs the pot.

"Hold on." I narrow my eyes. "What makes you think I won't order something else instead?"

She gives her long black hair a toss. "'Cause you know Mama knows best, hon." Laughing, she marches off to disappear through the swinging kitchen doors beside the bar.

Leaving me to wonder how best to make my approach. Time is

of the essence, but being too honest too soon might scare her off. The truth I bring isn't easy to bear, and it's scared away others before her...others who are no longer among the living.

As if to underscore the urgency of my mission, the news headlines on the TV above the end of the bar catch my ear. The ruler of a Middle Eastern country is threatening to nuke Europe back to the Stone Age. The U.S. is promising to nuke the nuker if he follows through, and Russia is ready to *super-nuke* the U.S. if that happens.

What would it take to kick that daisy chain of mass destruction into gear? Not too damn much, from what I can see. And what would it take to defuse it?

"Get ready for the biggest blast of flavor you've ever experienced!" Piri storms through the swinging doors with plates in hand. "You are *so* gonna thank me for this, even though Hector's the one who *cooked* it."

She puts the plates down in front of me--one with the *juevos*, one with tortillas--and sits across from me to watch me try the food.

"Awful." That's what I say at the first taste of over-easy eggs, *salsa verde*, and refried beans. "I can't stand it."

My smile says the opposite, and she laughs. "That'll teach you to try my recommendations!"

I taste another heavenly forkful, and my eyes roll with pleasure. "Never again. Ugh."

That's when I finally see my opening. Piri takes the salt and pepper shakers out of their wire rack by the window and plays with them--stacking one atop the other, then unstacking them, shuffling them, and restacking them again.

"I do that, too," I tell her between bites of the delicious mess on my plate. "Pretty much all the time with everything."

"Nervous habit." For the first time, she sounds a little embarrassed, but doesn't stop fiddling with the shakers.

I nod as I chew and swallow. "I make myself crazy sometimes. I get it in my head that if I don't do something a certain way, something bad will happen."

"Huh." She pours out tiny piles of pepper and salt, then swirls them in opposite directions with her fingertips--pepper clockwise, salt the reverse. "I used to get that sometimes."

Suddenly, my attention's even more laser-focused on her words. "Used to?"

She shrugs and reaches up to touch the ankh pin. "I got help." Then she scrambles the salt and pepper willy-nilly and flings her hands up. *Abracadabra.* "All better now."

Holy shit! I had no idea!

Just then, the front door opens, and an overweight bald guy with a vast, bushy beard lumbers in, carrying a laptop.

Instantly, she's up off the bench seat and heading for the door. My heart sinks to see her go.

"Hey, Big Daddy!" She grabs a laminated single-sheet menu and hands it to him as he heads for a barstool. "What'll it be?"

Big Daddy laughs. "The usual, Piri." His red tank top clings to his prodigious belly, and his baggy black basketball shorts hang to within centimeters of his high-top shoes.

"Irish coffee, hold the coffee?"

Big Daddy chuckles as he mounts the stool, which is more like absorbing it into his flab. "More in the mood for a blue plate special, actually."

"Got it." Piri zooms for the kitchen. "Hog jowls and possum fritters, easy on the tabasco."

"Gotta love that girl, huh?" Big Daddy says in my direction, but I'm not listening.

I'm too busy thinking about what she just told me and what it means to my mission. Because the truth is, her "getting help" is just about as bad as her getting killed.

Have you heard the expression, "burying yourself in your work?" Well, that's what I did after the playground massacre--though the work in which I chose to bury myself was something altogether new to me.

The world was falling apart; anyone could see it. The massacre had been just the latest outbreak of a general breakdown. But why? How much worse would it get? And was there any possible way to reverse it?

If only someone with deep experience in statistical analysis and massaging big data would take a swing at the problem--someone with a powerful personal interest in finding the answers to those questions. Who *knows* where the research might lead him? What unprecedented ideas he might find? What fresh *purpose* he might divine which could give his life meaning again?

That someone was me, of course. Flash forward three years, and I'm smack in the middle of a secret war between hope and those who seek to crush it. Between people like Piri and the pricks who want to kill them.

All over a small matter of *belief.* Because if enough people believe that certain seemingly superstitious actions can save the world, maybe they can.

At least until they're killed by the pricks (who, ironically, *also* believe) or, almost as bad, are "helped" to accept a new way of thinking.

Until someone like me comes along to guide them back to the fold...and keep them alive along the way, with any luck.

"Piri!" I approach her that evening at an outdoor concert in the Diamond--a little diamond-shaped park with a gazebo in the center of Ligonier. "Funny meeting *you* here," I tell her, as if my showing up here is purely accidental...as if I haven't been watching and following her from a distance all day, trailing her red Volkswagen Beetle on my motorcycle with a tinted helmet concealing my face.

Piri's sitting on a ragged quilt at the back of the crowd, sipping what looks like white wine from a plastic cup. She's wearing a beige sundress with white trim, again with the glittering ankh pinned to her bodice (the left side this time). She pats a spot beside her on the quilt. "The show's about to start, New Guy."

Grinning, I sit where directed, taking care to leave a *little* space between us. "Have you heard this group before?"

"They're okay." She tosses her jet-black tresses and leans back on her elbows. "*Comme ci comme ça.*"

"A wise woman once told me, 'Mama knows best,' so I guess I'll stick around."

I look around as more people file into the park with chairs or blankets. In such an exposed setting with the hope of the world by my side, I have to be watchful at all times, lest a killer get the drop on us. "And by the way, my name's not 'New Guy.'"

"Really? I *totally* thought it was."

"Call me Knock."

"As in door?"

"As in man."

"If your last name's Knock, too..."

"It isn't."

"Not Knock Knock?"

"It's Singer."

"Knock, who's there." She makes a face. "Nope, one Knock is not enough."

I laugh. "You think you can do better?"

"Are you kidding me?" She closes her eyes and speaks the next word slowly, with elegance. "*Pirouette.*"

I'm so mesmerized by her profile, I almost forget to speak. "Damn. You've got me beat."

"See?" She chuckles as she opens her eyes. "You can call me Piri."

Just then, Big Daddy catches my eye from across the Diamond, his monstrous girth clad in a white tank, shorts, beret, and high tops. It turns out he's in the band, as he heads up into the gazebo and settles his bulk behind the drum kit there.

"So what kind of stuff do you have to do a certain way?" asks Piri. "To stop something bad from happening?"

I smile to myself. What I told her back at the Liquorneer must have made an impression. She just saved me the trouble of bringing up the subject I most want to talk about.

"Different stuff." I pause, as if I have to think it over. "Like shaving. I have to use a certain number of strokes, or I'm afraid I might die." Another pause. "Or walking. I make sure I never step on a blue handicapped symbol in a parking space, because I don't want that fate to befall me or someone I love."

She's watching me with a sideways gaze. "What else?"

"When I say goodbye to someone I care about, I always do it three times. Otherwise, I might never see them again."

"You know what my shrink might say?" Piri lifts her head and affects a deeper voice. "You, sir, are a textbook example of OCD. Obsessive compulsive disorder."

"Is that so?" I raise an eyebrow. "Then what about the ones that *come true?*"

Piri frowns.

"For example." People are clapping, I need to wrap this up. "Once, I didn't say goodbye three times to a friend of mine. Two days later, he died in an accident."

"That's terrible." She winces.

"Did you ever have one that came true like that?"

Piri shakes her head, but I'm not convinced.

"Well, it's happened enough to me that I'm extra careful," I tell her. "Especially with the big ones."

"Big ones?"

"Like turning the TV news off and on three times while reciting 'Give Peace a Chance.'"

"And it works?"

I shrug. "World War III didn't break out *today*, did it?"

She stares at me for a long moment, as if trying to make up her mind about something. Then she smirks.

"You are *so* OCD." She laughs. "I'll bet my therapist would *love* to get his hands on *you.*"

"Aren't you even going to thank me for saving us all from World War III?"

"Is *that* all you did?" Again, she laughs. "*I* used to keep *all humanity* from kicking the bucket! How do you like *those* apples?"

"And you *stopped?* Because of your therapist?"

She grins at me as the band starts playing Clapton's "Let It Rain." I'm so lost in her smile, an assassin could probably walk right up and double-tap us both without setting off my alarm bells until it's too late.

Piri leans close and whispers in my ear, setting off bells of a completely different kind.

"I never said I stopped." Her breath is warm against my ear and cheek.

"But you said you don't believe anymore."

"I guess I still need a crutch." She touches the ankh on her chest. "Just because I no longer believe this pin keeps me safe from harm, that doesn't mean I have to stop *wearing* it."

"But your shrink cured you, didn't he?"

"What can I say?" She leans back and smiles as the music keeps playing. Big Daddy is a hell of a drummer, it turns out. "Old habits die hard, you know?"

People think they're crazy. They're driven by the unshakable belief that if they don't take certain steps in exactly the right way, something catastrophic will befall them, or their loved ones...or the world. Naturally, they think they're totally nuts.

You'd expect them to keep it to themselves, wouldn't you? To stay in the *closet* when it comes to their not-so-dirty little secrets. And maybe that was how it *used* to be back in the day, before *social media* was a thing.

On the Internet, everyone talks about everything, including superstitious obsessions--which is how I found Piri and the others before her. Using bleeding edge data mining techniques and statistical analysis tools, I combed social media, searching for people who fit the right profile...those who talked about performing certain classes of rituals and claimed they had a direct impact on current events. Then, I mapped the frequency of these rituals against actual events, searching for a causal relationship between them.

Guess what I discovered? The supposedly superstitious rituals of a specific population are *in fact* sustaining the *world*.

Is some supernatural force at work, inexplicably linking the rituals of a thousand or so people to the Earth's survival? Is there perhaps some kind of trans-quantum effect to blame, as these people's ritualized actions influence entangled particles in seemingly magical ways with a scientific basis? Or is the concentrated strength of belief itself the primary agent holding things together?

All I know is, it *works*...at least until the thousand Atlases with the world on their shoulders die or stop believing.

So many have been killed already by chaos-worshipping idiots who caught on to my research. The balance of the world is tipping in the wrong direction; losing even one more Atlas believer--like *Piri-*-could throw it over into wholesale destruction.

But I refuse to give up. I will do whatever it takes to stop the world from making even *less* sense than it already does.

No matter how crazy or extreme my actions might seem, rest assured, there is a method to my madness.

"I think you should stop. Just stop and see what happens."

That's what I tell her as we stroll through town after the concert, guided by the glow of streetlights and the chirping of a multitude of crickets.

"The OCD stuff, you mean?" She walks just close enough that our elbows occasionally brush.

Each contact is like a blast of fireworks to me. "Yeah, why not? You said you don't believe in it anymore. You just do it out of habit, right?"

"But why would I stop it?" asks Piri.

"To prove you don't need it anymore." Intentionally, I bump elbows with her. "I dare you."

She walks along silently for a moment. "Yeah, but *you* still do it, right?"

"Maybe I just need the right inspiration to quit. Sort of like an AA sponsor."

"So go see my shrink," says Piri. "I told you, he'll straighten you out."

"Come on. I *double*-dare you."

"I hardly *know* you. Are you *allowed* to double-dare someone you hardly know?"

"*Triple*-dare. *Quadruple*-dare."

"All right, all right!" She sighs. "*Maybe.*"

"Yes! I'm already feeling inspired!"

"*Don't!* I might still *chicken out.*"

"I'll do it, too, Piri. No rituals tonight, no matter what. We can compare notes in the morning at the Liquorneer."

She manages a nervous smile and taps the ankh pin with a finger. "I guess I could leave my pin at work tonight to avoid temptation."

"We don't *need* that OCD stuff, do we?"

"Not a chance." She's still nervous. "We *got* this."

My smile isn't the least bit nervous as we fist-bump under a streetlight.

Hours later, I break my promise. Watching her living room window from the brush, I pinch my outer thighs--alternating right, left, right--while chanting under my breath: *balderdash balderdash balderdash borealis.* To improve my chances of success, I perform one of my personal rituals.

But Piri, from what I can see, does not.

She puts on pajamas, makes tea, plays with her phone, watches TV--and lives up to my dare. At one point, she stands in the middle of the room and looks like she's thinking about turning in circles or walking backward...but she doesn't. She stares at the painting on the wall (*several* times) but never flips it upside-down.

The whole time I'm out there, I don't see her make a single wrong move. She's not wearing the ankh pin, and I don't see her execute a single ritual.

Why is this a *good* thing, if what I want to achieve is to get her back on track as a believer? Why would I dare her not to perform those rituals if they're helping keep the world from collapsing?

Let's just say I have my reasons.

Though it's true, part of me would be happy just to lurk out here and watch whether she follows my plan or not. Part of me wouldn't care if the world ends as long as I got to spend whatever time I have left gazing at her.

That same part of me almost hopes my plan *doesn't* succeed, at least not right away. Because the truth is, my mission doesn't end here. There's a reason I live in a motor home.

As long as other believers are at risk, so is the world and everyone in it. When I'm done with Piri, I'll have to move on to the next Atlas on my list.

The thought of it makes my gut twist. I haven't felt the way I do about her since before that gunman opened fire on the playground.

When the lights go out around eleven o'clock, I lose sight of her, yet I linger. I remember the touch of her elbow, the sound of her laugh, the twinkle in her eyes, and want only to experience then all over again. I want to *tell* her things. I want to *kiss* her, and the rest of the world be *damned*.

But eventually, I slip away in the shadows, off to do my duty and follow through with my plan.

It takes until 3:00 in the morning for the Liquorneer to completely empty out. I watch from the woods across the road, making sure that every living soul is gone, the lights are off, and the doors are locked by the bartender.

Fifteen minutes later, when all is dark and quiet along that stretch of rural road, I grab my gasoline cans and trot over to the Liquorneer's parking lot.

As far as I can tell, there are no security cameras outside the place, but I wear a black ski mask over my face just in case. Anonymity is crucial for this part of the plan to succeed.

My black gloves will help with that, too, since being overly careful isn't at the top of my to-do list tonight. After breaking in a window with a rock, I stick a rag in the spout of one gas can and light it, then heave it into the building. As flames start to dance inside the place, I do the same with my other can and another window, doubling my chance that the fire will properly catch.

Satisfied that I've done what I came here to do, I jog back across the road and into the woods. The orange glow of the rising flames from the Liquorneer's windows lights my way as I head for the motorbike hidden in the brush.

I don't hear any sirens when I get to Piri's neighborhood and park the bike behind a fence. Either the Liquorneer isn't wired with working smoke alarms, or the flames haven't built as fast as I'd hoped.

Things aren't the way I expect when I sneak up to her house, either. The lights are on inside, but as far as I can tell, nobody's home. There's no sign of life in the living room or anywhere else, and her red VW Beetle is gone.

Where could Piri have run off to at four in the morning? Expert statistical analyst that I am, it still takes a moment for me to run the possibilities.

When one particular answer jumps out at me, a blaze of adrenaline sizzles through my bloodstream with blistering urgency.

Without hesitation, I whirl with heart hammering and run as fast as I can for my bike.

If Piri is where I think she is, every split-second is of the essence. Even at that, I might very well have lost her, and the rest of the world along with her.

As I race up to the Liquorneer, I see that my worst fear has been realized. Piri's red VW is in the parking lot, and the driver's-side door is wide open.

So is the front door of the Liquorneer, which is ablaze all around with leaping flames.

She must have come back for the ankh pin. That's all I can figure. At some point after I left my post outside her bungalow, she must have decided she couldn't get through the night without it. Then...what? She ran in after it? Ran in to try to find a fire extinguisher and fight the blaze?

It doesn't matter. As I leap off the bike, letting it fall to the gravel, and bolt for the door of the place, all I can think about is rescuing her.

I call her name as I charge up the four front steps, but the roar of the flames is the only answer. Coughing from the smoke and fumes, I push through the wall of heat to peer inside. She *must* be in there somewhere, but all I see are rippling waves of orange and red flame and clouds of black smoke.

"Piri! Piri!" I scream my lungs out to no avail. She either *won't* or *can't* answer, and I think I know which it must be.

Horrified, I freeze. My goal was simply to convince her that the rituals were working after all, that her superstitious practices were averting disaster. The morning after giving them up, she was supposed to see the burned-down bar and resolve never to lose faith or slack off again. I never meant for her to get caught in the catastrophe like this.

"Oh God, oh God." I step back, gulping deep breaths, and get ready to plunge inside. Though there's no clear path through the flames, and I've got no kind of protection, there's no *time*, either. For all I know, her time might *already* be up.

One more deep breath, and I tense every muscle, about to charge. Realistically, I don't expect to come back out, let alone save her, but I've got to try.

I set my right foot on the planks of the porch. I clench my teeth and swing my left arm back.

Then, though I thought I was alone, someone grabs my arm and holds it fast. I'm locked in place like a nail driven into a board.

Looking back, I see it's Big Daddy standing there in a super-sized fireman's coat and red helmet. His face glistens with sweat as the glow of the flames ripples orange and crimson on his puffy cheeks.

"Follow me." He says it with a fierce confidence I haven't heard from him before. "Stay *right behind me*, understand?"

I think he's insane, but I nod.

He pushes past me without hesitation, without another word. I follow, fully expecting the flames to lash and sear me, to cook me alive.

But they don't. The flames part around his enormous girth, opening a pathway for us to walk unimpeded. Sweat is still gushing from my body, and I'm coughing from the smoke, but my flesh isn't catching fire and melting from my bones.

I have no idea how he's doing it, and I don't care. Determined not to waste this gift, I look all around for Piri as we walk, squinting against the flames.

Finally, he stops at the bar and turns. "Down there!" he shouts, pointing at the space behind the bar. "Hurry!"

I hesitate, because the bar is on fire, and he gestures impatiently for me to get moving. When my first nervous footfall lands outside the safe zone behind his bulk, the fire there winks out.

Emboldened, I take another step, and another. The path continues to clear as I move.

Sure enough, when I get to the end of the bar and look behind it, Piri is there. She lies unconscious on the floor, clutching the ankh pin in her left hand, surrounded by flames.

"What part of *hurry* don't you understand?" shouts Big Daddy. *"Grab her!"*

When I move behind the bar, the flames retreat, leaving Piri sprawled among the charred woodwork. Without another flicker of hesitation, I lean down and scoop her into my arms. Her body is warm, her chest rising and falling with breath.

Just before I follow Big Daddy back out, I kiss her on the forehead, so grateful for her life that I feel like my heart might explode on the spot.

I hear sirens in the distance, but there aren't any emergency vehicles outside when we escape. I don't ask Big Daddy how he got there in the first place, though I wonder.

I *do* ask him a question, though, as we spread his coat on the nearby grass and lay Piri down on top of it.

"How did you *do* that?" I jab a finger at the burning building across the parking lot. "How did you keep the flames *away* from us in there?"

"Beats me, but I'm not complaining." Big Daddy kneels and presses two fingers against Piri's throat, checking her pulse. "Are you?"

"Of course not." I brush the hair back from her forehead. "I'm grateful."

Big Daddy seems satisfied with her pulse and leans back. "Maybe some higher power got involved."

I get a strange feeling as I meet his gaze. "Anything's possible, I guess."

He nods slowly and pulls a red licorice twist out of his pocket. "She told me about her rituals, you know. How she was convinced they were keeping the world from ending."

"She did?"

"Seems to me everyone has superstitions of one kind or another." Big Daddy talks while he chews a bite of red licorice. "Somebody once said that even *God* has them."

"Like what?"

"Like if one little *world* ends, the whole *universe* might go with it." Big Daddy takes another bite. "No good reason to think that, right? But if He made us in His image, who knows? Who's to say He isn't subject to the same kinds of compulsions sometimes?"

I just nod. Fire trucks and ambulances are roaring into the parking lot as we speak.

"In which case, saving *her* might be something in *everyone's* interests." Big Daddy shrugs and smiles down at Piri. A trace of a smile flickers across her dreaming face as if in response. "Something to think about, huh?"

"Yeah." I touch her shoulder lightly, grateful beyond words to whoever made this possible. "Something to think about for sure."

What's it like to see Piri's living room from the *inside* instead of out in the bushes? Totally, utterly fantastic, take it from me.

Two nights after the fire, she invites me in for the first time, and I don't say no. I'm not sure where the future might lead, but for now I couldn't be happier to step inside her world.

"I'll get you a cup of coffee." She's still hoarse from the smoke inhalation, though she only had to spend one night in the local hospital.

"*I'll* get *you* a cup," I tell her, and then I add, "hon," which makes her laugh.

That in itself is all I need to feel complete. The sound of her laugh, the sparkle in her eyes, the smile on her face. My heart aches every time I think about how close I came to losing them all forever.

Do I deserve her? Big Daddy seems to think so. Whatever his deal is, he did *something* to help me rectify my mistake and give me another chance with her.

He gave me another chance to help save the world, too. It turns out the fire at the Liquorneer undid the damage from the shrink. Piri's belief in the power of the rituals is stronger than ever.

As long as she keeps me around, I will tend and protect that power--and with any luck, some kind of love between us.

When I come back from the kitchen with coffee, she turns on the stereo and gestures for me to join her. I put down the cups on a table and go to her.

She doesn't ask how I know the exact steps as we dance. Maybe she thinks we're just perfectly in synch, establishing a true love connection.

But the fact remains, I never miss a step. She spins clockwise in the middle of the room seven times, and so do I. Then we both spin counter-clockwise seven more.

The two of us walk backward diagonally, weaving our arms in complicated patterns behind our heads. We stop at the far corner and clap our hands three times at a framed black-and-white photo hung upside-down on the wall. Then, she moves the glittering ankh pin from the left side of her chest to the right and back again; I touch my own chest left-right-left as if doing the same.

And the whole time we're doing that, dancing and saving the world all at once, we're both singing at the top of our lungs...singing along with Stevie Wonder's famous song blasting at top volume from the speakers, making the windows shake.

The song is "Superstition," and I'm thinking we ought to add it to the ritual permanently, if she'll let me.

It might not make a bad wedding march, either, someday, if we ever get that far.

BLACKBEARD'S ALIENS

"Fire!" I have been called a Gentleman Pirate, and oft enough, the name suits. But on a day like this, Stede Bonnet is all pirate and no gentleman.

No sooner has the order to fire left my lips than the port side guns of the *Adventure* blast out their loads in clouds of roiling black smoke. Five iron balls leap through the air, heading straight for their target--a huge silver disk hovering thirty feet above the water.

Twin beams of red light flash out from the rim of the disk, burning two of the cannonballs into wisps of steam. But the other three make it through. They don't penetrate the hull of the silver disk as I had hoped, but they do make it rock in midair.

Take that, you hellspawn. "Reload!" I shout, though I know the men have already done just that. We are united in perfect rhythm after all our many battles as part of this fearsome flotilla. Our leader, much as I despise him, has taught us that.

Even now, not half a league away, I hear the guns of his personal flagship, the *Queen Anne's Revenge*, pound away at a larger target--another hovering object, this one triangular in shape. I don't have to look to know his banner yet flies from the mainmast, rippling in the Caribbean breeze.

There is no other flag like it: a field of black, with a skeletal, horned demon raising a toast to Satan whilst piercing a heart with a spear. All this time, I thought it was merely a symbol of evil designed to strike fear in the hearts of seagoing foes. And, for me, a personal symbol of a man I loathed, a pirate who'd taken everything from me and pressed me into service in his infamous fleet.

Little did I know it was a declaration of war on an unearthly enemy. Little did I dream, until recently, that Blackbeard had much more on his mind than wealth and power.

"Fire!" This time, the booms of the cannon begin before I cry out the word. It's not insubordination; the men know we must press the attack hard and fast.

But not one single ball connects with the target. This is because our one target has become many. The disk has split into twenty silver wedges, each leaping out of range of our guns.

And then streaking toward us like arrows from a brace of archers.

Raising the spyglass to my eye, I see spots of glowing light flare to life on the point of each wedge. The light is red, like the deadly beams that shot forth from the undivided disk a moment ago.

Their purpose is clear to me.

"Fight for your lives!" I pocket the spyglass and swing up my saber and pistol as I call out over the noise on deck. "Send 'em back to hell before they do the same to you!"

It's hard to believe there was ever a time when I'd not heard of these creatures. But that time was three months ago, true enough.

It was just then that Blackbeard's strange behavior began to arouse suspicions among his pirate captains, myself included. The way he started letting ships filled with goods from the West Indies pass without raiding them...the way he paced the decks at all hours, watching the inky darkness and muttering to himself...and then there were the treasure hunts.

I confronted him about it one night on Ocracoke Island, off the coast of Northern Carolina, as we watched the men dig. We had marched inland some distance and stopped in the heart of a grove of cedar trees. It was there he had instructed the crew to sink the first spade and dig until they struck something solid.

"Why are we pulling up all your old hoards?" I asked the question quietly under the rasp of sinking shovels and the grunting of the men. "New Providence, Nassau, Barbados, Oak Island--now here. Have you some grand scheme in mind?"

Blackbeard turned his fierce countenance upon me. It's true what they say about his fearsome appearance. With those glittering dark eyes and pitch-black beard, he looks like something more than man, something divine in a hellish way. "You'll know soon enough, Stede." He was a full head taller than me and had to look down to see my face. "And then you'll wish you didn't."

"Will you at least *open* this one?" It was stifling hot that night. I took off my broad-brimmed hat and wiped the sweat from my forehead with the back of my brown coat sleeve. "Or will you leave this chest padlocked in the hold of the *Revenge* like all the rest?"

He smirked behind his thick, braided beard, his namesake. "The ship's name is the *Queen Anne's Revenge*," he said.

I bristled, as he'd known I would. That ship had once been my own, christened *Revenge*, until he'd taken it from me. I despised him for it still, though I now served as captain of a smaller vessel in his fleet, the *Adventure*...waiting always for the day when I would regain what I had lost. *Working* for that day, too, always plotting and preparing. I was organizing a mutiny even then, taking advantage of Blackbeard's erratic behavior to sway key crewmen to my cause.

"Can you at least give me a hint, Edward?" I kept my voice low so the men would not hear me call him by his given name, Edward Teach...or as close to a given name as he'd admit to. "What plan do you have in mind for all that treasure?"

Blackbeard's broad face split in a pearly grin. "Who said anything about *treasure*?" He laughed and cuffed me on the side of my head.

Just then, the men struck something. They were several feet

down, up to their shoulders in the hole, when I heard the spades hit something solid.

"We have it, sir," said one of the men. He hit it again. "I think it's a chest."

"Bring it up, then." Blackbeard gestured impatiently. "And make it double-quick, lads."

Suddenly, his head jerked up, and he looked around. His hands found the butts of two of the six pistols stuffed into the bandoliers he wore across his belly.

"What is it?" I listened and looked, sensing nothing...and then I glimpsed a faint red light glowing among the cedars. It was steady, perhaps fifty yards distant--not flickering, not a torch, certainly.

"We must have been followed." Blackbeard cocked the pistols. "You're about to get your answers, Stede."

I drew my own pistol and saber. "Answers?"

Blackbeard spit on the ground and raised the guns. "You won't like 'em." Then, he fired both weapons into the woods.

As the brimstone smell of gunpowder filled the air, I heard a terrible shriek in the distance like the cry of a banshee. Suddenly, the red light flashed and divided, becoming three lights...and all three surged toward us.

"Stand your ground!" Blackbeard dropped his first two guns and reached for another pair from his bandolier. "Go for their *middle* heads!"

His words baffled me, but explanation came soon enough. The lights were fast upon us, and with them, strange creatures unlike any I'd ever seen.

To say they were nightmarish would not do them justice. They were skeletal things of polished bone--roughly human in that they each had two arms, two legs, and a trunk...but the similarity ended there. For the bones were covered with jagged spurs and points. And each creature had three heads like gleaming skulls: one atop the shoulders, with a crown of horns all around and sharp fangs in the jaws; one in the belly with a sharp beak; and one in the chest with a single glowing red eye and two mouths. Rays of crimson light shot out of those eyes, lancing right and left through the night.

Demons. That was the only word I had for them.

Chills leaped along my spine as they fell upon us. I heard the diggers scream, struck by the crimson rays, yet I did not flinch. I got off a shot at the demon nearest me, and my aim was true. The ball blasted dead on into the glowing red eye of the head in its chest. The thing went into a spasmodic dance, as if seized by St. Vitus, then spun screaming to the ground.

Blackbeard shot one, as well, but it still managed to throw itself around his legs. The third demon pressed the advantage, wrapping him in its spiny grip.

It was then I realized these things were more than mere skeletons. Their bones stretched and grew like vines, curling around Blackbeard as he grappled to free himself. Fresh spines and thorns arose and pierced his garments, anchoring themselves in his flesh.

For an instant, I was gripped by an impulse to leave him to his fate. It was the end I had hoped for from the start, since he'd taken my ship and convinced my own crew to turn against me.

And yet, I found myself running to his aid, hacking with my saber at the half-dead thing on the ground. Soon enough, it gave way.

Blackbeard, meanwhile, strained within the other demon's embrace. It continued to stretch around him, bones knitting a barbed cage as its horned skull craned back out of the way of his fevered head butts.

I slashed at its throat, taking the top head clean off--but the cage did not let go. The middle head was the vulnerable one, but it was pressed against Blackbeard, and I couldn't reach it.

Then, suddenly, a blaze of red light flared between them. The demon howled and shuddered, and Blackbeard burst free of the skeletal trap, sending fragments of bone flying everywhere.

But that was not the biggest surprise. I was far more stunned by what I saw before he pulled his tattered jacket closed to cover his exposed chest.

For there, over his breastbone, was a second head.

It was more like a face, not a fully formed skull as had jutted out of those demons. And it had two eyes, not just one--but those eyes both glowed with red light.

I sucked in my breath and backed away from him. He glared at me as he wrapped the coat tighter around himself.

"Into the pit with you." He gestured toward the hole the men had been digging.

I kept backing away. Did he intend to kill me?

Blackbeard rolled his eyes. "We're *both* going in. The beasties killed our diggers. We need to bring up the chest ourselves."

He stormed toward the pit, but I hung back. After all I'd seen, did I dare trust him?

"Get in the damn *hole*," he snapped. "Unless you *want* to stay out here alone and wait for more of those things."

He had a point. Swallowing hard, I slid my saber into its scabbard and followed him down into the ground.

After digging out the chest and hauling it to the beach, we rowed our skiff by moonlight toward the *Queen Anne's Revenge* and the *Adventure*.

At first, Blackbeard just glowered at his end of the boat, saying nothing. But after a while, my own stare seemed to wear him down.

"When I was a younger man," he said, "after sailing aboard a privateer's vessel in Queen Anne's War, I settled on an island in the Bahamas. It was called Shark Cay."

I frowned. "I haven't heard of it."

Blackbeard offered no comment. "I had a wife and two children there. Two splendid little boys." He pulled back on the oars, pushing the skiff forward. "I was happy."

Happy? I tried to imagine it. I'd seen him furious, vengeful, bitter, distant, and brutal, but never happy.

"Then, one night, *they* came." He bobbed his head toward Ocracoke, toward the demons. "They emerged from the heart of a raging storm, swirling with red, yellow, orange, blue, and black lightning. They swooped down out of a doorway in the sky in flying boats and landed on Shark Cay, which they laid waste to." Leaning forward, he met my gaze with eyes afire. "When they were done, I was the only living thing left on the island." His voice was like ice. "Perhaps this is why you have not heard of Shark Cay before."

I rowed my own oars a few strokes before daring to speak. "And you?"

Blackbeard sighed. "They took me with them. Back through the doorway." He gazed up at the stars. "They took me to the strangest place you can imagine. The skies were green, the sun was blue. Sounds were like smells, and tastes were like touches. There were beasties everywhere, some like the ones we just fought and some more terrifying still."

"It sounds like Hell," I told him.

"That's what I thought at first, but no. It was *another world*." He kept looking upward.

I nodded silently. If not for the battle we'd just been through on Ocracoke, I would have thought him insane.

"They...changed me. They thought I could be of use to them." He looked at me and sneered darkly. "They could not have been more wrong."

"You escaped."

Blackbeard smiled grimly. "They sent me back to do their dirty work, but I broke free. I've been waging war against them ever since, using the tools they gave me." He stopped rowing and patted his chest, where the second head glowed faintly under his coat. "I can *feel* them coming. I *know* what they want."

"How is that possible?"

"They *think* with one *mind*." He tapped his forehead with his finger. "I hear *echoes* and *whispers* enough to piece together their *plans*."

I stopped rowing too, then. "Which are?"

"The end of us all, Stede Bonnet." Blackbeard scowled. "Every man and woman on the face of the Earth."

I sat silently for a long moment, watching him. His words

sounded mad. I could not help but think that they were ample fuel for the mutiny I'd been organizing.

Yet how could I dismiss them after what we'd been through? "Armageddon?" I said. "When? How?"

"Very soon, Bonnet." Blackbeard closed his eyes. He'd woven fuses into his shaggy black hair, and the tips of them started to glow and burn as if someone had taken a match to them. "We won't have much time."

"Time for what?" I asked. "What do we have to do?"

His eyes shot open and the lit fuses flared. "Save the world, of course."

We set sail the next morning for Hispaniola to rendezvous with the rest of our pirate fleet--eight ships strong, counting the *Queen Anne's Revenge* and the *Adventure*.

The sun was shining bright, the wind gusting strong. We sailed in a southeasterly direction, making excellent speed over choppy sapphire seas.

Salt spray misted over me as I paced the deck, watching the horizons through my spyglass. As I walked, the events of the night before replayed in my mind. In retrospect, they seemed like an opium dream, wholly unreal. Had *any* of it actually happened? Or was *I* the one who'd gone mad, not Edward?

Just as I considered this possibility, I heard his familiar heavy footsteps clomping toward me. Turning, I saw him in glory restored--red velvet coat, black trousers and knee-high boots. Under the coat, as was his habit, he wore a white shirt with prominent ruffles from throat to waist. Already, his bandoliers were in place, plugged with six loaded pistols, and his cutlass was sheathed in the scabbard swinging at his left hip.

"'Morning, Stede." He stomped up beside me and leaned his elbows on the port bulwark rail. "You're looking in the wrong place."

"Am I now?" I tried sounding glib, but I was having trouble standing so close to him. Now that I knew what lay under his shirt, he seemed more fearsome than ever to me.

Blackbeard raised a finger to the sky. "Our next attack will come from up there. Especially now, as we cruise the waters between Bermuda and Hispaniola."

I looked up, shading my eyes against the sun. "And why is that?"

"This is where their doorways open," said Blackbeard. "In this wedge of deep ocean where Mother Nature lets down her guard." He smacked his palm on the bulwark. "The walls are thin here, Stede."

A chill shot along my spine. "Will they come for us, Edward? Are they on their way?"

He shrugged his broad shoulders. "I feel nothing, but they surprise me sometimes. We'll keep the crew on round-the-clock watch for just such an occurrence." Narrowing his eyes, he clamped a hand on my upper arm. "Now come along. I have a task for you as well."

He took me below decks, to a corner of the hold that was under watch by three armed guards. They were three of his most loyal men; I'd never dared approach them while recruiting for my mutiny.

"Here we are." Blackbeard spread his arms before the five wooden chests stacked in front of us. "Finer treasures no man has ever beheld."

I took off my hat and stood beside him. "What is this task you have for me?"

Blackbeard reached for a ring of keys that hung on his right hip. He singled out one cast iron key and shook it in my face. "The most important thing you have ever done and will ever do in your life."

Stomping forward, he inserted the key in the padlock on the topmost chest. He turned it, and I heard the lock snap open.

"Would you say the winds can blow us in unforeseen directions,

Stede?" he said as he unwound the chain from the chest. "That fate can lead us to places we never expected? Places we were destined to be?"

I thought of the day he first boarded my ship--*this* ship, now his. "Of course."

Blackbeard gazed at me with ferocious intensity from beneath his coal-black brows. "Then step forward, Stede."

Sweat ran down my back and sides. Had Blackbeard heard of the mutiny? Had he brought me down here to put an end to me?

"Come on now, Bonnet." He snapped his fingers.

Swallowing hard, I stepped forward.

"Do not be afraid, Stede." His words only made me *more* fearful. "This is what it has all been leading up to for you."

Then, he opened the lid of the chest.

I would have stumbled back away from it if he hadn't caught my arm and held me there. For the wooden box did not contain gold or silver or jewels, as I'd imagined.

It looked to me like a tub of guts--like someone had taken the offal from the day's catch of fish and dumped it inside.

The box was filled with glistening organs--deep red, pale gray, sickly green, onyx black. The mess *smelled* like guts, too, so rank and rotten it made me choke. I covered my nose and mouth with my hand, yet still the stench penetrated.

"Closer, Stede." Blackbeard forced me forward. "*This* is your *destiny*."

Standing so near, I realized that the guts in the chest were *still moving*--squirming and twisting before my eyes. The tip of a tentacle flicked up from the gruesome pudding, dragging a trail of slime with it. A flap of pink flesh rolled up, revealing a bloodshot eyeball the size of a breadfruit with a triangular pupil.

"*Listen* to it, Stede!" Blackbeard pressed me closer to the box. "*Hear* its voice in your *mind*."

"No, I..." Suddenly, I did hear something new. There *was* a voice--high-pitched and faint as the cry of a distant gull. It was saying something, speaking in a language I did not understand.

And though at first I thought I heard it with my ears, I quickly realized it was not reaching me that way at all. Somehow, it was *inside my head*.

"What...?" I listened, trying to pick out what it was telling me.

Then, I heard Blackbeard's gruff voice alongside it, whispering in my ear. "Put your hands in, Stede. Let it become *one* with you."

Another tentacle rose out of the mush and slithered toward me.

"Don't fight it, Stede," said Blackbeard. "This is what you must do to save us all."

He pressed me another inch forward--and then the ship lurched. A thunderous boom shuddered through the hull, as if the *Queen Anne's Revenge* had just slammed into another vessel.

"It's starting." Blackbeard shut the chest. "Our time has come."

"Time for what?" I said as we ran through the hold toward the ladders. "For me to become one with that *obscenity* back there?"

He grabbed a ladder and shot me a look. "You'll do it, Stede, or everyone you know in this world will die, and you'll be the cause of it."

The ship shook as we climbed above decks. I heard shots along the starboard bulwark, and saw the crew massed there with guns pointed down at the water.

As we hurried toward the men, an enormous green hump appeared alongside the ship, rolling forward. I quickly realized it was the back of a living creature, covered in glistening turquoise scales, cut by a red rill running along the spine.

"Sea serpent!" As the words left my lips, the creature's huge head reared up out of the water. It had the face of a dragon, with a long, reptilian snout, flared nostrils, and massive, jagged teeth. The red rill extended all the way to its forehead and stopped between its eyes, which blazed with telltale red light. "It's one of *theirs*, isn't it?"

"I was wrong about the next attack coming from above!" Black-beard dashed for the cannons, waving his cutlass overhead. "We must blow this thing to kingdom come!"

By the time we got to the five starboard cannons, the men had already loaded them. Matches burned in hand...but no fuses had been lit.

"We can't get a bead on it!" said one of the gunners. "Damn thing's too fast!"

As he spoke, the serpent dove into the water and disappeared. Seconds later, the ship lurched as the thing struck us from below.

Blackbeard grabbed the gunner's arm and shook him hard. "Get ready! You'll have your moment!" Then he released him and closed his eyes. The fuses woven through his hair began to glow and spark.

When the men hesitated, I stalked among them, bellowing. "You heard him! Get ready to point the damn guns! Matches at the ready, you bastards!"

As the men scrambled to prepare, the ship rocked once more and settled. I heard the sound of something huge emerging from the water.

"There it is!" somebody shouted.

"Light the guns!" I told them.

As matches touched fuses all down the line, the serpent's giant skull burst up before us. Like a snake charmed by a swami, it slid up above the bulwark and stopped, eyes locked on Blackbeard.

We had our moment. "Fire! Fire! Fire!" As I screamed out the order, the cannons belched forth their missiles amid great gouts of brimstone smoke. Three balls crashed into the head of the monster, smashing through flesh and bone alike with a sound like thunder and splintering trees.

With an ear-splitting howl, the beast collapsed into the water and sank from sight. The ship swayed in the wake of its passing, then steadied.

At which time, Blackbeard opened his eyes. The fuses in his hair were still burning.

For a moment, I wondered if the men might rebel with no help from me--if this display of supernatural power might be enough to turn them against him out of sheer terror.

Instead, they cheered him. He swung his cutlass overhead, and they cheered as one, not a shirker among them.

"The battle is begun!" he roared. "Who will join me in tearing the enemy's *throat* out with my *teeth?*"

Every man on the deck cried out in fervent assent.

"Then hoist the mainsail! Best speed to Hispaniola!"

We encountered no further sea monsters on the way to Hispaniola. Blackbeard said the demons weren't strong enough to fill the seas with them...yet.

We met up with the rest of the fleet at Port-au-Prince. It was then I realized that our force had more than doubled in size.

Instead of eight vessels, there were now sixteen, all heavily armed and sailing under black flags. By bribe or coercion, I know not which, Blackbeard had enlisted powerful pirate captains as allies in our war: Calico Jack Rackham, Charles Vane, Robert Deal, Israel Hands.

Blackbeard gave each of them a chest--myself as well--and instructions. Each captain would sail out to a different location along the rim of the Gulf of Mexico, taking along a second ship for support.

On the map, our destinations ringed the Gulf. When Blackbeard connected them with straight lines, they formed the points of a mystic pentagram star straddling the oblong sea.

"When the moment comes, open your chest," said Blackbeard. "The thing inside is your salvation. You must unite with it. Allow it to work through you."

I scowled as I stared at my own chest on the deck at my feet. I wanted nothing to do with its gruesome occupant.

"How will we know when the moment arrives?" said Calico Jack.

"Believe me, you'll know." Blackbeard stared at each of us in turn. "The bottom of the sea will rise and blot out the sun."

"These...things." Vane tapped his chest with the tip of his cutlass. "What exactly will they *do?*"

"The same thing all at once," said Blackbeard. "And this miracle will save us all, so long as no man refrains from his duty." He stomped his boot and glared at us. "So if doubts you have, speak up now!"

Not a one of us said a word.

Six days later, as Blackbeard predicted, the battle is in full swing. Did the other ships make it to their positions? I have no way of knowing, and no time to worry about it.

My crew and I are too busy fighting to defend the good ship *Adventure*--first against a flying silver disk, and now against the twenty wedges that the disk has split itself into.

The men fire their guns at the darting wedges, but they're no match for the deadly red beams that lance down to destroy them.

The wedges make several runs along the length of our vessel-- and then they stop and hover, ringing the deck. Doors open in the bellies of each of them, and skeletal, three-headed demons burst forth, screeching and brandishing fiery swords.

"Fight to the last man!" I howl as one of the demons scrambles toward me. "Aim for their middle heads!"

I follow my own advice, unleashing a shot at the red-eyed skull sticking out of my attacker's chest. My aim is dead-on; the head explodes, and the demon tumbles to the deck.

Heart hammering, I risk a look across the water at Blackbeard's ship--and what I see isn't good. The *Queen Anne's Revenge* is listing hard to port and giving off smoke. The triangular craft they've been fighting continues to batter the ship with fusillades of crimson beams.

How much longer can either ship hold out? When will the moment come--the one Blackbeard told us to expect?

As I think these thoughts, another demon bolts toward me. I run straight for it, slashing my saber at its chest...and the blade hacks through the bony middle head. The demon staggers back, clutching the cloven skull, and then it wails like a banshee and charges me again. I sidestep, barely, and the demon tumbles over the bulwark and into the sea.

That's when it happens.

I hear a thunderous rumbling from all directions. The gulf begins to churn and buck. Mighty swells toss the *Adventure* like a child's paper boat.

I see the *Queen Anne's Revenge* sway too, rolling violently from side to side. Whatever's happening, both ships are caught in its grip.

Suddenly, I see a vast, flat surface break the waves some five leagues hence. The sun glints on its silver skin as it rises from the deep.

I cannot see the far end of it. This thing, this *platform* is so massive, it extends beyond the horizon.

All along the curved edge, the sea pours off it in a wall of foaming white. The loudest roar I've ever heard booms across the gulf, like the sound of a thousand waterfalls crashing together all at once.

As the platform continues to rise, the *Adventure* and *Queen Anne's Revenge* are swept forward, drawn by the pull of a vast whirlpool swirling beneath it. I shout the order to drop anchor, but no one hears me over the rush of the falling water or the ongoing battle with the demons--guns blasting, swords clanging against bone.

As the monstrous object climbs higher, darkness washes over the *Adventure*. The sun has been blotted out.

The moment Blackbeard predicted has arrived. I know what I have to do.

Running to a nearby locker, I throw open the door and haul out the chest he gave me. Then I lift the lid and gaze upon the pulsating mass of organs and slime within.

How do I *do* this? How do I *become one* with this squirming, rancid sludge?

Suddenly, the darkness brightens. Looking up, I see red lights flaring to life in patterns along the underside of the vast platform. The light forms spirals, interlocking circles, rows of bars, clusters of pinpoints. It blinks and shifts and slides and spins, changing faster with each passing second.

As if the platform, whatever it might be, is awakening.

Just then, the ship lurches hard to starboard, and the chest starts to slide. I lunge to catch it--and my fingers touch the contents.

Without warning, the voice I heard in the hold pours into my head. At first, it still speaks a foreign tongue--but then, it becomes the King's English.

Not that I comprehend every word. *Do you wish to initiate the electromagnetic pulse?* That's what it says to me, in a woman's soothing voice.

What the hell is that? The thought comes to me unbidden...but it gets an answer.

The pulse will deactivate the World Machine, says the voice. *It will destroy all onboard systems permanently.*

Another question comes to me. *World Machine?*

The platform before you, says the voice. *It was sent here millions of years ago to reshape this hostile environment into one more suitable. It crashed, and remained ever since at the bottom of the impact crater, which became a sea.*

It was sent here from where? I ask.

Another world, says the voice. *The people there have been trying to reactivate it ever since. They created portals but could only come through a few at a time. They sent organic machines, like me...but we have been reprogrammed by Edward Teach. We stand ready to deliver an electromagnetic pulse that will destroy the World Machine's systems. We await your order.*

I hesitate. *What if I don't give it?*

All life on your world will be extinguished. And the purpose of your own existence will be unfulfilled.

Purpose?

You were chosen for this moment, says the voice. *Everything that Edward Teach has done to you was designed to lead you to this task. You are one of the few humans equipped to interface with our technology.*

The ship rolls and pitches. I suppose I should feel special now...grateful. I guess I should look at Blackbeard with new eyes.

But instead, I feel angrier than ever. I feel used.

All this time, he's been playing me for a fool, manipulating me because...why? Did he not imagine I'd agree to help save the world? Could he not have just *asked* me?

Suddenly, a thought flashes through my mind. *All this power. Could I use it to destroy Edward Teach instead?*

Yes, says the voice. *I can short-circuit the electrical impulses in his brain. However, I will not then be able to initiate the electromagnetic pulse that deactivates the World Machine.*

For so long, I've loathed that man. I've wanted nothing more than to destroy him and take back what's mine. Now, at last, I have the means.

But can I bring myself to do it at such a cost? Do I have hatred enough in my heart that I'd let the world perish for the sake of revenge against one man?

The lights on the underside of the platform flicker faster. A roaring tone, like the blare of a million foghorns, resonates outward, causing the decking under my feet to tremble. The *Adventure* and *Queen Anne's Revenge* rush closer to the whirlpool.

The voice speaks to me again. *Do you wish to initiate the electromagnetic pulse? Or do you wish to kill Edward Teach?*

I sink my hands deeper into the muck in the chest. I feel tentacles wrap around me, suckers attach to my flesh.

I'm becoming one with the organic machine. I know, without asking, that I have scant seconds to issue a command.

But I have to be honest. Right up till the end, I'm not sure what that command will be.

"Stede?"

I wake from a deep, dark sleep to the sound of his voice. To the rough grasp of his hand shaking my shoulder.

Blackbeard.

He chuckles and shakes me again. "Still alive, I see."

Much to my surprise, I am--and so is he. For that's the decision I made: to sacrifice my vengeance and save mankind.

Now look where it's got me. Washed up on the sand of an unknown shore like a tangle of flotsam--the pieces of a shattered ship washed up around me.

As I roll over and sit up, I see a section of prow on the sand twenty yards away. I can make out part of a name on the broken boards: ADVENT.

So this is what's left of the *Adventure*, the ship under my command. When the platform shut down and plunged back into the sea, tidal waves tossed her through the gulf and smashed her to bits here. It's a miracle I survived.

And more of a miracle that *his* ship survived. Gazing out at the now-becalmed waters, I see the *Queen Anne's Revenge* floating under a pristine red and orange sunset, heavily damaged but intact.

"Fine work, my friend." Blackbeard sits beside me, his glittering eyes taking in the sunset. "You, and Vane and Deal and Israel and Calico Jack...you saved us all." He laughs deep in his barrel chest, like a bear growling over a salmon. "A bunch of filthy pirates saved the world. How do you like *that* irony?"

"You son of a bitch." I shake my head. "How did you save the *Revenge*?"

He slaps me on the back so hard it hurts. "It's the *Queen Anne's Revenge*, Stede. I thought we'd settled that."

My eyes drift over her half-furled sails, glowing red in the light of sunset. My heart pounds at the sight of her masts, her guns, her softly curved hull--the dark-haired maiden carved in teak on her prow.

Nothing is settled. The only way it would have been is if the world had ended.

"How right you are." I elbow him in the side as hard as I can...wondering, at the same time, which men survived among the crew and if I can turn them to my mutinous cause.

Blackbeard pulls out a flask and takes a sip. "Beautiful evening, ain't it, ya' scurvy dog?"

I take the flask and raise it in a toast before I drink. "'Tis a shame it must be ruined by a scabby bilge rat like you."

A MAZE THAT IS A GREAT WHITE BULL

From the window of the helicopter, Andrea Tosca looked down at the vast stretch of red sand and gravel plain. She was amazed at the sheer nothingness of that expanse as it rolled off toward the horizon—especially because she knew what lay beneath it.

The very thought of it made her heart beat faster. She had traveled halfway around the world, and now she was here, with everything she had spent years searching for spread out below.

All she had to do was step through the door.

The pilot landed near a complex of khaki tents at the edge of a rectangular excavation. Red dust kicked everywhere from the whirling blades of the chopper, and personnel on the ground held on to their hats to keep from losing them.

"Thanks." Andrea had the door open before the skids had even touched down.

"Geez, hold on, lady," snapped the pilot.

But Andrea had already waited twenty-five years.

She grabbed her bags from behind the seat and jumped out, her gray-streaked, black hair flying in a nimbus around her head. It was the first time her feet had touched down in the Namib desert, the first time she had been in that sunbaked corner of southwest Africa.

But *not* the first time she had been to the site she had come to see.

A tall young Black man in an olive drab t-shirt and khaki pants approached her, waving in welcome. He was saying something, but she couldn't hear him over the noise from the helicopter's blades.

"Dr. Tosca." He reached for a handshake when they were close enough to communicate. "Good of you to come."

"Thank you for having me, Dr. Shilongo."

"Call me David." His smile was small, his accent the local *Afrikaans,* his manner reserved. "And I guess I should actually say, welcome back."

"Apparently," said Andrea. "As incredible as it seems."

"Yes." David nodded. "That is *one* word for it."

Dr. Shilongo wasted no time leading her into the biggest tent, and she was grateful. Being so close to what she'd come to see, she couldn't stand any further delays.

"Be it ever so humble." David spread his arms, taking in the cluttered contents of the tent. Every square foot was occupied by piles of gear, cartons of supplies, and folding tables overflowing with maps, books, microscopes, artifacts, and laptop computers.

"So this is where the magic happens." Andrea put her bags down and looked around admiringly, feeling right at home. "This is where you found what I lost."

"I hesitate to be definitive, given the level of sheer impossibility involved," said David. "But yes. It appears that's what we've done."

How many times had Andrea shaken her head in disbelief over the past two weeks since learning what had happened here? Yet she did it again, as sincerely as ever.

"Would you like coffee? Tea, perhaps?" David lifted a silver electric kettle from a table heaped with papers, chisels, brushes, and assorted mugs.

Andrea wanted only what she'd come for. "Show me," she said. "I want to see it now."

He looked like he might brew a beverage anyway, but then he put down the kettle. "All right." He crossed the tent to the least cluttered table, one with a beige drop cloth draped over some kind of low, large object. "Without further ado, then."

Clearing his throat, he took hold of one corner of the cloth, then whisked it away with a small flourish.

"Dear God." Andrea moved in close, her hands clasped at her chest. "That's it. That's perfect."

"Thank you." He took a little bow. "It's amazing what you can do with a 3-D printer these days."

The object on the table was a plastic model of what she'd come to see. Between her photographic memory and a lifetime of study, she knew its every convolution well enough to know, at a glance, that it had been reproduced in flawless detail.

"The Mithraic Maze." Reaching out, she lightly touched the thing, running her fingertips over the top edges of the walls. "Just as I remember it from the Po Valley 25 years ago."

"Except now," said David, pointing at the ground beneath their feet, "it is right here."

Fingers still touching the model, Andrea looked down with wonder. Could it be? She had already studied the data, gone over the images with a fine-toothed comb. She had already determined from afar that the findings of Dr. Shilongo and his team were valid. Otherwise, she never would have traveled the 8,000-plus miles from Austin, Texas to this desolate place.

But it was still so incredible, she was having a hard time wrapping her head around it. A big part of her, the part that was rooted only in science and its methods, simply couldn't believe it at all.

Because believing this meant believing in something that had nothing whatsoever to do with science.

"The ground-penetrating radar traced every pathway," said David. "Every unique characteristic. And they all matched up without fail. They all aligned precisely with your original measurements."

"And the beacon." Andrea's fingers shook as she ran them along the channels of the model. "After all these years."

"It is still sending out its signal," said David. "Every hour on the hour, in case there was any doubt."

"It's the same structure." said Andrea. "Right down to the tiniest flaw."

"It's the same maze you found 25 years ago," said David. "The *exact* same maze. Only it's *moved.*"

Andrea's hushed voice was almost a whisper. "From the Po Valley in Italy to the African Namib."

"More than 7,000 miles," said David. "And you, who discovered it the first time, have a second chance to unravel its mysteries."

Andrea stood at the edge of the dig, gazing down at the door in the earth.

It lay flat at the bottom of the pit that the team of archaeologists had dug—a metal door cast with a familiar image. In a square plaque occupying the middle section of the face of the door, a man was depicted cutting the throat of a bull, one knee braced against the great beast's heaving flank.

She knew it well, the casting on the door. It had haunted her dreams for 25 years.

"The tauroctony." She nodded as she stared. "The god Mithras killing the mighty white bull."

"The central icon of the Mithraic cult, yes," said David. "And the divine patron of this maze."

He led her down rough steps dug into the stone corner of the pit, moving with great care. With each step closer she came to that door, her heart beat faster, and her hands shook harder.

"Remarkable, no?" David stood at the foot of the door, hands clasped behind his back. "It looks no more aged or weathered than in the photos from your expedition."

"No one has been inside?" Andrea felt nervous, as if this were all a dream that might be suddenly snatched away. "That hasn't changed since your last communiqué?"

"We have kept armed guards in place at all times." David gestured at a man standing above them on the edge of the pit, brandishing an AK-47 rifle. "No *human* has crossed that threshold."

"What about the robot drone you sent in?" asked Andrea.

"It crossed the antechamber, which is rather nondescript. Then it ceased transmitting. It is dead, as far as we can tell."

Andrea crouched and ran her fingers over the edge of the door. Its metal was warm to the touch from the blazing heat of the midday Namib desert sun.

"I'm ready," she said. "I'm ready to go in."

"I had a feeling you'd say that." David smiled. "Why do you think the door is shut?"

"So open it," said Andrea. "Before it moves somewhere else and it takes another 25 years to find it."

"Nobody wants *that*." David chuckled good-naturedly.

"It happened once, that we know about," said Andrea. "Who's to say it won't happen again?"

"And what if it travels while you're inside? Have you wondered what will happen to you?"

She hadn't. All she had thought about since getting the news of this discovery was getting to it as fast as possible—that, and the face that haunted her mind's eye, growing clearer with each passing moment.

A face she hadn't seen for 25 years.

"One way or another, I'm going in." She pressed her palms hard against the door, cementing her claim. "I won't miss this."

"Don't worry, you won't," said David. "But there are protocols. We need to make sure you and your team are fully prepared."

Team? She glared up over her shoulder at him.

"You lost a man last time," said David. "Let's see if we can avoid any casualties *this* time."

Andrea marched through the desert that night, heading in the opposite direction from the dig. Even there, she knew the Mithraic Maze was just underfoot; as charted by the ground-penetrating radar, it fanned out for miles below the surface, just as it had in the Po Valley.

The expedition was leaving in the morning, organized by Dr. Shilongo...but Andrea did not want to wait. She just wanted to open that door right now and submerge herself in those long-sealed passageways—though the guards at the dig would never let her through. She knew because she'd already tried bribing every one of them.

Denied entry for now, she'd gone wandering through the red sands and gravel, wishing the ground would open up and take her directly into the maze. Given what the thing had done already, moving itself halfway around the world, was that really so impossible?

She'd even recited prayers to Mithras, though they were all of her own invention. The secrets of that ancient god were lost to history, the catechisms of his mystery cult erased and long forgotten. Hints yet survived—artifacts and occasional references in ancient texts—but no one knew just what it all meant.

That was one of the reasons there had been so much excitement over the discovery of the Mithraic Maze 30 years ago. Surely, in such a complex dedicated to Mithras, there would be evidence of the full breadth of his faith.

At least, that had been the expectation. The reality had been quite different.

Stopping, Andrea trained the beam of her flashlight on the sandy ground at her feet—seeing through, in her imagination, to the convoluted warrens of the maze under the surface. She remembered the gray walls, blank except for the occasional single-character hieroglyphic—none of it enough to tell any kind of story. She remembered how frustrating it had been, staring at those almost-empty surfaces, longing for some kind of illumination to shed light on mysteries as old as Ancient Greece.

Were they still as blank as they once were? If she could see down into them right now, would she still see the same absence of knowledge? Would the maze be as empty as she'd left it, occupied only by one lone figure? One lone man who'd stayed behind 25 years ago?

Part of her dreaded finding what was left of him...while another part held out hope against all sense that he had somehow survived. It was that part, the one that stubbornly clung to magical thinking, that had driven her here most fiercely.

Though given what the maze had accomplished so far, was that thinking so magical after all?

Suddenly, the ground trembled underfoot. The tremor was slight and brief—but it was enough to make her panic.

She whirled, looking back at the dig for signs of chaos...and there were none. Guards still paced the perimeter with rifles at the ready, and the lights around the pit remained steady.

If the ground had moved because the maze was taking flight, no one had noticed yet.

"No, please." Andrea fell to her knees, pawing at the sand. "Not yet. Don't go yet."

Again, the ground trembled slightly.

"O' Mithras, I beg you," said Andrea. "I've waited so long! I've come so far! Please don't deny me the chance to do what I've come here to do!"

Finally, the ground remained still.

"Thank you!" Andrea's voice was wracked with sobs. "Thank you, blessed Mithras, thank you for your benevolence!"

Stars winked above her in the velvety black sky as her tears dripped into the sand. Whatever was present in the halls of the maze below her, it gave no sign.

Early the next day, Andrea watched from the rim of the dig as three laborers set up a winch. With the morning sun flashing over the horizon, they spread the device's three legs so they straddled the door, then hooked the cable to the iron hoop of the handle and secured it.

Andrea's heart raced at the sight. The moment she'd been waiting for was fast approaching.

"Ready to go?" David strolled over from the tents, hands curled around the straps of the black backpack he wore.

Andrea wore identical gear—a black backpack, a white mining helmet with an LED lamp, a reflective silver body suit, and hiking boots. So did the other two members of the team, a young male grad student named Umberto and a young blonde woman named Greta.

As far as Andrea knew, however, none of them had a certain special surprise tucked away on their person except her. None of them could have even known they would need it.

"Yes, I'm ready," she said calmly.

With that, David leaned over the edge of the pit and shouted. "Raise it!"

The laborers did as he instructed, cranking the handle of the winch. The cord pulled taut, then hauled the door up by its metal hoop handle, opening a gap several feet high from the jamb in the red dust ground.

Andrea inhaled deeply, as if she could breathe the escaping ancient atmosphere all the way from the rim of the dig.

As she stood there, peering down into the darkness of the gap, she felt David's hand on her shoulder.

"Are you all right?" he asked softly.

"Yes." She nodded firmly. "Why wouldn't I be?"

"The last time you were in there, you were the only one who got out again," said David. "Dr. Clifton didn't make it."

"That was a long time ago," said Andrea. "I'll be fine."

"Seriously, my friend." David gave her shoulder a squeeze. "You don't have to go through with this. My team and I are perfectly capable of obtaining the intelligence you seek."

"This is *my* place. This is *my* day." She shrugged off his hand. "You would quite literally have to *kill* me to keep me from going inside."

"But it's been a quarter-century since you were inside the maze," said David.

"That's where you're wrong." She leaned toward him, staring grimly. "I *never left.*"

How much alcohol would it take to make her forget about losing Edward Clifton in the Mithraic Maze? Ten years after the incident, Andrea was still doing her damnedest to find out.

"Nope." She drained the last of a bottle of whiskey and tossed it off the balcony of her condo in Austin, Texas. "Still there." The shatter when it hit the parking lot three floors below was deeply satisfying.

The ring of her phone was somewhat less so. Contact with the outside world was not something she desired very much in those days.

Grabbing the phone from the little round table beside her, she opened the line. "Hello?" Booze and smokes had turned her voice to a croak, and she lit another one to show how little she cared.

"Dr. Tosca?" The voice on the line was that of a young woman. "This is Kelly Sandoval at Random Awk Publishing. Have you finished the manuscript yet?"

It took everything Andrea had not to hang up the phone on the spot. She was sorry she'd agreed to write the book about the maze. She just wanted to be done with it, done with everything.

"Are you still there?" asked Kelly.

"I quit." Andrea leaned forward and reached for the fresh bottle of whiskey lined up on the balcony's railing.

"You can't quit, you have a contract," snapped Kelly. "And you're already three months late on delivery."

"Who cares?" Andrea's head was swimming. She thought she might be sick very soon. "Get him to write it for you. Edward Clifton."

"Believe me, I would if I could," said Kelly. "Only nobody knows where he is, which is one of the mysteries of the vanishing maze of Mithras."

"There's another one?" Andrea felt a rush of loopy excitement. "Where is it? Tell me so I can write a book about it, too!"

"See, we're going in circles again." Kelly sighed with disgust and impatience. "Are you sure you're the one who got out of that place?"

Andrea stood, gazing down at the alleyway below. If she threw herself over the railing, would that finally do it? Would it finally set her free?

Because Kelly was right, she was lost.

She had been that way for the past ten years, wondering what had happened to Edward and why she had been the one to escape. Was he still alive somewhere? Would she ever see him again, the man she had loved more than life itself? Would she ever complete the unfinished business he had left behind ten years ago?

Day after day, she went over the same questions again and again, following the same well-worn paths. Wondering if every balcony or whiskey bottle or speeding car might be the exit she sought. Wondering if one last turn might bring her face to face with him again.

Instead of back to where she'd started when she'd last seen him, that singular moment ten long years ago when she had made the biggest mistake of her life.

That was something she would never write in any book. Her failure to act was what had left him lost in his maze, and correcting that failure was the only way she might ever get out of hers.

Hot wind scoured the pit dug into the Namib, whipping dust devils of red sand around the open doorway.

When the team had crossed the dig, David half-bowed and gestured for Andrea to take the lead. *After you.*

Shoulders back and head held high, she gladly marched to the head of the group. The moment she had waited 25 years for had finally arrived.

She paused for only an instant at the threshold, reveling in her long-awaited position—wondering what she would find beyond the front door. Then, she turned and stepped down onto the first rung of the ladder inside.

It creaked but held her weight as well as it had the first time she'd descended it. Bracing herself first on the door frame, then the sides of the ladder, she climbed down into the darkness without looking back.

Near the bottom, she switched on her helmet lamp. It lit up a circular patch on the floor, thick with gray dust. As soon as her feet touched it, they sent up glittering swirls of the stuff.

"Come on down!" she shouted up at the bright polygon of light at the top of the ladder. "All clear!"

As the next teammate followed, she walked further into the antechamber. The space, lit by her helmet lamp, was just as she remembered—a square, high-ceilinged room with scant inscriptions on the walls at eye level.

Walking to her right, she took a long look at the inscription there, thinking back to her visit 25 years ago. Eyes narrowed, she moved to the wall at her left and likewise scanned its inscription...then moved one more to her left and stopped there.

She pressed elements of the hieroglyphs in a sequence she remembered from a long time ago. Then, as she took a step back, the inscription glowed white, and the wall rumbled. It suddenly dropped away, revealing a doorway into the darkened maze.

As she peered inside, her helmet lamp lighting a cone of darkness, it took all her willpower not to charge in by herself. The smell of the stale air was like sweet perfume, summoning her to proceed alone.

She did do one thing that was against protocol, however. Before her teammates touched down at the base of the ladder, she leaned into the blackness and called out in a loud whisper.

"Edward?" she said, as if there were any chance at all he might somehow be alive in there. "Dr. Clifton?"

If anyone (or *anything*) heard her on the other side, they gave no sign.

Instinctively, she said a quiet prayer to Mithras—the bull-slayer, the god without a catechism, the patron of the maze—to aid her in her quest.

No sooner had the prayer left her lips than David stepped up beside her. He flicked on his helmet lamp, and its light joined her own in the shadows beyond the threshold.

"The hairs on the back of my neck are standing up," he told her. "I feel like someone's watching us from in there."

"You never know," said Andrea. "If we *do* come across anyone, it goes without saying that you should leave the interaction to me, yes?"

"You think you'll fare any better than the rest of us?" asked David. "Wouldn't you say there must have been a *reason* this thing left you behind the first time?"

"Let's go find out." With that, she adjusted the pack on her back, flicked on the walk-talkie radio strapped to her shoulder, and pointed her helmet cam straight ahead into the blackness. "Let's see what the old place has to say for itself."

Without further ado, she marched over the threshold, plunging into the darkness en route to the truth she had sought for so long.

Running. Panting. Sweating.

The last time Andrea had entered the maze had been at full tilt, arms and legs pumping so hard they were nearly out of control.

Helmet lamp flickering, she'd bolted through the passages like a madwoman, hell-bent on reaching the core. For she had only just realized that something was about to change in a big way...that quakes were building in the Po Valley, and the whole structure might be about to collapse in on itself.

Her second realization—that Edward Clifton had gone inside alone—had sent her racing into the underground complex. If Edward was in there when the walls fell, she would never see him alive again.

And that was unacceptable.

"Edward!" As she'd hurtled through the passageways, the tremors had intensified, driving her onward. Her thoughts had grown wild with worry, her focus

confused. If she hadn't known the map of the maze by heart, she never would have had any hope of getting through it and finding him.

Then, suddenly, the floor had lurched, and the walls had shifted around her. The path had changed, blocking her previous progress, shunting her into a pattern she no longer recognized.

Lost. She had no longer had any clue where she was going.

Not only had the layout dramatically altered, but the walls themselves had changed their appearance. It was as if, when they'd shifted, they'd exposed another side—a side covered with tile mosaics instead of plain gray plaster with scant hieroglyphs carved here and there.

In her confused and reckless flight, she had glimpsed scenes one after another in those mosaics—Mithras being born from a rock, Mithras slaying the white bull, Mithras dining with Sol Invictus (a man with a sun for a head). The images had flown past so fast that she had only gotten impressions of them, flashes of key details dancing past her eyes.

Then, darting around a corner, she had rammed into something standing in front of her—something flesh and blood—and had cried out in surprise.

It had taken only a split-second for her to realize it wasn't Edward. Stumbling back away from it, she had seen it had the body of a man...but that was where the resemblance to a person had ended.

It had been naked, covered with downy fur the color of light brown beach sand—and topped with the head of a lion. Something had been draped around its throat and shoulders, like a stole.

Or a snake. Its head had flicked around suddenly, and its jaws had snapped wide open, fangs dripping with glistening venom in the light of her helmet.

At which point, Andrea had run back the way she'd come, hearing the footsteps of the lion-beast padding swiftly after her in the darkness.

"Fascinating," said David, his face glowing in the light from his phone. "No surprises whatsoever."

Andrea frowned, annoyed at the interruption. "What?"

"Every turn you've made has aligned perfectly with the app." David pointed at the screen of his phone. "We developed it to map the layout of the maze, based on the data from the ground-pene-trating radar. So far, it has been *totally* right on the *nose*."

"Okay." Andrea had zero interest in the app or anything other than reaching her destination. "Thanks for the update." Her voice held the slightest tinge of sarcasm.

"Ms. Tosca?" asked Umberto, the grad student, who followed with blonde Greta at his side. "Has anything visibly changed since your last visit?"

"Not in the slightest," said Andrea, though the maze was very different indeed from the last time she'd been there. The truth was, she had never told anyone about the shifting walls or tile mosaics or the lion-man or...that *other* thing. Some details, she had kept to herself all those years; to do otherwise would have risked her profes-sional reputation—or much more than that, even.

"Are you suggesting no one has been inside for 25 years?" asked Umberto. "That the maze has been sealed all that time?"

"Who knows?" Andrea paused, searching her memory for the next turn—right or left? As clearly as she remembered the layout, she sometimes had to think about some of the intersections. "Per-haps we'll find evidence to that effect."

"I wonder if it landed anywhere else between the Po Valley and the Namib," said Greta. "Maybe it remained undiscovered until now."

Just then, Andrea froze. Had she felt a tremor underfoot, or were her nerves just bad?

"What is it?" David sounded instantly concerned.

If there had been a tremor, it was gone now. "Nothing." Andrea proceeded to make a right turn, then followed a short pass that led to a left.

A little further on, Umberto started running his mouth again. "Maybe this time, we'll discover the lost keys to the Mithraic mystery religion. Wouldn't it be wonderful to uncover the actual stories and prayers after two thousand years of speculation?"

"Of course, we *do* have the Mithras Liturgy from the Greek Magical Papyri," said Greta. "The Seven Tychal virgins, the Sword of Dardanos, and all that."

"Which may or may not be apocryphal," said Umberto. "I wouldn't bet money on the relevance of that material, though, if I were..."

"Shhhh!" Suddenly, Andrea threw back a hand to silence them —and not only because she couldn't stand listening to their blabber anymore.

She thought she'd heard something up ahead, though she couldn't be sure.

"What is it?" asked David.

Andrea's only answer was another emphatic shush. Slowly then, she stepped forward, edging into a path branching off to the right.

Skritch.

There, she heard it again, from not far away. The sound of a scratch or a twitch or a shift in what should have been dead stillness and silence.

Skritch Skritch.

Switching off her helmet light, she inched closer, listening, listening. Nothing this time except the pounding of her heart in her ears and the...

Suddenly, she heard a loud rustling noise, then a rush of rapid footsteps charging toward her. She flicked on the helmet lamp, filling the passage with light.

And saw a creature lunging toward her with the body of a man and the head of a lion, *roaring* like a jungle cat about to seize its helpless prey between razor-sharp teeth.

"Edward!" On that day 25 years ago, Andrea had run frantically through the corridors of the maze, her footing unsteady as the ground continued to tremble.

She'd taken as many sharp turns as possible, hoping to elude her pursuer...afraid to look over her shoulder in case the lion man with the snake was close behind and about to pounce.

She was running randomly now, utterly lost since the walls had changed formation. She no longer had any clue how to get to the core or anywhere else.

As if her situation wasn't bad enough already, the walls had started shifting again, swinging and sliding to redirect her route. As the landscape changed around her, she kept moving, terrified she might end up boxed in, unable to escape.

She paused for breath at an intersection, just for a moment—until she heard a booming roar that could only belong to the lion man on her trail. It didn't sound far away.

On the verge of blind panic, Andrea picked a direction to run and was about to launch herself onto that path—but then a sound from another direction got her attention.

Without hesitation, she spun and charged that way. She had no choice after hearing that sound...that voice, calling out a single word she could not ignore.

"Andrea!"

That voice, the voice of the man she'd run into the maze to find—the voice of Edward Clifton.

Andrea ran back the way she'd come, then suddenly sprinted left, changing course away from her teammates.

Running as hard as she could, she followed the bobbing light of her helmet lamp through what was otherwise pitch darkness. Her mind was in turmoil, but she was still well oriented, able to navigate the passages without completely losing track of her position.

She cut right, then left, then right again, evading the beast in pursuit. Every change of direction brought her closer to her destination, the center of the maze. What she was going to do when she got there, she didn't know, but she had no intention of going anywhere else.

The beast roared in frustration behind her. Sometimes, it sounded close enough to snag her with a fang; other times, it fell away and lost ground, getting caught in the wrong passage when she made an abrupt shift.

Somewhere in the distance, she heard David shouting for her, but she paid him no mind. Eluding the beast and reaching the core were the only things that mattered now.

Suddenly, the ground shook again, harder than ever. Andrea nearly fell but kept her footing and barely slowed.

But the latest tremor signaled a familiar change in the maze. The walls shifted and swung, grinding on ancient tracks in the floor. They turned their nondescript gray faces away, again revealing the colorful mosaics mounted on their opposite sides.

As Andrea ran, she saw Mithras on a mountain, Mithras in the sea, Mithras in the chariot of the sun. Some, she remembered vividly from her flight through the maze 25 years ago. Others were new to her, representing scenes from the Mithras legend that she had never known of until now.

As the walls had rearranged themselves, Andrea lost her bearings. She tried to keep running in what she thought was the right direction, but all she could really manage was to stay ahead of the lion-man.

Soon enough, she was utterly lost. Despite all her study and planning, everything had turned random again.

She wondered if it was all some kind of test. Maybe, if she turned and fought the lion-man, she could alter the outcome. It wasn't like she hadn't come prepared.

Just as she considered that move, she heard a familiar voice from not far away. It was a voice from out of the distant past, and it made her neck hairs stand on end with a wave of déjà vu.

She stopped in her tracks, zeroed in on the voice, and hastily doubled back, then bolted down a passage on her left. The beast stayed on her original course, however, running past the leftward turn she'd taken.

Again, Andrea heard the voice she knew so well, and again she changed direction, jolting right. She hung a quick left after that, then another—and suddenly slammed to a halt.

A bright light flared to life, illuminating the circular space in which she found herself. The light was coming from a man with a sun for a head, standing at the far side of the room.

But that wasn't what drew her attention most. Instead, her eyes locked on the man standing in the middle of the space—the dark-haired man dressed in the garb of Mithras, looking not a single day older than he had 25 years ago.

"Andrea!" he said, his face lighting with a smile of pure delight. "You found me!"

"Hello, Edward." Her heart hammered, and adrenaline blazed through her bloodstream. "It's wonderful to see you again."

Twenty-five years ago, Andrea had found Edward in much the same way—after ducking around corners on the run from the lion-man, following Edward's voice into the heart of the maze.

The man with the sun for a head, Sol Invictus, had lit up the circular room so she could clearly see Edward in all his glory, attired as the mystery god Mithras. He wore a pale green Grecian tunic and gold leggings, a bright carmine cape and matching Phrygian cap—a Persian-style hat with a single peak that drooped like the bud of a flower toward his forehead.

"Hello, my darling." The outfit, along with his curly black hair and deep tan, made him look much like the carvings and mosaics of Mithras from ancient times. It was a startling and unexpected thing to see.

But what worried her most was the figure of Sol Invictus in the corner and the lion-man charging through the maze somewhere behind her. What kind of bizarre magic had they stumbled into here?

Was this what had changed things between them? Did it even matter anymore?

"What's happening here, Edward?" she'd asked, doing her best to stay calm in the face of so many unknowns.

"A little active archaeology, sweetheart." He'd chuckled knowingly. "What better way to learn the secrets of Mithras than to become Mithras?"

She had nodded with feigned interest, hoping he didn't notice how forced her smile was. "How exactly did you manage this...transformation?"

"The maze took care of it," he'd told her. "It turns out the whole purpose of the thing is to resurrect the Mithraic archetype—to bring a new Mithras into the world when the world has fully forgotten the tenets of the original faith."

"And it told you all this, I suppose?" asked Andrea.

"It told me everything." *He'd stepped toward her, spreading his arms wide. "And I, in turn, will tell* you."

"Wonderful." Beaming, she had pushed aside her worries and embraced him. The man she'd fallen in love with at the start of the Po Valley dig two years ago, the man who'd miraculously absorbed the essence of the very mysteries they'd tirelessly sought together.

How she'd loved him, those nights in the tent, those days in the dig. How perfectly they'd fit together from the start, becoming their own transmutation of selves in much the same way as he and the maze of Mithras had done.

They'd been perfect together, so perfect. Their love had swept them along on a current of exotic mystery...at least until the final mystery had come along, the one she'd finally solved.

The one that had brought her here to this moment, wrapped in his arms.

"I love you, darling Andrea," he had said grandly. "You shall be my priestess, the shepherdess ushering new believers into the faith."

She had pressed herself against him, feeling the warmth of his familiar body and remembering what it had felt like just two nights ago.

Then, she had smiled up at him in his drooping red cap. And her hand had touched his face, then moved lower...and lower still...

Two nights ago, and not for the first time, Edward had landed a heavy punch in her belly. She had doubled over and stumbled backward, head spinning from the pain.

Insult after insult, threat after threat had flown from his lips. Again and again, he had hauled off and let her have it in every possible way, laying her bare before him.

How could she have been so stupid, thinking he had been a better man? And how could she have been so meek, letting him tear into her the way that he did?

Because none of this was for the first time. And to someone like her, with a photographic memory, the first time was as immediate as the last.

And the second, and the third, and the fourth, and the fifth.

The board of directors was going to take away his funding. The journal was going to kill his article on the find. His rival was going to steal his thunder and discredit him. These were the reasons he gave for flying into his rages the way he did...and none of them were enough.

Neither were the heartfelt apologies that came later, the lavishing of attention and gifts and hollow promises—anything to keep her from fighting back or leaving.

And she had stayed because of the dig, because of the mystery, because of her own deep feelings of worthlessness. An educated woman at the top of her game had let it happen.

At least until that final mystery she'd solved, the one that had changed everything for her.

Two days later, in the heart of the maze, her hand had dropped lower, lower...until it had found the hilt of the blade in the sheath at her hip, tucked under the waist of her jeans.

"Great Mithras," she had said, keeping her eyes locked with his. "I will consecrate this faith with a sacrifice. And I want you to ask yourself something."

"Yes?" he had said, smiling beatifically.

She had slid the knife from its sheath slowly, silently. "Would the other woman you've been screwing, the grad student girl, be so devoted that she would spill blood in your holy name?"

With that, she wrenched the blade high, intending to stab it into his throat.

At which point, the ground had quaked hard, throwing them both to the floor. The knife had jumped from her grip and clattered across the room, coming to a rest at the feet of Sol Invictus.

Just then, the lion-man had leaped out of the maze and sprung at her, fangs bared. He had landed on his haunches before her, hands flattened on the floor, serpent twitching at his throat.

Another quake had rocked the room. The lion man had raised one hand, poised to strike her.

Then, the whole place had shaken so violently, she'd thought it might crash down around her. The lion-man had thrown back his head and roared, even as Sol Invictus had flared like a nova, blinding her.

When her sight had returned, she'd found herself lying on the ground in the Po Valley, alone. Looking around, she'd realized that the dig at the entrance to the maze had collapsed.

And, later, she'd discovered that the maze itself was gone.

Twenty-five years had passed since the day the maze had vanished. Twenty-five years since Andrea had failed to kill the man she'd once loved.

The man who now stood before her, big as life, in his droopy red cap and cape, green tunic, and gold tights.

"You came back," she said calmly, though her hammering heart was anything but calm. "After all this time."

"You won't believe where I've been," he said, grinning. "I have *so* much to tell you. The maze *beyond* this maze—beyond this *world*—is so much more amazing than you can *ever* imagine."

"Wow, that's great." Andrea dropped her hands at her sides, thinking about the surprise she'd brought—the one that was especially for him, just in case he showed up. "How exciting for you."

"For *us*. For all of *humanity*." He stepped toward her, highly animated. "I bring a *new* message. A new *plan*. One that can *truly* change the world for the better. The *lost* plan of *Mithras*, reborn at last."

She listened, taking it all in. He sounded insane...either that, or enlightened. Where *had* he been? What had he experienced?

What if he was *right?*

"It all begins with forgiveness." He reached out, smiling, drawing closer with each passing instant. "Forgiveness and true *remorse*." Suddenly, he fell to his knees before her. "Remorse like that which I feel for the horrible things I've done to you."

Andrea's right hand touched the butt of the pistol in the pocket of her overalls. She slid her fingers over it, grasping the warm metal between them.

"I am so sorry, my darling," he said. "For *everything.* Please, can you find it in your heart to forgive me?"

Andrea hesitated. *What if he was right?* And what if he truly felt sorry? Did such redemption justify sparing him despite all he'd done?

Did the possible salvation of the world justify foregoing her revenge?

"The maze brought me back to you," he said, still smiling. "Our reunion was preordained. We were meant to save all mankind and pave the way for a glorious new age of harmony and..."

"Take your new age and shove it up your Mithr*ass*," she said, yanking the gun out of her pocket.

Then, as she swung it up and pulled the trigger, the room rocked, and Sol Invictus flared with the light of a nova, blinding her in the staggering flash.

Days later, Dr. David Shilongo stood at the rim of what had once been an historic and extensive dig, letting the hot wind of the Namib caress his face.

"Dr. Shilongo?" Umberto walked up beside him, clipboard in hand. "Everything's packed up. We're ready to move out."

"Thank you." David nodded, staring down into the collapsed pit. "We will leave momentarily."

Umberto nodded and followed his gaze. "It's like it was never here, isn't it? Not a trace of it."

"Just the body," said Greta, who'd come over to join them. "The body of Dr. Edward Clifton, freshly shot to death."

"Looking the same age as the day he disappeared 25 years ago," added Umberto.

"Just so," said David.

The maze was gone, utterly and completely. There was no hint of it on the ground-penetrating radar or any other type of scanning system. The door at the bottom of the pit had simply vanished, as had every artifact they'd pulled out of the site.

The disappearance had happened during their expedition, when a terrible quake had shaken the area. There had been a massive underground explosion, a blast that had left the three of them unconscious.

They'd awakened, without explanation, above ground. Teammates had treated them, and in the days that followed, helped them search for traces of the Mithraic Maze.

But their search had been in vain. The maze had simply vanished. It had moved on.

Just like 25 years ago in the Po Valley.

"Where do you think it went this time?" asked Umberto.

"And what about Andrea?" asked Greta. "Dr. Tosca? Do you think she went with it? Or is she still buried down there somewhere?"

David shrugged. "It's a mystery," he said, and then he turned from the dig site and headed for the convoy of trucks waiting to roll off over the vast red sand plain.

Somewhere else...

The lone figure clad in a green tunic, gold stockings, and a carmine cap and cape stalks through a cave on the trail of a great white bull.

Knife at the ready, eyes glittering in the darkness, the red-capped figure prepares to strike, reenacting the great hunt at the heart of the Mithras mystery. In seconds, the hunt will be over, and blood will run freely over the floor of the cave, lapped up by a man with the head of a lion, or is that a lion with the body of a man?

But the truth is, the cave is death, and the bull is the universe. The knife is knowledge, the seconds are eternity, and the lion-man/man-lion is destiny. The hunt is the cycle of existence, and the red-capped hunter, slashing the pale throat of the struggling, exhausted bull...the red-capped hunter slaughtering the bull to serve at a banquet that will surely please the life-giving sun god Sol Invictus in hopes of changing the rules for kith and kin forever...

The red-capped hunter is Mithras, who is also Dr. Andrea Tosca, who is also you.

And for her, it is enough to know the secrets. It is enough to become the secrets.

It is enough to add to the secrets with secrets of her own...his own...your own.

And, perhaps one day, she/he/you will emerge from the maze, or better said, emerge into another maze within a maze within a maze that's greater still. A maze that is a universe.

A universe that is a great white bull.

FUZZY DUCK

When they yank the hood from my head, I'm struck by how clean and sweet the air smells. I had forgotten, though I used to spend all kinds of time here back in the day. Back when I was the honest-to-God Secret King of the World, that is.

I stand for a moment with my eyes shut, drinking it in, savoring each crystal pure breath. If I didn't know better, I might think I'm in a mountain meadow on a beautiful Spring day. Not in a bar in a secret retreat that's at once the most powerful, luxurious, and corrupt places on Earth in the 21st Century.

Not in Xanadu, where the people who *really* run the world come to play and prey away from prying eyes.

"Mr. Nothing?" A short, middle-aged Chinese man in a dark suit steps in front of me. "Right this way, please."

As he leads me away from the goons who brought me in--a South African and a Russian with matching mouthfuls of gold teeth--I have a look around at the old familiar place. It all looks exactly the same as it did twelve years ago, when they fired my ass from the shadow government they call Apogee.

The room is enormous and designed with Olympus in mind,

from the towering Corinthian pillars to the Roman god statuary and brightly colored tile mosaics straight out of Pompeii. All the walls, floors, and furniture are built or carved from various shades of marble, dark as well as light and everything in between.

Elegant tapestries surround secluded niches overflowing with jewel-encrusted relics and satin pillows. Exotic gardens twined with fat jungle flowers and glistening green vines occupy raised circular beds situated under skylights. Fountains and little waterfalls burble everywhere.

The few patrons at this hour (Early morning? No idea.) stare back at me from couches in the shadows, sipping from golden goblets. I recognize one of these people instantly, then another. They are leftovers from my era, survivors of the terrible events that swept me from my throne forever.

Peering into a darkened alcove, I see another...and wish I hadn't. His name is Phineas Castor, and he looks every bit the brute and pervert I remember from my years on the throne. Some people were more responsible than others for my downfall, and that sick bastard was one of them.

He waggles his fingers in an mocking little wave as I go by, then returns his attention to the leather-clad boy at his side.

The next face I see is my own, reflected in an ornate gold-framed mirror occupying a wall that we pass. This place might not have changed much, but *I* have. I was forty-seven years old when I left, with an ever-present bronze tan, thick brown hair, straight back, and a fit, slender build. Twelve years later, I have the build of a couch potato or barfly--flabby and pale, with a soccer ball of a pot belly. My posture is slightly stooped, and my hair is gray, thin, and as shaggy as the veil of a weeping willow tree. My green eyes have perpetual wrinkles and bags, and the goatee I've taken to wearing is patchy and unevenly trimmed.

My footsteps echo in the cavernous chamber as my Chinese guide leads me on among the niches, booths, and gardens toward the answers that await. I still have no idea why the powers that be brought me here. They didn't tell me or ask my permission; they didn't have to.

My guide stops and points at an arched doorway. He provides no further explanation, and I don't ask.

My hackles rise as I walk past the Chinese man and through the archway. I find myself in one of the many private party rooms branching off from the main chamber. Looking around, I see signs of a struggle--broken glass, overturned furniture, scattered cigarette butts and drug paraphernalia. But none of that is the main attraction.

The most interesting thing is on the far side of the room: a man's body sprawled on the floor, stripped to the waist, motionless. A tall woman stands over him, scribbling notes in a small pad...and shooting me a stern look as soon as she becomes aware of my presence.

"Come in. Don't be afraid." Her voice has all the warmth of an ice storm in deepest winter. Her face, with its gray-eyed solemnness and high, chiseled cheekbones under a platinum blonde crewcut, intensifies the chill. "I'll protect you."

It's a cut, a jab, a gloat. She's one of the people responsible for exiling me in the first place. "What makes you say that?" I ask calmly.

"It's open season on kings of the world, obviously." The woman, Gerta Andersen, gestures off-handedly at the dead man on the floor at her feet. "Though I suppose you don't really count anymore, do you?"

I take a step closer for a better look at the body. I didn't recognize him at first, but now I see who he really is: King Prospero III, my successor.

"You see, everything worked out for the best." Gerta lifts one silver eyebrow. "If not for your downfall, that would have been *you* on the floor instead of him."

"His chest." I step closer, taking care not to disrupt any of the scattered debris. "Something's written there?"

"In blood, yes." Gerta tucks the note pad in the vest pocket of her black suit jacket. "What do you think it means?"

Two more steps bring me close enough to see over the debris and read the words on his chest. *Does he fuck?* That's what it says.

I shrug and look up to meet Gerta's gaze. "Why am I here? What do you want from me?"

"You're a private detective now, aren't you?" She spreads her arms wide. "So crack the case."

She's right, it's what I do. Turns out I have a knack for it. Stumbled into my first job not long after the exile and built a business from there.

Not that *this* is a case I would *ever* in my right mind take. "Don't need the work, thanks," I tell her. "Send me home."

"He's the *king of the world!*" She smirks like a boa constrictor ready to coil around me. "Aren't you even a *little* curious?"

"Not a bit." I turn and start working my way back to the doorway.

"What if it meant a chance to redeem yourself?" asks Gerta. "A chance to clear your name."

"You mean you'll give me my throne back?" I already know what the answer will be, and I keep heading for the door.

"Yes. You can have it back."

I was wrong, and I stop in my tracks. "You people would never do that."

"Try us," says Gerta.

I know better than to trust her. But what she's telling me is so unbelievable, I can't ignore it. "If I solve this murder, I become king of the world again? Just like that?"

"Yes." She nods.

"Seriously?"

She nods again. "For one day."

I knew it. The men and women of Apogee would *never* restore me to the throne.

But even the one-day offer is tempting. Thoughts of what I could do with 24 hours of absolute power flood my head.

"Will you call me by my real name, at least?" I ask. "If I agree to work the case?"

"Absolutely not." Her sharp-edged ruby lips curl in a sneer of disgust. "You'll always be Mr. Nothing to me."

I shake my head. She hasn't changed. But her current motives are still murky. "Why me? Why bring me in on this?"

"Your investigation skills," says Gerta. "And your unique perspective as an exile. You're an outsider, which brings a certain objectivity...yet you were on the inside once."

"You and your team couldn't solve this?"

"We weren't given much time." Gerta's eyes flash. "We were told to send for you almost right away. Meanwhile, we processed the crime scene and canvassed for witnesses but didn't come up with anything."

I'd wondered about that. They must have sent the collection detail to pick me up almost immediately after the king's death. Probably kept the room on ice to preserve the evidence, too. Extreme climate control is available in every part of Xanadu, after all, to cater to the most extreme and depraved tastes.

"So what's your decision?" Gerta sounds as if her patience has run out. "Man up or wuss out?"

I look at Prospero on the floor. My bullshit detector is going off like you wouldn't believe. I think it's possible that I might end up dead on the floor like Prospero, if things don't work out.

But then there's that king-for-a-day reward, which is probably bullshit...but maybe not. Most of all, there's one force in play that has a strong hold on me, though it has gotten me in trouble more times than I can tell.

Curiosity. It might be the death of me yet.

Until then, let's see where it leads. "Okay," I say finally. "Tell me what you know."

When Gerta's done talking, I spend some time alone with the body. I look for clues, anything that might inspire me now or later.

The cause of death, according to Gerta, was suffocation. Murder by pillow, to be exact. Though it would have taken someone physically powerful to hold Prospero down for long. The dead king is no small man; he's heavyset with a ponderous gut, but plenty of muscle mass beefing up his arms and legs. He would've put up a hell of a fight.

Which is exactly what happened, judging from the state of the private party room. Prospero fought back; the smashed glass and furniture is covered with his fingerprints. But there's no sign of anyone else's prints anywhere in the room.

And there's no other kind of trace in here, either. Gerta's forensics team has combed every millimeter of the place and found nothing but Prospero's DNA. The evidence says no one else was in this room during the murder.

Which is exactly what everyone in Xanadu says, too. No one was in here with Prospero that night, and no one saw anyone enter or leave. It was a busy night, the place was packed, yet nobody saw anything. The king of the world was murdered in cold blood in a side room of the most crowded bar in Xanadu, and nobody knows how it happened.

Which, incidentally, is total bullshit, but who can blame them? Everything is permitted in this secret pleasure dome, nothing is forbidden--except the murder of an Apogee VIP. Anyone found guilty of such a crime will be executed in a way you don't want to know about...*trust* me.

So back to the evidence, or lack thereof. *Does he fuck?* is scrawled on the victim's bare chest in his own blood. Some kind of condemnation? The suggestion of a sexual indiscretion? Everyone in Xanadu is a philanderer, no form of sex is forbidden--but jealousy can be a powerful thing. Maybe this was a crime of passion.

There's precious little else to go on. No trace of sexual activity on the body or in the room. No sign of poison in his bloodwork--just the usual booze and recreational drugs. No recordings, as this is a private room and he was the *king of the world.*

"The king is dead," says Gerta when she strolls back into the room. "Long live the *ex*-king."

"Poor son of a bitch." I stand and peel off the latex gloves I've been wearing. "Is he the first king to die in office like this?"

Gerta nods. "Hey, and *you're* the first to be dethroned and exiled! The two of you have something in common after all!"

Without answering, I head for the door. "Go ahead and get this mess cleaned up."

She falls in step beside me. "Where do you think you're going?"

"To sniff around. Talk to some folks. It's called investigation."

"Here in the bar, you mean?"

"Nope." I walk fast between the tables, gardens, and alcoves, aiming for the nearest door that leads to the corridors of Xanadu.

But when I get there, my gold-toothed Russian and South African friends step in to block the shit out of me.

"You can't go out there," says Gerta. "You're *persona non grata* in Xanadu."

I turn on her, mad enough to spit bullets. "I thought you wanted me to work on this *case.*"

"In *here.*" Gerta sweeps an arm around to encompass the bar. "Think of it as your headquarters."

"You have *got* to be *shitting* me."

"The good news is, unlimited drinks!" Gerta smiles and pats me on the shoulder.

As a recovering alcoholic and drug addict--three years clean and counting--this doesn't impress me. "I can't do the *job* sitting around a *bar.* I need to *circulate.*"

Gerta just shakes her head. "Not going to happen. Once an exiled traitor, always an exiled traitor."

For a moment, I think about rushing the two thugs and trying to fight my way through the door. But what would that prove, assuming I make it without taking *too* big an ass-kicking?

"Fine." I glare at both guards in turn, then Gerta. "So what say we quit pissing around and get some people in here to interview? If not eyewitnesses, at least people with some kind of motive and opportunity."

"Good plan." Gerta smirks. "Considering you have less than two days to slap a bow on this."

I stare at her like she just grew a horn out of her forehead.

"What?" She says it like I'm the biggest idiot who ever lived. "You think they'll let you stay here for the *coronation* of the *new king?*"

The man sitting across from me in my makeshift office in a booth at the bar looks like he just ate something rancid. His long, bony face is drawn down in a look of deep disgust, his sullen gray eyes staring sourly at me. Hard to believe he was once one of my staunchest supporters.

Good thing I don't let backstabbers bring me down anymore. "So you're telling me your alibi for the king's murder...is another murder?" I say it as pleasantly as possible.

Basque Almondine nods once. Hard to believe, back in the day, he was one of the funniest guys around.

"You were in your private rooms, killing a slave boy from the pits?" I ask him.

He holds up two fingers. Then a third. "More than one." His voice, with its indeterminate Southern European accent, is a hiss.

Then he smiles, and I want to be sick. I was once part of this fucked up culture, *king* of this twisted domain...but it still turns my stomach. I'm a different man now.

None of which changes the fact that technically, what he's telling me he did is perfectly acceptable. He hasn't broken a single law. Remember: killing an Apogee VIP is the *only* crime in Xanadu.

"You cost me a great deal of money. Did you know that?" Basque sneers and pokes a bony finger at me. "There was a pool after you left. I bet good money that you'd kill yourself within a week of your forced retirement."

"Did you have money on when *Prospero* would die?" I lean my elbows on the table and lock my gaze with his. "You were his biggest rival, weren't you?"

"We weren't *lovers*, if that's what you mean. But I would *never* kill a fellow member of Apogee. It's against the *law.*" He leans closer, and his parchment lips spread wide in a Venus flytrap grin.

"Speaking of which, *you're* not Apogee anymore, *are* you, old friend?"

Don't remind me. The pressure from the target on my back is impossible to ignore.

"Well, this has been special." Basque pushes his chair back, plants his knuckles on the table, and pushes himself to his feet. "I wish we had more time, but I have chores that won't wait another minute." He turns away, then sneers over his shoulder. "And by *chores*, I mean *murders*. Care to join me?"

"I'm busy." I drop my eyes to the list of interviews in front of me.

"Shame. I'll be sure to kill one for you, how's that?" Slowly, he raises a hand with two fingers erect. "Or more than one."

He raises a third finger, then a fourth, before shuffling his way out the door.

By the time I get through ten more interviews, with each subject more despicable and less helpful than the last, I'm ready for a smoke. (I don't count cigarettes when I talk about being clean for three years.) I'm also ready for some fresh air, so I go outside though I don't have to; there's no law against smoking indoors here, after all.

My guard detail walks out with me into the tropical sunshine, but the guys at least have the decency to give me a little space while still keeping me on a short leash. They wait by the door, keeping their eyes peeled for tomfoolery, while I light a smoke and walk a few yards away to the edge of a cliff overlooking the ocean.

I couldn't jump if I wanted to; there's a dome over Xanadu. But being the butt of so much undisguised loathing from my intervie-wees--and former subjects--makes me wish I could fly away.

"Excuse me?" My thoughts are interrupted by a woman's voice. "Nathan?"

I turn to see a face from the past approaching through the trees--but she's not scowling or sneering like the others.

417

"Hello." I manage a little smile.

So does she. "Long time no see."

"Much too long, Erin." I hold out my hand, the one without a cigarette, for a shake.

Erin ignores it. Instead, she throws herself forward and wraps her arms around me.

I wish I had a dozen flowers to give her. A dozen flowers for every second of that embrace.

Back by the door to the bar, the Russian and South African look ready to intervene...but I shake my head hard, and that keeps them at bay for now.

"I never thought I'd see you again." She whispers the words against my chest.

I flick away the cigarette and kiss the top of her head. "Same here."

If I could have taken one person with me into exile twelve years ago, it would have been Erin. In all of Xanadu, she was my truest friend, my most unflagging supporter. She stood by me right up till the end.

I can only imagine how hard that must have made it for her when I was cast out, and she was prevented from leaving with me.

Correction. I think I see traces of how hard it must have been. There are long-healed scars on her neck and shoulders, snaking out from the collar and short sleeves of her simple navy blue dress.

"What did they do to you, Erin?" No one's supposed to call her by her real name, which was stripped from her when she was abducted and thrown in the slave pits of Xanadu. But she told *me* her name and story, and I repaid her trust by lifting her into a better life as my assistant.

"That's not important right now." She lowers her voice. "They tried to keep me away from you, but I called in favors. I had to tell you the real reason you're here."

"What is it?" I lean closer.

"They think there's a conspiracy to bring you back to power," says Erin. "They think you planned the whole murder, and your supporters carried it out."

I shake my head, watching as the guards finally start toward us. "I had nothing to do with it."

"Which doesn't mean *somebody* didn't plan it that way." Erin hears the guards approach and grabs my wrists. "Someone *might* have brought you here to make you king again, whether you know it or not."

"Being king again is the *last* thing I'd want." I meet her gaze, ignoring the guards for one more moment. "Being with *you* is the first."

"Which would only make a damn bit of difference if either of us were free." Erin hops up to kiss me on my cheek. "*Be careful,*" she whispers.

And then she's gone, darting off along the cliff's edge and into the forest.

One by one, the slaves of Apogee filter into the bar, eyes down and hands folded in front of them. The men and women come to me in all skin colors, hair colors, eye colors, shapes, and sizes. They all have different QR codes tattooed on their left biceps, indicating their owners and medical histories. They couldn't be more different, though they all wear identical electronic shock collars, gray smocks, and black sandals.

To the VIPs of Apogee, they are property. To me, they are potentially a source of vital information.

After what Erin told me on the cliff, I knew I had to try something extreme, and I thought this might work.

If I can get them to talk.

That won't happen if a single VIP remains in the bar, so I shoo out the management and customers, even my guard detail...though Gerta drags her feet.

"Please leave," I tell her, pointing at the door. "And remember, you promised no recording."

"They're not your allies." She looks around with amusement at the downward-staring slaves. "And they *won't* do your bidding. You're as low on the totem pole as *they* are."

I see that as a blessing, not a curse. Maybe it will even help me solve this case. No Apogee VIP will tell me anything useful; maybe a slave will volunteer something.

"Maybe we should gas the whole lot of them and start over." Gerta finally heads for the door. "There's always more where *they* came from."

She storms out, leaving me standing among the ranks of the unfortunate. They are the missing, the castoffs, the forgotten from all over the world, scooped up like stray pets and broken to serve the sick whims of the men and women of Apogee.

"Hello, everyone." I stand in the middle of the room, and they slouch in a listless circle around me. "I come here seeking your help."

None of them looks at me, but all of them listen.

"Apogee is not in this room. They are not watching or listening." I spread my arms wide, then lower them to press my hands to my chest. "And I, as many of you know, am an exile, without power. I *swear*, I will not betray your confidence."

A few of them look up without raising their heads.

"I hope you will help me. I hope you will tell me what you know about the murder of King Prospero."

Some of the slaves shuffle and stir. The sound of their movements echoes through the room.

"None of you are suspects," I tell them. "According to the data in your collars and internal chips, you were all elsewhere at the time of the murder. But perhaps someone among you has heard or seen something that will help me find the killer."

Dozens of faces rise to look at me. Their expressions are uniformly dark. No one steps forward or raises a hand.

I start to question the wisdom of bringing them here like this. I thought that maybe, the strength of numbers and absence of Apogee might make them feel safe enough to tell me something that might turn into a lead.

But maybe they don't believe they're truly safe. I know *I* wouldn't.

More moments pass in total silence. Finally, I take a deep breath and say the only thing that seems to have a place here. The only thing that doesn't feel like total bullshit.

"I'm sorry." Another deep breath. "I'm sorry for everything I did to you when I was king. I'm sorry I never set you free." Another breath. "I've come to see how wrong I was."

The faces around me look just as grim as ever.

"Thank you for your time." The crowd parts as I start toward the exit, reaching into my pocket for a cigarette.

Then, a child steps in front of me.

He's Indian, perhaps 12 years old, with light brown skin and short black hair. "I will show you how to play a game," he says softly.

"A game?"

He points at the bar. "We will need beer."

I look up and see the adults watching closely, impassively. But no one steps forward to shut this down.

"Okay then." I nod, wondering what this has to do with the murder.

"The winner dies," says the boy as he walks toward the bar.

"Then that makes him the loser, doesn't it?"

The boy shakes his head. "The *loser* is the slave who sees it happen." He looks back over his shoulder with all the severity of a soldier in a war zone. "The loser is my *sister*."

That evening, the bar comes alive with a different kind of crowd. The slaves cleared out long ago, making way for a mob of revelers celebrating the holiday of Coronation Eve.

By six o'clock, the place is packed from end to end with Apogee VIPs, all of them dressed in colorful, dazzling outfits festooned with feathers, fur, and fortunes in glittering, gleaming jewelry. They've all come together to mark the occasion of a new king's ascension.

Is the new king a suspect in the murder of Prospero III? I thought so for a time; he certainly has a strong enough motive and ample power. But that was before I played the game with the slave boy (who says his name, which he's not allowed to have, is Dev. Now I know better than to blame the incoming king.

Now I know exactly who killed Prospero, and I'm about to reveal it.

"Buy you a drink?" Gerta sidles up to me on the dais in the middle of the room, where I've been observing the incoming guests. "Name your poison."

I don't dignify the offer with a reaction. "I need you to do me a favor," I say, keeping my eye on the door leading in from the halls of Xanadu.

Gerta smirks. "Barking out orders? You must've spent too much time with your slave buddies this afternoon."

More guests pour in through the door--but not the one I'm waiting for. "I need you to lock this place down on my signal."

Gerta laughs. "Now you really *are* tripping, Mr. Nothing. You expect me to *lock down* this bar with every high-ranking VIP in Xanadu inside?"

"If you want Prospero's *murder* solved, I do." Just then, I see the person I've been looking for enter the room. "And I expect you to do it *now.*"

Gerta glares at me. "*What* did you just say to me?"

I whirl on her. "Do you *want* to fuck this up? Or do you think you might *possibly* benefit from *cooperating* with me for a few minutes?"

"You know who did it? *Tell* me."

No way in hell will I back down at this point. I want *credit* for my work. "Lock it down. Do it now."

A moment crawls past. Then she folds. "You're unprotected, remember? Fuck this up, and you're dead."

"Just do it." I step away from her, watching as my target advances across the room.

Gerta storms off the dais and snarls orders at her security men. I watch as they fan out through the room, bunching up at the exit doors with weapons drawn.

I give the bar manager a prearranged signal, and he shuts off the music. Earlier, he gave me a wireless microphone, and I pull it out of my pocket and switch it on.

"Ladies and gentlemen! May I have your attention?" Elevated two feet from ground level on the dais, I'm able to make myself seen above the crowd. "Please, I need your attention!"

I hear plenty of grumbles and growls of irritation, mixed with boos and hisses of outright contempt.

When most of the crowd is looking my way, I continue. "Recently, your king was struck down by a cold-blooded killer. An *unknown* killer." I look at one face in particular. "Unknown *until now*."

"There have been many theories about this murder," I tell the crowd. "Some say Prospero was killed to bring a new king to the throne...or bring back an *old* king."

The room roars with catcalls.

"These theories could not be further from the truth!" I raise my voice to overpower the catcalling horde. "The reason for the murder was far more mundane. The killer was *not* a once *or* future king. But he *is* in this room right now!"

The crowd roars with outrage. I wait it out just long enough, then shout into the mic.

"I will now show you *why* and *how* King Prospero was murdered!"

There's chatter and scuffling as I gesture at a nearby, curtained-off booth. The black curtain parts, and Dev the slave boy walks out, carrying two mugs of water. He looks glum and a little scared as he approaches and steps onto the dais beside me.

I take one of the mugs from Dev with a reassuring smile.

"There is a game," I tell the crowd. "Perhaps you've played it yourselves. The goal is to repeat a set of simple words without making a mistake. Every time you make a mistake, you have to take a drink of beer--which increases the chance that you'll make another mistake and have to drink more beer, and so on.

"Allow us to demonstrate." I stand at one side of the dais, and Dev stands at the other. "Fuzzy duck." I say it loudly.

"Fuzzy duck," says Dev.

"Fuzzy duck," I say again.

"Duck fuzzy!" says Dev.

"There!" I look out over the crowd. "He made a mistake, and the game changes. Now I repeat after him, and he after me, until another mistake is made." I turn back to Dev. "Duck fuzzy!"

"Duck fuzzy!" says Dev.

"Fuzzy duck!" Again, I turn to the crowd. "Another mistake, you see? So now, we'll repeat the changed phrase until *another* mistake is made. But because of this particular arrangement of vocal sounds and the effects of alcohol consumption, it becomes increasingly likely that sooner or later, a player will say something *very* different. Go ahead, Dev."

"Fuzzy duck," he says.

"Duck fuzzy," I tell him.

"Duck fuzzy," says Dev.

And then I pause just a second for dramatic effect. "*Does he fuck.*"

At this point, the crowd is dead silent. I think I have their attention now.

"Those are the exact words that were scrawled on the chest of Prospero the night he was murdered!" I shout it like a preacher condemning a congregation. "They told us exactly *why* Prospero was killed, but we didn't see it until *today.* He was *murdered* because he *won* a drinking game, and his opponent was the ultimate *sore loser.*

"This child confirms it!" I gesture at Dev. "His *sister*, the only witness, *told* him who the perpetrator was, right before she was killed to keep her quiet. All trace of her presence was erased from the crime scene by the killer.

"And now, on the eve of the new king's coronation, I stand before you to reveal the killer's identity. His name is..."

Just then, I hear a loud crack from the crowd--the thunderclap of a gunshot. I duck, taking Dev down with me, as a second shot fires.

The crowd cries out and scatters. There's a third gunshot. I roll

Dev off the dais so he can hide behind it, then scramble to my knees and then my feet.

Before a fourth shot can be fired, I launch myself off the dais toward the shooter. I come down on top of him, knocking him back to the floor.

Heart hammering, I seize the wrist of his gun hand and slam it down hard, knocking the weapon free. He struggles, and I pin him as best I can; I hold him down just long enough.

Long enough for my Russian and South African guards to bulldoze their way through the chaos and take over. I roll off, and they hoist the shooter from the floor like a paper doll.

That's when I finally get to look the bastard in the eye. The asshole who was so used to getting his own way that he couldn't stand losing a simple drinking game. The shithead who killed his own king, then tracked down and murdered a 15-year-old girl who walked into the room at the wrong moment, a girl who ran but couldn't hide for long from the monster's wrath.

The killer, Phineas Castor, stares back at me with nothing but contempt, as if somehow, I'm to blame for all this. His disgust is palpable as it was earlier today, when he waggled his fingers at me from his alcove as I first arrived.

"Release me!" he wails. "I'm within my rights killing the ex-king and the slave boy! Neither of them is protected by Apogee!"

I just shake my head, because he hasn't changed since he helped bring me down twelve years ago. He's just as sick as he ever was, and I'm...not.

I knew it. I *knew* the offer of being king for a day was too good to be true.

The morning after the Coronation Eve drama, I tell Gerta I'm ready for my reward now. My first act as king for a day will be to free all the slaves.

"Yeah...no." Gerta shrugs. "You didn't think we'd actually let you do anything *important*, did you?"

We're sitting at the bar, side-by-side, having drinks. Mine is non-alcoholic, of course.

"But you said I could have the throne for one day," I remind her.

"Think of it more like you get one wish," says Gerta. "A *reasonable* one."

"I think freeing the slaves of Apogee is reasonable."

"Think smaller." Gerta clinks her glass against mine. "*Much* smaller."

I take her suggestion. I consider the possibilities, think about what I want that would make all the trouble worthwhile.

Then, I tell her, and she surprises the shit out of me.

She *agrees* to it.

When the hood is yanked from my head, I instantly recognize my surroundings. I'm finally home, back in my own apartment in Brooklyn.

I smell the mustiness and hear the traffic noise outside. I see my humble furnishings arranged in the tiny living room, from the beat-up old futon to the ancient black-and-white 19-inch tube TV on the stacked plastic milk crates.

I feel better than I have since I went back to Xanadu...especially when I realize I'm not alone.

Turning, I see two hooded figures behind me, one four feet high, the other more like five five. I yank the black cloth hoods from their heads and smile.

After Xanadu, I couldn't do everything I wanted, but I accomplished *something.* I got two people out from under the thumb of Apogee, with a promise that they will never be taken again.

"Nathan?" There are tears in Erin's eyes. "Did we really make it?"

"Yes." I nod to her, then pat the head of Dev beside her. "You're both free, and you're never going back."

With that, Erin wraps her arms around me, crying and squeezing me so tight that I almost can't breathe. Dev's crying, too, as he looks around in joyous disbelief.

And then I'm also crying, because we're together, and I'm not the man I used to be, and what's here in this room at this moment is all the kingdom I could ever want or dream of in this world.

FORCED RETIREMENT

Hericane was pursued by her murderously psychotic superhero father, Epitome, for over an hour before she finally realized that he thought he was chasing himself.

It was something he said that finally tipped her off, and it was not exactly hard to interpret. "You don't think I'll kill you because you're *me*?" he screamed as he flew after her at lightning speed. "Then you're *dead wrong!*"

This just brought up another question. Instead of asking herself, "Why is my father trying to kill me?" Hericane now wondered, "Why is my father trying to kill someone he thinks is *himself?*"

She asked herself this question as she felt Epitome's hand close around her ankle, catching her in mid-flight. As he hurled her out of the sky with a mighty swing, sending her plunging toward the city below.

It was a fall that her cape would not survive. With a great effort, Hericane managed to spin around and shoot back up, narrowly missing the lofty spire of the Scalzi Building...but an antenna on the spire snagged her white cape and ripped it from her shoulders. Not for the first time, she was glad that she had designed the cape as a tearaway piece; otherwise, it might have yanked her back to slam into the building.

The delay from such a collision would have given Epitome that one extra heartbeat he needed to catch up and pounce on her.

As powerful as she was, Hericane knew that once her father pounced on her, she might not survive for long. Hericane was easily one of the five mightiest super-powered people on Earth...but she had had a non-powered mother, so she was one generation diluted from the pure source of her father's blood. Epitome was the apex of the pyramid, the strongest of the strong, the king of the super-human gods.

And he had lost his mind. The man who had defeated such super-criminals as Heat Death, RNA, Noble Rot, and the Walking World War had fallen victim to his greatest enemy.

Alzheimer's disease.

Hericane flew as fast as she could away from the Scalzi Building and her father, though her seventeenth sense alerted her that he was following at high speed. Frantically, she tried to think of a strategy to escape him...but she drew a blank.

As often as she had succeeded in high-stress situations before, whipping the bad guys with ingenious impromptu battle plans, this time was different. This time, her opponent was her father, who was incredibly powerful even at the age of seventy-two...and even if she did come up with a plan to beat him, the last thing that she wanted to do was hurt him.

Hericane's hands were tied, while Epitome had the complete freedom of a disease which, in him, had led to something like insanity.

A sudden, sharp pain struck the middle of Hericane's back, knocking her from her beeline flight path. She recognized the effect of Epitome's "dagger eyes" power, which had already hit her at least ten times that day.

The key to neutralizing "dagger eyes," she knew, was to break out of Epitome's line of sight. Hericane did so by flashing down and hard to the left, putting a tall office building between her and her father. The pain stopped immediately.

Spotting an opportunity to escape more than just the "dagger eyes," Hericane stopped suddenly on the far side of the building and ducked back against the wall. Her costume—-a head-to-toe one-piece with chameleonic properties—immediately changed color and texture to match the brick surface against which she was flattened.

Epitome shot past in a streak of red and gold and kept going, as if Hericane were flying between the skyscrapers somewhere up ahead.

As she watched Epitome fly off, Hericane wanted to let out a big sigh of relief...but she remembered how acute his hearing was and puffed out a few tiny breaths instead.

Hericane was by no means convinced that Epitome would not see through her ruse and come back for her. Nevertheless, she took the opportunity to rest for a moment, regaining her strength while she tried to come up with a plan.

And tried not to think about her roommate, Mardi...otherwise known as the superheroine, Mardi Gras. Mardi Gras, who had taken the first hit when Epitome had blown down the wall of their apartment. Mardi Gras, last seen trapped under debris and bleeding from a head wound.

Mardi Gras, the woman Hericane loved.

Hericane's stomach twisted, and her heart hammered harder. She had to get back to Mardi fast, had to make sure that she was all right.

But before she could do that, Hericane had to stop her father. If she headed for the apartment, and Epitome followed her, she would just be endangering Mardi further. Mardi's powers enabled her to bombard people's senses with riots of noise and color and smell and texture...but indestructible, she was not.

Epitome, on the other hand, *was* indestructible. He had the strength to bench press North America, and he had hair follicles that could jump right off his body and drill through concrete or snip chromosome chains on command. He could fly like a jet fighter plane, just an eyeblink slower than Hericane in his old age. Then there was his trademark "Bonus Round," an adrenaline-burst crisis state in which he surfed the gamut of way-out powers, a new one every five seconds, as if he were surfing channels on a TV set.

With all that he had going for him, Epitome would have been unstoppable even if he had been in his right mind. Now that he had lost it to Alzheimer's—or most of it, anyway—Hericane had lost the option of talking sense into him, making him less controllable and more deadly than ever.

Epitome did not even have any weakness, other than whatever had brought on the Alzheimer's. His enemies had only ever managed to hold him at bay with threats against innocent civilians. Even if Hericane had been willing to employ such threats, she had a strong feeling that they would now be useless against her father. If he was delusional enough to try to kill his own daughter, what were the chances that he would stop his rampage to protect bystanders or hostages?

Not that he had ever seemed to care much for his daughter in the first place.

Hericane detached from the wall and decided to head for help. If she could make it to the Power Structure headquarters in nearby Paratown, the heroes stationed there would surely race to her rescue. Apparently, the heroes who were based in her own home turf of Isosceles City were all away on business or home sick in bed, as none of them had popped up to lend a hand.

Unfortunately, just as Hericane drew a bead on the route that would lead her to Paratown, she heard the telltale nails-on-a-chalk-board screech that heralded her father's approach.

The screech was a by-product of his use of certain powers simultaneously...in this case, flight and electro-breath. He had tried to have it "fixed" years ago, without success, but the truth was, it never interfered with his crimefighting.

By the time a target heard the screech, it was too late for the target to get out of the way.

This time was no exception for Hericane. Even expecting (dreading) that sound's recurrence if (when) her father figured out her ruse and doubled back for her, she still did not have time to get out of the way of the bolt of lightning bursting out of Epitome's wide-open mouth. Even possessing the gifts of super-fast reflexes and high-speed flight, she could not evade the sizzling electrical strike.

Searing current burned through her body like wildfire. Hericane stiffened and dropped like a stone, eyes fixed on the bright blue sky above her as she fell.

She saw her father plunging after her, fists bunched forward and face etched with fierce determination.

Sunlight reflected from his golden breastplate, throwing spots in Hericane's eyes. She had always thought that the breastplate had made Epitome look noble and powerful, like a Roman centurion...but now, it made him look mechanical and menacing to her.

The red fabric of Epitome's costume, which once had stretched tightly over bulging muscles, rippled in the wind over his shrunken, old man's body.

Shrunken, but nearly as powerful as ever. Nearly as deadly.

And his own daughter did not see even the faintest flicker of recognition in his eyes as he glared down at her.

Hericane soon realized that there was a positive side to Epitome's not remembering anything about her. Thanks to his memory gap, he was not prepared for the super-powered trick or two that she had up her sleeve.

Like the one that she called "the big breakup," which is what saved her life this time.

Fifty feet or so above the ground, Hericane had the presence of mind to trigger "the big breakup." In mid-fall, at the flip of a mental switch, she blew her entire body apart into its component cells. A fountain of red and pink leaped upward, streaming around and past plunging Epitome as he howled in surprise and anger.

Epitome was blinded for an instant, which was just long enough for him to crash into the street pavement below. Before he could rocket back out of the impact crater, Hericane's cells rushed back together, coalescing in their original form, and she bolted off toward Paratown.

As Hericane flashed across Isosceles City, she wondered yet again if Mardi was all right...and she dug deep for ideas on how to deal with Epitome. The only idea that kept coming back to her again and again was that Epitome would be impossible to deal with this time.

Not that that would be any different from any other time.

Hericane had only ever known him to be distant. Cold and remote. At best, he had been an unreadable, occasional presence in her life, unable or unwilling to make any but the most perfunctory connection with her.

She had guessed that it was because of her sexual preference for women, though that would only have applied to her in an obvious way since her teenage years. She did not have a similarly logical reason for why he had acted ambivalently toward her as a child.

Then again, he had not exactly been willing to make connections with anyone else, either. He had always been known as the greatest super-powered hero in the world, but he likewise had a reputation—especially in the hero community—as the unfriendliest guy in the business. He had never gone out of his way to socialize with colleagues or try to improve his image, and he had never seemed to care what anyone thought of him.

The truth was, he had never had to care. He was the mightiest man alive. No one could tell him how to act or what to do.

That was why, at first, Hericane had almost been grateful for the Alzheimer's. The intermittent memory loss of the disease's early stages had softened Epitome's sharp edges, even occasionally made him seem vulnerable. For the first time in years, he had phoned Hericane out of the blue and shown up at her apartment unexpectedly; though he had done so by mistake and had not seemed entirely certain whom he was talking to or visiting, Hericane's heart had still quickened at the sound and sight of the father who was finally turning to her in his hour of need.

Hericane had not been the only one to notice and appreciate the difference in Epitome. His super-heroic peers had noticed changes in him as well: overt friendliness; eagerness to partner with other heroes for adventures; and an unprecedented (for Epitome) willingness to let others take the lead in dangerous situations. None of this had been characteristic of the old Epitome. Behind his back, people had even joked that they had liked the new Epitome better than the old one...though some had not seen his changes as a laughing matter. Some heroes had realized early on that Alzheimer's and the mightiest man alive would be a volatile combination.

And they had turned out to be right.

Epitome had begun to have outbursts of anger in public. He had said and done inappropriate things without explanation or apology. He had begun to make mistakes, serious mistakes that would have killed civilians if not for the intervention of other superhuman heroes. Twice, he had forgotten who the bad guys were and had turned against his partners. Bedouin, Haiku, and Mr. Séance all had broken limbs to prove it.

By the time that the super community had seen enough and staged an intervention to convince Epitome to retire, it had been too late. He had become almost completely irrational. From the look on his face that day, Hericane had wondered if he had even understood a word that was said to him.

It was then that the superheroes had learned the answer to a question that they had never before thought to ask:

Who can make the most powerful man in the world retire?

Answer: Nobody but the most powerful man in the world.

Since Epitome's disappearance after the failed intervention, the superheroes had wondered what his next move would be. None of them had guessed that it would be to try to kill his daughter...and that he would seem to think, in some crazy way, that she was him.

Hericane had not guessed it, either...though, today, she had correctly predicted that she had not seen the last of him while slipping out of his crosshairs via "the big breakup." Even as she had been rocketing toward Paratown, she had known that eventually, Epitome would catch up to her again.

He did so just as Hericane crossed the city limits.

The instant she heard her father's trademark warning screech, Hericane veered hard to the left. Unfortunately, as always, hearing that screech meant that it was too late to avoid whatever attack it signaled.

This time, the attack came in the form of a nerve-wrecking synaptiquake and a two-fisted sledgehammer blow to her back. As soon as they hit, Hericane screamed in pain and shot straight down like a cannonball dropped from an airplane.

She plunged forty or fifty feet before shaking off the shock and rolling out of her fall. Swooping upward, she sprang into a fighting stance and spun around, looking for her father.

She could not see him anywhere. As she turned and scanned the heights, training all twenty-one senses on her surroundings, she wondered if Epitome had activated his Bonus Round of unpredictable powers, and one of those powers was a stealth mode.

Just as Hericane was thinking that, she felt waves of compressed air buffeting her from behind, pushed ahead of a dozen approaching, airborne objects. She whipped around in time to see twelve bricks hurtling toward her and pulverized each of them with a hyper-fast chop of her hand.

Hericane did not react quickly enough, however, to deflect or dodge the next mass to fly toward her. The bricks had been a diversion.

Epitome came next.

He blasted shoulder-first into her midsection, knocking the wind out of her and blowing her back and down. Before Hericane could catch her breath and retaliate, he slammed her at high speed against what felt like a slab of solid granite.

Then through it.

Looking out from her haze of pain, Hericane saw that Epitome had driven her through a power plant smokestack and kept on going. He was still propelling her backward, toward who knew what obstacles.

Toward who knew what pain.

"I won't let you kill me!" said Epitome. "I won't let you do what I did!"

Then, suddenly, the clear blue sky turned psychedelic.

Hericane squinted at the flashbulb bursts of light and the riotous swirls of pulsing color that bloomed all around her. A cacophony of discordant sounds, like an orchestra the size of a city tuning up all at once, exploded from nowhere at what felt like ear-bleed level.

Hericane's heart pounded, but not from shock or pain. Her heart pounded because she knew at once who was responsible for the chaos.

As Epitome let go of Hericane, snapping his eyes shut and clamping his hands over his ears to try to block the sensory assault, Hericane relaxed and let herself fall.

As she expected, Mardi Gras was there to catch her. Mardi Gras, who had let loose the storm of light and color and sound that had shaken mighty Epitome.

The instant she landed in Mardi's arms, Hericane threw her own arms around Mardi's neck and hugged her hard. The bells on Mardi's red and gold jester's costume jingled as Hericane squeezed.

"Thank God you're all right," Hericane whispered in Mardi's ear. "I was scared that he'd hurt you."

"He did," said Mardi, "but I still got your back, baby. And I got help, too. Look there."

Hericane turned and followed Mardi's gaze to a glowing disk of energy that was whirling nearby. As she watched, though the disk was flat, and no one hovered in the air behind it, a black-gloved hand punched out of the disk's center. The hand was followed by an arm strapped with timepieces from wrist to shoulder, and then a face emerged.

A face that Hericane recognized.

"Overtime!" said Hericane, watching as the familiar costumed hero slid out of the disk. The insignia on his chest was a stylized image of clockwork gears, representing his particular super-powered specialty: time travel.

When a second man began to emerge from the disk after Overtime, however, Hericane did not at first know who he was.

The newcomer was younger than she or Mardi or Overtime...in his early twenties, perhaps. He wore a gleaming white costume with ruby trim and a crimson cape.

The most striking thing about him, though, at first, was his hair. It was bright blonde, shining like spun gold, and cascaded in a perfect, smooth fall all the way to the middle of his muscular back.

"Who's he?" said Hericane, her eyes glued to the new arrival as he cleared the disk.

"A new recruit," said Mardi. "Courtesy of Overtime's latest time-chute. He's a real Epitome expert, you might say."

Hericane continued to stare at the long-haired newcomer...and then, suddenly, her attention was snatched away by a familiar blaze of pain in her side. Even as she realized what it was, she knew that there would be worse to come.

When "dagger eyes" struck, she knew that her father would not be far behind.

Sure enough, just as Hericane tried to twist away from the painful beam, Epitome flashed up from below and snatched her from Mardi's arms like a football. On his way past, Epitome cuffed Mardi on the side of the head, sending her spinning away toward the ground.

As Epitome clasped Hericane against the hard metal of his breastplate and carried her off, she hauled back one fist and hammered it into his jaw with all her strength. Epitome responded with a head butt that knocked Hericane senseless.

As Hericane struggled to regain control of herself, he raised her high overhead. He looked as if he were ready to hurl her to the ground below.

"I won't let you *kill* me!" he said, visibly shaking. "I won't let it happen again!"

Then, just as suddenly as Epitome had snatched her from Mardi, someone grabbed Hericane from Epitome.

It was the newcomer who had followed Overtime through the

chute. He flashed Hericane a blinding smile as he swept her away from her father.

Though Hericane had thought that he had looked handsome from a distance, she decided that he looked stunning up close. The smile, the bright green eyes, the creamy skin, the golden hair...all of it mingled in artful perfection, as impossibly ideal as a retouched photo or a painting.

He turned to her, and she was lost in his gaze. She was held firmly by his intense personal magnetism...and something else. Only after he had set her down on the roof of a factory where Mardi was waiting did she know what it was.

Familiarity.

The man leaped away before Hericane could say a word to him. He headed straight for Epitome, who hovered some distance away with a frown of deep confusion on his face.

"I know him from somewhere, don't I?" said Hericane.

"You might say that," said Mardi Gras.

At that moment, Hericane heard the familiar screech of her father's powers in action...and everything fell together. Her eyes widened and a chill raced up her spine as she figured out who the long-haired man really was.

Because her seventy-two-year-old father was not the one using his powers at that moment.

But the long-haired newcomer was.

"Oh my God," Hericane said in a hushed voice. "It's him."

Mardi Gras put a hand on Hericane's shoulder and squeezed gently. "Yeah, it is," she said. "We figured it was the only way."

"My father's younger self," said Hericane. "Overtime brought him from the past."

Mardi nodded solemnly. "He's the only one powerful enough to stop Epitome."

The sky flared as the young Epitome blasted his older counter-part with a bolt of electro-breath. The old man fell back fast, then caught himself and pressed forward against the crackling stream of energy.

The confused look was gone from his face, replaced by grim

determination. "How many times have I put you down today," he snarled, "and you just keep coming back for more."

Young Epitome cut off his electro-breath to answer. "This is the first time we've met," he said. "You don't remember because you're sick."

When she heard this exchange, Hericane understood another of the day's mysteries for the first time. Throughout Epitome's attacks, she had wondered why he had thought she was him...and further, why he was trying to kill her if he believed that she was him.

Now, she knew.

"He never kept pictures around the house," she said. "I never knew he looked so much like me when he was young."

"He sure did," said Mardi.

Hericane nodded slowly. "When he came after me, he didn't think I was him as he is today," she said. "He thought I was him from years ago. He remembered coming forward in time as a young man to fight himself as an old man."

"He knew this would happen all along," said Mardi, "but he ended up making it happen. By attacking us to try to head it off, he forced us to get help from the only person who could stop him."

"Himself," said Hericane.

As she and Mardi watched, old Epitome drove a fist at young Epitome's stomach, then another at his chin. Both blows glanced off seemingly without impact, as young Epitome hovered calmly in place without so much as a wince.

The next time that old Epitome took a swing, young Epitome caught his fist with one hand and held it effortlessly in place.

"Listen to me," said young Epitome. "You are sick. You need help. Let me help you."

Old Epitome struggled against his young counterpart's grip, working to free his captured hand. "You're a *liar*," he said. "You won't *help* me. I *remember* how this all *ends*."

"You have *Alzheimer's disease*," said young Epitome. "You don't know *what* you remember anymore."

"I *remember!*" said old Epitome, still straining to wrench his hand free.

Without a twitch of effort, young Epitome steadily pushed his older self's fist away from him. "You almost killed your own *daughter* because you thought she was *me!*" he said. "Still think you're in your right *mind?*"

For an instant, old Epitome looked down at Hericane and Mardi on the factory rooftop. Even from a distance, Hericane thought that she glimpsed a flicker of clarity in his eyes.

Then, it was gone, if it had ever truly been there. Old Epitome started to glow with an aura of hazy, golden light.

"No!" shouted Hericane, launching herself off the rooftop toward the action. "Don't *do* it, Dad!"

She knew exactly what that golden aura meant.

Old Epitome was not going to surrender. Instead, he was pulling out all the stops.

He was going into the Bonus Round.

So was young Epitome. With his older self activating a rapidly changing sequence of unpredictable powers, what else could he do?

For a moment, the young and old Epitomes hung in the sky, their combined auras swelling and brightening. Then, the auras shifted from gold to red, and the men exploded away from each other.

They charged back together immediately, each glowing with a different light and surging with a different power as the Bonus Round fully engulfed them.

Hericane intended to hurl herself between them and cut the battle short, but Overtime rocketed up to block her path. When Hericane tried to swerve around him, he grabbed hold of her and froze her in place with the Pause Inducer mounted in his gauntlet.

"I'm sorry," he told her. "That's a fight you don't want to be in the middle of."

Hericane wanted to correct him, tell him that she *had* to try to save her father, but she was on pause and could not speak. All that she could do was watch helplessly as the young and old manifestations of her father battered each other with a stream of destructive powers.

Both Epitomes changed powers in the blink of an eye, switching from one to the next every few seconds. It was a dizzying whirl of fire and ice and cyclones and explosions and body parts that multiplied and distended and vibrated faster than the eye could see. Even Hericane, who knew her father's abilities well, did not recognize some of the transformations and emissions on display in the heart of the duel.

One man grew to five times his original size, and the other man shot purple rays from his fingertips. Clouds of scalding steam hissed out of one man's nose, while the other man split into a dozen razor-sharp slices.

While Hericane watched, the two Epitomes flashed from nightmare vision to ink blot blasts, from plague breath to laser fists to slave rays to spike skin. Young Epitome's limbs disappeared, then punched back in from another dimension, glowing orange and seemingly detached from their owner, to pummel old Epitome from different directions. Old Epitome turned into a sheet of malleable golden metal and wrapped around young Epitome's head, sealing it in a sphere without a single opening.

Young Epitome thrashed in the air, pulling at the sphere, trying unsuccessfully to wedge his fingers between the golden skin and his throat. His body turned to rock, then steel, then ice, but he could not break open the sphere from within. He expanded and shrunk and stretched, but the sphere changed size and shape along with him.

Young Epitome wrestled with the smothering helmet for one more moment. Then, he stopped fighting it.

And became a blinding ball of energy like a new sun flaring to life in the sky.

Because Hericane was on pause and could not blink or shield her eyes, Overtime threw a hand over them to block the burst of light. When Overtime pulled his hand away, Hericane saw a single figure hovering in the sky, silhouetted against a pulsing rainbow nimbus.

For an instant, Hericane thought it was the seventy-two-year-old version of Epitome, because his hair was little more than stubble, and his costume was red with a gold breastplate instead of red and white fabric.

But as the halo faded, and the man drifted toward her, she saw that he was not the old man after all. He was not quite the same young man who had come from the past, either.

For one thing, the blinding smile was gone. "I'm so sorry," he said grimly, looking lost. He stared down at his costume, brushing it with his fingertips.

Hericane felt sick. She had always wondered how the impenetrable golden breastplate of her father's costume had been created, with its unearthly properties and unique, pebbled texture. It must have been forged in the heart of a volcano or a star, she had thought, or in another dimension where the laws of physics were different from those she knew. How else could an indestructible metal be shaped into body armor for a superhero?

Now, she knew. In addition to burning his long hair down to stubble, Young Epitome's nova blast had liquefied the metal sphere that had nearly smothered him. The metal had oozed down over his chest and adhered to his costume.

For fifty-odd years, Hericane's father had worn a costume sheathed in his own remains.

"Sorry," said young Epitome. The confusion on his face shifted to horror. Tears rolled out of both eyes. He drifted close to Hericane as if he knew her, as if she could help or reassure him in some way.

Hericane felt a mild zap like static electricity as Overtime took her off pause mode. Her body jerked as she regained the power of movement in her native time frame.

Even when she was able to move and speak again, however, she did not know what to say to young Epitome.

He continued to hover in front of her, alternately meeting her gaze and staring down at his newly minted breastplate. His expression shifted quickly, like super-powers in the Bonus Round, switching from anguish to disbelief to horrified rage to blank shock...though the overriding visible emotion was deep confusion.

"I think I owe you an apology," he said slowly, returning his gaze to Hericane. "I'm sorry for killing your father." He said it like a question, raising his voice on the last syllables.

"I only wanted to help him," said Epitome. His eyes narrowed and shunted to one side, staring into space. "I wanted to stop him from hurting people...but God knows I didn't want *this* to happen."

Tears rolled down his face, and his shoulders shuddered. He hung his head, then caught sight of the breastplate and quickly looked up again.

Hericane drifted forward and took him in her arms. She stroked the stubble on his scalp as he sobbed silently into her shoulder.

"I'm sorry he hurt you," said the man who was or had been or would be her father, trembling against her. He was younger now than she was, and she did not know him though she had known him all her life, and it was almost too strange for her to bear.

At that moment, Overtime bobbed into view behind Epitome and pointed to one of the fifty watches strapped onto his right arm. Then, he turned and waved at the rainbow disk of a newly opencd time chute spinning in midair behind him.

'Time's up,' he signaled. 'Time to send him back.'

Hericane shook her head and held on to her father.

"How can I live with this?" said Epitome. "Knowing I did this to myself? Knowing this is what's in store for me?"

"Don't close yourself off," whispered Hericane, giving him the only advice that she could think of...the advice that she had wanted to give him for decades. "Don't be afraid to reach out to other people. Maybe things will be different for you next time."

Overtime tapped Epitome on the shoulder then, and he drew back from Hericane. "I don't know if I can take that chance," he said, wiping the tears from his eyes. "I don't want to hurt you again."

He reached out then and ran his fingertips softly down the curve of Hericane's cheek. She had never known that he could be so gentle. His eyes widened and sparkled as he gazed at her wonderingly.

She felt tears of her own begin to fall.

Finally, she understood why he had pushed her away all her life. Not because of her sexuality. Not because he did not love her.

He had pushed her away because he had wanted to protect her from himself.

"I love you, Dad," said Hericane, her voice catching. It was the last time in her life that she would say those words to Epitome...though, from his point of view, it was the first time that she said them to him.

Then, Overtime took young Epitome by the hand and guided him into the swirling disk of the time chute.

Hericane should not have been happy, she thought, because, after all, she had lost her father that day. He had died right before her eyes.

And yet, her heart was full and her tears were tears of joy, for just before Epitome slid headfirst into the chute, he looked back over his shoulder and said the one thing that she had never heard him say to her before.

"I love you, too," he said. And then he was gone.

EVERYONE KNOWS HUMANS HAVE QUINTUPLE WIGGLE STICKS

"Officer!" shouts the crystal-breasted, green-spined Gargalumf, jabbing her glittering needle-fingers in my direction. "Stop that creature! He just *flashed* me his naked *wiggle sticks!* All *five* of them!"

The bubble-cluster cop turns my way, his milky eye pods focusing on the image of my fleeing form from across the diamond-lined plaza. "You mean *that* guy? With the blue goo body?"

"Yes!" confirms the Gargalumf. "That *creature!*"

The bubble-cluster cop makes a sound like a snort, which I with my six ultra-sharp ears still manage to hear even as I make my escape down a fluorescent pink alleyway. "That's no *creature*, Ma'am. That's a *human being*, is what *that* is!"

"A *human?*" She says it like it's some kind of terminal diagnosis.

"Why, sure!" says the bubble-cop. "Everyone *knows* humans have *five* wiggle-sticks!"

By the time I get back to my ship on the outskirts of town a few hours later, I've committed lots more mischief and had a blast every step of the way—randomly up-dumping garbage tubs, bungee-farting traffic to a standstill, flashing my wiggle sticks for thousands more Gargalumfs at a ginormous goof-rally, and more. I've been chased by the bubble-cops 16 times, shot at 24 times (with live—as in living, breathing, giggling—ammo), and cursed at hundreds of times besides...but it doesn't bother me a bit.

This is what I *live* for.

"Now *that* is what *I* call a great day!" The short silver gangplank of my spaceship—the *Human Racer*—lowers before me, and the bright white happy-lights strobe on either side to welcome me home. Even as I trundle inside on my blue goo pseudopods, I'm already thinking about the *vorp* I can get up to tonight, when I go out again.

"I got *you* beat, Skizzax!" Wompus, a blue goo buddy of mine, snakes his wiggle sticks through a rainbow heap of glittering glow-gems on the floor of the *Racer*'s cargo deck. "Grabbed *these* from an old gem-seller who'd heard all about *us humans.* He just handed them over and begged me not to *eat* him, the whimpering *blistula*!"

Chuckling from all 12 of my mouths, I join him in admiring the haul. "Nice, Wompie!" Today was all about mayhem for me, so I'm empty-handed, but tonight I'll bring home my own stolen goodies for sure. When you're *human*, you get what you *want*, and the *real* humans get the blame.

Whatever *they* are. Though the word "human" is well-known throughout the quadrant for striking fear in the hearts (or assorted similar organs) of multitudes of sentient beings, nobody seems to know what a *real* human looks like or even where they come from. Why else do you think my gang and others like us—originally known as Spigmagaxalons from planet Spigmagaxala—have had so much success appropriating the name for our own purposes?

"You think *this* is something, you should see what *Yogre* dragged in." Wompus fondles a huge red gem and chortles. "Folks here are *loaded* and *human-phobic*—the perfect combination!"

"I could get *used* to this place." I nod my gooey blue head in agreement, and my fishy orange parasites chitter and splash their tails excitedly all over my body. "It's a shame we gotta clean it out and leave at some point."

"All part of the job." Wompus tosses a green gem in his slimy maw and crunches it to bits.

Just then, the door to the rest of the ship pops open, and fellow gooey Freebo leans in from the hallway. "Hey! Did you see the news?"

My parasites squirt out a frown that smells like rotten *prawk* eggs. "What news?"

"Humans are on Eskalon Eight!" snaps Freebo.

"As in Eskalon Eight, the last planet we hit before this one?" I ask.

"Correct!" says Freebo. "And *humans* as in the *other* humans! The *real* ones!"

So much for extending our layover on planet Gargalumfa. As soon as the rest of our crew returns from their party-down hot times with wagging wiggle sticks in hand, we button the hatches and launch the *Human Racer* into space, heading for Eskalon Eight. Missing out on *real* human beings just *isn't* an option.

Though it's true, we might not even know them if we see them. Out of everyone on the ship, I probably know the most about human beings, but even *that* only adds up to a few vague nuggets my nanny told me when I was little.

Like, for instance, that humans are ugly, nasty creatures, possibly the worst in the universe. Nanny *hated* them with all her soul because of all the terrible things she said they'd done to her and her loved ones.

It's enough to make me nervous as we race out to meet them.

"I guess we had to cross paths with them sooner or later." That's what I say as I watch the stars streak by the big windows of the ship's command center. "Maybe they've even come looking for us."

"Not that it matters!" Wompus, who's steering the ship from the big central driver's seat, lets out a hoot of a laugh. "At this point, I'll bet more people know *us* as human beings than *them*!"

"You might be right, actually."

"Either way, we're the only humans who *count!*" says Wompus.

Just then, Yogre interrupts from the radio board. "Hey, I'm picking up some chatter from Eskalon." She twists glowing blobs on her board, which is made for blue goo creatures with pseudopod hands like us. "Oh, no." She listens to the chatter over wireless earpieces plugged into her six ears. "No way!" She sounds upset. "How *dare* they!"

"What?" I goo-flop a step toward her. "What is it?"

"You're not gonna like it!" warns Yogre, her female body goo— a brighter blue than any male's on the ship—popping and quivering like boiling *shenna* stew.

At that instant, the *Human Racer* lurches out of Garble Speed and slides to a stop. There in front of us, gleaming in the big main window, is a blue-brown-and-yellow world that's very familiar to me indeed.

Because we just *partied* down there a couple *weeks* ago!

"Back again!" barks Wompus. "Eskalon Eight. Second time's the charm!"

"The *harm*, is more like it." Yogre sounds worried. "You won't like what's going on down there, *trust* me."

I frown her a blue goo frown. "Why is that?"

"These *other* humans." Yogre shudders, sending the orange parasites scattering through her bright blue goo. "They're *worse* than *we* are."

Yogre was right.

Even as we bring our ship in for a landing at the spaceport outside the capital city, we see examples of the damage that's been done. Already, it's clear that this place is *not* the same as we left it.

"What happened to all the *graffiti?*" Wompus sounds horrified as he gapes at the view below. "Where's the giant image of my erect *wiggle sticks* that I painted on the runway?"

"And what about the mountain of *vorp* we dropped on top of the control tower?" asks Freebo. "The damn tower doesn't even have a brown *skidmark* smeared on it!"

"Not to mention, where's all the *wreckage?*" shouts Wompus. "I mean, our massive *metal sculpture* constructed from *space-junk?*"

"Space-junk that used to be *spaceships,*" says Freebo. "Until *we* tore 'em apart."

"What the *grife* happened here?" Wompus shakes his head in utter dismay as he lands the *Human Racer* on a pristine purple runway. "It's like a *nightmare.*"

"*Humans* happened." Yogre's voice is icy. "The *other* humans. The *real* humans."

"They cleaned up our *mess,*" hisses Wompus. "Those *bastards.*"

The story is the same as we wander through the city. Our excellent upgrades have been undone; it's as if we never came here in the first place.

At least the locals still keep their distance, regarding us with fear from their swirling bodies of lavender sand and razor blades. They *remember,* even if our good work has turned to so much total *vorp.*

Even if the flame-parks we extinguished with our voluminous piss are blazing once more...the screech-clouds we silenced are shrieking like pulsars again...the filth-pits we brought to life aren't devouring neighborhoods or even *crawling* anymore...and the Sea of Profanity has reverted to the Sea of Platitudes, just the way it was before we ever got here.

"This is *sick.*" I'm disgusted by what I see—and don't see— around me. "Why would they *do* something like this?"

Wompus sees a hovering street sign he once defiled—perfect now—and hawks steaming gray-blue goo all over it. "Looking for trouble, if you ask me."

"It took a lot of hard *work*, messing this planet up the way we liked it!" says Freebo. "That's our *mission*. It's what we *do.*"

"Yeah!" says Wompus. "We're *human beings*, damnit! *The* human beings!"

"That's where you're wrong." A deep, resonant voice suddenly speaks from around the corner of a pulsing white structure swarming with frenetic glowing bugs.

As one, we look in the voice's direction. At first, all I see is a faint shadow along the structure's bug-covered wall, cast by someone in the adjacent alleyway.

"Who *are* you?" I shout. "What's your game?"

"You cleaned up everything we did to this city!" adds Wompus. "What were you *thinking?*"

"Only making the world a better place." The shadow glides forward, growing larger. "That's what humans *do*...not that *you* would understand that."

Suddenly, the being casting the shadow steps fully into my line of sight, and I see him in all his bizarre glory. Eight feet tall and lanky as a stick bug, he towers over our blue goo selves, his shiny green scales glinting in the sunlight.

His eight spindly arms flicker and twitch, bending at six impossible angles each. His three heads bob on leathery yellow stalks.

Each of his faces is a single, multifaceted eye, a mirrored, honeycombed disk ringed by jagged gray teeth.

"*We* are the *true humans*," he tells us as a dozen others like him emerge from the alley. "And we are *done* letting the likes of *you* ruin *our* good name!"

I'm the first to laugh, which I know will push these guys' buttons. That, I'm guessing, will help us gauge their authenticity.

The rest of my blue goo gang follows my lead and cracks up right after me, howling with hilarity.

"That's a good one!" Wompus forces the words out between gales of laughter. "*You're* the *true humans?*"

"Absolutely," says the scaly green leader. "Anyone *else* making the claim is *obviously* an abject *impostor.*"

"Is that so?" Wompus is hooting so hard, he's doubled over. Even his parasites are laughing, making squeaky tittering sounds as they dive in and out of his gooey mass. "Well I guess you sure told *us.*"

His words set off a fresh explosion of jocularity among our group.

"Laugh all you like," says the leader of the so-called true humans. "Soon enough, you will learn that the legends of our *fearsomeness* are as accurate as they say."

"That's *our* fearsomeness, you phony!" shouts Freebo. "Those are *our* legends!"

"Yeah!" I holler. "Who do you think you *are*, taking credit for *our* reputation?"

"I am *Zork*," says the leader. "And I don't *think*, but I *know* I am *king of humanity!*"

The other blue gooies and I are quiet for all of half a second. Then, we burst out in the biggest laugh-quake yet.

"I advise you to take this more *seriously*," snaps Zork. "*True* humans are *not* to be trifled with."

"That's what we keep trying to *tell* you!" By now, Wompus is on the ground, gripping his gut and rolling back and forth.

Zork and his pals just watch us have our fun, their mirror-faceted faces unreadable. So much for "true humans" having a sense of humor.

"Laugh all you want, buffoons," says Zork. "You are not welcome on this world anymore. The natives don't even *think* of you as humans anymore."

"What *do* they think of us as, then?" asks Yogre.

"They call you *Ooshpah*." Zork makes a raspy sound that *might* be a chuckle. "Meaning, literally, 'worse even than offal, though at least offal has a reason to exist.'"

"Hey, it has a ring to it." I nod and point a blue goo finger his way. "It fits *you* perfectly."

Zork points his own seven-jointed finger back at me. "Get off this planet *now*. It is not your plaything anymore. It is under the protection of the *Human Empire*."

Wompus stops rolling. "The human *what* now?"

"The Human Empire," Zork says grandly. "Which now includes all the worlds *you've* laid to ruin, already *restored* to their former *glory* like *this* one."

"You have got to be *vorping* me." I spit out some blue-gray goo and shake my head. "What the *queeg* is your problem, *Ooshpah*?"

"*I'm* not the *Oosh*...!" He catches himself, takes a deep breath, and lets it out slowly. When next he speaks, his voice is calm again. "As I said, we are restoring the good name of our human species."

"To which *we* say, *thanks!*" I applaud, smacking my gooey hands together. The rest of my team does the same. "Thanks to *you*, we can enjoy *wrecking* the same planets *all over again*."

With that, my bunch and I turn our backs on the "true humans" and stomp away laughing, overturning and pissing on things along the way even as Zork and his dopes stare silently behind us.

"Time to get busy, my friends." I spread my pseudopod arms wide. "Screwing with planets is better the *second* time around, right?"

"Screwing with phony *humans* is even *better*," says Wompus.

"But hey." Freebo sounds a little worried as he looks back at Zork and the rest. "What if they *are* the true humans?"

I laugh and tousle his goo playfully. "Relax! *True* humans could never be *that* lame! They would *never* let us get away with laughing our *asses* off at them like that."

"*True* humans would be less *talk*, more *action*," agrees Wompus.

"Less talk, more *torture*, from what *I've* heard," I tell him.

I started pretending I was human at a very young age—playing in the pulsing black brain forests near my home on Spigmagaxala. I'd heard Nanny talk about how awful they were so often, how feared they were by people far and wide, that it felt exciting to pretend I *was* one.

I even found friends to join the game, other blue goo children who were only too happy to play at mayhem. What child *doesn't* want to imagine being bigger and meaner and feared, running rampant with no one to say otherwise?

At least until Nanny overheard me one day and shattered the illusion.

"You should *never* want to be like a *human*," she told me. "They *destroy* everything they *touch*. Everyone's *terrified* of them, because they know how *foul* and *selfish* they are."

"I'm sorry, Nanny." I was very contrite—on the surface, at least. "I'm very sorry."

"Do you *want* to be a creature with no conscience? One that does whatever it feels like with no regard for any other living thing?"

"No, Nanny," I told her, though the answer in my head was very different. Even then, I was getting ideas that would shape the rest of my life and the lives of the people who would someday join my gang.

Yes, Nanny. Oh yes, Nanny, I do want to be that creature.

How long will it take to undo the work of the "true humans" on Eskalon Eight? My team and I won't stop until we find out.

From the moment we walk away from Zork and his group, we hit the capital city in style, really *ginking* it up. We smash windows, break statues, turn around street signs, paint graffiti, release zoo animals. We piss out the flame-parks, silence the screech-clouds, bring the filth-pits back to life and drive them to feast on neighborhoods that got away the first time. As for the Sea of Platitudes, we don't settle for changing it to the Sea of Profanity; this time, we take it all the way to the Sea of *Perversion*.

If there's a prank to play or something to vandalize, we do it.

Everything clean is made dirty; everything fixed is made broken again.

Everything of value that isn't nailed down, we take. If it's nailed down, we take that, too, with more effort. If anyone gets in our way...they just *don't*.

Whatever we do, whoever we do it to, we make sure they *know*, make sure there's no *doubt*, it was *humans* who did all this, nasty *humans* deserving their fear and submission.

True humans, the ones made of *blue goo*.

But, eventually, there's pushback...from you-know-who, of course. Or as I like to think of them, *you-no-humans*.

"Hey, Skizzax!" Wompus stands in front of a bare beige wall, about to deface it with a huge can of spray-goo. "Didn't we already tag this thing today?"

He's right. "Those *queegs*." I touch the surface, which is still warm from a goo-stripping laser. "They're ruining our ruined stuff!"

"That's not the only thing they've cleaned up." Yogre points up at the tallest building in the city, which isn't tricked out like a giant, erect wiggle stick anymore. "Those boys have been *busy.*"

"Damn *Ooshpahs*." I shake my blue goo fist at the tower. "No *human* would pull this *vorp.*"

We pick up the pace, working faster than ever—pooping on this, tearing down that, screwing up these, those, and everything in record time. We move so fast, we don't take time for our usual loving attention to detail—getting the smears and scrawls and scribbles *just right*, artistic even. All that matters is staying ahead of the game.

Which we don't. Which we *can't*. As we discover, Zork and his gang outnumber us and have better equipment. They might not be true humans, but they're higher on the tech spectrum than we are.

I'll bet they're not higher on the spectrum of *doing-anything-to-win* than us, though.

"Enough!" I recognize Zork down the street (he's taller than the rest) and head right for him. "Hey, *Ooshpah!*"

Without a word, my team falls in behind me.

"Hello, pitiful non-humans," says Zork. "Ever get the feeling your work is all for nothing?"

"*You* tell *me.*" I stop a few feet away and lean toward him, glowering. "You gotta *know* we're just going to change it all *back* again."

"Until you get *bored* with it all, which you *will.*" Zork nods his three heads in rhythmic sequence—right, then left, then middle, then right again. "Non-humans can have such *limited* attention spans."

I lean closer, locking my gaze on his multifaceted disk of a face looming over me. "So what do *you* get out of this, really? Forget all that Human Empire *vorp* and reclaiming your good name *queeg.* What's your real reason for *ginking* with us like this? Are you looking for a payday here?"

Zork leans closer, too. "You remember what the legends say, don't you? About how we *true* humans came to live among the stars?"

"As a *true* human, of *course* I remember." I refuse to take my eyes off the many tiny reflections of myself in his mirrored facial facets. "We were *abducted* from our homeworld and made to work as *servants* and *slaves* until we *revolted* and seized control of our own *destinies.*"

"Bravo. You know *my* people's history." Zork claps his eight hands in intricate patterns. "Then you should *understand* why we *humans* refuse to let others—especially *pretenders* like you—rain down *suffering* and darken the *good name* we've worked so hard to bring *honor* to."

I narrow my eyes and scrunch up my blue goo nose at him. "But what's *really* in it for you? Because you sure as *blung* aren't human *vorpin'* beings."

Zork falls silent, breathing harder like he's stressed, which is perfect. Getting on his nerves is just what I wanted to do. Shaking these phonies up might be the only way we overcome them.

"Fine! Keep it to yourself!" I snap. "The only thing *I* care about is *you Ooshpahs* getting off this planet right *now* in the name of the *true* Human Empire! Ours!" I shake both blue goo fists in the air, and my teammates cheer loudly behind me.

"Get lost, triple-headers!" hollers Wompus. "*True* humanity hates your guts!"

"And so does everyone else!" agrees Freebo.

Even as my gang mouths off, Zork's up-to-now taciturn Zorkettes rustle and mumble themselves. The temperature's rising here, I can tell.

It won't be long now.

"*We're* the humans!" shouts a Zorkette. "*You* get off this planet!"

"*Make us!*" If anyone's ready for this, it's Wompus. His big blue goo chest is out, his parasites swirling like mad.

Another Zorkette joins the bad-mouthing. "Better watch what you *ask* for, *fake humans!*"

"I'm not *asking*! I'm *begging!*" Wompus' body expands with rage, then *subdivides* into multiple cloned copies, each just as angry and dangerous as the original.

The rest of my people do the same, angry enough to trigger the defense mechanism they're born with and fill the street with raging blue goo people. The Zorkettes do the opposite, folding and clacking together into towering combination creatures.

All except Zork, who's frantically waving and shouting at them. "Stop! Everyone, *stop* this!"

But even as he tries to head off what's coming, it's already underway. The blue goo army and Zorkette giants rush at each other, plunging headlong into a shattering, shuddering clash.

Leaving Zork in the midst of it all, befuddled—and me there with him, smirking like the son of a *queeg* I've always been.

"You piece of *vorp!*"

Zork lunges, clawing at my goo. But as big as he is, he's no match for my denser bulk and greater strength. Even without cloning myself, I easily swat him aside.

After that, he keeps coming for a while. Again and again, he charges, taking shot after shot. The best he manages, however, are a few passing grazes as I let him tire himself out.

Eventually, he gives up and slumps against the smooth gray wall of a building. I join him there, off to the side of the fight raging in the street between our peoples—the battle between the two claimants for the title of True Humanity.

From what I can see, it's not going well for either side. Battered clones and broken Zorkettes litter the throbbing pink pavement, and it's hard to tell if *anyone* is winning.

"I thought you people were going to clean up this place." I shake my head. "Looks to me like it's just getting messier."

"It does, doesn't it?" Zork's voice is no less deep and resonant, but some of the zing has gone out of it. "I hope you're satisfied."

"Meh." I shrug. "So tell me. What gave you people the idea to pretend to be humans?"

"Pretend?" He snorts with indignance. "But we *are* the true hu—"

"Yeah, yeah." I roll my eyes. "And *I'm* the Queen of Peedydink Minor."

Zork's multifaceted mirror face ripples, the gray teeth around it twitching—and then he relaxes and makes a sound like a sigh. "We bought the rights."

"What?" Bloody hell is going down a dozen feet away, but I still manage to laugh out loud. "From *who?*"

"The last surviving actual human. According to *her*, anyway."

I'm still laughing. "What did she *look* like? I'm dying to know!"

"It doesn't matter, all right? We had every reason to believe—"

"Come on, tell me! I've always wanted to *see* one!"

It's hard to tell when an eight-foot-tall, green-scaled creature with an unreadable mirror-disk face is embarrassed—but this might be it. "Well." He hesitates. "She looked kind of like a blob of foamy green mold with twelve stringy wings and five wormy protuberances squirming out of it."

"You are *vorping* me!" I laugh out loud again. "You mean humans *do* have *five wiggle sticks?*"

"Not *wiggle sticks* per se, no. Not in the sense of *external genitalia*. More like individual *heads*, each with its own sentience and—"

"I love it!" More laughter. "Just perfect!"

"I'm glad you're amused." He doesn't mean it.

"So why *did* you buy the rights, anyway?" I ask.

"We wanted to start a new business," says Zork. "We thought the human mystique would help our marketing."

"What kind of business?"

A building collapses nearby, brought down by fiercely battling combatants. "Damage recovery and keeping the peace." Zork shakes his heads.

At which point, my laughter is louder than ever.

For a while, then, I laugh, and Zork stays quiet. The fight keeps roaring away before us, just as undecided as ever.

"Listen," Zork says at last. "We have a contract for the rights, you know, but...who needs all this hassle?" He gestures at the ongoing battle. "Why can't we come to an agreement between us and just walk away?"

"An agreement?"

Zork makes an upper-body move that might be a shrug. "Who says there can't be *two* branches of the human race in this galaxy?"

I have to admit, I like the way he's thinking. Who says both sides can't give a little and stop the carnage? Didn't someone once tell me that even *humans* can be decent once in a while? "Two branches that stay the *gink* out of each other's way?"

He gives me a look I could never read in a million years if I tried. "Sure, why not?" Then, his mirror-faceted face turns back to the fight, implacably taking it in. "It could be tricky, though. The human brand is just so *toxic*. No one even *remembers* the last time they saw a *real* one, yet the name *alone* is enough to start a *brawl* like this."

"Those humans must've been some real mother pluckers, all right." I laugh, and so does he. "I just wish I could *meet* one of the bastards for once in my life and compare notes!"

"Are humans *all* bad, Nanny?" I remember asking that question once, as a blue goo boy back on good old Spigmagaxala.

Nanny, who was fixing me a brain-salad sandwich for midday meal, looked over coolly from the galley counter. "I wish you wouldn't ask so many questions about humans, Skizzax. Let's talk about something else for a change, like your lessons."

I rocked back and forth on the stool where I was sitting to watch her work. "Nanny, please! You know so much about them!"

"Which is why I'm *telling* you, they aren't worth your *time*. They don't deserve *thinking* about."

"But are they *always* so *awful?* I need to know!"

"*Do* you?" she asked. "Do you really?"

"Yes!" Even then, I was obsessed with human beings. Even then, I dreamed of becoming one—feared and respected and powerful, doing anything I wanted anywhere in the galaxy at any time.

Nanny opened her mouth as if she were about to answer, but then she hesitated. Narrowing her eyes, she gave me a long, considered stare unlike any look I'd ever seen her send my way before.

Slowly, she put down the knife she was using to chop brain bits. A shiver ran up my blue goo spine as she held my gaze.

"No." Her voice was calm and strange. "Humans aren't *all* bad. Once in a while, one will even surprise you.

"Once in a while, one will change her ways. Once in a while, she will do things that are kind or unselfish, things that make someone else's life a little better just because."

Nanny smiled then, her two green eyes glittering, the red lips of her mouth curling up at the corners. Reaching up, she brushed a single, glistening drop of moisture from her pale pink cheek, then pushed a lock of dark brown hair behind her left ear.

"And maybe," she said softly, "in spite of the dark side of human nature, the love in her heart will grow, and the change will be for good.

"Will that mean she isn't quite human anymore?" asked Nanny. "Perhaps, though some might say it will make her more *truly* human than *ever.*"

ROBBING THEM DOUBLE-BLIND

issuda of the Heelee:

When the door of the great silver orb slid open in the steaming purple jungle that morning, my people and I were mesmerized. As we slithered in for a closer look, we couldn't take our eyes off the upright, two-legged beings in identical black clothing, so different from any species on our world.

It was one of the greatest moments in our *lives*, in the history of our *world*, enough to make our forked tongues flicker and our fur stand on end. Finally, we were on the cusp; things were about to change for us in magnificent ways...even if we didn't understand a single word the three aliens said when they stepped out of their orb.

We hissed back at them in our own language, the height of futility--at least until the female with the long, dark hair raised a black box the size of her hand and pointed it at us. As we hissed, the box flashed and beeped...and when it stopped, and the female spoke, we *understood* her. It was a *miracle*...further proof that our momentous occasion was infused with true *magic*.

"Greetings." The voice from the box was similar to the female's, only stiffer, and the sounds didn't match the movements of her mouth. There was a delay as she spoke and the box translated her gibberish into words we could understand.

My people and I drew back in surprise, then pressed closer than ever, enthralled by the sight and sound of a completely alien creature speaking our language.

"We are called *humans*, and we come in peace." The female's red lips curled up at the corners, and she showed her gleaming white teeth, giving her pale pink face a look that I assumed, based on her calm tone of voice, was meant to appear non-threatening. It was a facial expression I soon came to realize was the human equivalent of a *smile*, which is *very* different among *my* people. "I am President Limi Tintinabula of the Humanish Connectorat, and I bring you the *sweetest* tidings of friendship and cosmic creaturehood."

"Presssident? What isss that?" As I spoke, I heard the human's talk box chatter with words from her language, presumably translating what I said so she could understand it.

"A *leader.* And these men are leaders, too." Limi gestured at the blond-haired male to the right of her, who had a strip of the same-colored hair above his upper lip. "This is Vice President Mannik Coopernecium. And this..." She gestured at the big, bald female to her left. "...is Secretary General Quayn Vesper."

"And what isss a *Connectorat*?" I asked.

"A group of worlds joined together to pursue common interests." Limi nodded her head. "And one of those interests is exploration and reaching out to peoples and planets we have not yet encountered. Which is why we are here." Her mouth curled and widened more to show more teeth. "To get to know you and your world. To see if you are worthy of membership in our grand interplanetary organization."

"*Membership?*" I was thrilled by her words. "Interplanetary organization?"

"So where do we start the tour?" asked Mannik. "When visitors come to your world, what do you show them first?"

"We have never had visssitorsss like you."

"Like *humans*, you mean?" asked Quayn.

"Like *anyone.*"

"Well then, even better." Limi bowed at the midsection. "It is our very great honor to be the first visitors to your world."

"Thank you," I told her. "You and your companionsss are mossst welcome, Presssident Tintinabula."

Limi straightened. "And what do they call *you*, my friend? What do your *people* call themselves?"

"My people are the *Heelee*." When I said it, as is our custom, the assembled crowd shook the chiming rattles on the tips of their tails in unison. "As for *me*, my name isss *Sissuda*."

"Excellent, Sissuda," said Limi. "Now show us the wonders of your world, so we may fully appreciate all that the Heelee have to offer."

Limi Tintinabula (Not a President):

How does it feel, being surrounded by giant, fur-covered alien snakes who could *easily* crush the life out of you, and instead having them offer you the keys to their kingdom? *Awesome!*

That's exactly how it went when the boys and I emerged from our spaceship, the *Anne Bonny*, in the jungle on planet Kaleidos that day and spooned out our usual line of B.S. The furry snakes--sorry, the *Heelee*--were so damn naïve, they bought in without any coercion or artistry whatsoever on our part. Communicating via our linguafilter translation device, we lied like crazy, from the part about my being a president to the part about us considering them for membership in the Humanish Connectorat, and they gobbled it up. Almost made me feel sorry for them.

Almost.

But the truth is, as Sissuda (the head spokes-snake) showed us around, I felt less and less sorry and more and more greedy. Because for a bunch of furry snakes, these Heelee sure knew how to keep up a treasure trove.

"Would you look at *that!*" My first mate, Mannik, practically slobbered in my ear when he caught sight of the giant golden egg in the middle of Slithertown (or whatever the Heelee called their little jungle settlement). "And it's *solid gold*!" He held up his scanner so I could see the readings on the egg. "That *alone* makes this our biggest haul *yet.*"

He was so right, it made my heart skip a beat. And it only got better from there.

"I'm glad you enjoyed sssseeing the *Olon.* Now come right thisss way, Presssident Limi." Sissuda led us down a winding path, his brown-furred body with its white polka dots sliding between purple-leafed bushes and yellow-trunked trees with shrouds of indigo flowers reaching all the way to the ground. "I will show you one of our holiest relics."

Jutting from a clearing surrounded by those indigo shroud-trees was a huge crystalline spike glinting with sunlight. It was jagged as a lightning bolt stuck in the ground and a meter higher than Quayn, the tallest among us.

And that wasn't all that was special about it.

"Solid *diamond*," whispered Mannik, sounding like he was about to have a coronary. "And there's another *two meters* of it wedged underground!"

"Wow." Coming from our woman of few words, Lieutenant Quayn, it was a mouthful and a half.

I felt a slight sweat on my upper lip and dabbed it away, struggling to conceal my own greedy excitement from our hosts.

"Thisss isss the *Obeliqua Fundimensis.*" Sissuda wound the length of his body around the giant crystal. "It isss where we come to worship the glory of our creatorsss, the *Drossa Ominosia*, and pray for delivery from their legendary demonic enemiesss, the Insidix."

"I must say, it's astonishingly beautiful," I told him, even as I worked to calculate the object's value on the open market. "Your people are lucky to have such a remarkable holy icon."

"It hasss kept us sssafe and in harmony for many thousssandsss of agesss," said Sissuda. "Ssso long asss it ssstandsss, nothing can diminish usss. Our prosssperity isss guaranteed."

Might not want to bet the farm on that. "Your gods and relics are powerful indeed," I told him. "How else have they smiled upon the Heelee?"

"Yeah," said Mannik. "What other goodies did they give you?"

"Come with me, and you will sssee." Unwinding from the crystal, Sissuda glided along a twisted path, and we followed. What other wonders might await us at our next destination?

The best yet, it turned out. Sissuda led us into a cave carpeted with furred snakes in a state of constant agitation. After he cleared a path to a darkened alcove, he flicked his tail against a switch on the wall, and the alcove brightened with patches of bioluminescent moss.

Bathed in that white light, an octagonal gemstone the size of a basketball turned slowly on a rotating metal stand. As it turned, I could see it contained many colors, from red to blue to yellow to green. I could *hear* it, too, ringing with high, jingling tones like a choir of bells.

"A *song stone!*" Mannik could hardly contain himself. "Only a *handful* have ever been found *anywhere* in the galaxy!"

As he gushed, the Heelee around us all raised their heads and hummed along with the stone, matching its tune perfectly. Their humming echoed in the cave, and the stone's song grew louder, too, as if feeding on their sympathetic vibrations.

"That's so *beautiful.*" I wasn't lying when I said it. The swelling song in the cave was probably the loveliest thing I'd ever heard in my life, aside from the singing sky-fish of Califraja. It made me think of growing up there, on planet Califraja, spending endless days and nights on bright green beaches by rolling scarlet seas. Now that I'd gotten away from there and traveled the stars with my crew of lowlifes, I sometimes wanted to go back there and forget all the bad shit I'd done.

"We call it the *Talimax.*" Sissuda stopped singing, though no one else did. "It isss sssaid the evil Insidix firssst entered our world by passsing through it. There are thossse who believe the only way to keep them at bay isss by joining our voicesss with that of the ssstone to interfere with their dark musssic."

"Well, it's remarkable," I told him through the linguafilter. "I've never heard anything like it."

"You sssee?" Sissuda flickered his tongue and tail in a way I've come to realize is the equivalent of a smile among his people. "We *do* have much to offer your Connectorat."

"You sure do!" Mannik chuckled. "I like what I see so far!"

"Impressive," said Quayn.

"And that's not even *all* of it. There's *so* much more to see!" With one last run of hums in tune with the stone, Sissuda looped around and slithered back the way we'd come.

As we all fell in step behind him, I couldn't help wondering how any intelligent being could be so utterly trusting. The snake had never seen us before that day; he knew nothing about us except what we'd told him. Was it possible such creatures existed, with no concept of suspicion? And further, that they'd look like *snakes*, of all things?

Not that I was complaining, mind you. Fleecing a pushover species would be a nice change of pace, after some of the slippery scoundrels we'd come up against recently.

"Gonna be a busy night, ain't it, boss?" said Mannik as we followed the snake through the jungle.

"How right you are," I said softly. "Good thing we've got plenty of laser diggers and antigravity lifters."

"Probably don't even need *stealth mode* for these trusting little snakes, though, huh?" said Mannik.

"Maybe not," I told him. "But *they're* not the only ones we need to worry about, are they? So let's not be *stupid* about it."

Sissuda of the Heelee:

At first, I didn't realize the next morning would be the most terrible I'd ever known. I never would have expected it, coming after our remarkable first encounter with intelligent life from beyond the stars.

The night before, we'd had a celebratory feast in honor of President Limi and her companions, which had left me exhausted. The rest of my people had likewise worn themselves out and were all still asleep when I awoke.

When I slid out of my burrow in Heeleetown Prime that morning, the sun was already shining brightly, and the air was warm. The breeze carried the smell of breakfast--rodents on the move not far away.

The breeze also carried another scent, which I recognized as the sweat of the humans. Slithering down a path, I found them walking my way through the purple vines, clad this time in red-colored clothing instead of black.

"Sissuda!" President Limi waved energetically. Her two companions were both waving, too--even the bald female who rarely spoke or made a friendly gesture.

I reared up and flickered my tongue in response. "Greetingsss, Presssident."

"How are you this fine morning?" As before, Limi carried the blinking black talk box that let me understand the speech of her and her fellow humans and vice versa.

"I'm well, thank you," I told her. "And what of yoursssselvesss?"

"Never been better!" Mannik's mouth with its upturned corners opened wider than ever. It was an expression that I now knew indicated great joy. "Must be something *special* about this planet of yours!"

"Wonderful to hear you sssay that," I said. "You enjoyed the feassst lassst night, I take it?"

"*Did* we!" Quayn's eyes widened, and she rubbed her belly.

"So where are you off to?" Limi asked me. "What do you typically do first thing in the morning?"

"Yeah," said Mannik. "And where can you get a good cup of coffee around here?"

"Coffee?"

"Never mind," said Limi. "But what *do* you do as part of your morning ritual?"

"Ah, ritual." I darted down a path through a copse of indigo shroud trees. "Thisss way."

"This way to what?" asked Limi as she and the others followed.

"My morning prayersss." A speckled rodent with four eyes and six furry legs scampered in front of me and froze. I resisted the temptation to gulp him down and instead scared him off with a nasty hiss and baring of fangs.

"Prayers?" said Limi. "To your gods? To ask for what?"

"We asssk for nothing," I told her. "We have all that we could ever need or want. Only good thingsss happen here. We pray only to thank the godsss for our paradissse of pure--"

Suddenly, I froze. What I saw up ahead was not right. I had come to the right place, I could *smell* it, but something about it was terribly wrong.

"No!" I shot away from the indigo shroud trees and crossed the clearing in a desperate flash. Sure enough, what I'd expected to see there was gone, leaving nothing in its place but a hole in the ground.

"What is it?" Limi sounded concerned. "What happened, Sissuda?"

I was in a blind panic, crawling around and around the empty hole. "The *Obeliqua Fundimensssisss* is *gone*! It hasss *disssappeared!*"

"You mean the giant crystal?" asked Limi. "The one you said was one of your holiest relics?"

"It hasss been here all of my *life!*" I stopped circling and went down into the hole, searching for some sign of the missing relic. "It *can't* be gone."

"Gee, little guy," said Mannik. "That's just *terrible*. That was one beautiful *diamond*, all right."

"Sure was," agreed Quayn.

"Where *isss* it? I don't *undersssstand!*"

"Sissuda, calm down," said Limi. "Is it possible it *sank*? Are there fissures or sinkholes around here?"

"None!" I combed the fresh dirt for remnants or clues but found nothing. The Obeliqua was gone without a trace. "The Drossa Ominosia who created it would *never* have placed it on fractured or weakened ground."

"Well, this is gonna sound kind'a crazy," said Mannik. "But is it possible someone might have *stolen* it?"

"Ssstolen?" I stopped squirming in the dirt and looked up at him. "What doesss *that* mean?"

"To *steal* something means to *take* what doesn't *belong* to you without permission," explained Mannik. "It's what *thieves* do. Surely, you must have *thieves* on your planet."

"Why would we need to *take* what doesssn't belong to usss if we already have everything we *need?"*

"You snake people crack me up," said Mannik, and then Limi gave him a dark look and he stopped talking.

Meanwhile, my heart felt like it would explode from all the sorrow. Raising my head, I cried to the sky, letting out a high-pitched wail of pure anguish. *Eee-lee, lee, lee. Eee-lee, lee, lee.*

"Sissuda?" Limi crouched at the edge of the hole, her features pinched in what I came to realize was an expression of great worry. "What can we do? Let us help."

But there was nothing they could do, so I kept singing...at least until I heard someone else singing from another place, not far away.

Springing out of the hole, I sped through the brush toward that song, focused only on reaching it. Because the one thing I knew at that moment was this: whoever was doing that singing had nothing to do with *my* song or the Obeliqua.

When at last I reached the singer and saw where she was, I wished I hadn't. Because seeing her there, at the mouth of that cave, and hearing the agony in every note of her keening song, meant the day was getting much worse.

I didn't stop to talk to her about it. Better, I thought, to get it over with and see for myself.

Racing inside the cave, I spotted the alcove instantly, bathed in the pale moss-light--and *empty.* Another precious artifact was gone.

"The *Talimax*, too?" Limi, who'd followed with her fellow humans all the way from the Obeliqua's clearing, sounded shocked at the mouth of the cave. "It's *gone?"*

I reared up, bobbing my head in dismay. "Gone." Then, I let out another howl of anguish, raising my voice to the heavens.

Only to hear yet *another* cry in the distance.

This time, following the wailing song took me back to the middle of Heeleetown Prime. Here, a dozen Heelee joined in anguished song, with more chiming in every minute.

Because the *Olon*, the great golden egg that always towered there, gleaming in sunlight, was gone as well.

"I can't believe thisss." As a crowd continued to grow, voices joined in mourning the inconceivable loss, I went limp at Limi's feet. "It'sss like the end of the world."

"Poor Sissuda," said Limi. "I'm so sorry this happened to you and your people."

"You can say that again," said Mannik. "It's a real tragedy."

As I glanced up, I wondered at the look on his face. He, unlike Limi, was smiling.

"Total tragedy." Quayn was also smiling. "Just the worst."

Was it possible? Did humans sometimes *smile* at times of great sadness? Because both Mannik and Quayn were smiling as they watched my people cry and thrash before them, mourning the loss of something so precious, its value could never truly be calculated.

Limi Tintinabula (Still Not a President):

Does feeling sorry for a bunch of hairy alien snakes make me a bad thief? If so, then maybe I am, because I *did* feel sorry for the Heelee after we took their precious shit.

We'd worked hard to get it the night before, using every high-tech trick in the book to keep quiet while hauling it all right out from under their noses. We'd busted our humps, no doubt about it-- but now that the treasures were stowed away aboard our ship, I couldn't stop feeling guilty for what we'd done to the snakes.

They were just so *distraught*, shrieking in anguish because their holy relics were gone. Every single *one* of them was howling at once with so much heartfelt pain, it seemed like it would *never* stop.

Meanwhile, my partners and I just stood there and let it wash over us. Though I felt a pang of regret for the poor snakes, Mannik and Quayn were tickled pink that we were getting away with the crime. It was all I could do to keep them from giggling out loud about the whole thing.

And why *shouldn't* they have been laughing? After all, we'd done *much* worse in the past and gotten away with it. So what if these snakes were the biggest bunch of rubes we'd ever encountered? So what if they were so dumb, they took the challenge right out of it for us?

The money we'd make from selling the things we'd taken would spend just as well, wouldn't it? All we had to do now was get off Snakeworld and cash in the goodies for a new life.

Though *that* might not be so simple if certain *complications* came into play, which we'd learned by now to expect in our line of work.

So being nervous made sense and came with the territory. "I think it's time to go." I looked around for the best exit lane through the mob of Heelee howling around us. There was no clear route, though I noticed the snakes were slightly sparser in one direction.

"But it's just gettin' good." Mannik was on the verge of bursting into laughter. "It's the whole reason we stuck around after last night, remember? To enjoy the reaction?"

"Well, I'm sorry I let you talk me into it," I said. "We should've left as soon as we were done."

"Lighten up, 'Prez.'" Mannik clapped me on the back. "They're freakin' *snakes.*"

"With *fur,*" added Quayn, sneering.

"I know," I told them. "But maybe wallowing in their sadness is over the top. Haven't we done enough, stealing their holiest artifacts?"

"If you feel that bad about it," said Mannik, "we can always leave 'em some of our holy *turds* to worship."

Just then, Sissuda stopped howling and slithered over to us. I had to elbow both Mannik and Quayn in the side to stop them from snickering.

"Presssident Limi?" Sissuda lifted his head and upper body to me and raised his voice to make himself heard over the Heelee's

473

howling. "Isss there anything you can do to help usss get our missssing thingsss back?"

"If only we could." I had to crank up the volume on the linguafilter so he could hear the translation. "We don't know *what* happened to them, do we?" I asked Mannik.

"We don't have a clue." Mannik pulled out his handheld scanner device and tapped the controls, watching the readout on the screen. "Not a trace of suspicious activity on our ship's sensors last night or this morning."

"Sissuda, do you or your people have any ideas?" I asked. "What about the Insidix you've mentioned? Didn't you say they emerged from the Talimax?"

"Yeah, the *Insidix*," said Mannik. "You said they're shadowy, right?"

"But they have never *taken* from usss before," said Sissuda. "They have never been so *brazen.*"

"It *had* to be them," insisted Mannik. "They're *messing* with you poor, innocent folks."

"But that would mean our creators, the Drossa Ominosia, have *forsssaken* us. That we have fallen from their favor. Otherwise, they would have intervened and stopped the Insidix." Sissuda slowly lowered his head to the ground. "Perhapsss it isss a sssign."

Sissuda fell silent, even as the crying of the hundreds of other Heelee around us grew louder. Their mourning seemed to be reaching a peak; the piercing shrieks were hurting my ears.

"We should be going." The linguafilter was barely audible over the shrieking. "Thank you for the hospitality, but we need to leave."

"Wait!" Sissuda popped up straight again. "Can't you ssstay one more night? We have ssso many other treasuresss yet to show you!"

"Treasures?" That got Quayn's attention.

"Hidden in other placesss," said Sissuda. "I can take you to sssee them tomorrow, if you can wait."

"Hell yes, we can wait!" Mannik grinned. "See you in the morning, snake buddy!"

"We need to leave, though." I gave him a meaningful glare. "We have to get to our *next stop*, remember?"

"Shame on you, President Limi." Mannik shook his head in apparent disgust. "Don't you think spending one more night here is the *least* we can do for these poor snake people?"

"Yeah," agreed Quayn.

Feeling Sissuda's expectant eyes upon me, I finally nodded. "All right. One more night."

"Thank you, my friendsss," said Sissuda. "I will show you many more wondersss, I promissse. Perhapsss you will show me sssome as well."

"Such as?" said Mannik.

"Perhapsss your magical ship might yet find sssome trace of the Insssidix and help usss retrieve our holy relicsss." With that, Sissuda flipped around and resumed singing with his people, adding his high-pitched cries to the chorus of keening howls from the Heelee around him.

Sissuda of the Heelee:

That terrible day of loss was followed by a terrible night. The singing of my people went on until long after dark; it never really let up until the Heelee started dropping into exhausted, restless slumber.

Even then, Heeleetown Prime was filled with anguished whimpers and moans. With our best-loved relics gone, none of us felt right anymore; we felt sick and exposed, unable to directly connect to our gods or resist the will of the shadowy Insidix.

It was hard to consider an existence without those things that had given our lives meaning. I couldn't imagine any of it feeling any less terrible, no matter how long we lived and got used to it.

But I was wrong. Things got much better after all, and soon.

The next morning, I expected to be greeted by a resumption of agonized singing. As emotional as my people are, I assumed their mourning would go on for some time to come.

Instead, I woke to a completely different sound--the chirping and whistling of *Heelee happiness*, coming from all around me.

At first, I thought I was hearing things. Happiness? So soon after pure *agony?* It made no *sense.*

But then, when I crawled out of my burrow and saw what was happening in Heeleetown Prime, I realized the world had changed again. What I heard was *no* hallucination.

Everywhere I looked among the mounds and nests and burrows, my fellow Heelee whistled and chirped with delight. Heads up and swaying, they danced with joy in the bright jungle sunlight, fur rippling in the gentle morning breeze. And every one of them was looking in the same direction, at the cause of their delight.

They were all looking at the giant golden egg towering over the middle of town.

Gazing up at its glittering skin, I marveled at the miracle of its presence. The Olon, which had been gone just a day ago, had *returned.*

Drawing closer, I puzzled at this turn of events. That it had been moved once before was hard enough to believe. That it had come back was *impossible* to accept.

Yet also *wonderful* beyond imagining. Like my fellow Heelee, I lifted my head off the ground and swayed with glee.

Then someone told me the Obeliqua Fundimensis and the Talimax had come back, too, and I whistled and chirped myself into a state of perfect ecstasy.

Limi Tintinabula (Not a President and Never Will Be):
"Limi! Lock and load!" That was what Mannik said when he woke me from a sound sleep that morning, turning on the lights in my quarters and tossing a rifle on my bed. "We've got us some *snakes* to kill!"

"What the *hell?"* I leaped out of bed in my black nightshirt, ratcheting into a state of instant readiness. "Are we under *attack?"*

"We need to *show* those damn reptiles!" Mannik was waving his own rifle around, livid. "We've gotta *teach* 'em!"

With that, he charged out of the room. I followed down the hall, not knowing *what* to expect. Had the Heelee invaded our ship? Were they trying to force their way aboard? Had we underestimated their suspiciousness and potential for violence *that* much?

"Here!" Mannik ran up to the door of the cargo bay and slapped the big red control button mounted on the wall beside it. "Just *look* what they've done!"

The door slid open from right to left. The lights flashed on automatically, revealing our cargo bay spread out before us. The cargo bay that should have been *full.*

But which instead was incredibly *empty.*

"Oh my God." I stepped inside and looked around. "What happened to the *relics?*"

"The damn *worms* must've gotten them somehow!" Enraged, Mannik cracked the butt of his rifle against the wall. "All their shit is *gone.*"

"But how is that *possible?*"

"Don't ask *me!* They couldn't have gotten *in* here, let alone brought in the heavy equipment they'd need to *lug* that shit with their primitive level of technology."

I looked at the surveillance cameras in the corners of the ceiling. "What about the ship's records? Anything on video?"

"Nothing! The haul was *here,* and then it was just *gone!*"

I shook my head. "So where *is* it? If the haul isn't *here,* where *is* it?" I did my best to sound baffled, though in truth I had a hunch about what might have happened. It was important, given the forces that might be at work here, for us to act our parts perfectly in this drama. If we weren't convincing, there was no way my plan could succeed.

Just then, Quayn broke in over the intercom. "Time for a walk, folks. You won't *believe* what I'm seeing on the spycams we planted in Snaketown."

Sissuda of the Heelee:

I was still caught up in the celebration for the return of our relics when President Limi and her companions returned to Heelee-town Prime. I darted over immediately, excited to see them in the midst of our happy occasion.

But the expressions on their faces surprised me. None of them was smiling. All three of them had the creased-brow look that I'd learned was the human version of a frown.

"Greetingsss to you all!" I lifted my head high and swayed before them. "Come and cccelebrate with usss! There'sss been a miracle!"

Limi spoke into her talk box. "What kind of miracle?"

"Our greatessst, holiessst relicsss have been *returned* to usss!" I told her. "Which makesss them even *holier!*"

"Is that so?" said Mannik. "And who exactly returned them to you?"

"Nobody knowsss!" I said joyfully. "And *it doesssn't matter.* All that mattersss is that the Olon, the Obeliqua Fundimensssisss and the Talimax have all come back to usss!"

I danced and cheered, hoping the President and her companions might join me, but they didn't. They just continued to stare with creased brows at the spot in the middle of town where the Olon now stood once more.

"No one saw anything unusual?" asked Limi. "There were no witnesses to the miracle?"

"It happened while we were all asssleep," I told her. "When we woke, all our relicsss had been returned to usss!"

"But doesn't it make you wonder?" asked Limi.

"Wonder about what?"

"Why were they taken in the first place? And why were they brought back?" Limi narrowed her eyes and walked through the swaying, whistling crowd toward the Olon.

I trailed after her, ahead of her friends. "What are you doing?"

"Making sure." Limi nudged her way through a cluster of jubilant Heelee.

"Sure of what?" I asked.

"The miracle." As Limi approached the egg, which was almost as tall as she was, she reached out to touch it. "Mannik, take a reading," she said over her shoulder.

Mannik slouched over, pulling out his scanner device. The scanner blinked and beeped as he ran it over the Olon's surface, watching the little screen closely.

"I don't undersssstand," I said as the beeping got louder.

"Do you *know* this is your original Olon?" asked Limi. "Do you know it for a *fact?*"

"Well of courssse it is," I said. "What elssse would it be?"

"A counterfeit," said Limi. "It happens all the time."

"Counterfeit?"

"Someone steals something valuable, makes a copy, and puts back the copy. Then they sell the original for a fortune." Limi nodded. "Many times, the original owners don't even know their treasure was replaced."

I thought about it, staring at the glittering golden Olon. The multitude of sparkling flecks in its surface seemed the same to me as they had ever been. "It sssoundsss terrible, but it didn't happen here," I said. "That is the sssame Olon I've known for my entire life."

"How can you be *sure?*" said Limi.

"He's right." Mannik shrugged his shoulders as he pulled the scanner away from the Olon. "Go figure."

"Okay then." Limi turned and headed back through the crowd. "We ought to check the other ones as well."

"Why can't you just accept the miracle?" I shouted as she walked away from me. "Why can't you *believe?*"

She stopped and spun to face me. "I believe *something* happened here, but it might not be what you *think*."

"Yeah!" said Quayn.

"What elssse *could* have happened?" I asked.

"You said the Insidix might have taken your relics," said Limi.

"What if they did it for a *reason?* What if they *tampered* with them in ways we can't *detect?* And if they *did* all that, you should *ask* yourself *why* they did it. How might it affect your *people?"*

I stared at her, processing what she'd said. Try as I might, I couldn't dismiss the possibilities and questions. *Someone* had stolen our relics for *some* reason.

"I'm just saying." Limi shrugged. "Maybe asking a few questions wouldn't be a bad thing."

Limi Tintinabula (Not Even Remotely Presidential):

"We should just *kill* all the snakes and take their shit again! I'll bet *then* it won't miraculously disappear from our cargo hold!"

That was what Mannik said when we got back to the *Anne Bonny*...and before that, en route to the *Bonny*, as well. As usual, he was ruled by a one-track mind--and this time, that mind was set on murder.

"Listen, calm down," I told him. "The *snakes* didn't take our haul, and you know it. We *all* do."

Mannik's rage shifted. I could tell from the look in his eyes that he knew what I was talking about. When I glanced over at Quayn, I could see that she understood, too...finally. By now, it wasn't something I should have needed to remind them about, but they weren't always quick on the uptake.

This truth they both recognized was not something to talk about openly. It could only be referred to indirectly, obliquely, in code.

Now more than ever, we had to play it just right.

As we continued down the corridor, I cleared my throat. "We're back on the same page, then?"

Quayn gripped my shoulder and whispered in my ear. "It's one of *those* deals again? We're on *their* radar?"

I rolled my eyes at her and shook off her hand. After all we'd been through over the years, she knew better than to ask those questions out loud.

"Now listen." I stopped and spun to face the two of them. I've got this figured out, okay?"

Mannik didn't look convinced. "But what about...?"

I shushed him with a sweep of my hand. "We won't go home *empty-handed,* and we won't need to *kill* the snakes, either. This is all going to work out fine."

"So we *are* going to take it back?" asked Mannik. "Steal all the goodies and get off this shitball planet before *we* get *robbed* again?"

"Sort of." I headed for the cargo bay with the other two close behind. "We're going to take *one* of the goodies."

"Just one?" Quayn sounded incredulous.

"Just one," I told her.

"Which one?" asked Quayn.

"And *why*?" asked Mannik.

"You'll see." I opened the cargo bag door and marched inside. "Now somebody give me a hand with the antigravity lifters, would you?"

Sissuda of the Heelee:

Though President Limi had gone back to her ship, I couldn't stop thinking about what she had said. Was it possible that the Insidix had tampered with our relics? If so, might it affect my people somehow?

It was scary to consider, especially because it made some sense. Why else would the relics disappear and reappear spontaneously, with no intervention from the Heelee or humans?

And it raised a question for which I had no good answer: How could I find out the truth about what was done to the relics and how it might impact the Heelee?

I went to sleep that night thinking I would never know the answers. Perhaps I would wonder about them for the rest of my life, always looking in vain for some sign of the truth behind what had happened. Always wondering if something dark had changed my people in ways I might not realize until it was too late.

Though the way things turned out, I *did* get another chance to seek the truth.

The next morning, when I woke and slid out of my burrow, I heard fresh cries of grief through the jungle. I followed them, racing through the purple brush in a state of fevered intensity, wondering what new distress had befallen my fellow Heelee.

When I reached the source, however, I found that the cause was not new at all. The cries of sorrow led me into a cave I knew all too well, the home of our holy relic, the Talimax.

Which was *gone. Again.*

Somehow, it had disappeared again in the night, vanished without a trace as it had two nights before.

And its disappearance could be explained no better this time than the first. No clues remained of whatever force or agent had taken it. Asking around among the mourners, I discovered there were no witnesses to the theft, either. The incident was just as inexplicable as the one that had preceded it; it was identical.

Except for one thing. This time, the Talimax was the only relic that had been taken.

I went from one site to the other and saw the proof with my own eyes. Though the Talimax was gone, the Obeliqua Fundimensis and the Olon were right where they were supposed to be.

Why this was, I had no idea. It made no sense, just as it had made no sense when all three relics had been taken the first time.

And it made me wonder what exactly would happen next. Would the other two relics be taken, so all three were gone again? Would one disappear each day, as another was returned? Would we go on like this indefinitely, with relics disappearing and reappearing in unpredictable patterns for reasons we could not fathom?

It would be enough to drive me crazy and take the rest of the Heelee with me. Or was that the purpose all along, from the beginning?

Perhaps, I thought, there might be a way to seek the answers I wanted after all.

The night after the three relics had disappeared all at once, we had not posted any kind of guard. What good would it have done? Our most priceless treasures had already been taken.

Perhaps, if we *had* put guards in place, they might have seen the truth behind the vanishings. They might have gotten actual *answers*.

And it might work that way *now* if we didn't make the same mistake twice. If someone waited at the vacant site tonight, and the Talimax was returned, he might get to see *who* or *what* returned it. He might get to solve the mystery and stop the cycle of disappearance and reappearance for good.

That was exactly my plan for that night, after the rest of the Heelee went off to sleep. That was why I alone reentered the vacant cave of the Talimax and hid myself in a crack in the base of the wall, waiting for something to happen. Waiting for an opportunity that might never arrive.

That was why I fought the urge to fall asleep with all my strength. Because I had to *see*. I had to *ask*.

I had to *know*. And, perhaps, I had to find a way to *end* this madness.

Limi Tintinabula (Homo Sapiens Non-Presidentus):

"Shouldn't we be *guarding* this thing?" Mannik smacked the side of the Talimax, which was back on display in the *Anne Bonny's* cargo bay.

"Absolutely not," I told him. We'd re-stolen the giant, singing gemstone from the Heelee and returned it to the cargo bay, where we'd kept it the *first* time we'd stolen it. But making the treasure harder for someone else to steal away from us was the *last* thing I wanted to do. Leaving the Talimax ripe for the taking was a vital part of my plan.

"I still think we should just take off and get paid for what we have." Mannik still had his grouch on about the whole situation, no matter how many times I'd laid it out for him. He and Quayn both had a tendency to argue against agreed-upon plans in the heat of the moment. "A bird in the cargo hold is worth three in the bush."

"This is how it has to be," I said firmly. "Trust me. It will all work out for the best."

Quayn grunted. "Define 'best.'"

"Let's go, guys." I hit the light switch on the wall by the door, and the bay darkened. "Nighty night, now."

"But I..." Quayn looked around with a scowl. "What if some-one...shows up?"

"We can only hope." I took her arm and guided her into the corridor. "That's what you call a best-case scenario."

Sissuda of the Heelee:

It was deep in the heart of the night when the elliptical blue glow began to flash in the middle of the cave. It was bright enough to wake me, thank the Drossa, though I'd fallen asleep in spite of my best efforts not to.

Inching my nose out of the crack where I'd holed up, I watched as the glow grew brighter. Part of it broke away, forming a second, smaller body of light that spun around the first a few times before zipping across the cave.

The smaller glow landed in the niche in the wall that the Talimax had once occupied, where it bounced around and flashed energetically. After a moment or two of that, it settled down, resting in the middle of the niche. Its glow gradually faded, revealing the stolen Talimax back in its rightful place, on display.

Meanwhile, the larger blue glow in the middle of the cave got brighter instead of dimming. Its flashing began to accelerate, which worried me. What if it was getting ready to disappear?

I lunged out of my crack in the wall and raced toward it breath-lessly. Had I hesitated too long to approach it? Was I losing my opportunity?

"Wait!" I swooped to a stop and flung up my head, flicking my tongue at the blue glow. "I need to talk to you!"

The glow backed away, and I followed. I didn't care if it was dangerous or not; I wanted answers.

"Just *talk* to me! Pleassse!" I rose up higher from the floor of the cave, demanding to be seen. "Tell me why you're *doing* thisss! Why do you keep *taking* our relicsss, then bringing them *back?*"

This time, the glow didn't move away from me. It just hovered there silently, flashing as I faced it.

"Tell me!" I said. "What doesss it all *mean?*"

After a moment, the central area of the glow took on a more solid shape, coalescing into what looked like a loosely coiled spiral studded with unblinking alien eyes of many colors, all directed at me. In the middle of the coils, a red-lipped mouth bobbed on a crimson stalk, finally opening to reveal copious white fangs with jagged tips.

"Why do we *do* this?" Though the coiled thing had no visible talk box, I understood its words instantly. Somehow, its rumbling, deep voice spoke perfect Heelee from the start. "We do it to clean up the *mess* left behind by the troublesome *humans.*"

"Messss? Humansss?" Confusion wracked me. "I don't under-ssstand."

"The humans are reckless," said the thing. "We protect the rest of the galaxy from their thoughtless and wicked behavior."

I shook my head hard as if that might clear it--but it didn't. "Who *are* you, anyway?"

"You may call us the *Vizigog*," said the coiled spiral thing. "You may think of us as humanity's *chaperones* and the galaxy's last *defense.*"

I continued to stare at the thing as it turned slowly within its elliptical cloud of blue glow. It seemed to warp and distend as I watched, as if I were seeing it move through a flawed lens or the rippling surface of water.

"I ssstill don't understand," I told it. "What doesss taking and bringing back our relicsss again and again have to do with the humansss?"

"*We*, the Vizigog, only *brought them back*. The *humans* are the ones who *took* them."

Wrapping my head around what I'd heard took some doing. "You mean Presssident Limi and her people?"

"Yes," said the Vizigog. "Though the one known as Limi is no president."

"But she *sssaid* she wasss, and..."

"She is a liar. A teller of untruths. It is a thing that humans do."

I thought about this for a moment. "How do I know *you* are not a liar?"

"You don't," said the Vizigog. "But I am not. If you are uncertain whom to trust, however, ask yourself which of us *brought back* the things your people treasure."

Again, I had to think. "What about the Insssidix?"

"They do not exist. Have you ever *seen* one? Has anyone you've ever *met* seen one?"

"But *why?*" I asked. "Why would the humansss *take* our thingsss and *lie* about it?"

"Because of *greed*," said the Vizigog. "The most powerful force motivating human behavior."

"Greed?"

"The desire to possess as much as possible," said the Vizigog. "To *take* what others have and get away with it. To exalt oneself over fellow beings by owning the greater share of resources."

"And thisss isss a bad thing?" I asked.

"The humans don't see it that way, but yes. Their greed has driven them to make terrible mistakes, forcing us to intercede again and again to prevent greater harm to other species of the cosmos."

"Which isss why you're here now, bringing back our Talimax."

"Yes," said the Vizigog. "To prevent harm to the Heelee. To give you back your rightful heritage."

"I sssee." This time, I was the one who backed away as I wrestled with all he had told me. If what he'd said was true, the humans had lied and taken our things because they were greedy. I knew I should be angry with them because of what they'd done.

But I couldn't. Try as I might, I couldn't hate Limi, Mannik, and Quayn. If anything, I realized I *admired* them.

Using only words, they had gotten away with stealing the most precious relics from my people. If not for the Vizigog's intervention, we never even would have *known* the humans were responsible.

"I ssstill can't believe humansss can do thisss," I said. "That they can lie and get away with it."

"Not just humans, unfortunately," said the Vizigog. "*Anyone* can do it."

"Anyone?"

"But the humans are very good at it." The Vizigog's blue glow dimmed. "They have fooled many beings and caused many problems, which is why they need chaperones. If not for us following them around, cleaning up their biggest messes, they might have destroyed *half the galaxy* by now...or *been* destroyed themselves."

"Half the galaxy?" How could simple, fleshy creatures with nothing visibly special about them be a threat on a *galactic* scale?

The more I thought about it, the more amazing it seemed. The more *powerful* and *different* from the always-honest, always-peaceful society in which I'd always lived.

"Ssso what are you planning to do next?" I asked. "Leave the Talimax here for my people to find? Make them wonder how it returned so mysssteriousssly?"

"Yes," said the Vizigog. "More or less."

"And what about *me*, now that I know the sssecretsss? Will you just let me tell my people everything I've learned?"

The Vizigog was silent for a moment. "That is a very good question. Our presence must always be concealed, especially from native populations."

I didn't like what he was saying or where this seemed to be heading. My mind worked fast to find a new path.

The humans' lies and thefts had stirred up my people and put me in danger. The Vizigog were lying and stealing, too, in order to undo and cover up what the humans had done.

Dealing with such strange ways and high stakes, I felt completely out of my depth. How could I ensure the well-being of my people and myself when I'd never even *known* of lies and thievery before the humans' arrival on my world?

Suddenly, an answer occurred to me. Maybe the best way to deal with those who lie and steal is to do the same thing in return.

And perhaps the best way to *beat* troublemakers is to *join* them.

"Well, I think I have a sssolution for you." I leaned toward him, feeling the heat of his blue glow. "Sssend the Talimax back to the humansss."

"Send it back?" He sounded surprised.

"Do it now, before any Heelee realize it'sss gone."

"But the humans *stole* it from your people!"

"It wasss all a big mix-up," I told him.

"Your statement is inaccurate," said the Vizigog. "The humans committed a *theft.*"

"You must be thinking of the Olon and the Obeliqua Fundi-mensssissss," I said. "The *Talimax* isss a *gift.*"

"Incorrect."

"It is a gift to our new friendsss of the Humanish Connectorate. A gesture of friendship and fealty." I was surprised at how easily my first lies rolled out of me. It helped that there was an essence of truth at the heart of them...and some very powerful motivation backing them up, as I believed my entire future depended on how convincing I could be.

"You want to return the Talimax to the people who first stole it?" asked the Vizigog. "Am I to assume you speak for all your people in this matter?"

"Yesss," I told him. "And I asssk that you do one more thing as well. One thing that will let usss all conclude thisss matter."

The Vizigog paused. "Will it involve more lies?"

I flickered my tongue and gave my rattle a shake. "Not to *you*, it won't."

Limi Tintinabula (For the Last Time, Not a President):

It felt good to be back in space again. As I gazed out the window of the *Anne Bonny*, watching stars streak by like blazing streamers in the velvety darkness, my soul was at ease, my mind relaxed and content.

Planet Kaleidos was behind us, and our work there was done. Our visit had been a complete success, and our payday was assured. In spite of an occasional hiccup, my plan had been perfectly executed, the outcome as predicted...in all ways but one.

"Hey, Boss." Mannik trotted up beside me, grinning like someone who'd just gotten a lot richer. "You going to take another look at it? I know that's where *I'm* headed."

"Sure, why not?" I smiled and shrugged. I hadn't been headed his way, but it couldn't hurt. After all, savoring the victories in life was just as important as learning from the defeats.

"I just can't get enough of this thing." As we marched around a bend, Mannik hit the big red control button on the wall beside the cargo bay door. "Know what I mean?"

"I do." As the door slid open, I stepped inside and flipped the light switch. The bay was flooded with bright light, revealing the precious cargo secured on a protective pedestal in the middle of the floor.

It was the Talimax, the huge octagonal crystal from the cave on Kaleidos. Its many facets shone and sparkled in the light, changing colors that ran up and down the spectrum and every conceivable shade in-between. It sang to us in high, ringing tones like the chiming of bells, a song that was all at once welcoming, lovely, and mysterious.

"We got it." Mannik beamed as he walked over to lightly stroke the edge of the crystal. "The last known song stone in the galaxy."

"We did." I nodded and joined him in stroking the giant gem. It felt warm to the touch, as if there were some kind of life or power source thrumming away inside.

"You were so *smooth* about it, too." Mannik lowered his voice to the softest of whispers. "The *babysitters* couldn't stop us. If anything, they helped make it *happen.*"

I just nodded. It was best not to talk about our babysitters, the

Vizigog, if we could help it. You just never knew when they might be listening.

But Mannik was absolutely right. We'd learned a lot from being thwarted by our self-appointed chaperones through the years. These days, we knew enough to not only work around their meddling ways, but to manipulate them into helping us achieve our goals.

Just barging in and stealing the Talimax would not have been enough. I'd known the Vizigog would simply return it to the Heelee, so a sneakier plan had been required. That was why we'd taken an impressionable Heelee under our wing, planting seeds of suspicion in his mind that a dark force other than our own was at work on Kaleidos. When he finally confronted the Vizigog, Sissuda was inclined to trust us over the stranger and gave us the Talimax as a gift, a gesture of friendship...and *payment*.

Because, by the time we'd gotten done with him, there was something Sissuda had wanted very badly to *buy* from us. Something the Vizigog couldn't stop us from selling, since there was no coercion whatsoever involved in the perfectly ethical and harmless transaction.

Suddenly, the *Bonny's* intercom crackled to life, and a now-familiar voice boomed into the cargo bay. "Bossss? Thisss isss the bridge. I was jussst wondering what our next ssstop should be."

I grinned at the sound of Sissuda's voice, translated by a linguafilter connected to the intercom system. In exchange for the Talimax, all Sissuda had asked for was to leave his homeworld as part of our crew. He'd had enough of his humdrum planet with its purple jungles and straight-arrow snake-bores. He wanted excitement and on-the-job training in the power of lies and misdirection, something he could never receive on crime-and-sin-free Kaleidos.

It was a small price to pay, in my opinion, for the priceless Talimax and all the good things it would bring. We might even come out ahead in the deal, if Sissuda proved his value, which he just might.

After all, he was already demonstrating he was a *natural* when it came to our business.

"Where do *you* think we should go?" I asked.

"Well, let'sss ssseee," said Sissuda. "How about a planet where the people posssesss pricelesss treasuresss and are even more naïve about lying, cheating, and ssstealing than the Heelee?"

"Perfect!" said Limi.

"I can think of a few," offered Mannik.

"Great! I'll pick one!" said Sissuda. "But you have to let me be part of the ground team. I've got an idea for a new sssetup, and I want to be there when we put it in play."

"What *kind* of setup?" asked Quayn, who'd just entered the cargo bay and caught the tail end of Sissuda's comments.

"You sssaid the one on *my* world wasss sssomething called a *double-blind*, right?"

"Correct," I said. It was much like a double-blind scientific experiment, only without the science. "Neither the Heelee nor our chaperones knew they were both being used. Two sides were kept in the dark about our true intentions."

"Well, *thisss* one will be a *double-blind* with *double profits. Half* the profits will come from our new alien friends, whoever we decccide to visssit."

"And the *other* half?" I asked him.

"Will come from the *chaperonesss*, of courssse," said Sissuda. "And they'll *gladly* hand it over by the time *I'm* done with them."

Mannik, Quayn, and I laughed our asses off, though there wasn't a chuckle from Sissuda over the intercom. Either he was dead serious, or an awesome freaking liar in the making--or *both*.

And *both* was exactly what that crafty son of a bitch turned out to be. He was a damn *prodigy*, the *best* I've ever known, and he put us all to shame in years to come, not that we minded.

Because by the time he got done with the Vizigog, *they* were the one who needed babysitting.

MONSTERS OF ICE CREAM

Slipping through the leafy forest by the light of the full July moon, I feel veils of hot, humid air part reluctantly around me. Wolfman that I am, I breathe deep of the loamy, fetid air, snuffling with delight at the myriad scents swirling in the stillness.

But one scent, more than any other, thrills me to the bone. My helpless *prey* is near, just up ahead. The subject of this night's hunt is almost within reach.

Throwing my head back, I let out a howl of delight. *AROOOO! This* is what I live for—the *hunt*, the *chase*, the *attack*. When I am in this form, part-wolf and part-human, *this* is the truest joy of my life.

Almost there. My heart hammers in my furry chest and my mouth waters. Excitement roars through my body from the tip of my nose to the tip of my tail.

Finally, just when I can hardly bear the anticipation another second, I burst through the last of the brush and erupt into a clearing. Ten yards away stands the place where I can seize that which I crave, that which will satisfy my monstrous hunger and make me feel complete for at least a short while.

The ice cream stand!

As a wolfman with a hyper-acute sense of smell, I can detect the soft-serve flavors in the air from here—chocolate, vanilla, teaberry. I also smell the other creatures—what the unenlightened might call *monsters*—gathered for their nightly fix. It's a familiar mix of scents, as this stand—Frostee Kurl outside Jameson, Pennsylvania—serves the likes of us nightly after midnight, after closing to more "normal" clientele (who, for the most part, don't even know we exist) at 11 p.m.

But there's something *unfamiliar* in the air tonight, too—unfamiliar at least in the context of this place. I smell something that isn't common here, something that isn't *allowed* here during late night hours, *ever*.

Spilled blood.

Something is *wrong* here; I can *smell* it...and *see* it, too. Instead of lining up to wait their turn on just another summer Friday night, my fellow self-proclaimed *abnorms* (short for "abnormals") crowd around the window on the back side of the stand, the one facing away from the road. Instead of chatting amiably to pass the time in line, they talk in urgent, worried tones.

This is *not* a typical late night at the Frostee Kurl.

"What the hell?" Sprinting forward, I push my way into the crowd. I'm not the tallest one here, so I clamber up the back of Frank, a patchwork reanimated man complete with flattop head and neck bolts. "What's happening? Who's bleeding?"

"Hi...Aaron. Mrs. Hoffman...fell." Frank's a little on the slow side. Not stupid, just slow. "Hit...head."

Peering over the crowd, I see what he's talking about. The old woman who owns the stand is facedown on the floor behind the window, unmoving. The blood I sniffed earlier pools around her forehead, glistening in the dim light inside the place. (Mrs. H. always keeps the lights low when serving us after hours so she won't attract surprise "normal" customers from the road.)

"Don't just stand there!" I leap off Frank's back and dart around the side of the little building. "She needs help!"

I get to the door first and try the knob, but it won't budge. Mrs. H. always keeps it locked, though no abnorm I know would dream of breaking the rules and trying to get inside on an ordinary night.

Tonight's a different story, though. "Frank!" I wave him over and point at the door. "Smash!"

Frank taps the door with a pinky, and it folds into splinters like it's made of balsa wood. Fragments are still clattering to the floor as I spring through the gap and charge toward Mrs. H.

Dropping to my knees at her side, I press my right index and middle fingers against her throat, searching for a pulse.

"Please tell me she's okay." My buddy Luther, who's a vampire, crouches beside me. Between his dark skin and black t-shirt and jeans, he blends in with the shadows so well I don't see him at first.

Holding my breath, I dig deeper for a heartbeat. Even as I'm half in a panic, I think about how strange it feels to actually *touch* her after all these years.

Give me a cat-flavored ice cream cone, please. How many times have I placed *that* order?

Sorry, we're fresh out. How many times has she said that and laughed?

"I can find a heartbeat fast, if there is one," says Luther. "But it might involve a *puncture* or two."

"Shhh." I lean closer and focus in, training all my enhanced senses on her body. She's still warm, at least, and I smell no rot. I hear *something*, but is it coming from her or one of us?

Please. Desperate, I do something I don't often do these days. I *pray*.

Please save her, God.

And suddenly, there it is. *T-dum.* A pulse in the throat of this 85-year-old woman.

T-dum.

"Somebody call 9-1-1!" I shout so the crowd outside can hear me. "Do it now!"

I see them all cheering at once out there, grinning and hugging each other at the window. The vampires, werewolves, golems, ghouls, lagoon creatures, sasquatch, wendigos, and all the rest are overjoyed that this one frail old lady might survive the night.

Am I the only one who realizes we might be about to lose a way of life here?

"Hey there, Mrs. H." I'm all human when I walk into her hospital room the next morning, bright and early on a Saturday, all blond hair, green eyes, navy blue polo shirt, and tan khakis. "How are you feeling?"

"Hello, Aaron." How she recognizes me when I'm not in my furry form, I'll never know. Other creature-types have said she does the same for them, as well. "I've got a real headache this morning."

"This is for you." I hold up a little purple vase with a few daisies and a spray of babies-breath in it.

"What? No *cattails*?" Her eyes twinkle when she smiles.

We both laugh. I put the vase on the bedside table and take her hand.

"You really gave us a scare last night," I tell her.

"*I* gave *you* a scare? Now isn't *that* ironic?" She chuckles.

"Did you slip on something or what?"

She shrugs. "I just had a little blackout. I'll be fine. But the doctors want to keep me here a while and run some tests."

I can't help frowning with concern. "What do they think *caused* the blackout?"

"Something about too many sprinkles." Mrs. H. laughs.

All I manage is a half-smile, because of all the worry. You know how some people are so important to your life that you can't afford to lose them? Well, she's one of those people for me, in spades.

Things were pretty crazy back when I first got scratched by a werewolf five years ago. My life was total chaos as the reality of being a wolfman settled in. I don't know what I would have done without Mrs. H. back then.

Frostee Kurl was the one place where I could be myself and be accepted as a wolfman, the one place where I could enjoy the one thing all abnorms have in common with each other and normal people...the one thing that makes us all feel *normal* again.

Ice cream saved my life, I don't mind telling you. Losing the woman who wasn't afraid to serve it to me would rip my damn heart out.

She's irreplaceable. Not everyone has it in them to be so compassionate toward creatures of the night. I've found that out the hard way the few times I've come face to face with normals while in my wolfman guise. Most of the abnorms, whether they shapeshift into monstrous forms or are just like that all the time, have had similar experiences. Good-hearted people are plentiful, sure, but too many others are more inclined to hate and fear us on sight. That's why we live our lives as a secret tribe, surviving under the radar... eating our ice cream after midnight and being grateful for every last lick.

"Aaron, I need you to do something for me," she says softly.

I lean closer. "What is it?"

"I need you to keep Frostee Kurl running while I'm gone."

"But I don't know how."

"The girls on the day shift will train you," says Mrs. H. "Then you'll train your own late-night crew."

I clear my throat, feeling the weight of her expectant gaze upon me. The last thing I want to say is "no," but... "You do know I have a day job, right? As a software developer?"

"This should only take a few days, Aaron. Can't you take just a little time off?"

My heart goes out to her, and Frostee Kurl means a lot to me. Still... "Isn't there someone else who could..."

Her hand shoots up and grabs hold of my wrist. "There's no one else I trust with the late-night shift," she whispers. "I can't ask just *anyone.*"

She's right and I know it. As much as I don't want to do it, as much of an inconvenience as it is, I can't argue with her logic. And I can't argue with one simple fact, either, that totally seals the deal whether I like it or not.

I owe her.

"All right, I'll do what I can," I tell her.

She pats my hand. "That's a good boy." There's that twinkle again. "That's a very good boy."

Some wolfman jokes just never get old, do they?

"Just move the cone like this, so the ice cream swirls into it," explains Carly, the brown-haired high school girl manning the soft-serve machine. "Build the layers like you're coiling a rope, understand?"

I'm a little annoyed, being trained by a kid to perform a menial task when I'm in my late 30s. I'm a *software developer*, for Pete's sake, and pouring a damn ice cream cone isn't exactly *brain surgery*.

But I'm training at Frostee Kurl as a favor to Mrs. H.—and all my abnorm kin, for that matter—so I fend off the attitude. It's not like I know how to do *everything* in this place, after all.

And it's not like the crack team of abnorms I've recruited can be trusted *alone* inside an ice cream stand.

"You're *sure* no one's ever spiked the soft serve mix with *blood?*" That's what Luther the vampire asks the pretty young blonde helping him refill the tank on the other server. The hoodie and shades he's wearing might make him fit to be outside during the day, but he really needs to learn some manners to work among normals like this.

"Brains!" That's what Gina the Zombie says as she scoops rasp-berry topping from a tub and gulps it down, thinking it looks like her favorite food. Another of the teenage girls has to snatch the tub away to stop her from digging out more.

Frank isn't faring so well, either. He's so tall, he keeps thumping his head on the ceiling. He's so clumsy, he keeps knocking things over and bumping into people. At least he's good at crushing walnuts for the sundaes with his bare hands.

And at least he hasn't alarmed the four teenage girls working the training shift this afternoon. None of them seem to suspect how far from normal we really are. It's funny how a little makeup and fast-talking can make people overlook the obvious—though it probably doesn't hurt that the girls are all teens and possibly somewhat oblivious due to hormones, high school, and YouTube.

Though I suppose it's also possible they just find us amusing.

Check out the smirk on Carly's face as I try to pour my own cone from the machine. Instead of nice, perfect swirls like the coils of a rope, I'm getting a floppy chocolate mess that is *all* the wrong shape.

"Nice job, boss-man!" Luther, who's still pouring mix in the tank of the other machine, cracks up at my effort. "That looks more like a *blob* I once knew that an *ice cream* cone."

Gina the Zombie's laughing, too, and so is Frank. Lucky for them, the next full moon isn't for another month, or I'd be wolfing out after dark and teaching them to show some respect.

"You think that's funny, huh?" I dump the cone in the trash and reach for another. "Let's see *you* do better."

Gina shambles over, takes the cone from my hand, and proceeds to make the perfect pour. She even gets the little curl on top just right, as if she's been doing this for years.

Though for all we know, maybe she *did* work in an ice cream stand before she turned into a dead-eyed zombie.

So maybe my team has more going for it than I thought.

"Nice job!" Carly claps for Gina's cone. "And just in time! It's almost noon, and you know what *that* means."

"Opening...time!" Frank pumps a fist in the air, inadvertently punching a hole in the drop ceiling tile.

As the girls scramble to keep the falling dust out of the toppings, I see a silver pickup roll into the gravel parking lot. A heavyset woman in a pink tank top and pale blue shorts with long, black hair gets out and ambles toward the closest service window, preceded by a flurry of wound-up little kids.

I can't believe it, but I'm actually *nervous*. The first customers of the day are here!

I won't lie. Team Abnorm gets off to a bumpy start.

As Frostee Kurl gets busier, and the girls place more demands on us, we drop the ball more than a few times. Luther spills half a bucket of soft serve mix on the floor, and Frank breaks the front counter in half. At one point, I set the milkshake mixer on the wrong speed, splattering the whole interior of the building with ice cream, blueberries, and milk. Even our ringer, Gina, has an incident, driving a bunch of dogs into a frenzy with her walking dead scent. (It's a good thing, being a wolfman, that I know the secret canine codes to shut that shit down before it gets *real* ugly.)

Hiccups aside, though, we eventually hit our stride and become the proverbial well-oiled machine. Customers come to the two service windows and place their orders with the girls, and the gang and I help fill them as fast as we can. Before long, we're making ice cream cones, sundaes, banana splits, milkshakes, slushies, floats, and sweeties (thick ice cream and candy concoctions in a cup) like a bunch of damn pros.

Do we get some funny looks in the process? Hell, yeah! Customers stare and point, and I can't say I blame them. After all, the staff is usually 100% teenage girls.

But no one in line seems overly bothered by our presence. Is it because they're eating or about to eat ice cream, the one thing we all love and that puts us all at ease? What do *you* think?

All that matters is that we get the job done...and enjoy doing it, in the bargain. Being on the other side of the window turns out to be a revelation; it feels like coming full circle, stepping into the shoes of the woman who saved all us abnorms at one time or another through the simple act of feeding us ice cream.

I never expected to like it, but I do. I really *do*...and I guess it shows.

"You guys are naturals!" Carly tells us at closing time, when the outside lights shut off at 11 p.m. "You did great! You are *totally* ready to cover shifts at this place."

"Stop, you're making me blush," says Luther.

"Now all we have to do is show you how to close up, and you're good to go." Carly shoves a mop in my hand with a smile. "Let's get this joint closed and call it a night."

"You heard the lady," I tell Team Abnorm, though this night is nowhere near over and done. Late-night hours—our whole reason for training to run the place—get underway in a little less than an hour. "Let's clean up so everyone can go home."

"But we're...not done yet." Frank frowns and points at the back of the place, where the late-shifters will soon gather from the shadows.

"That's right, Frank." I shove the mop in his hand with a wink and hope he catches my drift. "It ain't over till the ice cream lady sings."

I'm not convinced he understands, but at least he doesn't make any more references to the late shift as he slowly drags the mop across the floor.

Soon enough, it will all make sense to him.

Everybody leaves by 11:45...but Team Abnorm sneaks back moments later, when the girls are all long gone in their cars down the road. Using the key Mrs. H. slipped me in the hospital, I open the door and bring my crew back in, ready to start the next shift of the night.

This time, we work at the back of the building, setting up cones, toppings, and equipment in what the normals all think is a storage room. Creatures of the night that we are, we need nothing but a couple of green glow-sticks worn around our necks to light our labors—another way to keep our profile low.

Since the back of the place is surrounded by trees and brush, the front is deserted, and the main lights are off, Frostee Kurl looks empty and closed to all passing drivers, as if there's nothing of interest to see here, nothing at all. *If only they knew.*

Right on time at midnight, our fellow abnorms creep out of the shadows toward the back window, brutish and ravenous. They peer in at us with bulging, glittering eyes, probing expectantly for a sign that the treats they lust for will soon be theirs.

We don't hold them in suspense a moment more. Sliding up the service window, I lean out grinning and shout the two words they've been longing to hear. "We're open!"

Ever hear a round of applause from a bunch of misshapen abnorms? If you were here right now, you would—a macabre chorus of paws, claws, wings, fins, and mandibles clapping together, interspersed with the oddest yowls, howls, growls, groans, and hisses you've ever heard...sounds right out of your nightmares.

But all they boil down to, really, is *I scream, you scream, we all scream for ice cream!*

"We're covering for Mrs. H. till she gets back on her feet," I tell them. "Ice cream waits for *no one*, man or monster!"

Again, they all cheer...and then the orders start flying fast and furious. Trained up right as we are, Team Abnorm fills each one with speedy perfection, cranking out cones, sundaes, shakes, and all the rest like we've been doing it all our lives.

And for each delicious treat we hand through the window, we get cash—and effusive thank-yous—in return. I don't think *any* of them really thought this place would be open tonight after Mrs. H.'s incident; now that it is, they're beside themselves with joy—the Siamese twins and doppelgängers, especially.

As the ones doing the serving, I think those of us inside the place are even happier. When Luther and Gina hand out 8 large chocolate cones to each of the tentacles of the squidlike spawn of Cthulhu, both of them have big grins on their faces (which is something you don't see every day). When Frank hands over a banana split with extra bananas to Kong the Ape-God, it's hard to say who's pounding his chest with the most enthusiasm.

And when I give Sintilla the sexy succubus her cherry freeze-pop, I couldn't tell you which one of us is more turned-on.

Plain and simple, it's the best and biggest late-night shift I've ever seen at Frostee Kurl. The treats are delicious, nothing goes wrong, and everybody's happy.

At least until the six pickup trucks roar into the lot out front at two in the morning.

All the abnorms freeze at once, listening—waiting to see if they should scatter.

"Shouldn't be anyone out here this late," whispers Luther. "Except for us."

The chocolate-vanilla swirl I just poured is melting over my hand. "Probably just a couple drunk good-ol' boys stopping by to take a leak on the way home." It's happened before, after all. "They'll zip up and blow outta here any minute now."

But as the minutes drag on, I doubt my theory holds water. I still hear the rumble of engines and the sound of male voices out front...then the scuffing of shoes on gravel, getting closer.

I wave frantically at the back window, and the abnorms melt away into the shadowy woods. In a heartbeat, it's just me, Luther, Frank, and Gina alone in the ice cream stand.

Then, there's a loud knock on the front window, and we all jump at once.

"What the hell?" snaps Luther.

"Shh!" Raising my hands, I look around at my three friends, trying to calm them. "Be quiet!"

"Hey!" A man's gruff voice hollers from outside the front of the place. "We know you're in there, assholes!"

"Ass...holes?" Frank clenches both his fists. "I'll *show* him...who the *asshole* is."

"No!" I grab his wrist and hold on tight. "Stay here, all of you! I'll take care of this!"

"I don't like it, Aaron," says Luther. "How does he know we're here?"

"That's what I'm going to find out." I let go of Frank's wrist, tap an index finger against my lips one last time to remind them to stay quiet, then turn the corner and head out front.

"There you are!" A tall, muscular man with a bushy gray beard and a camouflage ball cap glares back at me. "About *time* you get out here, boy!"

I don't have to be in my wolf form to know this guy is trouble. "We're closed," I tell him, as if that'll make him go away. "Come back tomorrow after noon."

The guy's laugh is as mean-spirited as everything about him. "I'm not *here* for ice cream. I'm here to deliver a *message*."

"Is that so?" I stay a few feet back from the service window in case of surprises. "From whom?"

"From *me*," snaps the guy. "And every other God-fearin' person who lives around here."

"And *you* are?"

"Call me *Ram*," he says, "because that's what I'm gonna do to you and your weirdo friends as soon as the old lady dies. I'm gonna *ram* you all outta here for *good.*"

I hear laughter, and two more men ease up behind him. One's an overweight, middle-aged guy in a John Deere hat and ripped white t-shirt. The other's in his 20s, tall and lean, with curly blond hair and a tight black tank stretched over his muscular torso.

"Weirdo friends?" I frown, trying to figure out where this is headed. "You mean the girls who work here during the day?"

Suddenly, Ram smacks the window with the palm of his hand. "I mean the *monsters*, asshole!"

The blood runs cold in my veins. This confrontation just took an unforeseen turn.

"That's right, pal!" snarls Ram. "We know who you are! We know what you've got goin' on out here at night!"

I can't believe what I'm hearing. The late-night shift at Frostee Kurl isn't exactly public knowledge.

"The old lady might have let you get away with it, but *we* won't. *She* might have protected you, but that protection ends when *she* does."

I shake my head slowly, confused. "What in the *hell* are you talking about?"

"The old bat made a deal with the local leaders," explains Ram. "Like, *decades* ago. As long as she's alive, she can serve her *monster* friends at this dump, and they're safe. In return, *they* don't hurt anyone local or cause any damage around here."

It's the first time I've heard about this deal. "And when she dies?"

"We're puttin' a *stop* to it," says Ram. "No more *monster nights* at Frostee Kurl!"

"Why is that?" I ask. "Have these supposed monsters not held up their end of the bargain?"

Ram jabs the window with his forefinger. "They don't *belong* here."

"We don't *want* them here," says the young guy with the curly blond hair.

"They're dangerous," says the overweight guy in the John Deere hat. "They've gotta *go.*"

"What happens if they don't?"

A cold-hearted smile curled its way across his face, lifting his beard. "If *you* people don't hold up *your* end of the deal, neither will we."

I hate this guy so much, it hurts. I fight the impulse to call out the gang from the back room and let them tear him apart, as much as I'd love to see it happen.

"Okay." I clear my throat, and then I ask the question I'm most afraid to ask. "So is there a reason you're here tonight? Is Mrs. Hoffman...has she..."

"Not yet," hisses Ram. "But soon." He leers and snickers, enjoying the fun. "*Very* soon, from what I've heard."

When I get to the hospital the next morning, they're just getting Mrs. H. ready for surgery. She's already half out of it, slipping under on the drugs they've given her, but she sees me and begs to talk to me. The nurse already has me out the door, but she relents and lets me back in, if only for a minute.

"Hello, my puppy." Mrs. H. giggles. "Did you come to play fetch?"

I lean down and give her a quick peck on the cheek. Seeing her like this, I hesitate to ask the question I've come to ask...but I know I don't have much time.

"Mrs. H., did you make a deal to protect us?" I feel like a jerk bothering her with this at this particular moment.

"Why do you ask?" She frowns like a child who doesn't understand.

I lower my voice, though we're alone in the room just now. "Some men came to the Kurl last night. They said that if anything happens to you, the deal's off, and the monsters will all have to stay away."

For an instant, a look of deep concern—almost panic—flows into her eyes, and I regret coming here. Upsetting her right before she goes under the knife is the last thing I wanted to do.

But then that look melts away suddenly, completely replaced by an expression of dreamy bliss. Sighing, she slowly turns away, drifting off into some lovely nirvana that only she can know.

As much as I felt bad for intruding with my questions, I'm disappointed that the answers are denied me. The wolfman part of me wants to howl in frustration, keening at the sky in desperation.

But then Mrs. H. suddenly rolls her head back over and opens her eyes again. "I did make a deal," she whispers. "It was the only way to keep you all safe."

"Is there a contract?" I talk fast, before the drugs can kick in again. "Something on paper?"

She shakes her head once and smiles sadly. "No, I'm sorry. Just talk and a handshake."

I hear the nurse coming and talk even faster. "Is there some way around it? Some kind of loophole?"

Suddenly, she squeezes my hand with unusual strength. "Aaron, if I don't see you again...thank you. Tell the others I said that, too."

I forget my questions and start to choke up. "*We're* the ones who should be thanking *you.*"

"No." She squeezes even harder. "Your *friendship*...is what has made *my* life...worth *living.*"

Then her eyes flicker shut, and she slumps. Her grip on my hand is the last thing to relax.

The next thing I know, one nurse is pushing me out the door while two more sprint over to the bed. I'm there outside her room as they move her to a gurney and wheel her out fast, whisking her off to whatever surgery she's set to endure.

I find myself back at the ice cream stand though I don't really need to be here. Frostee Kurl opens in a half-hour, at noon, but Carly and the girls are perfectly capable of running the place on their own. I know I should rest up for the late-night shift instead—assuming there *is* one.

But I doubt rest will come easily to me now. Between Ram trying to drive off the abnorms and Mrs. H. fighting for her life, I'm a wreck inside.

All the more reason to come back to the place that almost always makes me feel better about life.

"Hi, Aaron." Carly opens the side door as I get out of my battered silver Chevy Malibu and lets me in with a smile. "Did you come back for more training?"

"Thanks." I step inside, where the girls are blasting music as they work. "I just thought I'd stop and see how things are going."

"They're going okay." Carly nods genially. "Any news on Mrs. H.?"

"She went in for surgery a little while ago," I tell her. "I'm not sure what her current condition is."

"We're all praying for her," says Carly. "At least she doesn't have to worry about this place."

I glance around and nod approvingly. "Looks like you've got it under control."

"Yep!" Carly pulls out a rag and dabs at a spot on the pour spout of one of the soft serve machines. "We're almost ready to open for the day."

"Now that we cleaned up the *mess* outside, we are." Emma, a pixie of a teen with short, black hair, hikes a thumb at the front window. "*That* was a fun way to start the day."

"What mess?"

"Beer cans and broken bottles *everywhere*," says Emma. "Plus all kinds of garbage. Somebody overturned the *trash bins*."

"Guess they figured they'd have some fun after closing time," says Carly.

More like Ram and his gang came back after the late-night shift and left a message. Because none of that mess was out there when Team Abnorm went home for the night.

"Did you call anybody about it?" I ask.

"The cops, you mean?" Tara the tall redhead nods. "We did, but they never came. We finally gave up and cleaned up the mess. We couldn't leave it that way for the customers, could we?"

"You did the right thing," I tell them.

"There are some real jerks running around, aren't there?" says Carly.

I think of the message and Ram and Mrs. H., and I wonder what's going to happen tonight. "You don't know the half of it."

I return to Frostee Kurl just before midnight, when the place is dark, and the girls are gone. I don't know why I bother; I can't imagine any of the regular crowd showing up to buy ice cream after what happened the night before.

But lo and behold, Team Abnorm surprises me, slipping out of the woods behind the ice cream stand as I head for the door.

"Hey there, Aaron," says Luther. "Nice of you to finally show up."

"Very...late...boss," says Frank.

"Setting bad example," says Gina the Zombie.

"What are you guys even *doing* here?" I ask them. "Do you really think we'll have *any* customers after what those *goons* did last night?"

Frank shrugs his massive shoulders. "Maybe. Maybe not."

"But what if the customers *do* come?" Luther's fangs glint in the moonlight when he grins. "Do you really want to miss what could be the last ever late-night shift at Frostee Kurl?"

I feel a surge of pride as I look at the three of them, so willing to take action in the face of danger...or at least sell ice cream. But there's a surge of worry, too. What if Ram and his gang return for another round of intimidation...or worse?

"Okay, good point." I pull out my key and unlock the side door. "Let's get set up just in case."

I lock the door behind us as the others head for the back room. They get right to work without a word from me, pulling out the toppings, arranging the cups and cones, and refilling the soft serve machine. They've gotten so good at their jobs that I'm starting to think I don't need to supervise them at all anymore.

Still, it might all be for nothing. I don't see anyone lurking outside, waiting for service. The usual line of hungry abnorms is nonexistent; the four of us are completely alone.

At least that's how it seems until I hear a sudden clang from the front room of the place.

Without thinking, I dash around the corner into the front room, expecting to face a violent intruder. Heart hammering, I look around frantically but see no one.

For once, I wish I were in wolfman form, able to sniff out any intruder and take him down with fangs and claws. Murphy's Law for Wolf-Men: There's never a full moon around when you need it most.

"Who's here?" I try to sound as intimidating as I can without a wolfman snarl and howl to back me up. "Show yourself!"

"Okay, okay." Instead of the hostile male voice I expected, a familiar female voice speaks up from behind the soft-serve machine. "Relax, it's just me. It's just us."

Carly steps out from her hiding place, followed by Emma and Tara. All three girls are smiling sheepishly.

"What are you doing here?" I ask. "It's after midnight."

"*We're* waiting for whoever trashed the parking lot, in case they come back for more," says Carly. "What are *you* doing here?"

Just as I'm about to try to explain, I hear the roar of pickup trucks hurtling into the gravel lot. We all look in the same direction as headlights blaze through the front windows with blinding intensity.

"That must be them!" shouts Emma. "Let's go!"

"No!" I stand between them and the door. "Stay here and let me handle it!"

"No way," says Tara. "We're not afraid of standing up to these assholes!"

"You don't understand." I get more nervous as I hear pickup doors open and footsteps on gravel outside. "This isn't about *you*. This is..."

Suddenly, I hear the boom of a gunshot, followed by the crash of shattering glass. The far front window explodes, followed by the front panel of the soda machine between Emma and Tara.

"*Get down!*" Even as I yell the words, and the three girls drop, another gunshot blasts through the far window and punches into the rear wall.

Crouching, I look toward the line of fire and see Ram taking aim with a rifle, midway between the building and the pickups.

"You're runnin' outta time, boy!" he shouts. "The old lady's in critical condition! She won't make it through the night!"

I straighten and step up to the window, daring him to blow me away. "Nice of you to be so concerned!"

"Only thing concernin' us is gettin' rid of *monsters* like you!" Ram takes another shot, which pings off the metal flashing between windows. "You oughta get a head start! You and your pals might not make it out in one piece if you keep makin' us wait!"

"Go screw yourself!" I tell him.

"Then again, maybe we'll just root you all outta there right *now!*" Ram starts forward, waving for the others to follow.

That's when I hear the side door of Frostee Kurl open, followed by a scuffle of footsteps. Instantly, I realize what's about to happen.

The abnorms are on the loose.

My gut clenches as I see Frank barrel around the front of the place, arms raised menacingly. Ram swings around and cranks off a shot in his direction—but it just bounces off and makes Frank madder.

Meanwhile, Ram's buddies take random pot shots at Luther as he swoops toward them in bat form. Every shot misses, but Luther doesn't; he drops on the face of the guy in the John Deere hat and claws him up good, then craps in his mouth and flutters up out of reach with a screech.

It's enough to make the bad guys run for their trucks. The bastards are lucky; Frank only manages to tear the front bumper off Ram's pickup before they hightail it out of here. Gina doesn't even get to bite a hunk out of one of them before they escape.

Even as one problem's solved—for the moment, at least— another presents itself. The girls stayed down during the fight, but not *all* the way down. Peering out the front window, they've seen the whole battle between the bastards and abnorms in all its scary brutality.

Now, as they slowly rise and turn to face me, their eyes are wide. There's no way I can hide or dismiss what they just saw.

I have some explaining to do.

When have I ever told a normal person about the secret world of abnorms? Never, actually. The fewer people who know about it outside my circle, the better. The more we keep it to ourselves, the less chance the angry villagers will show up outside our homes with tiki torches.

So talking about this with Carly, Emma, and Tara isn't easy. I know I'm rambling, and I know they're nervous. They ask questions, and I don't always feel like the answers are coming out right.

But all in all, they seem to take the news pretty well. By the time I get to the part about Mrs. H.'s deal and Ram's threats, they're frowning and shaking their heads sympathetically. None of them looks ready to run screaming, which is good.

As for me, I'm relieved when I get done. It feels liberating, getting all this off my chest, though I didn't have much choice in the matter. It's a big deal, actually, having someone else who's normal in the circle of trust besides Mrs. H.

But my soul-baring has another impact, too...one I hadn't considered.

"We need to do something," says Carly. "We need to help you and your people."

"It's what Mrs. H. would want," agrees Emma.

"She trusted us with this place," says Tara. "We can't let her down."

"Thank you," I tell them. "But Mrs. H. would also want you to stay out of danger."

"Some things are too *important* not to put yourself out there," says Emma.

Tara sticks her fists on her hips and looks defiant. "We can take care of ourselves, don't worry."

"But you were almost *shot* tonight," I remind them. "These people mean *business.*"

"So do *we.*" Carly folds her arms over her chest and nods. "And I know just what to do to *prove* it."

"No, listen," I tell her. "We need to let this go. You should be focusing on Mrs. H. and keeping the Frostee Kurl alive for her. That's what we want, too." I look back, and Frank and Gina nod. Where Luther is at the moment, I don't know. "We shouldn't do anything to upset the applecart right now."

"The hell with that," says Carly. "I've got a plan, and I know it'll work. Who's with me?" She reaches out for a fist bump.

Emma and Tara both bump her back...but when the fists come my way, I hesitate. I shouldn't encourage them at all, but what if?

What if these youngbloods have an idea that might just work?

I reach out as if to bump, then pull back my fist at the last second. "What's your plan?" I ask.

Ram was right. When I go to the hospital the next morning to see Mrs. H., the nurse at the desk tells me she is indeed in critical condition. There's been no improvement since yesterday, and no, I can't go visit her in Intensive Care.

I feel sick to the stomach as I stand there, thinking I might never see her again. After all she's done for me, I can't even be with her when she needs me the most, when she needs *anyone* to be at her side and give her strength.

But maybe, if the girls are right, I can still do something to preserve the dream she's built.

That's right, I've bought into Carly's scheme. So have Frank and Gina, though Luther's a question mark. He's been M.I.A. since last night, though maybe he's just flown off to avoid any fireworks headed our way. Luther's a decent guy, but he can be impulsive, to say the least.

Without Luther, the rest of us will have to take up the slack. Frank and Gina and I will have to double down and cover the task he would normally make short work of, flying like a bat and all. It's the most important part of the plan, when you get right down to it —spreading the word far and wide.

Just call us Paul Revere's Riders of the abnorm set.

We work like hell all day, *all* of us...and by midnight, we're ready. The girls and I unlock the service windows in the front and back of Frostee Kurl as the late-night shift gets underway for what might be the final time.

"Are you guys ready?" I ask as the digital clock on the wall counts the minutes after midnight.

"Of course we are!" Emma's wearing a crimson headband like she's loaded for bear. "Bring on the bastards!"

"Are *you* ready?" asks Carly.

"I hope so." Once again, I wish like hell it was a full-moon night, and I was surging with wolfman power...but no such luck. "We'll see."

Soon after I say it, I hear the sound of pickup trucks roaring into the parking lot. My heartbeat quickens, and I clap my hands together.

"Showtime!"

With that, I head for the side door, followed by Carly. We walk outside and around the front of the place, stopping midway between the windows and the semicircle of six pickups confronting us.

Ram hops out of the cab of his truck with his rifle over his shoulder. "Time's up, dipshits! The old lady's dead! Your precious deal's up in smoke!"

"So what?" Carly belts out the words without the slightest trace of fear.

Ram laughs gleefully. "Did you not *hear* what I *said?* Your *deal* is up in *smoke!*"

"We heard you the first time," I tell him. "And we've got the same answer."

"*So what?*" repeats Carly.

Ram swings his rifle down, pointing the barrel in the direction of the Frostee Kurl. "Maybe you oughtta come up with a *better* answer."

"No need. The old deal *is* done." I raise my right fist in the air, giving a signal to the girls inside the building. "The *new* one takes effect *now!*"

Suddenly, the interior and exterior lights all come on at once. The neon Frostee Kurl sign by the road flares to life as well.

"We finally *listened* to you, Ram!" I tell him. "You've been saying all along we need to end the *monster nights* at the Kurl...and you are absolutely right!"

Ram keeps his gun at eye level and looks around nervously. "No shit!"

"Starting now, the so-called *monsters* won't have their own special night shift." Sticking two fingers in my mouth, I let out a shrill whistle.

As the high-pitched sound echoes through the night, the woods rustle behind the ice cream stand. Figures emerge from the among the trees on either side of the place, moving from the shadows out into the light.

Humans of all ages, shapes, and sizes march alongside abnorms of equal diversity. Teenage girls walk with demons and vampires; middle-aged men stroll with witches and sasquatch. Chupacabra and lizard-men escort elderly couples while land sharks, phantoms, and human flies approach with housewives and children at their sides.

I see so many forms and faces that I know, and they just keep coming, pouring out of the forest. It's a genuine mob crowding into the parking lot, so I guess Frank, Gina, and I did okay spreading the word among the creature types, and Carly and the girls did the same among the normals.

To say the least, it is a stirring sight to see—all those normal and abnorms turning out on behalf of brotherhood...showing their true colors to save the one place they all love. If only Mrs. H. could be here right now, I think she'd have tears of joy in her eyes.

I *know* she would.

While the mob is still flowing out of the woods, I walk toward Ram. "We're ending the special monsters-only night shift effective immediately. From now on, *all* shifts will be open to *all* customers, no matter who or what they are!"

Ram looks like he just swallowed a turd. Eyes darting back and forth, he seems to be sizing up the odds...and then he lowers his weapon.

"All shifts for all customers, and *everyone* will be protected on this property!" Smiling, I spread my arms wide. "Everyone will be *safe* at Frostee Kurl."

Ram's top lip curls like he'd love to tear my throat out. Wolfman that I sometimes am, I'm familiar with the feeling.

"Everyone here agrees." I fling an arm back to indicate the mob behind me. "They are the Kurl's greatest fans, and they agree to protect all who come here, by day or by night."

The crowd roars with cheers and applause. The loudest shouts of approval come from good old Frank, who towers by the building with Gina beside him.

"Everyone here agrees on something else, too." Leaning forward, I narrow my eyes and poke a finger at Ram's chest. "You and your boys are *banned* from Frostee Kurl *forever*."

Silently, Ram glares at me, but he doesn't lash out. The mob is closing in around us, normals and abnorms alike, and he'd be stupider than he already is to challenge their authority.

"You know what that means, don't you, Ram?" I ask him.

That's when Carly jumps in and answers the question for him. "Hit the road!" she shouts.

Ram just stands there, fixed in place. His glare slowly becomes a broad grin. "This changes nothing, morons. The old deal is still over. It died with the old bat."

"Don't you understand English?" snaps Carly. "Get lost!"

"If we leave, we'll just come back later." Ram chuckles. "We'll take care of business when none of these fine folks are around to get in the way."

"Guess again!"

The new voice comes from nearby, in the thick of the crowd, and it's a shocker. People actually gasp when they hear it.

Everyone looks toward it at once, and a cry of surprise and joy rips through the mob. None of us can believe our ears and eyes.

But sure enough, Mrs. H. is standing right there in the flesh, her familiar face shining in the light of the neon sign.

"It can't be." The smug, nasty grin disappears from Ram's ugly face. "B-but you're..."

"A medical miracle, yes." Mrs. H. looks better than she's looked in ages. Her eyes are bright, her posture's great, her movements quick and smooth. How could she make such a turnaround so soon after being in critical condition? How could she recover so completely if she was declared dead not long ago, or close enough at least for Ram to make the call?

I get my answer, though I keep it to myself. My buddy Luther stands behind her, smiling like the vampire that bit the canary. He winks when he catches my eye, and I understand.

Mrs. H. is back thanks to him.

"Now you listen to me, Jerry Ram." Mrs. H. storms over and jabs Ram in the chest. "You take your good-for-nothing goons and get out of here. You're not welcome at Frostee Kurl anymore."

Ram stumbles back, and the crowd laughs.

"And get this through your thick skull," says Mrs. H. "Not only is there a *new* deal, but the *old* one is still in effect. Anyone who comes to this ice cream stand is protected, no matter who or what they are!"

Ram drops his gun, picks it up, and scrambles into the cab of his truck. The rest of his bunch are already in their pickups and rolling out of the parking lot.

"Now scram!" shouts Mrs. H. "Nobody wants monsters like you around here!"

Ram tears out of the parking lot, flipping the bird on his way up the road. Mrs. H. gives him a loud, sloppy raspberry, and everyone cheers, normals and abnorms alike.

Have I ever had a sweeter teaberry ice cream cone than the one I'm licking right now? Has the cold, minty flavor ever tasted so good or felt so satisfying? No way.

Now that the crisis at the Kurl is over, it's like the dark clouds have parted and the taste of every treat has been enhanced. It's like the feeling I get on a full-moon night when I'm charging through the woods, and the air is cool and fresh, and there are rabbits and chipmunks all around. It's like Heaven, or as close to it as we can ever get here on Earth.

The crowd around me is equally rapt, devouring frozen goodies with obvious delight. Most wonderfully of all, they're mingling with no regard for type or nature, with no trace of fear or prejudice. The scariest-looking abnorms chat and chuckle with the meekest-looking normals. The toughest-looking normals shake the hands (or paws or tentacles) of the most vulnerable-looking abnorms.

We're all together in this, which is just as it should be.

"Now this is what I call a party." Mrs. H. strolls over with a smile, the woman of the hour. "My kind of party."

I have another lick of teaberry. Letting such a good thing melt is *not* an option. "Great to see you up and around again, Mrs. H."

"Thanks." She gives my arm a squeeze. "It's good to be alive...or whatever." Her giggle sounds like that of a much younger woman.

"Well, welcome to Team Abnorm," I tell her. "Congratulations on the new you. It feels a little strange at first, doesn't it?"

"Yes, it does." She frowns. "Like nothing I've ever felt before."

I have another lick of the ice cream. "You'll get used to it. We all do."

Mrs. H. sighs. "I wonder if this how my big brother felt. He was turned in his early twenties, you know."

I look at her with surprise. "Turned to what?"

"Someone like you," she says. "Changing by the light of the full moon. But he didn't last long. The usual idiots hunted him down and killed him because he was different."

I nod sympathetically. After all this time, I finally understand why she's been such a defender of abnorms.

"It's always the same old shit," says Mrs. H. "Whatever they don't like or understand, they have to kill it."

"But maybe not here anymore." I look around at the crowd of humans and monsters sharing ice cream in the night, laughing and talking like the oldest of friends. "Maybe we've finally started a new way forward here tonight."

Mrs. H. grunts. "But it only feels like a drop in the bucket, doesn't it? *Every* town has abnorms of one kind or another in the mix. Who can save *them?*"

"Maybe it's enough that we've done it right here," I tell her.

"Maybe word will get around, and others will be inspired by our example. We've found the key, after all. We have the secret power that can bring us all together in spite of everything."

There's a twinkle of understanding in Mrs. H.'s eye. "The power of ice cream," she says with a firm nod.

"Alleluia!" I shout just before I take a super-long lick of the most delicious teaberry this side of God's own ice cream stand.

THE SPACEKISS SOLUTION

The alien who looked like a cactus blinked his prickly pear eyes and made a noise like a screaming cat.

At first, Dinah Ryan wasn't sure that this was a bad thing. For all she and her fellow Earthlings knew about aliens, it could have been a cry of pure ecstasy.

But then, the cactus puked chunky blue slime all over Ben Blakey, which tipped them off. With a noise like a dental drill running at full throttle, Mr. Cactus scooted off to the next booth.

So humanity was still screwed.

"Ah, man!" Blakey flicked slime from his gray jumpsuit and wrinkled his nose. "This stuff *stinks*!"

"You're telling *me*." Mahalia Davis darted away from him. "How the hell many of these species communicate by spraying shit at each other, anyway?"

Dinah grinned and shook her head, tossing her shoulder-length sandy brown hair. "I still say it's a joke. Initiation pranks for the new kids on the block."

"No," said Captain Alec Strayhorn. "We don't matter that much to them. Half of them don't even know we're here."

Dinah gazed out at the cavernous hall and realized Strayhorn was right. Every imaginable shape and size of alien being walked and bounced and flew and crawled and oozed across that giant crystal chamber. There were aliens with skin like stained glass, faces like mirrors, bodies like smoke, fur crackling with electrical current...and none of them were looking or sniffing or twitching in the direction of the Earthlings' booth.

"This is a *disaster*." Blakey used one end of the tablecloth to wipe slime from his arms and chest. "*Three days* at this debacle, and what do we have to *show* for it?"

"Lots of alien *freebies*." Mahalia shuffled the pile of bizarre devices, objects, and pocket-sized lifeforms on the table.

"Which we don't know what to do with!" Blakey bent down and wiped slime from his lumpy bald head. "For all we know, they're meant to kill and eat us!" Usually, Blakey was the funniest and most upbeat member of the team; his current surliness showed just how badly things were going.

Some Worlds' Fair this was turning out to be. The Fair was designed to give the inhabitants of many planets the chance to showcase their wares and attract investors. Plenty of other species were getting attention...but for the humans, the Fair had been an exercise in invisibility. They sat at their cobbled-together plastic booth playing old Earth movies on a TV pried out of their ship's cockpit, and nobody gave them a second or even a first look.

"We've done the best we could." Dinah tucked her hair behind her ears and shrugged. "We didn't exactly come prepared for this."

It was true. As the crew of Earth's first deep space exploration mission, the four humans had not expected to be setting up a booth at a glorified trade show on an alien space station. They hadn't even expected to *meet* honest-to-goodness aliens, for that matter.

Now, they'd been surrounded by so many wildly different varieties for so long, Dinah had to admit that the novelty was starting to wear off.

"I say we pack it in," said Blakey, dropping the slime-covered end of the tablecloth. "Let's go home."

"And tell the folks at home what?" Captain Strayhorn--a tall man with thick, dark hair, chiseled features, and haunted gray eyes--

straightened the tablecloth. "That everyone on Earth will *die* because our trade show booth was *half-assed*?"

That was enough to take the wind out of everyone's sails...and remind Dinah why she had a crush on him.

Strayhorn was a leader. While everyone else got bent out of shape over a little blue slime, Strayhorn kept his eyes firmly on the prize.

Which was saving humanity from extinction.

Blakey sighed. "I just don't know what else we can do. These bastards don't care about what we have to offer."

"Maybe you need to diiig deeper," said a familiar voice.

Just hearing it was enough to make Dinah's skin crawl. The voice had an oily, sinuous quality that curled around her brainstem and licked her fear center with a flickering, forked tongue.

The voice belonged to the alien who'd brought them to the Worlds' Fair in the first place. Dinah and the other humans called him "Heavy," which was derived from his endless, unpronounceable alien name.

"Surpriise them." Heavy looked like a five-foot long eggplant covered with writhing cilia topped with chattering faces. There were hundreds of tiny faces, every one of them representing a different alien species. Whichever face Heavy was using at a given moment-- the human face, in this case--inflated to life size and spoke the loudest.

Mahalia patted her curly black hair and snorted. "How can we *surprise* them when we don't even know what's *not* a surprise out here?"

Heavy's human face looked like Blakey's: pinched, puffy features and a lumpy scalp. The main difference was that the lip movements didn't always match the words. "Your homeworld wiiill be uniiin-habiiitable soon, yes?"

"You know it will," said Dinah. Hyper-accelerated climate change on Earth had already cranked up the heat and forced everyone underground. Scientists projected that humans would no longer be able to survive anywhere on or under the planet within five years.

"You came here looking for help to fiiix the homeworld, yes?" said Heavy.

Dinah nodded. The team had originally launched into space seeking new Earthlike homes for humanity. When all the inhabitable planets within reach had turned out to be taken, they'd jumped at Heavy's invitation to the Fair.

"You wiiill pay any priice for that help?" said Heavy.

"Of course," said Strayhorn. "But we don't seem to have anything anyone *wants*."

Heavy made a gurgling sound that the team had decided was his way of laughing. "Are you sure you have triied *everythiiing*?"

"Pretty much," said Blakey.

"Maybe you only *thiiink* you have," said Heavy. "Remember, somethiiing of no value to you could be worth a great deal to one of *them*." With that, he twisted his eggplant body around and waved every one of his faces at the crowd of aliens in the great crystal hall.

"What's that supposed to mean?" said Blakey.

"You tell me," said Heavy. "Iiit iiis up to you to fiiigure iiit out."

That night, Team Earth brainstormed in the cramped galley of their little spaceship, the *Diogenes*. They had only one day left of the Worlds' Fair, one day in which to make a deal to save humanity.

"Let's go over it again." Strayhorn tipped his chair back and propped the side of his leg against the edge of the round table. "What have we offered so far?"

Mahalia swallowed some coffee and lowered her mug. "Mineral wealth. Natural resources."

"Plant and animal specimens," said Dinah.

"A catalogue of genomes for life on Earth," said Blakey.

"What else?" said Strayhorn.

Dinah nibbled a chocolate chip cookie, then waved it at Strayhorn. "Food stocks. Pharmaceuticals."

Strayhorn nodded. "A database of all human knowledge."

"Strategic military rights," said Mahalia.

"Nuclear and biological weapons," said Blakey.

"Slaves." Dinah was exaggerating, but only a little; in desperation, they'd come up with an indentured servant scheme, offering a human workforce for offworld projects in return for Earth's salvation.

Even that extreme proposal hadn't drawn any interest from the oblivious aliens.

Strayhorn checked a list on a pad of paper in his lap. "That's everything, all right." He chucked the pad on the table and sighed. "So what else do we have to offer?"

Blakey laughed and slapped the table. "Absolutely *nothing!*"

"Heavy says otherwise," said Strayhorn.

"Right!" Blakey leaped to his feet. "And *that* asshole would *never* steer us wrong!"

"One more day." Strayhorn's quiet, steady voice locked in everyone's attention with high intensity. "That's all the time we have to make a deal. So let's *think*, people."

"We're like *amoebas* to them." Blakey's face was flushed. "Like *dust mites*. We've got *nothing* they want!"

"All right, all right." Mahalia scrubbed her fingers through her short, curly hair. "What *haven't* we offered so far?"

"Souls!" said Blakey. "We haven't offered them our *souls* yet!"

Mahalia grinned. "Careful. They might actually *want* those."

"Then I say let's *sell* them," said Blakey.

"But we can't prove they exist," said Dinah.

"All the better!" Blakey clapped his hands. "I say let's do whatever it takes to save Earth!"

Dinah looked across the table and caught Strayhorn's gaze. In the long trip out from Earth, she'd become addicted to that gaze. At moments like this, she felt like she would do anything to hold it, to keep it, to please him.

Strayhorn was a strong man, a good man, a leader. He wore a sense of mystery like a dark cloak, binding all his secrets in shadows deep inside. How could she ever hope to get at them?

"Wait." Dinah felt all eyes slide to meet her, but she didn't break Strayhorn's gaze. "Maybe you're onto something, Ben."

"Great!" Blakey rubbed his hands together. "Tell me about it!"

"What about imagination?" said Dinah.

Mahalia frowned. "How can we sell imagination?"

"Not imagination itself," said Dinah. "I mean we offer to sell something *imaginary*."

"Ah." Strayhorn nodded. "You mean lie."

Dinah shrugged. "More like exaggerate."

Blakey smacked her on the back. "You are such a con artist!"

"Could be dangerous," said Strayhorn. "All these aliens are more technologically advanced than we are. If we piss them off, they could *wipe out* humanity instead of *saving* it."

"We'll have to play it just right," said Dinah. "Keep them happy. Make them think they're getting what we promised."

"*If* we can even get them *interested*," said Mahalia.

"Right." Dinah searched Strayhorn's eyes for some sign of approval. At first, they were just as flat, gray, and inscrutable as always.

Then, she saw the light.

"Okay," said Strayhorn. "Let's see if we can make this work."

And Dinah's heart danced like a child in her chest.

The next day started out hopefully.

Team Earth set up early in the Worlds' Fair hall and attacked their mission with fresh enthusiasm. Strayhorn and Blakey manned the booth while Dinah and Mahalia traversed the crowd, using big smiles and chocolate from the *Diogenes'* stores to try to lure visitors.

The four teammates attacked the day as if it were their first at the Fair. Every one of them dug in with new energy and intensity, casting aside the pessimism of the previous day. Even Blakey gave it his all.

And they tried everything. Every line of bullshit they could imagine.

"Come one, come all!" said Dinah as she worked the crowd--wondering as she did so if any of the aliens understood a word she said. "Come see the vacation paradise of *Earth*!" Naturally, she left out the part about Earth being a global warming hellhole. (Though it *could* be a paradise to some of the aliens, for all she knew.)

"Follow me!" Mahalia said from the other side of the room. "Spiritual enlightenment awaits you on the holiest planet in the galaxy--*Earth*!"

"Visit the ancient world where all life began!" said Dinah. "Meet the seers whose visions foretell your future!

"Come to the miracle planet!" said Mahalia. "Heals all wounds, cures all diseases, and grants eternal life!"

"Your fantasies will come to life on Earth!" said Dinah.

"The gambling capital of the galaxy!" said Mahalia.

"Where golf is a way of life!"

"Be king of the world for a day!"

"Find lost treasure!"

"The streets are paved with gold!"

"Whatever you want!" said Dinah. "That's what you'll find on *Earth*!"

But it was all for nothing.

Throughout the day, only a handful of aliens came close enough to the booth to see the phony presentation whipped up by Strayhorn and Blakey--computer-generated images of a paradise that was nothing at all like the modern, dying Earth. The rest of the crowd was too busy gawking at other displays to take a look. Even the booth next-door, which featured a gray blob oozing green liquid in a silver bowl, attracted more attention.

By the time the Fair closed for the day, alien hordes rushing the doors like school kids on the way to summer vacation, Team Earth hadn't made a single deal. They hadn't fibbed up the slightest nibble of interest.

The four teammates slouched around the booth, shaking their heads and sighing. Aliens paraded past on their way to the exits, but none of them paused or even glanced over.

"No one can say we didn't try our best," said Mahalia, pushing alien freebies from other booths into a box. "It wasn't meant to be."

Blakey slumped on a folding chair with his lumpy bald head in his hands. "One good thing about the end of the world," he said. "When we go down in history as incompetent moron failures, at least there won't be much history *left*."

Strayhorn sat bolt upright, staring at the alien masses as they trooped past. "We'd better be on our way." His voice was cold and flat. "We're done here."

Dinah sat beside him and watched his face. He looked stern and impassive, unmoved...but she had a feeling that a lot more was going on inside.

He had failed to save the human race. How could that not tear him apart? How could that not *destroy* him?

"Well," said Mahalia. "How about a little clean-up music?" With a flick of her wrist, she popped a digital music player from the hip pocket of her red jumpsuit and laid it on the table. She pressed the surface of the thin, silver device, which was about the size of a playing card, and it started giving off music.

Jazz music, which was what Mahalia listened to the most.

"Come on." Mahalia tapped Blakey's shoulder. "Let's find a cart to haul this stuff back to the ship."

Blakey sighed. "Might as well," he said, and then he got up and went with her.

That left Dinah and Strayhorn sitting together in the booth. A trumpet ballad filtered from Mahalia's player, its slow, sweet notes adding to the melancholy mood.

Strayhorn rubbed his eyes, then placed his palms flat on the table. "I failed," he said. "It was up to me to save the world, and I couldn't do it."

Dinah laid her hand on top of his. It was the first time she'd ever touched him outside the line of duty. "Please don't give up," she said. "There must be something we can do."

Strayhorn didn't pull his hand away. His gaze remained fixed on the aliens parading past. "We can beg, maybe," he said. "But these people out here don't seem too inclined to charity."

"Then we'll change their inclination." Impulsively, Dinah cupped his chin and turned his face toward her. "Trust me, Alec. We'll do it together."

Then, Dinah surprised herself. Before she could think better of it, she leaned up and kissed Strayhorn on the mouth.

He didn't resist. In fact, after the first moment, he actively kissed her back, pressing his lips against hers.

The rest of the universe faded away. Heart pounding, Dinah reveled in the feel of Strayhorn's lips, the smell of his skin, the long-delayed contact between them.

The kiss went on and on, and Dinah wished it would never end. Nothing else mattered--not the crowd of alien lifeforms in the hall, not the impending doom of humanity, not Team Earth's failure. Not what would or wouldn't happen next.

For Dinah, it was a perfect kiss, a heavenly moment. She might never have broken the spell if not for the overwhelming new feeling that came upon her--the feeling that she was being watched.

Guessing that Blakey and Mahalia had returned to the booth, Dinah opened her eyes...and jumped. The kiss broke, and the perfect moment ended.

Dinah had been right about being watched, but not by Blakey and Mahalia. Instead of two pairs of human eyes, dozens of alien ones were trained on her and Strayhorn--eyes of all shapes and colors and sizes, eyes on stalks, eyes of crystal, eyes with wings.

For the first time all week, a crowd had gathered around Team Earth's booth at the Worlds' Fair.

"What the hell?" said Strayhorn. "What's going on?"

Dinah thought for a moment, then grinned. She thought she understood the situation. "Congratulations," she said. "We've finally found something they want to see."

And then she kissed Strayhorn again.

"Come one, come all!" Blakey stood on the table of the Team Earth booth and used his best carnival barker voice. "Experience the wonders of Earth's greatest treasure--*love*!"

Dinah and Strayhorn still sat behind the table, kissing...and the crowd of aliens watching them had grown into a mob. The aliens fanned out in all directions, hooting and babbling and jostling for a better view of the action.

Mahalia, meanwhile, acted as security, backing off any onlookers who got too close or made a grab for a body part. "The natives are restless," she said as she batted away an encroaching tentacle. "We'd better make a deal soon, or they're liable to rush the booth."

Strayhorn broke the kiss. "How do we market this? Earth as an interplanetary brothel?" His voice was heavy with sarcasm.

"If it saves humanity, *I'll* turn tricks!" Blakey said from above.

"Maybe they just like to watch," said Mahalia. "Performances, that is."

"Earth. Porno capital of the galaxy," said Blakey.

Mahalia shooed away a trio of flying yellow eyeballs. "Maybe we won't have to go that far. Maybe kissing's exciting enough for them."

Dinah kept pecking Strayhorn on the lips so they wouldn't lose the crowd. (Also because she was making the most of the situation.) "What about a kind of singles resort?" she said between kisses. "Humans could teach aliens about the concept of love and then match them up to experience it."

"I like it better than the brothel idea," said Mahalia.

"I say stick with the porno," said Blakey.

Strayhorn finished another kiss and nodded. "Try any and all of the above," he said. "Whatever it takes to trade for reverse global warming services--but start low and make the best deal you can."

"Roger that." Blakey winked at Mahalia. "Play something romantic, wouldja?"

"Will do." While wrestling with an alien's twitching feelers,

Mahalia switched the fast bebop coming out of her music player to a slow number with a lot of sultry sax.

Ben raised his arms and beamed at the alien mob. "Are you *lonely*, my friends? Do you want to be like *them*?" He gestured at Dinah and Strayhorn, who were locked in another kiss. "Would you give anything to discover the wonders of *love*?

"Then step right up!" Ben pumped his fists in the air. "This is your lucky day--if you have the technology to reduce carbon dioxide emissions in a planetary atmosphere, that is!"

"Hey," whispered Strayhorn. "Easy on the tongue."

Dinah leaned back and stared at him. They'd been kissing for at least two hours straight, mouth to mouth in front of an audience of gaping aliens.

So why was Strayhorn sounding *shy* all of a sudden?

Maybe, thought Dinah, he felt self-conscious with all the aliens watching him. Maybe he was getting tired. Maybe he was just stressed out about this being his last chance for a deal to save humanity.

Whatever the reason, Strayhorn didn't elaborate.

"Okay," said Dinah.

"Thanks," said Strayhorn, and then he licked his lips and leaned back in to resume kissing.

Dinah gladly rejoined him, though the moment had sapped a little of her fun. Even as she savored the warmth and pressure of Strayhorn's mouth, she couldn't help worrying in the back of her mind about why he'd nixed her French kiss.

"Thiiis being wants love," said Heavy, inflating his bald human face to speak to Team Earth. "He wants all the love he can get."

Heavy twisted his eggplant body and wriggled his cilia at the alien who had just pushed out of the crowd behind him. The new alien, who was seven feet tall, looked like an inside-out centaur covered in rough, blood-red crust and black bristles.

"His name iiis Ogog Lugofarloff," said Heavy. "Ogog wiiill buy the riights to all human love."

"Let's talk price then," said Blakey. "Can Ogog reverse global warming on our homeworld?"

Heavy rattled off a chain of rapid clacks and dings that sounded like an old manual typewriter in action. Ogog made the same kind of sounds back at him, mixed with the clomping of one black hoof on the floor.

"No," Heavy said when it was over. "But he *could* reengiiineer your species to surviive the new cliimate."

Ogog clattered and clomped again, ending with a decisive belch.

"Here iiis an example of hiiis work." Heavy fluttered his head-capped cilia in Ogog's direction. "Ogog has reengiiineered *hiiimself* multiiiiple tiimes."

Strayhorn broke the latest kiss and shot Blakey a glare that said it all.

Blakey nodded and winked, then turned back to Heavy and Ogog. "Give us your contact information, Ogog buddy. We'll have to get back to you on that."

After another hour of kissing while Blakey wheeled and dealed, Strayhorn pulled his lips back just enough to talk to Dinah. "I wonder what would happen if we switched with the others?"

Dinah looked out at the crowd of gaping aliens. "Do you want to take the chance?"

"No," said Strayhorn. "Not yet, anyway."

Dinah smiled and touched his cheek. "Just relax, Alec. Relax and enjoy."

Strayhorn scanned the babbling alien mob, then met Dinah's

gaze and held it. He stared deep into her eyes, searching for some-thing...and then his frown darkened.

"Why did you kiss me the first time?" he said.

Dinah shrugged. "To make you feel better."

"That's it?" said Strayhorn. "That's the only reason?"

Dinah hesitated, then decided to show her cards. "I wanted to," she said. "I've wanted to kiss you for a while now."

"I see." Strayhorn's frown smoothed out into his standard unreadable stare.

"Aren't you glad I did?" Dinah chuckled and rubbed noses with him. "Nobody came to our booth until I kissed you."

"Sure," said Strayhorn.

"In fact," said Dinah, "it might turn out to be the kiss that saves humanity, right?"

"Right," said Strayhorn.

"I'll bet they'll even make a movie about it someday." Dinah leaned close, brushing her lips against his. "A real love story."

And then she kissed him again, heart soaring with heat and delight like a butterfly or a dream.

"III have another customer for you," said Heavy. "She assures me she has the technical capabiiiliiitiies to reverse your homeworld's global warmiiing."

Dinah looked up in mid-kiss to see the gray blob from the silver bowl in the booth next-door bobbing in midair beside Heavy.

"Her name iiis Melliiicloriiis Myopa Quozahnna Non Zadacta." Heavy flicked his cilia in the blob's direction and made his human face smile. "She iiis empress of the Zlatyr Realm. The green fluiiid she iiis secreting means she iiis about to giiive biiirth."

"Tell her highness congratulations," Blakey told Heavy. "Ask her how we can be of service."

"Ask her yourself," said Heavy. "She iiis quiite capable of under-standiiing your language."

Blakey smiled at the gray blob as it hovered and dripped green fluid. "That's great. So how can we help you?"

"Melliiicloriiis wiiishes to buy all love," said Heavy, "and destroy iiit."

"Destroy it?" said Blakey.

"So she can market a cheaper, inferior substiiitute," said Heavy.

"Of course." Blakey glanced at Strayhorn but didn't seem to feel the need to wait for his advice. "Contact information, please. We'll have to get back to you on that."

After another hour of kissing, Strayhorn pulled away from Dinah and rubbed his jaw. "I can't keep this up," he said. "We need to switch personnel."

"I know what you mean." Dinah's lips were sore, and her jaw ached--not that she intended to stop the kissathon anytime soon. "I think we'll be okay if we just take a break for a minute."

"No," said Strayhorn. "It's time to switch." He started to get up from his chair.

"Really," said Dinah. "I'll be fine."

"You don't understand," said Strayhorn. "We *need* to switch."

Just then, Blakey let out a loud whoop. "We have a winnah!"

"Yay!" Mahalia grinned and applauded. "This is it, Captain! We found the real deal!"

Dinah had missed the latest flurry of negotiations. She looked over to see Blakey shaking the tentacle of a seven-foot-tall orange-furred squid-thing. "What is it?" she said. "What's the deal?"

"Kioska here will fix Earth's atmosphere." Blakey patted the orange squid's rubbery spear-point head. "He'll even terraform the planet to reverse the global warming damage to the ecosystem!"

Strayhorn walked around the table to Blakey and Kioska. "What'll it cost us?"

"You're gonna love this." Blakey threw an arm around Strayhorn's shoulders. "How would you like to be the first man to set foot on an alien planet?"

Two weeks later, Dinah blinked as light flooded the darkened stage where she and Strayhorn sat. She found herself gazing out at a huge crowd of orange-furred squid people, packed into a vast, upside-down theater.

Thousands of squid dangled by their tentacles from rungs in the ceiling. Each squid had one giant eye, blood-red and unblinking, fixed on Dinah and Strayhorn.

A chill rippled up Dinah's back as she felt their eyes upon her. Yet again, she marveled at where she was, so far from home, on an alien world that no human being before her had ever visited.

Kioska had led them here, to his homeworld, from the space station. It was here that the humans would hold up their end of the deal and earn salvation for dying Mother Earth.

Suddenly, a familiar figure tumbled onto the stage--eggplant-shaped Heavy, Team Earth's self-appointed manager. Stopping in the middle of the stage, he inflated an

orange-furred squid face on one of his cilia and turned it to the crowd. While Heavy unleashed a stream of wild squeaks for the audience, he puffed up a human face behind him and translated his words through it for Dinah and Strayhorn.

"Love!" said Heavy. "The new sensation! The most iiincrediiible experiience iiin the galaxy!"

The crowd responded with a deafening blast of whistles and squeals.

"Are you ready to liiive the dream?" said Heavy. "Are you ready for *love*?"

The squid things squealed louder. They swung back and forth on their rungs and smacked their bodies against each other with abandon.

"Then let the love begiiin!" As the noise and motion of the

crowd reached a wild pitch, Heavy hurtled off the stage, leaving Dinah and Strayhorn alone in the spotlight.

Backstage, Mahalia switched on her music player, which she'd tuned to broadcast through the theater's sound system. This time, instead of jazz, it played an opera piece--the Flower Duet from *Lakmé*, a sweet, soaring blend of two winding soprano voices.

That was Dinah and Strayhorn's cue. Smiling, Dinah leaned across the padded bench on which they sat. She slipped a hand behind Strayhorn's head, combing her fingers through his thick, dark hair, and pulled him close.

Their eyes met, and then their lips did, too.

They hadn't kissed since the end of the Worlds' Fair two weeks ago, and Dinah craved him. Returning to his lips felt like a fabulous culmination, an unimaginably perfect consummation. Every nerve in her lips flared with extraordinary sensitivity, magnifying every millimeter and millisecond of radiant contact between them.

Her pulse quickened, and her body warmed. Closing her eyes, she immersed herself in the building passion, the thrill of love on a grand scale, of legendary, history-making love.

Dinah was so caught up in the experience that at first, she didn't notice the change in the crowd. It took a few moments for the rising commotion to penetrate her romantic haze, to make her realize that the balance of the beautiful, dreamlike tide was shifting.

Opening her eyes, Dinah saw that the squid-people were jumping and bumping in the rafters. A growing racket rang out through the theater, a din of the shrillest,

highest-pitched squeals and whistles she'd yet heard from the orange-furred creatures.

As it got worse, drowning out the opera soundtrack, Dinah exchanged a look with Strayhorn. His typically blank expression had switched to one of fierce, alert intensity.

"What's happening?" said Dinah. "What do they want?"

Suddenly, Heavy jetted across the stage and jolted to a stop beside her. "What's goiiing on here?" he said with his bald human face.

"*You* tell *us*!" said Dinah.

"What are they saying?" said Strayhorn.

"'We want love!'" Heavy spun in a circle, every one of his heads and cilia quivering with agitation. "That's what they're sayiiing! They want love!"

The uproar from the crowd was so loud, Dinah had to shout to make herself heard. "I don't understand! We were *giving* them love!"

"Not liike before! Now try harder!" With that, Heavy whipped around and flashed offstage, leaving Dinah and Strayhorn alone.

As the crowd noise rose, Dinah gazed out at the hordes of orange-furred squid. "I guess we've got a tougher audience here," she said. "Necking isn't enough."

"We need to get out of here," said Strayhorn. "If they rush the stage, we're dead."

"No!" said Dinah. "Earth's depending on us!"

With that, she started unbuttoning her top.

"What are you doing?" said Strayhorn.

Dinah slid her arms from the sleeves of her blouse and tossed it to the stage. "What does it *look* like I'm doing?" With a shrug, she pressed closer to him, reaching for the buttons of his shirt. "If they want more, let's *give* them more."

Strayhorn grabbed her wrist, and Dinah pushed herself forward. With her free hand, she tore his shirt all the way open, then snaked an arm around his back and yanked him toward her.

"I say let's give them their money's worth," said Dinah, right before she lunged in for a ravenous, grinding kiss.

Strayhorn didn't get into the spirit of things at all, but Dinah kept working on him. She was convinced she could bring him around, especially once the squid-people started to settle down.

The problem was, instead of settling down, the squid-people grew more agitated. The clamor in the theater got worse with each passing second.

Dinah heard what sounded like falling bodies hitting the floor. When she looked out at the crowd, she saw squid dropping from the ceiling by the hundreds, bouncing to a landing on the theater floor on spring-loaded tentacles.

As soon as they landed, the squid started hopping toward the stage.

Yet again, Heavy zipped into the spotlight, spinning and quivering. "What iiis *wrong* with you two? They want *love*! Giiive them love love *love*!"

As Heavy darted away, Dinah shoved Strayhorn onto his back and pounced. Straddling his hips, she set to work undoing his pants while he gaped up at her in shock.

"I guess we have to take this all the way," said Dinah.

"No!" said Strayhorn. "Don't!"

"Give it everything you've got," said Dinah. "Remember, the future of humanity is riding on it!"

Before she could go any further, Strayhorn suddenly sat up and pushed her away. "I said *no*!"

Dinah fell back and rolled off the bench. She winced and cried out as she hit the hard floor of the stage on her side.

"Hey!" she said. "What was *that* for?"

"Even if we *weren't* about to be swarmed by alien squid-people," said Strayhorn, gesturing at the approaching audience, "I *can't* make love to you! I'm in love with someone else!"

"What?" Dinah leaped to her feet. "*Who*?"

"Look." Strayhorn pointed behind her, into the backstage wings. "That's who."

Dinah turned and saw Ben Blakey hurrying toward them. "*Blakey*?" she said. "You're in love with *Blakey*?"

Strayhorn shook his head. "Not Blakey."

Just then, Dinah saw Mahalia charge out after Blakey. "Oh." Dinah felt her face flush. "I get it."

Mahalia rushed past Blakey and grabbed Strayhorn's shoulders. A million little memories suddenly fell into place in Dinah's mind--a jumble of looks and touches and words exchanged between Strayhorn and Mahalia that she'd always chalked up to simple friendship.

Only now she knew better.

Why didn't I see it before?

At that moment, Heavy bolted over among them. "Where iiis

the love?" His voice was high and electric with fear. "Make the love! Make the love before iiit iiis *too late*!"

Dinah thought it was too late already. The orange-furred squid-people were hopping onto the stage, converging on the spotlight with deadly purpose.

"That's what we were *doing*!" said Strayhorn. "What else do you *want* from us?"

"No no no!" said Heavy. "No love! No love at all!" He flipped and spun and twisted in midair, giving off a smell like chocolate. "They want the *sounds*! The

dah-dah-dee-dah!"

"What the *hell* are you talking about?" said Blakey.

"*You* know!" Heavy flopped over and curled up, then uncurled and stretched out. "The *sounds* you made at the Worlds' Fair, when the two of you kiiissed! Liike

dah-dah-dee-dah-doo. The *love*."

Dinah shook her head. "I don't get it."

"Wait." Mahalia snapped her fingers. "You mean the *music*? The *music* I played in the booth when they kissed?"

"'Music'?" Heavy shuddered.

"Like this." Mahalia did a little scat-singing, improvising syllables over a jazzy snatch of melody. "That's music. *Jazz* music."

"'Music'?" said Heavy. "Don't you mean 'love'?"

Mahalia looked from Strayhorn to Blakey to Dinah, eyes wide with understanding. "Oh my God," she said. "This whole time, they wanted *music*, not *love*."

"They thought we made it when we kissed," said Dinah.

As the squid-people closed in, Mahalia dashed offstage. The squid were just reaching for Dinah and the others when the music playing over the theater's sound system changed from opera to jazz.

Just like that, the orange-furred squid halted their approach. As one, they swayed and squeaked in time with the music, tentacles rippling with the flow of a soaring, sparkling trumpet solo.

"Nothing like a little Miles Davis to soothe the savage alien," said Mahalia as she trotted back to the group. "And more where that came from." She held up her slim silver music player and tapped it with her fingernail.

Dinah let out a deep breath and slumped onto the bench. "That was close."

"You diiid iiit!" said Heavy, scooting around Team Earth in a jaunty circle. "You made the *love* again!"

"I still don't see what the big deal is," said Blakey. "Why don't you just make it yourselves?"

"We can't," said Heavy. "You are the fiiirst. Thiiis iiis something *new* to us."

"No kidding." Blakey laughed and clapped Strayhorn on the back. "I guess maybe humans are worth something out here after all."

"So now what?" said Dinah. "What next?"

"Contiiinue the Worlds' Tour, of course!" said Heavy. "Liiive up to your end of the deal!"

Blakey threw an arm around Strayhorn's shoulders. "So we'll just send around a recording, right?"

"Wrong," said Heavy. "We must have *live performance. Live love* on tour! The deal *says* so!"

"And us a bunch of non-musicians." Dinah blew out her breath.

"We'll just lip-synch." Mahalia shook her music player. "Play along with the recordings and pretend we're making the music from scratch."

"What happens when they get tired of the recordings?" said Dinah. "What'll we do then?"

"Same thing we always do." Mahalia grinned and winked at her. "Same thing Miles and Monk and Trane and all the rest always did.

"Make it up as we go along."

ONE AWAKE IN ALL THE WORLD

Pass Candle could not see the creatures, except as winking blips of light on the flash-brain screen mounted in the flesh of his left arm. He didn't need to look at the screen, however, to know that the creatures were all around him and his partner, Nona Stiletto.

He could feel their presence. Could feel their eyes upon him, staring from the shadows of the darkened and fog-shrouded city.

More than that, he swore he could feel their malevolence. Their savagery.

He stiffened his right arm as he swept it from side to side, covering an arc of the gray fog with the snout of the warflower dark energy gun peeping from under the skin behind his wrist. He followed the arc with the single beam from his headlight—the round, white disk mounted like a third eye in the middle of his forehead.

Candle narrowed his dark brown eyes and stared into the headlight's beam, but he still saw nothing moving toward him in the fog. Maybe, his feelings were the product of his imagination, and the creatures in the shadows would turn out to be benevolent toward cybernetically enhanced humans like himself and Nona.

But somehow, he doubted it.

Stiletto said nothing to suggest she felt the same way, but the posture of her slender frame as she walked alongside him was as stiff and guarded as his. Her head ticked from side to side, flicking her golden ponytail to and fro in the darkness.

The retractable sleeves of her slick black form-fitting flowsuit were all the way up, like Candle's, leaving her weapon-and-instrument-studded arms free for action. She aimed her warflower directly ahead, and Candle knew from experience that she was ready to whip it around in a heartbeat and use it.

"The humanoid's twenty meters ahead," said Candle, watching the readings on his flash-brain screen. "Distress signal's strong and life signs're steady. She's surrounded by non-humanoid life-forms, like we are."

Just then, Candle smelled an odor like strong vinegar and heard a sound like claws clacking on the pavement to his left. He and Stiletto swung in that direction simultaneously, lighting it up with the beams of their headlights. Candle saw nothing in the newly illuminated area but a building's stone wall and a scattering of what looked like splintered bones at its base.

"Playing hard to get." Candle nervously combed the fingers of his right hand through his wavy salt-and-pepper hair.

"Let's hope they stay that way," said Stiletto.

Candle started forward again, following the female humanoid's life signs. "Seventeen meters to go," he said. "Easy-peasy."

The sound of breaking glass echoed in the distance. Claws or something like them clacked not far away.

"Guess again," said Stiletto, sweeping her headlight toward the clacking, then forward again.

Candle thought Stiletto had a point. In the darkness and fog, it felt like they'd walked several kilometers rather than the half kilometer they'd actually traveled from their spacecraft, the *Sun Ra*, which was parked at the edge of the city.

Though Candle wasn't the jumpy type, he was having his doubts about what a good idea it had been to walk away from the *Sun Ra* at all...or land on this planet in the first place. Trouble was, he just hated ignoring a distress signal like the one that'd brought him here; some of his best jobs had come via distress signal.

He and Stiletto were first-class spacefaring exterminators, specializing in extra-nasty pests known as Squatters. Squatters ran people like puppets, remote-controlling them from somewhere beyond the Milky Way galaxy. Squatters reached out with their ultra-powerful minds and bonded people to them with over-whelming love and pleasure. Then, the Squatters sent these zombies, known as Wipeouts, on horrifically barbaric killing sprees.

Rumor had it the Squatters and Wipeouts were building up to something big, and people were scared. Contractors like Candle could make a living hunting the bastards full-time. Wipeout hunting was pretty damned rewarding for a top pro like Candle, in fact...es-pecially when he had a former Wipeout like Nona Stiletto for a partner.

Sure, Nona was still messed up from years of being possessed by the aliens. She had committed more violent crimes than she could remember, and she was marked forever by scars on the inside and outside.

But she knew everything about Wipeouts, and the Squatters had left her mean and strong. Just the fact that she had survived being separated from a Squatter showed what kind of a hardass she was. Candle had never heard of another Wipeout walking away from that ordeal alive.

And he couldn't think of anyone he'd rather have by his side today.

"Fourteen meters," he said, squinting into the ten-meter-deep cone of visibility that was the best his headlight could cut through the fog.

Candle and Stiletto pressed to within twelve meters of their target, then eleven. Finally, their headlights picked out a form in the gray soup.

At last, they got a look at the being they'd been seeking through the alien city...a being who, as far as they could tell, was the only remaining native humanoid on the planet.

In size and build, she resembled a human child, five or six years old...a little girl with glittering purple skin, multi-faceted red insect eyes, and not a hair on her head.

Candle and Stiletto lowered their arms so the beams of their headlights weren't flashing right in the little girl's face.

Candle told the girl his name, his flash-brain converting his speech into audio she could understand. "This is Nona," he added, hiking a thumb at Stiletto. "What's your name?"

"Luma," said the little girl. She wore a simple white shift and sandals. As she spoke, she hugged a ragged doll tightly against her chest.

On one wrist, Luma wore a gold bracelet set with a blinking amber crystal. A glance at the flash-brain screen confirmed Stiletto's suspicion that the bracelet was the source of the distress signal transmissions.

"Cool name," said Candle. "Nice to meet you, Luma."

Luma cocked her head to one side and narrowed her faceted eyes. "You look funny," she said. "What's wrong with you?"

Candle smirked at Stiletto. "There's nothing wrong with us," he said. "We're just not from around here."

"Okay," said Luma.

"We want to help you," said Candle. "Can you tell us why you're all alone here?"

Luma dropped her chin against the head of her doll and twisted slowly from side to side. As Stiletto watched, the little girl's skin changed color, shifting from dark purple to deep blue...signaling a mood change?

"I'm lost," Luma said softly. "I can't find my family. I woke up and went outside, and now I can't find them."

"Do you know where there're more people like you?" said Candle. "People who look like you?"

"You mean Sagrans?" said Luma.

"Is that what the people're called?" said Candle.

Luma nodded. "Sagrans."

"You know where they are?" said Stiletto.

Luma shook her head. "There's no one around except the Skil-la." As she said it, her voice dropped to a near whisper, and her skin shifted to deep purple again.

"The Skilla aren't people like you, are they?" said Candle.

"No," said Luma, shivering. "They're scary. Everyone says the Skilla are holy, but I think they're scary, too. I think they're going to get me."

Candle scooped the little girl up into his arms.

"Don't worry, Luma," he said, patting her back. "You're not alone anymore. We'll keep you safe."

"You will?"

"Yeah. That's why we came here. To help you."

"Will you find my family, too?" Luma's skin changed from purple back to deep blue.

"We'll do our best." Candle smiled and bounced her affection-ately in his arms. "I promise."

Stiletto's heart beat faster, but not because of any impending danger. It was the sight of Candle with Luma, the way he held her and reassured her.

Stiletto wished he'd do that for her, too. She wished he'd love her the way that she loved him.

She hadn't always felt this way. She'd been working with Candle since he'd freed her from the Squatter three years ago, and she'd only been sure she wanted him within the last six months.

She really didn't know if he felt the same way, though, and frankly, she hadn't been going out of her way to find out. The hardass routine that was so important to her job and just getting through the day was hard to push aside...plus which, her head was still a wreck from her time as a Wipeout. The Squatter was gone, but it had left behind a boatload of poison. Sometimes, Stiletto still felt echoes of the bastard swimming around in there, and she wondered if he was regenerating somehow.

That was what worried her the most and kept her from reaching out to Candle. What if she was still a danger to him, a sleeper agent with secret orders implanted at a deep level her deprogramming had missed?

Unfortunately, the more she tried to lock her feelings away, the stronger they grew.

And seeing Candle comforting Luma made them stronger still.

Candle put Luma down but held on to her tiny, green hand as he and Stiletto talked.

"Any ideas?" he said in a half-whisper.

Stiletto stared at the blinking lights on the flash-brain screen. "I've detected low-level mechanical vibrations."

"Where abouts?" said Candle.

"Center of the city. Four kilometers that way." Stiletto aimed her headlight into the murk.

"Where there's working machinery, there might be people," said Candle. "Shielded from sensors, maybe."

"There're a lot of non-humanoids between here and there."

Candle nodded. "And we can't take the *Sun Ra* in," he said, "because there's nowhere to land. Not even a flat rooftop." He sighed. "We'll have to keep going on foot."

Candle heard a whooping cry like hysterical laughter in the distance. Luma's hand fluttered, and he tightened his grip on it.

"Up for a hike?" he said to Stiletto.

She nodded. "I'm ready."

"How about you?" Candle gave Luma's hand a squeeze.

"Ready," said Luma.

"Then let's get going," said Candle.

Though Stiletto wasn't easily freaked, she felt the hairs on the back of her neck stand up way too often as she, Candle, and Luma trudged through the city.

She was being stalked. By something she couldn't see.

But she could hear it. The Skilla raised a constant clamor through the city, their distant whoops and yowls accompanied by the sounds of smashing and thumping and shattering. Close by, their claws clacked along the pavement, moving when Stiletto, Candle, and Luma moved...stopping when they stopped. Always, when the creatures were near, Stiletto smelled their heavy, vinegar-like scent in the humid air.

And the number of them that were close-by was growing. Flash-brain scans of the surrounding area revealed that more Skilla were clustering near Stiletto, Candle, and Luma with each passing moment.

"We're drawing a crowd," Stiletto said to Candle, keeping her voice to a whisper for Luma's sake. "Maybe a warning shot'll drive them off."

"Don't provoke them," said Candle. "Not yet. We're so outnumbered, let's put off a fight as long as we can." With that, he turned his attention to Luma. "So," he said, shifting his voice to a less serious tone. "What's your friend's name?"

Luma looked up at him, a puzzled expression on her glittering, deep blue face. She looked down at her doll then, and understood. "Her name is Gala," she said.

"How long've you and Gala been together?" said Candle.

Luma raised the doll to her ear. "Gala says we've been together since I was a little girl."

Candle smiled. "Cool." He still held on to Luma with his left hand and continually scanned his warflower back and forth with his right. "And how did the two of you meet?"

"Mommy and Daddy gave her to me," said Luma.

"The last time you saw your mommy and daddy, what were they doing?" said Candle.

"They were sleeping," said Luma.

"For a long time?" said Stiletto.

"I think so," said Luma. "I woke up and went for a walk. I wanted to go home to get my dreambook, but then I couldn't find home."

"So your family was somewhere other than home," said Candle. "What did this place look like?"

"Big," said Luma. "And dark." She raised the doll to her ear and listened for a moment. "Gala says Mommy and Daddy will be mad at me."

"Why is that?" said Stiletto.

"I wasn't supposed to open the door," said Luma. "I wasn't supposed to go outside."

"Because of the Skilla?" said Candle.

"Uh-huh," said Luma. "They're holy, but they can hurt you." Again, she listened to the doll. "Gala says they're going to hurt all of us, and it'll be my fault because I opened the door."

"Try to help Gala not worry so much," said Candle. "Tell her we're going to take good care of you."

"Okay," said Luma.

Just then, something heavy and hard hit the ground near Stiletto.

Everyone stopped in their tracks. Luma gasped and threw herself against Candle.

Spinning, Stiletto threw light in the direction of the noise. A block of stone, big as a human head, lay in the street barely three meters away.

Suddenly, Stiletto heard a clatter of approaching claws and caught the smell of vinegar in the air. A quick glance at her flash-brain screen confirmed the evidence of her ears, and she whirled around.

Two blips had disengaged from the unseen crowd of Skilla and were charging directly at Candle and Luma.

Without a word, Stiletto fired her warflower, shooting a crackling bolt of energy into the fog. Immediately, she heard a wailing screech, erupting loud and close enough to hurt her ears. Through a tunnel burned in the fog by the warflower's beam, she glimpsed shining silver eyes like a pair of coins suspended in midair.

Stiletto lashed the warflower around, seeking the second oncoming Skilla. She was rewarded with another raging screech. Then, with a flurry of clattering claws, the creatures hurtled away, their cries receding in the distance.

"So much for putting off a fight," said Candle.

"These creatures're pretty smart," said Stiletto. "They staged a diversion by throwing that stone, then came at us from the other direction."

Luma tugged on Candle's uniform then, and he and Stiletto looked down. The little girl's face was pinched in an expression of pure anguish. Her glittering skin was so fiery red that it looked like it would be hot to the touch.

"Gala says you lied!" Inky, black tears streamed down her face. "She says the Skilla *are* going to get us!"

"Tell Gala it's okay to be scared," said Candle, "but things can turn out fine no matter how scary they seem."

Luma shuddered with sobs. "Gala doesn't believe you!" Stiletto searched her mind for a plan to calm the child, then crouched down beside her. "That's because Gala hasn't heard the story of the girl with the invisible friend," said Stiletto. "Have you?"

Still sobbing, Luma shook her head. The inky tears rolled off her jaw and fell onto her white shift, staining it with spatters of black.

"You think Gala might like to hear the story?" said Stiletto, ignoring a whooping scream-laugh in the distance.

Luma shrugged.

Stiletto got to her feet and scooped up the child in one smooth motion. "Once upon a time," she said, "there was a lonely little girl. She didn't have any friends, because her parents kept moving from planet to planet all the time."

Luma's tears stopped flowing. "No friends at all?" she said, her skin shifting from bright red to maroon.

"None," said Stiletto. "Then, one day, she heard a voice. It seemed to be coming from thin air. 'I'll be your friend,' said the voice."

Luma's face relaxed from a frown to an expression of wide-eyed interest. Her skin went from maroon to violet.

"The girl couldn't see who was talking," said Stiletto. "She was scared, but she was so lonely that she said, 'Sure, you can be my friend.'

"So from that day on, the girl had an invisible friend. There was just one problem."

"What?" said Luma. "What problem?"

"The invisible friend was *mean*," said Stiletto, "but the girl didn't find out right away."

"When *did* she find out?" said Luma.

Stiletto raised an eyebrow. "To be continued," she said. "If you're good, I'll tell you the rest of the story later."

"But I want to know now!" said Luma, scowling.

"I'll tell you after we've gone a little further," said Stiletto. She lowered the child to the pavement and held her hand.

"But I can't wait!" said Luma.

"Later," Stiletto said sternly.

"All right," said Luma. Though she sounded unhappy, the dark green color of her skin revealed her true feelings. Her terrified panic was gone, replaced by a calmer composure.

Candle leaned close to Stiletto and whispered in her ear. "Way to handle the kid," he said. "I didn't know you had it in you."

Stiletto nodded without smiling, but she felt a rush of warmth at what he'd said.

Candle thought it was a good thing that Luma became obsessed with pestering Stiletto to continue her story. The Skilla were growing bolder, and he was glad the little girl's mind was on something else.

Again and again, the creatures raced close and bolted away. They dropped stones and bones and shingles from above, littering the route with debris.

And their numbers, according to the flash-brain, continued to grow. Candle wondered how many more of the creatures would join the pack over the kilometer and a half that he, Stiletto, and Luma had yet to walk. He wondered what other surprises the Skilla would spring.

Unfortunately, he didn't have to wait long for the next one. It happened just as Stiletto was about to continue her story.

"All right," she said, finally giving in to Luma's repeated requests to know what happened next. "I'll tell you a little more."

Luma's skin was pale green, which Candle knew by now meant the child felt at ease. "Tell me!" she said.

Before Stiletto could get out a word, the rocks started flying.

Candle felt something strike his arm with a stinging impact. As he whipped around, he felt another solid object collide with his kneecap.

A shower of rocks followed, hurtling straight toward him from out of the fog.

Candle opened fire with the warflower, punching the searing beam through the murk. "Get down!"

Behind him, he heard the whine of Stiletto's warflower firing at the same time as his, lashing out at the other side of the street.

Another volley of rocks leaped out of the fog from a different spot. Candle spun and fired there, too, then combed the beam along the street to pick off any additional ambushers lying in wait.

The bombardment ended, giving way to a deafening chorus of shrieks and screams from all directions.

"Everybody all right?" said Candle.

Even as he said it, he could see the answer to his question.

Luma was sprawled on the pavement, eyes closed. Her skin was white as a bedsheet except for a blazing red welt above her left eye.

"How is she?" said Candle, standing guard while Stiletto scanned Luma's head with her fingertip sensor pads.

"Lots of swelling in there," said Stiletto. "She might have a concussion."

"Can we treat her?"

Stiletto removed the first aid kit from a hip pocket of her black flowsuit. "Just the surface wound," she said, yanking a tubular spray applicator from the kit. "The deep swelling's another matter." Stiletto ran the tip of the applicator over the welt on Luma's forehead, administering a spray of antiseptic, anesthetic, and anti-inflammatory agents. "Her body's different from anything I've worked on before. Trying to treat the internal injury could do more harm than good."

"Should we keep her awake in case there's a concussion?" said Candle.

"Damned if I know. If she was human, I'd say definitely."

"Let's risk it, then," said Candle. "*If* we can wake her up."

"Roger that," said Stiletto, brushing a strand of blond hair out of her face.

The Skilla continued to howl and scream-laugh as Candle bent down by Luma's right ear. "Luma," he said. "Wake up. It's time to wake up."

Luma didn't twitch.

"Please, Luma," said Candle, raising his voice. "We need you to wake up."

Still nothing.

Stiletto leaned close to Luma's left ear. "Do you want to know what happened next?" she said.

Finally, Luma stirred. Her snow-white skin fluxed pink, then shifted to pale orange.

And her red, faceted eyes flickered open.

"Yes," she said softly. "Please tell me."

As the Skilla kept circling and raising a ruckus, Candle and Stiletto continued toward the source of the mechanical vibrations.

Stiletto carried Luma in her arms and told her more about the little girl with the invisible friend...in other words, the story of Stiletto herself and the Squatter who had made her a Wipeout. Luma's skin shifted from pale orange to deep green, a change that Stiletto took as a good sign.

Stiletto told Luma how the little girl's invisible friend had played tricks on her and gotten her to play tricks on other people. (She didn't mention the fact that the "tricks" consisted of bloody killing sprees that claimed the lives of her own family and countless strangers.) Though the tricks the girl played were mean, Stiletto said, the invisible friend fooled her into thinking they were fun.

When Stiletto got to the part where the policeman showed up, Candle interrupted.

"What's our status?" he said.

Stiletto scanned their surroundings with her left-fingertip sensor pads. "Same as before."

Candle sighed. "How long till dawn?"

"About an hour," said Stiletto. "You thinking they're anti-daylight?"

"Hoping," said Candle. He looked at Luma. "What's the word on you-know-who?"

"Swelling's worse," said Stiletto.

"Let's hope those vibrations lead us to a doctor," said Candle.

Stiletto smirked. "What a day, huh?"

"Easy-peasy." Right after Candle said it, he winked one dark brown eye and gave Stiletto's shoulder a squeeze.

As his fingers pressed and released, Stiletto felt her face warm with a blush.

Candle was surprised, a little later, when Luma asked him to tell her a story.

She probably just wanted him to kill time while Stiletto took a break...but he figured he'd give it a shot. Anything to keep Luma awake, especially since she'd been yawning more and more often lately.

"Okay," said Candle. "Let's see." He thought for a moment, scrubbing his fingers through his wavy, salt-and-pepper hair. "I know," he said at last. "Have you heard the story of the lonely policeman?"

"No," said Luma, shaking her head. "Please tell me."

Candle cleared his throat. He'd decided to pick up Stiletto's story where she'd left off, but from his point of view.

"Once upon a time," he said, pacing the floor, "there was a lonely policeman. He was always busy, because these mean invisible friends kept making people play tricks on each other."

Luma yawned and rubbed her eyes. "You mean like the lonely little girl?"

"Yeah," said Candle. "As a matter of fact, he went to see that little girl one time. He said, 'Don't listen to your invisible friend, little girl. He's not nice.'"

"What did the girl say?"

Candle thought he'd skip over the part about Stiletto trying to kill him while under the Squatter's control. "To be continued," he said. "I'll tell you later."

"*This* is *dawn?*" said Candle, looking around at what was really just a brighter version of the same old fog.

"I guess it's better than *dark* fog, at least," said Stiletto.

"Not much of a silver lining if you ask me," said Candle.

As they walked, Stiletto and Candle combed their warflowers from side to side, ready to open fire at the first hint of aggression from the Skilla.

Stiletto knew the creatures were out there, lurking all around in great numbers...but they didn't make a sound. She heard neither the clack of a nearby claw nor a distant, screaming cry.

The hairs on the back of her neck wouldn't stay down. She

thought the silence was a lot harder to take than the cacophony of the night before.

Fortunately, Luma perked up enough to interrupt it. Her glittering skin switched from pale gray to turquoise, and her yawns became less frequent.

As she walked along between Stiletto and Candle, Luma tugged Stiletto's hand. "What happened next?" she said. "When the policeman told the little girl her friend wasn't nice?"

"Well," said Stiletto. "The invisible friend told the little girl the *policeman* was the mean one, so the girl tried to make the policeman go away."

"Did he?" said Luma.

"No," said Stiletto.

"But then what?"

Stiletto heard something crack nearby. "To be continued," she said, staring intently in the direction from which she'd heard the sound.

Instead of pleading with her, as usual, to keep telling the story, Luma turned right around to Candle.

"Did the policeman go away?" she said.

Candle smirked. He kept his eyes and warflower trained on the fog as he picked up the story.

"No," he said. "He made the invisible friend go away instead." *With forbidden drugs and hardcore psychic acupuncture*, he could've added, but he left that out.

"Did the policeman and the little girl make friends then?" said Luma.

"The opposite. She hated him." Candle couldn't resist taking his eyes off the fog long enough to glance Stiletto's way. She looked aloof as always, but he was sure he spotted a trace of a smile on her face.

"She hated him?" said Luma.

"Not forever," said Candle. "As time went on, they got to be friends."

"Better friends than the invisible friend was," said Stiletto.

Candle grinned. "Even though they didn't always get along."

"You can say that again," said Stiletto.

"The next thing you know, they were partners," said Candle.

"And no matter what happened," said Stiletto, "the little girl was glad the policeman had found her."

Candle was surprised. He'd caught a flash of emotion in her voice that he hadn't noticed before.

He looked in Stiletto's direction. She was looking down at the flash-brain screen on her left forearm, but he had the distinct feeling that she had been looking right at him just an instant before.

Suddenly then, she stopped in her tracks. "The Skilla are gone," she said.

Candle stopped. "What do you mean, gone?"

"I mean *gone*," said Stiletto. "No sign of them on flash sensors."

Candle looked around at the murk. "Maybe they hate daylight after all."

"It's possible." Stiletto didn't sound convinced.

"Well," said Candle, "let's not look a gift Skilla in the mouth. How far are we from the source of the mechanical vibrations?"

"Less than a kilometer," said Stiletto.

"Then let's get moving." Candle hoisted Luma off her feet and set out at a brisk jog to cover the remaining ground. Stiletto fell in beside him, watching the flash-brain screen for signs of renewed danger.

Luma wrapped her arms around Candle's neck and held on tight. "Guess what?" she said in his ear.

"What?" said Candle.

"I know what the names are," said Luma. "The names of the little girl and the policeman."

"Okay," said Candle. "What are they?"

"Nona and Pass," said Luma, and she giggled.

Candle smiled. "Cool," he said.

"Cool," said Luma, and then she squeezed her arms more tightly around his neck.

"Stop," said Stiletto. "This is it."

Squinting into the fog, she saw a gray metal door set into a low stone bunker at the end of the street.

"Ventilation system," said Stiletto. "That's what's been making those vibrations. It's pumping stale air out of an underground chamber and pumping in fresh."

"Sagran bio signs?" said Candle, gently bouncing Luma until her eyes opened. In spite of the run through the streets, Luma's sleepiness was coming back in force.

"Lots, but faint," said Stiletto, watching the flash-brain screen on her arm. "We didn't pick them up earlier because there's some kind of interference signal."

"Invisible fence, maybe?" said Candle. "A signal tuned to a frequency that keeps the Skilla out?"

"Beats me," said Stiletto, "but I think I found a way in." She pointed her fingertip sensors at the windowless stone bunker. "There's a shaft on the other side of the door, leading underground."

As Candle started for the bunker, he bounced Luma on his arm. "Look familiar?"

Luma grinned sleepily. "Yes!" she said, pointing an index finger at the bunker. "This is where Mommy and Daddy take me every year. This is the place I couldn't find when I got lost."

"Cool," Candle said with a smile. "Guess you're not lost anymore."

When the three of them reached the bunker, Stiletto gave the metal door a push. When it wouldn't open, she turned her attention to what looked like a release mechanism.

The release mechanism consisted of a keypad at eye level with ten push buttons. Each button was imprinted with an alien symbol; Stiletto's wild guess was that the symbols corresponded to the numbers zero through nine.

"Numeric code lock," she said, aiming her fingertip sensors at the mechanism. "Normally, I could crack this puppy open in a heartbeat."

"But?" said Candle.

"The device isn't electronic, so it'll take my flash-brain longer to analyze it."

Candle sighed. "What about you?" he said to Luma. "Have any idea how to open the door?"

Luma frowned and rubbed an eye with her fist. "Mommy taught me a song, but I don't know if I can remember all the words right now."

"You remember the tune at least?" said Candle.

"Maybe."

"How about giving it a try?" said Candle.

Stiletto was about to say something when she caught the smell of vinegar in the air. Before she even looked at the readout of the flash-brain, her heart started to pound.

Raising her warflower, she turned away from the door.

"Pass," she said, keeping her voice perfectly even. "Multiple Skilla life signs, coming in *fast*."

Candle nodded. "Guess our friends aren't so nocturnal after all."

In the distance, Stiletto could hear the clattering of claws. Hundreds of them.

Getting closer every second.

"How about if you work with Luma on remembering that song?" said Candle. "Music isn't my strong suit."

Stiletto moved in and took Luma, balancing the little girl's weight on her hip.

"Try to make it a fast number," said Candle. "Not that I expect much trouble at all whatsoever."

With a wink, he walked off to face the horde of creatures stampeding down the street.

Candle stationed himself twenty meters from the bunker and immediately opened fire. He blasted his warflower into the fog for a full minute before he finally caught his first glimpse of the Skilla.

One of the creatures slipped through the field of fire and lunged toward him. It was as big as a rhinoceros, with six lean legs and claws like scimitars. A huge scorpion's tail arced over its body, tipped with a spiked stinger as big as a man's head. Its torso was covered in long, crimson spines that glistened as if they were wet.

It had a face like an open wound lined with razor-sharp teeth.

As the warflower's beam lashed into the Skilla, Candle was disappointed. He had hoped that seeing the enemy would have made it seem less intimidating.

Now, he wished that the Skilla had stayed out of sight.

Stiletto would've thought, with the legion of Skilla attacking, that her biggest challenge would be calming Luma down. Instead, she had to fight to keep the little girl awake.

"Luma," Stiletto said sharply, shaking the girl in her arms. "How did the *song* go?"

Luma hummed three notes and closed her eyes.

Stiletto shook her. "Sing the *song*. The one about the door."

Luma's eyes drifted open. "Five laughing children standing in the rain," she sang softly, and then she stopped.

"Luma!" The sounds of battle filled Stiletto's ears.

Luma's eyes dropped shut, then popped open. "Five laughing children standing in the rain," she sang. "One of them's a three-year-old and two are six and ten."

Stiletto memorized the sequence of numbers from the song: five, one, three, two, six, one, zero.

"Number one is six feet tall and always gets the door," Luma sang without opening her eyes. "But Mommy says the ones she loves the best are two and four." Luma yawned and lowered her head back onto Stiletto's bare shoulder. "The end."

Stiletto added the numbers from the last two lines to the earlier sequence. She typed them into the keypad on the door, as if the top three keys were numbers one through three, the second row four through six, the third row seven through nine, and the bottom key zero.

She entered the sequence in a hurry: five, one, three, two, six, one, zero, one, six, one, two, four.

Nothing happened.

Candle didn't think he could hold off the Skilla for much longer.

As his warflower fire dropped the creatures at the front of the horde, more rushed up from behind. The pile of bodies kept rising, forcing Candle to aim upward at increasingly sharp angles. Then, the onrushing Skilla started using the pile as a diving platform.

As they hurtled through the fog from above, claws and stingers extended, Candle picked them off one after another...but the terrible rain wouldn't end. When one shrieking Skilla went down, another one or two always took its place.

They just never stopped coming. Candle knew, as each moment flew by and the bunker door stayed shut, that things were probably going to get much worse very soon.

As Stiletto went over Luma's song again, she found a place where she might have screwed up.

When Luma had sung, "But Mommy says the ones she loves the best are two and four," Stiletto had added the numbers one, two, and four to the sequence. What if the plural "ones" meant she should have added more than a single "one" to the string?

Stiletto puffed strands of blond hair out of her face and punched in the number sequence on the keypad again, this time adding another number one before the final two and four.

A second later, she heard the clicking of tumblers inside the door. Then, a clang and a scrape.

The door slid open, releasing a blast of musty air that overpowered the vinegar stink of the Skilla.

"Pass!" shouted Stiletto. "It's open!"

Candle was already backing toward the door when he heard her, but not because he had any idea that it was opening.

Two Skilla lunged at him, claws and stingers carving through the space where he'd stood only an instant before. He swept the beam of the warflower from one to the other, dropping them both...and as soon as their bodies collapsed to the pavement, three more leaped into the gap.

Candle unleashed another spray of fire from the warflower and backed into the doorway. Out of the corner of his eye, he saw Stiletto behind the door, waiting to pull it shut.

"On three!" said Candle. "One! Two!"

The last thing he saw before Stiletto slammed the door was one of those faces like a ragged, open wound, oozing saliva or mucus and crammed with a forest of teeth like shards of broken glass.

"Three!"

Even as the door crashed shut, Candle knew he'd see that face again in his nightmares.

Stiletto led the way down the spiral metal stairwell in the middle of the bunker. She didn't have to switch on her headlight, because the well was lit by an incandescent strip set into the stone wall.

Candle followed, carrying Luma. He talked to her and bounced her in his arms, though keeping her awake had become a losing battle.

At the base of the stairwell, Stiletto stepped onto a dirt floor in front of a pair of metal doors. A video monitor was mounted at eye level on one of the doors, and she activated it by twisting a large knob underneath it.

An adult male Sagran appeared on the screen. Like Luma, he had red, multifaceted eyes and no hair. He wore a sky blue tunic, and his glittering skin was pale green.

"Shhh," said the Sagran, touching his mouth with the tip of a finger. "Don't wake the sleepers."

Stiletto started to ask a question. The Sagran talked right over her, which clued her in that the video was strictly playback, not interactive.

"You are welcome to take your place among us," said the Sagran, opening his arms wide. "But first, please join me in a prayer."

The Sagran closed his eyes and solemnly bowed his head. "O gods of destruction," he said. "We freely offer the fruits of our labors to you. You bless us by tearing down what we have built, clearing the way for us to rebuild and be reborn.

"O Skilla," said the Sagran, "cleanse our cities with your sacred storm. Remind us that the physical world is fleeting, that we may cherish every breath of our lives.

"When at last you rest at the end of these three holy months, and our people awaken, may we find that you have left even less intact than the year before. May we continue to find fulfillment in the eternal cycle of creation and destruction."

The Sagran opened his eyes and lifted his head. "Enter," he said with a serene smile. "Dream of the storm above and the work ahead."

With that, the video screen went dark.

The double doors swung open on a pitch black space. Stiletto activated her headlight and stepped inside.

The first thing she saw by the beam of the headlight was the body of a woman, curled in a fetal position on blankets on the floor. The woman's eyes were closed, and her skin was pale gray. She wore a simple white shift like Luma's.

As Stiletto played the headlight over the floor, she saw that the woman wasn't alone. Everywhere Stiletto looked, the floor was covered with the bodies of Sagran adults and children, all with gray skin and eyes closed.

Stiletto scanned them with her fingertip sensor pads. "They're hibernating," she said.

"'Three holy months,'" said Candle, quoting the prayer from the video. "It's the only way they can coexist with the Skilla. Hibernate while the Skilla are on the rampage."

"They should wipe out the Skilla and be done with it," said Stiletto.

"Not if the Skilla are sacred to them," said Candle. "I guess the Sagrans see them as gods of destruction, like the Hindu god Shiva on Earth."

Stiletto crouched beside a sleeping Sagran and scanned his head with her fingertip sensors. She scanned two other sleepers the same way.

"They've got the same internal swelling as Luma," said Stiletto. "Could be a normal part of the hibernation process."

"Not a concussion after all," said Candle. "Luma was just trying to go back to sleep like everyone else."

Stiletto gazed at the little girl in Candle's arms. Luma was fast asleep, drooling on his shoulder.

"We should find her parents," said Stiletto.

Candle nodded. "Time to wake up, Luma," he said, gently bouncing the child in his arms. "Just one more time, and then you can finally get the rest you deserve."

After a long search by headlight through the vast underground chamber, Luma pointed out a man and woman sleeping side by side on a multi-colored quilt.

"That's Mommy and Daddy," she said drowsily.

Candle smiled and lowered her to the quilt, placing her between her parents. "There you go," he said. "Now promise me you won't wander off again, okay?"

Luma yawned and nodded. "I promise," she said. Now that she had been returned to her parents, the amber crystal in her bracelet stopped blinking.

"Good night," said Candle. "Sleep tight."

Luma lay down on her side and curled up between her mother and father. Now that she was perfectly relaxed, her glittering skin took on a pale green hue. "Finish the story first. What happened next?"

"I have a better idea," said Candle. "Why don't *you* finish it?"

"Okay." Luma thought for a moment, then grinned. "Pass and Nona fell in love and lived happily ever after. The end."

Then, hugging her doll, she closed her eyes and fell asleep, her skin color shifting from pale green to pale gray.

"Cool story, huh?"

Candle said it as he and Stiletto followed a network of tunnels under the city, bypassing the Skilla on the way back to the *Sun Ra*.

He caught Stiletto by surprise. Instead of bouncing right back with a typical wisecrack, she didn't answer.

The truth was, of course she thought the story was cool, since she was crazy about him...but she was afraid to go further because of her lousy past. Her Wipeout career had ruined everything else in her life, so why not ruin this, too?

On the other hand...

She couldn't escape the feeling that something had changed between her and Candle on Sagra. He'd said some nice things about her, and the way he'd touched her that one time had been amazing.

Or maybe it was all in her imagination. After all, it wasn't as if he'd said anything that couldn't be interpreted more than one way. If only he'd said something with no room for misunderstanding, then maybe...

"I think we should end the story the way Luma did." Candle

grinned, his deep brown eyes twinkling in the glow of her headlight. "How about you?"

So much for misunderstanding.

It was up to Stiletto now, and the moment couldn't have been more perfect. The man she loved had given her the kind of opportunity that might never come her way again.

And yet, on the brink of a new beginning, Stiletto hesitated. What if the Squatter who had once possessed her managed to return? She couldn't bear the thought that she might one day hurt Candle.

Then, of course, it was always possible that Candle might hurt *her*...that he might *leave* her. She thought it would be a lot worse to have him and lose him than never to have him at all.

"Well?" he said, eyebrows raised expectantly. "What do you say?"

Then again, she'd already been with him for three years, and he'd never let her down. They'd been through a lot together, and she thought she knew him well enough to know he wouldn't hurt her.

So what was she waiting for?

Candle sighed. "Okay, then. Can't blame a guy for trying."

Aw, what the hell.

"No, no," said Stiletto. "I want to know what happens next. To be continued." Then, she grabbed his hand and held it like a trophy as they hiked toward the distant light at the end of the tunnel.

MONKEY SEA, MONKEY DO

Have you heard the one about the woman who turned into a water-breathing Sea Munky creature just as the world's bodies of water mostly dried up?

Hilarious, right? Unless *you're* the woman, in which case...

"How many times do I have to *tell* you idiots? Quit *pissing* in one of the last pools of water on *Earth*. Some of us have to *breathe* in here, y'know?"

In which case, you guessed it--*major suckage*.

And yes, I *am* that woman slash Sea Munky, she of the poorly-timed wish. My name is Ida, and I was a teacher in my human days...a teacher with a desperate need to get away and a lifelong fascination with Sea Munkies.

Yes, *those* Sea Munkies--the ones sold via misleading ads in the pages of comic books back in the day. Some people collect knick-knacks with frogs or pigs or cows on them; me, I *became* the object of my freakish obsession.

And look where it's gotten me. Sure, I'm five foot five with neon pink scales, webbed flippers, a ridged back, and a long, prehensile tail. Sure, my skull is topped with four stiff spikes...a kind of crown accented by a bright red bow and an upswept fan of blonde hair. Sure, my gills enable me to stay underwater indefinitely.

But what good does all that do if I'm stuck in the same shitty oasis pool in a dried-up world with a bunch of other water-wish misfits?

The answer is, no good at all. I *hate* my life.

Oscar the Merman floats a few feet away, looking sheepish. "Sorry, Ida. I had to pee so bad, I couldn't get ashore in time."

I smack my hands flat on the surface. "It's a *thirty-foot diameter pool*, Oscar! It's not that *far* to the *edge.*"

Oscar shrugs. "Does it *matter*? The pool is *mostly* piss at this point, isn't it?" With that, he combs his bony fingers through his long brown hair and submerges.

"That *doesn't* mean we should stop *trying!*" Angrily, I whip my tail, spraying precious piss/water onto the sandy shore. Immediately, I regret the move; given the worldwide über-drought conditions, there's no replacement moisture on the horizon.

Any stray water gets instantly soaked up by the palm trees that ring our desert oasis. I'm grateful they keep the worst of the blazing sun off us, but I also hate that their roots drink up the liquid we so desperately need.

Just then, a long green neck sways up out of the pool, supporting a head like a football with a blunt nose and big, dark eyes. This is Vanessa, another wisher like me--though *she* wished to become a Loch Ness Monster type instead of a humble Sea Munky. (Lucky for her, the pool is much deeper than it is wide, since she's a good bit bigger than I am.)

"Why *shouldn't* we stop trying?" Vanessa swings her head over and stares, inches from my face. "It's only a matter of time for us, Ida Mae."

"I refuse to accept that," I snap.

"Sooner or later, this pool will dry up," Vanessa says in her sing-song voice. "Or the surviving humans--as few as they are--will come for it. Thirsty people will finally figure out it's here and will come for it."

"They'll have a fight on their hands." I nod defiantly. "But in the meantime, we have to make sure it's *worth* fighting for. Not just a puddle of piss in the desert!"

"*That* ship has sailed," says a male voice from the far side of the pool. "Don't you think?"

I don't answer. I have nothing to say to him, though technically he's one of my kind--the *last* male Sea Munky in the world.

And he's part of the *family*, too. He's my *husband*, the one I haven't said a word to in the past nine years of the Drypocalypse.

The only other Sea Munky in the world, my long-estranged husband Lee, leans back on his elbows on the shore like he's having a soak in a hot tub. A shaft of bright sunlight streams down between the fronds of the palm trees, making his neon pink scales glitter and gleam.

"If you could have one wish granted, I wonder what it would be?" Lee knows I won't answer, but he keeps talking anyway. "Bet you can't guess what *mine* is."

Vanessa won't talk to him, either, though she *has* been known to *bite* him on occasion. She's my best friend, after all.

"It *might* involve being the *last* Sea Munky on Earth," says Lee. "Or the last *anything.* At least *then* I wouldn't have to overhear your incessant *whining.*"

Sometimes it's hard to remember that I used to feel guilty about Lee. After all, when we caught that magic whelk twelve years ago, I was the one who wished it would turn us into Sea Munkies.

Since the change made me happier than I'd ever been, things between us were fine for a while. But once the Drypocalypse kicked into high gear, and the oceans, lakes, and rivers started evaporating, our relationship soured. Staying in human form would have been stressful enough, as humans were dying of thirst in droves and killing each other over what water was left...but being aquatic creatures was even harder. Though we were magically attuned, able to find and swim through secret portals between the remaining bodies

of water we needed to sustain us, those bodies were quickly disappearing in the most terrible drought of all time.

As we went from one watery refuge to another, only to have
them all go up in steam, Lee got progressively grouchier, and I got
sick of his attitude. Life in the vast ocean turned into life in a tiny
pool in a desert oasis, and I finally broke it off.

Trapped in such close confines, it isn't easy to ignore him, but I
do. "Vanessa, I'm going to clean this cesspool up some." Reaching
out, I pat her Loch Ness Monster neck. "I respect your opinion, but
you're welcome to..."

Suddenly, there's a splash, and Lee pops up between us so there's
no longer any way we can ignore him. "What would you say..." He
clears his throat and speaks louder. "What would you *say* if I told
you..."

Vanessa swats him away with a flex of her neck, tossing him
head over flippers across the pool. He barely misses colliding with
Tina the Nymph, who has just surfaced over there with a couple of
pals.

Lee splashes down but quickly comes back up between us.
"What if I told you there's an *unused wish* floating around in this pissy
little pond?"

Lee grins. "The possessor of said wish assures me it has most
definitely not been cashed in yet, magically speaking."

Vanessa decides the time has come to break her silence. "How is
that even *possible?* We're all on the verge of *extinction* here. If
someone *had* a wish, they sure as hell would've *used* it by now."

Lee shrugs. "Saving it for a *rainy day,* so to speak. Or a *not-so-rainy*
day, is more like it."

"That makes no sense whatsoever," says Vanessa. "If this
supposed wish-keeper had just wished us and the world back to
normal, he, she, or it wouldn't *need* to save the wish for a rainy or
not-so-rainy day."

"What's the hurry?" Lee's long pink tail emerges from the water and twitches slowly. "This wish is like a get-out-of-jail-free card. The bearer can wait till the last minute to use it, if he or she so desires. Meanwhile, this individual can see if a better purpose comes to mind."

"*Better purpose?*" sputters Vanessa. "What *better purpose* could there be than reversing the *Drypocalypse* and saving *everyone?*"

"Yeah, but why be hasty?" Lee spreads his scaly pink arms. "Especially if we're talking about what might be *the last wish in the world.* There aren't too many *wishers* left, so I can't imagine there are too many *wishes.*"

Suddenly, a single word emerges from my lips, the first word I've said to him in a full nine years. *"Who?"*

His eyes widen with delighted surprise, as if he can't believe his luck and doesn't know just what to do about it. "Who what?"

"This supposedly unused wish," I say coldly. "Who has it?"

"I can't believe you don't know already!" says Lee. "It's..."

Before he can finish, a white-skinned creature leaps from the sandy bank and engulfs him in its huge maw. Lee's fizzy pink Sea Munky blood sprays everywhere as the creature's jagged teeth clamp down on his shoulder and throat.

Thank God Vanessa takes swift action. Stunned by the attack, I just gape as her vinelike neck snaps around, and she sinks her own razor-sharp fangs into the creature's pale hide.

The beast roars and thrashes, heaving Vanessa aside. As it lurches around to face me, I get my first clear view of the thing.

Though the creature launched itself from the bank, it is nearly identical to a fierce oceangoing predator (from the days when there *were* oceans): the great white shark. If not for its gnarled, needle-tipped claws, it could *be* such a shark, from its oblong nose to its triangular back fin.

The shark-thing roars, about to pounce on me--until Vanessa

charges across the pool and slams her bulk into it. Belly up, the beast skids toward the shore, claws clacking helplessly.

That's when I finally snap out of my state of shock. Lowering my head like a bull, I brace myself and bolt toward the invader as fast as I can. Just as the shark-thing flops against the bank but before it can right itself, I drive the four spikes atop my skull into the meat of its belly as hard as I can.

This time, the blood spilling into the pool is the shark-thing's. It rushes out and slicks the surface of the water, and there's more to come.

Howling with rage, I tear my spikes free, then drive them in again. And again.

I'm furious, a Sea Munky possessed. Lee was an asshole, the two of us were over, but seeing him slaughtered right in front of me was too much to bear.

Again I wrench out my spikes, and again I drive them in. I manage one more strike, then another, before the glistening gray tentacles of Scott the Mer-Squid slither up from below to wrap around the shark-thing's corpse and drag it down into the depths of the pool.

"What the hell *was* that thing?" Milky white shark-thing blood runs from my crown spikes down over my face. "Since when are there *land-sharks?*"

"Maybe a *shark* wished it could survive without an *ocean?*" Vanessa boosts her body onto the bank and stretches her neck high like a periscope, gazing out at the desert. "Oh, dear." Bracing her back against a palm tree, she stretches higher still. "It isn't *alone*, Ida Mae. I see triangular fins cutting through the sand at a high rate of speed...and they're coming *this way.*"

My heart's still hammering from the fight. "How many of them?"

"Six," says Vanessa. "Make that *seven*. They'll be here in *minutes*. The first one must have been a *scout* or something."

Just then, several pool inhabitants poke their heads above the water's blood-slicked surface.

"What's *happening* up here?" Jenny the Nymph looks scared. Her long blonde hair picks up a little red from the blood. "We just saw Scott hauling some *shark* with *claws* down to his burrow."

"Oh my God!" Rick the Sea Horse catches sight of Lee's carcass floating nearby. "Did you finally *kill* him, Ida?"

"It was the *land-shark*, and there are more on the way!" Vanessa slides back into the pool. "We all need to *go deep*, right *now*, or we'll end up like *him.*"

"Don't have to tell *me* twice!" Jenny climbs on Rick's back, and the two of them plunge out of sight into the depths. So do the others--Philosophical Water Bear and Jilly the Mer-Jellyfish.

Vanessa and I are the only ones left above water.

"Are you all right, hon?" she asks.

I take a deep breath and let it out slowly. Lee deserves a decent burial, but there's no time for that now. Though maybe there *is* a way to save more than his remains.

"I *will* be," I tell Vanessa. "Just as soon as I find out who has that last *wish* Lee told us about. Assuming he wasn't just being full of shit like he was ninety-nine percent of the time."

Speaking underwater is very different from talking above the surface. It requires extreme mastery of airflow, vocalization, scent, movement, and even taste. To a human, it wouldn't make any sense...though after twelve years as a Sea Munky, I understand it perfectly.

Which, in this case, is unfortunate, because my interrogations in search of an unused wish are getting me nowhere fast.

"I know you were a good friend of Lee's." That, more or less, is what I say to Oscar the Merman. *"You spent a lot of time together, didn't you?"*

Oscar shrugs, looking jumpy...but I can't hold that against him, because we're *all* jumpy right now. The land sharks are still up above us in force, hungrily circling the shore around the pool.

At least they haven't dived in after us, yet. They might be able to race through sand as if were water, but they don't seem too inclined to jump into *actual* water.

"Did Lee ever mention an unused wish to you before?" I ask Oscar, watching for any twitch that might suggest I've struck a nerve.

Oscar shakes his head and swishes his scaly green tail, which doesn't sparkle much here in the deeper, dimmer water.

"Oscar, please." I try to sound sympathetic. *"This wish, if there is one, might be the only way any of us survives this."*

"We're already on borrowed time," says Oscar. *"The whole world is."*

"What if it doesn't have to be?" I reach over and lower a flipper-hand onto his shoulder. *"Think about it, Oscar. If there's a wish, and we use it right, who's to say we won't be able to* fix *all that?"*

Oscar looks more and more skittish. *"The only wish I ever had was the one I used to become a merman."*

This interview is so much like the other three I've done so far, I want to scream. No one can (or will) help me with Lee's secret.

"Are you sure, Oscar? He never said anything about an errant wish that someone in here was holding onto?"

"All we did was hunt bugs and minnows together, says Oscar. *Most of the time, he was off with his girlfriend, Jilly."*

Finally, someone tells me something I don't *know*...as hard as it to *believe* it. *"Jilly the Mer-Jellyfish? They were..."*

Just then, a fat bug with gleaming, silvery wings drops down between us. We both fall silent, mesmerized as the bug gently weaves through the water.

I know we're both having the same thought. We're starving, and that bug looks delicious.

But before either us can make a play for it, Chuckie Tuna lunges up from below and snaps it up. It's only then, as Chuckie drags the bug away past a fish with a glowing lantern hung from its head, that I see the danger.

The light reveals a line stretched through the water, attached to the bug in Chuckie's mouth.

"Chuckie, no! Spit it out! Spit it out!"

Even as I shout the words, I know it's too late. His mouth opens wide, but nothing comes out. The line tightens, dragging Chuckie up toward the light.

He's been *hooked.*

He struggles with all of his might, but it's for nothing. The line keeps pulling him higher, ever higher.

"Oh my God," says Oscar. *"They got him, they got him!"*

Other denizens of the pool crowd around us, watching Chuckie rise. When he reaches the surface, his body is hauled out of the water by seven pairs of scrabbling pale claws.

"It's the land sharks!" says Jenny the Nymph. *"They're fishing for us!"*

At first, there is panic in the pool. Water folk swim this way and that as the fishing continues, dodging hooks and lines with the speed that terror brings.

But after a while, when no one else takes the bait, the number of lines decreases. When we water-breathers start tying lines together, the novelty wears off even more quickly. The land sharks reel in everything, leaving us to mourn our lost Chuckie.

Or, in my case, to see a jellyfish about a wish.

I find Jilly drifting ten feet below the surface--a little too close for comfort to the shark gang, but still out of their reach. Her glistening bubble of a body floats near the middle of the pool, frilly tentacles hanging languidly as hair or Spanish moss.

"A wish?" says Jilly. *"Lee never mentioned a stray wish to me."*

Can I expect honest answers from Lee's girlfriend? If I were her, I'd probably hate me for not saving him or dying instead of him. I'd probably hate me just because I was once part of his romantic life.

"He never talked about someone saving a wish for a rainy day?"

Jilly bobs silently for a moment, considering. *"Never."*

Not getting any traction, I try a different approach. *"Was there anything that made you curious? Anything he did that seemed mysterious or off?"*

Jilly's tentacles undulate with growing agitation. *"Why do you care? Aren't you happy you finally got rid of him?"*

I don't dignify her question with an answer. *"Jilly, if there's a loose wish around here, it could save us all. Maybe it could even bring back Lee."*

She swims closer, interested. Maybe I'm finally getting through to her.

Then, suddenly, a huge rock crashes into the water right on top of her, plunging her into the depths with all the speed of a lightning strike.

"Jilly!" Looking up, I see more rocks drop into the water, thrown into the pool one after another. Apparently, the land sharks have abandoned fishing and taken up a new mode of attack.

It's a simple approach, yet brutally effective. The rocks shoot through the water like depth charges, colliding with anything in their paths--like Jilly...

Or *me*. Just as I'm diving to seek refuge, one of the rocks smashes into me, catching my ridged spine and hurling me down into the darkness like the anchor of a ship.

When was the last time I hit bottom?

It's been a while, but the silt still feels as soft as I remember. I come in fast, weighed down by the heavy rock, but the downy silt cushions the impact, protecting me from injury.

I lie there for a moment after I hit, gazing upward. In the brighter water above, I see dark shapes plunging downward--more rocks pitched into the pool by the land sharks, all plummeting in my direction.

Galvanized by the sight, I heave aside the rock that brought me down and scramble upright. A big rock splashes down right where I was just lying, sending up clouds of brown and green silt.

Propelled by my webbed feet and tail, I race for the stone wall of the pool in a flurry of bubbles. Rocks fall behind and to either side of me, blasting into the bottom with far more force than I did when I landed.

One grazes me, striking my hip, which sends me tumbling. Head over shoulders I go, coming to rest on my back at the base of the wall.

When I look up, I see another rock barreling toward me, too close to evade. I realize the moment of my death is upon me, and there's nothing I can do to escape it.

I snap my eyes shut, bracing for the collision...but it never comes.

Instead, someone grabs me from behind and drags me out of the way through a hole in the stone wall. As the rock crashes down, and the hole fills with swirling silt, I get dragged further down a tunnel by someone I still can't see.

The next thing I know, I'm being hauled out of the water into an air-filled cave, then lowered onto a wet slate floor.

Whoever brought me here speaks with a high-pitched voice, like that of a female child. "Are you all right?"

Coughing, I brace my webbed hands on the floor and push myself up to a seated position. I can see my surroundings, as the place is lit with glowing white moss clinging in patches to the rock walls.

Before saying a word, I turn for a look at my rescuer--or captor, depending on my luck.

And I do a double-take.

Standing not three feet away is a kid with scaly pink skin, webbed hands and feet, a long tail, and five head spikes that look like a crown.

I never knew. "What the...?" I never knew.

I never *knew* there was a *third* Sea Munky living in a cave at the bottom of the pool.

It takes a long moment for the shock to wear off and the words to start coming. "Who *are* you?"

The Sea Munky child frowns. She doesn't look older than nine or ten years old. "Who do you *think* I am?"

I get to my knees, mystified by this secret made flesh. "You're like *me*. A Sea Munky."

The child touches the black bow between her two front head spikes, then adjusts her hair. It's upswept like mine, but it's bright red instead of blonde.

"You're not supposed to be here," she says. "But you were in trouble. I had to bring you in."

"What's your name?" How long has she been here, I wonder, hidden away? How many times have I swum overhead, never guessing she lived down below?

"My name is Mira," says the child. "And you should leave. I don't want him to be mad."

"Him who?"

"Daddy," says Mira. "He lives here with me."

A thought occurs to me. "Your Daddy. He looks like *we* do, doesn't he?"

"Like a Sea Munky, you mean?" Mira nods briskly. "Of course! He's my Daddy, isn't he?"

I hesitate to ask the next question. "Mira." But I know I need to hear the answer. "Who's your mommy?"

"It doesn't matter," she tells me. "Don't you know Sea Munky *daddies* are the ones who have the babies?"

I didn't, but I don't want to admit it. "There has to be a mommy *somewhere* along the way, doesn't there?"

Mira narrows her eyes. "Where's Daddy? You know where he is, don't you?"

Given who her father *has* to be, I hate to answer. I hold back.

But Mira tunes in to the truth anyway. "Something *bad*

happened to him, *didn't* it?" Her voice rises with anger and fear. "He always said that was the only way *you'd* ever get in here."

"Mira..." I'm having trouble finding the right words. The truth is, I'm struggling just to wrap my head around all this.

Because it's clear to me now. Her. Him. Me.

Us. I know what we are.

As hard to believe as it is, I *know*.

"He's *gone*," says Mira. "*Isn't* he?"

Though I only met her moments ago, I want to reach for her. I can't stand to see the pain on her little face, hear the sadness in her voice.

I want to take her in my arms and comfort her, help her get through this. Because as strange as it seems, the only logical explanation here...

Is that we are *family*.

Suddenly, there's a tremendous *boom* from the direction of the pool, and the cave trembles around us.

"What was that?" asks Mira.

"Let's go see," I suggest.

The two of us dive into the water and swim back out the way we came. Quickly, we reach the end of the tunnel and peek out of the hole into the depths of the pool.

Just in time to see a hand grenade drop on the far side of the pool and explode.

Everything shakes violently as Mira and I duck back into the passage. Our wide eyes meet, and we retreat, darting into the air-filled cave.

"Now they're *bombing* us." I shake my head in disgust. "Where they got the *explosives*, I'll never know, but they're *using* them."

"Who are *they?*" asks Mira.

"Land sharks. They're trying to kill everyone in the pool."

Mira nods thoughtfully. "Did they used to be people, too? Like the other people in the pool? People who wished they could be something else?"

"Or sharks, maybe. I don't know." I shrug. "They're not natural, that's for sure."

Mira paces to the wall, to a niche in the rock. "Where do people get these wishes?" Her back is turned to me as she talks.

"Different places, I guess. Genies, magical creatures, falling stars, magic spells..."

She glances over her shoulder at me. "Is that where you got yours?"

"From a creature, yes. A magic *whelk*, if you can believe it. Like a snail."

Mira reaches for something in the niche. I can't see what it is.

"What happened to the magic whelk?" she asks quietly. "After she made your wish come true?"

"I don't know."

"I do." Mira turns so I see what's in her hands...and I gasp.

She's holding what looks like a conical snail shell, pale yellow, banded with gray and brown speckles. A black-mottled foot extends from the shell's opening, and a pair of fleshy white hornlike appendages slowly twitch in my direction.

"I have her right here." Mira smiles. "*This* is the magic whelk."

There's a blast outside the cave, and our refuge shakes around us.

"Is this possible?" I walk over and crouch in front of Mira, gazing at the whelk in her hands. "I think...I must have just let go of it when the wish took hold."

"*Her*, not *it*." Mira sounds indignant. "And you *did* let go, but *he* caught her. *Daddy* held onto her."

"He did?" Wonderingly, I reach out one index finger, and the whelk's horns gently graze it. When they do, I feel the slightest zap, like static electricity jumping between us. "But why?"

"Just in case." Mira raises the whelk to her eye level and stares at it. "He said he had his doubts about the wish. About becoming a Sea Munky. It was never *his* wish, was it?"

"No." How many times did he remind me of that? Even now, beyond the grave, his words haunt me.

"It was a good thing he *did* save Ethel here," says Mira. "It turns out, if she grants a wish, and a person who wasn't the wisher gets dragged into it, that person gets a wish of their own. It's only fair, isn't it?"

Now I get it. I understand what Lee was hinting around about before the land shark got him. *He* was the one with the unused wish all along.

But if that's the case... "Then the wish is useless." The hope I've been clinging to fizzles out.

"I knew it." Mira's eyes narrow. "Something bad *did* happen to Daddy. He *is* gone."

My heart goes out to her. This world the two of them shared is quickly fading away. Nothing will be the same after what I say next...but I feel like I owe her the truth anyway. "Yes. Your father is gone."

When Sea Munkies cry, their tears turn to bubbles swirling with color and float away. That's why little bubbles drift from Mira's eyes now.

"I'm sorry." Is it because I'm her mother that I want to rush over and comfort her? Or is it just because she's a child, and I've taken someone from her forever with a handful of words?

"It was the land sharks, wasn't it?" Just as she asks the question, there's another explosion outside the cave.

"Yes," I tell Mira. "It was the land sharks."

More tears bubble up from her, gently wafting on the still air of the cave. Sniffling, she wipes them away with the back of her arm. "That's all right," she says softly.

"Why is that?"

"Because." She nods firmly. "I inherited his wish."

581

There's another explosion, but its shockwaves don't reverberate nearly as long as the implications of what Mira just told me.

"You mean..." My mind is racing. "You mean, *you* can use your Daddy's wish since he's gone?"

"Mm-hm." Mira holds the whelk closer and strokes the curve of her shell. "Because I'm *special*. That's what Ethel says. I wouldn't be the way I am without *your* wish, just like Daddy. I didn't have any *say* in the matter...so now I *do*."

Another grenade explodes, continuing the countdown to the end of our watery little world. It might be mostly piss, but I still hate to see it go.

"Do you know what you're going to do with the wish?" I ask Mira. "Have you given it any thought?"

She shrugs. "What do *you* think I should do?"

The answer has been taking shape since Lee first told me about the unused wish. "I think you should fix the world. Put it back the way it was."

"Wet and green, you mean?" says Mira. "Like Daddy told me?"

"Yes." I walk over and lay my hand on her shoulder. "Before it all dried up."

"Before Daddy died, too?"

"Before that, yes. And before I made the wish that changed us." I gently flick my tail. "Can Ethel do all that? Can your wish make everything right again?"

Mira stares hard at the whelk. The little creature's horns flex as if they're beaming a message to her mind, or communicating their own delicate sign language.

"Y-yes," Mira says finally. "But you have to do your part. You have to make up for the suffering you caused with your selfishness."

"Is that so?" I don't like hearing it.

"Will you?" asks Mira. "Will you do your part?"

I want to resist, but whatever that sea snail asks, it's a small price to pay. "Yes, of course."

"Okay." As another grenade booms beyond the cave, Mira closes her eyes tight and bows her head. Her lips move, but I don't hear whatever it is she's saying.

Meanwhile, the whelk pulses with amber light in her hands. The pulsing quickens, and the light expands outward--then shoots off in all directions in a shower of blazing sparks.

"It's done." Mira opens her eyes and looks up at me. "There's just one thing you have to do for me before it happens."

"What's that?"

Multicolored bubbles fizz from her eyes. Reaching out, she takes my hand.

"Show me," she says. "Mommy, I want you to show me."

I tell Mira to close her eyes before we swim out of the cave, and I'm glad I do. The water is full of bits and pieces of friends and neighbors, blown apart by the bombardment.

I hold her close with one arm, and she clings to me. With my other arm, I guide us through the debris, dodging familiar faces and body parts.

Propelled by my tail and webbed feet, we spiral up from the depths, rising toward the light. A long, green neck I know all too well twists in our path, and my heart catches with hope...but it is no longer connected to the monster who was once my best friend and defender.

I push past it, and still we rise.

Building momentum with powerful kicks and thrashes, I cruise ever upward. I see the stubby snouts of the land sharks ringing the view, and I grit my teeth, climbing harder.

When we break the surface, they all roar and reach for us. We're past them in an instant, carried by our momentum, shooting skyward.

I squeeze Mira, and she opens her eyes, looking around at everything--our sad little oasis, the sadder desert of pale sand all around it. She's never seen the world above the surface, never glimpsed daylight or blue skies undistorted by rippling water. It's something she wanted to see more than anything, especially now.

Because she knows what will happen after the wish takes effect. Ethel told her.

Ten feet up, twenty, we go...and hit the apex of our flight. Our momentum fades, and we're a breath away from falling.

Mira knows what that means. It's time to keep up her end of the bargain.

"I love you, Mommy." She gasps out the words, then closes her eyes tight.

"I love you, too," I tell her, as her lips move and Ethel glows brighter on her shoulder.

Then, her last wish, maybe the last wish in all the world, comes true.

I blink, and everything is different.

The warm salt water parts before me, yielding to my enormous bulk in vast, foamy swells. The size of a major city, I plow onward through the skin of the ocean, through sun and storm alike, never flinching.

My giant tail swoops behind me, churning the sea like a hurricane's gust. My massive flippers steer me, turning me like a carrier along the curls of the tidal flows and streams.

Call me a whale at your peril. The biggest whales are dwarfed by my enormity, splashing like sunfish alongside an atoll. I am more like a *place* than a *thing*, dominating the briny kingdom such that nothing natural or otherwise can come close to matching me.

Except him. Roaring up beside me, he is my equal in *every* way, and my *love*. Like me, his emerald bulk is colossal, the force of his passage powerful to the point of godlike. Ships and creatures give him a berth so wide, it is like he is in a sea by himself.

Like me, he inhales immense clouds of polluted air and purifies them, devouring the excess greenhouse gases pumped out by human life. Like me, he cleanses the atmosphere, devours the waste, and breathes out epic draughts in perfect balance, staving off the apocalyptic transformation of the weather of the world.

Like me, his sole purpose and greatest joy is plying these glittering blue seas, making music with each fresh billow from the monumental emerald chimneys that tower on his back like giant organ pipes.

But unlike me, he does not remember the *other* world, the one that was drying up around us. The one that was drawing to a desiccated, whimpering close until someone made that one last wish that changed everything.

To him, this is the only world that ever was. These are the only selves that ever were, the only "us" we've ever known.

He does not remember that he was once Lee, or I was once Ida. He does not know the significance of the pink spines jutting from our titanic skulls, that they are the remnants of the fragile Munky forms we once wore in that pitiful pissy pool in the desert oasis.

And he does not remember the name or face or voice of the one who wished this glorious new world into being in the first place. He has no recollection of that person.

But to me, it is as if I last saw her only moments ago. And though I knew her only briefly, the memory of her good, sweet soul lingers in every tear that rises as a multicolored bubble from my eyes the size of mountains.

WHY YOU SHOULD THINK TWICE BEFORE ADOPTING AN ALIEN BABY

As I stand on the narrow ledge, back tight against the mountainside, geysers of superheated steam erupt from the cleft below. I press the purple-skinned Iskani baby against my chest, shielding her with my arms as best I can from the scalding heat…though, as humans, my wife and I are more in need of protection than this extraterrestrial child is.

Squinting through the steam, I see a flight of Iskani warriors approaching astride their giant, leopard-furred dragons. Each flap of the dragons' wings brings them closer, their warrior riders taking aim at us with their glittering, electrified javelins.

For what must be at least the millionth time, I find myself wishing we had never agreed to the adoption of the baby in my arms, an adoption that has made our lives terrible and led directly to this moment of imminent peril.

"Paul!" shouts my wife, Maeve, who is pressed against the mountainside next to me. "The ledge is shrinking!"

Looking down, I see it's true. The thin shelf of orange stone is slowly squeezing back into the mountain.

It is then I realize we stand not on a rocky formation, but on one of the living bioliths that inhabit the Iskani landscape. The locals call them *chorlak*, which translates into English as "hungry mountains."

I feel the ledge tremble and know it will soon disappear, sending us plunging into the gaping cleft that has opened below.

Sweat pours down my face. The Iskani baby shrieks and gouges my chest with her jagged claws. The toxic green sludge that passes for baby excrement on Isk oozes over my arms and stomach, burning my skin.

As I stare into the child's huge, indigo eyes, anger wells from deep in my heart. We've been through so much because of her, and now it seems we're going to die. There is no way out.

KRA-BOOOOM

We aren't the only ones in mortal danger, either. A massive explosion draws my attention skyward, where the Earthfleet star carrier *Lewis Puller* is engaged in low atmosphere combat with three smaller but no less deadly Iskani warships. The *Puller* has taken a massive hit; even from a distance, I can see the carrier wobble as clouds of smoke and debris billow from her lower hull. If she goes down, the hundreds of men and women aboard her will perish, and the Iskani warfleet will face no opposition in launching an attack on Earth's nearby outpost, Hammurabi VII.

It will all be because of her, the baby...her and the Star Stork organization that brought us together and enabled the disastrous interstellar adoption.

It is then, in this dark moment, as the warships pound the *Puller,* the dragonriders prepare to release their javelins, the ledge narrows, and the steaming maw of the living mountain widens to swallow us, that I think about throwing the child into the depths.

It's an idea that's been growing in the back of my mind, in one form or another, since the moment we first met baby Oyo.

"And *smile!*" A bright light flared in my eyes, briefly blinding me.

Maeve, in the window seat beside me, gripped my arm a little tighter. Though we'd been traveling through space aboard the gravity liner *Starbright* for weeks, making our first trip ever out of Earth's solar system, the truly stressful part of our journey—facing the media—had just begun.

As the light cleared, the photographer—a hologram projected from Hammurabi VII—grinned and flashed a big thumbs-up. *"Perfect! Our readers will love that shot!"*

"Mr. and Mrs. Carter." The hologram of an ebony-skinned reporter from a top-rated video news feed shoved in front of us the instant the photographer got his shot. Her three little camera orbs zipped in with her, focused on me and Maeve. "How does it feel to make history?" She gave her head a toss, and her glowing golden nimbus of hair crackled softly. "How does it feel to be the first human couple to adopt an alien child?"

"It feels amazing." Maeve brushed a strand of bright red hair from her eyes. "It feels like the most wonderful thing that's ever happened to us."

I smiled in complete agreement. This was a day we'd hardly dared expect would ever come, yet now it was upon us...the culmination of the hopes and dreams we'd shared from the start of our marriage.

We were going to have a *family*.

"The odds were certainly against you, weren't they?" The reporter, like the photographer, was a hologram beamed from afar, yet she looked vividly solid and present in the ship's passenger compartment with us. "More than 500,000 couples competed in the lottery for a chance to adopt this child."

"We were very lucky." Maeve gave my arm a squeeze. "Very blessed."

The reporter narrowed her eyes and tipped her head to one side. Her camera orbs floated toward us, lenses pushing forward as they zoomed in closer.

"Some people claim you cheated," she said. "That you made a payoff or knew someone on the inside. What do you say to those people?"

"I say we did nothing of the sort," I told her. "And we are

rooting for every one of those people to get their chance as well. We will do everything in our power to make a good impression so the Iskani will welcome them on future adoption missions."

"Hmm." The reporter's eyes narrowed even more. "And what about those who say such adoptions are a form of unjust social engineering and cultural displacement?"

"I'd tell them it's nothing to do with all that." Maeve smiled, stealing a glance out the window as the surface of the planet grew nearer. "It's just love. That's all. Love and family."

Hours later, not long after the *Starbright* had landed, Maeve and I stood on a balcony of orange stone, waving at a sea of cheering, purple-skinned Iskani spread over a vast plaza before us.

"What do you think?" A tall, slender Iskani stood between us with a hand on each of our shoulders. Dressed in bright yellow robes, he'd introduced himself to us as Menomenee Quellid, governor of whatever city-state this was. "How does it feel to be adored by so many beings on a world you're only now visiting for the first time?"

"It feels incredible!" Even as I said it, the cheering got louder, and the spectacle grew more exciting. Some of the Iskani puffed what looked like colorful soap bubbles out of blowholes on their foreheads, sending them wobbling upward, where they popped with flashes of colorful light. Others threw flowers onto the balcony—six-legged flowers that skittered in circles, then hopped back into the crowd again.

I took a deep breath, drinking in the overwhelming sensory bombardment. There were so many bubbles, so many purple-skinned aliens bathed in the light of the three bluish suns—so much strange and joyous song unlike anything I'd heard before, a kind of music that sent shivers up my spine and stirred the deepest corners of my heart.

The warm air smelled like cinnamon and roses, the familiar

scents intermingled with others I didn't recognize. Though I'd eaten nothing since arriving, the taste of bitter chocolate lingered on my tongue. My skin tingled faintly, snapping off little sparks of static whenever I touched anything or was touched.

"We have declared this a worldwide holiday!" Though Quellid spoke in his native tongue of buzzes and whistles, I heard his words in English through a translator earpiece. "The two of you, and all your people, are now considered part of our Iskani family."

"It means so much to us to hear that." Maeve dabbed tears from the corners of her bright green eyes. "This couldn't possibly be a more wonderful day!"

Just then, our handler from the Star Stork organization—a stern, slim woman named Sidra Beck with short gray hair and a snappy white pantsuit—stepped up and cleared her throat. "Having said that…any word on our main attraction, Governor Quellid?"

"As a matter of fact…" Quellid fluttered one seven-fingered hand at the crowd. "Here she comes now."

It was then I got my first glimpse of our new child in the flesh. Off in the distance, a purple infant bobbed just over the heads of the crowd, passed from one pair of hands to the next.

"Oyo!" Transfixed, Maeve called out her name and stepped forward. "Oh my God, there she is!"

Joining her at the edge of the balcony, I watched as the tiny alien crowd-surfed toward us, rolling and turning among the singing, dancing Iskani like a beach ball at a rock concert back home. Even then, from a distance, I thought I could feel a connection with her…but maybe it was just wishful thinking.

"Is that *safe* for the child?" asked Maeve. "Being bounced around like that by all those people?"

Quellid chuckled. "I assure you, she is perfectly fine. All infants undergo this ceremony of presentation, and it never, ever damages them."

"Just the same," said Sidra, "this wasn't something you mentioned in the briefing."

"Didn't think it was relevant." Quellid shrugged. "Consider it a bonus."

Sidra asked if there would be any other surprises, and Quellid said something snarky, but Maeve and I weren't really paying attention. The two of us stood at the balcony's edge, watching as our child was buoyed closer with each passing second.

"Oh, please be careful!" Maeve winced. "Don't hurt her! Not after all it took to *get* her."

I put my arm around her shoulders and squeezed gently. "She'll be fine, honey. Everything will work out fine, I know it."

Suddenly then, a crowd member threw the baby higher and further than ever, sending her tumbling toward us. Maeve and I both gasped...but at the last instant, another Iskani leaped up, his long, limber body outstretched, and snagged the child as if she were a fly ball on a baseball field.

The Iskani who'd caught her landed lightly on his feet and turned to face the balcony. The crowd parted, opening a clear path all the way to the balcony, and he started down it, holding Oyo aloft.

Maeve jumped and jittered with excitement. She was right, it had taken a lot to get here, to get *her*; winning the adoption lottery had been only the first step. It felt like a miracle that we'd made it so far and were finally about to accept that precious gift.

Just as the Iskani carrying Oyo reached the balcony, the entire crowd fell silent. Quellid stepped up, arms upraised, and emitted a high-pitched, fluttering cry that echoed across the plaza.

"From our abundance of life, we reach out across the heavens!" His voice shifted from a wail to a roar. "We share our gift with these distant kin, bringing them the familial hope and joy they crave. We present them with this child, knowing full well the glorious experience and enlightenment they will find in the raising of it!"

With that, Quellid clapped his hands, and the Iskani reached toward us. Just as I was wondering how he could possibly reach us, some five meters above, I saw the answer.

The Iskani's ropy purple arms stretched all the way up to the balcony, telescoping ever longer to push Oyo in our direction.

I gaped, having briefly forgotten how the Iskani could distort and extend their malleable bodies. Until then, it was something I'd only read about and seen online.

"Go ahead," said Sidra as the baby topped the balcony's railing. "Take her."

"She is yours now!" howled Quellid. "Will you accept her?"

The baby gazed at us with huge indigo eyes. The little blowhole on her forehead irised open and shut.

Unexpectedly, after all her eagerness to make the adoption a reality, Maeve hesitated.

As seconds ticked away, I took action and reached for the child. As soon as my hands made contact, the crowd went wild.

Everyone in the plaza sang and danced with abandon, whirling and leaping with ten times the enthusiasm they'd shown before. The Iskani revelers stretched and twisted, wrapping together in complex knots and combinations that made it hard sometimes to tell where one of them ended and another began.

As the frantic celebration swirled before us, I cradled the purple baby in my arms, smiling down at her. The warmth and weight of her were welcome against me, the exact shape of a void that had existed within me for far too long.

Finally! In an age when human reproduction had become a rarity, limited by the ravages of a worldwide pandemic, I possessed what so many on Earth wanted, yet so few had. The potential for happiness and fulfillment squirmed against me, giant indigo eyes fixed on my face like magnets on an anvil.

I had a child. *A family.* So what if she wasn't human?

Beaming, I reached out with a finger to tickle her soft purple belly. In that moment, I wasn't thinking of how we were making history or what the future might bring or anything else. I just wanted to make her giggle.

Instead, as my finger touched down, she let loose a high squealing sound and puffed inky black vapor from her blowhole. It smelled like burning plastic and made me dizzy as soon as I breathed it.

I felt my legs crumple under me, and I couldn't control them. My last thought as I fell and darkness welled up over me was that I hoped the baby wouldn't get hurt when I went down.

The next thing I was aware of was Maeve's voice calling my name, as if from a distance. *Paul...Paul...Paul...*

Her voice grew closer as I crawled toward consciousness, dragging myself out of the dark stillness. Details trickled in, reminding me of my last moments of awareness before the collapse.

Suddenly, one thought exploded in my head. "Oyo!" My eyes shot open. "Please tell me she's okay!"

Maeve smiled down at me, nodding. "The baby's fine, hon. She couldn't be better."

"What the hell happened?" I turned my head on the medical table where I lay and saw Sidra and a tall Iskani female in a silver uniform huddled around something, blocking my view of it. "Some kind of black gas...?"

"Nothing to worry about, according to them." Maeve bobbed her head toward Sidra and the Iskani.

"Except for the uncontrollable passing out part, you mean," I said sarcastically.

"It's a defense mechanism," said Sidra from across the room. "Not common, but not entirely unexpected, either."

"It was to me," I said.

"Well, it shouldn't happen again." The silver-uniformed Iskani female smiled. "I've inoculated her with some cells from you and your wife, so she ought to recognize you both as non-threatening from now on."

"Okay." Her reassurances weren't exactly making me feel better, especially because I didn't know who the hell she was.

Sidra corrected that promptly. "Paul, this is Dr. Anemolee Cogix, a physician we work with as a consultant here on Isk. She assures me there will be no permanent damage from the child's emission."

"Definitely harmless to your human physiology," said Anemolee. "Other than, as you say, the passing out part."

I propped myself up on my elbows and shook my head hard,

trying to dislodge the cobwebs inside. It was then I could see what Sidra and Anemolee were huddled around—a silver metal tub with baby Oyo's hands and feet visible, twitching above the edge.

Satisfied that I was fine, Maeve drifted toward them, eyes fixed on the tub. "Can I hold her now?"

"Absolutely." Anemolee reached in, lifted out Oyo, and handed her toward Maeve. The baby was clad in a bright yellow onesie printed with white flowers, plus white booties on her feet.

As Maeve took her, her big indigo eyes were locked on me.

"What I want to know is this." I sat up and turned, swinging my feet off the edge of the table. "What other surprises might there be in store for us?"

"Raising a child is always full of surprises, isn't it?" said Anemolee.

I frowned. "You know what I mean. Knockout-gas-from-the-forehead kind of surprises."

"None that we're aware of," said Sidra. "Nothing evident from the detailed data provided by the Iskani or our own intensive studies of their species' biology. Our xenobiologists and theirs agree that you should be absolutely in the clear from here on out."

"Correct," said Anemolee. "And of course, you'll have a planet-side trial period under close supervision, if that makes you feel better."

Maeve cooed at the baby in her arms, utterly lost to her charms. "I'm sure that isn't necessary."

"We'll follow through with it just the same," said Sidra. "Just in case you come up with any questions or concerns."

Anemolee nodded. "We'll be available at any time."

"You've both been thoroughly briefed, but remember," said Sidra. "This *is* the first program of its kind...and the two of you are first-time parents. Your lives are about to change dramatically."

"Oh, we'll be fine." Maeve couldn't stop smiling or fiddling with Oyo. "Won't we, Paul?"

"Absolutely," I said with a confidence I didn't entirely share. "As long as our family is together, we'll be totally fine."

Hours later, it seemed my doubts had been for nothing.

Maeve, Oyo, and I were in the bungalow we'd been assigned, on a scenic spot on the estate of Governor Menomenee. The incident at the presentation ceremony was forgotten; the three of us were bonding as if we were all from the same species, with no differences that mattered between us.

So what if Oyo excreted four different kinds of waste (two liquid, two solid) instead of two? We learned how to contain and clean it up without injury, which was tricky, since both liquids and one solid were toxic.

So what if the pitch and volume of Oyo's crying, at its height, could make our ears ring and even cause sharp pains? We learned to keep her soothed and kept earplugs handy for the rest of the time.

So what if the claws on her hands and feet popped out when she was unhappy and slashed up my arms and chest? Keeping her happy solved that, and Sidra promised she'd provide us with claw-resistant clothes to save our skin the rest of the time.

Somehow, none of the inconveniences bothered us at all. We'd known what to expect, and we'd decided long ago to accept it. Didn't the same kind of contract hold every family together, what-ever their species or origin? Wasn't that agreement at the root of every family's shared identity and story?

By the time we put her down for the night in the cradle beside our bed, then slid into bed ourselves, I had only positive feelings about the situation. My fears had been for nothing; the knockout gas incident had been a fluke.

"I've never been happier in my life," said Maeve.

"Me either," I said, and I meant it. The dream of a family we'd shared was finally a reality. We were together, and the future lay before us with all its promise, unlocked at last.

We fell asleep in each other's arms, smiling serenely, unable to stay awake a single moment more.

The first thing I tried to do when I snapped awake was scream...but I couldn't, because my mouth was covered.

So was my entire face.

Thrashing on the bed, I grabbed at my head, clawing at the rubbery substance wrapped tightly around it. Whatever it was, it wouldn't come loose, not even the slightest bit.

Panicking, I flung myself off the bed and came down hard, my left knee cracking on the stone floor. The pain cut through my terror as I dropped on my side, pulling my thoughts into focus...but it did no good. Whatever had a grip on me, it felt like it was vacuum-sealed in place.

As I flopped and twisted helplessly, I saw sparks in the darkness and felt a wave of dizziness. Desperately, I fought to suck in the slightest breath of air, but it was impossible. Nothing was getting under that rubbery wrapper.

Finally, my strength left me. My fingers scrabbled weakly at the choking film, and I went limp.

Then, suddenly, I heard a burst of voices and footsteps, muffled by the clinging substance. I felt hands grab hold of me, forcefully dragging me over the floor—then great heat, concentrated on my head and upper body.

As the heat rose, it quickly became unbearable under the wrapper. Already on the verge of passing out, I felt myself plunging ever faster into the darkness.

Then, I was gone.

Again, I drifted up from the depths of unconsciousness to the sound of someone calling my name—not Maeve this time.

"Paul?" It was Anemolee. "Can you hear me, Paul?"

My eyes flickered open to the sight of her gazing down at me with concern. Maeve was there, too, peering at me from alongside her.

"Oh, thank God!" said Maeve. "You're alive!"

"Are you...sure about that?" I felt awful. My head was throbbing, and my throat was raw. I still lay on the floor where I'd fallen. "What the hell...happened?"

"Something unexpected, actually." Anemolee cleared her throat. "Given the age of the subject, that is."

"What subject?" I asked.

"Oyo." Maeve looked deeply worried as she stroked my cheek. "The baby nearly smothered you."

"How the hell...?"

"It's rare, but not completely unheard of," said Anemolee. "Most often, we see it in Iskani when they undergo pubescence. The body's morphic properties activate, and a spontaneous transformation can occur. In this case..."

"Oyo suddenly gained the ability to stretch," interjected Sidra, who'd been lurking out of my eyeshot. "Then she wrapped herself around your head and cut off your air supply."

I closed my eyes and sighed. "Defense mechanism again?"

"We don't know," said Anemolee. "We're running tests on the child to find out."

"Great." All I wanted at that moment was to return to unconsciousness—shut out the bad news and what it suggested about the rosy future we'd dared to imagine. After all we'd been through and the bonding we'd done as a family, baby Oyo had two strikes against her.

"We're thinking an allergic reaction might be to blame," said Anemolee. "Perhaps a response to the inoculation of cells from you and your wife."

"Seriously? The so-called cure almost killed me?"

"We hope to have answers soon," said Anemolee.

I sat up, leaning back against the bed. "Where is she?"

"Don't worry," said Sidra. "Oyo's in the med lab. She can't hurt you now."

That wasn't what I was worried about. "Is she okay? Whatever you did to get her off me…"

Anemolee nodded. "The child is perfectly healthy. We applied a heat beam to relax and dislodge her, but it didn't harm her in any way."

"Good." I met Maeve's gaze, and she smiled. "I'm glad to hear that."

"Are you?" Sidra looked grim. "If you've changed your mind, you don't have to go through with this, you know. No one would blame you if you chose to terminate the adoption."

There was a clear spark of panic in Maeve's eyes at that.

"Thanks," I told Sidra. "But let's not get ahead of ourselves. When will the test results come in?"

"Within the hour, we hope," said Sidra.

"That's great." I wasn't surprised. Iskani medical technology was at least the equal of our own. "So let's talk when the data's been baked and see where that leaves us, okay?"

"And bring Oyo back with you either way, okay?" Maeve's voice held a tinge of desperation.

"Will do," said Sidra, though I thought she might be lying. "We'll bring her to see you no matter what."

Half an hour later, there was a knock on the bungalow door…and both of us jumped to answer it.

Maeve got there first, grabbed the handle, and flung the door open. "They must've finished the tests early!"

I held my breath, worried about what we might hear and the impact it could have on our lives.

But neither Sidra nor Anemolee was out there. Instead, a group of Iskani gaped at us, looking hostile.

"Hello?" Maeve stared back at them. "Did you bring us the test results?"

The hulking male at the front of the group swung his muscular arms, reaching for her.

"Hey!" Instinctively, I hauled Maeve back out of reach, then heaved the door around toward the jamb.

By then, though, the male's shoulder blocked the gap, stopping the door from shutting.

I stepped back, pulling the door with me, then pitched myself forward, plowing hard into the male Iskani's chest. Caught by surprise, he stumbled into the crowd, knocking those next in line off balance, buying me precious seconds.

With the doorway clear, I leaped back and hurled the door shut, then slammed the deadbolt into place. We were safe for the moment.

"What's happening?" asked Maeve. "What do they want?"

Just then, we heard Sidra's voice behind us, from the kitchen area. "This. They want this."

Turning, we saw her standing in the kitchen doorway, holding Oyo.

Looking behind her, I saw Anemolee climbing up from a hatchway in the floor, one I hadn't even known was there until then. The throw rug that had covered it was cast aside in a crumpled heap.

"I don't understand!" Maeve rushed toward the kitchen with arms outstretched. "Why do they want Oyo?"

"Honestly?" Sidra shrugged. "We have no idea."

"How is that even possible?" As I said it, the crowd started shouting and pounding on the front door.

"It just is." Sidra handed Oyo to Maeve. "And the problem is much bigger than it may at first appear."

Maeve cradled Oyo in her arms and rocked her back and forth. "What do you mean?"

"The crowd outside extends *far* beyond Governor Menomenee's estate," explained Anemolee. "There are *thousands* of people converging from across the capital city, all massing on this location, chanting the child's name. They *want* her."

"But I thought the Iskani people were okay with this adoption," I said. "They just got done throwing a big *party* to celebrate it."

"We don't understand it any better than you do," said Anemolee.

"And it only affects Iskani," said Sidra.

"Like you?" I asked Anemolee. "Is it affecting you, too?"

She shook her head. "Not yet. I feel nothing at all unusual."

I wasn't sure I believed her. "So you're saying thousands of people just suddenly changed their minds, and they want to take back Oyo...and then what? What do they plan to do with her?"

"We don't know," Anemolee said grimly.

The shouting and pounding outside was growing steadily louder, and I was growing more nervous with each passing moment. "What do we do next? Just hand her over?"

"No!" snapped Maeve. "We have no idea what they might do to her!"

"We have another option." Sidra half-turned and gestured at the hatch in the kitchen floor. "An escape route, if you want to take it."

"There's a tunnel," said Anemolee. "It will lead you to a wilderness outside the city."

"Then what?" I asked. "Go off the grid and live off the land until this blows over?"

"We'll arrange a rendezvous," said Sidra. "We'll extract you as soon as we can and get you all off-planet."

"So it's either that or hand over Oyo and hope for the best?" I said.

Sidra looked around as the ruckus from outside got louder still. "Whatever you choose, you should it do it while you still *have* a choice."

I knew what Maeve wanted to do before I looked in her direction. As crazy as it seemed, there was only one choice we in our right minds could make.

"All right." I headed for the hatch. "Now tell me how you're going to make contact when the time comes."

The sky was gray when I threw open the door at the far end of the escape tunnel. It looked like early morning, with two of the three suns still low on the horizon, though it was true I'd lost track of time; it felt like we'd been in the tunnel for ages, hurrying through the dim light cast by glowing red lichens on the ceiling and walls.

"All clear." Thankfully, no one was waiting for us on the other side, ready to snatch Oyo from our grasp. All I saw nearby was tangled crimson foliage; all I heard were the stuttering cries and yelps of whatever passed for wildlife out there.

As soon as Maeve emerged, Oyo started on a crying jag, her piercing wails drowning out all other sound.

"So much for staying low key." I looked around worriedly, hoping no one was listening. According to Anemolee, the wilderness area where we'd ended up was sparsely populated, but not deserted.

"Give me her bottle," shouted Maeve, wincing against the shrieking as she rocked and patted Oyo.

I swung the pack off my back, plunked it on the bright orange ground, and unzipped the front compartment. The supplies, provided by Sidra, wouldn't last more than a day or two, but I hoped that would be enough.

I pulled out a purple plastic bottle filled with pink nutrient broth and handed it over. Maeve pushed the nipple toward Oyo, and she chomped down on it without hesitation.

"Thank God." My ears were ringing, but at least the crying was over…for now.

"She's settling down." Maeve continued to hold the bottle as Oyo gulped greedily.

"I hope it lasts." Reaching back into the pack, I pulled out the handheld radio Sidra had given us, checking the glowing display— but no messages had come yet. We were still in the dark, waiting for information…but what if no information arrived? What if we'd made the wrong call and were trapped on a one-way path to disaster?

"So here we are, on the surface of an alien world." I gave up on the radio and dropped it in the pack. "We're on the run from hostile aliens, and we have an alien baby with demonstrated dangerous capabilities in our possession."

"Wrong," said Maeve. "This is *not* just some alien baby. She is our *daughter.*"

"I stand corrected."

"Let me ask you something, Paul." Maeve glared. "If she wasn't an alien, if she was just an average, everyday *human being*, and she had 'dangerous capabilities,' as you put it, what would you do about her then?"

She was hitting too close to home, and I didn't like it. "Let me ask *you* a question, Maeve. What if *she*..." I pointed at Oyo. "...is somehow responsible for thousands of people coming after us all of a sudden?"

Maeve looked hurt, then puzzled. "But that's not possible."

"For a *human* baby, maybe."

"But how...?"

Just then, we heard a roar overhead and looked up—just in time to see a needle-nosed, silver-skinned aircraft punching past at high speed.

"What the hell?" As I said it, another plane shot past after the first...then banked left and peeled away on another course.

At that moment, something chimed in the backpack, and I dove for it. The noise was coming from the radio, signaling a text message that flashed on the little square screen.

Warning! Iskani forces converging on your location!

"What is it?" asked Maeve. "What does it say?"

As she asked, another message appeared. *Earth forces en route. Go to rendezvous point ASAP.*

"We need to get moving." Stuffing the radio in my pocket, I grabbed the pack, shoved my arms through the straps, and swung it onto my back. "Somebody's coming our way."

"Somebody who?" asked Maeve.

"Those guys." I pointed up, where the planes had been—and

another streaked past as if on cue. "So much for our top-secret escape route."

Maeve and I hurried through the overgrown landscape with Oyo, three fugitives from a world that had turned against us. We avoided clearings as much as we could, veered away from voices and the sounds of heavy machinery, dodged potentially hostile wildlife and threatening foliage whenever we came upon them.

The whole time, we followed the glowing white arrow on the face of my wrist-mounted location finder (another gift from Sidra) pointing the way to our rendezvous site. If we straggled off-course because of natural obstructions or enemy patrols, we worked our way back on track. If we got turned around, the device quickly recalibrated and guided us out of confusion.

If we grew tired or lost hope, the beeping of the location finder's built-in proximity sensor kept us going, signaling that we were getting ever closer to the rendezvous point.

Occasionally, text updates came in over the radio, too, giving us news about our situation. Oyo's adoption, we learned, had turned into an interstellar incident. The Iskani planetary government was threatening action against Earth's outpost on Hammurabi VII if the baby wasn't turned over to them immediately. Earth had responded by sending the star carrier *Lewis Puller* to intercept any assaults by the Iskani warfleet...and rescue us in the bargain.

Oyo, meanwhile, was oblivious as always...though it seemed there might indeed be more to her than met the eye. According to a text note from Sidra, the results of Oyo's tests were inconclusive... but certain genetic abnormalities and metabolic fluctuations were evident. Continued study would be warranted once the crisis was over, though of course that didn't help us now, on the run with our lives in the balance.

Especially as the odds against us kept getting worse. More planes flashed past by the hour, and the troops we spotted seemed to multiply by the minute. As we climbed a hill, we saw new opponents in the distance—huge leopard-furred dragons flapping across the valley, piloted by Iskani warriors armed with electrified javelins.

"What next?" I snapped, setting off another crying jag from Oyo. "What the hell else can they send after us?"

Maeve blew out her breath, looking exhausted. "They'll get us sooner or later. We're too outnumbered."

Leaning against the rough trunk of a blue-leafed tree, I shook my head. "Screw that, honey. They'll never win. We've got an ace in the hole."

I pointed at shrieking, kicking Oyo, and Maeve and I laughed.

"I'll bet she could kick *all* their asses," I said.

At that moment, the radio buzzed, and I saw another message appear on the screen. "'Get to higher ground.' That's what they're telling us. 'As high as possible.'"

"Maybe it's for the extraction?" said Maeve. "So they can fly down and pick us up?"

Pushing away from the tree, I eyeballed the craggy orange peak rising behind the foothill we'd ascended. I took a few steps toward it, and the location finder let out a rapid series of beeps.

"That looks like the obvious choice." I gestured at the peak. "And the watch says it's in the right direction. Might even be the actual rendezvous point, from the sound of it."

Maeve took a long look at the dragons in the distance, all twelve of them flapping implacably in a zig-zag search pattern over the valley. Oyo looked, too, and stopped crying, as if the sight comforted her.

"Well, we better get moving," said Maeve. "Make it a little harder for our friends on the dragons to spot us."

"It's for their own good," I said, ushering her to join me on the next stage of our trek. "Somebody has to protect them from Oyo, after all."

From the foothill, we worked our way up that mountain, leaning into the strenuous climb through shaggy red brush and spiky orange crags. Always, we were on the lookout for approaching threats, since we were fairly exposed—but no menacing force seemed to have us in their crosshairs. I was starting to think the higher ground plan was the best advice I'd gotten all day.

It had its limits, though. The slope grew steadily steeper the further we went. Without climbing gear—and with Oyo in tow—we could only get so far.

The good news, however, was that we seemed to be heading for ground zero, the exact rendezvous point. The location finder beeped so fast, its signal became a constant, high-pitched tone…and I switched it to silent mode.

"Almost there," I said, helping Maeve up onto a ledge that skirted the face of the mountain. "Then we hunker down and wait."

"Hopefully, we won't have to wait too long." Maeve frowned at Oyo, whose indigo eyes had fallen shut. "Our supplies are pretty skimpy."

And the dragons are still out there, searching. I kept the thought to myself; there was no need to restate the obvious. *If they reach us before pickup, we have no way to fight them off.* There was no need to say that aloud, either. The outcome of such an encounter would be obvious, too.

We paused there for a moment, gazing out at the surrounding valley with its lush red vegetation. A soft breeze flowed over us, carrying a heady mixture of alien floral scents and late-day warmth.

"Are you sorry we did this?" asked Maeve. "Are you sorry we came all this way to adopt her?"

I noticed she looked tired and reached for Oyo, gently taking her in my arms. Watching as she slept, it was easy to forget the craziness and danger she'd brought into our lives…easy simply to marvel at the little purple face that had become so familiar.

"I should be," I said softly, trying not to wake the baby. "I mean, we wouldn't be in this mess otherwise, right?" I smiled at Maeve, and she reached over to touch my cheek. "But the funny thing is, when you come right out and ask me…"

Before I could finish my sentence, the radio buzzed for attention in my pocket.

Quickly fishing it out, I read the series of messages that flashed on the screen, each more surprising than the last. "Oh my God." I could hardly believe what I was reading…and the implications were staggering.

"What is it?" asked Maeve.

Shaking my head slowly, I lowered the device. "They lied to us."

Maeve's frown deepened. "Who? About what?"

"The Iskani." I looked down at the child in my arms. "They lied about her."

"Lied about her how?"

"They never told us what she really is," I said. "They never told us she's a weapon."

Maeve looked at me as if she thought I'd lost my mind. "That doesn't even make sense," she said. "Oyo's an infant, not a weapon."

"She's both, apparently." As I said it, Oyo shifted in my arms, swatting the air with her tiny purple fists. "The lab results confirm it."

"But Anemolee said the results were inconclusive…"

"And Anemolee was lying," I said. "She was part of a conspiracy, according to Sidra…covering up Oyo's true nature until we could get her home to Earth."

"I still don't understand," said Maeve. "What kind of weapon is she supposed to be?"

"You know all those people coming after her all of a sudden? Demanding we hand her over? She *called* them here. She's *that* kind of weapon. She controls *minds.*"

"But she's a *baby*…"

"Which is why she's only able to give very simple instructions," I said. "Like 'Come and save me from these two scary aliens trying to take me away.' She just broadcasts whatever she's feeling, and people come running."

"Or flying." Maeve looked out at the dragons, which had given up their zig-zag search pattern and were on a direct heading for our mountain.

"Exactly." Oyo stirred again, and I rocked her, hoping to keep her asleep. "She's genetically engineered, meant to serve as a first-strike weapon against Earth. They wanted her to pave the way for an invasion by the Iskani warfleet."

"Anemolee confessed to all this?"

I nodded. "She said the child's abilities activated prematurely. I guess she *really* doesn't want to leave Isk."

"Wow." Maeve rubbed her temples. "This is a lot to take in. This whole adoption was nothing but a *trick?* And the people coming after us…that's all *her* doing?" She stared at Oyo.

"According to Sidra." Gazing at the child, I almost couldn't believe it was true. She still seemed blissfully innocent…putting aside the time she knocked me unconscious and the other time she almost killed me, that is.

But the news from Sidra answered so many questions…except one.

Maeve was the first to say it aloud. "So what do we do now?"

Before either of us said another word, the ground rumbled under our feet.

"What the hell?" The rumbling quickly intensified, shaking the ledge on which we stood. "An earthquake?"

Maeve and I stepped back, steadying ourselves against the slope. "I thought you said things couldn't get any worse!"

"I never said that!" Just then, a memory came back to me, something I'd learned from our studies of Isk before our trip. "Oh, shit." I looked around as pebbles and dust trickled down from up-slope. "I think I know what this is."

I could see the light dawning in her eyes at the same moment. "A *chorlak*, right? Isn't that what they call them?"

"'Hungry mountains.'" A sinking feeling took hold in my gut and wouldn't let go. "Living bioliths."

The rumbling got stronger with each passing second. Oyo squirmed, and I saw she was awake, her glittering indigo eyes gaping at me. I wondered how long she'd been awake. If she, a genetically engineered living weapon, could control thousands of Iskani minds...

"She's doing this," I said. "Oh my God, I think she's controlling the mountain."

At which point, she opened her little mouth and let loose what I could have sworn was the most blood-curdling shriek she'd managed yet.

The mountain continued to rumble with ever-increasing force. Parts of it broke open below our ledge, shooting up geysers of scaldingly hot steam...cutting off any descent we might have made to lower ground.

The dragonriders, meanwhile, flapped ever closer with javelins at the ready. They were moments away at most.

Oyo may have sensed all this, because she got more agitated than ever. Still screaming bloody murder, she raked her claws through the flesh of my chest, drawing blood, and churned out clouds of rancid green smoke from the blowhole in her forehead. Every orifice in her body opened wide, overwhelming her diaper and pumping out toxic excrement in all its Iskani forms to sear and blister my skin.

Just when I thought I couldn't take anymore, Maeve pointed at the sky. "Look! They're here!"

A massive vessel dropped down from above, a streamlined giant studded with heavy weaponry. I recognized her profile instantly as that of the *Lewis Puller*.

"Thank God." As I said it, Oyo swung a clawed hand at my face, but I ducked away in time. Finally, I dared feel the spark of hope in my heart.

Unfortunately, it didn't last.

Just as the *Puller* appeared, three Iskani warships zoomed toward it with guns blazing.

"No!" I howled.

The Iskani craft were much smaller but no less deadly for it. Dancing around the *Puller*, they got in shot after shot, blowing holes in her hull—not enough to bring her down, but enough to hold her back from coming to get us.

Or at least to get us before the dragonriders or living mountain did.

KRA-BOOOOM.

The *Puller* takes a massive hit; even from a distance, I can see the carrier wobble as clouds of smoke and debris billow from her lower hull. If she goes down, the hundreds of men and women aboard her will perish, and the Iskani warfleet will face no opposition in launching an attack on Hammurabi VII.

It will all be because of the maniacally screaming purple baby in my arms. All because of little Oyo.

"Paul!" says Maeve, who is pressed against the rock wall beside me. "The ledge is shrinking!"

Looking down, I see it's true. The shelf of orange stone we've been standing on is slowly squeezing back into the mountainside.

"We're dead, aren't we?" Tears pour down Maeve's face. "There's no way out."

It is then, in this dark moment, as the warships pound the *Puller,* the dragonriders prepare to release their javelins, the ledge narrows, and the steaming maw of the living mountain widens to swallow us, that I think about throwing the child into the depths.

It's an idea that's been growing in the back of my mind, in one form or another, since the moment we first met Oyo.

From the start, Maeve threw herself unreservedly into loving her...but I held back. I was always afraid of the dangers or troubles she might pose, simply by being an alien; then, when my fears turned out to be true, I pulled away even more. Always, I knew I might need to take drastic action to survive—especially when she nearly asphyxiated me. Always, I knew it might come down to her or us...and my choice in that situation was never really in doubt.

Now here we are, in the very moment I expected to face all along. It is literally her or us, a matter of simple survival.

If Oyo is the cause of the attacking Iskani warriors and the quaking mountain, then getting rid of her should end the madness. If I remove the source of the mind control, the minds being controlled should snap back to normal. Maeve and I should be able to walk away unscathed.

It's only logical. And it is literally in my hands.

How can I not save my wife if I think salvation is possible?

"They're almost here, Paul!" shouts Maeve. "The dragons are almost here!"

Turning, I grip Oyo by the shoulders and wrench her away from my chest, taking strips of my flesh along with her. All I need to do is let go, and she will drop into the blistering volcanic heat surging below. Everything should be over in a matter of seconds.

Does Oyo sense what's about to happen? Suddenly, she stops howling and locks eyes with me.

Then she opens her mouth, and something other than a piercing shriek comes out.

"*Da.*" A single syllable, that's all...and then she says it again. "*Da.*"

My heart pounds, and I feel a strange rush of feeling from deep inside. Is it triggered by Oyo's power? Has she finally figured out how to control our alien minds? Is this a last-ditch attempt to save her own skin?

Or perhaps, is it something more?

"*Da.*"

What if she's no different from any human child? What if all she really wants is the love of her parents...*both* parents? The love I've been withholding from the start.

What if all the rest of it was only ever about the same thing? An infant's desperate cry, magnified and weaponized a thousand times over.

"*Da.*"

I flex my hands, all too conscious that time is running out. The safest bet is obvious. My duty to my wife is clear.

But against all common sense, I pull Oyo toward me again. Her eyes stay locked with mine, and she trembles in my grip.

Then I kiss her cheek gently and whisper "I love you" in her ear. Toes hanging over the rim of the dwindling ledge, I rock her in my arms with absolute acceptance of whoever she is and whatever comes next.

However much or little time we have left, we will face it together.

HAMLET WITH A BOMB INSTEAD OF A POODLE

"To be or not to be," said Joji Fak, leaning over the fire in the back alley burn barrel so it nearly singed his bushy black beard. "And by *not*, I mean I'll blow the living *fuzz* outta you with my hot pink *machine gun*, ya' dopes."

Two of the guys around the barrel laughed out loud, and three others grinned big grins in the firelight. Joji's one-man performance of the classic play *Hamlet* was every bit the smash hit he'd expected.

"I just *love* Shakespeare's dialogue." Rotten Robin, a stooped and haggard crone on the fringe of the little crowd, flipped the end of her moldy green scarf with a flourish. "It's so *poetic*."

Joji felt a surge of pride and infused his next lines with extra oomph. "What a shame that all this *blood* should go to waste! Somebody bring me the effervescent *mop of tongues!*"

"Not the mop of tongues again!" Pupa, a little blond boy in front, smiled with gap-toothed delight.

"What about the *bomb*?" asked a cockeyed, trash bag-clad bruiser who went by the name Laughing Boy. "The one Hamlet said he'd use to blow up King Lear's wicked daughters?"

"You'll never guess." Joji made a hissing sound and raised a filthy index finger. "Ariel the fairy swooped down and *grabbed* it from him, then used it on her ex-boyfriend, Pucky, who was just about to have a go at his mistress, Bianca the Shrew!"

Everyone cracked up at once, hooting and howling and clapping.

"The end!" Joji bowed, doffed his threadbare red cap, and held it out, as was the custom—though no one living in that alley had anything to offer but the pure gold of laughter and applause.

All except one tall, dark-skinned stranger in the back, draped in a hooded black cloak. Blended with the shadows as she was, Joji hadn't noticed her during the telling of his tale.

Not until now, when she shouted one word above the ruckus.

"Poodle!"

The joyous clamor faded as all eyes turned to the cloaked woman.

Joji frowned. "Excuse me?"

"Hamlet had a *poodle*, not a *bomb*." The woman's voice was as throaty and authoritative as the voice of Pious Leader that was broadcast every hour on the hour from the city's loudspeakers. "Everyone who has ever read *Shakespeare* will tell you that!"

Joji was instantly on guard. The written word was forbidden from all eyes, lest it poison the saintly soul. "None of us has ever read *his* work or anything *else*, I'll have you know!"

"Everyone who has *heard* Shakespeare, then," said the cloaked woman. "What you've performed here is no closer to the writings of the great *Bard* than the oinking of a hundred *hogs* in a pen!"

Laughing Boy clapped his hands and giggled. "Speaking of hogs, Joji, could you do the *Hamlet* with the dancing pigs in yellow tutus again? I *love* that one!"

"Or the one with the white whale who climbs Mount Doom?" shouted Rotten Robin.

"Or the *Macbeth* where the creature explodes out of the queen's chest?" said Pupa.

"You people know *nothing* of literature!" snapped the cloaked woman. "The dancing pigs are from *War and Peace!* The white whale on Mount Doom is from *Lord of the Dick!* And the chest-bursting creature is straight out of *Animal Farts* by Orwell!"

For a moment, the only sound in the alley was the crackling of the flames in the barrel. Then, as one, the street folk burst into uproarious laughter.

"What are you *laughing* about?" the cloaked woman snarled.

"You!" Laughing Boy howled so hard, he had to hold on to his sides. "*You're* the one who has it all wrong!"

"We know it isn't your fault, though." Joji shook his head, smiling sympathetically. "You must come from a district where the great stories of ancient times were handed down all wrong, where the great books were poorly preserved and distorted by defective storytellers."

"Not *everyone* is lucky enough to have a *master* teller like our *Joji*," said Rotten Robin.

"Clearly, you've been a victim of unscrupulous improvisers, the kind who value their own authorial voices above those of the greats," Joji told the cloaked woman.

"They wouldn't know *To Kill a Strangelove* if Atticus Grinch turned into a cockroach right in front of 'em!" said Laughing Boy.

"Yet even the most misguided of storytellers may have a poignant tale to offer." The cloaked woman smiled darkly and glided toward Joji. "I have a story of my own to tell, in fact—one you are going to want to hear."

"It better be good," Joji said with a smirk.

"Once upon a time," said the cloaked woman, "there was a little teller who played fast and loose with the great works of literature, infusing them with an abundance of his own creative touches. That in itself was not a crime.

"However," said the woman. "*All* stories were *judged* in that world —in *this* world—by the *harshest* of standards."

"Judged?" Joji's smirk faded. "By whom?"

"Me, and those like me." The woman opened her cloak, flashing a golden, star-shaped badge that was pinned to the chest of the red tunic underneath. "We street-critics are *everywhere*...our word is *final*...and *I* have found you *exceedingly wanting*." Her hands shot out and grabbed Joji's arms with strength that surprised him. "*Your* fate shall be like that of the prince in the *true* tale of *Hamlet*...the one with the *poodle* you so blithely disregarded."

Rotten Robin frowned. "You mean the one where Ernest Hemingway and Stephen King get blasted and raise poor Yorick from the dead for shits and giggles?"

"Or the one where Gatsby falls for Holden Caulfield and ends up dead because of a tragic mix-up between their feuding cliques at Beverly Hills High School?" asked Pupa.

The cloaked woman swept steel cuffs from a pouch at her waist and clamped them on Joji's wrists. "More like the one where Hamlet ends up *dead* for not realizing that telling the audience what you *think* they need to hear can get you *killed*."

"No, please!" wailed Joji. "I meant no harm!"

"Shh!" snapped the woman. "Quiet! Remember Hamlet's last words? 'The rest is violence.' "

"Don't you mean, 'The rest is silence?' " asked Joji.

"Not in *this* version of *Hamlet*," said the woman as she dragged him away by the cuffs. "The one with the *guillotine* instead of a *poodle.*"

THE COP WITH A ROSE FOR A HEAD

The woman with a daisy for a head--her name is Gravelina Scalding--runs out the front door of her townhouse with a pair of pruning shears pointed in my direction. The silver-shining blades are scissored open wide, ready to snip my green throat with a squeeze of the handles.

Myself, I have a red rose for a head, but not for long if I don't make a major move right this instant. Then, who'll find the killer of things roselike, the man, woman, or thing the papers call the Pruner? Who'll avenge the murders of my dear darling wife and seedlings?

The very thought of their deaths is enough to fill my red red heart and my green heart too with rage.

My partner, Chub, is nearby, but I know better than to look to him for help. While I have the head of a rose and the body of a man, Chub has the head of a man (though it's a fat, pasty man's head like a pile of mashed potatoes) and the thick-stalked body of a sunflower. He gets around on flippery roots, but he's useless in a pinch because he just can't run.

So it's up to me, as usual.

Since I'm more interested in questioning Gravelina than killing her, I don't reach for the pistols in the pockets of my lemon yellow suit jacket. Instead, as Gravelina charges, I grab a nearby lawn chair and charge right back, jamming the aluminum frame into the blades of the shears. Gravelina keeps pushing--she's stronger than I expected--but I hold her off. One last shove and I knock her back off her feet, sprawling on the cobblestone walk.

The shears fall from her grip, and I kick them away. Dropping on top of her, I pin her wrists to the walk and cough a cloud of ester vapor in her face. This particular ester is meant to tranquilize and bring out the truth.

"We know you're connected to the Pruner," I say in the language of the flower-headed people, the play of scents and the rustling of petals. "Now tell me the killer's name."

Gravelina thrashes violently beneath me, nearly freeing one arm. "The weeds must be pruned if we are to touch the sun," she says.

The blood and chlorophyll syrup in my veins freezes. She is quoting the message that was left hanging in wisps of fragrance in the air at each of the Pruner's twenty-one known murders.

I press the thorns in the palms of my hands more deeply into the meat of Gravelina's wrists. "Tell me! Who is the Pruner?"

"The question you should ask, Inspector Glisten," she says, "is who *isn't?*"

"Daisy-heads suck," says Chub, wrapping a dark green frond around a mug of beer. He hoists the beer from the bar and downs the contents in one swallow. Drinking is one thing he does fast.

"Gravelina won't crack," I say in flower-speak. Though Chub has the head of a man, he understands my rustling/scent language, which makes my life easier. With some difficulty, I can eke out a whispery approximation of man-talk with vibrations of my stamen, but Chub saves me the trouble.

Whatever I did to deserve him as a partner, I'm glad I did it.

Chub's no rose-head, so he'll never be promoted, but he's been my loyal, reliable helper for seventeen years. He hated me at first, but I won him over by saving his life, and we've been crime-busting best buddies ever since.

Not that we've been busting much crime since the Pruner came along.

"Maybe the aphids in the crime lab'll dig something out when they get a taste of her," says Chub. "Sniff out trace information from her petals."

I shrug, displaying my lack of confidence in this possibility. Though aphid bugs have been known to find evidence when we let them gnaw on a suspect or a victim for a while, the technique has been as useless as everything else we've tried so far to track down the Pruner.

A girl with a marigold head drifts by, carrying a water mister on a tray. I want a spritz and wave her over. "In the meantime, what do we do next?" I say. "Gravelina was our best lead. Aromacams picked up her scent in the lobbies of two hotels where murders were committed. We found the pollen prints of five victims on her pistils."

"Hmm," says Chub, thoughtfully swaying from side to side. "She said the question we should be asking is who *isn't* the killer. Does that mean the process of elimination?"

The marigold girl lifts the blue-tinted mister bottle from the tray and directs the nozzle at my rose-head. I lean forward as she squeezes the trigger, spraying my crimson petals with fine droplets of water.

I feel instantly refreshed and tip her generously. As she bows and glides away, I admire the bobbing of the sepals at the base of her blossom, the sway of her buttocks under her filmy white skirt. She reminds me of my wife, Zwilla, though my wife has a rose instead of a marigold for a head.

Had. I mean she *had* a rose for a head before the Pruner killed her.

For the umpteenth time today, I feel a stab in my gut at the thought of dead Zwilla. Though she has been gone for a month, the pain is as fresh as if she had been taken only this morning.

To dull that pain, I return my attention to talk of investigating her murder. "One other possibility, Chub," I say. "Could she have meant that the least likely suspect is actually the murderer?"

Chub thinks for a moment, then sighs and shakes his fleshy jowls. "Maybe she just wanted to throw us off track," he says.

"You might be right," I say, reaching for a plant food spike from the jar on the bar. "We know Gravelina has a connection to the killer. Perhaps we should take a closer look at her personal life."

"She works for a rhododendron-head who arranges humans," says Chub. "Miss Carionette. Maybe we should drop by her shop."

I kick off my right shoe, peel off the sock, and nibble the food spike with the tiny toothy maws on my toes. "Now you're thinking, man-head," I say as the nutrients rush into my system. "We'll clip this weed yet."

I flash Chub a confident smile, but it's all fake. We've been looking for the Pruner for over a year now, and all we have to show for it is a longer list of victims.

A list that now includes my wife and children. They bring the grand total to twenty-one.

That means that more is at stake in this case for me than personal revenge for the death of my family. For any police inspector like me to leave twenty-one murders unsolved in one year's time, that individual won't be inspector for long

The word on the grapevine is that I'm just about out of a job, and I believe it. I've seen better cops than me get the old heave-ho for lesser failures than this. My nineteen years of distinguished service on the force don't mean much next to my last year of shitty underperformance

If Chub and I don't produce a perp soon, the axe will fall hard and fast on yours truly. What comes after that, you don't want to know.

Let's just say that they're probably not saving me a spot in the garden of honor.

Not that anyone needs to punish me for failing. I'm doing a great job of that all by myself. Whatever the department does or doesn't do to me, I'll *never* forgive myself for not saving my family.

This does *not* mean, however, that I will go any easier on the criminal rot that I am about to tear into. If anything, it means I've got that extra, bloodthirsty *zip* that comes with having almost nothing left to lose.

The kind of zip that'll make the Pruner wish he'd never put it there...*if* we manage to find him.

"Gravelina is my finest arranger," says Miss Carionette as she puts the finishing touches on the latest masterpiece at her shop, Fleshlovers. The masterpiece is a bouquet of six humans done up in spring colors. "I refuse to believe she had anything to do with any murders."

"What do you know about her personal life?" I say, admiring Carionette's work as I question her. The tall woman in the center of the arrangement, jet-haired and smooth-skinned, is draped with veils of pastel chiffon in pink, mint, and lemon.

The mauve petals of Carionette's rhododendron-head ruffle with an affected highbrow accent. "Very little, Patrolman Glisten," she says, giving me the wrong rank on purpose. (I can tell from her scent.) "She had a keen interest in composting and expressionist animal grafting...not necessarily in that order."

Strolling away from Carionette, I look at the framed photos on the walls of the shop, examples of her past work. In one, three dark-haired human males dressed as farmers hold watering cans over a naked blonde human female huddled on the ground like a furled shoot. Something about the image makes me feel warm inside, and I linger in front of it.

"Did Gravelina ever talk about roses?" I say, moving on to a photo of three human females in brightly-colored leotards, standing back-to-back with arms stretched skyward.

Carionette's tone changes. Her scent, aloof until now, sweetens with false servility, and a barely perceptible nervousness excites the flutter of her petals. "Only when a rose placed an order," she says, "and then only in a businesslike manner, I can assure you."

I come to a photo of a single human male, a young one, covered head to toe in a red silk bodysuit. He holds his arms straight out, red-gloved hands folded together in the foreground of the picture.

Suddenly, I realize that all is not as it seems at Fleshlovers.

"I'd like to see your back room," I say, giving Chub a meaningful glance.

"I'm afraid I don't have time to show you gentlemen around," says Carionette, brushing at the veils on her subjects. "You'll excuse me, but I have to deliver this arrangement within the hour."

"We won't take up your time," I say. "My partner and I will have a look-see ourselves."

"There's nothing of interest back there," says Carionette.

"Not according to this," I say, pointing at the photo of the red-bodysuited human male. "How about it, Chub?"

Chub shakes his head and wags a frond at Carionette. "You oughtta be ashamed, Miss Carionette."

"It's not what you think," says Carionette.

I lift the photo from its place on the wall and wave it at her. "You can't openly advertise illegal trade," I say, turning my scent bitter and stiffening the flutters of my petals. "But this, the Red Boy, is a well-known sign of certain criminal activities."

Agitated, Carionette stops working on the human bouquet. "That's not an advertisement of illegal merchandise. It's a photo of a specialty item that's very popular with our hipper clientele--the Red Boy bouquet. It's meant to capitalize on public awareness of the Red Boy image."

"Capitalize this," I say, hurling the photo to the floor. The glass pane in the frame shatters on impact.

Storming past Carionette, I sweep around the counter at the rear of the shop and heave open the door to the back room.

What I see in the back makes my stomach churn and my petals wilt. Though I knew what to expect as soon as I spotted the Red Boy, the sight of such perversion is still hard to take.

On one side of the workbench, a translucent plastic bin brims with deep crimson petals. More of the petals are scattered over the bench, each a graceful curl from lip to cup.

And on the center of the bench...

"Rain, sun, wind, and earth," I say softly, making the sign of the cross over myself to ward off the evil in this place.

On the center of the bench, half-finished, is a replica of a face...the face of a rose, assembled from the same crimson petals. As if that were not bad enough...

I can tell from the texture and scent that the petals are real. This mask is being glue-gunned together with petals from someone with a rose for a head.

Someone like me.

"Let me explain!" says Carionette as she charges into the room. "These are all castoffs purchased from donor plants!"

"As if I care where you got the petals," I say, turning to face her. "As if you don't know that the true crime here is the manufacture of rose-head masks." I step toward her, emitting one of my special ester vapors. This one is designed to instill terror in whoever inhales it.

"B-but this is a special commission," says Carionette. I can tell from the way her petals flicker that my ester is taking effect. "It's a death mask for a rose-head whose face was t-terribly damaged in the accident that k-killed him."

I continue to move closer. Carionette remains frozen in place. "Do you know how many times I've heard that story before?" I say slowly.

Then, I pounce, throwing her back against the wall and pinning her arms to the plaster with my palm-thorns.

Chub has finally managed to flipper into the doorway, and I say to him, "Partner Man-Head? What is the penalty for making, distributing, or wearing rose-masks?"

"Everyone knows that," says Chub. "Death by lethal injection of herbicide."

"Mandatory death penalty," I say, pressing my petals to within inches of Carionette's rhododendron-head. "But you never know, Miss Carionette. Maybe, if you tell me *everything* I want to know, I'll

623

cut you some slack."

"W-what do you w-want to know?" says Carionette.

"A name and address," I say. "Who ordered this mask?"

I am surrounded by roses who are not roses.

Men and women dance under the flashing colored lights in the warehouse, and at first glance, everyone appears to have a rose-head. A closer look, however, reveals that every rose is a mask, and behind every mask are petals of white or gold or pink or purple or orange.

There must be at least a hundred people who look like roses in the warehouse, and the only one among them who is an actual rose-head is yours truly.

And I'd thought seeing the rose mask in progress at Fleshlovers had been sickening. This twisted masquerave, in violation of the most sacrosanct of our laws and moral codes, is off the charts when it comes to sick-making.

Masking oneself as a daffodil or petunia is one thing. Lower species are fair game when it comes to dress-up.

But the rose is sacred. The rose is most beautiful. The rose is above all others.

And imitation of the rose is forbidden.

Under other circumstances, I would call in a strike force and fumigate this noxious den of pretenders...but my job tonight requires different tactics. Forcing down my revulsion with great effort, I circle the dance floor in search of the man described by Miss Carionette.

Fortunately, my authentic rose-head enables me to blend in as I explore, though I am certain no one around me imagines that a true rose is among them. Chub waits outside; there was no way that mashed-potato man-head could have entered this exclusive "roses-only" event.

It doesn't take me long to locate my target. He is seven feet tall and wears the only black rose mask in the place. His name is Carotid Aficionado, and according to Carionette, he is the man who ordered the rose-head mask she was making in the back room at Fleshlovers.

He is also the organizer and host of this nightmarish masquerave.

Carotid stands by the bar at the back of the room, a rose-masked woman on either arm. His scent puffs at me like clouds of smoke from a fire--powerful, capricious, and arrogant.

As I draw near, he turns his attention to me. I wisp out a scent of my own, designed to project non-threatening respect.

"Mr. Aficionado?" I say in flower-speak. "May I have a moment of your time?"

The fragrance of his voice is just as abrasive as his personal scent. Even muted by the rose mask, the

flutter-talk of his petals is loud with hyperconfidence. "What'll you pay me for it?" he says, and the ladies on his arms giggle behind their masks.

"I can't afford to pay you what it's worth," I say humbly (though I want to snap his head off). "How about you make it on the house and call it your good deed for the day?"

Carotid chuckles and nods. "Just so you don't take more than I'm willing to give. I don't tolerate *anyone* stealing from me."

"It's about Gravelina Scalding," I say. "She's out of the picture."

"Is that so?" says Carotid.

"My name is Rooted Capsule," I say, "and I'd like to offer my services."

"Outstanding," says Carotid. "The question is, can you measure up to dear Gravelina?"

"Let's find out," I say. "Give me a chance."

Carotid sheds his chippies like the sleeves of silk pajamas and rests a hand on my shoulder. "You've talked me into it, Cappy," he says, then gestures at a guy wearing a yellow rose-mask behind the bar. The guy runs up metal stairs to an elevated booth, and a minute later, the pulsing music cuts out. The dancers stop moving all at once.

Instantly, my guard goes up, as I realize that the whole scene has just gone bad.

One of Carotid's men hands him a microphone. As he flower-speaks, his flutters and scent are amplified and cast out over the crowd, nice and loud.

"Hello, roses!" says Carotid, and the mob on the dance floor flutter-roars and applauds. The obscenity of it, of all these low-growing species wearing rosy masks and cheering as he calls them roses, makes my toe maws snap angrily in my shoes.

"Are the stamens of your rose-heads heavy with pollen, guys?" says Carotid. The rough, insistent flutters of male flowers charge the air. "Ladies, are your pistils crying out to be dusted with hot, surging pollen?" The room ripples with a wave of lighter fluttering as the women chime in. "Then it's your lucky night!"

I try to slide away from Carotid, but he keeps a tight grip on my shoulder. Undesirable outcomes are hurtling toward me, and I have no weapon to blow or cut or spray my way out of here.

But I do have a man-head up my sleeve, and how sweet is that? Smoothly, I drop my hand in my pocket and press the button on the secret weapon I call the Chub Signal, otherwise known as a pager.

As Carotid pushes me forward into the hands of two goons, I take heart that any minute now there'll be fire in the hole.

"Gravelina can't be with us tonight," says Carotid, at which the crowd rustles with disappointment. "But your Uncle Carotid won't let you down! Put your hands together for our very special guest, Rooted Capsule!"

Everyone but me and the goons claps wildly.

"Nobody leaves a Carotid party unfertilized!" says Carotid, and then he spins around like a rock star and punches an index finger toward the elevated DJ booth. "Hit it, Goomie! Make it a love song!"

The guy in the booth scratches a record on the turntable three times, then lets it spin. A hip-hop version of "Flight of the Bumble-bee" explodes from the amps.

One goon holds me while another raises a mask toward my face. The mask is a rounded cone striped gold and black, covered with fuzzy bristles...an instantly recognizable icon of sensuality and life-giving for every greenblooded blossomer.

It's a replica of the ass-end of a bee. Now I know why Gravelina Scalding had so many pollen samples on her.

Like Gravelina, I'm meant to go person to person and rub my masked snout in their flower-heads, picking up pollen from the males and smearing it on the pistils of the females. This is not just a masquerave, it's a pollination orgy...and I'm "it."

At least, that's what's in store for me until the roar of an engine fast approaches outside and the doors of the warehouse blow in like autumn leaves in a wind-gust.

Thankfully, in addition to drinking, there are two other things that slow-moving Chub Man-Head does fast, and one of them's driving.

The other is evident as the machine gun turrets on the roof and hood of his squad car burst to life. Chub might take a half-hour to flipper across a room, but he's a speed demon when it comes to shooting people to death.

Chub's guns chew up the crowd with deafening, random fury, filling the air with plumes of green and red syrup. Rose masks fly apart like feather pillows, petals of red and pink and yellow and white spraying outward as if magnetically repelled from the depraved scum who wear them.

As the crowd scatters in a panic, I haul up a leg and kick back hard into the shin of the guy who's holding me. His petals and scent flare with pain, and he loosens his grip just enough for me to tear my arms free.

When the other goon, the one who was going to put the bee mask on me, charges, I dive at him with palm thorns extended. My thorns slide into his chest like meat thermometers into a roast, and then I drag them downward, gashing him open. Red and green fluid pours out like wine, and the goon drops away...just in time for me to spin around and finish off the first guy.

Goon One barrels at me with steaming petals and fists clenched like he's squeezing mice to death in them. To the sweet sound of Chub's blazing gunnery, I swirl my yellow suit-coat off and whip it over the goon's head bullfighter-style. While he wrestles with the coat, I drive a knee-thorn into his belly and slash him open with joy in my hearts. His guts smack the dance floor before he does, so it's a job well done.

All the while, the gunfire rages, and dancers pelt the floor like hailstones. One of the few people left standing is Carotid, who runs out the back door without his arm candy chippies.

Weirdly enough, when I chase him down and pin him to the alley wall with my thorns, he doesn't look the slightest bit rattled. I tear the black rose-mask off his red carnation-head, and he just stares at me like I'm no more threatening than a pizza delivery guy.

"Alone at last," he says. "Let the games begin."

"What do you know about the Pruner?" I say, twisting my thorns deeper into his flesh with much satisfaction.

Carotid laughs, the multitude of fine red petals in his bloom fluttering with delight. "What's a Pruner, pray tell?" he says.

I hoist him away from the wall and slam him back hard against the bricks. "Drawing a blank?" I say. "Fortunately for you, I'm an expert at shaking loose blocked memories."

"Unfortunately for *you*, I'm a card-carrying masochist," says Carotid. "In fact, I'm having a party in my mind with you right this minute."

"Tell me what you know!" I say, enraged by the smartass answers. I feel like my wife and kids are watching, disappointed that I am failing again to find their killer. By now, I am ready to do just about anything for just one lead that will point me toward the Pruner.

Actually, I have a pretty good idea that killing Carotid on the spot will make me feel better, too...but I hold back.

Instead, I spike Carotid's thigh with my longest knee thorn, then slowly drag it downward, opening a furrow in the meat of his leg.

He stiffens, and I know I've finally hurt him. "The drama is completely unnecessary," he says. "All you had to do was say 'pretty please with sugar on top.'"

I hesitate, glowering up at him. "Tell me what you know about the Pruner," I say...and then, grudgingly, I give the vermin almost what he wants. "Pretty please."

"Come on now," he says. "Give your daddy some sugar."

"With sugar on top," I say, jamming every thorn deeper to drain some of the sweetness from his freaky little victory.

Carotid leans down close enough for me to hear and smell his whisper. "I'll do better than tell you," he says. "Uncle Carotid will *show* you."

As Carotid leads me among the wildflowers in their foul-smelling camp, I am yet again overcome by disgust.

I have been here before, in this sordid domain of rootless scum, when duty called me to quell a disturbance or show the cop flag when they had murdered one of their own. Each visit filled me with a superstrong urge to raze the place with a bulldozer and pulverize everyone here.

These people of the streets and shadows huddle around barrels of burning compost and squat in makeshift tents of trash bags and scavenged cardboard and plastic sheeting. They dress in stinking rags infested with parasites and water themselves from stagnant puddles. The adults shuffle drunkenly and the screaming children scramble through the mud like animals, filthy and unsupervised.

It is like a vision of the end of the world. It is what happens when people abandon the rule of law and the time-tested virtues of civilization.

And it is only one of many such camps festering in the heart of this fair city and too many others across the land. I am ashamed that we allow such places to exist without plowing them under or blowing them up.

"You said the Pruner would be here," I say to Carotid, stroking the grip of the automatic handgun in the right-hand pocket of my lemon-yellow suit jacket. "So where is he?" Next, I stroke the grip of the gun in my left-hand pocket, too.

"I spy, with my little eye," says Carotid, "the certain someone you're dying to meet. Over there!" Flinging out an arm, he points a skinny finger dead ahead.

Looking where he indicates, I see two dandelion-headed people sitting on the ground by a campfire in front of a ragged bedsheet tent. One is a full-grown man, cooking something in a tin can, and the other is a little girl, maybe eight years old.

"That's the Pruner?" I say, tightening my grip on the guns in my pockets.

"Seek and ye shall find, dear Cappy," says Carotid. "Or would you rather call it a night? I can't say I blame you for being a little timid."

"Move it or lose it," I say, giving him a shove forward. "Introduce me to this madman."

Carotid starts toward the dandelion-heads. "You say 'madman,' I say 'to-mah-toe,'" he says.

I follow without answering, my nerves vibrating like overcharged power lines. All I see ahead is a grubby

yuck-man cooking dinner with a sooty waif...but the shadow of the Pruner looms oilslick black, and my man-head backup is parked a block away.

As we draw up on the man and the little girl, I catch a big whiff of sweet and sour stench that makes me want to turn away. Body odor mixed with raw sewage and dandelion scent sticky with sickness.

The dandelion-heads look up as we approach, and Carotid gives them a jaunty wave. "Hello to you!" he says. "You're about to meet someone terribly annoying, and I apologize in advance. His name is Inspector Firstbreath Glisten."

I flash Carotid a look because he somehow knows my real name even though I never let it slip. It is now that I realize that this scoundrel is playing a deeper game than I imagined.

"Inspector," says Carotid, extending a hand toward the dandelion-heads by the fire. "You wanted to meet the Pruner. Allow me to introduce Gristle Skinbone and his daughter, Medium."

I nod, which is as far as I'll go with pleasantries given the circumstances. Gristle nods back and wisps out amid the stench a scent with a touch of courtesy and a bucketful of thinly disguised contempt.

In that moment, I have no trouble at all believing that this scabby scat is responsible for the murder of my family. His rancid odor leaves no room for doubt that he is capable of far, far worse than raising a child in this squalid cesspit.

More than anything, I want to kill him. My fingers twist like snakes around the guns in my pockets.

I barely manage to restrain myself. "All those murders," I say to Gristle, thinking of my dead sweet wife and seedlings in particular. "Why did you *do* it?"

Carotid loops an arm around my shoulders and pulls me close. "'Scuse me, Mr. Jumpy-to-Conclusions," he says, "but what makes you think I was *only* talking about *him?*"

Confused, I look to the wilted little girl in the dancing firelight. "You must still think we're playing a game," I say, "if you're trying to tell me *she's* the Pruner."

Carotid moves so close his petals brush up against mine. "What gave you the idea there's only *one* Pruner?" he says, the scent of his voice thick-sweet with wicked amusement.

"Tell him, honey," he says to little Medium. "Tell him what you did to the pretty rose-head. Tell him how you won your medal."

Medium touches a tarnished silver disk pinned to her stained and putrid sweater. "Okay," she says timidly. "Daddy and I met the rose-man walking in the park. I told him a joke while Daddy hit him with a stick and knocked him down."

Medium hesitates, and Carotid coaxes her to tell the rest, sweetie.

"Then Daddy and I cut him up with clippers," says Medium. "I just did the small stuff on account of I'm small."

"And you won yourself a medal, didn't you?" says Carotid.

Medium nods shyly, fingering the disk on her sweater.

"What do you say to the nice man, honey?" says Gristle.

"Thank you for the medal, Uncle Carotid," says Medium.

"You earned it," says Carotid, ruffling her petals playfully.

I am speechless. Something inside me flips over like a vegetable that looks fine on top and is crawling with insects underneath.

"Okey-doke, lawface," says Carotid, clapping his hands together. "You got your confession of sins. Happy now?"

"I don't understand," I say. "Why would they...how could they do it?"

"Look at how they live," says Carotid, gesturing at the squalid bedsheet tent. "Destitute, undersunned and suffering while the high-faluting rose-heads prance in unobstructed daylight and sip the purest water out of gold decanters. Can there be a nobler motive than the end of oppression?"

"You mean to tell me...they killed twenty-one roses...out of resentment?"

"Shame on you," says Carotid. "Do these two look capable of murdering twenty-one roses?"

I say nothing.

Carotid laughs. "This is just our first stop! There's more to the Pruner than two unwashed wildflowers."

Again, Carotid presents me with seeming impossibilities in a place that reeks like I'll never stop smelling it.

"I'd like you to meet Mrs. Marinade Flypaper," says Carotid, pressing me toward a shriveled tulip-head in a creaky rocking chair. "She's got a groovy story I'll bet you're itching to hear."

Ancient Mrs. Flypaper is so crinkled, she looks like she's been freeze-dried. Her withered purple tulip-head trembles atop a haystick body swimming in a sweat-yellowed dressing gown. I think she will crumble into dust if I breathe too hard in her direction...but the real reason I try not to breathe much is that she stinks like urine, sour milk, and rotting flowers.

In fact, the whole place smells that bad if not worse, filled as it is with decaying running-out-of-timers. In this seediest of low-rent nursing homes, the used-up carcasses of too-late bloomers slump together in pre-death putrescence, regretting that they didn't save enough money in smoother years to afford a better fadeout.

"Go ahead, Mrs. Flypaper," Carotid says cheerfully. "Tell Inspector Glisten about Hedgerow Diadem. Don't leave out the good parts, sweetheart."

The old tulip-headed woman looks at me nervously. "But he's a...he's a..."

"A policeman?" says Carotid.

"A rose," says Mrs. Flypaper, and as rancid as her odor is, I taste the same whiff mingled with her fear that I inhaled from Gristle Skinbone in the wildflower camp.

Contempt.

"Don't worry, Marinade," says Carotid, patting her scrawny hand. "What's he going to do to you? Put you in prison? Kill you? Like you're not in prison already! Like you're not as good as dead right now!"

Mrs. Flypaper's tulip-head petals crackle as they unfold slightly in a weak smile. "You're right as always, dear boy," she says. "What do I have to lose?"

Carotid tucks down a wedge of petals atop one side of his red carnation-head, winking at me. "Can you say 'recurring theme,' Inspector Glisten?" he says.

Tempted as I am to say the hell with Carotid's revelations and give him the shooting he's been begging for, I keep the cage door closed on my pacing tiger temper and listen to the old woman's raspy storytelling.

"Hedgerow Diadem was the doctor who provided our medical care here at the home," says Mrs. Flypaper. "Only he didn't do a very good job of it."

"He was a louse!" says an old man behind me with a wretched blue pansy for a head. "He thought he was so much better than us because he was a high-and-mighty *rose-head*!"

"It's true," says Mrs. Flypaper, nodding. "We were all terrified of getting sick, because his patients often died...and who's going to question it when a poor old tulip or pansy in the county home passes away?"

633

"No one, that's who!" says another old man, this one with a white gardenia-head with hardly any petals left on it.

"All he wanted was to milk our medical insurance," says the pansy man, rapping his ashplant cane on the floor.

"One day, a good friend of ours died because Dr. Diadem gave her the wrong medication," says Mrs. Flypaper.

"Her name was Quartzie Ossobuco!" says the gardenia-head. "I was in love with her!"

"We heard about the Pruner," says Mrs. Flypaper, "and we got an idea. A group of us cornered Dr. Diadem in the parking lot, and we killed him."

"With knives," says the pansy-head.

"We might not look like much," says Mrs. Flypaper, "but you'd be surprised what seven of us can do when we work together.

For a long moment, I stand and absorb the unreality of Granny's vile bedtime story. Withered coots and biddies ganging up on a rose physician is nearly as unthinkable to me as an eight-year-old girl helping Daddy cut down a stranger in the park.

And yet, I come to believe that it happened. These people are not roses, after all, or my faithful man-head. As harmless as they appear, I know that they are untrustworthy and capable of anything.

And deserving of no mercy.

I resist the impulse to dole out swift punishment, however, in favor of pressing for more information. "How many others did you kill?" I say flatly.

"Only Dr. Diadem," says Mrs. Flypaper, rocking in her chair. "But we like to think we did our part."

"Did your part for what?" I say.

"Pruning's a team effort," says Carotid. "If everyone picks up just one piece of garbage, the streets will be litter-free in no time!"

"You're pretty brave to be talking trash about rose-heads," I say coldly, "considering a rose-head policeman's standing right here with the firepower to shut you up forever."

"Then who would answer the big question on your tiny little mind?" says Carotid, dousing me with a fragrance thick with arrogant spite. "Namely, 'Which Pruner chopped my family into little pieces, Carotid?'"

With a major effort, I force back the impulse to do what I know is the righteous thing--in other words, capping him here and now. The scumwad is right: I need to know. I need revenge.

"All right then, compost," I say to him, grabbing his arm and digging in a palm thorn nice and deep. "Since you're Mr. Know-it-all, let's quit beating around the bush. What's the answer to the big question?"

The grinning masochist doesn't even flinch a little from my thorn-stab. "You'll see, Cappy," he says. "Cross my heart and hope you die."

For the next two hours, Carotid continues to lead me around town, introducing me to one self-confessed Pruner or group of Pruners after another.

The parade of psychopaths quickly wears me down. For one thing, none of them admits to killing my so-very-loved ones, and that's the Pruner or Pruners I most want a

face-to-face with (though I'm coming back later, make no mistake, to extinguish every other Pruner I meet along the way).

For another thing, I quickly sicken of the toxic anti-rose-head sentiment spewed out by the whole rotten crew.

I hear the same crap from the band of housewives who murdered a rose-head city councilman that I hear from the men's church group who cut down a rose-head newspaper publisher. The teen street gang who killed a rose-head attorney and his family sing the same song as the janitor who hacked up a company vice president.

This, to say the least, is a real bud-opener. I've been a cop for over a decade, dipping my roots over and over in the filthiest shit-pools...and I never knew how far and wide the poison had spread. Until this night, I never knew how much the non-roses hated us.

As an educated man, I can dismiss this hatred as the sour grapes of the ignorant and the unsuccessful, the disenfranchised, unlucky, and unattractive.

What I can't dismiss or deny is the sheer breadth and depth of this blight. This hatred of the greatest of us all, the benign and divine rosy beauties who lift up all society with our achievements and wise guidance, has infiltrated further than I ever could have guessed.

And I know, in my green and red hearts alike, it has the potential to do far more damage to our precious world than any single serial killer ever could.

Or, perhaps, the damage has already been done. It certainly has been for me.

When my wife and children were killed, my world was flipped upside-down...but at least it was still recognizable. The social order remained intact. People seemed to know their place in the scheme of things.

Now, the only scheme that I see is madness. All that stands between order and chaos is the thinnest of shivering membranes, ready to pop at the touch of a light breeze or a hard look.

This is what is going through my mind as Carotid directs our driver, Chub, toward the last stop on our tour.

As Carotid and I enter the lobby of the stadium, the roar of the crowd is deafening. The mingled scents of many flower-heads in close proximity are overpowering; individual signals are impossible to identify, though a single shared sentiment dominates the chaotic broadcast. Hatred like an avalanche, a tidal wave, a firestorm, out of control.

"Stay close, Cappy," says Carotid, marching toward the open gate that yawns before us, pulsing with brilliant red light. "This is one place you don't want to wander off in."

My sweating hands are tight on the guns in my pockets. Though

I do not yet see the full picture of what I have stumbled into, it is clear to me that something terrible awaits.

"Why?" I say to him. "What's going on here?"

Carotid spins and throws his arms up in the air. "A spectacle years in the making!" he says, walking backward. "The grand finale or brave new beginning, depending on your inclination!"

"What the hell are you talking about?" I say, following him through the gate. The roar and fumes of the crowd beyond are so strong that I can barely hear his scent and have to sight-read the flutters of his petals.

"The greatest show under the sun!" says Carotid, silhouetted in flame. "Behold, *Red Night!*"

As I step out of the gate, all I see at first is fire, leaping up from the green turf of the playing field. An enormous bonfire blazes at dead center of the stadium, orange and red and yellow tongues lashing in the wind.

Staring deeper into the flaring surge, I see a solid form at its core, tall and straight like the trunk of a tree or a telephone pole. I follow it up along its height, rising far above the field into the night sky.

When I get to the top, I realize that it is meant to be more than a tree or a pole. The spar in the heart of the blaze is supposed to be a stem.

Atop it, an enormous effigy of an open rose blossom burns.

Suddenly, the crowd explodes with a roar of clapping and stomping, and I drop my gaze to the field to see what the excitement is about. It is then that I know conclusively that the giant burning rose was not erected and lit as a worshipful gesture.

Gangs of flower-headed men parade onto the turf to the thunderous music of a marching band. At first, I see geraniums, marigolds, begonias, violets, asters, chrysanthemums...no roses.

But as the men get closer, I see roses among them after all. Each gang carries a rose-head, raised overhead like a coffin or a luau pig.

And when they get to the bonfire, the men throw the rose-headed people in with a flourish.

And the flames shoot higher.

Carotid leans close, his petals brushing against mine. "Here are some more Pruners for you," he says as the men throw another rose-head into the fire. "Aren't you going to arrest them?"

I flash back to the words of Gravelina Scalding when I asked her who the Pruner was. "The question you should ask, Inspector Glisten," she said, "is who *isn't?*

At last, I understand what she meant.

A rose-head drops to the field from above, and I look up into the packed stands. I see roses among the thousands of flowers there, struggling and screaming as they are beaten and tossed over the railings.

Petals of rose red and pink and yellow and white swirl in the air like autumn leaves on a windy day.

"Don't feel bad, Cappy," says Carotid, throwing an arm around my shoulders. "You know as well as I that it takes a fire to clear the way for new growth. How else can the overgrown species get their day in the sun?"

Another rose is dumped on the bonfire. The men who threw him high-five and hug each other in celebration.

As I watch, I realize that I recognize them. A chill shoots up my spine as the last flakes of sanity peel away from my world.

They are cops out of uniform. Not just any cops, either, but cops from my precinct.

They are my coworkers.

The six of them are non-roses all, but I never doubted their devotion to the law and to me until now. I always thought that we were on the same team, though I as a rose was of course the leader.

"Friends of yours?" says Carotid, following my dumbstruck gaze. "Let's not be antisocial." Before I can stop him, he detaches his arm from me and jogs forward, waving at my supposed teammates by the fire.

They turn and look. At least two of them, I am certain, look past Carotid and see me.

For an instant, I am frozen in place. One thought blazes in my mind like a desert sun.

Did one of them kill my family? One of my own *colleagues?*

Or, worse, was it a *team effort*? Did *all* of them do it *together*?

Hearts jackhammering in my chest, I turn and run. As I charge through the gate, I hit the Chub Signal in my pocket and draw my guns.

When I bolt out the front doors into the parking lot, I feel the start of true panic build inside me like a bud about to burst. My secret weapon who has never let me down and who I fully expected to see waiting at the curb in the revving Chubmobile is nowhere to be found.

By far, it is my darkest moment in a night of nightmares. After seeing my fellow policemen front and center in the cold-blooded murdershow of Red Night, I guess I should have expected that even stalwart Chub might turn against me...but the thought never crossed my mind. Now, it seems, betrayal is the only explanation for my partner's absence, and death by kill-crazy mob is my only likely destiny.

As the stadium doors crash open behind me, I run straight ahead into the parking lot because there's nowhere else to go. Stealing a look over my shoulder, I see the six traitor-cops hurtling toward me, and that's not all; flower-heads of all description swarm out after them, shaking knives and scythes and ball bats and fists in the air.

I run for my life between lanes of parked cars, barely outpacing the onrushing army. Feet thunder across the pavement like the pounding hooves of stampeding cattle; a cloud of choking stench rolls over me, scents mingled in a single transmission of murderous rage.

How far I'll get, I don't know, but I know if I stop I'll be dead in an instant...or worse, dragged back to the stadium alive and conscious.

Unfortunately, just as I know too well the fates that await me if I stop running, I know that I can't keep running forever. Eventually, I will run out of steam, and they will get me.

The heat and pungence of their stench-cloud intensifies as they gain on me. I begin to think that I won't have to worry about losing steam after all, because they will overtake me long before that happens.

Then, just as I have consigned myself to a terrible Red Night death, I hear the screeching of tires.

Looking over my shoulder, I see the glorious Chubmobile leap out of a parking space, directly in the path of the oncoming mob. As the car jolts to a stop, the machine gun turrets on its roof and hood chatter away, spraying the crowd with a shitstorm of fiery bullets.

As the nose of the mob explodes with blossoms of red and green fluid, I bolt toward my beloved savior-buggy. The door handle jitters in my grip with the supersweet vibrations of the stuttering guns.

"Couldn't you park any closer?" I say as I dive into the passenger seat.

"I was in a towaway zone," says Chub. "The asshole parking attendant would've made his own crippled grandma move."

It's not like me to give with the mush, but I pat Chub's shoulder as he keeps firing into the mob. "Thanks, man-head," I say. "I knew you'd never let me down."

"How can I," says Chub, "what with all the dirt you've got on me?"

"Works both ways," I say, watching the sap-and-bloodbath beyond the driver's side window. "What say we make like bananas?"

"Where to?" says Chub.

"Given recent developments," I say, "I think we ought to pay a visit to Miss Carionette."

Months later, Chub Man-Head sits at the bar in our favorite joint, one frond wrapped around a freshly-refilled beer, and waves me over. For a moment, it's like old times again, my partner and I bellied up to shoot the shit after a long day of shooting lawbreakers.

But I can't fool myself for long. The old times are ancient history.

"Hey, waiter!" Chub says to me. "How about a mist for my partner here?"

These days, I'm not the one on the receiving end of the mister spray.

A man with a lily for a head turns from beside Chub at the bar and extends his glossy white petals to receive the refreshing spritz. I lift the mister bottle from the silver tray I carry and let him have it-- not with bullets like I want to, but with the sweet spray of droplets from the mister's nozzle. His petals ruffle smoothly with delight.

The full-head azalea mask Miss Carionette made me is so good, the lily-head doesn't know I'm a rose underneath. Chub has my number, but that's okay; he'll never rat me out. To keep his job with the Department, he badmouthed me, blamed me for every screw-up in history, and signed oaths of loyalty to the new, non-rose government, but I gave him the go-ahead for all that and I know it was just for show. He did so well at it, in fact, that he got promoted to *my* old job as *inspector*, which is something that *never* would have happened in the old days of rose dominance.

Not that success has gone to his man-head. Not that it ever will.

This is the one thing that has not changed in my inside-out life: Chub Man-Head, who I now realize is my best friend and not just my partner, will never let me down. Looking back, I am glad that when I was on top, I bothered to treat this one non-rose with respect, and that he was worthy of it.

Not that Chub's new partner seems as willing as I was to befriend the little people.

"Don't be so stingy with the mist next time," the lily-head says in flower-speak, dropping a lousy tip on my silver tray. Even on my hardest-up days money-wise, I was a better tipper than this cheapskate.

Inspector Chub, at least, adds another bill to my tray. "Take care," he says with a wink on his mashed potato puss.

I linger for an instant, more grateful than ever for the good and faithful man-head. Now that the other flowers have killed every rose they could get their hands on, and I can never show my true rose-head face in public, Chub is my only connection to the life I once knew. Without his support, even from afar, I know I would have gone insane long ago.

I smile to myself as my former partner drains his beer in one gulp, and then I move along to serve other customers. To say the least, I hate doing it, spending my days misting the petals of the inferiors who troop through the door like they own the place, like they own the whole world.

But it keeps me alive. I make enough money that I don't have to live in a wildflower camp or peddle my ass as a street pollinator. I blend in and watch for other flower-heads who might be roses under masks, just in case there are some Red Night survivors around...though I haven't found any yet.

Also in the plus column, my job isn't my life anymore like it was back when I was an elite lawman. I have time for a life away from work these days.

Some nights, I go on hunting expeditions, ambushing wealth-flaunting nightlifers fattened on the kill-gotten gains of the Red Night massacre. I call myself the New Pruner and aim to beat the record for hacking up non-rose flower-heads...but only after I've interrogated them for information about the murders of my wife and kids.

That's the one secret I never discovered while investigating the original Pruner killings. I'm still no closer to figuring it out, but I'm nowhere near giving up, either.

Neither is my friend in high places, Inspector Chub. Though he hasn't found a single lead in the case, he says he's all over it in his spare time. His man-head's intuition keeps him believing that the Pruner who struck down my family has not flown far. Recently, in fact, Chub said he had a feeling that the killer was so close that he could reach out and touch him.

It makes me feel good that Chub's taking this case as personally as I do. It gives me hope that someday, in spite of my reduced circumstances, I'll track down and punish the animal who snuffed out Zwilla and the girls.

Some people might say it's unimportant now, given all that's happened...but to me, it has never been *more* important. Sometimes, it's the only thing that keeps me going.

And sometimes, there is one other thing.

On certain nights, I go to Carotid's club. I put on a rose mask over the azalea mask over my rose-head, and I pretend I'm dancing among rose-heads again, not lesser flowers masked as roses. Sometimes, I pretend my wife and seedlings are among them, swaying and waving and smiling in sunlight, telling me everything's going to be all right.

And for a while, at least, I feel like I'm on top of the world again.

ABOUT THE AUTHOR

Robert Jeschonek is an envelope-pushing, *USA Today* bestselling author whose fiction, comics, and non-fiction have been published around the world. His stories have appeared in *Clarkesworld, Galaxy's Edge, StarShipSofa, Pulphouse,* and many other publications. He has written official *Star Trek* and *Doctor Who* fiction and has scripted comics for DC, AHOY, and others. His young adult slipstream novel, *My Favorite Band Does Not Exist,* won the Forward National Literature Award and was named one of *Booklist's* Top Ten First Novels for Youth. He also won an International Book Award, a Scribe Award for Best Original Novel, and the grand prize in Pocket Books' Strange New Worlds contest.

Visit him online at www.bobscribe.com. You can also find him on Facebook and follow him as @TheFictioneer on Twitter.

Subscribe to the Blastoff Books Newsletter: http://newsletter. blastoffbooks.net/